'Mother of God
Velasquez. 'It's

As his terrified brother Benito flung his rifle aside and took to his heels, a bullet from Annie's Winchester hit Nicosia in the centre of his forehead. Quickly reloading, she took aim and dealt Arnaldo de Ulloa an equally fatal blow before he had time to defend himself.

Revised List of J. T. EDSON *titles in chronological and categorical sequence.*

Ole Devil Hardin series

YOUNG OLE DEVIL
OLE DEVIL AND THE CAPLOCKS
OLE DEVIL AND THE MULE TRAIN
OLE DEVIL AT SAN JACINTO
GET URREA

The Civil War series

COMANCHE
YOU'RE IN COMMAND NOW, MR. FOG
THE BIG GUN
UNDER THE STARS AND BARS
THE FASTEST GUN IN TEXAS
A MATTER OF HONOUR
KILL DUSTY FOG!
THE DEVIL GUN
THE COLT AND THE SABRE
THE REBEL SPY
THE BLOODY BORDER
BACK TO THE BLOODY BORDER

The Floating Outfit series

THE YSABEL KID
·44 CALIBRE MAN
A HORSE CALLED MOGOLLON
GOODNIGHT'S DREAM
FROM HIDE AND HORN
SET TEXAS BACK ON HER FEET
THE HIDE AND TALLOW MEN
THE HOODED RIDERS
QUIET TOWN
TRAIL BOSS
WAGONS TO BACKSIGHT
TROUBLED RANGE
SIDEWINDER
RANGELAND HERCULES
McGRAW'S INHERITANCE
THE HALF BREED
WHITE INDIANS
THE WILDCATS
THE BAD BUNCH
THE FAST GUN
CUCHILO
A TOWN CALLED YELLOWDOG
TRIGGER FAST
THE MAKING OF A LAWMAN
THE TROUBLE BUSTERS
THE GENTLE GIANT
SET A-FOOT
THE LAW OF THE GUN
THE PEACEMAKERS
TO ARMS! TO ARMS! IN DIXIE!
HELL IN THE PALO DURO
GO BACK TO HELL
THE SOUTH WILL RISE AGAIN
THE QUEST FOR BOWIE'S BLADE
BEGUINAGE
BEGUINAGE IS DEAD!
MASTER OF TRIGGERNOMETRY
THE RUSHERS
BUFFALO ARE COMING!
THE FORTUNE HUNTERS
RIO GUNS
GUN WIZARD
THE TEXAN
OLD MOCCASINS ON THE TRAIL
THE RIO HONDO KID
OLE DEVIL'S HANDS AND FEET
WACO'S DEBT
THE HARD RIDERS
THE FLOATING OUTFIT
APACHE RAMPAGE
THE RIO HONDO WAR
THE MAN FROM TEXAS
GUNSMOKE THUNDER
THE SMALL TEXAN
THE TOWN TAMERS
RETURN TO BACKSIGHT
TERROR VALLEY
GUNS IN THE NIGHT

Waco series

WACO'S BADGE
SAGEBUSH SLEUTH
ARIZONA RANGER
WACO RIDES IN
THE DRIFTER
DOC LEROY, M.D.
HOUND DOG MAN

Calamity Jane series

CALAMITY, MARK AND BELLE
COLD DECK, HOT LEAD
THE BULL WHIP BREED
TROUBLE TRAIL
THE COW THIEVES
THE HIDE AND HORN SALOON

J. T. Edson

IS-A-MAN

CORGI BOOKS

IS-A-MAN

A CORGI BOOK 0 552 12663 2

First publication in Great Britain

PRINTING HISTORY
Corgi edition published 1985

Corgi Books are published by Transworld Publishers Ltd., Century house, 61-63 Uxbridge Road, Ealing, London W5 5SA, in Australia by Transworld Publishers (Aust.) Pty. Ltd., 26 Harley Crescent, Condell Park, NSW 2200, and in New Zealand by Transworld Publishers (N.Z.) Ltd., Cnr. Moselle and Waipareira Avenues, Henderson, Auckland.

Made and printed in Great Britain by
Hunt Barnard Printing Ltd., Aylesbury, Bucks

Author's Note

To save our 'old hands' from repetition, but for the benefit of new readers, we have included in the form of an Appendix various Western terms which we have received frequent requests to be clarified and an explanation of certain Comanche words. The spelling of the latter is phonetic.

We realize that, in our present 'permissive' society, we could use the actual profanities employed by various people in the narrative. However, we do not concede that a spurious desire to create 'realism' is any excuse for doing so.

Lastly, we refuse to pander to the current 'trendy' use of the metric system. Except when referring to the calibre of certain weapons traditionally measured in millimetres – i.e. Walther P-38, 9 mm – we will continue to employ miles, yards, feet, inches, stones, pounds and ounces, when quoting distances or weights.

J. T. EDSON
Active Member, Western Writers of America
MELTON MOWBRAY
Leics.,
England

Prologue

To an observer experienced in such matters, although someone uninitiated might have been mislead, the clothing and accoutrements of the rider who was bringing a fourteen hand blue roan gelding to a halt within the walls of a dried up water course that made its descent through a cliff on to more open land in North-West Texas, were those of a young and probably not yet fully trained Comanche warrior.

Dismounting on the right side, as was the habit of all North American Indians, brought more clearly into view the most important indication of the nation to which the rider belonged. Being considered indispensable by every *Nemenuh* brave-heart regardless of age or social status,[1] this was the breechclout. Made from a broad piece of cloth of the traditional blue colour, it was drawn up between the legs and passed under a belt around the waist so the ends, one in front and the other behind, extended almost to knee level.[2]

Instead of the rider wearing trousers, attached by straps to the waist belt, close fitting buckskin 'leggins' offered protection to the lower limbs and reached from hip to

[1] *The meaning of* 'Nemenuh' *and various other Comanche terms, spelled phonetically, which appear in this narrative can be found in* Item One *of the* APPENDIX.

[2] *The breechclout is still worn by present day Comanches of a conservative nature. It is nothing more than a form of 'g-string' made from braided cord, passed between the legs and wrapped around the waist. While it cannot be seen, nor is it decorative, it is accounted magically protective of the male wearer's sexual organs.*

foot. Beyond the seam, the border of the material was left loose and presented a wide, flapping margin to show off fringes of a length which distinguished them from those worn by members of the other Plains Indian nations. Ornamentation, such as small pieces of silver, bits of other metal, beads, shells, teeth from *wapiti*—erroneously called 'elk' by Europeans—and black or, more highly prized, grizzly bear, were attached to the fronds of those intended for ceremonial occasions. However, having been made for everyday use, the pair which the rider had on were unadorned.

Every authority on Indians claimed it was possible to identify the tribe by the moccasin tracks they left; because the heel fringes, the nature of the soles and the form of the toes imprinted distinctly different marks.[3] Generally being short and stubby, the foot of a Comanche created 'sign' that provided an additional clue. Having buckskin uppers and a seam down the heel, with the lower border sewed to a stiff sole of tanned buffalo hide, the moccasins were decorated in a similar fashion to the borders of the leggins. Running from the lace to the toe and along the seam at the heel, the fringes were relatively short on top. However, fifty or so in number, those on the heel were almost eight inches in length.

Conforming to the natural contours of the skins and torso of the wearer, a long sleeved shirt had its neck cut in a simple V-shape. Hanging to below the top of the leggings outside the waist belt, it almost concealed the dangling flaps of the breechclout. It was made from the soft yellowish red-brown hide of a doe whitetail deer. Apart from fringes extending to over a foot in length around the collar and along the seams of the sleeves, being worn for work and not ceremonial, it too was without adornment of any kind.

While a metal bit was considered necessary by almost every equestrian race elsewhere throughout the rest of the

3 *For example, the heel fringes of the Cheyenne were made from either two small tails of whitetail deer, a strip from the tail of a buffalo, or its beard, which trailed behind.*

decorating it with one or more eagle feathers, or other insignia of success, had not been earned. Although the *Pahuraix* generally tended to be taller and more slender than others of their nation,[7] she had inherited her curvaceously buxom build of the more typical Comanche from her white mother. The fit of the masculine shirt over her torso in particular indicated she was powerfully muscled and firmly fleshed, not fat. Her hair, instead of being black, cropped to shoulder length and parted down the centre—as was the usual style for one of her age and sex—was rusty reddish-brown and formed into two braids after the fashion of a warrior. While pretty by European standards, her coppery bronze face was broad and the brown eyes were somewhat slanted in the close to Mongoloid way of the *Nemenuh*. However, her nose was snub rather than aquiline, making the features closer to Caucasian in their lines.[8]

At birth, the mother of the rider had called her 'Annie Singing Bear'!

However, translated into English, the name—although mostly shortened for convenience to '*Tuinep*' —she had acquired from her father and the other members of the *Pahuraix* Comanche band was, 'Should-Be-A-Boy'!

What was more, regardless of sex or birthright, by training and upbringing, the rider *was* a Comanche warrior!

[7] *According to Comanche folklore, being inveterate gamblers, the* Pahuraix *had acquired their uncharacteristic physical conformation as a result of having to stand and reach high to pile up the large amount of property they invariably used as stakes for bets.*

[8] *'Caucasian': a member of the white sub-division of the human race. The name was derived from a skull found in the Caucausus which was taken as establishing the type.*

Part One

The Making Of A Comanche Warrior

1 *Something Of A Tomboy*

'Mr. Brackley, I'd like to challenge one of your ladies!'

Hearing his name spoken in a feminine voice with a local accent, the tall, burly and white haired man wearing a black Derby hat and three-piece brown suit ran his gaze over the poster he had just attached to the wall of the Journey West Saloon in St. Joseph, Missouri. It was large and announced in bright red letters:

HERE TONIGHT
FOR ONE NIGHT ONLY
PUG BRACKLEY
FORMER HEAVYWEIGHT CHAMPION WRESTLER OF THE WORLD
(Retired Undefeated)
Presents
HIS TROUPE OF INTERNATIONAL LADY WRESTLERS
COUNTESS FRITZI von HAMBURG, Germany
VICOMTESSE FIFI de VERSAILLES, France
DUCHESS MOLLY of CONNEMARA, Ireland
LADY LAVINIA of SHEFFIELD, England
CONTESSA ROSA of MILAN, ITALY
DONA CONCHITA ALVAREZ of MADRID, SPAIN
Challenges From Local *FEMALE* Contenders Welcomed
NO CHALLENGES FROM GENTLEMEN ACCEPTED
Try To Beat My Ladies, Ladies, And Win
A TWENTY-FIVE DOLLAR PURSE

Then, swinging around, Horace 'Pug' Brackley looked the speaker over with a calculating and knowing gaze!

No more than five foot four in height, Brackley

estimated her to be a girl not yet into her twenties. Sitting upon rusty reddish brown hair, a mass of ringlets cut shorter than was dictated by current fashion, was a brown felt hat with a low round crown and fairly wide brim turned up at the sides. Ornamented by a spray of red egret feathers, it had a yellow ribbon passing under her chin to frame a face which was pretty without being outstandingly beautiful and had a tan implying she spent much of her life out of doors. She had on a long sleeved russet coloured day dress, V-necked and filled in high to the neck by a frilled white chemisette. Gathered at the waist, its skirt was long to the ground and gave no indication of what kind of footwear she favoured. Its lines suggested her build was curvaceously close to buxom, but offered no clear sign whether the 'hourglass' curves were created by artificial aids to nature. In her bare left hand, which bore no rings to indicate marital status, she had a vanity bag and the equally unadorned right was empty.

There was much about the girl which aroused speculation and curiosity for Brackley. It was not the first time he had had such a challenge issued, but mostly these had been delivered by a man on behalf of the woman concerned. Even on the rare occasions when the offer had been made in person, the challenger was invariably from much the same stratum of society as his contenders and not, unless he was mistaken in the summations he had drawn from her voice and appearance, the somewhat more affluent one to which he believed she belonged.

The six female members of Brackley's Troupe did possess the ethnic origins he ascribed to them. However, the aristocratic sounding titles and names of their respective cities on the poster were no more than products of his imagination. He had selected the latter because they were generally known by the audiences as being situated in the countries each of the women was supposedly representing. Regardless of the nations from which their 'roots' had stemmed, all came from poor immigrant families. Without exception, they had joined him to obtain a better standard of living and, despite the rigorous training he insisted was carried out to ensure the high standard of performance he demanded, considerably easier working conditions than would have been available to them in the communities from which they hailed.

Every instinct Brackley possessed, including a well developed judgement of human nature, told him the same did not apply to the speaker!

While the girl was hardly a 'princess in rags', the burly white haired man felt sure she had not been born into an impoverished immigrant family. Her attire was of good quality and well cut, although not made from the most expensive materials available. What was more, it was in much better taste than was worn by any of the women with whom he generally dealt. Certainly it no way resembled the somewhat garish clothing and ostentatious amounts of cheap jewellery with which his 'ladies' tended to announce their improved circumstances. She wore the ensemble without any trace of self-consciousness, which implied she was used to doing so and was not just wearing it to persuade him that she belonged to a 'better' level of society than was the case.

A further suggestion of the girl's status was provided by her voice. It had a well modulated timbre indicative of a better education than was usual amongst his 'ladies' and their general run of challengers. The latter were always either 'good' women from poor backgrounds, or prostitutes, who had earned themselves a reputation locally for toughness and competence as fighters. He did not believe she came into either category. She was pretty, as were all the members of his Troupe and some of their opponents. However, she was healthy and fresh faced in a way which implied a country dweller's life with a fairly affluent background. Furthermore, while not exactly ingenuous, her features were far from being hard or brash either by nature, or because of an impoverished upbringing. On the other hand, there was something about her which suggested she had known what she was doing when she addressed him and was not just acting upon some momentary girlish impulse.

All of which, Brackley told himself, raised the point of why the challenge had been issued?

It seemed unlikely, the man felt sure, that the girl had sought him out because she believed participating in a wrestling bout offered an easier way of obtaining money than would be available to one of her class by conventional means. Nor did she strike him as being the kind of over-indulged wealthy 'spoiled' brat' who could be looking for an unusual form of excitement to relieve boredom, or was perhaps trying to win a bet, or was motivated with a desire to draw attention to herself by adopting behaviour which would embarrass her family when their associates heard of it. If he had believed the latter to be the case, knowing the sufferers of the embarrassment were liable to try and bring down repercussions on the indirect cause rather than the real culprit, he would have dismissed her request out of hand. As it was, he felt he should at least find out why she had decided to issue the challenge.

'You would, would you, young lady?' Brackley asked, having thought quickly and arrived at his inconclusive decision. And then, seeking to satisfy his curiosity, he asked 'And do you mind if I ask why?'

'For the money, of course,' the girl admitted.

On reading one of the posters she had seen Brackley putting up, and hearing a passing man address him by his name, she had concluded she was being offered an opportunity to make a badly needed addition to her financial condition. The would-be challenger had silenced that part of her which tried to insist she was being ill-advised to say the least. Nevertheless, she had not been so impulsive as to make her proposal immediately. She had decided to take the precaution of trying to learn more about him before committing herself, and had succeeded in remaining undetected as she followed and studied him with a gaze as discerning as his own. Then, deducing correctly that he was returning to the saloon, she had known she must delay no longer and, hoping she sounded more confident than she felt, she had spoken.

During the conversation, the girl had been convinced by her scrutiny at close quarters that the summations she had already formed about Brackley could be correct. Towering above her though he was, she found his demeanour more reassuring than menacing. He had rugged, yet pleasant, ugly features with a suggestion of a sense of humour in their lines. There was none of the loud and 'flashy' clothing she would have expected from somebody in such an unusual line of work. Rather he dressed and looked like the moderately well-to-do local farmers with whom her father had associated and in whose company she had spent much of her time as a teenager without coming to any harm. Furthermore, his voice was suggestive of a Southron upbringing and better education than she would have expected. All in all, he gave her the impression of being trustworthy and could be counted upon to deal honestly rather than try to take advantage of her.

'The twenty-five dollars' purse, you mean?' the burly man suggested, reaching out with his right hand to tap the appropriate place on the poster.

'That's what I mean,' the girl confirmed. Then, throwing a glance in each direction as she had done twice before since starting the conversation, she continued, 'However, could we go somewhere off the street to talk, please.'

'Of course,' Brackley assented, his curiosity aroused. After he had led her into the mouth of the alley separating the saloon from the next building on the street, he enquired, 'So you think you can beat one of my ladies?'

'I'm willing to *try*—Besides—!'

'*Besides*?'

'From what I've heard about you,' the girl said with a friendly frankness which its recipient found refreshing and flattering. 'There is a collection taken for the loser of the bout, which means either way I'll have something for my efforts.'

'I do and you *would*,' Brackley replied.

'Would you mind telling me how much that will be?' the girl asked.

'That always depends on how good a show you—the challenger's put on,' Brackley answered. 'It can be as high as twenty dollars if she's done well and the crowd like her.

But where did *you* hear about what goes on at my shows?'

'Two of the men who were staying at the rooming house where I was living in Surbiton had seen your Troupe when you visited there,' the girl explained. 'I heard them talking about it over breakfast next morning.'

'So you live in Surbiton, huh?' the burly man said, the visit to which her companion had referred having taken place some two months earlier. 'That's a pretty long way from St. Jo.'

'I know, I've made the journey,' the girl answered, but her tone and demeanour had become wary, 'Not that I *live* there, I was just staying for a vacation and I haven't run away from home, if that's what you're thinking.'

'I wasn't,' Brackley lied, the possibility having crossed his mind. 'But, if you'll pardon me for saying so, you're not the usual kind of challenger I get for my ladies.'

'Going by what the men were saying about the woman who took on your German Countess in Surbiton, I thought I might not be. But I'm still making the challenge.'

'Why?'

Brackley considered the question was justifed. He had noticed that the girl constantly glanced about her while speaking and awaiting his answer. However, even if she had not run away from her home, he was willing to admit this could have been motivated by nothing more significant than a desire to avoid being seen whilst engaged in a conversation with somebody like him. On the other hand, should she be a runaway and knew her parents were looking for her, it seemed unlikely that she would want to let herself become involved in something which would attract attention to her.

Of course, the man told himself, there was another possibility. The girl might be a criminal on the run from the law. However, studying her, he felt sure this was not the case. What was more, if she was a fugitive from justice, she would be just as disinclined as a runaway to draw attention to herself by engaging in a wrestling match.

'I need some extra money,' the would-be challenger replied, meeting the speculative gaze of her interrogator without flinching. 'And your offer strikes me as being a good way of getting it.'

'That *sounds* reasonable,' Brackley admitted, in spite of his misgivings. 'But do you have any idea of exactly what you're getting yourself into?'

'I think so,' the girl replied, then raised and bent her right arm. 'I've always led an active life and haven't forgotten what I learned as a child. Feel my muscle and I think you'll find I'm not exactly puny.'

'You're not, I'll give you that,' Brackley admitted, having made the experiment and found a very firm bicep under the material. He had already noticed, whilst entering the alley, that his companion moved in a sprightly fashion suggestive of more agility than might be expected from one of her build. However, realizing she had misunderstood his question, he continued, 'But I still want to know if you've any idea of *exactly* what you're getting into?'

'I've ridden almost all my life and know how to take a fall,' the girl asserted. 'On top of which, I was always something of a tomboy and learned how to take care of myself in scuffles with boys as well as other girls. And I'm not afraid of taking some knocks and collecting a few bruises, if that's what you mean.'

'That's part of it,' Brackley declared. 'But I'm more thinking about *where* you'd be. It'll be in a *saloon*, with a whole crowd of *men* looking at you.'

'At the risk of appearing boastful,' the girl asserted with a smile, 'I've noticed men *looking* at me for a few years now and it hasn't done me any *harm*.'

'I don't doubt you have had them look,' Brackley answered, running a far from disapproving gaze over his companion. 'But I'd say that'd only be while you're on the street and *dressed*.'

'It was,' the girl conceded. 'But I don't recollect the two men in Surbiton saying your ladies were *undressed*.'

'They *weren't*, at least not the way I reckon you mean,' the burly man affirmed quickly and definitely. Concluding there was no point in saying the women of his Troupe did occasionally wrestle stripped to the waist at select private functions, as the event under discussion was not in that category, he went on, 'And they won't be tonight, but they'll be wearing a whole lot *less* clothes than I'll bet you've ever let yourself be seen in.'

'I had an idea what I'm wearing wouldn't be suitable,' the girl claimed, glancing at and running her right hand over her skirt. 'But I've a pair of riding breeches and a man's undershirt I can put on.'

'The breeches'd be a mite rough on whichever lady you was up against,' Brackley pointed out, hoping this would prove a deterrent.

A shrewd businessman, the manager of the Troupe could see the advantage of accepting the challenge. Good a show as his wrestlers put on amongst themselves, the response from the audience was always far better financially when one of them was taking on a member of the local community. He sensed, due to the girl being so different from the usual type of challenger, this would be even more so if he consented to her participating. Nevertheless, because of an inborn sense of what was right, the supposition was in conflict with a feeling that somebody with her background did not belong in such an atmosphere and he was hoping the implications of his remark would cause her to change her mind.

'I guess they would,' the girl conceded. She was silent for a moment, then looked at the poster and, clearly having arrived at a decision, gave a shrug. 'All right, as they won't do, I'm willing to borrow the same kind of clothing your ladies wear if they'd lend me some.'

'It sounds like you've thought this out pretty good,' Brackley commented with a grin suggesting admiration.

'I have,' the girl confirmed and, while it had become friendly again, there was a timbre of grim determination in her voice. 'Including something I felt sure that *you* would have to take into account.'

'What would that be?'

'What the men around town would think and say if they heard you'd *refused* to accept my challenge.'

'By golly, young lady, you *have* thought it out real good,' Brackley stated and there was still more admiration than animosity in his tone. Then, giving a shrug redolent of cheerful rather than resentful resignation, he went on, 'All right, on *your* head be it. I'll have—I reckon Annie—*Lady Lavinia of Sheffield* will be the safes'—*best*—to take up your challenge.'

'I'll leave *that* up to you,' the girl declared, giving no sign that she had noticed the way in which the selection of her opponent was worded although she decided it justified her assumptions with regards to the character of the man she was addressing. 'How do we do the wrestling?'

'The bout'll be a single fall, with no time limit,' Brackley explained. 'It's won when one of you has her shoulders pinned to the mat, is made to say she submits, or gets knocked out. Do you know what I mean?'

'I've a pretty good idea,' the girl admitted. 'Those were the rules when I've seen men wrestling at fairs and such back home.'

'And you're willing to go along with those rules?' Brackley inquired. 'Even though you could get hurt so much you'll have to say you submit, or perhaps be knocked *unconscious*.'

'I'm willing to take a chance on either!' the girl asserted 'I don't really expect to win, but I promise I'll do the best I can.'

'I reckon you will at that.'

'Then you'll take the challenge?'

'Just as long as you're *sure* you want to go through with it.'

'I'm *sure*!'

'All right then, your challenge's accepted,' Brackley affirmed. 'I'll have to know your name, so that I can announce you.'

'Syl—Reb—Becky Hind—*Becky—Ingraham*,' the girl supplied and, despite having somewhat mixed feelings over having achieved her purpose, silently promising herself that she would do her best to surprise the white haired man when the time came.

'Becky Ingraham of Surbiton, Missouri,'[1] Brackley suggested, having noticed the slight hesitation with which the introduction was made and deducing the name he had finally received was an alias.

'Oh no!' the girl replied, the vehemence of the response giving strength to the supposition. 'Don't mention *Surbiton* whatever else you say. I wouldn't want *anybody* from there to find out wher—what I'm doing!'

[1] *Although we have received the general background of 'Becky Ingraham', neither we nor the world's foremost fictionist genealogist, Phillip Jose Farmer—author of, amongst numerous other works,* TARZAN ALIVE, The Definitive Biography Of Lord Greystoke *and* DOC SAVAGE, His Apocalyptic Life'—*with whom we have consulted, have been able to discover her real identity or even the true location of the town called 'Surbition' in the documents from which we produced this narrative. Therefore, we will continue to use her alias in the interests of avoiding confusion. J.T.E.*

2 *I* Killed *A Man*

'Wh—Wha—What—?' Becky Ingraham gasped, as the spinning sensation inside her head subsided and conscious thought began to stir. Finding herself looking up at an unpainted wooden ceiling which she did not recognize, she also realized she was lying on something far harder even than the less than soft bed at the rooming house which was her temporary accommodation. Lowering her still blurred gaze to a lower level, she discovered there were two vague masculine and a female shape near her, but she was unable to identify any of them. Despite a growing realization that every muscle and fibre of her shapely young body was throbbing with a persistent aching pain, she tried to shove herself into a sitting position, staring about her in a dazed and close to frightened fashion. 'Wh—Where am I?'

'Take it easy, honey!' Horace 'Pug' Brackley requested, gently restraining the girl. 'Your head hit the mat with a helluva bang, but the doctor here says you've got nothing worse than a bump on it the size of a goose egg.'

'It was your own fault, duck,' claimed 'Lady Lavinia of Sheffield, England', having hurried forward on seeing Becky was regaining consciousness. Her accent was not what might have been expected from one with such an aristocratic name and she employed a term of friendly endearment common in the working class areas of the British city from which she had originated. Despite her exhaustion and physical suffering, she had refused to go to her own changing room at the rear of the Journey West Saloon until she was sure she had not inflicted any permanent damage to the girl. Hoping this was the case, there was an expression of relief on her face and her tone became redolent of that emotion as she went on, 'You was so good, I forgot I wasn't working with one of the regular girls and used the routine I would've with them to get the bout over.'

Despite the conviction with which she had spoken when issuing the challenge, Becky had needed to call upon all her resolution and strength of will to go through with it.

She had been helped by the friendly way in which she was greeted when being introduced by its manager to the International Troupe Of Lady Wrestlers and its other two male members, Percy Pulbright—who was to act as referee—and the 'advance man', Sidney Colkiss, responsible for going ahead to make the arrangements for the bouts in the towns they visited. Nevertheless, on being taken to one of the rooms at the rear of the saloon and shown the clothing she was to wear, she had begun to realize what Brackley had meant when asking if she realized exactly what she was getting into. Not only did the sleeveless white cotton blouse have an extreme decollete, but it, and the black tights, clung like a second skin to her otherwise—except for a pair of heel-less black cloth shoes—unclad curvaceously buxom body. It was attire of a brevity far exceeding anything she had worn in the presence of members of the opposite sex since her tomboy childhood. Even then, those who had seen her skimpily clad were cousins and friends of the same age as herself, not total strangers.

While crossing the crowded main bar-room, accompanied by 'Contessa Rosa of Milan, Italy' who was to be her second, the girl had discovered that the scrutiny of the all male audience was far more disconcerting than when she was fully and conventionally dressed. She told herself that, due to the drastic way the style of her life had been recently changed, in all probability, if she wanted to survive, this was only the first time she would be compelled to depart from the standards in which she had been raised. Therefore, by forcing herself to remember what was at stake, she had been able to enter the ring at the centre instead of yielding to an inclination to run away.

Once the bout had commenced, Becky had soon forgotten her misgivings. She discovered that her faith in Brackley's character was justified and she realized why Lady Lavinia had been selected to meet her challenge. Although she had gathered some knowledge of holds and throws as a child, having been taught by her father who was a skilful amateur wrestler, she could not have lasted for long by her own endeavours against such an experienced opponent. Almost twice her age, matching her in height and build, with yellowish-red hair styled in a similar fashion, the Englishwoman had whispered instructions which allowed her to escape the first time she had found herself in a grip she had not encountered during her childhood tussles. Helped by her natural agility and fitness, the advice which continued to be given had enabled her to put on an exhibition which the crowd had found enjoyable and believed to be completely genuine.

The end had come when, forgetting she was not in contention against another member of the Troupe, the red head had set into motion a routine they often employed to produce a spectacular finish. Not only had the girl been close to exhaustion and unaware of what to expect, but she was distracted by having seen two men from Surbiton who she had reason to believe were looking for her sitting at a ringside table. Therefore, she had failed to break the fall she had taken with the skill she had displayed up until then. Without realizing the back of her head had struck the padded floor of the ring hard enough to knock her unconscious, Lady Lavinia had doubled her body over at the waist and, lying across her legs, held her pinned against the 'mat'.

When Pulbright had completed the count of three and told the red head to rise, she had done so with the intention of carrying on with her usual display of 'aristocratic' arrogance by supposedly gloating over having attained victory. However, both she and the referee had realized something was wrong when Becky's folded body had straightened involuntarily then continued to sprawl supine, unmoving and with eyes closed. Despite the rigorous bout in which they had engaged and occasional genuine suffering to which she had been subjected due to the inexperience of the girl, Lady Lavinia had been alarmed and very concerned when she realised what must have happened. It had taken all her will power to commence acting in a manner far different from her true inclinations. However, she had restricted herself to stalking back to her corner and donning the cloak handed to her by her second, behaving all the time as if completely disinterested in the fate of her beaten opponent.

Subsequent events had also taken a more serious turn than was intended. The manager of the Troupe of International Lady Wrestlers and Sidney Colkiss had hurriedly left their ringside table and entered the ring. Joining Pulbright and 'Contessa Rosa of Milan, Italy', they had been diverted before they could conduct an examination of the girl. Taking a glance at the hostile response being displayed by the crowd, who had clearly taken Becky to their hearts, Brackley had been aware of the danger. All around the bar-room, men were standing up and indignantly shouting. However, he had encountered a similar situation more than once and knew how best to cope with it. Although he knew doing so would entail neglecting Becky for a short while, he had put the scheme into effect in the interests of avoiding an incident which would bring him into conflict with the local peace officers, and with William Flanagan, the owner of the saloon.

Before any of the spectators could decide to take physical action against the girl's victorious assailant, Brackley had hissed an order to her second. Knowing what was wanted, the Contessa had started screaming abuse in her heavily accented English and dashed across the ring. She was prevented from 'attacking' Lady Lavina by 'Countess Fritzi of Hamburg, Germany', who was equally cognizant with the situation. Leaving the girl where she lay, the three men had crossed to where the pair were locked together in a hair pulling struggle and dragged them apart.

The sight of the altercation between the Contessa and the Countess had served its purpose by holding the attention of the crowd. Nor had it ended with their separation. Following the routine in which both had participated on several occasions during their travels, they had both demanded they be allowed to settle their disagreement without interruption. First making it seem he did not approve, Brackley had allowed himself to be 'persuaded' by the shouted demands from the onlookers that they were allowed to do so. With the promise of a 'grudge' fight between the 'enraged' seconds agreed upon for later in the evening, the spectators had quietened down and returned to their seats.

Taking advantage of the distraction, Doctor Oswald Plunkett—the local medical practitioner selected by Colkiss as most suitable to attend in case there should be any accidents involving the combatants, a precaution which Brackley insisted upon having taken even when there was no local contender likely to cause the need for such attention—had entered the ring to examine the unconscious girl. On being told that it was safe for them to do so, Kolkiss and the Contessa had carried Becky back to the changing room. They had been accompanied by the doctor, who wished to be present when the girl recovered so that he could carry out tests to ensure she was not suffering from any serious effects.

While this was happening, Brackley had declared the Englishwoman the winner of the bout. Due to the prospect of further action being forthcoming shortly, disregarding the fact that it had been promised and would have happened anyway, there was some applause from the audience. Satisfied he had removed the danger of trouble, as Lady Lavinia and her second took their departure, Brackley had requested that 'all gentlemen present' showed their appreciation for a *very* gallant loser by contributing to a collection to be taken in her behalf. Leaving this to Pulbright and the as yet uninvolved female members of the Troupe, who had been watching the bout from the rear of the crowd, he had hurried to the changing room to which the girl had been returned. Watched by the clearly anxious red head, who had bluntly refused a suggestion that she went to take a rest, Becky already had been laid on the table in the centre—its top padded with the clothing of all the occupants—and the doctor was continuing his ministrations. Before she had regained consciousness, 'Duchess Molly of Connemara, Ireland', had brought in the results of the collection. Having delivered it to Brackley, who saw it was a larger sum than usual, she had gathered up her costume and left to change in the other back room for her bout with 'Dona Conchita Alvarez of Madrid, Spain'. Just after the door was closed, much to the relief of Lady Lavinia and the burly, white haired manager, the girl had started to stir and asked the incoherent question.

'Wha—? Why—?' Becky gasped, again trying to rise, and this time, on receipt of a confirmatory nod from the local medical man, she was allowed to sit up supported by Brackley's hand on her back. Shaking her head, which caused it to throb still more, she continued with no greater coherency, 'How—Wha—?'

'How many fingers am I holding up?' the doctor asked, as the girl's words came to an inconclusive halt and he presented his open right hand before her gaze.

'Wh—What?' Becky responded, puzzled by the question.

'Try to tell the doctor, duck!' Lady Lavinia requested in a worried tone, knowing the purpose of the test.

'Three and your thumb,' Becky obliged, making an effort to focus her gaze and thoughts upon supplying the information.

'That's *good*, my dear,' Plunkett said reassuringly. Big, heavily built, prosperous looking and hearty, he exuded an aura of confidence and possessed an ability in his profession which made him liked and respected throughout St. Joseph. Having satisfied himself that the vision of his patient was not impaired, knowing such a fall as had rendered her unconscious occasionally caused a loss of memory, he continued, 'Do you know *who* you are and where you're at?'

'Who I a—?' the girl began. About to give the information, her wits resumed their normal functioning and she recollected enough to warn her against supplying her real name. 'I—I'm "Becky Ingraham".'

'What have you just been doing?'

'Wrestling with Lady Lavinia there.'

'Where do you come from?'

'Bra—*Surbiton*,' Becky began and hurriedly corrected. Then other remembrances of her recent activities flooded back, including the one she realized was in part responsible for the mishap which was causing her present interrogation. Gazing around the room, she asked in a strained voice, 'Where are Shipley and Archer?'

'Who?' the doctor asked.

'Two of—,' the girl commenced, then revised what, just in time, she realized would be information she should not divulge. Mentally cursing herself for having behaved in a way which brought her to their attention, she elaborated truthfully as far as it went, 'They're two men I used to see around Surbiton.'

'Have they followed you here?' Brackley asked, guessing the reason for the alteration.

'Ye—,' Becky started, again preventing herself from completing what she realized was an ill-advised admission. 'I wouldn't say *followed*, but I'm sure they recognized me and I wouldn't want people in Surbiton—!'

'Is she all right, doctor?' Lady Lavinia asked, concluding that the girl was becoming disturbed by the way in which the conversation had developed.

'Well, Your Ladyship,' Plunkett replied, looking at the red head with a twinkle in his eye. Before settling in St. Joseph, he had met enough genuine members of the British upper class to feel sure she did not originate from it. However, he liked what he had seen of her during their short acquaintance and, despite having seen the flaw in the girl's amended comments he accepted the reason for the intervention. 'I don't reckon she's up to taking you for the best of three falls right away, but there's nothing wrong a good night's rest won't put right, even though she'll be—in medical terms—as stiff and sore as hell comes morning.'

'I'm ever so *sorry* we can't have another two falls right off, duck,' Lady Lavinia claimed, beaming in a mixture of relief and delight at the girl. 'In fact, unless it's being run over by a couple of horses and carts with *heavy* loads, there's nothing I'd like better. But, seeing as we can't and unless the doctor says different, what about you and me getting cleaned up and dressed?'

'You've prescribed the very treatment I would advise, Your Ladyship,' Plunkett asserted, noticing Becky had managed a weak smile. Satisfied he was correct in his diagnosis and sure the girl was in good hands, he turned his attention to Brackley. 'Well, Pug, I reckon the bar's done enough business to keep Will Flanagan happy. So how's about you going out and getting the next bout started?'

'*You've* prescribed the very treatment *I* would advise, Doctor,' the manager of the Troupe declared. 'Look after Miss Ingraham, please, Annie, while I get the show going again.' Turning his gaze to the girl, who was now sitting without needing support, albeit still showing signs of suffering and exhaustion, he went on, 'By the way, young lady, I reckon you'll be pleased when you see how much was collected from your supporters out there.'

* * * * * * * *

'Now ain't *this* a piece of *luck*, Milt?'

'Luck *nothing*, Bernie. Seeing's we'd dogged her from the saloon and this ain't where she's staying, I telled you's, happen we waited a spell, she'd come out for us!'

Looking at the speakers as they moved towards her, Becky Ingraham realized she had compounded the error made when she sought out Pug Brackley in her desire to obtain more money for continuing her flight!

After they had collected their clothing, the girl had been taken by Lady Lavinia from the Journey West Saloon to the small boarding house not far away in which the members of the Troupe were staying. On the way, acting upon whispered instructions from her employer, the red head had suggested that Becky joined their party. Despite it being a way of life which, she felt sure, would not have met with her mother's approval, she had considered accepting. However, remembering she had been found by Milton Shipley and Bernard Archer, she had formed such a liking for her companion and the burly retired wrestling champion in particular that she considered it was unfair to let the friendly people of the Troupe become involved any deeper in her *very* serious personal problems.

Instead of refusing outright, or explaining the situation, Becky had promised to think the offer over. Before any more could be said, she was shown and had used the douche bath with which the Troupe had equipped one of the rooming house's outbuildings. Refreshed by the shower of cold water, she had dressed while the red head was taking one. However, she had not waited until Lady Lavinia was finished. Satisfied that the red head and Brackley did not know where to find her, although regretful of behaving in such an ungrateful fashion after all their kindness, she had set out with the intention of returning to her temporary accommodation.

The interruption had come shortly after the girl had passed through the picket fence surrounding the darkened and, except for Lady Lavinia in the outbuilding, what she had been told was the unoccupied boarding house!

While speaking, the men were eyeing Becky with malicious satisfaction!

Wishing there were other people nearby, the girl was staring at them in return!

There was sufficient light from a full moon for the girl to be able carry out her scrutiny with reasonable clarity. The pair struck her as being just as unprepossessing as they always did when she had seen them around Surbiton. Both were tall, lean and had unshaven features which gave an accurate indication of their vicious natures. Clad in cheap and equally grubby riding clothes, each carried a Colt Model of 1849 Pocket Pistol—a five shot revolver in spite of the name—tucked into the waistband of his breeches. Rumour had it they were skilled in handling the weapons, which they were said never to hesitate to use when this was required by a situation.

'Keep away from me!' Becky commanded, convinced the most unsavoury reputation they had acquired was well deserved.

'What'll you do happen we *don't*?' Shipley challenged. 'Rough us up like you done with Bobby Clay 'n' his lil ole loving boy friend that night in the schoolhouse?'

'Mr. Clay wouldn't be any too *pleased* to hear you talk like that about his son,' the girl warned.

'We ain't worried none about *that*!' Archer asserted, darting a grin at his companion and reaching across with his right hand to lay it on the butt of his Colt. ''Cause we don't aim to tell him's we have and *you* won't be able to snitch on us neither, what we've been told to do with you.'

'Don't go a-scaring the gal that ways, Bernie,' Shipley ordered, also fingering his weapon. Although a glance around failed to locate anybody near by, he wanted to avoid causing a commotion which would bring people to investigate and he continued with his attempt to remove any misgivings aroused by the incautious comment of his companion. 'We'n's've been deputized by the town constable to fetch her back to Surbiton to stand trial is all.' His gaze swung to Becky and he went on in what he hoped would be a convincing tone, 'So, happen you don't give us no fuss 'n' come along quiet-like, you'll not get hurt no ways.'

'I don't *believe* you!' Becky stated.

'It don't make no never mind to us'n's whether you do or not,' Archer declared, lacking his companion's grasp of the situation. ''Cause you're *coming* regardless,'

Listening to the remark from the shorter and more uncouth of the pair, and realizing it nullified Shipley's declaration, Becky felt frightened. However, the fear did not prevent her from realizing the ramifications of her predicament. Taken into account with what Archer had said and considering the circumstances, she began to suspect that Robert Clay did not want her returning to stand trial in Surbiton. Instead, he had given them orders to find and kill her.

In spite of the deduction, the girl found herself upon the horns of a dilemma!

On the surface, in view of the supposition, the obvious course was to scream as loudly as possible for help!

Even as the thought came, Becky saw the serious objections to carrying it out!

Should she attract such attention, the girl felt sure Shipley had the means to support his claim of having been deputized by the town constable. Clay possessed sufficient influence in Surbiton to have this done. It might also carry enough weight in St. Joseph to make the local authorities discount her belief that she was to be murdered and not merely taken back to stand trial.

Before Becky could decide what action to take, there was an interruption!

'Are these fellers bothering you, ma'am?' inquired a masculine voice which was also Missourian in timbre, yet less harsh and repelling than the tones of the hard-cases from Surbiton.

Instantly, the girl and the men accosting her swung their attention to where the speaker was striding purposefully from the mouth of a nearby alley!

Something over six foot in height, looking to be in his late 'teens, the newcomer had wide shoulders and a clearly powerful physique. His clean shaven face was good looking, apart from having a somewhat large and curved nose above a short chin. However, these did not give any suggestion of weakness to his expression. Rather his demeanour was one of grim determination. Clad in a wide brimmed and round topped black hat, a collarless white shirt and a not too expensive brown swallow-tail coat, he had the legs of his yellowish-brown Nankeen trousers tucked into knee length black riding boots.

'Get the hell out of here, you duck-bill faced son-of-a-bitch!' Archer snarled, never being of a discerning nature and, ignoring external suggestions to the contrary, drawing the conclusion that the interloper was merely a country dwelling youngster paying a visit to what he regarded as a very large city and seeking to impress the girl with supposed gallantry and courage.

'I asked the lady a question,' the newcomer pointed out, his voice becoming cold and hard as he shoved open his coat to show two Colt Model of 1851 Navy Belt Pistol revolvers carried in a black silk sash about his waist with their butts turned forward. 'And I don't take it kind to be called what you called me.'

More intelligent than his companion, Shipley saw how the latest development could be turned to their advantage. Despite what he had told her, the orders they had received were to kill the girl when they found her. While having no moral scruples against doing so, he possessed a greater awareness than Archer of the dangers involved. Should they be caught in the act, justice would be swift and deadly final. However, as there did not appear to be any witnesses in the vicinity to deny an explanation that they had come to the rescue on seeing the young man molesting the girl and he had shot her before they were able to kill him, the intervention offered solution.

'Sounds like you've got tangled with a tough one here, Bernie,' Shipley commented, deciding to put his conclusions into effect. 'He for sure *talks* that way.'

'Talks easy, Milt,' Archer answered, eyeing the young man in disdain. 'It's doing's counts!'

'Back off, ma'am!' the newcomer said quietly, standing in a seemingly relaxed fashion although the girl sensed he was as tense as a spring under compression.

'Watch out, Milt!' Shipley shouted. 'He's pulling a gun!'

With the excuse supplied, both hard-cases grabbed at the revolvers they wore!

Even though Shipley's declaration was premature, the young man acted upon it with promptitude. Turning palms out, his hands flashed to and wrapped about the butts of the two Colts. Moving with the speed which implied considerable practise, he twisted them from the silk sash. Not until the seven and a half inch octagonal barrels were clear and beginning to turn away from his body did he start to draw back the hammers with his thumbs and slip his forefingers into the triggerguards.[1] Nevertheless, even though the revolvers were longer than those carried by the pair, he was the only one to get off a

[1]*An example of how dangerous a failure it is to take such a precaution when drawing a single action revolver is given in:* THE FAST GUN. *J.T.E.*

shot. What was more, despite the speed with which he was moving, he selected the antagonist who was the more dangerous and acted upon his conclusion.

A sudden appreciation of his peril brought shock to Shipley's face. Instead of concentrating upon Archer as the instigator of the trouble, giving him an opportunity to carry out his scheme no matter what happened to his companion, the young man's gaze was on him. Even as the realization of what this meant came to the taller hard-case, flame ripped from the muzzle of the right hand Navy Colt. Any further thoughts were ended by a .36 calibre round ball of soft lead driving between his eyes and killing him instantly. Twirled around, his hand released the revolver it had just extricated and his body toppled to the ground.

Amazed by the deadly speed his intended victim was showing, Archer could not prevent himself from freezing momentarily. Nor was he allowed to resume his draw. Cocking the discharged Colt deftly, the young man fired the other before the move was completed. In spite of this, the shot proved as effective as its predecessor. Taken in the left breast by a bullet which reached and tore apart his heart, the second hard-case followed his companion and landed lifeless a moment later.

A gasp of horror burst from Becky. Although it was the first time she had seen human beings killed, she neither fainted nor went into hysterics. Nevertheless, she could not prevent herself from turning away. Hearing footsteps approaching, she concluded the attention she had wished to avoid had been attracted. It was with mixed emotions that she saw it was only Lady Lavinia, Brackley and Doctor Plunkett hurrying towards her.

'What's happened?' the retired champion wrestler demanded, skidding to a halt.

'These pair was mean-mouthing and frightening the young lady here,' replied the rescuer, nodding at his victims then swinging his gaze to the girl. 'They tried to throw down on me when I cut in.'

'They didn't show good sense in that,' Plunkett

claimed. 'You're James Butler Hickok from over to La Salle County, Illinois, aren't you?'

'That's me, sir,' confirmed the young man. 'I've been back there visiting with kin 'n' was heading for Kansas again when I saw the lady needed help.'

'Thanks for giving it, sir,' Brackley said, then looked at the girl. 'Are they the pair who you asked about, Miss Ingraham?'

'Yes,' Becky confessed, sensing the burly man wanted to help her.

'Have they been sent to take you back to Surbiton?' Brackley demanded, even though his tone was gentle.

'They *said* they had,' Becky replied. 'But, from remarks they made, I'm sure they really meant to kill me.'

'Why'd they want to do that?' Brackley inquired.

'I *killed* a man there,' the girl explained.

'Did he need killing?' the former wrestler asked, glancing around as there were sounds indicating others were coming to investigate the shooting.

'He was attacking me,' Becky replied. 'But, because of how it happened, Mr. Cla—his father—doesn't want me taken back to stand trial.'

'Here comes the law!' Plunkett put in, seeing badges glinting on the jackets of two armed men among the crowd who were running from between various buildings. Helped by his knowledge of Surbiton's population, he guessed the identity of the seeker after vengeance. Therefore, he was eager to discover what had happened and willing to help her if, as his every instinct suggested, she was speaking the truth. 'Leave me do the talking and go along with what I say.'

3 *YOU'll Never Be Safe* Anywhere *In Missouri*

'Well, we've got *that* cleared up,' Horace 'Pug' Brackley declared, returning to the sittingroom of the boarding house in which he and his Troupe Of International Lady Wrestlers were staying as the only guests. His gaze flickered from the other male and single female occupants as he joined them at the table, continuing, 'And it's all thanks to *you*, Doc.'

'Shucks,' Doctor Oswald Plunkett answered, giving a mock self-depreciatory shrug. 'It was all done by kindness and just *bending* the truth a mite.'

Although only half an hour had passed since the shooting, much had happened!

However, some of the events which had just been concluded had commenced shortly before that!

After Becky Ingraham had received the promised payment for her participation in the bout and had been escorted from the Journey West Saloon by 'Lady Lavinia of Sheffield, England', Brackley had gone in search of the men she had mentioned and of whom he believed she had reason to be afraid. Remembering having noticed her staring in alarm at the pair he now suspected just before she was thrown backwards from the ropes, failing to break her fall correctly, he had been worried when finding they were no longer at the table they had occupied. One of the other spectators at it had told him they left the barroom shortly after she was carried from the ring.

Telling Percy Pulbright and Sidney Colkiss to keep things going in his absence, Brackley had confided his misgivings to the doctor and they had set off to find out whether the girl was in any danger from the pair. Arriving at the outbuilding behind the rooming house and discovering she had already taken her departure, the sound of the shooting had caused the former wrestler and the doctor to go and investigate. They had been accompanied by Lady Lavinia, who was so alarmed on learning why they had come from the saloon while a bout was in progress that she had not waited to don more than her cloak over her underclothes. Having reached the scene of the incident before the two deputies belonging to the town marshal's office, who were also brought there by the shooting, they had learned enough to realize that Becky would almost certainly have need of their help. Although for different reasons, each of the men had been willing to supply it.

Realizing Plunkett was best suited for the task, Brackley and the others had accepted his advice and allowed him to do most of the talking!

It had soon become apparent that the peace officers had sufficient liking and respect for the doctor to allow themselves to be influenced, even guided, by him. Neither had argued when he pointed out that Becky was still not fully recovered from the strenuous bout of wrestling and had just been through a very trying experience and suggested the senior of them left the other with the corpses and questioned her in the privacy of the rooming house.

Before the suggestion could be put into effect, there had been a bad moment for the girl. Learning they were strangers to the man who had killed them, the older deputy had set about trying to discover the identity of her assailants without asking whether she knew them. However, she had had no cause for serious alarm. Despite what Milton Shipley had told her, a search of their pockets had not produced anything to even suggest where they had come from, much less indicate they might have been temporarily appointed to carry out an assignment in behalf of the town constable at Surbiton. Prompted by the doctor, who had pointed out how villainous they looked, the senior peace officer had stated a belief they were a couple of the worst kind of visitors attracted to the town and had paid a well deserved penalty for having tried to force unwanted attentions upon a young 'good' woman.

On arriving in the sitting-room of the boarding house, its owners and all the other occupants being absent for various reasons, Plunkett had continued to do most of the talking.

When discussing the affair later, Brackley frequently claimed it could not have been handled better!

What Plunkett had told the deputy was basically the truth.

The doctor had begun by explaining how the two men had accosted Becky and, when James Butler Hickok came to her assistance, had reacted in such a hostile fashion he was left with no alternative but to kill them. Due to St. Joseph being a major staging point for wagon trains and other kinds of travellers between the East and the Western frontier country, gun fights were sufficiently frequent for members of the town marshal's office to know what to look for when one occurred. As each dead man had completed the drawing of his weapon, even though neither was allowed time to get off a shot, the peace officer had asserted it was his opinion that their killer—who was clearly known to him as well as the doctor[1]—had acted in justifiable self defence.

Furthermore, on raising the question of her presence, the deputy had accepted Plunkett's explanation that Becky had come to St. Joseph on vacation from an unspecified town elsewhere in Missouri and belonged to a good family. They would, the doctor had elaborated, suffer considerable embarrassment should it become known to the other members of their community that she

[1] *Although James Butler Hickok had not at the time of this narrative acquired the sobriquet, 'Wild Bill', he had already started to make his name known as a competent gun fighter in Illinois, Missouri and Kansas. Some details of his later career are given in*, Part One, 'The Scout', UNDER THE STARS AND BARS *and* Part Seven, 'Deadwood, August the 2nd, 1876', J.T.'S HUNDREDTH. *He also makes a brief 'guest' appearance in*, Part Six, 'Eggars Try', THE TOWN TAMERS.

had succumbed to an impulsive whim and engaged in a wrestling bout at a saloon; which, in turn, had resulted in her inadvertantly becoming involved in the shooting.

Such was the trust in which Plunkett was held by the lawman, his version of the facts was accepted. Becky had not even been asked for her name and address. Instead, drawing the required conclusions from the doctor's suggestion of influential connections who would not wish for her to be connected with a killing under such circumstances as apparently prevailed, the deputy had promised he would put in a report which would preclude her from needing to appear at any 'hearing' held on the matter. Then, ascertaining that Hickok would be remaining in St. Joseph for a few days, and where, he had taken his departure.

After the peace officer left, responding to a hint from Plunkett, Lady Lavinia had offered to take Becky's rescuer to the Journey West Saloon where they would be in time to see the final bout of the evening and was accepted. As soon as she had changed into suitable attire, she and Hickok had taken their departure. Asking the girl to wait, in a manner which warned she must do so, Brackley had seen them off the premises. Coming back into the sitting-room, despite the apparently light-hearted comments which had passed between him and the doctor, Becky had known there was something much more serious to come.

The supposition was quickly proven correct!

'Thank you both for all you've done,' Becky said, looking from one man to the other.

'You're welcome,' Plunkett replied, from the chair he was occupying at the table opposite where the girl was seated. Then, his manner changing subtly to imply he was getting down to important business, he continued, 'Now Pug and I want to know *all* about you.'

'Yes, "Miss Ingraham",' Brackley supported, the way in which he said the name indicating he knew it was an alias. 'We do.'

'You have to understand *our* position,' the doctor continued, his manner gentle. 'We've saved you from being asked some questions I'm sure you'd rather *not* have answered. Which could prove embarrassing, to say the *least* for us. Which being, we want to know exactly what kind of trouble you're in. That way, we'll not only know where we stand, but can figure out how much more help you're likely to need.'

'I'm *very* grateful for all you've done already,' the girl stated. 'But I'd rather you didn't take the chance of doing anything more.'

'I don't know about Pug,' Plunkett asserted. 'But I don't like Robert Clay—!'

'You know *him*?' Becky gasped.

'We've met and I don't like him, or anything he and his liber-radical soft-shell bunch stand for,' the doctor declared, remembering the hurriedly changed reference which the girl had made about the man in question before the deputies came on the scene. 'And, as he's mixed in this from what you've said so far, I'm willing to take cards myself. So tell us about *everything* else, then we'll decide whether we need to know your *real* name.'

'Very well,' the girl assented, accepting she owed the two men an explanation. What was more, knowing the affair was far from over even if the local peace officers did not take it any further as far as she was concerned, she felt sure they would give her sound advice should she be frank with them. 'Firstly, as you've guessed, my name *isn't* Becky Ingraham—.'

'And, like Doc told you,' Brackley interrupted. 'We'll let you know if we want to be told who you really are. There's one thing I would like to know, though.'

'What is it?'

'Who taught you how to wrestle the way you can?'

'My poppa,' Becky replied. 'I told you I was a tomboy as a child. Well, he was a good wrestler and, as momma couldn't give him the son he wanted, he taught me some of his tricks.'

'You learned good,' Brackley praised.

'That's what brought me here,' the girl answered and shuddered at the recollection aroused by the words.

Sucking in a deep breath, she went on, 'I grew up in the back country near—!'

'Don't tell us *anything* that could help me to find out things about you I'd rather not know,' Plunkett requested. 'That way, I won't be able to give you away should I be asked.'

'As you wish, sir,' Becky accepted. 'Well, although I grew up and ran a mite wild in the country, momma managed to force enough book-learning on me so I could get work as a schoolteacher in Surbiton after she and poppa were killed in a bad storm. Hoping you don't think I'm bragging, but I was pretty good at it. After the children found out I hadn't forgotten what I learned from poppa, we got on just fine and I decided this was the kind of life I wanted to lead. Then Vernon Clay came back from college in the East and brought a friend with him. With his father's help, they were both hired as teachers.'

'Robert Clay's got a whole heap of say around there,' the doctor informed Brackley, as the girl paused, then swung his gaze back to her. 'Although I'd have thought he'd have wanted something better for his boy than teaching in a small place like Surbiton.'

'Could be that's the best he figured the boy was capable of?' the former wrestler suggested.

'Could be,' Plunkett conceded, thinking the conclusion was probably correct. 'No matter why, though, he'd only have to pass the word for them to be taken on and they would be.'

'Yes!' the girl said shortly.

'I get the feeling you didn't reckon they was much shucks as teachers, Miss Ingraham,' Brackley remarked, eager to hear the rest of the story.

'I *didn't*,' Becky confirmed vehemently. 'And it wasn't just because they took a dislike to me from the start. I didn't like the way they went about their teaching. Instead of giving their classes the lessons they were supposed to be, they spent their time talking about how wrong it is for some folks to be rich and others poor, or explaining about Abolition and how bad rotten *all* Southrons are for opposing it.'

'I've heard their kind!' Plunkett rumbled, his face taking on grim and bitter lines. 'Good damn it, Pug, they always use the same kind of talk to try and get the poor folks ready to vote their way and, figuring it'll serve their ends, they won't rest until they've stirred up real bad trouble between the North and the South.'

'I can see it coming like you do,' Brackley replied, in an equally sombre fashion. 'And, when it blows up, folks favouring both sides in Missouri and Kansas'll be the first to get to shooting. That's why I'm taking the Troupe down through Arkansas to Texas. I don't hold with slavery, but I'm a Southron and that'll make the girls likely to be picked on by Abolitionists as well as me if we stay north of the Mason-Dixon line.'

'It will,' the doctor conceded. 'Like the soft-shells, there's getting some real bad scum taking up as Abolitionists for what they figure'll come their way out of it. Anyways, Miss Ingraham, was it what they was teaching what stirred up the fuss between you and young Clay?'

'Not directly,' Becky replied. 'Like I said, the two of them took a dislike to me right from the start, but that didn't bother me. What caused the trouble was—well, how he and his friend tried to treat two boys. I was going by the school-house late one afternoon and saw the side door was open, so went to shut it. Then I heard voices and, as there shouldn't have been anybody inside, went to find out who it was—!'

'Go on!' Plunkett encouraged gently.

'Vernon Clay and his friend had two of the older boys bent across desks,' the girl obliged, moving restlessly on her chair and showing distaste at the disclosure she was making. 'With their trousers down—!'

'I've heard tell schoolteachers having that done when they're figuring on using a switch to punish misbehaving,' the doctor remarked, as the explanation trailed to an end once more.

'It *wasn't* a switch they were meaning to use,' Becky corrected, her face reddening in a blush. Gesturing in the appropriate direction, she went on hesitantly, 'They had the front of their trousers unfastened and—!'

'I can *guess*!' Plunkett growled, having suspected what was taking place in the classroom despite his previous comment. 'A lot of soft-shells are so inclined. What happened then?'

'I went in and told the boys to haul up their trousers and go home,' the girl explained, keeping her head lowered so she did not have to meet the gaze of her audience. 'Which they right quickly did. After they'd gone, Vernon Clay started yelling like a crazy man that he was going to teach me not to interfere in his affairs and came at me. The look on his face frightened me, so I ducked my head and charged him in the chest. It send him backwards over a desk and his friend ran across to look at him, then shouted his neck was broken and I'd killed him.'

'Was it broken?' the doctor asked.

'I didn't look,' Becky replied. 'But he had fallen heavily and, hearing what his friend said, I just turned and ran.'

'What did the constable say when you told him how it happened?' Plunkett inquired, although he could guess the answer.

'I didn't wait to see him,' the girl admitted. 'He's Robert Clay's man, body and soul. Which being, I knew he wouldn't believe *anything* I said. And I also could imagine what chance I would have of being given a fair hearing if I was brought to trial for the killing, so I decided my only hope was to get away before I could be arrested. Luckily, I enjoy riding and kept a horse at the livery stable. So I bundled up some of my clothes, the month's pay which I'd collected that afternoon and the other money I had in my room, went and got him and started running. When I got to—!'

'No names of towns!' the doctor reminded.

'A *nearby* town,' Becky amended, 'I went in on foot and bought a boy's hat, jacket, shirt, pants and boots. Dressed that way, I managed to pass without attracting too much attention until I arrived here in St. Jo. On the way, I'd decided to try to get on a wagon train heading West. Knowing I'd need extra money, I sold the horse and—Well, you know the rest.'

'Not *all* of it,' Brackley denied. 'Or didn't Annie—Lady Lavinia—tell you I'd like to have you join the Troupe?'

'She did,' the girl confirmed, managing a weak smile. 'And she told me her real name is Annie Tolcher.'

'And you weren't interested?'

'I was, but I didn't think it would be fair to you if I did after having been seen by Shipley and Archer.'

'Why not?'

'They work for Mr. Clay—!' Becky commenced.

'So you've told us,' Brackley replied. 'I didn't meet him when the Troupe was in Surbiton.'

'Then you probably don't know him, but I *do*.' Becky countered. 'And, going by all I heard about him after I went to live in Surbiton, I felt sure he'd want me arrested for what I did to his son. But, unless I'm *wrong*, he wants more than just *that*!'

'How do you mean?' Plunkett asked, remembering other comments the girl had made suggesting much the same.

'From what they said,' Becky explained. 'Although Shipley tried to make me believe they'd been deputized by the constable to take me back, I think they'd really been told to *kill* me when they found me.'

'You *could* be right,' Brackley admitted. 'I don't reckon he'd want what you caught his son doing being told in even the Surbiton courthouse.'

'That's for sure,' the doctor agreed, then he frowned. 'How long ago did it happen?'

'Twelve days,' Becky replied.

'Twelve days, huh?' Plunkett said, thinking of the distance to Surbiton. 'It wouldn't take you that long to get here. Did you go to try to get help from your kinfolks?'

'No, I don't have any in Missouri and I didn't want to get any of momma and poppa's friends mixed up in it,' the girl answered. 'It took me so long because I didn't come here direct, but used a roundabout route to try to throw off whoever was sent after me. I arrived last night.'

'That's strange,' Plunkett commented, seeming to be

addressing the remark more to himself than the other two.

'What is, Doc?' Brackley inquired.

'No word's reached St. Jo about young Clay being killed,' the doctor explained. 'And, his father being such a coming man in the State, even if it wasn't given out how he died, I'd expect to have read he was dead in the newspaper.'

'So would I,' the former wrestler supported, remembering how he had discounted the possibility of the girl being a fugitive from justice as he had not heard of a crime of any significance in which she might have been involved. Then he realized what could be implied by his companion also lacking information. 'You mean he might not be *dead*, but was only knocked out and his friend said he'd broken his neck to scare Miss Ingraham off?'

'It's possible,' Plunkett pointed out.

'Then why would Clay send those two fellers after her?'

'I told you, he's a coming man politically. Having it known that his son got up to bug—such games could lose him a helluva lot of support and might even ruin his career. So the last thing he wants is to have a witness around who saw it.'

'Then I might not have killed him after all?' Becky gasped.

'Like I said,' Plunkett replied. 'It's *possible*.'

'Then why would his father have sent Shipley and Archer after me?' the girl asked. 'If you're right in what you think, the last thing he would want is for me to be fetched back.'

'According to you, they hadn't been sent to take you back,' the doctor reminded. 'He not only doesn't want you there, you know too much for him to even want you left alive.'

'What Doc's saying makes good sense to me,' Brackley declared. 'Which means you'll never be safe *anywhere* in Missouri. Do you have kin some other place you can go to?'

'I've an aunt somewhere in Texas,' the girl replied. 'But I've no idea where exactly.'

'We're headed for Texas,' the former wrestler stated. 'So why don't you come along with me and the Troupe?'

Once again, the girl found herself considering the good points of the offer. Not only would she be supplied with transportation and companionship while continuing to travel, but she was convinced accepting would prove financially beneficial. Before leaving the saloon, she had been given her share of the collection taken whilst she was unconscious. Although she was informed that the full amount was to be divided amongst all the wrestlers, as would the result of similar collections after each other bout, the sum had been higher than the twenty dollars quoted by Brackley on their first meeting. Furthermore, regardless of the considerable exertion and suffering which engaging in the bout had entailed, she had found the appreciation she earned from the spectators most stimulating and satisfying.

However, Becky also remembered her reason for deciding to decline the first time the offer was made and felt it was still valid!

'I still don't like the idea of getting you mixed up in my troubles,' the girl objected. 'Robert Clay isn't a man to forgive and forget. He's going to keep having me hunted.'

'With his hired men dead, it'll be two or three days at the soonest before he finds out what happened,' Plunkett countered, realizing Brackley had offered a good solution to the problem. Much as he admired the girl for the way in which she had handled what must have been a most trying situation, he knew she would have a far better chance of continued survival if she accepted the offer. 'You'll be heading for Arkansas by the time he can get anybody else on your trail and I'll do all I can to steer them off the wrong way by claiming you've gone West.'

'But that will get Mr. Clay angry at *you*!' Becky pointed out.

'I reckon I've got enough friends around and about for him to think more than twice about making fuss for me,' the doctor answered, exuding confidence. 'And if you'll be ruled by me, Miss Ingraham, you'll go along with Pug and the Troupe. They're all good folks and they'll stand by you no matter who Clay sends and might catch up with you.'

'You can count on *that*!' Brackley asserted, his liking for the girl having increased as he listened to how competently she had behaved in the terrifying state of affairs with which she had been confronted. 'Come with us and, even if you can't find your aunt in Texas, by the time you get there you'll have saved enough money to take you well beyond Clay's reach if you're so minded.'

'Very well,' Becky assented, after turning the matter over in her mind for a few seconds and concluding she was being given a chance which was unlikely to be bettered. 'You've got yourself another wrestler, Mr. Brackley.' Seeing the glances of relief and satisfaction passed between the men, she managed to put a more light-hearted timbre into her voice and went on, 'What am I going to be, a Duchess, Countess, or Lady?'

4 *Indians!*

There was no sign of anybody other than the three male and all but one female members of the International Troupe Of Lady Wrestlers in the vicinity of the clearing by the banks of a stream on which they had made camp the previous night. Nevertheless, an arrow came from amongst the fairly dense fringe of flowering dogwood bushes and buried itself almost fletching deep in the massive chest of Horace 'Pug' Brackley. The hoarse cry of pain which burst from him as he was spun around was echoed by other noises.

On seeing what had happened from the opposite side of the trail, Becky Ingraham coming to a halt at the edge of the undergrowth in which she had been answering the call of nature, concluded that certain suspicions she had had were being confirmed in no uncertain fashion!

Almost two years had passed since the events of the night in St. Joseph, Missouri, which had resulted in the girl joining the Troupe!

Despite it being a way of life *far* different from anything Becky had known previously, she had never regretted the decision!

As the girl had expected, there had been more to the work than just appearing in the wrestling bouts!

Although Brackley always had arrangements made for them to stay in rooms at a boarding house when they were appearing in a town, the Troupe travelled from place to place in their own transportation. The two wagons used by them were the type known as 'prairie schooners'. Designed to carry a maximum load of around two thousand, five hundred pounds, with tyres not more than two to three inches in width, they were somewhat smaller than the massive Conestogas used by companies engaged in hauling bulk freight. Nevertheless, each was constructed with sufficient dimensions to carry their personal belongings and the necessary equipment for the bouts.

Regardless of the weather when travelling, which anyway grew milder the further the Troupe had moved southwards, their living conditions on the trail were not as bad as might have been expected. In addition to providing adequate mobile accommodation for the party, the white canvas canopies which helped to create the popular name for the vehicle offered a good measure of protection against inclement elements. Being built for the purpose, guided by the knowledge of the essential requirements acquired by the makers, such wagons were ideally suited to the needs of people travelling across the often considerable distances over roads which were generally poor—often being comprised of little more than the wheel tracks of previous users—between towns west of the Mississippi River.

Everybody was expected to lend a hand with the various chores of their nomadic existence. These had included repairing damage to their costumes, taking care of the horses which pulled their wagons, maintaining the vehicles, cooking meals when travelling and helping to erect the ring wherever the bouts were to take place.

Being of an adaptable, friendly nature and showing she was willing to take her full share of the work, the girl had had no difficulty in gaining the acceptance and friendship of her travelling companions. She had been taken under the wing of Annie 'Lady Lavinia of Sheffield, England' Tolcher, but all the others were equally amicable. On learning she had been a schoolteacher, far from resenting her superior education, the women had been willing to make use of it. She had often been asked to read what was said about the bouts in local newspapers, sometimes having to act as pacifier of ruffled tempers when the comments were less than flattering or even adverse. Another task which earned friendship and approbation had been, without flouting her superior education, to write letters for those who could not to their respective kinfolk. Ever willing to exercise her mind, she had passed more of her leisure time in trying to increase her knowledge by learning their languages. Of them all, she had become most proficient in the lessons she received in return for improving the English spoken by 'Dona Conchita Alvarez of Madrid, Spain'.

The time was to come when the knowledge of Spanish acquired by Becky was to be *very* helpful!

From the beginning of their association, in spite of her concern over the possibility of her affairs bringing danger to her companions, Becky had been determined to repay Brackley for his kindness by becoming a worthwhile member of the Troupe!

The desire had been fulfilled!

Possessing excellent physical health and helped by her unconventional childhood training, Becky had quickly learned to employ all the 'tricks of the trade' and developed a few of her own. Not only had she been a regular participant in the rehearsed and, to a certain extent, staged bouts with the other members—generally posing as an unconnected challenger rather than a supposed scion of the European aristocracy—but it was not long before she was considered good enough to take her turn at meeting some of the genuine local contenders to come their way. In spite of the lack of skill possessed by such opponents, or rather because of it, these events often developed into serious and violent fights. However, she had found she was able to cope with such events. Like her companions, she had the advantage of more skill acquired by constant training, and greater physical fitness due to the daily routine of exercises Brackley insisted upon being carried out. As the genuine challengers either lacked these qualities, or possessed them to a lesser extent, she had always emerged victorious.

Even when suffering the after-effects of having taken on an aggressive local challenger, which were invariably more severe than those acquired in contention against the other members of the troupe, the girl had considered time was passing in a satisfying and far from unenjoyable fashion!

Nor had the threat which Becky feared arisen!

Much to the girl's relief, as time passed following her departure from St. Joseph, no further pursuers sent by Robert Clay had put in an appearance. Nor had another eventuality she envisaged occurred. When the successors of Milton Shipley and Bernard Archer reported failure to produce the desired result, knowing him to be vicious and vindictive, she had thought he was unlikely to give up his desire to have her silenced. Instead of continuing to rely upon local and unofficial means to bring this about, which were costly and proving ineffectual, he might enlist properly appointed law enforcement officers to the task of locating and capturing her, with the intention of ensuring she did not live long enough to reach Surbiton for trial.

On Becky having confided her supposition with Brackley, he had said he did not believe there was any cause for concern. Even if there should be a warrant for her arrest issued by the local constable at Clay's instigation, she would be moving further away during the time which would elapse while it was being circulated to other law enforcement agencies. Furthermore, once the Troupe entered Arkansas—because of a general disinclination towards co-operation, due to the peace officers in each State being comprised of supporters of the 'North' and 'South' in the continually worsening political situation—she would have little to fear from a warrant originating in Missouri.

Either the assumption had proven to be the case, or—as he had promised—Doctor Oswald Plunkett had been successful in throwing any hired seekers after vengeance off her trail so effectively that Clay had concluded there was no longer any way of having the cause of his animosity located and killed!

Whichever the reason, the girl was not subjected to any further attempts at revenge!

By the time the Troupe had reached Texas, Becky was a competent and popular performer. Although she had made a few inquiries about the aunt she believed to be living in the State, she was not distressed when these produced no results. Instead, despite having become convinced she was no longer being hunted by the law or Clay's hirelings, she had been pleased to have a reason for staying with her friends. Not only did she find their company congenial and the acclaim she received when in the ring most gratifying, it was also a more profitable way of making a living than being a schoolteacher. In addition to providing excellent entertainment, being a novelty, they had drawn good crowds everywhere they went and the collections 'for the gallant loser' were well supported. Brackley was a generous employer and, as she had few expenses to meet, she was building up a useful nest-egg against the day when she decided to settle down in a more conventional employment.

Following most lucrative appearances in several North Texas' towns, the Troupe were on the trail to Fort Worth; where they had been assured that equally enthusiastic and generous audiences would be found. They were travelling alone, but this had generally been the case and none of them were unduly worried by the lack of company. Ever watchful for their welfare, Brackley had asked the marshal of the last town they had visited about the dangers they might encounter. He had been informed that, being a well armed party, they should not run into any difficulties. There were outlaws, but these preferred easier prospects than a group of people obviously well able to take care of themselves. Raising the matter of another possible threat, he was assured that—due to the punitive activities of the United States' Cavalry and the Texas Rangers—there had been no Indians along the route they would be following for at least five years.

Having covered about half of the distance to their next destination and halted the previous evening at a spot much used by travellers along the trail, the Troupe had been preparing to continue the journey. While Lady Lavinia was helping the men to hitch up the four-horse teams, the rest of the woman had been doing the other work involved in breaking camp. On completing her chores, Becky had crossed the trail to relieve herself in the bushes at the other side.

As usual when the Troupe were not accompanied by other people and were travelling during the appropriate climatic conditions, the girl was clad in the same general fashion as her female companions. Although none of them would have thought of dressing that way when other people were present, it was utilitarian attire for wearing in pleasant weather and well suited to the needs of an active life, but also flattering to each figure and appearance.

Apart from her footwear, Becky's clothing comprised of only three garments. A snugly fitting cheap white cotton blouse with its neck unfastened and sleeves rolled up was all that covered her torso. To offer extra mobility and let it be easily removed or donned, her skirt was improvised from a length of black material. It was wrapped around and fastened at her waist. Below, its sides overlapped so that decorum was retained even though an unconnected flap was formed at the front. Beneath it, she had on a pair of the black tights and cloth sandals she wore when in the ring.

Even before she had set off into the undergrowth, Becky's instincts had suggested something was wrong. While she was drawing up the tights and fastening the waistband of the skirt about her midriff, having been born and grown up in the country, although further north and east than her present location, she had realized what she felt to be amiss. Being so soon after sunrise on a bright and warm late spring morning, she would have expected the surrounding woodland to be ringing with the calls of birds. However, while she could hear some singing in the distance, everything was silent in the immediate vicinity. What was more, despite having failed to obtain any visual verification, she had had the feeling of being watched while starting back towards the trail.

The arrow which struck Brackley and what happened next indicated beyond any shadow of a doubt to Becky that her misgivings were justified!

Before any of the party near the wagons could recover from the surprise caused by seeing their manager struck in such a fashion, several Indians burst into view from amongst the bushes flanking two sides of the clearing. Anybody better versed in such matters than were the members of the Troupe would have known from the style and decorations of their attire that they were Kiowas. All were wearing war paint and, although none were carrying firearms, they held more primitive—albeit, equally effective in their hands—weapons of various other kinds. Giving whoops intended to frighten their proposed victims into immobility, making the counting of coups easier, they charged towards the white people.

'*Indians*!' screeched Dona Conchita, an avid reader of sensational literature whether in newspapers or the more lurid cheap 'blood and thunder' fiction of the day, turning from where she had been about to pour the remains from the coffeepot on to the dying campfire.

'*Sauvages dangereux*!' 'Vicomtesse Fifi *de* Versailles, France' screamed in the same breath, always more ready than the others to revert to her native tongue in moments of stress, letting fall the two bed rolls she was carrying towards the wagons.

'Holy, Mother of God!' echoed 'Duchess Molly of Connemara, Ireland', dropping the large wooden box filled with cooking utensils she was carrying.

Regardless of the shock they too had received, the rest of the group in the clearing did not react vocally!

However, to give them their due, even the three who spoke recovered from the frightening surprise quickly enough to respond before they could be reached by their attackers.

The next few minutes were filled with violent and confused action!

Nor were the casualties restricted to the white people!

In fact, the attack was far from being the unopposed massacre—apart from such of the women taken alive for the pleasure of the braves before being killed—which the raiding party was anticipating!

Since leaving St. Joseph, following the example of Brackley—who was prevented from making use of his—Percy Pulbright and Sidney Colkiss had taken to carrying a Colt Model of 1851 Navy Belt Pistol revolver readily accessible on their persons at all times. Originally these had been intended mainly for the protection of Becky should she be found by Clay's men, but they had continued to be worn as the terrain being traversed had become increasingly more sparsely populated. Although neither man could have laid claim to being the equal of James Butler Hickok, they had practised enough to possess some skill in handling the weapons.

Unlike their male companions, none of the female members of the party were carrying weapons. Although two of them sought to rectify the situation by arming themselves, the rest in the clearing were compelled to rely upon their bare hands to try to fight off their attackers. This did not mean any proved to be a helpless victim. They were, after all, well trained in defending themselves with bare hands and started to put their knowledge into effect instead of merely surrendering to their fate.

Colkiss was able to draw and fire, taking the nearest of the charging braves in the body, but he learned too late the weakness of the revolver he was holding. Unlike the much more powerful Colt Dragoon Model of 1848 revolver he had declined to buy in St. Joseph because of its size and weight, the Navy Belt Pistol discharged a .36 ball with a powder charge which was too light to generate the great stopping power of its .44 calibre contemporary from 'Colonel Sam's' Patent Arms Manufacturing Company in Hartford, Connecticut.[1] Therefore, instead of going

[1] *Although Samuel Colt—whose honorific arose from his having been appointed a Colonel of State Militia by the Governor of Connecticut—commenced production of his firearms at Paterson, New Jersey, he transferred operations first to the Whitneyville Armoury, Hamden, near New Haven, in the same State and then to Hartford, Connecticut, where the company is still in operation. J.T.E.*

down, his assailant was able to keep coming.

The largest of the International Lady Wrestlers, whose blonde hair and Teutonic appearance gave some credit to her title, 'Countess Fritzi von Hamburg, Germany', was one who had no weapons. Nor was she holding anything which could be improvised as such. Accepting the situation and leaping forward with the kind of yell she gave when launching an attack upon an opponent in the ring, she felled the brave closest to her with a blow to the chin from her clenched right fist. All her weight and power was behind it. Combined with his forward impetus, the impact was sufficiently enhanced to seriously damage her hand. Nevertheless, breaking his jaw and snapping his head to the rear, the blow flung him unconscious to the ground. Unfortunately, she only gained herself a very brief respite. A moment later, before she could continue her defence, her skull was crushed by another Kiowa wielding a war club.

Slower than the Troupe's advance man, who would have gone on ahead to make arrangements for their appearance when nearer to their destination, Pulbright had not quite got the revolver clear of his waistband when he saw a brave thrusting his way with a war lance. Instantly, his instincts as a fist fighter took over. Releasing the Colt, his right hand deflected the spear-shaped head of the weapon and his left lashed across with a blow to the side of his attacker's head. However, as the Kiowa went reeling aside without dropping the lance, an arrow sent by the man who killed Brackley ploughed through his throat. Sent in a twirling stagger, dropping his revolver and clutching involuntarily at the shaft protruding from his flesh, he collapsed coughing his life away.

Instead of using the coffee to help douse the fire, a precaution which none of the party ever failed to take when breaking camp, Dona Conchita flung it into the face of the brave closest to her. A howl of pain burst from him as the still hot liquid flooded over his features and into his eyes. Hurling the metal pot after its contents, she darted over and snatched up a razor sharp butcher's knife from amongst the utensils dropped by Duchess Molly. Putting it to use in the way she had learned as a child in the less than salubrious district of New Orleans where she had grown up, she inflicted a mortal injury upon the brave who had come to a stop and was aiming a bow and arrow at Duchess Molly. Even as she did so, a tomahawk was sunk into her back and she sprawled face down on the grass.

The warrior shot by Colkiss was filled with eagerness to gain the acclaim of counting coup by personal contact before any of his companions, such a feat always being more highly regarded than when acquired as a result of a weapon striking a mortal blow from a distance. He was also given encouragement by still feeling the stimulation derived as a result of drinking some of the 'rotgut' trade whiskey they had purchased from a white renegade and which had inspired the raid. Despite receiving what proved to be a fatal injury, the lead did not hit any vital organ capable of causing instant death. In fact, he hardly felt it in his aroused state of mind and was not even slowed down. Reaching his intended victim before another shot could be fired, although bleeding to death internally, he swung his tomahawk with deadly effect.

Tall and slender, yet strong as whipcord and agile to boot, Vicomtesse Fifi elected to employ the skill at *savate* she had acquired and which was her specialized style in the ring. She was successful in kicking aside her first assailant. However, as she was trying to deal with the second in a similar fashion, the one she had already attacked spun around and flung a tomahawk which buried into her side. Stumbling with fingers trying to extract it, she was struck down by the second man.

Having failed to acquire the requisite skill needed to thumb back the hammer of the Colt quickly, Colkiss might have fared better if he had duplicated Pulbright's reliance upon bare handed fighting skill. As it was, while he was still fumbling in his attempt to perform the vitally necessary function required by the single action mechanism, the blade of the more primitive weapon buried deep into his uncovered head and toppled him lifeless at the feet of his assailant.

Despite having been on the closest and most intimate terms with Brackley of all the Troupe, Lady Lavinia did not allow her feelings for him to slow down her reaction to the sight of his fate. Rather it gave an added inducement for her to move with rapidity. Making for the wagon which she and he shared with half of the Troupe, she was reaching for the double barreled ten gauge shotgun on the driver's seat when a brave leapt on the box from the opposite side. Snatching up the weapon before he could do so, she was starting to cock the hammers as he sprang at her. Lacking the time to complete the necessary action, she stepped aside and, caused to miss her, he collided with a second Kiowa who was rushing her way from the other direction.

Moving with all the speed she was capable of, which—as was the case with all the buxom Lady Wrestlers—was far from sluggish, Duchess Molly leapt to where a muzzle loading rifle was leaning against the side of the wagon used as mobile accommodation by herself and the other half of the Troupe. Catching it up, having learned how to handle one as a girl in Kentucky, she hauled back the hammer while swivelling around. There was no time for her to raise it and take aim. Nevertheless, unaware that she had been saved from a Kiowa bowman by Dona Conchita, she fired from waist level and managed, by instinctive alignment, to send the bullet into the side of the brave kicked towards her by the Frenchwoman. Although she inflicted a mortal wound, it was just too late to prevent him throwing his tomahawk and killing Vicomtesse Fifi.

Spinning around, the red head saw what she had caused to happen and appreciated the chance she was being offered. Realizing she would not be able to bring the heavy weapon to shoulder level, aware of its potential, she also knew there was no need. Elevating the muzzles, she squeezed the forward trigger. Flame erupted from the right side barrel in the wake of the lethal load of lead shot. Engulfed by the nine .32 calibre buckshot balls, which had barely started to spread, neither Indian survived. Already staggering from the collision, they were thrown onwards helplessly.

Having been on the point of dousing the fire with the water used for washing the breakfast utensils, 'Contessa Rosa of Milan, Italy', hurled it and its container at the brave making for her. Before he could recover from this, she followed it up with a powerful kick to the most vulnerable portion of the masculine anatomy and toppled him in a writhing heap on the ground. Sent her way by Pulbright's blow, the warrior armed with the lance drove it into her back before she could take any further action. However, he was not allowed to feel more than a momentary elation over his action. Realizing what he was intending while firing at the pair, Lady Lavinia was unable to use the second charge from the shotgun quickly enough to stop him. While the buckshot balls divided sufficiently to strike the man and break the shaft of the lance, they arrived too late to prevent him from driving its head between the Italian woman's shoulder blades with such force it emerged from between her breasts.

Aware there would be no time to reload, Duchess Molly swung the barrel of the weapon in a sweeping arc at the Kiowa who was closing in upon her. Although he was knocked aside by the blow, another warrior laid open her stomach with a raking slash from a tomahawk. As she was going down, a similar weapon was thrown to sink into the red head's back and bring to an end all resistance in the clearing.

It less than five minutes from the release of the first arrow, with one exception, Pug Brackley's International Troupe Of Lady Wrestlers had ceased to exist!

However, the Indians responsible had not achieved their purpose without loss to themselves!

5 *Die, White Bitch!*

Staring horrified at what was happening in the clearing, Becky Ingraham was torn between two conflicting emotions. Incensed by rage at the sight of first Horace 'Pug' Brackley then other members of the International Troupe Of Lady Wrestlers being struck down, part of her wanted to dash across the trail and do everything she could to help fight off the attacking Indians. Countering the desire was the inborn trait of sturdy common sense which had guided her when faced with the possibility of suffering the consequences of having protected herself so effectively against Robert Clay's son in far off Surbiton, Missouri. This warned there was little she could do, being unarmed, so to go across would avail her friends nothing and bring about her own death. Nevertheless, being a person of strong loyalties, she found it difficult to accept such a practical and sensible point of view.

Before she could reach a decision, the matter was taken out of the girl's hands in no uncertain fashion!

Despite the commotion in the clearing, a rustling sound from the bushes close behind her came to Becky's ears!

Swinging around, the girl discovered she had been correct in her belief that she was under observation!

* * * * * * * *

Despite the high hopes with which they had set out and the boasting of anticipated successes, after having been out for fifteen days, dissension had arisen amongst the fifteen Kiowa warriors who formed the war party. In fact, some of them had begun to question the wisdom of making the raid into territory left untouched for a long time because of the speed with which white retribution was delivered against previous expeditions. For one thing, regardless of the promises made by their self appointed leader, Plenty Coups, their travels had been practically non-productive until the previous evening when scout had returned to report locating two wagons.

The news could not have been better timed as far as the leader of the party was concerned. There were several amongst the braves who had begun to suggest the enterprise was not looked upon favourably by the Great Spirit and he was badly in need of something to reinstate his claim to having divine support for suggesting it be carried out. For one thing, the supply of 'fire water' obtained by Plenty Coups,[1] which had been used as a major inducement to persuade the others to accompany him and had ensured his leadership was accepted, was almost all gone. Even while he still had some of the liquor left, there had been another cause of discontent. The sole success so far attained had benefited only three of the warriors. Finding a Comanche woman alone while scouting ahead on the sixth day, they had raped and killed her instead of bringing her alive to be shared with the rest of the party.

Such had been the resentment of the leader over what he had regarded as a deliberate flouting of his authority that, when giving his instructions for the attack upon the white people, he had told the fortunate trio they must cross the trail and make their approach through the woods on the opposite side to the wagons. Also still incensed at having been excluded from the pleasures described at length—if less than tactfully—by the participators in the rape, the rest of the party had given support for the decision. Therefore, despite knowing they were selected to reduce their chances of counting coup or getting an early choice of the loot, the three had grudgingly concurred. While their companions were taking up positions closer to the intended victims, they were making their way there by a much longer route.

[1] *The name 'Plenty Coups' was given by many Indian nations to warriors who had been successful on the war trail. J.T.E.*

Filled with a sense of grievance against their leader, Long Wolf and Steals Food had come into sight of a white girl as she was concluding her reason for being in the woodland. Watching as she adjusted her attire, they had found the appearance she presented most attractive. A glance around had suggested their companion, Chases Antelope, was not close enough to have seen her. Instead of signalling for him to join them, they kept silent and set off after her. Although deciding she would offer them an opportunity to indulge in sexual pleasures which their leader had hoped to make them either miss or be late in taking, they realized they must not offer to do so prematurely.

Despite their resentment over the task they had been given, the older of the pair had been aware that it would provoke reprisals of a painful nature if they were responsible for a commotion which caused the element of surprise to be lost by the main body. Therefore, even though doing so could allow Chases Antelope to find out what was intended and join them, he had reluctantly concluded that they must wait until the attack was launched by their companions before closing in to make their capture. Having formed the summation and passed it in a whisper to his companion, who had reluctantly accepted his decision, they had stalked their quarry with the intention of taking her by surprise as soon as there was no need to worry about her making a noise.

Before the two braves had been able to get near enough to grab and silence her, their intended victim started walking in the direction of her companions. Believing they had even less to fear from a single paleface squaw than the Comanche woman who had fallen into their hands and whose spirited attempts at defence had left all of them marked by her teeth or fingernails, they followed. However, they were still not within reaching distance when she came to a halt near the edge of the trail.

Hearing the commotion which told him the main attack was being launched, the taller brave rested his bow against a bush. While he was removing the quiver of arrows, he discovered his companion had reached the same conclusion. However, much to his annoyance, he realized that Steals Food was able to put it into effect more quickly.

Noticing the third of their party was coming in their direction, instead of continuing to make for the white people beyond the woodland, the younger and shorter brave realized there could be a further threat to his desire to reach the intended victim first. Sticking the head of the lance he was carrying into the ground, he continued his advance without waiting for Long Wolf to discard the archery equipment or bothering to draw the Green River hunting knife out of the sheath at the right or the tomahawk from the two loops of rawhide on the left side of his weapon belt. However, his eagerness and a belief that it would not make any difference to the result caused him to be less cautious than he had been taught was advisable when stalking an intended victim. He felt certain that, even if the paleface woman had not become absorbed by seeing what was happening to her friends, she would never hear the slight noise he was making as he advanced with hands reaching to grab her.

* * * * * * * *

Steals Food was only partially correct in his assumption!

Although the approach had been quiet, there was just sufficient noise to warn the intended victim!

Nevertheless, swinging around, Becky Ingraham was only just in time to prevent the stalk achieving complete success!

Despite the shock of finding herself confronted at such close quarters by an Indian brave whose face was decorated and rendered even more hideous with what she had heard described as 'war paint', the girl was almost numbed into terrified paralysis!

However, feeling the greasy fingers closing upon her throat and seeing two more warriors approaching, Becky regained control of her wits fast!

Catching Steals Food by the wrists, one of which was decorated by a bracelet of Indian manufacture, the girl had reason to feel gratitude for the way in which she was attired. Her freedom of movement would have been seriously hampered by conventional outer garments and underclothing. As it was, neither the skirt nor the tights offered the slightest impediment. Rising through the flap, her sturdy right leg was completely at liberty to deliver a powerful kick. Passing beneath his raised arms, the top of her foot struck her assailant's ribs with enough force to make him release his hold. Nor was he allowed to regain it. Knotting her left fist as her leg descended, she delivered a punch to his jaw which sent him sprawling headlong into a bush.

Surprised by the obvious ease with which the paleface victim had escaped from his companion, Long Wolf nevertheless continued to approach without offering to arm himself. However, his expectation that she would run away proved incorrect. Instead of doing so, Becky employed the method which had sent Vernon Clay backwards over a desk and either killed or rendered him unconscious. Despite knowing what the previous effect could have been, she had no compunctions over repeating it.

Bending at the waist, the girl darted towards her second assailant like a bighorn sheep ram meeting the challenge of a rival. Taken unawares by such a tactic, Long Wolf could not avoid receiving the top of her head against his chest. Powered by her sturdily curvaceous body, the impact threw him backwards. Almost completely winded, he was unable to retain his balance and sprawled on to his back. However, carried onwards by her impetus, his attacker could not halt. As her lightly shod feet trampled over him, he grabbed and caught her by the left ankle. He failed to retain the grip, but it was held for long enough to achieve some success.

Finding herself being tripped, but not held on to by the hand which caused it, Becky reacted as she had frequently done under similar conditions in wrestling bouts. Going down, she threw herself into a forward roll. What was more, she was travelling with sufficient momentum to allow her to complete it by regaining her feet and resume control over her motions. This was most fortunate, for she came upright in the path of the third Kiowa as he was charging recklessly forward.

Having seen what happened to his companions as he was approaching, Chases Antelope did not lay aside the lance he was carrying. However, wanting to take the girl alive, neither did he strike with the steel head. Instead, he slowed his pace and swung the weapon upwards to chest level in front of him. His intention was to knock her over by shoving with the sturdy ten foot long wooden stave. However, assisted by the training she had received over the past two years, she was able to ensure this attempt too came to nothing.

Catching hold of the stave with her hands between his, Becky appeared to be trying to fend off the Kiowa by pushing against it. For a moment, it appeared they were engaged upon nothing more than a trial of strength. Then, waiting until she felt him increasing his attempt to counter her actions, she showed her actual intention. To the brave, becoming aware that she was going backwards and towards the ground, it appeared he was succeeding. Unfortunately for him, the withdrawal was not entirely caused by his extra weight and greater strength.

Knowing she could not oppose her attacker by brute force and muscle power alone, the girl had had no intention to do other than give the impression of trying. When satisfied she had achieved the objective she was seeking, she started to slip backwards without releasing her hold on the lance. Bringing up her feet as her weight compelled him to tilt forward, she got them against his stomach. As her shoulders struck the ground and she felt the pressure of his body against her soles, she straightened her bent legs. Helped by the shove he was exerting and a pull forward on the lance with her hands, she catapulted her assailant over her. Turning a half somersault, he alighted on his back with a thud which jolted all the air from his lungs.

While delighted by the third success in a row she had achieved, Becky was too intelligent to devote even a moment in well deserved self congratulation. Aware that none of her assailants were likely to have been rendered *hors de combat*, she wasted no time in bounding to her feet. A glance informed her that, although neither of his companions were doing so as yet, the youngest brave was already able to resume hostilities. Emerging from the bush into which he had been knocked, if the expression on his face was any guide, he was furious over having been subjected to such treatment at the hands of a woman. What was more, the way he was snatching the tomahawk from the slings on his weapon belt indicated the delivery of his next assault would not be restricted to bare hands.

In spite of having experienced little difficulty in dealing with the young warrior on his previous attempt to attack her, the girl knew the next would be a vastly different proposition. For one thing, she would no longer have the element of surprise. Furthermore, he would be coming at her holding a weapon which he was certain to have been taught to use with some skill. If her assailant had been alone, aided by her greatly improved knowledge of fighting with bare hands—even though dealing with an armed assailant had not formed part of her training—given sufficient room to manoeuvre and the goading of desperation, she might be able to cope and, perhaps, even render him *hors de combat*. However, the time required to do so would allow his companions to return to the fray. With those thoughts in mind, she decided the only safe course was for her to run away.

The problem was, in which direction to go?

Continuing to think fast and clearly, aware what little hope she had of survival depended upon it, the girl realized that making for the wagons was not the solution. In spite of the better surface for running it would offer, even appearing on to the trail would worsen rather than improve her desperate situation. Furthermore, judging by what she could see as she looked across, there was no help to be had in that direction. What few of her companions were still alive had far too much demanding their attention to be able to give her any assistance. On the other hand, to go towards them would bring her into view of the Indians attacking the camp and was likely to add to her pursuers.

That left the woods on either side!

Turning to her left, unfastening and throwing off the skirt as a possible impediment to her future movements, Becky darted through the undergrowth as fast as her legs could carry her. While doing so, she silently thanked providence for the strenuous kind of occupation she had been engaged upon since leaving St. Joseph, Missouri, which ensured she was now in an even better physical condition than on the last occasion when she had faced a threat to her life. She was aware that this alone offered her only a slender hope of salvation.

Without needing to look back, the girl could hear enough to warn her that the young brave was following in hot pursuit. Her awareness of what to expect if she was caught gave her an inducement to keep going such as she had never known before. However, although the circumstances were *vastly* different and the stakes were *much* higher than the acclaim of the other players if she was successful in eluding them, it was like a game at which she had excelled during her tomboy childhood. With relief, she discovered that she still retained much of the skill she had acquired and this had never stood her in better stead. The nature of the terrain did not allow her to run in a straight line. Instead, she had to weave through gaps in the undergrowth following tracks made by animals and remain constantly ready to duck beneath low hanging branches of the trees.

Brushing inadvertently against the foliage while swerving around a bush, Becky felt it clutch at the bodice of her blouse beneath her left arm. Even as a momentary alarm close to panic gripped her, to the accompaniment of a ripping sound, her momentum split and snatched the flimsy material free from the thorny clutches before it could slow her down. For all that, she knew the tremendous strain of having to keep running at such a pace was beginning to tell upon her. However, if the savage exclamations she could hear but not understand, and the other sounds which came to her ears were any indication, her pursuer was suffering from the same disadvantages and meeting with even less success in avoiding them.

Reaching an area of open ground with a large cottonwood tree roughly in the centre, the girl concluded that crossing it would add to her danger even though realizing she had no other choice. Although she knew little about Indians, she had heard that a tomahawk could be thrown as well as used to deliver a chopping attack. Glancing back, despite seeing nothing to suggest the warrior meant to act in such a fashion, she was startled to discover how he had succeeded in closing the gap between them. However, despite feeling sure they were following, she also drew consolation from discovering neither of the other braves were as near.

Running into the open, Becky could hear the footsteps to her rear drawing ever closer. Every instinct she possessed warned she could not stay ahead until reaching the other side. Accepting the inevitable, on arriving at the big tree, she spun around with her back to the trunk. While it was only a small consolation under the circumstances, a glance told her there was still only one of her attackers to be seen. Against that, the speed with which he was moving proved she had been correct in her assumption that she could not hope to go much further before he caught up. Therefore, pressing herself against the hard bark of the trunk, she tensed. Sucking in gasping breaths and watching the way in which he was rushing at her, she tried to decide how she might turn his obvious anger and impetuous behaviour to her advantage.

Enraged at having suffered the humiliation of being felled by the girl in front of his companions and by the pain suffered during the dash through the bushes, the young brave was no longer giving any thought to the sexual pleasures earlier envisaged. Nor, incensed by a burning sensation where a branch had whipped the cheek already bearing the still unhealed scratches from the fingernails of the Comanche woman, was his desire for revenge changed by the sensually attractive sight she presented.

This was in some part enhanced rather than detracted from by her physical condition. Discarding the wrap-around skirt had brought into view her shapely buttocks, hips and legs now covered in perspiration which caused the black tights to cling like a second skin. Similarly soaked and torn open at the front by the contact with the bush, the blouse no longer covered her well developed bosom as it rose and fell in accompaniment to the efforts of her lungs to replenish themselves with air.

Coming into reaching distance and giving a bellow of, 'Die, white bitch!', Steals Food swung the tomahawk in a vicious horizontal arc intended to inflict a suitable revenge!

However, at the last moment, the proposed victim took most competent evasive actions!

Timing the moves perfectly, Becky thrust herself aside just before the weapon reached its target!

Unable to halt the blow, Steals Food received a jolt which threatened to numb his arm as the blade buried deep into the wood. A moment later, before he could try to pull it free, he was again struck by a punch to the side of his jaw delivered with the precision learned to counter similar attacks by untrained opponents. This time, coming with all the power of the muscular buxom body of the girl, the force not only sent him sprawling sideways, caught even harder than previously, he was unconscious before he landed on the ground.

Opening and shaking her fist in an attempt to relieve the throbbing caused by the impact of the blow she had struck, Becky saw the other two braves racing into the open. Even as she thought of jerking the tomahawk from the tree and making a stand, the futility of such behaviour struck home. Not only was her right hand still partially numb and she had no desire to undertake so desperate a venture handicapped by using the left, she was completely unfamiliar with such a weapon. The latter stricture did not apply to her assailants and they would know how to defend themselves against it. Furthermore, while the other was bare handed, the one in the lead was still carrying his lance and this gave him a much longer reach than she would have with the tomahawk.

Concluding that her only slender hope was in a renewal of the flight, leaving the weapon embedded in the wood, the girl spun and darted towards the other side of the open ground!

Seeing their quarry setting off again, the braves let out angry exclamations. Sharing a trait of Texas cowhands and Mexican *vaqueros*, along with most other so-called 'horse Indians', they had little liking for such strenuous activity when on foot. Already they were breathing hard and were far from enamoured of continuing the chase in such an energy draining and exhausting fashion. However, only one of them was in a position to do anything about it. Knowing how fleet of foot Steals Food could be, Long Wolf had expected only a short chase. Therefore, wanting to enjoy the anticipated pleasures when the capture was made, he had not waited to collect his bow and arrows before setting off in pursuit.

Being just as eager for what he considered would be shortly forthcoming, Chases Antelope had nevertheless taken up the chase with the lance still in his hands. What was more, while not at his best as a result of the stomach throw he had suffered, he had gained his name by his competence as a runner. Therefore, although carrying the weapon had prevented him from catching up with Steals Food, he was able to leave Long Wolf behind. Nevertheless, seeing the girl resuming her flight, he was disinclined to let her keep going. The commotion from the other side of the trail was dying away and he did not want too much of a delay before going there to claim a share in the loot from the wagons.

Releasing the lance with his left hand and drawing back his right arm, the brave skidded to a halt. However, despite being too far away to be able to make a thrust, he did not throw it after the fashion of a spear. Experience had taught him this was not the best method of employ. Instead, he sent it through the air in a way which he had learned increased the chances of making a hit on a moving target. Twirling around and around in its flight, it was not dependent upon the pointed head to make contact and bring down the intended objective. Instead, flying parallel to the ground, the ten foot long wooden shaft covered a much greater span than the point and reduced the chances of missing.

Struck behind the knees just as she reached the edge of the clearing, Becky might have counted herself grateful that the missile was almost at the end of its flight. If it had arrived at full speed and power, she could easily have suffered a broken leg. Even with its momentum diminished, it still arrived with sufficient force to achieve its purpose. Feeling herself struck and tripped up, she let out a cry of mingled pain and alarm. With her equilibrium destroyed, arms flailing wildly she found she was plunging helplessly towards a tree. Despite all her efforts to avoid it, her head struck the side of the trunk. The blow was only glancing, but the impact was hard enough to knock her unconscious.

Flopping limply face down, the girl was not aware of the two Kiowas hurrying towards her!

6 *It's A* Tshaoh!

Although she had managed to avoid letting her captors realize she was conscious for longer than she had dared to hope would be possible, at last Becky Ingraham was compelled to inadvertantly give a sign that she was at least recovering her faculties. Given a heave on her feet by the young brave she had twice knocked down and toppled from the bare back of the horse, across which she had remained flaccidly draped whilst on the move, she had contrived to stay just as limp as she was falling to the ground. Unfortunately, she had landed on what felt like a small roundish rock. Before she could prevent herself from doing either, she gave a gasp of pain and her body jerked convulsively. The sound she inadvertently emitted was not loud, but proved sufficiently so to be heard by all the men in the vicinity.

Having turned to walk away, believing the captive was still unconscious, Steals Food glanced over his shoulder. Calling to tell the rest of the braves that she would soon be ready for their pleasure, he swung around in eager anticipation of what he had been waiting for ever since he had recovered from the second blow he had received to find she had been captured. Looking past him as he started to return, guessing what he had said, Becky concluded that the fate she had succeeded in avoiding so far was about to befall her. Attracted by her groan, the other five Indians forgot what they were about to do and, putting down their assorted weapons, duplicated his action by beginning to move her way.

On regaining consciousness several hours earlier, the girl had had a few seconds of confusion. Then, fortunately before she had done anything to betray her return to sentience, the recollection of what had happened had flooded through her mind. The memory was frightening and had made her feel as if she was touched by an icy cold hand, but she had been able to hold her fear in check. Her every instinct had warned this was no time to panic or act before she had ascertained the exact nature of the situation. Although the earlier mixture of yells, screams and shots had ended, indicating that the attack upon the International Troupe Of Lady Wrestlers was over, the sounds of conflict had been replaced by guttural masculine voices speaking a language she could not understand. Looking up cautiously as her vision cleared, she had discovered she had been carried to the clearing in which her party had set up camp the previous night.

Instead of continuing the examination of her surroundings, while she had sufficient presence of mind to prevent herself from groaning, Becky had started to reach up instinctively with a hand to feel at and give some solace to her throbbing head. Before she could do so, the realization of how such an act could also have undesirable repercussions had caused her to refrain. Although she felt sure she had been taken captive by the three men who pursued her through the woodland, the movement had established that she was not bound or otherwise restrained in any way. However, with her faculties having returned, she had concluded she would be advised to ascertain the full ramifications of her predicament before attempting to capitalize upon any advantages she might have.

Raising her head a little so as to obtain a better view of her surroundings, but otherwise remaining motionless, the girl had quickly satisfied herself that there was little relief to be gained from her hands and feet being free. Until that point, she had been hoping—futilely, she had told herself—that being at liberty suggested rescuers had come upon the scene. One glance was all she had needed to ascertain that this was not the case. The only other living beings in sight were Indians and she recognized the three who had chased her in the woodland.

Subsiding to lie motionless at the conclusion of her undetected scrutiny, the girl had been both distressed and relieved by having discovered neither Horace 'Pug' Brackley nor any of the other members of the Troupe had survived the onslaught. Although her first inclination had been to scream her hatred at the cause of her companions' deaths, she had also envisaged, just in time to prevent it, how she would be affected if she yielded to the impulse. To do so could not bring them back to life. It would only draw attention to her and, at that moment, she was being totally ignored. Nauseated as she was at the sight of how all the bodies—male and female—had been mutilated, the sight had at first stopped her from realizing the implications of being alive in the hands of the men responsible for the slaughter.

When the thought of her own predicament had occurred, Becky had made an effort and kept her disturbed emotions under control. Even before coming to Texas, she had read of the horrible fate awaiting white women who were taken prisoners by marauding Indians. That she had been kept alive indicated her captors had such treatment in mind for her. Wondering why she had not already been subjected to it, she had deduced being unconscious had spared her. The conclusion had shown her how she might hold off the commencement of the molestation for long enough to be offered either an opportunity to escape, or try to ensure she was dead before they could start.

Continuing to keep the braves under overt observation, making sure she remained still and closed her eyes as soon as any of them showed signs of looking her way, Becky had quickly concluded the cause of the controversy was helping to prevent them forcing their malevolent attentions upon her. In addition to the little interest being taken in her, the tones and gestures being employed offered sufficient indications to support the supposition.

Convinced that the braves were all absorbed in the acrimonious debate, the girl had thought their preoccupation with one another might offer her an opportunity of making an attempt to escape. However, once again, her common sense had come to the fore and pointed out the folly of the idea. There were, she had quickly realized, serious objections to even trying to take any kind of action along those lines. For one thing, while she had regained her wits sufficiently to be able to think clearly, she was still feeling the effects of the collision with the tree and had not yet recovered from the strains imposed by her previous flight. Should she rise and run, one or more of the warriors were certain to see her and she was in no condition to endure the rigours of another pursuit.

Nor would wriggling away on the ground be likely to offer a better chance of success than setting off at a run, Becky had reluctantly decided. She had often noticed how even slow movements could catch the corner of the eye and bring the full gaze in their direction. One of the reasons she had not yet been subjected to the kind of attention she felt sure was intended by her captors was they wanted her conscious and aware whilst having their way with her. To let it become obvious she was recovered might cause them to forget the disagreement at present occupying them.

With the conclusion drawn and acted upon, Becky had also realized there was only one way in which she might hold off what was intended and, perhaps, be granted some more viable chance to make a bid for freedom. If she could convince the braves that she was still unconscious, she believed they would leave her alone until she 'recovered' and could increase their enjoyment by her frantic response to their attentions. It was only a *very* slender chance, she had warned herself, but better than any other alternative she had been able to call to mind. For one thing, the respite would allow her to rest and replenish her energies ready to make the most of any opportunity to escape which might arise.

Accepting she had no other choice, the girl had continued to lie where she had been put down!

The ploy had worked!

In the first place, as Becky had deduced, the Kiowa braves had been involved in such an acrimonious discussion it had continued to keep their attention from her!

Furthermore, while the girl had not been aware of the fact on her recovery, some time had passed before the majority of the Indians learned of her presence!

On arriving at the edge of the trail, Long Wolf had seen enough to let him assume he might achieve his ambition to gain control over the party. Telling his companions to wait in concealment with the girl they were carrying, he had crossed over. From his closer examination of the clearing, he concluded that his impression that the attack had been far from an unqualified success was correct. For one thing, with the exception of the captive who had fallen into the trio's hands, not a single living prisoner had been taken. Furthermore, despite having the element of surprise in their favour, the main body had suffered several casualities and the loss of six lives. Among the dead braves was Plenty Coups, having succumbed to the bullet wound shortly after he had struck down the white man who inflicted it.

However, basing the assertion upon the grounds of being the brother of the deceased leader, there had been another claimant for the position of his replacement!

Hearing his rival commenting upon arriving from the other side of the trail that it seemed the medicine of his sibling had gone bad, Travels Far had set about attempting to refute the suggestion!

Already, the would-be leader had pointed out, a search of the wagons had revealed some worthwhile loot. There were four more rifles and the number of double barrelled shotguns was now four, but the three small firearms highly prized for being able to shoot several times without needing reloading which had been taken from the dead white men were all of their kind that were available. Lessening the impact he had sought to create by referring to the weapons having been acquired, he was compelled to concede there was not much black powder to be used with them, and percussion caps, moulded bullets and the lead to make more were also in extremely short supply.

Regardless of the improvement in the armament of the party, Travels Far was unable to deny that other things had turned out less successfully than had been anticipated!

There was a quantity of clothing in the wagons, but the majority were garments for women. Unfortunately, little of this was attire that men could wear and the masculine clothes would not be suitable for the kind of rugged usage to which it would be subjected. Furthermore, the expected food and, much more eagerly sought, hard liquor had not been forthcoming. Although their killers had no means of knowing, the slaughtered white people having meant to re-supply on arrival in Fort Worth, had only a small amount of food left and never carried liquor. Sampling the contents of what he had assumed to be a bottle of the white man's 'firewater', but was actually a liniment used by Percy Pulbright, the taste had proved so unpleasant the brave making the test had smashed all the others he had found without investigating what they contained. Of the five horses taken, four were too large and heavily built to be of much use for riding and the one which would have been had injured its leg while trying to bolt in fright during the commotion.

Eager to use any means to discredit Plenty Coups, in addition to commenting adversely upon the various deficiencies in the loot, Long Wolf had drawn attention to another promise which had been made and clearly had failed to materialize. When learning how their intended victims' party was comprised, their late leader had spoken eloquently about the small risks likely to be involved and the pleasures which would be forthcoming from the white women who fell into their hands. Indicating the wounded and dead, Long Wolf had remarked that it seemed the risks had proved much greater than was suggested. On being informed that the paleface females had proved more dangerous as fighters than their men, he had concluded their spirited resistance had caused the attackers to react with a violence which caused death instead of trying to capture them alive. Commenting that he had never heard white women were so fierce, he had pointed out wryly that as a result of their ferocity there was no enjoyment to be had unless it was to be obtained from their corpses.

When Travels Far had tried to counter the assertions by reminding the others how Long Wolf and his companions had played no part in the fighting, he had replied that Plenty Coups had clearly thought there should be no need for their assistance. Therefore, doing as they were instructed, they had achieved one thing where the rest of the raiding party had failed. Calling for Chases Antelope and Steals Food to come over, he had been gratified by the response to the sight of their burden.

Although Becky had not realized it, her condition on arrival had prevented Long Wolf from gaining immediate acclaim for her capture. What was more, even after she had regained consciousness, her behaviour had prevented him from exploiting the result of the pursuit through the woodland. In spite of having been handled and fondled in a way which she had found revolting, she had had sufficient self control to continue to give the impression she was still comatose. Fortunately for her, circumstances had ensured such treatment was not protracted, or frequent.

When the intended recipient of their lust had continued to show no signs of recovery, seeing an opportunity to belittle his rival's success in providing her, Travels Far had played upon the animosity aroused as a result of the earlier ommission to bring in a living female prisoner by asking how the other spoils of the raid should be divided. Taking a cue from him, indicating the bracelets worn by Steals Food and Chases Antelope and the necklace also made of Navajo silver and turquoise around Long Wolf's neck, one of his cronies had reminded the others that the trio had not even offered to share the jewellery taken from the body of the Comanche woman. Then he had suggested ownership of what had just been collected should be restricted to those who had actually participated in the fighting.

Naturally such an arrangement had not met with the approval of the trio who would be excluded. What was more, mindful that expressing concurrence could establish a precedent to their detriment on future expeditions, there were sufficient dissenters to the suggestion to ensure a more equitable arrangement was reached. As was only to be expected, none of those fortunate to have acquired the firearms would give them up. Nevertheless, they had agreed to allow Long Wolf, Chases Antelope and Steals Food to take a share of the other property.

With the loot shared and the girl showing no indication of her true condition, a further bone of contention had arisen. This was on the subject of what the party should do next. Knowing to keep going would almost certainly entail a further clash of interests with Long Wolf and not relishing the prospect for all his bluster, Travels Far had indicated his belief that they had done enough and should return home with the spoils they had gathered. The warriors injured in the fighting had been in agreement and there were others, no longer having the inducement supplied by the white man's firewater, who were of the same mind.

However, mainly because the proposal to go home had originated from his rival, Long Wolf had declined. Pointing out they had little to show for their endeavours, he had stated his intention of seeking further coups and loot before returning. Although he had failed to win over the entire party, his two companions and three more of the braves, two of whom had acquired rifles, elected to accompany him. Aware that it would not be advisable to remain in the vicinity of the trail, Travels Far and his adherents had not even been inclined to suggest remaining until the white girl could be revived so they too could have their way with her. Nor, as Becky had still showed no sign of having recovered, had the other party taken the time to try and bring her back to consciousness. Instead, loading her across the back of a horse belonging to their victims and selected by the brave who had failed to obtain a firearm, they had separated from their companions.

Never had Becky's fortitude and courage been put to such as test as during the following hours!

As the girl was to realize later, she had been fortunate in more ways than one!

In the first place, the horse across which Becky was being carried had been bred for draught work. Its broad back and plodding gait offered less discomfort than she might have experienced if it had had a physical conformation suitable for conventional riding. Although warm, the weather was not excessively so. Therefore, the heat from the sun created neither a burning sensation upon her thinly covered back nor added greatly to her thirst. Having relieved herself in the woods before being captured, that need did not arise either. On the other hand, she had been able to obtain some water by scooping up a double handful unnoticed as the party were allowing the animals to drink while crossing a stream.

At first, in the hope of finding some way of returning to the trail should she succeed in escaping, the girl had tried to remember the route being taken by her captors. She had soon found that the terrain they were traversing made this impossible from the position across the horse she was compelled to retain. With the men all around, she dare not raise or turn her head even briefly in case she should be seen and her deception exposed. Every movement she made brought one or another of the braves closing in to check on whether she was 'recovering consciousness' and she had been all too aware of what to expect if she allowed them to discover this had already happened.

Despite having been passing through woodland as well grown as that through which she had fled earlier, Becky had not attempted to escape. As was the case in the clearing where the massacre of her friends had taken place, she had realized the inadvisability and futility of trying. The moment she moved, she would have been seen by her captors. By the time she was off the horse, they would be commencing their pursuit. Even if she had succeeded in eluding them, which she had felt sure was *extremely* unlikely, she would be left on foot and unarmed in terrain she suspected would prove far more dangerous than the Ozark Mountains where she had roamed in her childhood. However, neither that possibility, nor the fact that she was poorly attired for survival would have deterred her if she had considered her surroundings offered a chance of avoiding the braves.

Before passing any suitable physical feature, such as a cliff over which the girl could throw herself and thereby gain a start upon her pursuers, the party had arrived in a clearing with a small stream running across its centre and Long Wolf had told them to stop. While the others were preparing to take a rest, carrying out the instructions of their self-appointed leader, the young brave she had twice knocked down had removed her from the back of the horse with a most undesirable result.

Realizing there was no longer any point in keeping up the pretense of being unconscious, Becky scrambled upright as quickly as she was able. She found she was too unsteady on her feet to think of flight. In fact, she was poorly conditioned to even try to fight off the warriors. Nevertheless, she silently swore she would do everything possible to resist. If she had an opportunity, she would get possession of a weapon and kill herself before they were able to have their way with her.

Before the need for the girl to take any action arrived, there was an interruption!

An ear-splitting and awesome yell rang out from the direction in which the party had reached the clearing!

Swinging her gaze around, Becky stared at an Indian who burst into view from amongst the trees!

'It's a *Tshaoh*!' Long Wolf yelled, forgetting his intentions towards the captive as he deduced from various signs to which Indian nation the new arrival belonged.

Lacking the knowledge required to make such an identification, Becky stared at the new arrival with as much interest as her captors were showing!

Looking to be in his mid-twenties, taller and more slender in build than the Kiowas, the approaching man was also more scantily attired. A red cloth band inscribed with some kind of blue, white and green symbols was fastened around his forehead. Below it, his black hair—parted down the centre on top of his skull—hung in two shoulder long braids. He had on moccasins and almost knee high buckskin leggings. These and what looked to the girl like a length of blue cloth hanging to form flaps at the front and behind over the weapon belt around his waist completed his attire. While slightly Mongoloid in lines and set in an expression of grimly savage determination, his coppery-brown features were not bad looking even by European standards. In spite of his clearly aggressive demeanour, there was no 'war paint' on his face. However, in the centre of his bare chest was the scarlet print of a hand.

Everything about the newcomer, including the reaction of her captors to his appearance, suggested to Becky that he was not coming with peaceful intentions. Knowing the United States' Cavalry employed Indian scouts to help deal with redskin marauders, she wondered whether this could account for his presence. He might have been sent by the commanding officer of a troop which arrived at the scene of the massacre to track down the men responsible. Having done so and discovered they were about to start molesting her, he was coming to the rescue instead of waiting for reinforcements.

However, if she was correct in her suppositions, the girl considered her would-be rescuer was poorly equipped to carry out his intentions. The only arms he had were a big Bowie knife in a sheath on his weapon belt and the war lance he was carrying. Neither of them struck her as being adequate to deal with six enemies.

Therefore, while Becky was grateful for the thought behind the intervention, she did not believe it would save her!

7 *Against Odds Of Six To One*

Being better informed than their captive on such matters, none of the Kiowas discounted the newcomer on the grounds that he appeared to be unaccompanied!

The sight of the lance in the hands of the rapidly approaching man gave warning that he could and almost certainly would prove a *very* dangerous proposition!

Although he for one had needed the information given by Long Wolf to appreciate what his party were up against, even Steals Food was aware that any *Tshaoh* was a worthy foe and none of that race went armed in such a fashion unless possessed of great courage and a determination to succeed in battle or die trying. Therefore, in spite of the belief he had often stated regarding his competence as a warrior, he found it was disconcerting and alarming to realize he was the closest of them to one of that particularly efficient type of brave from a traditionally hostile nation and who could have good cause for taking vengeance upon him.

However, in spite of suspecting what had brought the *Tshaoh* to the clearing, the youngest of the Kiowas was given no chance to take any kind of either offensive or defensive action. He had left his lance stuck point down in the ground when coming to remove the girl from the horse. Instead of trying to retrieve it and get on something closer to an equal footing with the approaching man, he grabbed at the tomahawk on the slings of his belt. Before he was able to bring it out, he inadvertently provided Becky Ingraham with verification for the theory she had formed about the disadvantage of trying to protect herself with the same weapon.

Showing no sign of concern over being up against odds of six to one, the newcomer let out another of the savage yells and used his lance without breaking stride. Seven foot in length, with a sturdy shaft made from *bois d'arc*—regarded by members of every Indian nation as being one of the hardest, finest and most durable of timbers—to which an obviously sharp edged and pointed leaf shaped steel head was securely bound with sinew of rawhide thongs and glue at the forward end and a similarly fitted short metal spike on the other.

Driven forward in a thrust from under the arm which told of deadly skill, the user having been taught that wielding it overhand and downwards was far less effective, the point impaled Steals Food's stomach before he would have been in reaching distance with the tomahawk even if permitted to draw it. Just as deftly, having helped to gain admittance, the cutting edge of the head was manipulated to disembowel him while slashing out again through his flesh. Taking his right hand from the tomahawk, he clutched with both right and left at the mortal wound. Screaming in agony, he stumbled aside and collapsed face forward.

Passing the stricken youngster and still employing the same devastating rapidity, the *Tshaoh* sent the head of his lance between the ribs and into the left side of the chest of a Kiowa who had elected to accompany Long Wolf instead of returning home. The moment that the weapon was snatched free, in a smoothly flowing continuation of the movement, its direction was altered and the metal shod butt was driven against the face of the second brave to make the decision to continue on the raid. With blood gushing from his cut mouth and shattered teeth, he let the knife he had drawn slip from his grasp and his dart towards the attacker was turned into an involuntary retreat.

Bringing around the lance, the newcomer deflected the chop with a tomahawk being made at him by Chases Antelope. Then, slipping the shaft between his intended assailant's legs at knee height, he moved quickly to the right without removing it. Doing so caused the Kiowa to trip, but he managed to retain his grip on the fighting axe. However, as the *Tshaoh* slid the weapon free, he was not allowed to render his latest victim *hors de combat*. Instead, he was compelled to sweep it around and make Long Wolf, coming into the attack holding a tomahawk, leap clear of its arc. The retreat was done so hurriedly and with such vigour that the leader of the party went several steps before being able to bring his movements under control.

Once more, the newcomer was prevented from dealing a *coup de grace*!

Seeing the third of the recruits from the main body had taken warning from the skill he was displaying and was making towards where a rifle lay on the ground, the *Tshaoh* wasted not a moment before following. Nevertheless, regardless of the speed with which he was moving, it seemed to the watching girl that he would arrive too late. He was still beyong thrusting distance when the brave was snatching up the firearm and starting to turn. Despite her concern, the newcomer proved to have a better grasp of the situation than she anticipated.

Sliding his right hand to just below the steel head and the left to the centre of the shaft while still striding forward, the *Tshaoh* lowered the butt to the ground at an angle in front of him. Then, he bounded into the air as if performing a pole vault. Using the lance as a pivot and support, he swung around on the shaft with his body almost horizontal to the ground. Flexing and straightening his legs in midair, he drove both feet into the shoulder of the warrior before the turn could be completed. The impact flung the man in a twirling reel and cause him to lose hold upon the firearm.

Despite his successes, there was no respite for the *Tshaoh*. No sooner had he alighted from the leaping kick, than he had to take his right hand from the lance and knock aside the tomahawk flung at him by Chases Antelopes. While he was doing so, Long Wolf was rushing at him from behind and the man with the damaged mouth was returning to the fray from one side. By accident rather than deliberate intent, they were timing their respective approaches so there was no way he could deal with one before the other was upon him.

Appreciating the extent of the danger which was threatening her rescuer, Becky was not the kind to stand passively by and let it happen. On the point of rushing forward to tackle the closest of the assailants, deriving some satisfaction from the thought that he had helped capture her and was leading the party, the throbbing ache in her side acquired on landing after having been tipped from the horse suggested there was something better than her bare hands available. Glancing at the cause of the pain, she decided it would be ideal for her purposes. About the size of the baseballs she had thrown with some success as a child and while a schoolteacher in Surbiton, Missouri, it was roughly the same shape although having ridges something like those on a turtle's shell instead of being smooth.

On snatching the object up, the girl discovered it was not a small boulder as she believed. Instead, she was holding what she guessed from memories of reading books on the subject of natural history must be a young armadillo which was rolled into a defensive ball. Being country-born and raised, she had no fear of even unfamiliar animals. Nor, while never cruel under normal conditions, did she let herself be deterred by the thought that her intended missile was a living creature and not the inanimate piece of rock she had envisaged. Swiftly 'winding up' as she had when pitching at baseball, she hurled the creature with all her strength. Not only was her aim good, there was an added bonus resulting from her having selected it.

Finding itself suddenly lifted and flung through the air, the armadillo unwound its protectively coiled body. Going where it was meant to, it did more than just strike its objective. Finding itself suddenly coming into contact with something solid yet which yielded slightly, it immediately started to carry out another instinctive defensive measure. Like all its species, it had sturdy forepaws and long sharp front claws which gave it the ability to dig its way underground very rapidly and this it attempted to do. Just how effectively it was equipped for such a task was proven by the screech of pain which burst from Long Wolf as the skin of his face was ripped open from forehead almost to mouth level. Finding itself unable to burrow out of sight, on dropping to the ground, it scuttled away with a surprising speed for such an apparently ungainly creature.

Blinded by involuntary tears and blood pouring into his eyes, which had not been touched by the claws, the leader of the Kiowas spun around to reel away with hands clasping at his ruined features. He was helpless to protect himself and paid the penalty. Letting out a shout, the *Tshaoh* plunged the head of the lance into his chest and gave a surging heave which swung him around. Although the motion dislodged him from the weapon, its shaft was grabbed by the other brave as he went blundering away dying on his feet.

Granted an opportunity to do so, Chases Antelope had risen and retrieved his tomahawk. Yelling for the brave with the injured mouth to hang on to the lance, he hurried forward. To add to the newcomer's problems, the brave who had received the leaping kick was returning to the fray.

Glancing around while resisting the attempt to wrest the weapon from his hands, the *Tshaoh* ascertained the extent of the danger and acted upon his rapid summation!

Realizing he could not liberate the lance by wrenching it from the grasp of the Kiowa quickly enough to serve his needs, the newcomer did not waste time and energy in trying. Instead, he released his hold and took a quick step to his rear. Before the brave could turn his other weapon on him, he snatched the bowie knife from its sheath with his right hand and brought it around in a rising arc. Taken completely unaware by the change in tactics, the Kiowa was unable to evade the blow. Raked across the throat by the razor sharp clip pointed blade of the big knife, he gave a strangled gurgling cry. The lance slipped from his grasp and he too went away from his assailant for a few staggering steps before collapsing with his life blood flooding from the severed arteries and veins of his neck.

In spite of having removed another of his enemies, the *Tshaoh* was once more in dire straits. Not only was one attacker darting towards him armed with a tomahawk, the other surviving Kiowa would soon be able to retrieve and use the rifle. However, again the white girl came to his aid and provided the respite he desperately required.

Concluding her rescuer would require further assistance, Becky did not hesitate to supply it. Not for the first time since she had had to flee for her life from Surbiton, she had cause to be grateful—on this day in particular—for her tomboy childhood. Memories of another sporting activity from those days, which had also served her well on occasion in the wrestling bouts, suggested how she might best render the necessary aid. In spite of still feeling the effects of the long hours spent hanging across the back of the horse, calling upon every reserve of strength and energy she could muster, she set about putting the idea into effect.

Running to gather the necessary momentum, on converging with Chases Antelope, the girl launched herself bodily through the air to cover the remainder of the distance separating them. Because he was giving his full attention to the *Tshaoh*, whose deadly competence had caused him to forget how well she had fought against himself and his companions before they had been able to subdue and take her prisoner, her arrival was completely unexpected. Despite catching a glimpse of her body diving towards him, he was just too late with his realization that she was intervening. Given no time to think of avoiding her, the force of the kind of tackle she had learned as a child produced the result she was seeking.

Not only was the Kiowa struck on the buttocks by the full weight of Becky's solidly fleshed and curvaceous buxom body, which arrived with the considerable impulsion her running had built up, but her arms wrapped around his legs just above the knees. Jerking his legs together by the constriction she applied, she ruined his equilibrium and felt him going down. She might have derived satisfaction if she had noticed that the tomahawk flew from his grasp, regarding the loss as a bonus to her efforts, but things were happening too rapidly and she had other things to occupy her attention. Unable to halt her forward momentum, or unwind her arms quickly enough, she was compelled to accompany him. Landing before she was able to untangle herself, the impetus she had built up caused them to roll over.

Finding himself once again granted a respite by the prompt action of the white girl, the *Tshaoh* was aware that he must make the most of the opportunity with which he was being presented. Although by training and inclination he would have preferred to continue the fighting with his lance, he realized this was not possible under the circumstances. Already bending to gather up the rifle, the other surviving Kiowa would be ready to fire before he could retrieve the weapon and cover the gap which separated them. Nor, he also concluded, would he be able to get there in time to deliver a blow with his knife.

Still locked together, the impact of their arrival having failed to make them separate, the girl and the brave involuntarily exchanged the upper position twice as they rolled across the ground. Brought to the bottom just as the impulsion of the tackle came to an end, the girl found herself in a position which had occurred in childhood scuffles and more recent wrestling bouts. Having had his legs released as they were turning, he was able to thrust himself into a kneeling posture and straddle her torso as an aid to holding her supine beneath him.

Under less demanding circumstances, Chases Antelope might have derived a sensual satisfaction and pleasure from the sight Becky was presenting. Left exposed by the damage her blouse had sustained earlier and framed between his thighs, her breasts rose in firm bare white mounds which he would normally have started fondling. At that moment, however, he had no desire to do so. Instead, realizing he was involved with somebody who was seriously hampering his freedom of movement at a time when it was vitally important he remained unhindered, he gave not a single thought to her physical attractions. Reacting as he would have done if in contention against a masculine adversary, he grabbed her by the throat and raised her head with the intention of crashing it against the ground.

In spite of being well beyond striking distance, the *Tshaoh* knew he had the means to protect himself without the need to take the time required to get close enough. It was not a measure he would have cared to employ in different conditions, but he accepted he had no other choice. Pivoting on his left foot to supply added momentum and swinging around his right arm, he opened his hand the moment his well trained instincts told him was most suitable to his needs. Released, the massive knife hissed through the air with its two and a quarter inch wide blade turned parallel to the ground over which it was passing almost too swiftly for the human eye to follow. However, its departure left him without a weapon of any kind in his grasp.

Deducing from past experience what was intended by the man pressing upon her stomach with his buttocks, Becky was equally aware there was only one way in which she might counter it. Although she had instinctively grasped his wrists, she knew her attempts to pull away his hands would not save her. However, she did know something else which would help except that putting it into effect was a very different matter. Not only was she up against a heavier and stronger antagonist than any she had fought in the past, but the exertions to which she had been subjected throughout the day were taking their toll. Conscious that she was growing weaker by the second, she braced her neck and, striving to thrust upwards with her body, she contrived to lessen the force with which the back of her head was driven against the short turf beneath her. Nevertheless, the impact hurt and she knew its repetition would eventually render her *hors de combat*.

Straightening with the rifle in his hands, the Kiowa saw the way in which the newcomer had elected to deal with the threat he posed. However, the realization that doing so had left the *Tshaoh* empty handed did not arouse any elation for him. As the girl was finding out not too far away, awareness of a possible advantage being presented was one thing, but dealing with the situation proved to be a vastly different proposition. Even as he tried to deflect the rapidly approaching missile with the weapon he had retrieved, it was too late.

Thrown with skill and all the power of the wirily muscular body of the slender newcomer impelling it, the knife arrived as it was intended. Copied from a design perfected for Colonel James Bowie by the Arkansas master cutler, James Black,[1] the blade was made of finest steel produced in Sheffield, England. Although its present owner neither knew nor was even interested in its origins, being aware of how potent a weapon it was, he had always taken care to maintain it in excellent condition. Not for the first time since it had come into his possession, he had reason to consider the time and effort spent in doing so well worthwhile.

Driving into the Kiowa's body, the way in which the throw was made allowed the eleven inch long, two and a quarter inch wide blade to pass between the rib cage at the left side. Slicing onwards, the clip point was driven deeply enough to inflict a mortal wound. A shriek burst from him, but he neither fell nor released his rifle. Guessing he was dying, he was impelled by a desire to take revenge upon the man responsible. Snarling what were meant to be words expressing his hatred, but emerged as only incoherent sounds, he tried to bring the weapon to his shoulder. However, strong though the desire for vengeance might be, the terrible injury was weakening him too rapidly for him to achieve his purpose. Reeling on buckling legs, he crumpled without even having managed to draw back the hammer much less take aim and fire.

Having made the throw, the *Tshaoh* did not wait to watch whatever result he might achieve. Instead, he lunged for the lance lying in front of him. Gathering it up,

[1] *Further information about Colonel James Bowie and his knife is given in:* Item 4a *of the* APPENDIX.

he swung his gaze around to ascertain what further action he must take. Discovering the white girl was in a difficult and dangerous situation, letting out a roar of rage, he immediately darted to her assistance. However, he was motivated by more than gratitude for her having intervened twice in his behalf. Seeing the bracelet worn by the Kiowa, he knew his mission was not yet accomplished and he intended to complete the quest for vengeance which had brought him to the clearing.

On the point of slamming Becky's head against the ground for a second time, Chases Antelope heard the fury-filled yell and looked around. Concluding the *Tshaoh* was a far greater danger than the girl he was straddling, he took his hands from her throat. However, his desire to rise hurriedly was impeded by her grasp on his wrists. Snarling an imprecation, he tried to set his arms free while thrusting to bring himself to his feet. Seeing what was happening, Becky did her best to impede him. While she was now too weakened to prevent him from rising, or retain her hold, she nevertheless provided a hindrance which was to prove fatal for him.

Applying added vigour in his attempt to escape from the grasp which was putting a serious impediment to his freedom of movement, the Kiowa discovered to his cost that succeeding proved less than beneficial. On wrenching himself free, his wrists were released so suddenly that he was thrown off balance. Nor was he allowed to regain control of his motions. Lurching upwards more quickly than he had intended, he saw the blood smeared head of the lance sweeping towards him in an upwards swing. He made an ineffectual grab at the shaft, but had not touched it when the point took him in the stomach. Such was the power with which the blow was struck, the head of the lance sank onwards until it emerged at the rear. Lifted from his feet, he was thrown over backwards and landed supine. Writhing like a like a snake impaled on a thorn and screaming in torment, he was pinned to the ground alongside the girl he and his companions had hoped would provide them with enjoyment.

Having instinctively started to sit up, Becky felt her senses reeling as she turned her gaze to her rescuer with the intention of thanking him. However, giving her not so much as a glance, he put a foot on the Kiowa's chest and jerked out the lance. The sound made by the weapon as it emerged was the last straw for the girl. Giving a horrified gasp, first time in her life, she fainted.

Flopping limply on to her back once more, the girl neither saw nor heard the victorious warrior as he bent over and, striking the stricken man on the cheek with his open left hand, completed a ritual highly thought of amongst his people by saying, '*A:he*!'

8 Woman Of Spirit

'Look,' the *Tshaoh* said in a language he and the girl he had rescued had found they had in common,[1] albeit only to a limited degree, as they rode side by side over a rim. 'My home!'

Gazing in the direction indicated, Becky Ingraham felt a sinking sensation as she received confirmation of the suspicion which had been plaguing her for the past three days. Although there was an Indian village on the banks of a stream down below, she could see no sign of white people's habitation anywhere in the vicinity.

On recovering from her faint and looking about her, the girl had come close to repeating it. With a sensation of horror, she had discovered that her rescuer had been engaged in an activity which she had read was frequently performed by members of his race after a fight. All the six men who had been abducting her were dead, which had not come as any surprise. Nor, having had no doubt over what they had intended to do to her, had she felt remorse over their fate. What had shocked her was seeing that their long black hair was gone and the top of each head was red with blood caused by the forcible removal.

Getting to her feet, struggling to control the nausea which threatened to engulf her, Becky had stumbled to the river and taken a drink. With her thirst quenched, she had felt somewhat better. Looking at her rescuer, she had found that the expression of rage was gone and he was far

[1] 'Tshaoh', *'Enemy People'; the name given by Indians of other tribes, often with good cause, to members of the Comanche Nation.*

from being menacing or unprepossessing. Although he was gazing back at her and she had become conscious of the discrepancies of her attire, there was none of the lewd and lascivious scrutiny to which she had been subjected by her captors. What was more, although he had come over, it was to present her with a red satin blouse and green wrap-around skirt which she recognized as having belonged to 'Lady Lavinia of Sheffield, England'. For a moment, she had been puzzled to account for him having the garments. Then she had realized he must have found them amongst the other loot taken from her dead friends by their murderers.

Accepting and donning the clothing, the girl had told herself that her rescuer having scalped the dead warriors did not preclude the possibility of him being employed by the Army. According to what she had heard around camp fires whilst hunting with her father and those of his friends who had had experience in the West, such scouts were not prevented from treating hostile Indians they killed in such a fashion. Nor did discovering he did not understand English when she tried to thank him cause her to change her mind about his occupation.

Seeking for a way of communicating with the warrior, so as to be able to satisfy her curiosity, Becky had thanked him for clothes in Spanish. Her delight at finding she was understood had been tempered by the limitations caused by their respective knowledge of the tongue. The dialect she had learned from 'Dona Conchita Alvarez of Madrid, Spain' was different to the one in which he had replied and, because she had not learned the appropriate terms needed to pose the questions, there had been much which she could not have explained.

On being asked and having admitted she was hungry, the *Tshaoh* had formed the correct deduction from the way the girl's face had twitched in revulsion as she gazed at the scalped bodies of the Kiowas. Telling her to accompany him, he had led the way to where three horses which had clearly seen recent considerable hard use were standing 'ground hitched' by their dangling reins. Collecting pemmican and jerky from the buckskin *parfleche* bag fastened to the cantle of one of the saddles, he had offered some of each to her. Having partaken of both when on hunting trips with her father—except the meat used to produce them had always been beef and not, although she was unaware of the fact, the flesh of buffalo with which she was presented[2]—she had eaten ravenously.

By the time the meal was over, the sun had been sinking beyond the western horizon. After helping her rescuer to bring the property of the dead Kiowas to the woodland and to tend to the horses, she had been so tired from the stresses of the day that she had made an extemporized bed from fallen leaves and slept without being disturbed until morning. Over a breakfast of pemmican and jerky, hoping the name would be familiar to him, she had asked the *Tshaoh* if he would take her to Fort Worth. Although it was obvious he had not understood the name, he had inquired whether she could ride and, receiving an answer in the affirmative, told her to select a horse so they could be on the move.

It was not until the pair had left the woodland and were heading across more open, rolling terrain in the middle of

2 *'Pemmican' and 'jerky' were staple foods much used by the North American Indians of all tribes, although each had its own way of making them. They were portable, long lasting and, containing much nourishment in a small compass, ideal for carrying as emergency rations when travelling long distances with the possibility of not being able to hunt for fresh food.*

2a *'Pemmican', often referred to as 'Indian bread', was made of venison, buffalo or pronghorn meat—as available—which was dried, mixed with tallow, pounded and pressed tightly into cakes. Sometimes a few serviceberries were added to improve the flavour.*

2b *'Jerky', dried meat. The process was accomplished by stripping the hams of an animal in a manner which left a thin membrane covering each piece and cutting other portions of the carcase into slices about an inch thick. In either case, the pieces were dipped into a strong boiling brine. Then they were smoked briefly and the curing process was completed by exposure to the sun. Despite looking unpalatable, in addition to being lighter to carry than pemmican, it was even more sustaining against fatigue and, if cooked into a soup, the portions swelled to considerable proportions and served as a most nourishing meal.*

the afternoon that the girl had realized they were heading in a westerly instead of the more southerly route she had been travelling before the massacre. On asking why this was, the *Tshaoh* had pointed to their rear to where a small party of riders were following in the distance and explained they were the rest of the band responsible for the murder and mutilation of her friends. Assuming he was taking a roundabout way of returning to whichever Army post he belonged, instead of rejoining the soldiers who had sent him to her rescue—unless he had been on a mission alone and acted of his own initiative—she had not been unduly worried by him continuing to lead her in the same direction.

After making camp at sundown, without the pursuers having closed the distance more than marginally, the *Tshaoh* had satisfied himself that Becky knew how to load and shoot a rifle. Then, telling her to watch over the animals, he had set off on one of his horses and armed only as he had been when she first saw him. This time, having witnessed how efficiently he was able to use the weapons, she had had no misgivings. Nevertheless, something else had puzzled her and it went unexplained. While making preparations to leave, he had taken a pair of old and obviously worn out moccasins from his *parfleche* and tucked them under his waist belt.

Left alone, the girl had forced herself to remain awake, ready to use the two rifles if necessary. The need had not arisen. Returning as daylight was starting to lighten the sky, it was obvious her rescuer's expedition had not been without success. He had brought three horses with him and there was another scalp hanging from his belt. However, he no longer had the old moccasins. Nor had there been any further sign of the pursuers as they continued to ride to the west.[3]

Finding their mutually restricted knowledge of Spanish did not extend to posing the main questions which plagued

[3] *The significance of Singing Bear's behaviour is explained in:* OLD MOCCASINS ON THE TRAIL.

her, Becky had taken consolation from the thought that her rescuer had not tried to molest her in any way. Rather he had treated her with a consideration she would not have expected from all the information she had acquired about Red Indians over the years. Not only did he show no interest in her as a woman, but he never offered to keep any of the captured weapons out of her reach or to restrict her freedom of movement in any way when they were camped for the night. Therefore, she had told herself that he must be taking her to the Army post at which he served instead of returning to the trail. The supposition had grown weaker with the passage of time. Nevertheless, realizing she would have the greatest difficulty in even finding her way back in the direction from which they had come, she had made no attempt to do so.

When she saw the Indian village, Becky realized her belief that the rescuer was a scout for the Army might have been completely wrong. However, she told herself that there was just a chance that he was a scout and had come home to dispose of his loot before taking her back to her own kind.

Accompanying her rescuer down the slope, leading four of the captured horses, the girl studied her surroundings. Constructed of animal hides—buffalo, she was to discover later—over a conical framework of long, straight poles,[4] they looked much the same as she had seen depicted on paintings of Indian villages although she felt certain the decorations painted on the walls of the *tipis* must differ from tribe to tribe. Fires were burning outside them, some with cooking pots bubbling as meals were being prepared for the occupants. Elsewhere, men and women sat or stood around performing a variety of tasks. Beyond the stream which flowed through the centre of the camp, in addition to mounts picketed close to the

[4] *While the number might be more, or less, generally a Comanche* tipi *was supported by twenty-two poles—pine or cedar being the woods most favoured—peeled, seasoned and pared down to a suitable diameter. A more detailed description and how one was erected is given in:* COMANCHE.

dwellings of their owners, many horses and ponies were grazing under the watchful gaze of boys approaching adolescence.

No matter what was occupying them, with the exception of the horse herders, the people started to hurry forward as the newcomers reached the edge of the village. All were tallish and slender in build, clad in clothing made of buckskin and with the men wearing blue breechclouts no matter what else they had on. Asking questions in their own tongue, some of which Becky realized must be about her, it was obvious they were delighted by the arrival of her rescuer. Signalling for her to dismount, he slipped from his saddle and, she assumed, started to explain what he had been doing and how she came to be with him.

'How'd he take you, girl?'

Hearing the words, spoken in English which was hesitant as if from lack of recent use, Becky turned towards the speaker. She proved to be an elderly and white haired woman clad like the other females in the crowd, but whose features were undoubtedly European in spite of being tanned to almost the same shade as the Indians.

'Take me?' the girl repeated in puzzlement. 'I thought he was a scout for the Army and had been sent after some Indians who'd massacred my friends.'

'I can tell you're not a Texan,' the woman stated, her accent that of a Southron. 'But what in the Good Lord's name made you think a thing like that?'

'He risked his life to save me from some of the Indians who did it,' Becky explained, the tone in which the question had been posed giving further evidence that she had been wrong in her assumption.

'Seeing's he's come back, I figured he'd caught up with them,' the woman admitted. 'But it wasn't to save your life. Three Kiowa bucks took his wife while she was out food hunting and had their way with her afore they killed her. So he took him a blood oath to get revenge and, from the looks of things, he'd done that and *more*.'

'He *did*!' Becky confirmed and she could not restrain a shudder as she thought of the bodies she had seen on recovering from the faint. 'But, if he isn't a scout for the Army, who is he?'

'His name's Singing Bear,' the woman replied. 'This here's the Waterhorse Band's, so they're called. Honey, he's a *Comanche*.'

* * * *   * * * *

'A *Comanche*?' Becky Ingraham gasped, putting the same emphasis on the name of the tribe as had her informant.

Even before she had reached Texas, the girl had heard of the Comanches. They had a reputation for ferocity and hostility towards white people which no other tribe yet possessed. Many and lurid were the tales told of their skill at waging war and the atrocities which followed every victory they achieved. Yet she could hardly reconcile such stories with either the way in which she had been treated by her rescuer, or the appearance of the people who were gathered about her.

While Singing Bear had killed and scalped six men in the fight following his first appearance, then taken the life of another to dissuade the remainder of the war party from following them, the girl had no complaint about the way he had treated her. Not only had he refrained from molesting her in any way, but he had fed her and helped with the chores such as tending to the horses. Nor did the people look in any way filthy, vicious and depraved. Their appearance was cleanly and their behaviour reminded her of the villagers amongst whom she had grown up when welcoming one who had been absent for some reason and returned in triumph.

'They're Comanches all right,' the elderly woman confirmed.

'But he's treated me *well*,' Becky objected, unable to reconcile her rescuer's conduct with what she had heard. 'He didn't—didn't—!'

'He loved his squaw and's still in mourning for her,' the woman pointed out. 'And, even happen he wasn't, he's not bad mean like some's you could've got took by.'

'Have you been—badly treated?' the girl asked, deciding her informant looked nothing like the ill-used and abused drudge she would have expected a captive of savages to be.

'Not over bad,' the woman admitted, then looked around as the newly return brave spoke to her. Returning her gaze to Becky, she continued, 'Singing Bear says I've got to take you to his *tipi*.'

'Then I'm—?' the girl gasped.

'You're to stay here,' the woman affirmed and her voice took on a timbre of warning. 'Don't refuse to come along with me, nor start acting foolish, honey. You can't do nothing, 'cepting make things bad for you happen you even try.'

'But—But—!' Becky gasped, gazing about her and needing to call upon all her self control to prevent herself from leaping to and mounting a horse so as to take flight.

'Come on,' the woman said, gently yet firmly, taking the girl by the left arm. 'I know how you feel, honey. I did the same when I was brung here.'

'You mean—?' Becky began, as she was urged by a gentle tug to start walking away from the horses, having concluded from what she had been told that her informant was living with the Indians by preference and free choice.

'My name's Annie Wishart,' the woman introduced. 'I was the only one they took alive from a village they massacred. They'd come looking for revenge, 'cause some lousy scalp-hunters'd killed a dozen or more of their women and kids, I found out later. I felt real bad about being took at first. Then, after a spell, I got around to figuring I wasn't all that bad off at all.'

'You mean you *like* it *here*?' Becky asked.

'Took a spell, but I come 'round to just that,' Annie replied. 'I was still alive and in some ways better off. I'd been took from a husband's worked me finger-raw 'n' got mean drunk and whipped me at least once a week, and I wound up with one's worked me no harder, fed me better and never laid a hand on me. Yes, honey, I've knowed *worse* than living with the Comanche and, was I you, I'd try to start thinking along them same lines. 'Cause you're likely like me, to *stay*.'

'You mean there's no hope of being rescued, or escaping?'

'The first just *might* happen, only it hasn't during the six years they'd had me. But was I you, I'd give up all notion of escaping. This's the furthest east I've been with 'em and, 'less'n I'm mistook, we're still a far piece from the nearest white folks and it's all bad mean land along the way to get there. Even happen you got a hoss, lit out and they didn't run you down—which ain't *likely*, way the bucks can follow sign 'n' ride—there's some worse things than living among 'em's you'll be like to meet out there.'

Engrossed in the conversation, Becky suddenly became aware that she and Annie were being followed. Not by any of the men, but by five Indian girls forming a half circle about them. All were younger than her, not bad looking and simply clad in undecorated buckskin dresses which were tight enough to show off each's trim figure to its best advantage and moccasins. However, she was less interested in their looks and clothing than in their attitude. Moving closer, they were passing remarks between themselves to the accompaniment of gestures her way which she sensed were far from complimentary or friendly.

'Keep going, honey,' Annie instructed, after saying something in what Becky assumed to be the Comanche language which failed to either stop the girls following or reduce their all too obvious hostility.

Doing as instructed, the brunette felt her temper rising as hands reached out to push and grab at her clothing. Then one of the girls, made bolder by her apparently meek acceptance of their abuse, snatched a slender branch from outside the *tipi* they were passing and lashed her across the shoulders.

Such was not, anybody who knew her could have warned, the kind of treatment which the girl who called herself 'Becky Ingraham' would allow to pass without retaliation!

Letting out a gasp of pain mingled with anger, the brunette quickly spun on her heel until locating who had struck her. Bringing around her knotted right fist, she delivered a power packed punch to the jaw of her assailant. It was a beautiful blow, sent with skill and precision. The kind which she had learned could end hostilities before they could go any further. Certainly it had that effect as far as the recipient was concerned. Sent in an uncontrollable twirl, the branch flying from her grasp, she did not stop until sprawling limply and unconscious on the ground.

Angry yells burst from the rest of the girls. Two of them were delayed by having to shove the white haired woman aside as she tried to stop them, but the other pair were able to leap straight at Becky with hands reaching for hair. Their attack was purely feminine and far less skilled than she had become accustomed to dealing with in the ring. Darting between them, she dealt each a backhand slap to the face which spun them away before either's fingers could take hold. Having done so, she twirled to meet the rush towards her being made by the first two. Ducking her head, she charged to ram it into the midsection of the closest and, emitting a startled squawk, the girl was thrown backwards by the impact.

As Becky came to a halt and was straightening up, the other Comanche threw both arms around her biceps and pinned them to her sides. Only for a moment, however. Putting to use all the strength in her sturdily curvaceous body, the brunette threw off the restraining grip with a force which caused her attacker to stumble away. Turning to continue the offensive, Becky was seized in a similar manner from behind. This time, before she could try to escape in the same fashion, two of the girls rushed towards her. Bracing herself against the one to her rear, she swung her legs up and, getting a foot against each of the approaching pair's breasts, she gave a thrust which sent them reeling backwards. Having done so, feeling the arms around her relaxing as her feet returned to the ground, she reached over her shoulders. Grabbing two handsful of black hair, she bent at the waist and catapulted the girl in a half somersault over her.

Although she had liberated herself once more, the freedom gained by Becky was only brief. Almost as soon as she escaped, still gasping in air to replace that driven out by the force of the butt, the girl not involved in the latest attack returned to the fray. Tackled around the waist, the brunette was starting to deal with the one responsible when the two she had thrust away came rushing back. For a moment, there was a confused staggering scrimmage with hands grabbing hair or clutching at clothing. Then their legs became entangled and, locked together, they went to the ground and engulfed the fourth Comanche before she could recover from being dumped supine.

Churning over and over, the five girls formed an incredibly interwoven, yet ever altering mound of furiously struggling female flesh from which arose a variety of screeches, yelps, croaks, gasps, groans and screams to give testimony to how much pain was being inflicted upon every one of them. Attracted by the commotion, everybody who had gathered to welcome back Singing Bear hurried up. However, none made any attempt to intervene. Instead, they formed a large circle and made it plain they were enjoying the spectacle. What was more, following the trait common amongst members of the *Pahuraix*—Water Horse—band of the Comanche nation, many of them soon started betting upon what would happen next as well as the eventual outcome.

However, it was doubtful whether the spectators—or the combatants, for that matter—could have said exactly what was being done by any of the quintet at a given moment!

Regardless of what was taking place, to Becky, it seemed she was constantly being mauled by dozens of pairs of hands and at least a similar number of legs were also assailing every portion of her body. Fists and flat palms pounded her head, shoulders and body from groin to bosom, back and front. Soon blood was flowing from her nostrils and her right eye started to swell and discolour, but she had no idea whether knuckles or some other portion of her attackers' anatomy was responsible for either. Her limbs were jerked, twisted and tugged at. While this was going on, knees and feet too inflicted suffering wherever they made contact and this too was happening with great frequency. Nor was her brunette hair ignored as a means of adding to her pain and there were moments when she thought not only handsful, but her very scalp would be torn away.

Nevertheless, the punishment was not being delivered without retaliation!

There was no opportunity for Becky to make use of the training she had received and skill acquired as a member of Horace 'Pug' Brackley's International Troupe Of Lady Wrestlers. Instead, she too was instinctively using fists, knees and feet with completely impartial abandon. What was more, no matter where she hit, clutched, or otherwise attacked, it was upon the person of an enemy. To her advantage, due to the indescribable confusion and continual tangling of their bodies, each Comanche was frequently—if inadvertantly—causing pain and damage to the others. In fact, such was the state of confusion and their continued close proximity, she was only responsible for one of the four Indians' noses being bloodied and two of the six blackened eyes sustained by her assailants.

Furthermore, the combatants were not always fighting as a single group. On one occasion, the mound separated with three of them rolling away and, oblivious of their efforts being directed against one another, battling just as furiously together until coming up against Becky and her single attacker to make the mound complete once more. Later, another separation found her for a short while entangled with two of the girls before they and the other pair all merged again.

In addition to what was being inflicted upon her person, the brunette's attire was subjected to equally indiscriminate damage. The wrap-around skirt was soon gone and her blouse disintegrated to leave her bare to the waist. Not only were the legs of her tights torn away, one completely and the other at knee level, the whole of their seat was wrenched out by wildly clutching hands. However, in spite of this, she faired better than two of her attackers. All four's clothing was also severely damaged, not all of this being inflicted by her, but the loss of their dresses left the two completely naked without inducing them to quit the fray.

A full ten minutes of such unceasing combat thrilled and entertained the spectators!

Towards the end, inevitably, the strain began to take its toll upon the embattled quintet!

Movements became slower, grips weakened and blows diminished in force. Although all five continued to be hurt, none had sufficient breath to spare for crying out. Instead, croaking wheezes alone gave audible evidence of the punishment to which all were continually and indiscriminately being subjected by one another. In addition to diluting and partially washing away the blood each had flowing from nostrils and, in three cases, lips, the perspiration all were copiously shedding made their bodies slick and slippery. However, by rendering their breasts in particular difficult to retain when grasped, the wettening of their skin proved a blessing in disguise. On the other hand, regardless of their mutual suffering, not one of them showed the slightest indication of giving up the struggle.

'That's quite a wildcat you've brought back,' a brave commented to Becky's rescuer, watching the struggling girls for the third time separate into two mounds and, coming to their knees, she delivered a punch which landed sufficiently hard to stretch her totally naked opponent unconscious across the first attacker she had felled and who had been kept from returning to sentinence due to having been rolled on by all five during the struggle. 'She's a woman of spirit.'

'Yes,' Singing Bear agreed, knowing the white girl's attackers to be unmarried maidens who he suspected were respectively motivated by a desire to become his wife and were resentful of the possibility of an outsider having been selected to fill the position. 'I saw that when she helped me against the Kiowas.'

Looking around instinctively, Becky discovered that the number of her attackers was reduced still further without requiring any effort on her part. One of the trio was sprawling on to her back and lay, arms and legs thrown apart. The only movement from her was the rise and fall of her bosom as her lungs automatically sucked in air. Seeing the other two were still feebly fighting with one another and paying no attention to her, the brunette was able to appreciate the opportunity she was being granted in spite of the exhaustion which welled through her. Forcing herself to get up, staggering in exhaustion, she went to where they were kneeling with interlocked fingers and engaged in a mindless test of strength. Grabbing them by the scruff of the neck and jerking them a little way apart, giving neither a chance to resist, she banged their heads together. Stunned by the impact, they went limp in her hands and, on being released, collapsed on to their backs rendered *hors de combat*.

Forcing herself to remain erect, in spite of hurting in every fibre of her being and reeling from exhaustion, Becky felt the elation she had come to know when emerging victorious in a serious wrestling bout against a local contender. Although she was unable to understand what was being said, gazing around, she realized the spectators were giving her the same kind of enthusiastic and admiring reception she had received even when it was a woman from the area she had defeated. Then the reaction set in and she crumpled to the ground. Nevertheless, she was just sufficiently conscious to feel herself being lifted and carried—by Singing Bear, she discovered later—through the enthusiastic crowd.

9 *Hello, Annie Singing Bear!*

The scene lit by the red glow of the nearby flames was much the same as had been enacted a countless number of times since human beings first learned how to make use of fire for warmth and illumination!

Laying supine on an extemporized bed of soft dry grass under the stars, held spread-eagled by Annie Wishart and three of her closest friends amongst the Indian women, Becky Ingraham felt the movements she had created by her muscular spasms descending lower in her abdomen. From what she had witnessed when other mothers-to-be were on the point of giving birth, she deduced the functions which had taken place within her during the past nine months were coming to fruition.

Just over a year had gone by since the brunette was brought to the village of the *Pahuraix* Comanches by Singing Bear!

Carrying Becky to his *tipi* at the conclusion of the fight, her rescuer had left her in the care of Annie and the medicine man and woman of the band. After stripping off her ruined tights and bathing her in cold water, they had stopped her nose bleeding and applied an oily lotion which smelled sweetly and did much to soothe away the pain resulting from the bruises which mottled her whole body. The problem of replacing her attire had been solved by selecting from the garments which had belonged to the warrior's murdered wife and who, perhaps accounting for his behaviour towards the brunette, had had a shorter, and more slender build than those of the more typical Comanche. Therefore, they were both much the same dimensions and few alterations had proved necessary to obtain a fit. While Becky had not been enamoured of the prospect of wearing the dead woman's garments, she had accepted there was no other choice. Her own clothing had been ruined in the fight and there was no other female attire amongst the loot taken from the Kiowas. An examination had established that the buckskin dresses were clean and, as time went by, she had grown accustomed to making do with the underclothing—little more than a simple loincloth for the rest of spring and summer—which was all that was available to go beneath them.

While seeming primitive in concept, the treatment had proved sufficiently effective to allow the brunette to accept an invitation by Singing Bear to a special kind of celebration the following evening. Acting as interpreter, Annie had explained it was known as a 'Give-Away' dance; being chiefly to thank *Ka-Dih*, the Great Spirit of the Comanches, for looking favourably upon him and allowing the successful conclusion of his quest for vengeance, but partly to honour the victory she had had over the five girls. From what she was told, the latter had proved most beneficial to him. Remembering how she had come to his aid against the Kiowas, he had had confidence enough in her ability to bet heavily on her and the winnings, supported by the loot with which he had returned, ensured he could provide a good quantity of gifts to be presented on her behalf as well as his own to their guests.

The affair had been accounted a great success and had done much to start reconciling Becky to her future. Not only had she found herself treated with respect and kindness, particularly after her rescuer had described the part she played in the fight with the Kiowas, but it had given her an insight into the way in which the Comanches relaxed and enjoyed themselves. She had discovered they were far from being the dour and vicious savages she had always heard was the case. Rather they had thrown themselves into the festivities with a gusto and amiability which had equalled anything she had seen displayed by people of her own race. What was more, at the conclusion, she had not been faced with one situation which she had been envisaging with dread. Taken back to the *tipi* by Singing Bear, despite her grave concern over them being its only occupants, he had made no attempt to press attentions upon her. What was more, they had continued to sleep in separate beds until a growing mutual respect and liking had turned to genuine affection.

On recovering from the effects of the fight, Becky had found herself faced with the most serious test of courage she had ever known. Her upbringing in Missouri had at first revolted at the thought of being compelled to live on terms of intimacy with a man who was neither of her race nor creed, but she had soon come to realize she might have been far worse off. What was more, accepting that any attempt to escape was almost certain to be thwarted and would probably result in changing Singing Bear's attitude of kindly consideration to something much less pleasant, she had put the idea from her thoughts. She had also refused to listen to an inner voice claiming death was better than dishonour. Not only would such an act have gone against the religious principles with which she was imbued as a child, but nothing in the way she had been treated was sufficient inducement for her to contemplate seeking release by committing suicide. Therefore, being the kind of person she was, she had forced herself to adjust to what she sensed could be a long period—perhaps even being permanent—during which she would have to accept vastly different standards of behaviour even than had been the case when she joined Horace 'Pug' Brackley's International Troupe Of Lady Wrestlers.

Having reached the conclusion, with Annie Wishart acting as willing guide and mentor, the girl had set about getting the best out of her new way of life. Except for incidentals such as the stays being somewhat longer, it did not change in one respect. Like all the Plains Indians, the *Pahuraix* never remained in one location for more than a few weeks at most. While almost as nomadic, despite there being no wheeled transport available, she had found travelling was not excessively more difficult and uncomfortable than it had been as a member of Brackley's Troupe. She had also discovered her new accommodation might appear more primitive, but it offered some advantages over the wagon in which she had lived when moving from town to town. Developed as a result of the experience gathered by many generations of Comanches, in addition to being portable as was required by their mode of existence, a *tipi* could easily be kept cool in the heat of summer, was waterproof and well able to withstand the elements during winter.

Nor had she lacked companionship. Regardless of what she had expected, she had not been subjected to abuse or cruelty by the majority of the Indians. In fact, she had found herself able to make friends amongst the Comanche women and the girls with whom she had fought became the staunchest of them. Nevertheless, on three separate occasions during the first few weeks she had been compelled to defend herself against attacks by other female members of the community. In each case, being in contention against only a single adversary, her superior knowledge of wrestling and the use of her fists had brought her victory with an ease which did much to increase her status around the village. To ensure this remained and as a precaution to remove the desire of any others who might have harboured similar hostile feelings, she had let it be seen that she meant to keep up her fighting skill by giving instructions in bare handed combat to the young males as part of their training as warriors.

As the band moved from place to place, always seeking to make camp near water in the fashion which had produced one of its names, Becky had been taught by Annie and the others how to erect a *tipi*. They had shown her which kinds of vegetation and roots were edible and could be used as supplements to meat of various kinds when making a meal. Instruction had been given about gathering the necessary fuel, starting a fire without using the matches she had previously considered indispensible, and cooking on it. Her knowledge of needlework had been expanded to let her cope with the materials from which the

Pahuraix made their clothing. She had also learned about the primitive, yet efficient, means of giving first aid for injuries and the employment of various herbs and plants for medication. All in all, although she had accepted it would be futile to try to put the various skills to use in an attempt to escape and return to her own kind, she had gathered much knowledge useful as an aid to surviving on the vast range which was still being traversed by the *Pahuraix* and other bands of Indians.

Ever eager to attain knowledge and quick to learn, the brunette had soon acquired competence at the various duties expected of her. In addition, by proving willing to carry out her share of whatever work was being done, she had increased her popularity. What was more, being constantly amongst people speaking nothing else—with the exception of the elderly white woman and half a dozen Mexican captives—she had quickly become fluent in the *Pahuraix* dialect of the Comanche language. Having a natural dexterity, helping to develop her acceptance and popularity, she had gained competence at the *Nemenuh* women's sport of 'kick-the-ball'. In a short while, her skill had developed to such an extent that she could soon compete against the best in hopping on the left foot while keeping a ball made of rags in the air by 'dribbling' it off the ground with the instep of the right until it was dropped when either remaining 'on the spot' or moving forward.

One problem Becky had faced, particularly as their own relationship had warmed, had been coming to good terms with an important member of Singing Bear's family. As she had expected and had felt sure would have been equally the case if the roles were reversed, they clearly had reservations about his taking a white woman as a replacement for his murdered squaw. With the passing of time and the exhibition of her good qualities, his grandparents, father, brothers, sisters, aunt, uncles, nieces and nephews had grown to consider her as one of their own, albeit not in that order. However, as would probably have proved the case no matter what race was involved, gaining the approval of her Comanche mother-in-law had been more difficult. That she had achieved it eventually was a tribute to the effort she had put into doing so.

On the whole, while life had not been idyllic, it was far from the horrible nightmare Becky had been led to assume was the fate of a white woman taken captive by Indians. She worked harder than ever before and lived in an even more primitive fashion than when travelling with Brackley's Troupe, but it was not a life of constant drudgery and misery. What was more, the hunting and other food gathering being good, she remained as well fed—albeit on food cooked in different ways and employing some ingredients she had not previously encountered—as she had ever been, no matter what her previous situation. Once she had grown accustomed to mounting from the right side, as was the custom of most American Indians regardless of their tribe, she had found her equestrian abilities were equal to the calls made upon them.

Discovering she was pregnant had proved a shock for Becky, although her closer relationship with Singing Bear had warned her of the possibility. Nevertheless, she had endured the travelling from location to location with a stoicism she had seen shown by other women in a similar condition. With the passing of time, although some of the heavier burdens were taken over from her by her friends as the development of the child inside her body had began to make itself more obvious, she had been grateful for the rugged state of her constitution and the work which had ensured she remained in excellent physical condition. Because of this, she had been able to continue riding a horse when on the move and to perform her less strenuous chores until receiving the signs which warned the birth was imminent.

The indications had started late on a pleasant afternoon. Called for by Becky, the medicine woman and Annie had pronounced the time was at hand, then made their preparations. Accepting pointed comments with good grace, although usually a warrior—particularly one who elected to accept the responsibilities and prestige of selecting the war lance as his main weapon—was at other times very much the 'master of the house', Singing Bear had taken his departure to spend the waiting period in the company of his closest companions. With the weather being so clement, it had been decided by the experienced helpers that the event should take place in the open. Everything had been made ready, including there being other female assistance available. These had proved necessary. The birth was not easy and the mother-to-be required support and restraint in the later stages.

After much pain, suddenly Becky felt something which moved thrusting itself between her parted thighs. There was a final convulsive motion and the firm, wriggling lump was gone. Despite a sensation of relief and a cessation of her suffering, she lay spent by the exertions of the delivery. She was too weak to even try to wipe away the perspiration which clouded her vision, much less attempt to sit up and find out if all was well with the baby. Before she could ask after its welfare, she heard a slapping sound and something which put her in mind of the yapping of a distant coyote. Then she realized it was originating from much closer and an understanding of what it must be flooded through her.

With the realization came anxiety!

For all their love of children, the Comanches did not allow an infant born deformed, diseased, or a weakling, to live!

Therefore, should the baby be other than healthy after its long struggle to leave the womb, it would be put to death regardless of how its mother felt upon the matter!

Alarmed by the prospect, Becky tried to sit up. Gentle hands raised and supported her shoulders. Somebody wiped away the sweat with a piece of cloth. With her vision restored, her gaze focussed upon something small and reddish which writhed and squalled in the hands of the medicine woman.

'I—Is it all right?' the brunette gasped, speaking in English.

'It's a fine healthy girl, Woman Of Spirit!' the medicine women replied before Annie Wishart could supply the information in the same language, guessing what the question had been and using the name by which Becky was known to the *Pahuraix*.

'A girl!' the brunette gasped. Taking the baby, she looked at it. From the first moment she had realized she was pregnant, she had wondered how she would react to the sight of a child which was illegitimate—even unacceptable—by the standards under which she had been raised. Feeling and watching its movements, she realized she did not care how its birth might be regarded by others. It was *her* first born and she loved it. Wanting to express her gratitude to the woman who more than anybody else had helped her adjust to her new way of life, before lowering the baby to suckle at a breast, she went on in tones of rapturous delight, 'Hello, Annie Singing Bear!'.

Part Two

The Finished Product

10 Should-Be-A-Boy

Like any healthy child born in a Comanche village, Annie Singing Bear was given the care and treatment befitting a valuable addition to the *Pahuraix* band. During her first days, she was kept swaddled by robes in the *tipi* where Becky Ingraham—the *Nemenuh* did not use surnames and she was known among them as 'Woman Of Spirit'—was 'lying-in' to recover from the rigours of the birth. From the beginning, not only did the baby receive constant loving attention from her mother, but the distaff members of her father's family, Annie Wishart and other women friends supplied it too. What was more, although he would have preferred a boy for his first born, Singing Bear lavished just as much affection upon her and did everything he could to ensure her well being.

When Becky was able to get up and about, Annie spent the next period of her life on a '*papoose* board'—which could be stood up out of harms way, or carried easily on her mother's back—during the hours of daylight.[1] Until attaining a size and weight which precluded the former, she was transported either by her mother when moving around on foot or suspended from a saddle or travois pole if the band were on the move. No matter whether in camp or travelling, particularly when the return of cold weather caused her to be wrapped inside the cradle by a cocoon of blankets with just a small hole left to allow her to breathe

1 *The* 'papoose *board' was also called a 'cradle board'. It was either a basket made of rawhide fastened to a flat, angular plank, or a soft buckskin sheath that laced up the front and was securely anchored to a back board.*

and through which only her peering eyes were visible, removing her from the container to keep her clean after she had carried out her bodily functions would have been a laborious and time consuming task. It was avoided by inserting a draining tube between her legs and out of the container at the front and having her excrement caught in soft, dry moss. Despite these precautions, she still got wet and messy. However, before being transferred to sleep in her 'night cradle',[2] she was thoroughly washed, greased and powdered with the pulverized dry rot of cottonwood which experience had proved was of all the material available most suitable for the task.

Almost ten months elapsed before Annie was allowed liberty to experience the exploratory pleasures of crawling about on the floor of the *tipi*. From then until she was able to walk without needing constant supervision, she still continued to be returned to the *papoose* board or night cradle as conditions demanded. Nevertheless, despite the confinement, her education was commenced. The first lesson was that crying would not cause her whims to be gratified and soon, no matter what the conditions, she kept silent. As she grew older and more able to understand, she learned to do some things and avoid others which would not have been to her advantage. She was also taught that she could benefit by acting in a certain way, but not from another. Scolded by her parents when necessary and praised as deserved, she was never subjected to corporal punishment at either's hands. On the occasions when such additional discipline was required, it was supplied by a female member of her father's family, or one of her mother's friends, all of whom took an active part in her upbringing and her mother performed a similar service for them.

In accordance with Comanche tradition, the next step in Annie's education should have been learning the duties of a woman. She began conventionally enough by helping

[2] *The 'night cradle' comprised of a stiff rawhide tube which was sufficiently sturdy it allowed the baby to sleep between its parents without the danger of either rolling upon and suffocating her.*

her mother to carry water and progressed to assisting in gathering wood. However, even while doing so, she started to show a greater propensity for masculine activities. More and more when the time came for her to perform such feminine chores, she would be found playing the games which were usually considered the province of boys. Another aspect also became increasingly noticeable.

Commencing shortly after her birth, like every *Nemenuh* since *Ka Dih* had seen fit to bring them into contact with the 'god dog' which changed them from comparatively harmless wanderers on foot to mounted warriors second to none, the girl had become used to the horses and their motions as a result of being carried strapped to a saddle, hanging on her mother's back and, later, clinging to Becky or the mane of the animal carrying them. From these beginnings, she gained confidence, learned balance and graduated to riding by herself upon a gentle old pack horse at a somewhat earlier age than was usual for one of her sex. On reaching her fifth birthday, she was capable of handling the pony presented to her by her grandfather. Before two more years passed, she was as capable as any boy her age at sitting a colt bareback.

Nor did the attainment of masculine achievements end with riding!

As was the case during Becky's tomboy childhood, if Annie had been raised in the society and ways of her maternal kinfolks, every effort would have been made to turn her proclivity away from masculine activities. Instead of adopting such an attitude, having accepted as valid the pronouncement on the subject made by the band's medicine man and woman, the *Pahuraix* had considered the deviation from normal behaviour was ordained by *Ka Dih*. Therefore, they did not feel there was any stigma attached to it. Rather they had believed it was an honour that she was selected by the Great Spirit to follow the life-style—if not necessarily in a sexual sense—of a male. Nor had her mother raised any objections to the arrangement. Rather it had been welcomed by Becky as, if the predilection continued, one situation she had envisaged for the future might be forestalled even if not completely removed.

In keeping with the ways of the Comanche, due to her father being occupied by the duties of an active warrior, Annie's education was put into the hands of her grandfather, Brother To The Hawk. Thereafter, instead of receiving instruction suitable to a *tuepet* from the distaff side of the family, she started to acquire the same upbringing as would any *tuinep'*. Furthermore, in spite—or rather *because*—of its 'medicine' significance, not only was she allowed to discard feminine costume, her adoption of masculine attire was permitted to extend to the breechclout.

One other matter had arisen as a result of the drastic alteration to Annie's way of life. Her name was changed to 'Should-Be-A-Boy'—generally shortened to '*Tuinep*'' —and everybody waited to find out whether she could live up to the proud heritage of her father and grandfather. Although the latter had given up the honour, both had attained considerable fame as lance carriers.

Once the girl's future had been settled, presenting her with a bow and some blunt arrows, Brother To The Hawk had taught her how to shoot. Spending much time in practice, she hunted small birds and animals with the boys of her age. As she gained competence, she ranged farther from the camp in search of larger quarry. From the beginning, she was made to realize that hunting was a serious duty rather than a pleasurable pastime and how her ability might mean the difference between having food, shelter and clothing instead of suffering from starvation and exposure. As time went on, she progressed to attaining the necessary skills of hunting and the war trail. These had included all aspects of horse handling, living off the country, silent movement through any kind of cover, locating hidden perils, following tracks and becoming adept at concealment. Also taught was how to wield and make the most of every kind of weapon a warrior was able to select from.

Not all the training was by actual practice and participation. When the weather was unsuitable for outside activities, the girl and her male companions were told about tribal history, religious beliefs, traditions, legends and other essentials. Prominent in the instruction was the procedure to be carried out when a wrong inflicted by an enemy demanded personal vengeance be taken. This entailed swearing an oath to *Ka-Dih*, painting a red hand on the bare chest and riding out with the intention of only returning when the quest was completed.[3] They were also taught that there was no greater honour to be achieved than to become a lance carrier and uphold all doing so demanded.

To imbue Annie with the sense of pride and purpose which made the difference between remaining an average member of the community and becoming a warrior of renown, the ambition of every *Nemenuh* boy, she was frequently told of achievements which had brought acclaim to members of her family. The story which impressed her most was how her father had saved her mother after having tracked down and, in spite of having along a three-horse relay, stalked the killers of his former wife without being detected, then counted coup on six of them.

The story of Singing Bear's achievement helped Annie to understand why her mother and she differed in such ways as the colour of their hair and build from the rest of the band. When she expressed concern over how this might affect her future, she was assured that having a parent who was white—particularly one as courageous

[3] *Although the sign of the red hand was also made when a Comanche brave elected to ride* pukutsi, *there was a difference. Such an action could only be taken when there was to be a battle with warriors from another nation. Having made the hand print on his bare chest and shouted*, 'Pukutsi!', *so all might know his intentions, the brave charged forward alone and carrying whatever weapons he chose, with the objective of being first into the fight and, unless victory was won, dying instead of withdrawing. An explanation of how a lance carrier differed from a warrior electing to ride* pukutsi *can be found in* Item 2 *of the* APPENDIX.

and wise as Woman Of Spirit had proved to be—would not prevent her from achieving the ambition of every *tuinep'* to become a name warrior. According to news which reached them, visits by members of other Comanche bands being a not infrequent occurrence, a *Pehnane* youngster named *Cuchilo* and also of mixed blood had attained such competence he had had two Give-Away dances in his honour before the age when he qualified to be a *tuivitisi*.[4] Not only did learning of his exploits give her an added inducement to succeed, she was to hear of him again and make his acquaintance at a later date.[5]

For the next fifteen years, Annie's life followed the course which would have been taken by a boy. Always on the move, she acquired competence in everything a warrior would need to know. However, having inherited her mother's passion for learning, she also gained knowledge in subjects which none of her pure blood companions of either sex obtained. Nor did this stop with becoming fluent in English and passable in Spanish under the tuition of Becky, Annie Wishart and the Mexican captives. Seeing her mother obviously engrossed in one of several books which her father had brought back from a raid, meaning to have the leaves used as packing for a shield, her inborn curiosity caused her to inquire what made it so interesting. Being told the black markings on the white pages were used to convey information, she asked to be taught their secret and added reading and writing to her other accomplishments.

However, acquiring learning of white means of communication was an occupation of the late fall, winter and early spring. Once the weather started to improve,

[4] *Among white men,* Cuchilo—*the Spanish word meaning knife and granted because of his skill in wielding one as a weapon—became known as 'the Ysabel Kid'. How he achieved the distinction of the two Give-Away dances at such an early age is told in:* COMANCHE. *Information about his career in later life is given in various volumes of the* Civil War *and* Floating Outfit *series.*

[5] *Two of Annie Singing Bear's meetings with* Cuchilo *are described in:* WHITE INDIANS *and* BUFFALO ARE COMING!

Tuinep' and her masculine companions were allowed much freedom to do things which would help them with their future lives.

Throughout their pre-adolescent period, when not receiving instruction from their elders, *Tuinep'* and boys of her age group went their own way. Unlike the girls, they were never expected to perform any of the menial tasks about the camp. Instead, they were left to their own devices and any discomfort caused to their elders as a result of their high spirits and mischievous activities was overlooked on the grounds that, 'He is going to be a warrior and may die young in battle.' It was a system which taught self reliance, while also fostering a spirit of manly comradery which Annie absorbed regardless of her sex.

When camp was set up in a new location, the youngsters sought out a nearby portion of the stream where they could play all day. Occasionally, they would be joined by girls. In which case, they would build shelters of various kinds and establish a village in miniature complete with a 'chief' and 'families' comprised of a 'warrior'—with Annie always considered in that category—and his squaws. While the boys hunted to provide meat, the girls gathered berries, edible roots and eggs to supplement the meal.

However, with the approach of adolescence, such 'family' gatherings and other childish games were forgotten by *Tuinep'* and her age group. Instead, they joined and took to roaming in gangs already formed by older boys. Racing on foot or horseback, attaining other forms of equestrian skill, hunting, swimming and wrestling occupied more and more of their time. Given instruction by her mother, including how to make the best use of a clenched fist as a means of winning a bare handed fight—a tactic never developed to any great degree by the *Nemenuh*, or any other Indian nation—Annie quickly acquired a reputation for her prowess at the latter.

As their fathers 'raided' for horses and other loot, the gangs stole food from around the camp. At nights, armed with ropes—in the skilful throwing of which they could compare favourably with any cowhand or Mexican *vaquero*—they cut out mounts from the herd, regardless of ownership, to joyride on across the open range. Should they be detected, they would dismount and scatter to avoid the humiliation of being captured. Such escapades were not encouraged by their elders, but neither was any attempt made to prohibit them from participating. It was considered a part of the training to fit them for their future services as warriors and their marauding activities provided a useful extra guard against enemies seeking to reach the village.

With the passing of time, Becky Ingraham had grown from a girl frequently experiencing misgivings about her new way of life to a mature woman who had accepted it was the only one she was likely to have in the future. Whatever slight hope had remainded of escaping and returning to her own people ended with the birth of her first—only, as events proved—child. While she had accepted that Annie would almost certainly grow up as a Comanche, encouraging a working knowledge of the English language and passable standard of literacy had been precautions in case her summation proved incorrect.

Not only had the brunette accepted her situation, but being the kind of person she was, she had been successful in her desire to better it. Her natural intelligence and some of the things she had learned before meeting Singing Bear had served her well. Even before it had become obvious she could not provide him with the son he desired, in accordance with Comanche custom, he had taken three other wives. Being a successful warrior and consistently fortunate gambler, giving them high social standing in the community, he provided each with her own *tipi*. Furthermore, far from having been discarded, Becky was granted the special device—a decorative tongue-like appendage, which hung at the front and rear from the neck of her dress—indicating she was the *pairaivo*.

Reconciling herself to a marital situation which would have been regarded as abhorent by her own family, Becky had performed her duties as senior wife in a way which won her the confidence, respect and affection of her subordinates. What was more, the discovery that her only child appeared to have been specially selected by *Ka-Dih* for some purpose as yet unknown, she was able to attain added prestige by becoming associated with the band's spiritual advisers. From the medicine man and woman, she had acquired knowledge and wisdom which would not have been made available to an outsider lacking what was apparently a connection with the Great Spirit. All in all, regardless of her race, she had grown to be considered a person of worth and importance in the band.

There had been few contacts with her own people during the sixteen years Becky had spent amongst the *Pahuraix*. Nor had any of the white or half breed traders who came to the village struck her as offering a means of leaving. In fact, after the first of them had come and gone, she had kept out of the way when others put in an appearance. Nevertheless, as Annie Wishart had no such inhibitions, she had learned something of events taking place in the outside world. Other information had been brought by visiting parties of *Nemenuh*.

Although members of other bands occasionally told of conflict with 'long knife blue coats', who the brunette had guessed were members of the United States' Cavalry, the *Pahuraix* never crossed their path. This was partly because their terrain was not yet close enough to the ever spreading white settlements to bring them to the attention of the Army. Furthermore, the commencement of the War Between The States had caused the withdrawal of Union troops and the Confederates had none to spare for hunting Indians who were causing no trouble. The only contact with the civil war raging further east had come when Singing Bear and other warriors were invited by a trader to attend a meeting of all nations which was intended to persuade them to join together and drive the hated white man from the land. Nothing had come of the suggestion. The delegation had returned telling how a white haired, yet young looking, paleface *giant* had arrived and proved the medicine of the 'devil gun' supposed to help them attain victory was false.[6]

Even with the cessation of hostilities, news of which filtered through to Becky, there were no drastic changes to the situation at first. However, there were growing references by visitors from various bands to large herds of the white man's 'spotted buffalo'—as the half wild longhorn cattle were known—being driven towards the north by 'ride plenties' possessing a fighting ability which made attacking them a hazardous proposition.

Oblivious of the misgivings her mother was now experiencing about the way in which the world in their vicinity was developing, just past her fifteenth birthday as the maternal side of her bloodline regarded the passage of time, Annie well justified the name, 'Should-Be-A-Boy'. In appearance, apart from the colour of her hair and certain aspects of her features, she looked like a typical Comanche rather than a *Pahuraix*. Giving no thought to a figure which was becoming increasingly feminine in its development, her hair style and attire was masculine from head to foot.

Trained by having received the upbringing which was considered necessary to produce a potential warrior, *Tuinep'* was judged competent at everything she might be called up to do in that capacity. Anybody who questioned her right to either wear masculine attire or bear her name quickly came to regret having done so. Regardless of her phsyique becoming curvaceously buxom in a way which displayed her sex beyond any doubt, there was not an ounce of surplus fat on her body and powerful muscles lay beneath the skin to supply the means by which she could put her objections to the suggestion into effect. Nor did she lack the ability to do so. Skilled in the use of various weapons—including such firearms as came into the possession of the band—due to the lessons she had received from her mother, she was also probably better able then

[6] *Although the participation of Singing Bear is not recorded, what took place at the meeting is told in*: THE DEVIL GUN.

any of her male contemporaries to defend herself with bare hands if the need arose. Furthermore, albeit only in practise against other members of the band as yet—who, nevertheless, had done their best to catch her out—she had proved to the satisfaction of her elders that she was capable of everything a warrior riding a war trail would need to know and do.

Having attained such a status, like all those of her generation who had reached a similar stage in their development, Annie longed for an opportunity to gain acclaim and social advancement. Before this could happen and almost certainly lead to her being brought into contact and conflict with either the 'ride plenties' or the soldiers who also were appearing in increasing numbers, events occurred which were to shape her destiny along lines different to those which she envisaged.

Natural exuberance and rivalry caused Should-Be-A-Boy and others of her age group, now the leaders of the various gangs of roaming *tuinep'*, to compete more actively to bring themselves to the notice of their elders. By doing so, they frequently caused the village to be thrown into a state of uproar. While they could not be ordered to desist, long experience had taught the population how to gain a respite from their activities. This was done by taking advantage of them still being required to continue the training intended to turn them into seasoned and experienced *tehnap*.

In the company of the half a dozen boys who shared the responsibility for the disturbances with her, Annie was sent on a training expedition under the guidance and command of Feeds Many; a *tsukup* noted for his long experience and success as a hunter. They were not allowed to take along any provisions, but were expected to live off the land. Finding suitable sustenance proved far from easy. Over the past few years, the great herds of buffalo which had once formed a major portion of their food supply and source of other close to essential materials had diminished. What was more, while the area in which the band was currently making its home had not yet been taken over by the white man's cattle—which had been allowed to roam and breed without check during the four years of the War Between The States—some other reason had reduced the wild life to a fraction of its former quantities.

After four days which failed to produce anything larger than jack rabbits, selected to ride scout ahead of the others, the girl had located what would provide a far more substantial meal. Furthermore, although not as large as the buffalo, the creatures she had located were considered almost equal to that great shaggy beast in the matter of acclaim to be gained from them being hunted successfully.

From birth, especially as her proclivity for masculine rather than feminine activities had manifested itself, Should-Be-A-Boy had been encouraged to be completely self reliant. Her education had tended to stress individual rather than group effort, particularly where the gaining of acclaim was concerned. Nevertheless, if the animals she had discovered were buffalo—aware that they could be approached and run down on horseback without too great difficulty—she would have returned and enlisted the aid of her companions so as to increase chances of making several kills.

Knowing that such tactics would not be suitable for dealing with the kind of creatures she had found, Annie had decided that she must conduct the hunt without assistance. She had also concluded that, although the bag would be smaller, doing so would be within her capabilities. Not only would the nature of the terrain allow her to ride closer without being detected in the early stages, but she was carrying the means of making the final approach across open ground attached to the cantle of her saddle. However, the method she was meaning to employ could only be successful if used by a single person.

There had been an inducement even more potent for Annie than a desire to obtain food and the approbation of the party with whom she was travelling. If she was to be successful, she would have taken a long step towards leaving her days as a *tuinep'* behind and being accepted first as a *tuivitsi*, then, in the course of time, a *tehnap*, perhaps even a lance carrier, to continue the proud heritage of her family.

Realizing the situation was offering her a chance to achieve something which had so far eluded her companions, the delight *Tuinep'* had experienced over the possibility was tempered by knowing that making anything of it was going to prove far from easy. Regardless of the thought, she had not hesitated before setting off to see if she could prove herself worthy of the advancement.

11 *Go Home,* Tuivitsi

There was nothing in the mouth of the draw that she had descended to reach the open ground to which Annie Singing Bear could fasten her blue roan gelding. However, this did not worry her. She knew it was sufficiently well trained to remain where she left it without needing to be secured in any way. In fact, there was not even the necessity to 'ground hitch' it by allowing the one-piece reins to dangle down from the hackamore. What was more, it being her favourite mount, she had taught it to come in answer to her whistle and she could bring it to her when needed.

Leaning her bow against the right side wall of the gap, Should-Be-A-Boy removed and hung her quiver on the sharply forward curved horn of her saddle. Then she unfastened the bundle attached to the cantle and shook it open to reveal the hide of a buck whitetail deer with the skin of the legs, the head and its antlers still attached. Slipping the hollowed out skull on to her rusty-red brown braids, so the horns rose in almost a natural fashion, she draped the skin around her shoulders. With this done, she continued with her preparations.

Despite having laid aside the bow and arrows, *Tuinep'* had no intention of leaving them behind. Since having been presented with it and the holster by her parents, she had acquired the ability to handle the Colt Army Model of 1860 revolver on her weapon belt fairly well. This included having learned a variation of a technique which her mother had told her was used by white men for bringing it from the holster with reasonable speed. However, it was not the means in which she intended to try and bring down the largest quarry yet to come her way.

Although Singing Bear had never come into contact with a Western gun fighter, he had instinctively adopted a gun expert's policy and had taught his daughter to regard the six-shooter as a readily accessible defensive weapon, for use only at close quarters. Therefore, she considered the bow was far more suitable to her immediate needs. In addition to having a greater effective range, she could dispatch a succession of arrows, without being restricted to six, just as quickly as she was able to cock the hammer of the single action Colt and squeeze the trigger to discharge bullets.

Selecting an arrow from the quiver, Annie checked that its shaft was absolutely straight and the vertical hunting head was very sharp. Having assured herself upon these vital issues, she retrieved the bow and quiver. Holding the former with her left hand, she nocked one arrow to the string with her right thumb and forefinger. Having done so. She curled the other three around the carrying strap of the latter so it could be dropped if the need to use the bow should arise. Contriving to keep them all concealed beneath the hide, she advanced a couple of paces. Then, showing great caution, she surveyed her surroundings to check that everything was ready for the final and most difficult part of the approach to within shooting distance of her quarry.

As Should-Be-A-Boy knew all too well, although she could not have put the thought into exact words, she was in contention against creatures ideally suited by selective breeding over thousands of years for survival upon the kind of terrain which formed their natural habitat.

However, while the *Pahuraix* did not hunt them as regularly as the *Kweharehnuh* Comanche band, Annie had been taught enough about the habits of the animals she would be stalking to believe there was a chance of her efforts meeting with success. On the other hand, she did not delude herself into considering the task a sinecure. Regardless of contriving to arrive undetected at the mouth of the draw, the hardest part of the task still lay ahead. There was a small clump of flowering dogwood bushes no more than fifty yards from the nearest of her intended quarry, but it was almost a quarter of a mile away. Reaching the shelter it offered would be far from easy.

In spite of the kind of hide being used as camouflage by *Tuinep'*, the animals she had located were not whitetail deer!

When first coming into contact with the vast herds of American pronghorn, early white trappers and buffalo hunters called them 'goats'. With no greater justification, laymen of later generations referred to the species as being an 'antelope'. Naturalists, studying the animals with greater attention to detail, in spite of classifying the species, *Antilocapra* 'Goat-Like Antelope' *Americana*, found it to be very much of an anomaly. While having some of the habits of both types of creatures to which it been erroneously related by less knowledgeable people, and regardless of having an appearance resembling the antelopes of Africa and Asia and sharing the same predilection for open spaces, it was related to neither them nor the goats. Furthermore, while it had characteristics of other animals, it was closely related to none.

Branched forward in a distinctive fashion, growing around a blade-like boney core permanently attached to the skull, the protruberances rising from the head of the pronghorn were shed annually like the antlers of a deer. Nevertheless, being comprised of hair, whereas antlers were bone, they classed as horns. No other animal had branched horns capable of being shed. Like the sheep and goat families, the species possessed a gall bladder and the females of all three had small horns. To further confuse the naturalists, it shared with the camel the distinction of having no dewclaws. However, the anomalies which plagued white scientific students notwithstanding, it was ideally suited for its way of life.

Neither knowning nor caring about the problems of classification caused by the pronghorn for white naturalists, Should-Be-A-Boy studied the herd she had located with the gaze of a predator seeking food. With a mature buck standing between thirty-two and forty inches high at the shoulder, being about four to four and a half feet in length, it had a weight of anything from one hundred to one hundred and twenty-five pounds. The does averaged about ten per cent smaller. Although she hoped she would be able to bring down at least two regardless of sex, allowing the surplus meat to be taken back to the village, even one of either sex would provide a more adequate meal than jack rabbits for herself and the other members of her party.

The problem Annie was seeking to solve was how to arrive at the shelter offered by the flowering dogwood bushes from which she hoped to make at least one kill with the means at her disposal. While a very skilful Comanche archer could send an arrow with accuracy over greater distances, she knew the limits of her ability were somewhat less than a hundred yards. However, she was convinced that—provided she could avoid putting her quarry to flight before having approached to within that range—she ought to be able to achieve her purpose. But, she had to get much nearer to the fifty or so pronghorn loosely scattered on the open land which offered no other cover. Doing so was not made easier by nature having equipped them to detect and avoid stalking predators in such terrain.

Should-Be-A-Boy was aware that the pronghorn had sharp hearing and a keen sense of smell. Nevertheless, according to all she had heard, it was the most remarkable eyesight which she considered would pose the greatest threat. Set wide apart and deep in boney sockets, the eyes of a pronghorn had a diameter of around one and a half inches. Far seeing, with spherical vision, she had been told they had a power so great that on a clear day moving objects could be located at distances ranging to three or more miles. If any member of the herd detected possible danger, two muscular discs contracted and caused the mass of white hair on the rump to rise abruptly and reflect a remarkable amount of light. What was more, twin glands in the discs released a pungent odour which served to draw further attention to the maker of the alarm signal. As the flaring disc patches of the one locating a potential threat were seen, they were immediately repeated by others until every pronghorn within visual distance was alerted and on the lookout, ready to take flight if necessary.

Talking of the 'good old days', before the coming of the paleface brother, *tsukup* claimed there were times when the plains as far as the eye could see would be dotted with the alarm signals. It was also told how inexperienced *tui-vitsi* sometimes mistook the flashes emitted by the pronghorn for the sun glinting upon the shiny metal worn by enemies such as white 'long knife' soldiers.[1]

However, regardless of their superb means of self preservation, there were ways by which the pronghorn could be hunted successfully. Unlike the buffalo still to be found in the northern part of the band's now reduced territory, albeit in much smaller numbers than were known to previous generations, they could not be approached and run down in a chase on horseback. There was, in fact, justification for the claim that the pronghorn was the fastest creature on four legs.

Nevertheless, although the girl had never heard of such a term, she had been taught there was a vital chink in the armour of the species' otherwise well developed instincts for self preservation. This was the trait of curiosity and she was intending to exploit it to her benefit. She had heard of hunters having been able to hold the attention of the creatures while moving closer by waving a blanket or hide over the head, but she was relying upon a disguise which she had been told was even more likely to lead to success.

Pausing for a moment before leaving the concealment offered by the mouth of the draw, knowing she would almost certainly be located almost as soon as she stepped

[1] *White men too sometimes made a similar mistake when first seeing the heliographic signalling of pronghorn. See*: Chapter Six, 'The Yap-Eaters're Tough *Hombres*' FROM HIDE AND HORN.

on to the open ground, Should-Be-A-Boy silently breathed the appropriate prayer asking *Ka Dih* to look kindly upon her efforts!

With the precaution taken, Annie stepped forward to attempt to make possible the acquisition of food for her companions, and for her to receive the acclaim of the rest of the *Pahuraix* band when they returned to the village. Instead of trying to avoid being detected, knowing this would be impossible, she walked from her hiding place openly. However, she bent at the waist and allowed the hide's legs to dangle down as if they were still being used as a means of locomotion.

Grazing on the tender green shoots of grass and range weeds such as chicory, onion, larkspur or dandelion, the master buck, even more than the others in the herd scattered across the open ground, did not allow eating to override vigilance. Between plucking up food, he kept darting repeated glances all around. However, aware that such a growth could offer shelter for a predator, he never let his gaze stay long away from the clump of flowering dogwood bushes which was the only piece of sizeable cover in the immediate vicinity. The need for such frequent scrutiny was increased by the undergrowth being downwind and, therefore, no warning smell would be forthcoming if some dangerous beast was lurking in concealment.

Catching sight of a movement, the buck was ready to give the warning which would cause his family to take flight. However, the grazing hereabouts was good and, before warning he wanted to be certain the departure was necessary. Therefore, he turned his very keen gaze upon the source of the movement. From all appearances, the creature which had attracted the attention was horned and was moving on four legs. There was no wind borne scent to help form conclusions, but the actions were not suggestive of a predator trying to approach its prey unnoticed. They were, nevertheless, sufficiently unusual to arouse interest. With his curiosity stirred, the buck elected to hold back the signal until certain whether flight would be necessary. With that in mind, while resuming his grazing, he kept darting looks at the slowly advancing creature.

Peering from beneath the head-piece of her disguise, *Tuinep'* was elated by her success so far. However, knowing her task was still nowhere near completed, she kept her eagerness under a tight rein. Each step took her nearer to her goal, but she realized any undue haste could ruin all she had so far achieved. Once she attained the concealment offered by the bushes, she could discard her disguise and be ready to use the bow from a distance over which she was confident she could make a hit even if her quarry started moving away.

Step by step, occasionally causing the head and antlers to jerk upwards and, hopefully, add to the belief that she was some harmless kind of animal, the girl advanced across the open ground in her crouching posture. She was ready to stop if any of the pronghorns, more of which had noticed her, showed signs of becoming alarmed. However, judging from appearances, they were just as curious as the master buck and, following its lead, were doing nothing more than keeping her under intermittent observation while carrying on grazing.

At last, *Tuinep'* was behind the shelter of the bushes!

A sigh of relief burst from Annie as she realized she was now hidden from her quarry and need no longer remain bent over beneath the hot and far from comfortable disguise. Lowering the quiver to the ground, she rested the bow and nocked arrow against the branches. Then, easing off the hide, she draped it over the foliage so the antlers would be in view from the other side. With that done, not hearing or receiving any other indications that the pronghorns were alarmed by her actions, she swung the strap of the quiver over her head and suspended it across her back. Picking up the bow and arrow, she started to ease herself into a position from which she would be able to use them.

Still partially concealed by the dogwoods, having found a point at which two were sufficiently far apart for their foliage to form a shallow U-shape instead of being at practically the same height, the girl was delighted by what she saw. One of the antelope, a doe approaching its prime, had grazed closer than she realized during her approach. It was standing broadside on no more than twenty-five yards away and offered as near a perfect target as any *Nemenuh* hunter could desire. Moving with all the caution she could muster, struggling to control her excitement and eagerness to take up the challenge offered by the largest animal she had so far sought to kill, she concentrated all her attention upon making the smoothest draw of her life.

With the stave of the bow at its maximum flex, and arrow held against the tension of the string, Should-Be-A-Boy made certain of her aim. When satisfied, she uncurled the fingers of her right hand and felt the missile being propelled forward. Never had time seemed to be passing so slowly. Her heart was pounding against her ribs so hard she felt sure the pronghorn must hear it and be frightened into taking flight. What was more, the arrow seemed to be travelling in such slow motion it was certain to be detected and evaded long before it arrived.

Neither eventuality occurred!

Speeding across the intervening space far more swiftly than the girl's emotional state led her to assume, the arrow made contact exactly at the position she intended. Passing between the ribs, the vertical sharp pointed head impaled the heart. Giving a bound as it felt the impact, the doe was dying even as it alighted. Its legs crumpled and it toppled on its side to kick spasmodically a few times before becoming still.

Regardless of the wild elation which flooded through her, the training in archery received by Should-Be-A-Boy had been so thorough it caused her to react instinctively. Without the need for conscious guidance, while bending her legs slightly to crouch almost completely concealed behind the foliage, her right hand reached up to fetch an arrow from the quiver and nock it to the string with the shaft resting on the shallow V where her left thumb encirled the handle of the bow.

By the time the doe had fallen, with her head raised no higher than was needed to let her keep the animals under observation, *Tuinep'* was already making her draw and picking out the next of the herd which she intended to try and take. Waiting to find out what the reaction to the collapse would be, Annie was confident that she could fell it as easily as she had the doe provided they did not take flight. While several yards further away from her place of concealment, her objective was somewhat larger and offered a similar aim at the chest cavity.

Although Annie realized other of the pronghorns would produce more tender meat, she had no intention of selecting such a one for her next target. Trophy hunting was not the sole province of the white sportsman. Desiring to acquire something with which to give an indication of her ability in the future, she chose the master buck of the herd as best suited for the purpose. His horns were as long and massive as any of their kind she had ever seen, having a length almost equal to that from the tip of the nose to the crown of his head. Not only would they and the skull look most impressive surmounting the coup pole which she would place outside the entrance to her *tipi*, adding scalps and other indications of her prowess as a warrior which she had no doubt would be forthcoming on being accepted as one, but they would serve as a lasting reminder of her first successful hunt.

Judging by appearances, *Tuinep'* considered she would be able to achieve her ambition. Although the herd buck gave a startled grunt and bounded into the air, he stopped on alighting. Looking all around, because of the position behind the bushes she had taken, he failed to locate the cause of the doe's collapse. Nor, as the girl was downwind from him, was he given a warning by catching her scent. Having let out startled grunts, the other members of the herd were moving about restlessly and staring at the stricken creature. Then, as their leader gave no sign of taking flight, they resumed their feeding.

Satisifed it would be all right to do so, Should-Be-A-Boy straightened her legs and eased herself slowly until once more able to draw and line the arrow waiting to be loosed. Before she could attain this, she heard human whoops ringing out. Glancing over her shoulder, she discovered they were originating from further along the top of the cliff down which she had descended, where it made a gentle curve which would allow her and the pronghorns to be seen. On returning her gaze to the front, a surge of anger flooded through her as she saw almost every member of the herd looking towards the source of the sound. The white hairs on their rumps started to erect and flash. At the same time, the acrid warning scent they were emitting was carried to her by the wind.

While the smell was far from pleasant and she possessed a keen pair of nostrils, the girl paid it not the slightest attention. Her only thoughts, which were not of endearment, were given to the stupidity of her companions. Already disturbed by the doe going down, the herd buck let out an explosive snort which she concluded was a signal to inform the others of what he wanted them to do. Having made it, he twirled and ran with the rest following.

Even as Annie was thinking of what she would say and do when her companions joined her, she realized all might not be lost. Because of the position from which the commotion had occurred, the pronghorns were cutting across at an angle leading them past her hiding place. What was more, they would be going past much closer to her than they were before.

There was no time for Should-Be-A-Boy to feel mollified by the discovery!

Realizing she would still be offered a broadside shot at her objective as he went past, concluding that *Ka-ih* was still regarding her favourably, Annie felt sure she would still have a chance of achieving her ambition!

Already travelling at a very fast pace, the buck led his herd into view!

Aware of what was needed when shooting at a moving target, the girl turned her bow until she was leading the big buck by a good twenty-five feet. Satisfied she had made sufficient allowance for the various factors involved, still swinging at the waist, she released the string. As the stave vibrated, he heard the sound and put on a spurt which his followers duplicated.

There was a muffled thud as the arrow connected with hide and flesh!

Nevertheless, Annie was amazed and even mortified by what she saw!

Instead of achieving her objective, Should-Be-A-Boy watched the third animal behind him going down as a result of what—but for one thing—would have been a perfect neck shot. Despite hardly being able to believe any animal could be moving at such a speed, she realized she must have underled her intended quarry by at least ten feet and her victim had inadvertantly run into the path of the speeding arrow. However, while disappointed at having missed such a prime trophy, she drew some consolation from noticing her victim was a buck of fair dimensions.

Not that *Tuinep'* wasted time in regretting the loss, or giving self congratulation!

Even as she was arriving at her conclusions, the girl was sliding another arrow from the quiver. Nocking it, she drew and, aiming swiftly yet as carefully as circumstances allowed, she loosed it after the departing herd. Despite the urgency and her desire to make another kill, she had not sent the missile in the hope of procurring an indiscriminate hit. Instead, she had directed it at the buck bringing up the rear of the herd. Flying as directed, the arrow caught him just in front of the left hipbone. Despite the distance it had covered, it still retained sufficient driving power to range forward and down until the head come out at the right side of his neck.

The elation which Annie felt over having made such an excellent shot changed to disappointment as, in spite of her believing the arrow was well placed, the buck showed no sign of even breaking stride. Knowing he and the others were now beyond any distance at which she could hope to achieve anything further against them, even if she should whistle up her horse and set off in pursuit, she watched in growing amazement as he ran on. Then, after having covered about seventy-five yards, his front legs suddenly gave way. Going down, he rolled over and over in a series of somersaults until halting. When he came to a halt, it was obvious to her that he was dead. To her further gratification she realized that she had for the second time hit the animal at which she had aimed.

'Which of you started yelling?' Annie demanded, her tone and demeanour menacing, looking around from her task of eviscerating the second of the pronghorns as the rest of the hunting party rode up.

'I did,' the elderly man in the lead replied.

'*You*?' Should-Be-A-Boy gasped, letting the blood smeared blade of the Green River knife sink until it was dangling by her side instead of being retained in the threatening fashion.

'Yes,' Feeds Many confirmed. 'Although the chief of the herd started feeding again, he was alert to the danger and would have seen the movement of your bow no matter how carefully you tried to use it. Then, knowing where the danger lay, he would have led them away from you. By shouting, we caused him to go past you at shooting distance.'

'We'll eat well tonight,' commented Always Hungry, the youngster who Annie had suspected of causing the disturbance. 'You have done well, *Tuinep'*.'

'*Very* well,' the *tsukup* seconded and the others rumbled their excited concurrence. Then his seamed brown face creased in a smile and he went on, 'Go home, *tuivitsi* and take the pronghorns to your family that all may know just how well you've done.'

'My thanks, *naravuh*,' the girl replied, realizing the term employed by Feeds Many had not been a mere slip of the tongue. Trying to keep the pleasure she was experiencing from being obvious and knowing what was expected of a warrior, even a *tuivitsi*, under such circumstances, she continued, 'However, the two bucks will be sufficient for that. Keep the doe and may you and your party enjoy as good a hunt as I have had.'

12 *You Did That Well,* Tuivitsi!

Despite contemplating with pleasant anticipation the festivities which would celebrate her first successful efforts as a grown up hunter, Annie Singing Bear did not allow it to make her lose the watchfulness she had been taught was essential at all times when travelling. Therefore, as she was riding along, she was constantly gazing about her. No small animal darted away without her noticing it and birds taking flight also drew her attention. Even as recently as that morning, the sight of an armadillo, a raccoon or a few Eastern cottontail rabbits scuttling for cover would have sent her after them. Neither would prairie chickens gathered on their booming grounds, with males indulging in their elaborate courtship antics, nor a flock of considerably smaller bobwhite quail, have been overlooked in the growing urgency of the quest for food.

Because of her sense of elation, such small creatures no longer aroused any interest in the girl!

As a reward for her activities earlier in the day, Should-Be-A-Boy had been allowed to take one of the pack horses which the *tuinep'* on the training expedition had brought to transport the results of their efforts and it was carrying the two pronghorn bucks lashed to its saddle. With such trophies to display and her elevation to the status of *tuivitsi*, which would be accepted by everybody on seeing her triumphant return to the village, she felt she could ignore lesser quarry.

Nevertheless, the sight of a dozen or so whooping cranes on a distant slope was sufficient inducement for *Tuinep'* to decide to turn in that direction. Largest of all the birds which came the way of the *Pahuraix* during the changing seasons of the year, because of their size, comparative rarity and being extremely difficult to take, their flesh was regarded even more highly than that of the smaller sandhill crane, wild turkey, or various kinds of water fowl, hunted by the *Nemenuh* when available.[1] Therefore, they were not to be despised by one who had at last been allowed to leave behind the childhood quest for more insignificant creatures. To be able to kill even one of them, in addition to the three pronghorns she had brought down that morning, would add to the acclaim she had already earned.

Telling herself that *Ka-Dih* was clearly giving a sign of continuing his favour, Annie also knew she would need as much skill as she had shown when stalking the pronghorns if she was to benefit from it. Never one to shirk a challenge, she started to ride slowly in the direction of the big birds. Satisfied she was still beyond the distance where they might decide she was dangerous and fly off, she kept the pack horse following her blue roan gelding. It was her intention, when closer, to leave both animals in some convenient shelter and complete the stalking on foot.

Before arriving at the position she had selected for dismounting, Should-Be-A-Boy had her attention distracted. Regardless of her desire to add to the approbation already acquired that day, she did not forget her training. Between studying the cranes, she also kept her surroundings under observation. While doing so, certain marks on the ground caught her eye and, drawing nearer, what she discovered put thoughts of the birds from her mind.

Swinging from her saddle so as to be able to carry out a closer examination of the tracks which had come to her notice, having acquired considerable skill at reading sign, *Tuinep'* drew conclusions she did not care for. They had been made by three horses, one of which was probably being led and carrying a lesser load than the others. The

[1] *One method employed by the Comanche and other Indian nations for hunting wild fowl is described in*: OLD MOCCASINS ON THE TRAIL.

animals and their riders were not in sight, but that offered little inducement for her to relax. From the direction the hoof marks had come and were going away, it seemed likely that the makers were selecting a route by which they could travel without allowing themselves to become too obvious. Furthermore, she estimated they were not very far ahead.

There were two disturbing factors about the discovery and about her summation!

Firstly, although the other horse was unshod, the signs proved that one ridden horse and the animal being led had on the pieces of metal which white men and Mexicans were said to consider necessary to attach to the hooves of their mounts, whereas the *Nemenuh* and the rest of the Indian nations did not.

Secondly, unless they turned aside, the direction being taken by the riders would lead them to the *Pahuraix* village!

Considering the message she had read from the tracks, Should-Be-A-Boy was not enamoured of the conclusions which were suggested!

Over the years, the girl had seen white and Mexican traders accompanied by Indians paying visits to the village. However, they invariably arrived in greater numbers and with either wagons or several pack animals carrying their wares.

On the other hand, while *Tuinep'* could not claim personal contact, she had heard the 'soldiers'—as her mother described such warriors in the English language they and Annie Wishart employed when together or if wishing to talk privately in the presence of other members of the band—being discussed by braves who could. By all accounts, they frequently made use of Indians of various tribes as well as white men, Mexicans and mixed bloods to scout for them when riding the war trail. Nor did the presence of the led horse rule out the possibility that two of them had been sent with orders to locate her people. No Comanche would need to do so when riding on such a mission, but the pair ahead probably lacked the skills of the *Nemenuh* and needed to carry provisions to sustain them if their search was expected to be long in duration.

Deciding that she was getting nowhere by merely standing and wondering what the riders might be up to, Annie was not alarmed by the realization that there was only one way she would be able to satisfy her curiosity. Nor did she experience any disappointment over knowing that doing so would compel her to call off the attempt to collect one or more of the whooping cranes. Rather she was pleased with the latest turn of events. She considered they were proof that *Ka-Dih* was presenting her with a chance to win acclaim beyond any which would be forthcoming as a result of a successful hunt. If she should be correct about the two men being scouts seeking the village, she would gain far greater approbation by either preventing them from doing so or giving a warning of their presence.

If circumstances presented her with a choice, because she would be offered an opportunity of counting coup on an enemy, Should-Be-A-Boy concluded she would prefer the former contingency!

Swinging astride the blue roan gelding, Annie glanced at the pack animal. Because of what it was carrying, she had no desire to leave it behind. A bear, a cougar, or pack of wolves, any of which might be in the vicinity, would be all too willing to obtain such an easy meal as the tethered horse and its burden. After a moment's thought, she concluded there was nothing as yet to prevent her taking it along. It was sufficiently well trained to follow without fighting the lead rope, or needing any attention, so she could keep it with her until she came into sight of her quarry and was able to form an idea of what kind of opposition she would be facing.

Riding forward, following the tracks, *Tuinep'* alternated between glancing at them and studying the terrain ahead with an even greater care than she had previously shown. After covering about two miles, she received her first sight of the riders. She was still too far off for her to make out more than the basic details, such as the third animal being a loaded pack horse. Noticing each man was carrying a rifle of some sort across his lap, she decided they were an Indian with white hair suggestive of one no longer young and a somewhat taller white man with a similar stocky and thickset build. At such a distance, being aware that the other bands of *Nemenuh* were not the only ones with that kind of physique, she was unable to see sufficient to even guess at which tribe the former belonged. However, the clothing worn by the latter was more like that she had heard described when warriors were speaking of 'ride plenties', rather than the blue coloured attire of the soldiers.

Whoever the pair were, Should-Be-A-Boy soon concluded she had little to fear from either as far as her presence being discovered was concerned. She was putting to use all she had been taught about such matters to lessen the chance of being detected and, although each glanced behind on a couple of occasions, neither gave any indication of having seen her. Nevertheless, she did not let herself be lulled into a sense of over confidence. Nor, in spite of their lack of vigilance, did her eagerness to count coup for the first time cause her to behave in an impetuous fashion. Having learned the value of patience and planning before taking action whenever possible, she put the precept into practice and considered the ramifications of the situation. As a result of the conclusions she formulated, being satisfied they could not arrive in the vicinity of the village before the following afternoon at the earliest, she decided against moving in to deal with them while the daylight lasted.

Continuing to follow the pair, making skilful use of every natural feature to keep them from realizing she was on their trail, the girl found she was gradually closing the distance without any attempt on her part to do so. Unfortunately, with the sun sinking below the western horizon, the light was failing fast. Under such conditions, although a *tehnap* might have detected the necessary indications, she lacked the experience needed to pick out anything which would help her to ascertain the Indian's tribe. However, as they clearly remained oblivious of her presence, she saw no reason to lengthen the gap between them. It would, she decided, make her final stalk less difficult.

Shortly after dusk, halting the roan and pack horse, Should-Be-A-Boy sat listening for a moment. Although the arrival of darkness prevented her from being able to keep her quarry under visual observation, she was not greatly perturbed. Even if they should turn away from the direct line they had taken ever since she first learned of their presence, she did not consider there would be any danger of her losing them. Among the other subjects she had been taught to fit her for life as a warrior were ways of following enemies at night. While doing so was not easy, she felt sure the need would be fairly short in duration. If her quarry acted as she anticipated, they would soon be making camp and she did not envisage any difficulty in locating it.

Finding she was unable to hear even distant hoof beats, Annie slipped from the saddle. Lying down, she placed an ear against the ground. For a moment, failing to detect the sounds she expected, a sensation of alarm filled her. Then she realized the slight scuffling noises carried through the soil might be the horses moving a little while being unsaddled. With relief, she told herself this suggested the two men were no longer riding through the darkness. Her next problem would be to find out where they had halted. Standing up and gazing ahead, she failed to acquire any indication. Nor was she any better informed at first when she mounted the gelding.

Concluding she had no other choice, Should-Be-A-Boy signalled for the roan to move forward. However, she held it to a slow walk. Although she applied all her senses to seeking for anything that would help her to locate her quarry, she detected only the usual sounds of the night. Then a sudden and disturbing thought struck her. Perhaps the men had not been as unaware of her presence as their behaviour had led her too assume. If such was the case, they would be lying in wait for her to come within range of their weapons. What was more, as they would be remaining still, they would have more chance of hearing her approaching than she would have of receiving any warning of their presence.

Just as the girl was deciding the time had come for her to leave her horses and continue the advance on foot, she saw a faint red glow ahead. Instantly the misgivings which had started to plague her disappeared. It was obvious that the men had not discovered they were being followed. What was more, either because they believed they had nothing to fear or they were sufficiently lacking in the basic precautions required when riding scout in the domain of an enemy, they had made a fire. No matter which was the reason, it was giving her the information she required.

Despite her eagerness to acquire the prestige of counting coup and gratitude of the rest of the band for having stopped two enemy scouts locating the village, Annie did not forget something else she had been taught. From the moment it was accepted that *Ka-Dih* intended she was raised as a *tuinep'* and not a *tuepet*, it had been impressed upon her that a *Nemenuh* brave needed more than just courage to become a name-warrior. Whilst bravery was essential, except when electing to ride *pukutsi*, it must be tempered with discretion to achieve greatness. She remembered her *tawk* telling her, 'While it is good to die for your people, there is greater credit in making an enemy die for his.' He had also frequently asserted the most successful warrior was the one who was willing to dash straight into the attack when conditions were favourable, but was ready to employ stealth if necessary. With those precepts to guide her, bearing in mind that the odds would be against her even though she hoped to have surprise on her side, she realized that she must curb her impatience. To make her victory more certain, it was advisable to pick the most appropriate time to come upon them.

Dismounting, Should-Be-A-Boy's first thought was for the welfare of the roan and pack horse. Aware that it would be some time before she would be able to make use of them again, she removed their saddles so they could enjoy a roll on the grass. With the task completed, she lay down and rested while waiting to give the two men an opportunity to settle down for the night. When she considered a sufficient period had elapsed, she replaced the rigs. Knowing she could trust the gelding not to wander far even though at liberty to do so, she fastened the other horse's lead rope to the horn of its saddle. Having taken the precaution which would allow both to graze while preventing the loaded animal from straying so that she could have it brought up when she had accomplished her mission, she completed her preparations. Donning her quiver and picking up the bow, she set off on foot to follow the guidance which was still given by the faint glow of their fire.

Moving through the darkness, achieving a silence which would have gladdened the hearts of her grandfather and father if they had been present, the girl was delighted by what she saw when granted the first view of her quarry. Having made camp at the bottom of a small hollow with its sides coated by bushes, they lay sleeping on opposite sides of the fire. She could not locate the rifle each had been carrying, but presumed it must be hidden by the blankets in which they were wrapped. However, the pack was in plain sight and the three horses hobbled close by were of a good quality. All in all, there would be much worthwhile loot in addition to the prestige of having counted coup and taken two scalps.

To add to Annie's satisfaction, it was obvious that the pair believed they had nothing to fear. Although having taken the precaution of selecting a place which should have offered them protection against being seen by a chance passer-by, they had compounded the error of having lit the fire by keeping it going when they would have been advised to let it die out. Therefore, both were illuminated as well as any stalking enemy could have wished them to be.

Studying the scene while moving closer, taking even greater care to avoid noise, Annie decided there was only one problem to be solved. However, she did not consider it would prove insurmountable. In fact, it might even be beneficial. Using his saddle for a pillow, each man was so completely covered by his blankets that only the general shape of his body could be seen. Being wrapped in such a fashion was almost certain to restrict the speed with which he could throw them off should he be aroused by her actions.

Wanting to be certain of being close enough to deal with the other after killing the first, the girl took no action until she arrived at the edge of the bushes. Deciding it would be unwise to go further and being at what she felt was a satisfactory range for the bow, she came to a halt. On the point of drawing back the arrow she was carrying nocked to the string, she noticed an object with which she was familiar draped across each shape and annoyance flooded through her.

Although she did not own one as yet, Should-Be-A-Boy was familiar with the kind of fringed buckskin 'medicine' boot used by braves to cover their rifles when travelling and which was far more than merely decorative. The colouring and pattern of the symbols painted upon one served as a means of identification. Having received instruction in such matters, she decided from the insignia that they had been made respectively for members of the *Pehnane* and *Tanima* bands. What was more, while the saddle of the man with the Liver-Eater boot was of the kind taken from white 'ride plenties' by *Pahuraix* war parties, the other was unmistakably an excellent and costly example of Comanche manufacture.

The significance of the conclusions Annie reached came as a bitter disappointment!

No matter what had brought them to *Pahuraix* territory, there were indications which informed the girl that the Indian was *Nemenuh*. Even though the other was a white man, it seemed he had sufficiently close connections with the *Tanima* band to be displaying one of their medicine boots to give notice that he enjoyed their protection. Therefore, despite having made such a successful stalk, she could neither attack them nor take any of their property as loot.

On the point of turning away in disgust, Should-Be-A-Boy threw a baleful glare at the shape beneath the *Pehnane* medicine boot. Deciding such a lack of precaution did not speak highly of his ability as warrior, no matter how good a saddle and horse he owned, she saw a way by which she could prevent her efforts being a complete waste of time. Although she had yet to engage upon a successful hunt for buffalo, her family were sure to give a dance to celebrate her having brought down the three pronghorns. What she decided to do would not achieve the acclaim she would have attained if the pair had been enemies, but it would gain a lesser approbation when she described its successful conclusion and the response it elicited from the pair.

Returning the arrow to her quiver, with a gesture redolent of indignation over being prevented from attaining the higher praise she had envisaged, the girl leaned the bow against the nearest bush. Then she dropped on to her stomach and started to wriggle across the open ground. Watching the two shapes, ready to freeze into complete immobility if either showed signs of stirring, she made her way towards the *Pehnane*. Going by appearances, both were in a *very* deep sleep. There was no movement whatsoever from either. Not even the restless movements which her appearance was causing the horses to make was disturbing them.

Arriving within touching distance of her objective, *Tuinep'* came to her feet. After gazing for a moment from one to the other of the unmoving figures, she let out a hiss of disgust. Then, sucking in a deep breath to fill her lungs, she gave the loudest war whoop she could produce. Its volume shattered the silence of the night, causing the three horses to snort and show signs of alarm. However, it was the response from the blanket covered shapes which held her full attention.

Or rather the complete lack of response of any kind!

Despite a noise which should have woken up anybody who was not totally deaf, neither figure made a movement!

'You did that well, *tuivitsi*!'

'Almost as well as *Cuchilo* could have done at that age, *haints*!'

Even as Annie was on the point of bending to snatch away the blanket she had believed was covering the Indian, the sound of masculine voices came to her ears. The first speaker was employing the somewhat slow tongued dialect of the *Pehnane*. Despite being a white man and having used the term implying his companion was a sufficiently close friend to qualify as a blood brother,[2] the second was almost as fluent in the accent of the *Tanima* band. However, both were giving their words a ventriloquial quality which prevented her from being certain of the exact position of either.

Suddenly the full implications of what she had done struck the girl and she had never known such a sense of mortification!

It was all Should-Be-A-Boy could do to resist an impulse to run away!

Brought to a full awareness of her folly, Annie realised she had been too eager to count coup and gather loot. Instead of remembering her training and being on the alert for any signs of treachery, she had overlooked and failed to draw the correct conclusions out of the complete absence of any movement whatsoever from the two blanket covered shapes. Such an omission might have been excusable while she was concentrating the majority of her attention upon moving in silence down the slope. It was *not* after she had allowed her disappointment to lead her into what, she now realized, was a piece of folly more suited to a child first allowed to run with the other *tuinep'* than one who had attained the status of *tuivitsi*.

If the men had been sleeping without being disturbed by her arrival, the yell given by the girl would have woken them up and either might have shot her instinctively before she could identify herself as *Nemenuh*. Nor would even her father and grandfather have blamed whichever had done it for reacting in such a fashion. Rather they would have been ashamed that a member of their family, to whom they had given instruction as a warrior, was killed as the result of a stupidly ill-advised piece of behaviour.

2 *The Comanche also used the word*, 'haints', *to mean a brother-in-law.*

13 *What's In Store For Us?*

Although one part of Annie Singing Bear was impelled by a desire to take flight and avoid facing the two men, the rest refused to do so. Such a craven response was not the act of a *Pahuraix tuivitisi* who was born of and *tawk* to the lance carriers, Singing Bear and Brother To The Hawk. She had already brought enough shame to their name without adding more. With that in mind, being as close to tears as she had ever come since she was a baby, she made no attempt to discover whether she was correct in her estimations of where the men might be. Instead, hoping to gain some measure of forgiveness, she ran across to calm down the plunging pack horse which was showing more fright than their mounts.

Hearing movements amongst the bushes, Annie looked around without releasing the headpiece of the horse's hackamore. She drew some small consolation from noticing she had been very close in her estimation of where the voices had originated.

Striding into view from the right side of the clearing, the Indian moved swiftly despite the suggestion of age given by his shoulder long white hair and leathery features. Although travel stained, his attire was that of a wealthy Comanche and the red cloth headband bore the medicine symbols of the *Pehnane*. A massive knife was sheathed on the left side of his weapon belt and there was a Colt Model of 1848 Dragoon revolver in an open topped holster at the right. In his hands, he held a rifle of a kind the girl had only seen once before. It was one of the wonderful 'many shooters' which she and every other warrior wished to obtain.

Appearing just as quietly from the left, the white man was somewhat younger than his companion. He had a low crowned, wide brimmed tan coloured hat shoved back on a head of grizzled brown hair much shorter than the girl had been told she might expect from a scout for the soldiers.[1] What little of his face was not covered by a neatly trimmed short beard was burned a deep brown which made a contrast to his blue eyes. As Annie had guessed, apart from the Comanche moccasins and leggins he was wearing, his attire was that of a 'ride plenty' Texas cowhand. The most unusual item was a vest made from the black rosette-spotted yellow hide of a jaguar. Around his waist hung a gunbelt with two rosewood handled Colt Model of 1866 Army revolvers in contoured holsters and he too was carrying a repeating rifle.

'You knew I was following you and what I'd do,' Annie said, looking from the older to the younger of her intended victims and back.

'We saw you a couple of times,' the Indian replied and, although his face was impassive, there was a twinkle in his eyes. 'When we slowed down and you didn't catch us up, knowing what my *tawk*,[2] *Cuchilo*, would have done at your age, we guessed you'd decided to do the same. Are you the one our *Pahuraix* brothers call "Should-Be-A-Boy"?'

'I am,' the girl confirmed, releasing her hold on the pack horse as it had quietened down and trying to conceal her pleasure at learning her name was known to a *Nemenuh* from another band, particularly one of the quality she suspected the speaker to be from the reference to his connection with *Cuchilo*. 'And I apologise for what I tried to do, Chief Long Walker of the *Pehnane*.'

[1] *Although long hair was generally regarded as unacceptable for men throughout much of the Old West, legend has it many civilian scouts for the United States' Army allowed theirs to grow so it offered a better trophy should they be scalped by Indians.*

[2] 'Tawk', *the name by which a Comanche grandfather and grandson addressed one another. Because of the way in which her life had developed, Annie Singing Bear was entitled to use it in conjunction with Brother To The Hawk.*

'There's no need for that, *Tuinep*" the elderly Comanche claimed. 'A *tuivitsi* must practice stalking and other skills so as to become a *tehnap*.'

'He must also learn not to take anything he sees for granted,' the white man supplemented, glancing to where he and his companion had used branches and leaves to make the shapes concealed beneath the blankets in the expectation of what the girl would do.

'*Chaqueta-Tigre* speaks truly, *Tuinep*',' declared Long Walker, once a noted lance carrier and now respected as senior 'old man' chief of the *Pehnane* band. 'You moved well, but I wouldn't make a habit of waking sleepers the way you tried with us, even if you know they are friends.'

'I never will again,' Annie promised and meant it, realizing her reception would have been less cordial if she had failed to respect the indications left to inform her that she was dealing with a *Nemenuh* and a white friend of the *Tanima* band. 'May I share my food with you?'

'It will be an honour,' Long Walker replied, guessing why the girl had been riding alone and leading the pack horse. 'We saw your hunting had been good.'

'It has,' Should-Be-A-Boy agreed, then cupping her hands around her mouth she gave a series of piercing whistles. Having done so, she went on in the politely deferential tone of one addressing a person of importance, 'I took three pronghorn.'

'That is a worthy feat,' the chief asserted. 'Brother To The Hawk has cause to be proud of his *tawk*.'

'Did you train your pony too?' the white man inquired, nodding towards where the sound of approaching hooves came from the darkness.

'Yes,' Annie admitted, but the hint of pride in her voice changed as a realization that something was *very* wrong struck her. 'Only it *can't* be him and there's more than just him and the pack horse coming!'

'And they aren't those you've been hunting with?' Long Walker suggested.

'Not from that di—!' Should-Be-A-Boy began.

Before the girl could finish, something which she could not understand was yelled and the hooves changed their pace from a walk to a gallop as the riders started to rush down the slope.

'Back to the bushes!' Long Walker commanded, his tone urgent.

Although the chief and *Chaqueta-Tigre* darted in the direction from which the former had come, Annie did not accompany them. Instead, she turned and, despite being compelled to go towards the approaching riders, ran to collect the bow she had left behind. Before she could reach the bush against which it was resting, an Indian holding a war club and round shield similar to those used by her own people, but which bore the insignia of the Kaddo tribe, stepped into view between her and her objective. He was accompanied by another of that nation carrying a carbine of the kind she had seen brought to the village as loot taken from soldiers. Letting out a whoop of delight, the former sprang forward with the shield held so it offered protection for his head and torso. Keeping silent, the latter brought his weapon to his shoulder.

Despite the shock she received, Should-Be-A-Boy had been sufficiently well trained that she responded to the danger instinctively. What was more, offering testimony to the thoroughness with which Brother To The Hawk had instructed her, she did not even need to think which of the weapons on her person was best suited to her immediate needs. Nor, despite it being the first time she had to put her lessons to serious use, did she panic or become flustered.

Turning her right hand palm out, with its thumb coiling over the spur of the hammer, Annie closed it about the walnut grips and, while twisting the short barrelled Colt 1860 Army Model revolver from its holster,[3] caused the action to be cocked. Turning the muzzle forward, she squeezed the trigger and released the hammer. There was

[3] *As the hook which retained the loading lever beneath the barrel when not in use had been repositioned, we suspect the shortening had been done by a white gunsmith before the Colt 1860 Army Model revolver came into Annie Singing Bear's possession.*

no need for her to aim. Already the brave was very close and swinging up his war club for a blow. In doing so, he inadvertantly let the shield move aside.

Not much, but enough!

Bellowing loudly, the revolver dispatched a .44 calibre bullet at waist level and aimed by instinctive alignment. Snipping off a couple of the feathers on the rim which served as decoration and a distraction when the shield was being wielded in a fight,[4] the lead tore into the brave's chest. With the whoop of triumph turning to a scream of agony, he was spun far enough for his blow to miss its intended target. However, the margin was so close that the girl was compelled to step hurriedly aside to avoid being struck by his body as the impetus of his attack caused him to blunder past her.

Despite having saved herself from the first of the Indians, Should-Be-A-Boy found she was far from out of danger!

If anything, the girl decided, her position was even more perilous!

Belonging to a small party hired to prevent Long Walker and *Chaqueta-Tigre* from reaching the village of the *Pahuraix*, the two warriors had been sent ahead to locate them. On the point of rejoining their companions, they were saved from having to report failure by seeing the glow of the fire. Sending a younger warrior who was with them to fetch the rest, they had left their horses and began to move in on foot.

While descending the slope with all the caution they had not doubted was a vital requisite of staying alive when dealing with two such efficient enemies, the scouts had seen somebody else—a half breed, going by the colour of the hair—approaching the blanket covered shapes. However, before they could take any action, they had observed the result of the yell. Each had concluded that, having made a similar error, they had been saved from falling into

[4] *A description of how an Indian shield was made and used in a fight is given in*: Chapter Eleven, 'It is Their Right To Kill You', GO BACK TO HELL.

a trap laid by their intended victims. Accepting there now would be no hope of taking the chief and the Texan by surprise and aware that the carbine held only a single cartridge, they had decided to wait until reinforcements arrived before allowing their presence to become known.

Pure chance had brought the pair to where Annie had left her bow. Before either could envisage the possibilities offered by it being there, the incautious approach of their companions caused the alarm to be raised. Seeing the girl darting in their direction, the discovery of her sex notwithstanding, neither discounted her as a potential danger in the forthcoming fighting. The fact that she had reached the clearing without them detecting her suggested *very* thorough training in the ways of a warrior. Furthermore, the reception she had received from the two men warned they considered her to be a friend. All of which meant the scouts would have to deal with her before giving any attention to their main quarry.

Although the second brave had halted and brought up his Springfield carbine, his objective was not either of the men they had been seeking. However, he had been prevented from using it by the man with the war club coming between him and what he had realized, regardless of the obvious indications of female gender, presented all the danger to be expected from a Comanche brave. One who had not long been a *tuivitsi*, maybe, but already capable of proving a *most* dangerous antagonist. The way in which the revolver was used gave unmistakable proof of that. However, he was in an ideal position to open fire as his stricken companion stumbled out of the way.

Fortunately for Annie, although making for the shelter of the bushes, Long Walker and *Chaqueta-Tigre* had been looking over their shoulders towards the source of what each realized was almost certainly a threat to their lives. Discovering the girl was not accompanying them, they had concluded she was going to retrieve the bow she had left behind when making her approach across the clearing. However, even as they were mentally praising her for acting in such a clear thinking fashion by going to collect the weapon, they saw the Indians burst into view.

Swivelling around more swiftly than his older companion, albeit not by any great margin, *Chaqueta-Tigre* was already cradling the brass butt of the Winchester against his right shoulder by the time he came to a halt. The girl had saved herself from the first attacker, but he knew the second would be too much for her. Sighting and firing, he threw the lever through its loading cycle. Without waiting to see what result he had, turning the barrel slightly between them, he dispatched four other shots as swiftly as he could operate the mechanism. By the time the second was on its way, Long Walker too opened fire.

Caught by one of the bullets, the brave was flung from his feet. As he went, he was squeezing on the trigger of the Springfield when another struck its lock. The action was wrecked, but not before the hammer descended hard enough to discharge the percussion cap. Although the powder charge sent the soft lead ball out of the muzzle, the barrel had been knocked from its alignment. Not much, but just enough. The margin was so close that, if there had been the slightest delay in the damage being inflicted, the shot would have taken effect.

For the first time in her life, Should-Be-A-Boy heard a sharp 'splat!' and felt the wind of the lead passing just above her head. However, instead of being disconcerted by the eerie sound, she kept her wits about her. On the point of giving her attention to the second brave, she realized there was no need. Turning her gaze to the first, she discovered he was still on his feet. What was more, although the shield was dangling by his left side, he was showing signs of returning to the fray.

Thumbing back the hammer, Annie raised the Colt with both hands to take sight. This time, she tried to send the bullet into the centre of the man's forehead. Although she discharged it a fraction earlier than she intended, she had no cause to feel disappointed by the result. Hitting the man just below the chin, her lead shattered the bones of his neck. Pitched backwards, the club and shield dropped from his hands. However, he sprawled backwards against a bush and hung dying upon its foliage.

'Get out of the firelight, *Tuinep'*!' Long Walker barked, acting upon the instructions as he gave them and narrowly being missed by a bullet which flew from the darkness.

Even as the chief spoke and moved, the action already being anticipated by his companion, the first of the mounted attackers arrived at the edge of the clearing. He was a tall, buckskin-clad half breed with a vicious face and carrying a most effective weapon. Nor did he leave the two men in doubt as to which of them he had selected as his victim.

'I've got you now, Goodnight!' the man bellowed, allowing the one piece reins to drop across the neck of his horse and starting to bring up the double barrelled ten gauge shotgun.

Looking back and recognizing the speaker, *Chaqueta-Tigre* knew he could not spin around and use his Winchester swiftly enough to save himself from the swathe of lead which would be hurled his way. However, even as the thought came, he heard the crack of the short barrelled revolver. An instant later, the half breed jerked under the impact of lead. Although he only received a minor wound, his weapon was deflected and its lethal charge of shot flew harmlessly into the air. Seeing his intended victim disappear into the bushes, he concluded discretion was the better part of valour and spurred his horse onwards without trying to repeat his murderous intentions.

Having taken his briefly interrupted departure from the clearing, Long Walker swung around just in time to see the girl fire and save his companion from the shotgun. Then she followed his advice although many a *tuivitsi*, particularly after having done so well in what was probably a first fight, might have become too excited to accept it. However, he also noticed she did not miss the chance to carry out the ritual of counting coup upon the first enemy with whom she had been compelled to deal.

'*A:he*!' Should-Be-A-Boy hissed, as she had been taught was required, tapping the dying Indian with her left hand in passing.

Swivelling around and coming to a halt on arriving amongst the shelter offered by the bushes, Annie was in a state of elation. Not only had she achieved her first coup, it was attained by her bare hand touching the man upon whom it was counted while he was still alive. Her only regret was that she had been unable to collect her bow. Despite having achieved success with her Colt, she would have preferred its longer range for use in the fighting which she knew was forthcoming.

Following closely upon the heels of the half breed, spread out in a rough line, were half a dozen Indians. They were carrying a variety of weapons, all of which they were just too late to use. Brought into the light of the fire, they were instantly assailed by the Winchesters of the two men and the girl's revolver. The first to appear went backwards over the rump of his horse and two more of the braves followed him to the ground. However, much to her annoyance, Should-Be-A-Boy knew she had not accounted for any of them. What was more, in addition to keeping his horse racing across the illuminated area, the man she had hit managed to retain his hold on the firearm he was carrying. He still had not dropped it as he disappeared amongst the bushes ahead of the others who had escaped the deadly fusilade.

In spite of being delighted at having counted coup, Annie was disappointed by the way the rest of the affair had turned out. Two of the braves shot by her companions were armed with bows and the other a lance. Even if the carbine which had nearly killed her was not ruined by the bullet, it was the loot of whichever man caused the hit. Therefore, unless he was generous and presented it to her, she would not acquire a firearm as she had hoped to do and provide a most fitting climax to her first fight.

Listening to the sounds of the hooves fading into the distance, although there was no suggestion that the riders were even slowing down, much less starting to return, the girl hurried through the bushes. Holstering the revolver she had emptied, having no means of reloading until her gelding brought the pack horse with her spare ammunition, she gathered up the bow. Then, seeing the two men were returning to the clearing, she concluded it would be all right for her to follow their example. However, before going to join them, she went to where the man she had shot was hanging lifeless on the bush. Shaking him to the ground, she set aside the bow and, taking out the Green River knife, she deftly removed his scalp.

* * * *   * * * *

'What do you think, ma'am,' *Chaqueta-Tigre* asked in English, knowing Chief Long Walker could understand. 'Will the *Pahuraix* join the other bands at Fort Sorrel and talk about signing a treaty to go on to a reservation?'

'I think they might,' replied the woman to whom the question was directed, speaking the same language in a way which showed she did not often use it. 'They were certainly impressed by what you said and seeing what one of those repeating rifles of yours are capable of doing. By the way, thank you again for giving Annie such a fine present.'

'She earned it,' the bearded white man declared with the accent of a well educated Texan. 'That damned 'breed would have killed me if she hadn't shot him in time.'

At the conclusion of the dance given by Singing Bear to celebrate Should-Be-A-Boy's first success as a warrior, being his *pairaivo*, Becky Ingraham had been told to escort the guests of honour to the *tipi* provided for them. She had found the business which brought them to the village most interesting, albeit disturbing, as she had seen how it might affect the future for herself and her daughter. Therefore, she had been pleased to be given an opportunity to discuss the situation.

With the surviving attackers departed and those left behind found to be dead, Annie had thanked Long Walker and his companion for saving her from being shot. In turn, to her amazement and delight, she had received from *Chaqueta-Tigre* an expression of his gratitude for her quick action in dealing with the half breed which far surpassed anything she would have envisaged. Opening the pack, he had taken out and given her a Winchester Model of 1866 carbine and two boxes of cartridges.

Over the meal they had when her horses arrived in response to the whistle, the girl had learned that the half breed and the Kaddo Indians he had hired had been sent to prevent the two men delivering a message of importance to the *Pahuraix* band. However, it was not until half way through the dance to honour her achievement that she had learned what this was. After having described how competently she had stalked them, without mentioning the error she had committed, Long Walker had praised her for her conduct during the attack and she had been accorded the acclaim such a feat deserved. With the story told, at the request of Brother To The Hawk, the *Pehnane* chief had explained the reason he and *Chaqueta-Tigre*—known as a brave warrior, albeit one against whom some of the braves had occasionally been in contention—were paying the visit.

At the request of the United States' Government, the Long Walker and—although he had never been in the Army, but was actively engaged in the cattle business which was of major importance to the economy of Texas[5]—Colonel Charles Goodnight were trying to persuade all the other Comanche bands to attend a meeting at Fort Sorrel and discuss making peace. Speaking eloquently, Long Walker had explained the advantages of being taken on to a reservation. He had also warned that the good old days of raiding and riding the war trail were coming to an end. Not only did the white men have far larger numbers of soldiers available than ever before, even though the medicine of the Devil Gun had failed to produce the promised effect when put to the test, but they were now armed with much more efficient weapons. The

[5] *The title 'Colonel' was honorary and granted by his fellow Texans to Charles Goodnight as a tribute to his ability as a fighting man and a leader. His sobriquet had originated after he had started to wear the vest made from the skin of a jaguar—called* 'tigre', *'tiger', by Mexicans—which had strayed north into Texas and he had hunted it down when it took to killing his cattle. Details of his career are recorded in*: GOODNIGHT'S DREAM, FROM HIDE AND HORN, SET TEXAS BACK ON HER FEET, SIDEWINDER *and* THE MAN FROM TEXAS.

demonstration of how rapidly a Winchester rifle could be fired and reloaded had been a telling argument. Every experienced warrior had realized such a device could be carried by a horseman and give him a potential far beyond anything their own arms could attain. Having been promised by the 'old man' chiefs that the matter would be discussed at length in the morning and they would be informed of the decision, the guests had relaxed and the festivities had continued without further reference to the matter until it was raised as they were being taken to their sleeping quarters.

'How will my daughter and I be affected if the treaty is signed?' Becky inquired, the death of Annie Wishart a few weeks earlier having left her the only white person in the village.

'You'll be able to go back to your own people,' Goodnight replied.

'Our own people,' Becky said, looking around her. 'We won't be *compelled* to do it, will we?'

'Don't you *want* to go back?' the rancher queried, although he could guess what lay behind the conversation.

'I've lived with the *Pahuraix* for a long time and *Tuinep'*—Annie—has never known any other life,' the woman replied quietly, yet just a trifle defensively, wondering what the bearded man would make of her reaction to the possibility of returning to live amongst her own kind. 'Do you think Annie in particular would be accepted, *Chaq*—Colonel?'

'I've known some of mixed blood who are,' Goodnight answered and, although he knew there was one *very* important difference, went on with a gesture towards his companion. 'Long Walker's grandson is for one.'

'*Cuchilo* was mixing with white people from an earlier age than *Tuinep'* is now,' the chief pointed out. 'She would find it *very* difficult to change her ways.'

'That's for sure,' Goodnight supported. 'The way she fought in that clearing yesterday and took the scalp of the brave she killed, she lives and thinks like a Comanche brave even more than *Cuchilo* did.'

'Then what's in store for us?' Becky asked. 'Will we be made to leave the village?'

'Not if you don't want to go,' the rancher claimed, being able to envisage how difficult it would be for the still good looking woman to adjust to living amongst white people and that her daughter would find the change even harder to accept. Remembering he owed the girl his life, he went on, 'I'll promise you one thing. Whether you want to come back amongst white folks, or stay with the *Pahuraix*, I'll see your wishes are respected and will do everything I can to see you're all right no matter which way you decide.'

14 *Her Blood Cries For Revenge*

Listening to the rumble of angry voices which came from around the great council fire, Annie Singing Bear hurried to the wooden cabin in which she had lived with her parents since their arrival on the reservation. She realized that what she was intending to do would be the most momentous act of her life. What was more, if she was allowed to carry out her intentions, she would be given an opportunity to follow a tradition of the Comanche nation which she had believed would never again be needed.

Much had taken place to alter the life of Should—Be-A-Boy since the night she counted coup upon the Kaddo brave!

After long debate, the elders and medicine makers of the *Pahuraix* village had agreed to attend the peace treaty gathering at Fort Sorrel. On arriving, the delegation had found that although equally large contingents of the *Pehnane, Yamparikuh, Dertsanayehka, Tanima, Mutsane* and *Kweharehnuh* bands were present, the *Wawai* had followed the advice of their medicine woman, Fire Dancer. Not only had they stayed away, they were actively involved in trying to ensure the meeting ended in failure.

Having accompanied Singing Bear, Becky Ingraham at the request of the elders, had ensured that she and her daughter kept out of sight of the white people who were attending the gathering. In spite of this, the girl was present amongst the crowd assembled to witness the signing of the treaty. Although she had seen *Cuchilo* offered an opportunity to achieve the ambition of every *Nemenuh* warrior by riding *pukutsi* successfully and also fulfilling an oath of revenge he had sworn years earlier,[1] she had not been given an opportunity to make his acquaintance.

Like the others bands who attended, the *Pahuraix* had seen enough to warn them that Chief Long Walker was correct in his references to the changed state of affairs. Therefore, receiving assurances of good treatment by *Chaqueta-Tigre* and other white men who had earned their trust, Brother To The Hawk and the other 'old man' chiefs had concluded there was more to be gained than lost by making peace and going to live on a reservation. With the exception of the *Kweharehnuh*, whose domain was sufficiently wild and isolated for them to feel safe from the encroachment of the white people, the other bands had been of the same mind.

Although keeping what a later generation would refer to as a 'low profile', Becky had contacted other white women who were living in a similar fashion to herself. What she had heard about their experiences when coming into contact with members of their race who had gathered for the meeting warned her that her suppositions were correct. Even if she should give up her present way of life, return and become accepted in a white community, she had felt that—if ever achieved—the process would be very lengthy and filled with hardship. She had doubted whether such an acceptance would be achieved by Annie. Raised not merely as a Comanche, but a male warrior of that race, the girl would be quick to resent insults or even slights and her response was almost certain to bring her into conflict with the law.

Talking over the matter with Singing Bear while Should-Be-A-Boy was absent, Becky had received no argument to her suggestion that they should seek out and ask *Chaqueta-Tigre* for further advice. There was more than the affection he had for his *pairaivo* and daughter behind his acquiesence. Having retired from the honour

[1] *Why the Ysabel Kid elected to ride* pukutsi *and the reason he swore the oath of vengeance is told in*: SIDEWINDER.

of being a lance carrier, even though suspecting the need would be lessened when they reached the reservation, he had no desire to lose the warrior he and Brother To The Hawk had raised to carry on the proud traditions of their family. Nor had he seen anything out of the ordinary in requesting counsel from one who was not a *Nemenuh* and had acquired a second sobriquet, 'Dangerous Man', when in contention against his people. One of the factors which had made him such a successful warrior had been the possession of intelligence as well as bravery. Therefore, as he had in the past, he had been willing to go to somebody with greater knowledge of the situation than he possessed when faced with a difficult problem.

Also aware of the reception accorded to other white women who had lived with various of the bands, Colonel Charles Goodnight had agreed there was justification for Becky's misgivings. Knowing she was happy with Singing Bear, which he had a strong suspicion would not prove the case if they parted under such conditions, he had considered there were no moral or ethical reasons why she should change her situation for no better motive than a desire to conform with the conventions of her own race.

Sharing Becky's belief that her daughter was unlikely to be able to make the adjustments necessary to adopt an entirely different way of life, the rancher had pointed out how both of them could help the *Pahuraix* by letting their status remain unchanged. Being able to converse in English and Comanche, as well as knowing how to read and write in the former language, they would be well suited to act as liason between the band and the white men responsible for managing the reservation to which they were assigned. Seeing the validity of the proposition, Becky had stated her intention of remaining with her husband.

Remembering how Should-Be-A-Boy had already killed a man and taken his scalp, despite conceding the first had been unavoidable in the prevailing circumstances, Becky had still retained sufficient of her white upbringing to find satisfaction in the thought that going on to a reservation should prevent the need from arising again. She had believed *Chaqueta-Tigre* had the means to guarantee that the terms he described to herself and Singing Bear were honoured should the treaty be signed. Conditions were going to be sufficiently good to ensure there would be no need for further hostility between the two races.

Subsequent events had justified Becky's faith!

Goodnight had not been without allies in his efforts to bring about the treaty with the Comanches. Very important and perceptive men such as General Jackson Baines 'Ole Devil' Hardin and his clan, Temple, son of General Samuel Houston—commander of the greatly outnumbered force which defeated *Presidente* Antonio Lopez de Santa Anna at the Battle of San Jacinto and won independence from Mexican domination for Texas[2]—John Slaughter[3], Big Ranse Counter,[4] others equally prominent in the cattle business and various Army officers who were not of the glory hunting kind, had rendered their considerable support. With the negotiations brought to a satisfactory conclusion, they had been equally determined to ensure the exceptionally competent warriors of the various bands were encouraged to remain at peace.

Together, Goodnight and his supporters formed a group with influence which extended throughout the Lone Star State and was sufficiently potent to be acknowledged in Washington, D.C. Therefore, when they devoted their

2 *Some of the events leading up to the victory and how it was brought about are recorded in the* Ole Devil Hardin *series.*

3 *Some details about the career of Texas John Slaughter are given in*: Part Eight, 'Affair Of Honour', J.T.'S HUNDREDTH; GUN WIZARD *and* SLAUGHTER'S WAY.

4 *As yet, we have only recorded a few of the events in the life of Big Ranse Counter. However, we have the honour to be biographer for his youngest son, Mark, whose career is recorded in various volumes of the* Floating Outfit *series. We also have the privilege of serving in the same capacity for two more of his descendants, Sergeant Ranse Smith of Company 'Z', Texas Rangers and James Allenvale 'Bunduki' Gunn. Details of their careers can be found respectively in the* Alvin Dustine 'Cap' Fog *and* Bunduki *series.*

attention to avoiding problems caused elsewhere by the Bureau of Indian Affairs, they were able to have their wishes given *very* careful consideration and to be put into effect. Among other things, at their instigation, decent land was placed at the disposal of the *Nemenuh* bands. Just as important, they had insisted agents were provided who had the interests of the people at heart rather than the lining of pockets which was the rule rather than the exception on some reservations elsewhere.

In accordance with the terms of the treaty, the delegation had rejoined and led the rest of the band to the rendezvous arranged by *Chaqueta-Tigre*. Escorted by a company of Cavalry, whose task was to prevent interference by anybody—red or white—who might have wished to prevent the transfer being completed, he had guided them to the tract of land assigned as their reservation. It had proved much better than they had been led to expect might be the case by members of other tribes in similar circumstances.

Although the band would be restricted to an even greater degree than during the last few years of their independence, having clearly defined boundaries and being away from any route over which trail herds of longhorn cattle would be driven north to the railhead markets of Kansas, the land they were given was not the arid and unproductive terrain often supplied for such a purpose. While it had been arranged for an adequate supply of beef and other staples to be provided free of charge, there were still a number of deer and other animals to be hunted. Furthermore, to lessen the need for them to move around, permanent accommodation in the form of sturdy wooden cabins had been erected on the banks of a stream. There had been some scoffing at the suggestion of living in the buildings, but finding they had offered even better shelter from the elements than a *tipi* during the first winter had caused all except the most conservative of the population to make the change and continue to live in them.

Making the transition from being nomads to remaining in one location had not been easy. However, that the

Pahuraix were able to do it was to a great extent the result of Singing Bear having brought back Becky from his quest for vengeance. From their arrival on the land assigned as the band's reservation, in addition to having already been accepted by the Indians as a person of wisdom whose offspring had been singled out for special attention by *Ka-Dih*, she had established a friendly rapport with Agent Moses H. Dillingham and his wife which did much to smooth over such problems and difficulties as invariably had arisen. What was more, not only had the white couple also taken her daughter to their hearts, the feeling was soon reciprocated and this too proved beneficial to relations between the Agent and his charges.

Despite being disappointed by the realization that she would in all probability be prevented from achieving her ambitions as a warrior, to count many more coups and gather much loot, to even becoming a lance carrier to replace her father and *tawk*, Annie had settled down quickly and followed the new standards of conduct required by living on a reservation.

Ever a quick learner and possessing something of her mother's facility to adapt to changed conditions, although probably not to a sufficient extent to have been able to adjust so radically as would have been required had they gone to live permanently amongst white people, Should-Be-A-Boy had settled down quicker than the full blood *Pahuraix*. During the early days, this was to a great extent due to her participation in the frequent meetings with various authorities connected with the reservation which her mother had attended in the capacity of interpreter. Not only had she kept herself occupied by increasing her vocabulary in English, but with the help of the Dillinghams and encouraged by her parents, she had improved her skill at reading and writing. What was more, she had soon found something else to demand her attention.

Seeking to allow his charges to retain some control over their affairs, although no such organization had ever been regarded as necessary in normal daily life in the village, one of the earliest innovations Dillingham had introduced was the formation of a force something like that which was employed to act as regulators during the annual buffalo hunts. Supplied with blue tunics and *kepis* of the United States' Cavalry pattern, also a limited supply of ammunition for their firearms, their duty was to keep watch over the reservation and to ensure its rules were respected.

Singing Bear was no longer a lance carrier, but the memory of his achievements in that capacity was sufficiently fresh to give him the necessary authority when he was put in command of what amounted to being the *Pahuraix's* police department. Being aware of the consequences, he had done all he could to prevent incidents arising out of braves committing acts which would have been contrary to the conditions of the treaty.

Although the rest of his force were *tehnaps* who had already acquired such a status they no longer felt the need to seek ways of adding to it, Singing Bear had enrolled Should-Be-A-Boy to act as interpreter when they were required to deal with white people of any kind in the line of duty. There had often been need for her ability to speak English. An important part of their activities had been to control the traders who came to the reservation, particularly those bringing cheap, yet potent, whiskey in defiance of the law which wisely prohibited its sale to Indians.

However, despite being in as near a position to act as a warrior as was possible in her new way of life, Annie did not have any opportunity to acquire the acclaim she had hoped might be possible. There was one event which threatened to send her riding a vengeance trail, but the need for her to do so was prevented before she could set out.

Remembering how white men's liquor in the hands of Kiowa braves had led to the rape and murder of his first wife, and having seen the adverse effects drinking caused elsewhere, Singing Bear had been in complete agreement with Dillingham's desire to keep its curse from the *Pahuraix*. From the commencement of his duties, he had applied vigour to suppressing the iniquitous trade and was so successful that, after six months, it resulted in him being killed by two of the men involved. Having fled beyond the boundaries of the reservation before his body was discovered, the pair had believed they were safe from retribution.

Seeing the way in which Should-Be-A-Boy and the rest of the police reacted when they learned the murder had taken place, despite his own anger at the death of a man who had come to be a good friend, the Agent had warned that any attempt to follow and take revenge upon the killers would be in contravention of the treaty. Whether the attempt was successful or not, he had pointed out, it would give fuel to those elements in the white community who were for ever on the lookout for anything to the discredit of the Indians on reservations. Although the girl might not have been deterred by either factor, or even her mother stating agreement with Dillingham, matters were taken out of her hands. Acting swiftly at the request of the Agent, a newly appointed United States Deputy Marshal, Solomon Wisdom 'Solly' Cole,[5] had gone after the guilty men and killed both when they tried to resist arrest.

Singing Bear had not died in vain. Following the lead set by her father and their respected leader, Should-Be-A-Boy and the rest of the force he had imbued with his abomination of whiskey peddling continued the work he had started with such vigour that other whiskey traders left the *Pahuraix* alone and sought safer markets elsewhere.

Genuinely mourning for her husband, Becky had increased the involvement she had developed over the years with the village's spiritual practitioners. Because she was not born Comanche, she was unable to acquire the mysterious powers which some makers of 'medicine' attained, inexplicable though the effects they produced

[5] *Some events in the career of United States Marshal Solomon Wisdom 'Solly' Cole can be found in*: CALAMITY SPELLS TROUBLE; Part Seven, 'Deadwood, August 2nd, 1876', J.T.'S HUNDREDTH *and* Part Six, 'Mrs. Wild Bill', J.T.'S LADIES.

might be to non-initiates.[6] But she had found her acceptance into the society of Talks To Birds and his small, yet exclusive and influential, coterie gave her an even stronger voice in helping the Agent ensure that the even tenor of life on the reservation was not disturbed by violations of the treaty.

Almost eighteen months had elapsed since the murder of Singing Bear without any further incidents of a sufficiently serious nature to threaten the peaceful existence of the *Pahuraix*. There had been restlessness amongst the younger braves, but the good faith Dillingham had created, the continued efficiency of the reservation police and the influence Becky helped the elders to apply had held it in check.

For her part, guided by her mother and the Agent after the death of her father, Should-Be-A-Boy had matured even more rapidly than might have been the case if the old way of life was still being followed. She had the intelligence to appreciate how the *Pahuraix* could be affected adversely by breaches of the treaty and was always active in helping to prevent them occurring.

At last, however, a threat to the peace more serious than any which had previously occurred had arisen!

Returning alone from a patrol, having ascended just high enough to be able to look over a rim, Annie had seen four Mexicans. Despite having no reason to mistrust them, the instincts she had acquired during her formative years had caused her to halt before she would have been observed in return. Always interested in anybody other than the *Pahuraix* she encountered on the reservation, her curiosity had been further aroused by realizing they had come out of, rather than just passing, a distant clump of bushes. What was more, not only were they clearly in a hurry, they constantly glanced about them as if fearing pursuit.

[6] *Examples of the power of Comanche 'medicine', particularly the ability to transmit messages by thought to a receptive subject over long distances, are given in*: SIDEWINDER, GO BACK TO HELL *and* WHITE INDIANS.

Riding onwards with the intention of finding out what had brought the quartet on to the reservation, having had her suspicions aroused by their behaviour Should-Be-A-Boy rode straight to the place from which they had appeared rather than follow them. What she had discovered shocked her. Lying on the ground, was the prettiest and most popular of village's *naivi*, Loves Dancing. The pony tethered near by and various signs indicated she had come in search of berries and had been ravaged and seriously injured by the Mexicans.

Enraged by the sight, Annie's first inclination had been to set off after the quartet immediately. However, she was no longer the headstrong *tuinep'* who had endangered her life on the night she met Chief Long Walker and *Chaqueta-Tigre*. Therefore, the powers of self control she had developed pointed out she could not ride away and leave the badly hurt girl unattended. Taking comfort from feeling certain she could identify every one of the quartet, despite the distance which had separated them her eyes being keen enough to have picked out details, she had put aside thoughts of pursuit and made a *travois* upon which to transport Loves Dancing. Despite having worked and travelled as quickly as possible, night had fallen before they reached the village. What was more, regardless of the prompt action she had taken, she had arrived too late for medical attention to save the life of the brutally treated girl.

News of what had happened spread with the speed of a wind-swept prairie fire!

The outrage could not have come at a worse time!

In spite of Dillingham having ensured that all aspects of the treaty were fulfilled by the white men, the approach of summer always evoked memories for the braves of the greater freedom they had known before coming on to the reservation. As had happened each preceding year, there were already those who spoke loudly about returning to the age-old ways of roaming at will and seeking acclaim by riding the war trail. However, a lack of sufficient inducement, backed by bellies filled without the need to expend effort, and sound counsel from the elders, had so far been able to hold such desires in check.

Such was the popularity of the ravaged girl, there were many who demanded, that an immediate pursuit should be launched and an appropriate revenge taken. However, aware of what would happen if this was done, Brother To The Hawk had pointed out that the perpetrators could not be tracked in the darkness and would have crossed the boundaries of the reservation before they could be located. Although the wisdom of the first part of the statement had been accepted without argument, the second was not.

Listening to the angry declarations from many members of the crowd around the great council fire that revenge must be extracted, Should-Be-A-Boy had been in favour of the general view. However, her mother and Dillingham, who had heard the news and came to try to prevent what he was certain would be proposed in retaliation, had shared the summations of her *tawk* where the full ramifications of any such action being taken was concerned. What was more, on having the situation explained, she had found herself in agreement with what she was told. Being one herself, she knew the temperament of a Comanche warrior well enough to realize there were those who would not be content with merely going on the quest for vengeance. Instead, they would want to seek out more acclaim and acquire loot by attacking people who were not involved in the incident. Once that happened, there were white men who would be only too willing to consider the treaty had been broken without cause and demand reprisals.

Possessed of an inborn perception, Annie had realized she was the one most suitable to try and avert the peril. The days when Brother To The Hawk would have been listened to as a lance carrier, one of the bravest of the brave and with a status considered even higher than a chief, were too long past for him to be able to command the respect required to turn the warriors from their intentions. Although Woman Of Spirit was known to be shrewd, she was not Comanche by birth and could never attain the medicine powers which might have helped her enforce her will. Well liked though the Agent had come to be on account of his fair dealing, he too was not *Nemenuh* and could have little influence upon the intentions of the braves.

Which meant Should-Be-A-Boy, accepted by every member of the *Pahuraix* band as *Nemenuh* and a competent warrior who had already counted coup, alone might be considered suitable to prevent a disastrous course of events!

Nevertheless, in spite of the changes which had been made to her outlook since arriving on the reservation, Annie was unable to overlook the enormity of the action she was contemplating!

The plan envisaged by Should-Be-A-Boy would take her into the regions of medicine which no warrior approached without qualms!

However, the girl could not envisage any other way by which the undesirable state of affairs could be averted!

Fortunately, all that was needed for Annie to try and set her scheme into motion was in the building!

Silently offering a prayer for *Ka-Dih* to give His blessing to what she was planning, the girl swiftly began to make herself ready for putting her scheme into operation!

* * * *   * * * *

Having stepped forward, one of the leading exponents of the demands for riding after the Mexicans found his words were being ignored. Turning his gaze in the direction where more and more of the crowd were looking, he discovered the reason for the loss of attention.

Walking into the glow thrown by the big fire, Annie Singing Bear would not have gone unnoticed in any society. However, there was a special reason for the way in which the assembled members of the *Pahuraix* band were looking at her. It went beyond her being clad only in a blue breechclout, her weapon belt and moccasins. Nor, despite the feminine aspects of her physique having developed to a most noticeable degree, was this the reason every male eye was turned her way. Plainly visible between and partially on each of her firm bare breasts was the imprint of a red hand. Silence fell as she raised her arms and turned so every body present could see the sign she had made on her torso.

'I am Should-Be-A-Boy!' the girl announced in ringing tones, following a ritual she had been taught. 'It was I who found Loves Dancing, but could not deal with the men who ravaged her. Now her blood cries for revenge and *puha* has come to me from *Ka-Dih*. He says that I—and I alone—must take it for her. Therefore I, born of Singing Bear and Woman Of Spirit, *tawk* to Brother To The Hawk, give my solemn oath that I will go after them and will not return until I have repaid them for what they have done!'

15 *I Don't Want To Kill Him*

A startled exclamation burst from Don Ruiz Caraballeda as he stared at the rider on a small blue roan gelding who, having either accidentally or deliberately avoided the guards he had put out to the west, in spite of there being a full moon to assist them in keeping watch, came unannounced into the firelight!

Tall, lean and hard featured, Caraballeda was no better dressed than the *vaqueros* he hired. Even before the newcomer put in the unannounced appearance, he had been in a far from amiable frame of mind and was seething with a sense of annoyance which had not decreased to any great degree in spite of its original cause having occurred three days earlier. Having just returned from ensuring the trail herd he had brought from his *hacienda* in Mexico was bedded down and well guarded for the night, regardless of the extra precautions he had taken for its protection having proved unnecessary so far, he was no less worried by the potentially dangerous situation than when it had been forced upon him. Therefore, even if the visitor was only passing by chance and taking an opportunity to obtain a meal, he was far from being in the mood to offer hospitality.

Every instinct possessed by the *haciendero* warned that the arrival might not be for any such innocent reason!

The supposition did nothing to put Caraballeda in a better frame of mind!

Driving some three thousand head of longhorn cattle from Northern Chihuahua to the *gringo* railroad in Kansas, which offered a far more lucrative market than anything available in Mexico, was far from being a sinecure even if nothing else was involved. When one had also brought a large sum of counterfeit United States' dollars over the *Rio Bravo*[1] concealed in the chuck and bed wagons,[2] to be sold at a *very* healthy profit to an *Americano* criminal at the town where the herd would be sold, there was an even greater necessity to avoid attracting unwanted attention.

It was the latter reason, rather than being afraid of coming into conflict with cattlemen living in Texas and objecting to his herd crossing their range, or encroaching upon their market, which had caused Caraballeda to select a route he had considered should keep him clear of such competitors. Unfortunately, because of circumstances which he had not foreseen, his desire to avoid any confrontation which might cause the *Americano* peace officers to take an interest in him had resulted in the possibility of it happening.

While making preparations for the trail drive and its secondary—albeit potentially more profitable—purpose, Caraballeda was acting as a reluctant host to two of his nephews, Nicasio and Benito Velasquez and a pair of equally dissolute, but just as well connected, companions. They had been sent from Mexico City to save them from the consequences of some unsavoury activities. Far from mending their ways, continuing to behave in the irresponsible fashion which had resulted in what they regarded as a banishment, they had been abusing his reluctant hospitality by doing as little work as possible and generally causing disruption around the *hacienda*. If the matter had been left in his hands, suspecting they would prove even more of a nuisance on the trail, he would have refused their

[1] 'Rio Bravo'; *the name given by Mexicans to the river which Americans call the 'Rio Grande'.*

[2] *Used when there were sufficient men to justify it, in addition to carrying the belongings of the trail crew, the 'bed wagon' transported various pieces of equipment such as a rope to make temporary corrals for the* remuda *and spare 'ready-made' horse shoes which would otherwise have had to be packed into the chuck wagon.*

suggestion of accompanying him. However, he had yielded with misgivings when they had elicited the support of their parents and produced requests which were closer to commands under the circumstances, their father having financed the transaction in counterfeit money, that they and the de Ulloa brothers should be taken along.

Because Carabelleda had stayed well away from human habitation as the herd was moved northwards across Texas, the two sets of brothers had no chance to make mischief amongst the white men. Nevertheless, despite knowing of his illegal activities and the necessity to avoid arousing interest in the trail drive, they had finally proved as much of a liability as he had anticipated might be the case.

Claiming they were tired of living on no better diet than the simple provisions carried in the chuck wagon, without having asked for permission from the *haciendero*, the four young men had left the herd with the stated intention of hunting for some wild animals as a change from beef. It was not until after they had taken their departure that Caraballeda discovered they had bottles of *tequila* with them. On their return, in addition to all being the worse for drink, Benito Velasquez and Ruben de Ulloa each had four freshly made scratches on their faces. Having had them thrown into a stream to sober them up, the *haciendero* had been furious when he had compelled them to confess how the injuries had come about.

Normally, having done the same in his youth, Caraballeda would have regarded the molestation of an Indian girl as nothing more than an understandable piece of high spirited fun. On this occasion, he knew enough about conditions in Texas not to regard it in such a light. Instead, he was all too aware that both his endeavours could have been put in jeopardy.

Although Caraballeda had been informed that most of the Comanche bands were on reservations and were honouring the terms of the treaty signed at Fort Sorrel, memories of their war-like nature were still much too fresh for him to take comfort from having heard the *Pahuraix* in particular appeared to have settled down and were living in peace. What was more, he realized that it was not only the Indians in the village of the ravaged girl who he must worry about. Even in the unlikely event that they should restrict themselves to nothing more than reporting the incident to the Agent for the reservation, the matter was far from being over. Moses H. Dillingham had a reputation for taking *very* good care of his charges and being determined that nothing should be allowed to happen that might cause them to take the war path. It was common knowledge that when white whiskey peddlers murdered one of *Pahuraix* braves, to prevent others seeking vengeance, he had caused them to be hunted down and, proving there were people of influence who shared his resolve, there had been more praise than criticism when they were killed by a peace officer while resisting arrest. Therefore, on being informed that a girl had been raped, he could count upon the authorities being just as willing to co-operate in bringing the perpetrators to justice.

If nothing else had been at stake, the *haciendero* would have been indifferent to the fate of his nephews and their no more likeable companions. However, aware that Nicosia and Benito Velasquez were privy to his illicit secondary business interest, he felt sure they had let the de Ulloa brothers share the secret. The supposition had prevented him from telling them to go home by the shortest route and as quickly as possible. Knowing them, he had been disinclined to allow them out of his sight. It was a considerable distance to the safety they would be offered by crossing the *Rio Bravo* and he doubted whether they could traverse it, even knowing what was at stake, without making more trouble along the way. Should any of them be arrested before arriving in their native land, from which an internationally accepted convention would prevent them being extradited, he did not doubt they would try to avoid the consequences of their actions by informing the arresting lawmen about the counterfeit money he was transporting.

The period which elapsed since he had learned of the rape had been very worrying for Caraballeda. To make their behaviour all the more dangerous, the quartet had ridden ahead of the trail herd in their search for game. While he was not on the reservation, the route he was taking meant his party must travel parallel to its boundary and he had concluded he would not make any great improvement to the situation should he turn westwards instead of continuing north. Furthermore, regardless of the direction they took, there was no chance of putting so much distance between themselves and any pursuers that they could not be caught. There was a limit to how fast a herd could be pushed and it was much lower than the speed at which riders without the encumbrance of the cattle could follow.

Being experienced in all aspects of handling a herd on the trail, Caraballeda had taken every precaution he could think of as soon as he had heard of the quartet's behaviour. Although he would have preferred to avoid giving such an indication of their location, it had been too late to prevent the cook lighting a fire. Instead of having it put out, which would have caused even more smoke no matter how carefully the dousing was done, he had doubled the guard on the cattle and kept sentries posted all around the camp. On moving out the next morning, he had sent his most experienced men to act as scouts ahead, to the rear and on each flank. Not content to rely solely upon them, making use of a pair of powerful field glasses, he had frequently scanned the surrounding terrain.

Either due to the precautions, or because the ravaged girl had not been found, nothing out of the ordinary had happened on the first day. However, even though there had been no sign of human life until the rider had come into view that evening, the *haciendero* had insisted that care must still be taken. Therefore his mood was not improved by realizing there had been no warning that somebody was coming through the sentries he had posted.

Studying the newcomer, as was everybody else in the camp, Caraballeda felt puzzled.

The clothing was masculine and so was the saddle of Indian origins on the small blue roan gelding. However, despite the loose fit of the cheap dark red cotton shirt tucked into well worn yellowish-brown nankeen trousers—from the legs of which emerged bare ankles above moccasins—the body was unmistakably that of a young woman. No hair showed from beneath the rounded crown of her somewhat too large wide brimmed black hat, but her darkly bronzed and good looking features were suggestive of mixed blood. No weapons hung on the plain leather belt around her waist, but there was a Winchester Model of 1866 carbine, its woodwork decorated by patterns made from brass tacks, lying across her knees.

'How did you get here without my guards seeing you,' Caraballeda demanded in good English.

'Twasn't hard for somebody's been raised Comanch',' the girl replied, bringing the roan to a stop a short distance from the *haciendero* and remaining in the saddle. 'But I'm rightly pleasured's you talk American, 'cause I don't speak no Mex'. You'll be the big chief of this here outfit, I'm reckoning?'

'I am,' Caraballeda confirmed. 'Why have you come?'

'To see you,' the girl answered. 'You're some closer in this way than I expected, so I'm right pleased I heard you and I reckon you'll be just as pleasured when you hear tell why I've come.'

* * * *   * * * *

Taken with the other alterations to her usual appearance Annie Singing Bear had made before she left the cabin, the sight of the red imprint on her bare bosom and her announcement had created a considerable sensation around the council fire!

Even those too young to have ever seen the ritual which Should-Be-A-Boy had enacted were aware of its significance!

However, the girl had not acted on a spur of the moment impulse!

While returning to the village with Loves Dancing on the *travois*, Annie had known there was going to be serious trouble when it became known what had happened. What was more, having learned enough during her time on the reservation to appreciate the consequences which could arise if any of the other braves undertook to avenge the girl—whose popularity was certain to arouse such a desire—she had decided they might be reduced if she was allowed to do so.

Discussing the idea with her mother and *tawk* on her arrival, Should-Be-A-Boy had found they were in agreement with her summations. Nor, on Brother To The Hawk having pointed out there would be objections to the solution, had Becky Ingraham allowed thoughts of the danger her daughter would be facing to deter her from trying to help bring about its acceptance. The talk she had with Agent Dillingham had verified the points raised by Annie without disclosing to him what was being contemplated. Therefore, Becky had forced herself to think as *pairaivo* of the late Singing Bear—whose offspring was a Comanche warrior, with all that entailed—rather than a widowed white woman faced with the daunting prospect of her only progeny being committed to going on an exceptionally dangerous mission. Adopting that philosophy, even though she had never heard the term, she had been able to accept that only such desperate measures might prevent the repercussions which were sure to take place should the murdered girl be avenged by the *Pahuraix* themselves in any other way.

Gaining the approval of her family had been one thing, but the girl had discovered extending it to the rest of the band was less easy!

The warning that there would be opposition given by Brother To The Hawk had been proved valid!

Regardless of her assertion that she was guided by having received medicine *puha* from *Ka-Dih*, the girl's rendition of the vengeance oath had not been allowed to pass unchallenged. However, it had not been considerations of her sex which caused the objections. Everybody present had long since accepted she was a warrior and would soon be worthy of attaining the status of *tehnap*.

Despite having conceded such was the case, members of Loves Dancing's family had said it was up to them to deal with those responsible for her rape and death. There were several in the crowd who had genuinely considered that, regardless of the ability she displayed, *Tuinep'* was still too inexperienced to be able to handle the situation adequately. Some of the younger braves, having hoped to use the incident as an excuse to ride the war trail, had stated a similar reason for disputing her claim.

Having spoken up in behalf of Should-Be-A-Boy, Becky—as was her right as Woman Of Spirit, even though she was born white—and Brother To The Hawk had received influential support. Whether Talks To Birds and the band's other spiritual advisers had accepted the girl's claim to divine guidance as valid or not, they too had appreciated how agreeing to her proposal might avert a situation they were equally desirous of avoiding. Being just as perceptive, the other 'old man' chiefs had added their weight to the argument in her favour. However, although she was given permission to carry out the wishes of the Great Spirit, it was not unqualified. Instead, she had been allotted no more than five days to carry out the quest and warned that, should she not have completed it by the end of that period, others would be sent to do so.

Should-Be-A-Boy had followed tradition by wearing only the prescribed clothing for swearing the oath of revenge. Furthermore, she was expected to be dressed in the same way when confronting those responsible for her making it. However, she was not restricted to such scanty garb while searching for her quarry. Taking advantage of this, before leaving the village, she had donned attire—including a hat large enough to conceal her warrior's braided hair inside its crown—which she had hoped would make her less obviously of Indian extraction than her usual clothes if she should be seen outside the boundaries of the reservation.

Riding a three horse relay, which naturally included her favourite blue roan gelding, the girl had commenced her search at the bushes where she had found Loves Dancing.

As they had made no attempt to conceal the signs of their passing, following the four Mexicans had been easy at first. However, when their tracks had joined and become mingled with numerous others, suggesting they had joined men engaged in driving a herd of cattle north, she had realized her task would be even more difficult than she had envisaged.

Circling the area of the camp where the quartet had gone the previous night, Annie had not found the tracks of their horses—or any others they might have received in exchange—going away from it and she assumed they were travelling with the herd. Riding after the cattle, in spite of the precautions she had taken to avoid being seen, she had made sufficiently good time to catch up late in the afternoon. On coming into sight of them, she had discovered that all the men were Mexicans. However, while they were on the move, the presence of the scouts had prevented her from being able to approach close enough to ascertain whether the four in whom she was interested were there.

Being clad in the required fashion in case she should be given an opportunity to complete her mission, and having employed the skill at silent movement she had acquired to evade the sentries, Should-Be-A-Boy had scouted the Mexican's next camp after night had fallen. Although she had satisfied herself that her quarry were present, she had decided there was no way she could be sure of killing all four if she should open fire from her place of concealment. What was more, with her presence betrayed, the added precautions which were certain to be taken would remove any chance of getting the survivors in the limited time at her disposal.

Showing a wisdom and patience which her *tawk* and dead father would have regarded as praiseworthy, Annie had accepted she must refrain from trying to carry out her mission until a more suitable opportunity was presented. Acting upon the conclusion, she had withdrawn from the immediate vicinity of camp as silently as she had approached. Continuing the pursuit when the herd moved on at dawn, despite hoping she would not be identified as

Nemenuh if seen briefly at a distance, she had taken sufficient care to ensure she remained undetected all day.

Taking into consideration the advantages she could be offered by the changes she had made to her appearance, the girl had concocted a scheme which she hoped would allow her to bring the quartet on to ground of her own choosing. However, as it was not her intention to attempt anything against them immediately if she succeeded in producing the result she required, she had retained the attire worn during the day. Having circled around well beyond the range of vision of the scouts, leaving behind the other two horses and riding the well trained blue roan gelding, she had made her way towards the camp.

Once more contriving to elude the men put out as guards, a more difficult task than when on foot and in darkness, Should-Be-A-Boy had only located three of her quarry while selecting and addressing the Mexican she had concluded, from watching them, was the leader of the party. For the first time in her life, she was making use of her sex instead of trying to conceal it. She was gambling that discovering she was a girl and hearing her cryptic comment would arouse his interest sufficiently for him to want to learn more about her.

'Well now!' Benito Velaquez remarked in his native tongue, coming out of the bed wagon before his uncle had a chance to continue the conversation with the newcomer. He had gone inside to drink *tequila* in defiance of the orders he and the other three had been given and liquor always aroused his baser instincts where the opposite sex was concerned. Forgetting everything they had been told about improving their behaviour on their return from raping the Comanche girl, he swaggered forward and, extending his right hand towards her, went on, 'Look at what we have he—!'

About to ask what the girl had meant, Caraballeda swung his gaze in the direction of his nephew!

The angry reproof which the *haciendero* was about to utter went unsaid!

Even without having identified the tall young man by

his distinctively decorated expensive *charro* attire, as had been the case with the other three—all of them being better dressed than the rest of the party—the raw scratches on his left cheek would have supplied Should-Be-A-Boy with an indication that he was one of those she sought. Controlling an inclination to raise and fire the Winchester at his leering face, she brought his words and gesture to a halt by launching a kick with all the power her sturdy right leg could muster. Caught in the centre of the chest with considerable force and unexpectedly, Benito was propelled backwards. Tripping and sitting down with a thud which jolted most of the breath from his body, he spluttered a profanity and made a fumbling grab at the ornate handle of the Colt Model of 1860 Army revolver in the tied down holster of his gunbelt.

'Tell him to stop, mister boss man!' Annie commanded, pleased to be able to continue using English as she did not want to let it be known she spoke enough Spanish to be able to follow whatever might be said in that langauge. Swiftly swinging the carbine from its place across her lap and pivoting the lever through its loading cycle, she turned its barrel into alignment upon the younger Mexican while directing the words to the *haciendero*. Although she would have liked nothing better than to do so, she went on, 'I don't want to kill him, but I will if that gun comes out!'

'Leave it!' Caraballeda bellowed, spinning on his heel and glaring furiously. Seeing his order was being ignored, he darted forward and kicked the gun out of Benito's hand as it emerged from its holster. Then he turned his attention to his other nephew and the de Ulloa brothers who were showing similarly hostile intentions. 'Stop that right now, you three. *Madre de dios*, don't you know shooting might make the cattle stampede?'

Despite being just as surprised to see the girl, on her arrival, the *vaqueros* had followed the example set by their employer in reacting to her appearance. Now, sharing his appreciation of the dangers which a commotion could produce, the nearest of them moved just as quickly to prevent any of the trio drawing a weapon.

'I don't know what you said, mister,' Annie remarked, returning the carbine to across her knees without changing its condition of immediate readiness for use, or removing her right hand from the wrist of the butt and leaving its forefinger curled through the triggerguard. Wanting to keep up the pretense of not being conversant with Spanish and yet to show she too appreciated the danger which shooting could create for the herd, she continued, 'But it's right lucky for you it worked. I don't know over much about them critters we call "spotted buffalo", 'cepting they get scared and take to running *real* easy should there be any loud noises like guns going off near 'em.'

'She knows what will happen if there's shooting, so don't any of you do anything to frighten her into starting!' Caraballeda snapped over his shoulder, having noticed how the Winchester was held and reaching the conclusion which Should-Be-A-Boy had hoped to produce. Swinging his gaze back to her, he resumed speaking English. 'Who are you and what brings you here?'

'They call me Annie Singing Bear,' the girl introduced, feeling sure the name she had been given by her mother was not known to the Mexicans even if they had heard of her as 'Should-Be-A-Boy'. 'And I've come to tell you what kind of trouble you're in on account of that son-of-a-bitch and those other three young bastards over there.'

'How did you know it was us who—?' Benito began, increasing the girl's satisfaction by proving he too could speak sufficient English to be able to follow the conversation and, if their reactions were any guide, the same applied to the other three.

'Shut your mouth!' Caraballeda thundered, spinning around with such obvious anger that the incautious question was ended before being completed. Then, once more returning his attention to Annie, he decided to try a bluff, 'I don't know what you mean.'

'Then it could just be I've come to the wrong place,' Should-Be-A-Boy answered, having inherited her father's skill as a gambler and having been a successful competitor in games which depended upon the use of deception.

'Which's a pity's I was counting on getting paid well for what I've got to tell.'

'Paid?'

'Paid, with American money. I've seen the way white women live and conclude it'll be a whole heap easier'n staying with pappy's folks on the reservation. Only I'll need some cash to buy clothes's'll let me get started among momma's kind.'

'And what is it that you have to sell?'

'You show me a hundred dollars in American money and I'll tell.'

'That's a lot of money.'

'Not's much's you'll lose should those spotted buffalo of your'n get scattered to hell 'n' gone,' the girl declared, confident she had aroused enough interest to give her plan a chance of succeeding. 'Which's what'll happen 'less'n you find out *all* I know.'

'Here's the money,' Caraballeda said, taking a thick wallet from the inside pocket of his *bolero* jacket and counting off the appropriate number of ten dollar bills. 'But I don't hand it over until I decide you've earned it.'

'They don't know it, but after they'd done bad wrong to a gal from the village, those four was seen from close enough for them to be described so well they can be picked out easy,' Annie supplied truthfully. She continued, with less veracity, 'Everybody was all riled up, but the old man chiefs and the Agent talked 'em out of coming after you. All 'cepting her two brothers, that is. They've tooken them an oath of revenge and're after making good on it right now.'

'That doesn't worry *me*,' the *haciendero* claimed, but he could not prevent a trace of his concern from showing to the perceptive girl. 'I've more than two men with me.'

'Sure, but those braves won't come at you with head down 'n' horns a-hooking,' Should-Be-A-Boy countered. 'Fact being, happen they get what they want, they'd sooner leave the rest of you be so's they don't get the rest of the band in fuss for them breaking the treaty.'

'And what do they want?' Caraballeda asked, although he knew the answer.

'Those four jaspers,' Annie replied, indicating the quartet with a disdainful motion of the carbine. 'Just them, not anybody else, but they're bound and determined to get them even if it means tagging along and cutting down anybody who gets in their way, or scattering the herd so's they can be had while the rest of you're trying to stop your spotted buffalo from getting clear away.'

'That's interesting,' Caraballeda admitted, having suspected the seekers after vengeance would adopt similar tactics. 'But not enough to be worth a hundred dollars.'

'Would you be willing to pay it for knowing where to find 'em?' Annie inquired.

'Give her the money, Uncle Ruiz!' Nicosia Velaquez requested and the de Ulloa brothers muttered their concurrence. 'Then you can send men to get them.'

'Like hell will I send any of the men!' the *haciendero* stated bluntly. 'I'll pay the girl for what she knows, but you four brought this trouble on yourselves and you're going to deal with it the same way.'

16 It's *Her* Who's After Us!

'You see!' Benito Velasquez hissed, his tone and manner redolent of the triumph which came through being proved correct. 'They're where she told us that we'd find them and they're doing just like I said they would!'

'Why don't you go over and shake them awake?' Arnaldo de Ulloa suggested in a *sotto voce* snarl, scowling at the two shapes lying in the centre of a clearing on either side of a fire which had almost died away.

'Don't start arguing!' Nicosia Velaquez commanded, also holding down his voice yet managing to induce a note of savage urgency into his words. Starting to bring up his Winchester Model of 1866 rifle, he went on, 'Let's shoot them from here and get it over with!'

Accepting the wisdom of the suggestion, being satisfied by the way in which the situation had developed, the other three young Mexicans also brought the rifles they were carrying to shoulder level!

Seeking additional proof of the danger before parting with the money requested by the girl, Don Ruiz Caraballeda had gone further into the matter of how, if the *Pahuraix* sought revenge, it could bring them into conflict with the white authorities for breaking the terms of the treaty they had signed. Confirming that the point had been taken into consideration by the council of elders, she had noticed he seemed more disturbed than pleased when she said they were considering asking Agent Dillingham — who had coped successfully with a similar situation — to have his people's law deal with the men responsible for the rape and subsequent death of Loves

Dancing. In fact, he had appeared relieved when she had gone on to explain how two braves had claimed to be instructed by *Ka-Dih* to take the oath of vengeance and that it had been decided they must be allowed to carry it out before other measures were contemplated. Thinking about what had followed, she had concluded he had some reason for wanting to avoid official intervention.

The leader of the Mexicans had shown much interest in learning where Should-Be-A-Boy claimed to have seen the two braves who, before preparing to spend the night, were seen making 'medicine' to prepare them for carrying out their quest. Clearly knowing of the *Pahuraix* prediliction for living near water, and hearing they were in a clearing on the banks of a stream, he had felt sure this too was the way of the Waterhorse Comanches when engaged upon such a spiritual activity. Wanting to estimate the extent of the danger, he had asked what would happen if the men being sought killed their pursuers. He was informed that, under the circumstances, the population of the village would regard it as the will of *Ka-Dih* and would not allow any further action, even the reporting of the incident to the Agent, to be taken. Satisfied and relieved by the latter information, he had paid her the promised hundred dollars and allowed her to depart unhindered.

Giving thought to what he had learned, being unable to envisage any reason why it should not be the truth, the *haciendero* had concluded that to allow anybody other than the errant quartet—who were clearly known to the *Pahuraix*—to deal with the braves authorized to seek revenge could lead to the herd and the counterfeit money being endangered by the rest of the band. Being cold bloodedly ruthless by nature and having a serious need of the profits which would accrue from the trip, he had decided the safety of the cattle and illicit merchandise far outweighed family ties, especially to the far from likeable sons of a second cousin, in the decision of what was his best line of action.

After the girl had left, much to the consternation of his nephews and their companions, Caraballeda had repeated his assertion that they alone would have to cope with the threat to their lives. Nor was he swayed by the Velaquez brothers pointing out how their family had financed the illegal aspect of the enterprise upon which he was engaged, but he had reminded them that he had more to lose than anybody in Mexico should things go wrong because of their drunken misdeeds. Furthermore, having alienated themselves from the *vaqueros* by their arrogance and idleness since leaving Chihuahua, they had been just as unsuccessful in their attempt to persuade volunteers to accompany them. Knowing them, he had taken a precaution against their running away by giving a warning that their only hope of survival was to dispose of the men who were seeking them. If they should try to escape by taking flight, they would be tracked down and, lacking the knowledge they now had of where their enemies could be located, they would be caught and killed long before they reached safety.

Accepting they would have to act unsupported, the four young men had followed the instructions given by the girl. On reaching the woodland, she had directed them to, they had heard chanting in a foreign language and had seen the glow of a fire amongst the trees some distant ahead. Remembering they had been told their quarry would be making 'medicine', they had deduced the voice was praying.

Although Arnaldo de Ulloa had said they could ride up shooting and end the threat straight away, Benito Velasquez had pointed out the folly of such a course. This could not be accomplished without a great deal of noise which would warn the braves that somebody was coming. The only sure way to deal with them, he had claimed, would be to wait until after they had gone to sleep. Supporting his brother, Nicosia had suggested the attack be held off until day was breaking. By doing so, they would be able to see more clearly where they were going and keep down noise which would serve to alert the Indians to their presence. Although the de Ulloa brothers had not cared for their companions doing all the planning, neither had been able to come up with a better scheme. Passing a bottle of *tequila* around to help keep up their spirits, they had waited until dawn was starting to lighten the sky before continuing their advance.

Going forward on foot, given a spurious confidence in their abilities by the potent liquor, the quartet had felt sure they were moving too silently to be detected by their intended quarry. Certainly there was nothing to suggest the contrary when they had come into sight of the small clearing. Two horses were standing hobbled and grazing on the banks of the stream which ran through it. Covered by blankets, their owners appeared to be sleeping deeply and unaware of any danger threatening.

More by accident than deliberate intent, the four rifles crashed at the same instant, different targets having been selected. Both the blankets jerked and holes appeared where the torsoes of whoever might be lying beneath them would be. However, although the hobbled horses snorted and showed signs of alarm, neither shape made any movement.

'We've got them both!' Benito Velasquez enthused.

'Let's make sure!' Arnaldo de Ulloa commanded, working the lever of his rifle and walking forward.

Just as eager to see the results of their efforts, the other three Mexicans duplicated the actions. Noticing how completely motionless their targets continued to be, each was convinced the braves were killed instantaneously. Eager to collect proof that they had ended the threat to their existence without needing to be helped by anybody, they had eyes for nothing else. Separating as they approached the fire, each pair of brothers went to a shape.

'Let's take a loo—!' Nicosia Velasquez began, jerking aside the blanket.

'Shall we take their sca—?' Ruben de Ulloa commenced, in the same breath, also pulling away the covering he and his brother had selected as their target.

What was brought into view produced four *very* startled exclamations at the same instant!

'*Madre de dios*!'

'What's thi—?'

'There's nobod—!'

'This isn't a ma—!'

Before any of the Mexicans could respond in a more positive way to the discovery that each blanket was draped over only a pile of leaves and branches, another voice spoke!

The tone had such a timbre of hatred and loathing it could hardly be discerned as feminine in gender!

'*Namae'enumh*!'

Without realizing that they had heard the most profane and deadly insult any Comanche other than a member of the *Wawai* band could utter, the Mexicans brought up their gaze to locate the speaker!

Doing so was not a difficult task!

The slight was in some ways even more alarming than the discovery that the targets at which the quartet had fired were not sleeping human beings, but inanimate decoys!

Under different circumstances, being lecherous and licentious by nature, the Mexicans would have derived pleasure from the appearance presented by Annie Singing Bear!

Since they had seen her last, the girl had discarded the hat, shirt and trousers. Clad only in her breechclout, weapon belt and moccasins, as was demanded by tradition for the carrying out of an oath of vengeance, the feminine attributes of her shapely buxom figure were all too obvious. Nevertheless, at that moment, not one of the quartet gave a thought to her sex. Not even the firm mounds of her bare breasts, with the mark of the red hand showing in contrast to her bronzed skin, could distract them from realizing the implication of her reddish-brown hair in its warrior's braids and the vivid slashes of white, green and blue 'war paint' which gave an added savagery to the lines of her otherwise attractive face. If further proof of her hostile intention had been needed, it was supplied by the Winchester Model of 1866 carbine she cradled in a firing position against her right shoulder as she stepped from her place of concealment at the other side of the clearing.

In spite of being compelled to revise her original suppositions, everything had gone as Should-Be-A-Boy hoped and planned!

Knowing there was no human habitation for many miles in the direction taken by the four Mexicans as they rode away from the bushes where they had left their victim, the girl had felt sure she could catch up with them before they could reach safety. However, before she set off on her quest, her mother had warned that she must do everything possible to avoid letting it be obvious that anybody from the village was responsible for their deaths. Despite realizing that to do so would mean she could not take back anything to prove she had carried out her oath of revenge, it had been her intention to catch up with and kill them by the most convenient means at her disposal. Having done so, unsaddling and turning loose their horses, she would conceal the bodies and their belongings in some secluded place. She hoped so long would elapse before anybody missed them and tried to find out what had happened that it would prevent any suggestion of the truth being established.

Discovering that the quartet had joined and were travelling with a trail herd had warned Annie that her task would be far more difficult than if they had been alone. For one thing, she had concluded it would be almost impossible for her to carry out the oath of vengeance without Indian involvement being suspected. She had also realized that, should she be fortunate enough to come upon one or more away from their companions, their absence would be noticed very quickly and a search instituted. Even if the bodies were not found, knowing what had happened on the reservation, the party would suspect that revenge for the molestation of Loves Dancing had been taken. Furthermore, the survivors would take such precautions to protect themselves, she would not be offered any further opportunity to complete the mission in the time at her disposal and others would set out to do so. This in turn would ensure that the involvement of the band was made public.

Keeping her quarry under observation from a distance and noticing how they were dressed in what she guessed to be a more expensive fashion, Should-Be-A-Boy had deduced they were different from the other Mexicans in the party. Instead of riding with the cattle or the *remuda* like everybody else while on the move, they had remained close to the two wagons. Yet this had not been to help the drivers with their work. Nor had the four taken any part in the tasks being carried out at the camps either in the evening or before moving on the following morning. Allowed to carry out a closer observation during the hours of darkness, she had formed the impression that their companions did not care for them.

Based upon what she had seen and deduced, aware that the details were widely known of how Agent Dillingham had reacted to the murder of her father, Annie had formulated a plan which she considered might allow her to carry out her mission without the other Mexicans wanting to be involved. Although it was beyond the boundaries of the reservation, the knowledge of the terrain they would be traversing, which she had acquired as a result of hunting on it—and the memory of what had led up to the only coup she had yet counted—had suggested the means by which she could achieve her purpose. In fact, thinking how the various factors were combining to help, it had seemed to her that *Ka-Dih* was looking favourably upon the enterprise despite her having obtained permission to participate without actually having received the *puha* she had claimed to come from Him.

Riding ahead of the trail herd, the girl had selected the most suitable place in the woodland and made her preparations for what she hoped to bring about. Natural inclinations rather than prescience had caused her to have two indispensable items in her possession. Although inured to hardship, like every Indian brave, she saw no reason to suffer more than was needed. Therefore, she had brought along blankets in which to keep warm at night while on the mission. Everything else she had needed to create the two 'sleeping braves' was readily available close by and leaving her two reserve horses hobbled in the clearing had given support to the illusion she was seeking to create.

Having set the scene for what she hoped would be the confrontation she was seeking, *Tuinep'* had ridden to the Mexicans' camp to try to bring it about. Although she had been ready to explain her motives for the supposed betrayal at greater length, the need had not arisen. Nor, due to the leader she was addressing having known something of the *Pahuraix* band's prediliction for living near water, had she been required to give an explanation of why the 'two vengeance seekers' would select a clearing by a stream to make their 'medicine'. However, she had been pleased with the interest he had shown in her claim that the herd would only be endangered if he and his men interfered in the quest for revenge. She had laid stress upon the point that, provided nobody else became involved, the rest of the men and the cattle would be left unmolested. Because her pretense of not being able to understand Spanish was accepted, she had heard enough pass between the quartet and the leader to assure her that he had no wish for the white authorities to become involved. She also deduced the quartet would receive no help from their leader.

Having laid her trap, Should-Be-A-Boy had taken her departure and returned to the clearing to see whether it would be sprung!

Concealing her blue roan gelding amongst the undergrowth a short distance away, relying upon her faculties being sufficiently keen to detect the approach of her quarry long before they were in a position to see her, the girl had remained by the fire. In addition to keeping it going, she had chanted in Comanche to help guide the quartet to her. However, what they had believed to be a prayer was actually a bawdy song. Despite having laid a false claim to receiving *puha* from *Ka-Dih*, her religious beliefs were too strongly held to permit further irreverence.

Hearing them arrive in the woodland and then stop long before they reached the clearing, Annie had guessed what was intended and elected to let them come to her instead of seeking them out. While she did not doubt she could stalk them without being detected, she had known there would be less chance of one or more getting away if the confrontation was to take place on the ground she had prepared.

Waiting with the patience she had been taught was essential for a warrior, as she had only the two blankets needed to cover the decoys, Annie had been grateful for the excuse to keep the fire going and ward off the chill in the night air. Kept warm during the period of waiting, as much a precaution against becoming stiffened by cold as for comfort, she had concluded her estimation of the quartet's intentions was correct when she heard them resuming their approach at daybreak. What was more, she had quickly decided the leader of the Mexicans had not changed his mind and given them assistance. The noise they were making had satisfied her that only four men were coming and they were those she sought. She had felt sure the other men with the cattle would have proved much more competent at silent movement and her summation had proved correct.

Despite the hatred she had developed for the quartet, Should-Be-A-Boy had controlled her inclination to start shooting the moment they came into view. She wanted to wait until they were out in the open before taking action against them. However, she had wanted to let them know at whose hands vengeance was to be meted out. Instead of taking the fullest advantage of their error by opening fire immediately, she had spoken the profanity and caused them to become aware of her presence.

Tuinep' achieved her intention!

'Mother of God!' Nicosia screeched, chilled by horror as the realization of what he was seeing struck him and speaking a moment before a similar conclusion was drawn by the other three. 'It's *her* who's after us!'

Just as numbed as his sibling and the de Ulloa brothers had been by the discovery that they had fallen into a trap, while the comment was being made fear brought a reaction from Benito Velasquez. However, it was one of self preservation rather than action taken to help the others escape the consequences. Without even waiting to see how Nicosia and their companions fared, he flung his rifle aside and took to his heels. Although he heard shooting to his rear, he did not so much as glance back to find out what was happening.

The words were the last conscious act of the elder Velasquez brother's life. Just after he said 'us', Annie sent a bullet from her Winchester into the centre of his forehead. Throwing the lever down and up with the deft skill acquired through considerable practise since the carbine had been presented to her by Colonel Charles Goodnight, she sent the spent cartridge case spinning into the air and replenished the chamber. Turning and sighting along the twenty inch barrel, she squeezed the trigger to deal Arnaldo de Ulloa an equally fatal wound as he was lifting his weapon to defend himself.

Such was the ability Should-Be-A-Boy had attained, her third shot took Ruben de Ulloa before Nicosia's lifeless body arrived on the ground. However, this time the speed with which she aimed caused her to inflict only a minor wound. Pain combined with terror to distort his scratched face. Acting in the fashion of a cornered rat, he began to raise his rifle.

Seeing there was no such response from the last of the quartet, the girl continued to give her attention to the surviving de Ulloa brother. Moving with all the speed she could muster, aware that a slightly injured and enraged enemy could prove far more dangerous even than one who was unharmed, she put the little carbine through its reloading and firing cycle five times in very rapid succession. Although only two of the bullets she discharged found their mark, they proved to be sufficient. Flung backwards before he could shoot in return, Ruben was dead by the time he fell across his lifeless sibling.

Darting forward, holding the Winchester ready for instant use, the girl concluded she had achieved her oath where three of the Mexicans were concerned. However, although they were dead, the fourth was unscathed and had already reached the edge of the clearing. The bullet she sent after him missed and he disappeared between the trees before she could correct her aim. Nor did he offer more than fleeting glimpses as he continued his flight in the direction from which he had come. Therefore, having counted the shots she had instinctively fired and being aware she had no replacements on her person, she was too wise to squander the three which remained in the chamber and magazine against such a difficult target.

Accepting pursuit was unavoidable, like every Comanche brave, Annie would never walk when it was possible to ride. What was more, she suspected the fleeing man would reach and mount a horse before she could catch up with him on foot. Giving a whistle, she caused the blue roan to join her at a run. She had not taken off the saddle when leaving it the previous evening. Nor did the construction of a hackamore require it to be removed to allow the animal to graze while waiting to be used. Catching hold of the horn as the gelding joined her, she vaulted astride its back and sent it onwards without any break in its rapid gait. Before she had covered many yards, she was given proof that her supposition with regards to the young Mexican was correct. Not only did he continue to avoid offering a target suitable for the circumstances, she saw him reach and mount one of four tethered horses and gallop away through the trees.

Watching Benito as they left the woodland, Should-Be-A-Boy quickly concluded she might have to end the chase with her carbine from a greater distance than she would have preferred. She did not doubt that her mount could catch up with his, even thought he was doing everything he could to achieve greater speed, but she felt waiting for this to happen could be ill-advised. From the direction he was taking, he was making for where he believed the Mexicans who had remained with the cattle could be found. If they considered the herd might be endangered by the pursuit, or the discovery of how she had tricked them aroused their anger, they would intercede in his behalf and drive her away. If that happened, she doubted whether she would be granted another opportunity to complete her mission.

Certainly she would not be able to do so in the time she had been allocated, or without resorting to methods which would cause the man with whom she had talked to complain to the white authorities.

Even as *Tuinep'* was drawing her conclusion, the need to act upon it was removed!

Racing across more open country, being ridden by a man in a state of blind fear caused the fast running horse to have a mishap it might otherwise have avoided. Trying to turn aside and avoid going through a gap between two bushes it realized was too narrow for its body, the control being applied so painfully by the bit in its mouth forced the horse to remain on its path. Feeling the resistance to his wishes, panic caused Benito to seek all the more determinedly not to be turned from the most direct route back to the herd. Attempting to enforce his will, he was caught unaware by the violent resistance of the horse as it finally swerved. Such was the force of the animal's efforts, his feet lost the stirrups and he was precipitated from the saddle.

In one respect, Benito might have counted himself fortunate. Thrown into the foliage, he was saved from crashing face first to the ground. However, he was aware only that he had been deprived of his means of escape. Hearing the drumming of rapidly approaching hooves, while another set went away at a slower pace, not even the suffering caused by his arrival against the bush could prevent him from appreciating what the sounds implied. Twisting himself around, he stared in horror at the rider coming towards him. Once again, he gave not the slightest thought to her appearance or sex as she sprang from the saddle. All he knew was that he was at the mercy of one of the dreaded Comanche warriors whose reputation for savagery and brutality were still an all too often mentioned memory, even amongst the kind of society to which he belonged in Mexico City.

'No!' Benito screeched, dropping to his knees and clasping his hands before him in an attitude of prayer. Forgetting that the girl had claimed she did not speak

Spanish, he continued in that tongue, 'D—Don't hurt me. It was the others who attacked the girl. As the Holy Mother is my judge, I never even went near much less laid a hand on her!'

Staring at the cringing young man, being able to understand his words, a feeling of even greater revulsion filled Annie. Although he had thrown away his rifle, he still had a revolver and fighting knife on his weapon belt. What was more, he clearly had not been sufficiently injured to be rendered unable to defend himself. If he had the courage to offer resistance, she would have killed him instantly. However, her training and upbringing had no sympathy with cowardice regardless of why it might be shown. Repeating the profanity with which she had announced her presence in the clearing, she swung around her carbine to lash its barrel against the side of Benito's head. The impact knocked him sideways from his knees. He was rendered unconscious, which proved fortunate for him in one respect.

'Those scratches on your face make a liar of you!' Should-Be-A-Boy stated, going to lean her carbine against one of the bushes which ended the pursuit. Drawing the Green River knife from her sheath, she went on in a tone as savage as any male comanche warrior could have produced, 'But when I've finished, you'll never again treat another girl that way.'

17 Is-A-Man

'Good evening, Colonel Goodnight,' Agent Moses H. Dillingham greeted, trying to keep the concern he was experiencing from showing. 'It's over then?'

'Yes,' *Chaqueta-Tigre* confirmed, glancing from the small and bespectacled white man to Brother To The Hawk, Talks To Birds and Annie Singing Bear who were present in the office of the Agency's building. However, his bearded face showed nothing to indicate whether the news he brought was good or bad. 'It's over.'

'Was the verdict—*favourable*?' the Agent asked, too worried to spend time on unnecessary conversation.

Despite hopes to the contrary, there had been repercussions from the successful conclusion of Should-Be-A-Boy's quest for revenge!

However, the problems which had arisen were not created by Don Ruiz Caraballeda!

Employing the skill she had acquired castrating colts, having all she would need in the small buckskin pouch she had fastened to the cantle of the blue roan's saddle the previous evening, the girl had rendered Benito Velasquez incapable of ever again committing rape. She was using a sinew to suture the gash through which the 'seeds' of the testicles were removed from their bag of flesh, having stopped the bleeding with a liberal application of powdered witch hazel leaves, when she had seen four riders in the distance. Recognizing them as *vaqueros* who had been with the herd of cattle, she had left the still unconscious young man lying where the operation was performed. Keeping the Mexicans under observation while withdrawing towards the woodland, she had felt sure they had not noticed her.

On arriving, the *vaqueros* had examined Velasquez and, while one remained with him, the other three had started to follow the tracks he and the girl had made. Seeing this, she had made her way to the clearing. Collecting her other two horses, she had moved them some distance away. Leaving them and the roan in concealment, after reloading her Winchester Model of 1866 carbine from the supply of ammunition in her belongings, she had returned on foot to find out what the trio would do when they saw the other results of her ambush. Although the Mexicans had approached through the woodland on foot and in a very wary fashion, perhaps because they were more concerned with what they found in the clearing, they did not detect her in her hiding place.

Until she appreciated the implications, what had happened next came as a surprise to Should-Be-A-Boy!

Instead of loading the bodies on to the horses which had been collected in passing, the trio had stripped off their weapon belts and clothing. Then they had been buried in a shallow grave dug by the *machetes* two of the living Mexicans were carrying. While this was being carried out and the excavation covered by the turf which was removed, obviously to make it less noticeable, the other *vaquero* had gathered a couple of saplings. They had been of the size and kind used to make a *travois* and the watching girl had guessed this was the purpose to which they would be put. Then the trio had loaded the belongings taken from the corpses on to the horses. However, they did not leave immediately.

'Comanches!' the man who had gathered the saplings had called in his own language. When receiving instructions from his *patron* he had been told that, although the half breed girl who was taking an opportunity to get away from the reservation had said she did not understand Spanish, most members of the *Nemenuh* possessed some knowledge of that language. 'Can you hear and understand me?'

'We hear and understand,' Should-Be-A-Boy had replied in the same tongue, pleased to be offered an opportunity to prevent her involvement from being suspected. Continuing to keep a gruffly masculine timbre to her voice, she had hoped her pretence at not knowing the language would prevent them suspecting the truth. She had also employed the close to ventriloquial skill she had acquired since meeting Chief Long Walker and *Chaqueta-Tigre* to lessen the chances of betraying her position, she had asked, 'What do you want?'

'Are you satisfied with what you've done?' the Mexican had inquired.

'We are,' the girl had declared truthfully. 'Tell your leader we will give him and his spotted buffalo no trouble now we have taken our revenge upon those we wanted.'

Apparently convinced by the assurance, the three Mexicans had ridden away on the horses. Returning to and using another of her relay, wanting a fresher mount than the roan in case fast moving should be required, the girl had followed them from a distance with her relay. Rejoining their companion, having retrieved their horses in passing, they had constructed a *travois* with the poles and a couple of the dead men's *serapes*. Putting her living victim on to it, they had set off in the direction from which they had made their appearance. When they reached the herd, they had talked with its leader and the injured man was placed in one of the wagons.

Taking the precaution of keeping after the herd until noon the following day, accepting the discomfort caused by a heavy fall of rain throughout the night, Should-Be-A-Boy had satisfied herself that nobody was turning back with the idea of avenging her victims. Because the time allocated to her was running out and she wanted to report her success to the rest of the band, before anybody else was sent to take on the mission, she had not continued the observations for longer. She had made her way back to the village feeling certain that, for reasons of his own, the man with whom she had spoken was willing to forget what had happened to the quartet.

Annie's assumptions were correct with regards to Caraballeda. Accepting they and their companions had met a fate he would have meted out in similar circumstances, he had considered the death and serious injury inflicted upon his nephews a small price to pay for the safety of his herd and illicit cargo.

Unfortunately, the matter was not allowed to pass unnoticed as the *haciendero* and the *Pahuraix* would have preferred!

Three days after the incident, a party of white men from Claxton, seat of Gareth County and the town nearest to the reservation, had arrived in the woodland to hunt for raccoon. After they had made camp in the clearing, which struck them as ideal for the purpose, one of their hounds had started digging into the shallow grave. Before its owner could call it off, it had uncovered enough of a body to cause a further examination to be made. Discovering there were three naked corpses, death having been caused by bullets, they had gone home immediately and reported their find to Sheriff Home Tomlinson.

Hearing of the discovery and having connected it with the response of the *Pahuraix* to the return of Should-Be-A-Boy after several days of unexplained absence, Agent Dillingham had suspected she had taken revenge upon the men responsible for Loves Dancing's rape and death. He had also been aware of the danger to his charges, no matter how justified the killings undoubtedly were, if his suppositions were correct. There were white people always on the lookout for anything which could turn public sympathy against the Indians living on reservations, especially those like the Waterhorse band who occupied land suitable for ranching or other development.

One such faction were very vocal in Claxton. Although the investigations of the county sheriff had been to no avail, the rain having washed away any traces which could have served as a clue, they had started to make pointed comments about the shooting having happened so near the reservation. In fact, although nobody had been accused of the killings, they had brought to bear pressure for a Grand Jury to be convened and conduct an inquiry with the intention of establishing who was responsible.[1]

Even before he learned of the moves being made in the county seat, seeking to counter any threat which might arise from the killings, Dillingham had telegraphed for Colonel Goodnight to come to his assistance. Responding with alacrity, having already been on his way with a herd of cattle to fulfil a contract for supplying the reservation with beef, *Chaqueta-Tigre* had been quick to act when told what was happening and of the suspicions harboured by the Agent. Equally alert to the danger and soon having become better informed, as a result of his being accepted as a blood brother of the *Tanima*, he had used his influence to ensure the scales of justice would be tilted on the side of the morally right.

Being on good terms with the rancher and having no liking for the faction who were trying to blame the *Pahuraix*, but nevertheless being aware they were a political force to be reckoned with locally who could make the performance of his normal duties difficult, the sheriff had been eager to seek his advice. He had pointed out that—as the corpses were obviously Hispanic—there was a possibility the people involved did not reside in Texas, much less Gareth County which had no *Chicano* population. Furthermore, the suspected participation of the *Pahuraix* made it a Federal rather than a local issue.

By letting it be known that he was throwing all the considerable influence he and his friends could command behind the citizens who did not share the viewpoint of the anti-Indian faction, Goodnight had helped to ensure the investigation for the benefit of the Grand Jury was taken out of the hands of the sheriff's office. What was more, Judge Mannen Blaze had been selected by the State Attorney General to officiate and he belonged to the most

[1] *'Grand Jury': under the legal system of the United States of America, a special jury formed of a statutory number of citizens—usually more than twelve—to investigate accusations against persons charged with, or suspected of, a crime and indict them for trial before a 'petit' jury if there is sufficient evidence.*

powerful group of *Chaqueta-Tigre's* supporters. Having been acting upon a rumour from a generally reliable source that there was something illegal about a trail herd from Mexico which had passed through the area, United States Deputy Marshal Solomon Wisdom 'Solly' Cole had been in the vicinity. Learning of his presence and knowing he possessed the necessary jurisdictional qualifications to take on the chore—including the right to conduct inquiries on the *Pahuraix* reservation, which the sheriff did not—the Judge had telegraphed his superiors and he was ordered to put himself at the disposal of the Jury.

'I'll give young Solly Cole his due,' Goodnight declared. 'He did the best he could to learn what happened. But the rain had washed away all the signs. So he could do nothing more than testify that the bodies had been stripped clean and their horses were gone, but they hadn't been scalped and there wasn't anything else to suggest it was Indian work. He also told how he'd questioned the leaders of the *Pahuraix* and they'd all sworn the Sun Oath that no *man* of the band had done the killing. There were a couple of the jurors tried to claim that them saying so didn't mean it was the truth, but the Judge pointed out no Comanche would go against such a thing so sacred to their beliefs by lying and he was supported in it by those two Army scouts who he'd had come along as expert witnesses where Indians were concerned.[2] Then, Cole said he was satisfied none of the braves from the reservation knew anything about it and was going to look into a possibility of somebody who might know the answers. As there wasn't any more witnesses to give evidence, the Judge sent the jury off to consider what they'd been told. They were out for a fair spell and came back with a verdict of, 'Murder By A Person, Or Persons Unknown', but that they didn't think any of the *Pahuraix* were involved and recommended the investigation be continued to find whoever did it. So it's over, unless Solly Cole

[2] *The Comanches did not attest to the truth of a statement by invoking the name of* Ka-Dih, *but said, 'Sun, Father, Earth, Mother, do not let me live another season if I am lying.'*

can find the fellers he's after and prove they did it, or learn something from them to let him know who did.'[3]

'Thank heavens for that verdict!' the reservation agent breathed, realizing the danger to his charges had been averted. While he only suspected the truth behind the oath sworn by the council of elders, knowing of Annie's unconventional background and upbringing, he turned his eyes to her and went on, 'There's good cause for a celebration in the village tonight.'

'That there is, seeing I reckon the truth will never be known,' Goodnight seconded. He was in agreement with the supposition expressed to him by Cole at the conclusion of the Grand Jury that the Mexicans could have a good reason for not reporting the death of the three men to the authorities and might even disclaim all knowledge of it when questioned. Also directing his gaze to the girl, he went on, 'And, if I may supply the gifts, I would like there to be a Give-Away dance to honour a *warrior* of the *Nemenuh* whose name is "Is-A-Man"!'[4]

[3] *Another investigation, the details of which we know nothing, prevented United States Deputy Marshal Solomon Wisdom 'Solly' Cole from catching up with the trail herd. However, after Don Ruiz Caraballeda had completed the transaction and left Kansas, the man to whom the counterfeit money had been passed was betrayed by a colleague before it could be put into circulation. He did not tell the authorities from whence the money had come and the* haciendero *returned to Mexico. Although Benito Velasquez survived the journey, neither he nor his uncle ever disclosed the reason for the injury he had inflicted.*

[4] *The granting of a 'man-name' to commemorate a meritorious deed was not solely the province of people related to the person who received it, but could be done by somebody who was not a member of the family and, particularly if the donor was considered to be of importance, it would receive acquiescence. Therefore, although Colonel Charles Goodnight was white, his connection with the* Tanima *band and reputation as a warrior made him eligible and Annie Singing Bear's* Pahuraix *name was accepted by all the Comanche nation as being changed from 'Should-Be-A-Boy' to 'Is-A-Man'.*

Appendix

Throughout the years we have been writing, we have frequently received letters from readers asking for various Western terms to be explained in greater detail and for clarification of certain assertions we make. While we do not object to receiving such correspondence and always *reply, we find it saves much time consuming repetition to include those most often requested in each new title. We ask all our 'old hands', who have seen most of the inclusions many times, to remember there are always 'new chums' coming along who have not and to bear with us.*

1. The following are the meanings of the Comanche words most frequently encountered in this volume:
Nemenuh; 'The People', the Comanche nation.
Pairaivo; senior, or favourite, wife.
Ona; baby.
Tuinep'; a boy up to adolescence.
Tuivitsi; a young, unmarried, generally inexperienced warrior.
Tehnap; seasoned and fully trained warrior.
Tsukup'; old man.
Naravuh; familiar, or joking, term for an old man.
Tuepet; girl up to adolescence.
Naivi; adolescent girl.
Hevi; a grown woman.
Pu'ste; old woman.
Pahuraix; Water Horse band.
Pehnane; Wasp, Quick Stinger, Raider, band.
Kweharehnuh; Antelope, Sunshades On Their Back, band.

Yamparikuh; Yap-Eater band.
Dertsanayehka; Wanderers Who Make Bad Camps band.
Tanima; Liver Eater band.
Mutsane; Undercut Bank band.
Wawai; Wormy band.
Namae'enuh; 'One who has incestuous intercourse', a deadly insult derived from the alleged practice of the *Wawai* band.
A:he!; 'I claim it!'. The declaration made by a Comanche warrior in a fight, when delivering a fatal blow or—regarded as more praiseworthy—touching a living enemy with an empty hand, to announce he had 'counted coup'.
2. 'Lance carrier'. Because the war lance had such a high and special 'medicine' significance, when a Comanche warrior elected to carry one, he was expected to be the first into battle and the last to leave the field no matter how adversely the fighting might be going for his band. However, providing he had discharged this responsibility honourably—and survived—he could decide to stop being a 'lance carrier' whenever he wished without detriment to his reputation.
3. 'Hackamore': an Americanised corruption of the Spanish word, '*jaquima*', meaning 'headstall'. Very popular with Indians in particular, it was an ordinary halter, except for having reins instead of a leading rope. It had a headpiece something like a conventional bridle, a brow band about three inches wide which could be slid down the cheeks to cover the horse's eyes, but no throat latch. Instead of a bit, a '*bosal*'—a leather, rawhide, or metal ring around the head immediately above the mouth —was used as a means of control and guidance.
4. Although the military sometimes claimed it was easier to kill a sailor than a soldier, perhaps tongue in cheek, the weight factor of the respective weapons had been responsible for the decision by the United States' Navy to adopt a revolver with a calibre of .36 while the Army employed the heavier .44. The weapon would be carried upon the person of a seaman and not—handguns having been originally and primarily developed for single-handed use by

cavalry—on the person or saddle of a soldier who would be doing much of his travelling and fighting from the back of a horse. Therefore, .44 became known as the 'Army' and .36 as the 'Navy' calibre.

5. 'Clip' point: where the last few inches of the otherwise unsharpened 'back' of the blade—when laid in a horizontal position with the 'edge' down and the handle to the left of the viewer—joins and becomes an extension of the main cutting surface in a concave arc. This is the characteristic which many authorities claim identifies a 'bowie knife'.

5a. What happened to the knife possessed by the alleged designer of such a weapon, James Bowie—many claim this was actually his older brother, Rezin Pleasant—after his death during the final attack upon the besieged Alamo Mission at San Antonio de Bexar, Texas, on March the 6th, 1836, is told in: GET URREA and THE QUEST FOR BOWIE'S BLADE.

5b. A 'spear' point, which is less utilitarian than a 'clip', is formed by the two sharpened 'edges' of the blade coming together in symmetrical curves. It was generally used for purely fighting knives such as the 'Arkansas toothpick' or assassin's weapons.

6. We consider at best specious—at worst, a snobbish attempt to 'put down' the myth and legends of the Old West—the frequently repeated assertion that the gun fighters of that era could not 'hit a barn door at twenty yards'. While willing to concede that the average person then, as now, would not have much skill in using a handgun, knowing his life would depend upon it, the professional *pistolero* on either side of the law expended time, money and effort to acquire proficiency. Furthermore, such a man did not carry a revolver to indulge in shooting at *anything* except at close range. He employed it as a readily accessible *weapon* which would incapacitate an enemy, preferably with the first shot, at close quarters, hence the preference for a cartridge of heavy calibre.

6b. With the exception of .22 calibre handguns intended for casual pleasure shooting, those specially designed for

Olympic style 'pistol' matches, the Remington XP100—one of which makes an appearance in: Case Two, 'A Voice From The Past', THE LAWMEN OF ROCKABYE COUNTY—designed for 'varmint' hunting at long distances, or medium to heavy calibre automatic pistols 'accurized' and in the hands of a proficient exponent of modern 'combat' shooting, a handgun is a short range *defensive* and not an *offensive* weapon. Any Old West gun fighter, or peace officer in the Prohibition era and present times expecting to have to shoot at distances beyond about twenty *feet* would take the precaution of arming himself with a shotgun or a rifle.

7. 'Up to the Green River': to kill, generally with a knife. First produced on the Green River, at Greenfield, Massachusetts, in 1834, a very popular type of general purpose knife had the inscription, '*J. Russell & Co./Green River Works* on the blade just below the hilt. Therefore any edged weapon thrust into an enemy 'up to the Green River' would prove fatal whether it bore the inscription or not.

8. 'Right as the Indian side of a horse'; absolutely correct. Derived from the habit of Indians mounting from the right, or 'off' and not the left, or 'near' side as was done by people of European descent and Mexicans.

9. Americans in general used the word, 'cinch', derived from the Spanish, '*cincha*', to describe the short band made from coarsely woven horse hair, canvas, or cordage and terminated at each end with a metal ring which—together with the *latigo*—is used to fasten the saddle on the back of a horse. However, because of the word's connections with Mexixo, Texans tended to employ the term, 'girth', usually pronouncing it as 'girt'. As cowhands from the Lone Star State fastened the end of the lariat to the saddlehorn, even when roping half wild longhorn cattle or free-ranging mustangs, instead of relying upon a 'dally' which could be slipped free almost instantaneously in an emergency, their rigs had double girths.

THE END

PARADI

Mary Minton has been a t
Leicester Education Centr
include sailing and designi
been an avid reader. She has had seven previous novels published by Century and Arrow. She now lives in Leicestershire with her family.

1

Alistair MacKay put on his top hat, gave it a tap and turning, smiled at his wife. 'Well, Mrs MacKay, and are you ready for Paradise?'

Jessamy laughed, adjusted her squirrel necktie and slipped a hand through her husband's curved arm. 'Ready and waiting, Doctor! Have been for the past five years.'

They left their lodgings and went out into the crisp air of the January morning.

They had arrived late the night before. Then, moonlight and frost had beautified the street. Now Jessamy saw how shabby the houses were. But then they had not expected luxury; they were in a part of the East End of London, where there was poverty and sickness.

Alistair said, 'If we go down here it will bring us into the main thoroughfare, then we can perhaps get a cab.'

'No, let us walk then we can become acquainted with the district. You said it was only streets away.'

When they turned the next corner a cacophony of sounds reached them – the iron-rimmed wheels of carts and barrows on the cobbled road and the raucous shouting of traders.

Alistair laid a hand over Jessamy's and eyed her solemnly. 'I had hoped to take you to Italy for our honeymoon. Instead you have this.'

'Italy can be for the future,' she said softly. 'We are about to fulfil a dream of years and that will be most rewarding – would you not agree?'

'Yes, Jessamy, I do agree. It's just that...' He shrugged and by then they had reached the main street with all its activities.

One part of the road, which was narrowed by a number of stalls lining it, was occupied by drivers shouting abuse, but they were ignored. Many of the stalls sold secondhand goods – clothes, shoes and boots, and there was one piled with chipped crockery – cups, saucers, plates, pudding basins and pie-dishes. Next to it a stall was packed with boxes of nails, screws, pieces of wire, rusty tools, screw-drivers, awls and so on. Then there was a fruit and vegetable stall, with the next one displaying pigs' trotters, black puddings, polonies and saveloys; from a large bowl, steaming pease pudding was being ladled into jugs or basins brought by the customers.

Each side of the street was also lined with small shops, with some of the proprietors trying to persuade people passing by to step in and see their bargains. None took up the offers. Nearly every woman had a dark shawl over her head, while the men wore cloth caps and mufflers; children were ragged, many of them barefooted. One woman said to a tubby man in the doorway of a bakery, 'Blimey, Alfie, where d'you think we'll git money to buy cakes? We ain't even tasted a crust of bread for a coupla days.'

The man grinned. 'Yer ship'll come 'ome someday, gal. Every cloud 'as a silver lining.'

'I only 'opes as I'll live to see it,' replied the woman who, to Jessamy's surprise, was smiling. Her face was colourless and she was bone thin. Two skinny children clung to her skirts.

When Jessamy asked Alistair how the young mother could possibly manage to smile he said, 'Because she's a survivor. The majority have to be in the East End.' He took some coppers from his pocket. 'Here, slip these into her hand as we pass.'

Jessamy did so and the woman called, 'Ta, love, good to know there *is* a silver lining. Bless the both of you.'

When Jessamy said she was afraid that pride might have made her refuse the coppers, Alistair said quietly, 'There's no such thing as pride when children have to be fed. Unfortunately, we're unable to do that often.' They were silent for a while. The road had narrowed and refuse from the gutters overflowed on to the pavement. Jessamy picked up her skirt. The small houses nearby were no more than hovels, with few people in sight. Although Jessamy and her husband were wearing dark grey she thought they might have drawn attention to themselves by the quality of their clothes, but they could have been invisible for the notice anyone took of them.

When they turned left into Paradise Street, Alistair explained that this street and Paradise Road formed a V, and that their house was on the corner. This street was wider than the others and they passed some derelict houses and buildings that could once have been warehouses. In between were spaces where weeds pushed through piles of rubbish.

Jessamy's spirits sank a little and she waited with a feeling of apprehension to see the house. Although Alistair had warned her not to expect too much she was appalled at its condition. It was double-fronted and three-storeyed, with a basement. The four steps leading up to a massive oak door were broken and so were many windows. The paint had peeled from window-frames and from the railings that enclosed a small front garden. A path had been swathed through the tangled undergrowth to the steps.

Alistair said on a cheerful note, 'I know there's a lot to be done but the house has great possibilities.' He guided her up the front steps, warning her to be careful. He had difficulty in turning the key in the lock and the door had to be coaxed over tiles which had risen with the damp. Nothing, however, dampened Alistair's enthusiasm.

'Look at this staircase, Jessamy – see how broad and shallow the treads are. It'll make it easier to carry patients to an upper floor.'

Jessamy was eying the hall floor, which was covered in dead leaves, filthy pieces of paper and a few old boots and bits of rags. No doubt the boots were responsible for some of the broken windows. Alistair picked up a stocking on the end of his stick. 'Now where did this come from? Not the most romantic place for a tryst, is it?' He let the stocking fall then, walking with brisk steps to the nearest wall, pressed a button; a part of the oak panelling slid open to reveal shelves. 'What do you think of this, my love? Isn't it a wonderful innovation? There are three more parts of the panelling that do this – think of all the medicines they will hold.'

It was then that Jessamy was caught up in her husband's enthusiasm. She had been behaving foolishly: the house at Paradise Corner was to be a dispensary, not their future home. She said, 'It's a splendid idea, Alistair.' She looked about her. 'This hall is large enough to be split into two rooms. There is a fireplace at either side.'

'I thought three, Jessamy.' Alistair walked about waving his stick. 'The staircase is in line with the door, so we could have walls built making a passage towards it. The left side can be split into a waiting room and a dispensary.' He lifted his stick. 'This side will be a ward.'

Jessamy shook her head. 'No, it would be too noisy.'

'Jessamy, my love.' Alistair spoke gently. 'We are not planning a private nursing home but a dispensary and treatment centre for the poor.'

'Oh, so because they're poor the sick must not only be prepared to suffer pain but noise, too?'

Alistair apologised. 'It was a stupid thing to say, Jessamy. Of course they must be considered. We shall have a ward on the first floor along with the operating room and my laboratory. Shall we take a look at the kitchen and other rooms while we're downstairs?'

The kitchen was large; the black cooking range and grate massive. Every cooking utensil that had been left behind was rusted. There was a big walk-in pantry and a door that led into a laundry room and store-rooms.

They were on their way upstairs when Alistair remarked, 'We shall have to decide which part of the house will be our living-quarters.'

Jessamy stopped dead and eyed him with surprise. 'You surely don't intend us to *live* here? You would be on call twenty-four hours a day.' When Alistair smiled and told her this would be impossible, as he would be working at Guy's Hospital part of the time, she continued, 'Then that is all the more reason for us to live somewhere else. Don't forget we have a small daughter who needs our care, too.'

Alistair put an arm about her waist and walked her up the rest of the stairs, saying softly, 'Did you really think I could forget about our darling? Is any child more loved, more cared for? Look at the number of people who fight to have her with them – your mother, your Aunt Verity, your Cousin Louise and your other cousins, Rebecca and Anne.'

On the landing he took her by the shoulders and said, 'Jessamy, dear, you know that you and Romy have all my love. If it was possible I would be with you all the time, but I have work to do and...'

'And I have too, Alistair. It's just that we were parted from you for so long. I wouldn't care if it was a hovel we lived in as long as we could close our door at night and be alone.'

'It would only be for a few months.'

'No, the months would run on, I know. It could end up being a year, maybe two.'

Alistair gave a small sigh. 'Can we talk about this later? I want you to look at all the rooms before Mr Saunders arrives to see what has to be done.'

Jessamy agreed, but suspecting that Alistair secretly hoped she would change her mind once she saw the rooms on this floor, had difficulty in pretending to show an interest. They had just decided that the first room they went into, a large one, should be the ward when there was a tat-tat at the front door. Alistair said, 'Ah, Mr Saunders,' and went down to let him in.

Jessamy stayed behind, angry that Alistair seemed not to understand how important it was to her to have their own home. For years they had had to meet in secret until her divorce came through from Fabian Montague, her former husband. These were years during which Romaine had known Alistair as her uncle, while she was really his child. Why could he not understand her need for them to be in their own home, not in a busy dispensary-cum-hospital, where there would be sick and dying people?

Alistair called to her to come and meet Mr Saunders and so she went downstairs.

Mr Saunders was an elderly man whose three sons worked with him. What Jessamy liked about him especially was that whatever Alistair suggested in the way of alterations, he would weigh it up, agree, or if he disagreed, would give a good reason. He even suggested fitting up a pulley on the staircase so that people having trouble climbing stairs could be transported on a seat or a stretcher.

'Splendid!' Alistair exclaimed, his face alight with pleasure. 'You are a man after my own heart, Mr Saunders. We shall get on well.' They went over the rooms on the first floor with Alistair explaining about their plans for a ward, to lead through into a small room where files could be kept, and showing him the rooms which were to serve as the laboratory and operating theatre.

They then went up to the second floor, with Alistair explaining that these rooms were accommodation for staff who would live in. Mr Saunders was full of praise for them both. 'My word, Doctor, you and your wife are doing a good job. There's a great need for a place such as this. Folks haven't the money to buy medicine from the doctors as it takes some of them all their time to feed their family.'

Jessamy said, on impulse, 'I wonder, Mr Saunders, if you could suggest a small house nearby which we could rent? Our daughter is only six and I don't want her to know pain and suffering at this age.'

Jessamy knew she had done an unforgivable thing by taking it out of her husband's hands and avoided looking at him, but it was Alistair the old man addressed. 'Well now,' he said, rubbing his chin, 'I could make a suggestion. I have a little cottage just round the corner in Paradise Street and it's empty just now.'

At that moment there came an urgent knocking on the front door. Alistair glanced at Jessamy then hurried downstairs. She followed. A girl of about twelve stood on the step, a shawl over her head. 'Oh, please come,' she begged. 'Me Mam's 'aving the baby any minute.'

When Alistair asked where her mother was she jerked her head over her shoulder. A woman was coming towards them, holding on to the railings. She, too, had a shawl over her head; her face was paper-white and she had difficulty in getting her breath. Alistair and Jessamy went immediately to help her. Jessamy said, before they reached her, 'We have no facilities, Alistair! What can we do?'

'Get her off the street for a start.'

Mr Saunders appeared and told them, 'I can fetch some blankets, sheets and towels. Is there anything else you need?'

Alistair asked him if he could obtain some hot water and he said yes, and turning went hurriedly around the opposite corner.

They assisted the woman into the house and Alistair suggested taking her into the kitchen, where at least all the glass was in the windows. The woman, who had gone into another spasm of pain, bit so hard on her lower lip she drew drops of blood. Alistair took off his overcoat and was about to lay it on the floor when Jessamy pointed out two wooden benches that would do as a makeshift bed. They had dragged them over and placed them together when Mr Saunders returned, laden down with blankets, a quilt, sheets, a tin bowl with soap and flannel, newspapers, a bucket of sea coal and some kindling.

He said, 'I'll get a bit of a fire going. A lad will bring some hot water shortly.'

By the time Alistair and Jessamy had got the woman settled on blankets covered with newspapers, the sticks were beginning to spark. Mr Saunders was about to withdraw when he paused and said, 'What about the little lassie?'

Jessamy, who had momentarily forgotten her, turned to see the girl pressed fearfully against the wall. Her mother whispered, 'Send her to her gran's. She doesn't like seeing babies born, she's already seen ten into the world.'

Ten? Jessamy mentally cringed. The girl darted out, and Mr Saunders disappeared, too.

Alistair had just taken off his jacket and rolled up his sleeves when Mr Saunders reappeared with two buckets of hot water. He set them down and said he would be nearby if they needed anything else. Jessamy poured some water into a tin bowl and handed Alistair soap and towel. After washing his hands he began to examine the woman, who was now emitting a keening, pain-filled sound.

Alistair had díscussed obstetrics with Jessamy many times. She knew that a woman who had had a number of children could give birth very quickly, and that care had to be taken to protect the baby's head as it slipped into the world. She knew how to cut the cord and how, if a baby was choked with mucus, to hold it upside down by the ankles and rub its back so that the matter could drain from throat and nose. She knew many things but despite this, and having given birth herself, had never actually seen a baby being born. Oddly enough, it was not the pain she remembered from her own experience but the joyous sound of Romy's first shrill cry, an absolutely wonderful sound.

She watched now with interest as Alistair moved his hands over the woman's abdomen. He said in a low voice, 'We have twins,' and added as he moved one hand higher, 'there's a little head here that ought not to be there.'

Jessamy swallowed hard – a footling presentation? It could be a difficult birth if the baby's feet came first. It was not often that happened.

Alistair said to the woman, 'You're carrying twins, Mrs – '

'Fuller,' she whispered. 'Twins run in the family.'

'The first baby is on its way, Mrs Fuller. Don't push any more.'

A few minutes later the baby arrived and Alistair handled it gently. Jessamy, excited, said to the mother, 'You have a son – he's lovely.' There was no response.

After Alistair had cut the cord he handed the baby to Jessamy. His little red face was crumpled and when she had wiped it gently he began to scream, as though in protest at leaving his nice warm world. Again she thought the screaming a wonderful sound and didn't know whether to laugh or cry. After making a bed for him with two of the fleecy white towels, she tucked a piece of blanket around him then turned to Alistair, wanting to see the next baby come into the world.

This was not an easy birth. When the tiny feet showed, Alistair had to find an area behind the knee to straighten the leg and then do the same with the other. It was a girl. She was stillborn, the cord tied so tightly around her frail little neck her face was blue.

Jessamy felt grief-stricken. Poor little thing. When the afterbirth was disposed of Mrs Fuller said in a flat voice, 'It's dead, isn't it? What was it?'

Alistair told her it was a girl. Jessamy brought her son to the woman and laid him in her arms and she drew the cradled baby closer. 'She would have been loved like the others.'

While Jessamy cleared up Alistair and the mother talked in low voices. He had just straightened and said, 'Have some rest now, Mrs Fuller,' when the door opened and a woman came storming in.

'I'm Daisy Bodger,' she announced. 'That's me daughter there.' She had a tight, bitter face. 'Has the babby come?'

Alistair took her aside, explained the situation and she sniffed. 'Pity they both weren't stillborn.' She went over to her daughter. 'When are you going to leave that drunken good-for-nothing 'usband of yours, our Nancy? He's an animal. You can't feed the kids you got now and you'll go on adding to 'em. I'll tell you this – '

Alistair interrupted. 'Mrs Bodger, your daughter needs rest at this moment, not recriminations. I must ask you to leave.'

She was suddenly deflated. 'I'm sorry for going on so, but someone 'as got to knock some sense into that Jack Fuller. He'll kill her, that's what, giving her all these kids, one after another.'

Alistair took hold of her arm and began to lead her to the door. He was about to open it when she stopped and said, 'The little lass – can I take 'er?' There was a tremor in her voice and Jessamy felt a lump come into her throat. When she handed her the tiny body, wrapped in sheeting, Mrs Bodger said, 'She'll be buried proper, not chucked like rubbish on a muck 'eap.' And with a 'Ta,' in Alistair's direction, she left.

Seconds later Mr Saunders looked in and held out a linen bag. 'Mrs Bodger said to give you this. Her brother will come later to collect Mrs Fuller and the baby and bring them home.'

In the bag was a nightdress and baby clothes, all well-worn but clean. Jessamy washed mother and baby and a few minutes later both were asleep. Alistair and Jessamy stood looking at them. The fire was now giving out some warmth and with blankets and quilt over them, there was at least some degree of comfort. Jessamy murmured, 'What awful lives some people have to suffer that others don't know about.'

'Yes, indeed, but thank goodness we were able to help. I never thought we would be dealing with our first patient before we had moved into Paradise Corner.'

'No, and what a fiasco.'

He shook his head. 'No, Jessamy, an achievement. A baby was brought into the world and the mother is still alive.'

'And for what?' Jessamy asked, a bitterness in her voice. 'To carry on in poverty, to be a slave to a drunken sot, the child to know only hunger, live a life of hell on earth.'

'Are you then God?' he asked gently, 'to have the life of this child all mapped out? Many a boy brought up in poverty has made his mark in the world.' When Jessamy made no reply Alistair put his arm around her. 'I'm sure we shall have many a crisis in our new lives. You coped splendidly this morning, so don't let this setback discourage you.'

'No, it was just that I can't help feeling sorry for Mrs Fuller, whose husband treats her so badly.'

'But he doesn't, Jessamy. He drinks, yes, but when I was talking to her earlier she told me that I was to take no notice of any gossip, that Jack was not a bad man. She said he loved her and the children and added that she would never leave him. He needed her.' Alistair paused then added softly, 'Just as I need you, my love.'

He gave her a hug and a kiss then said he must have a word with Mr Saunders. When the two men came back in Mr Saunders pulled one of the other wooden benches forward, saying to Jessamy in an undertone, 'I'm sure you'll be ready to sit down, ma'am.'

'You've been a tower of strength, Mr Saunders. I don't know what on earth we would have done without you. All that bedding you brought and the rest of the things – did you borrow them from someone?'

'No, they were in the little cottage around the corner in Paradise Street. I bought it for my youngest lad and started to furnish it for him when he was going to get married but, unhappily, his fiancée changed her mind and Robert emigrated to Australia.'

'Oh, how sad. I'm sorry.'

'When you mentioned wanting a house nearby I thought you might be interested in it. The rent would only be nominal.' He addressed this to Alistair, who did not look pleased.

'I must explain, Mr Saunders, that it may only be for a short time,' he said stiffly.

The old man smiled his gentle smile. 'You can rent it for as short a time as you wish, Doctor. I would just be glad to have someone in the cottage.' He paused then went on, 'I'll be over there later if you want to take a look at it, working out the estimate for your dispensary. And now I'd better be going. I'll see you later, perhaps.'

Alistair did unbend sufficiently to thank Mr Saunders for all he had done, but Jessamy was furious and turned on him when the old man had gone. 'How could you behave in such a way to that kindly man?'

'I thanked him.'

'So grudgingly. You took your ill-temper out on him because I asked if he knew of a house nearby.'

'No, you're wrong.'

There was a sudden shouting and Jessamy realised someone was calling through the letter-box. Alistair went into the hall and came back with a huge, brawny man who said,

'I've come for me niece and babby. I'll just bundle them up and take 'er 'ome.'

When Alistair protested that Mrs Fuller needed to rest he boomed, 'Don't you worry, Doc, she'll be fine. She's tough. Our Nancy loves kids an' so does me sister Daisy. We all do, the more the merrier.' He swept up mother, baby and bedclothes and before Jessamy could say that the bedding was borrowed, he added, 'I'll let you have this lot back tomorrer. Ta for yer trouble,' and away he went with Alistair following, still protesting.

The door slammed and Alistair came back slowly, pushing his fingers through his hair with quick thrusts of frustration. 'What can one do with a person like that?'

'Nothing.' Jessamy untied the sheeting from around her and put on her jacket. 'I think the best thing we can do at the moment is to get away from here.' Alistair said he agreed and shrugged himself into his overcoat.

When they left the house they met Mr Saunders again, who had heard the shouting and come back to investigate. Alistair explained the events, to which the old man said in his philosophical way that it might be wise to accept the whole incident as an initiation ceremony. Alistair nodded. 'Yes, indeed.'

Taking the bull by the horns, Jessamy suggested they have a look at the cottage now. Alistair bridled for a moment, then his shoulders went slack. 'Yes, why not?'

They went round the corner into Paradise Street and were immediately faced by a roofless building which the old man said was the coachhouse in days gone by; the house next to it was known as the Coachman's Cottage. It appeared to be a two-up and two-down, in good repair. Even the soil in the small garden had been dug over and cleared of weeds. Mr Saunders opened the front door and stepped aside for them to enter.

Narrow stairs rose from the small passage and at once it brought back memories to Jessamy of the house where Alistair had lodged after leaving his job as assistant in her father's pharmacy. He had quitted St Peel near Newcastle because she had met and fallen in love with Captain Fabian

Montague. Mr Saunders opened a door on the left saying it was the living room. There was a faint smell of tobacco and an armchair stood by the fireplace where a fire burned brightly. He ran a hand over the back of the chair. 'I've been in the habit of calling in now and again. I didn't want the house to feel rejected – I think that buildings have feelings, too. After all, they're built from living things, aren't they? They come from the earth, stone, wood...and go back to it.' There was a moment's silence then he said, 'Well now, this door here leads into the scullery.'

Another across the passage took them into the parlour and there Jessamy gave an 'Oh' of pleasure. She turned to Alistair. 'Look at the big window and the garden!'

The garden was long, walled-in. The soil had been levelled and Mr Saunders said he was going to grass it over for children to play on and install a swing on the oak tree. They then went upstairs, where there were two bedrooms and a small boxroom. When they went into the first bedroom Jessamy was once more reminded of Alistair's bedroom in his lodgings, where they had made wild passionate love and...where Romaine had been conceived. Jessamy tried to still the sudden racing of her heart. She had been married to Fabian then but had felt no guilt because he had treated her so coldly. Why, then, should she be feeling guilty now?

The men were talking and Jessamy forced herself to concentrate on what they were saying. Mr Saunders was explaining that he had some furniture stored if they needed it. He had bought it as a wedding present for his son and bride, had they married.

'It's all so perfect,' Jessamy declared. 'We must take it. Surely you agree, Alistair?'

Alistair hesitated a moment then said to Mr Saunders, 'My wife and I will talk it over.'

'Of course, Doctor. It's here if you want it.'

Jessamy could not resist saying quietly, 'I think it might have been waiting for us, Mr Saunders.' Although he made no reply, a smile played about his lips and she thought he gave an imperceptible nod.

When they left the cottage and walked back in the direction of the other house, Jessamy had a sudden feeling that all was going to turn out right. Alistair must see the advantages of moving into the cottage. She slipped her arm through her husband's and smiled up at him. 'Have you any need to go back into the house?'

'No, why?'

'Well, Mrs Brunt told me she would be out visiting this afternoon. She said she would leave a cold lunch and we could have our dinner at five. And, as we are on our honeymoon I thought...'

A broad grin spread over Alistair's strong face. 'So why are we dawdling? Step out, witch.'

There was a joyousness between them then that not even the poverty of the district could quell. It was the freedom of being able to make love when they wanted, instead of the long waits they had suffered when they could only meet in secret.

2

The little maid let them in, bobbing a curtsy and telling them that the lunch had been laid in their room. They thanked her and went upstairs.

Although their landlady had a prim and proper manner she was not mean in any way, and a cheery sea coal fire was burning brightly in their room. After Alistair had helped Jessamy off with her coat and she had removed her hat she held out her hands to the fire and said over her shoulder, with a teasing smile: 'Could Italy have had more to offer?'

Alistair came up and turning her to face him, began to undo the buttons on her blouse, which made her catch her breath and sent delicious shivers through her. By the time he had undone the last one his breathing was ragged. 'Jessamy, Jessamy...' He had just buried his face against her throat when there was a tap on the door. They sprang apart. Jessamy grabbed her coat and was trying to get her arms back into it when a hoarse little voice enquired if Madam wanted her to make a pot of tea.

Jessamy gave a little cough. 'Not yet, Maggie, but we would like some later.' Feet pattered away.

Alistair flung out his arms and said dramatically, 'Thy serving wench has killed all passion stone dead between us, noble lady. Can it be rekindled?'

Jessamy replied in like vein, 'Knowing your appetites, my lord, it should offer no problem.' Then she collapsed into laughter and Alistair picked her up and threw her on to the deep feather bed.

'With or without thy raiments, sweet lady, I shall have my way with thee.' He clambered up beside her, but it was no use, they could not get back to their former mood.

Alistair slipped his arm around Jessamy and drew her head against his shoulder. 'It's guilt, did you know that?

When Maggie was downstairs you were not conscious of her presence but once she came upstairs you thought, my goodness, she'll know what we're doing. Not to worry, my darling, we have this evening.'

Jessamy raised her head. 'We'll come to bed early while the lodgers and Mrs Brunt are still downstairs.'

Alistair laughed softly. 'They'll know why we came to bed early. We are not the only married couple to make love.'

'Aren't we?' she asked, her eyes full of mischief. Then she said, 'I think I'm hungry,' and made to get up.

Alistair grabbed her hand. 'I'm hungry for you, my darling.'

'Not hungry enough, dear husband, or you would not be talking about it.' She slid off the bed. 'Come along. Get up so I can straighten the bed. I wouldn't want our landlady to jump to the wrong conclusions.'

There was a knock on the door: it was Maggie with the tea. Alistair shot off the bed and Jessamy frantically straightened the top cover before he opened the door. He helped Maggie with the pot and after she had gone he raised the covers of their lunch. 'Mmm, cold roast beef, sliced potatoes with horseradish sauce and portions of gingerbread. We shall have to leave room for dinner at five o'clock.'

They both did justice to the fare and afterwards Alistair suggested a walk. They strolled in the opposite direction from the one they had taken that morning, seeking a park that Mrs Brunt had mentioned, but were disappointed to find it was no more than a square of open land with a few trees and four wooden benches.

Jessamy, used to moorland and sea air, began to realise what she was going to miss as they pursued their dream. And what about Romaine? Would she be homesick for all the people she was used to, her grandparents, great-grandparents and other doting relatives...?

Alistair, stopping at one of the benches, pulled out his handkerchief and flicked it over the boards. 'Madam, pray be seated.'

She sat, staring straight ahead and Alistair asked quietly what was wrong. Jessamy explained her fears and he took her hand. 'Children are adaptable, my love, Romy no less than any other child. Louise has offered to live with us and help take care of her, and your cousins Rebecca and Anne want to help with the dispensary. We also promised your parents that we would visit them from time to time and they would visit us. I don't think that Romy will feel estranged in any way. It's impossible to do more – she must not dominate our lives.'

'I don't want her to, but at the same time she must be considered.' There was an edge to Jessamy's voice.

Alistair turned to her. 'Jessamy, there is something that has to be settled here and now and I do not want it to be brought up at any other time in our lives.'

'I don't like your tone,' she retorted.

'Like it or not you must listen. I will not have Romy dominating any decisions that we might have to make in the future.'

'And what if she were ill?'

'Then, naturally, she would take priority, but as long as she's young and healthy and full of high spirits she adapts to our lives.'

'And if I refuse?'

'Then we shall go back to Mrs Brunt's and pack your bags. I shall take you home where you can be with Romy every hour of the day if you wish.'

This was an implacable side of Alistair that Jessamy had never seen before and, although she was seething at his attitude, there was a part of her that respected him for his firmness. If her father Chadwick had shown more firmness with her mother Esmeralda they would all have spent a happier life together. But then, she was in no way like her mother. She said, her tone cold, 'And what would your plans be?'

'To return here. I have a wife and child to support and a dispensary to open.'

'So you would abandon us?'

'Isn't it the other way around, Jessamy?' Alistair's voice

had softened. 'I would come and see you both as often as I could, but too many sacrifices have been made in the past to allow my life to be dictated by what you feel are the imaginary needs of our child.'

'Perhaps you are forgetting that I have made sacrifices too,' she said sharply.

'That is something I could never forget, Jessamy. Shall I tell you what prompted me to bring this up about Romy now? Your mother's obsessional love for your half-brother Ralph. She cut you and your father right out of her life.'

Jessamy turned her head. 'But surely you must know that I would never cut you out of my life because of my love for Romaine?'

'Isn't that what you were planning to do?' he asked gently.

'No, I think I was testing you, wanting to know how far you would go, wanting to know how much you loved me.'

'I'm surprised you found that necessary after all we've gone through over the past few years,' Alistair said, a sadness in his voice.

'And I thought you were behaving unreasonably over the cottage. I expected you to be pleased to have the opportunity for the three of us to be together, with Romaine away from the awful poverty and sickness.'

Alistair sighed. 'I'm having to think of money all the time. Yes, even the saving of a few shillings rent a week. I have to also find a practice in a good-class district to rent, to earn money to keep the dispensary going.'

'We have money, Alistair. People have been generous.'

'It's still not enough. Do you remember the list we made of all the things we would need to set us up – beds, bedding, crockery, cutlery, towels, medicines and medical supplies of every kind. I could go on and on.'

'But we'll get more money. We've only touched the fringe. Fabian promised a large sum.'

'No!' Alistair got up and thumped his cane on the ground. 'I will not accept a penny from him. Never.'

'So – for the sake of your petty pride you would refuse

money to help the sick and needy. And I really thought you cared about them, believed it was a dream with you as it is with me. I would take money from the devil himself if I thought it would help someone such as that poor woman we attended to this morning.' Her voice had risen as she spoke, but now she said in a lowered tone, 'You once told me that it was impossible to know a person through and through, and then you asked if we really knew ourselves. I thought then that I knew everything there was to know about you, but now I can see I've never really known you.' Jessamy got up. 'I never wanted to be parted from you, nor would I have kept Romaine from you. She adores you. We shall live in Paradise Corner and hope it won't be for too long...for our daughter's sake.' She started to walk away then stopped as she heard Alistair laughing softly.

When she glanced over her shoulder he held out a hand. 'Come and sit down again.' She wanted to resist but found herself putting her hand in his. When they were seated he turned to her and his eyes held a merriment.

'You are a witch, Mrs MacKay. You knew exactly how to get your own way. I'll look again at the cottage, I can't be fairer than that.'

'All right, but I don't think I should have to beg for something that will be beneficial to all of us. It doesn't show much love.'

'Jessamy, be reasonable. You know I love you very much, have done from the first moment of meeting you. When you married Fabian I was bereft, then, when I knew you were to be divorced my hopes soared that my two dreams might be fulfilled. Yes, Jessamy, *two* dreams. What I didn't bargain for was my jealousy but I too, like many others, am plagued by the baser elements of nature.'

'Surely they are the natural elements! I too knew jealousy when young ladies in Papa's pharmacy would cast glances in your direction.'

'Then there is only one punishment to fit the crime.' His expression was solemn but his eyes were dancing. 'Stormy loving – the punishment to be carried out later this evening.'

Alistair had only to mention 'stormy loving' for Jessamy to be back with him in the cottage on the moors, or in his lodgings. Alistair had the ability to convey sensuality in a single word. Every pulse in her body had begun to throb. She said, a catch in her voice, 'You choose the most unlikely time, Doctor MacKay, to make known your punishment for the offender.' Then they were both laughing, with Alistair nuzzling his cheek against hers.

Jessamy was glad they were on their usual loving footing again. If they ever lost this the dispensary would be doomed.

When they got back to their lodgings Mrs Brunt came up, wanting a word. Alistair and Jessamy exchanged glances then Alistair said, 'Yes, of course, Mrs Brunt,' and drew out a chair for her.

'Well, Doctor, it's like this. I've been hearing what you did this morning for Mrs Fuller and our group applaud the action of you and Mrs MacKay.'

'Your group?'

'Oh, sorry, I'm not explaining myself. A few of us several years ago started a group whose aim it was to try to collect money for various charities. The group was small at first, and we used to meet at one another's houses for musical evenings. Then we began to grow and now we rent a small hall.'

Mrs Brunt paused. 'Now, we had arranged to hold a show for one of our charities tonight but we've since unfortunately discovered that the money was going into the pocket of a certain person, no names mentioned, and so we all decided at our emergency meeting today that we would like to give the proceeds to benefit your dispensary instead.'

'Well, that's very kind of you all, Mrs Brunt, isn't it, Jessamy?'

'Yes, indeed.' They both waited, with Jessamy thinking it was obviously a religious group and they would be faced with attending and singing hymns and listening to various platitudes.

Then Mrs Brunt went on, 'We had planned to make it

a more convivial affair than usual.' She leaned forward in a confidential way. 'Not exactly music hall, but at times a little bit...saucy.' There was an imp of mischief in her eyes and Jessamy wondered how she could ever have thought their landlady prim and proper.

Alistair smiled. 'It sounds *most* interesting.'

'It is, Doctor. We shall have a young lady performing who is very popular. Her name's Kate Keller. She's a lovely girl, teases the men but the wives don't object because they all know how straight she is. Would you and your wife like to come?'

Jessamy looked at Alistair and still smiling, he nodded. 'How could we refuse? What time does this concert start, and where is it?'

'At seven o'clock, and the hall is just three streets away. Now I'll go down and see to the dinner.'

'I wonder what this concert will be like,' Jessamy mused. 'Mrs Brunt offered tempting snippets. I've never been to a music hall in my life.'

Alistair grinned. 'She tempted me, I must say. I've been to several during my student days and I would say that the word convivial just about summed them up.'

'You didn't tell me you had been to music halls!'

'Of course not. You would have thought I was on the road to hell and worried yourself sick, whereas it was just a little light relief from those endless nights of study when I usually didn't go to bed until three or four in the morning.'

'Oh, but you *did* tell me about your hard work, my love. Many times.'

'And now they are gone,' he said softly, and made to draw her to him. There was a tap at the door and Jessamy giggled as she went to open it.

Maggie staggered in with a laden tray. 'The missus says to 'ave it while it's 'ot, ma'am.'

Jessamy assured her they would. It was a beautiful evening when they set out for the concert later, the stars pinpoints of ice and small pools crackling underfoot. Mrs Brunt did most of the talking, telling them about the various other concerts they had held, then Alistair commented that after this evening he and Jessamy would have to get down to some really hard work going round warehouses for supplies.

To their surprise Mrs Brunt proved a mine of information on this subject. She and her husband had set up and run two hotels in their time but after his death she had decided to have just a few lodgers. 'You mustn't accept the prices of the warehouse people right away,' she warned them. 'You must bargain with them.'

When Alistair protested, she said, 'You must! It would spoil all their pleasure if you didn't. Let your wife do the bargaining if you don't fancy it, as women have a knack for it. You tell me what you need to buy and I'll tell you the best warehouses to go to. You want to deal with amiable men. Mind you, amiable or not, once they've reached rock bottom price they stop there and not even a lovely attractive woman like your wife could make them change their minds. We'll have a nice long talk after we get back from the concert. We're nearly at the hall – that's it, on the left.'

They could hear lively chatter and some bursts of laughter before they reached the doorway. When they did arrive Mrs Brunt was greeted with genuine pleasure and Alistair and Jessamy with a lively interest.

'Isn't this nice. It's not often we meet the people who the benefit is for...and what a splendid venture it is...a dispensary is needed in these parts...desperately needed... You're both from the North? We have members from several parts of London.' Alistair and Jessamy were taken into the hall to meet the chairman. Jessamy, who had expected just a small hall, was surprised at its size. There were tables and chairs set out and many of them were already occupied. The hissing of gas-jets mingled with the buzz of talk. There were waiters serving drinks and girls selling 'fluffy baked potatoes, all 'ot'. Jessamy was fascinated.

They were introduced to people from different walks of life. Some were well-dressed, some not, but all seemed dedicated to charitable work, and Alistair whispered to

Jessamy that he didn't think they would have to look far for volunteer helpers, should he need them.

A table had been reserved for the couple and their landlady, and they were joined at it by a stout jolly man who was introduced as Mr Adler, the Master of Ceremonies. He bought them drinks, and Jessamy felt very adventurous accepting a small port. Mr Adler left them then to open the proceedings. He introduced Alistair and Jessamy, talked about their venture then asked the audience to contribute what they could to help it when the box came round. There was great applause.

The first performers were then announced – a baritone and tenor who were to sing a duet. There was no stage as such, just a raised platform with a pianoforte. Entrance to the platform was from a door at the back covered by a gold velvet curtain. A young man made a feature of pulling back the curtain and sketching a deep bow as the two men came out. They were obviously well-known, to judge by the warm response from the audience.

The couple, who looked to be in their thirties, were in evening dress; their shirts and gloves snow-white. Mr Adler announced that the men were going to sing a favourite from their repertoire, *The Moon Has Raised Her Lamp Above*, which brought considerable applause.

Mrs Brunt whispered to Jessamy, 'Oh, you're in for a treat. They have beautiful voices.'

Jessamy was entranced by the quality of the singing and felt all romantic at the words: 'The moon has raised her lamp above to light the way to thee, my love...'

Alistair pronounced the singers superb and said he hoped they would sing another song. They did, but unfortunately they chose *Greensleeves*, which had unhappy associations for Jessamy. It took her back to her grandparents' house, Beacon Hall, where her Cousin Lillian used to play the pianoforte while the family sang.

Lillian...who looked so angelic and yet had so much evil in her. Jessamy tried to concentrate on the present duettists but it was impossible to shut out the image of her cousin, who had caused so much havoc.

At last the men were bowing themselves off the platform with Mr Adler announcing they would return later.

The next turn was a magician, but Jessamy was only partly aware of playing cards being conjured from the air and of a rabbit being brought from a top hat, which seconds before had been shown to be empty. The image of Lillian dominated her thoughts as she had dominated her life years ago. It was she who had been indirectly responsible for the breakup of her marriage with Fabian.

Jessamy was brought abruptly back to the present by a burst of clapping.

Mr Adler made a big performance of announcing the next turn. 'Wait for it, wait for it,' he said with a broad grin. 'And who are you all waiting for?' There was a shout of '*Kate*!' and he said, 'Of course, the one and only, your very own favourite...*Kate Keller!*'

The pianist struck several dramatic chords then the curtain was drawn across and a girl appeared, a very unexpected kind of girl.

Dark curls danced from under a cerise satin hat, the plumes in it swaying as she walked from side to side of the platform blowing kisses. Her dress, also cerise satin, was low-cut with a short, many-frilled skirt. From a cape of white swansdown, cut short at the front and long at the back, stepped a pair of shapely legs. The applause was deafening.

Jessamy was aware of an aura about the girl, which she knew was more than the effect of the low-cut dress and daringly revealed legs.

Mr Adler handed Kate a tiny green parasol and she put it up, stepped from the platform and came down among the audience, casting saucy glances from man to man.

Then, stopping in front of Alistair, she pursed her mouth as though to kiss him, but instead began to sing the song, *Daddy Wouldn't Buy Me A Bow Wow*. She leaned towards him, her bottom thrust out in a pert way. Her eyes were liquid velvet, her voice so seductive it would have to be heard to understand the inflections.

Jessamy, who was suffering for Alistair, sure he would

be terribly embarrassed, stole a glance at him and was astonished to see a look of pure bliss on his face. Her Alistair...good heavens!

Although Kate moved away she kept coming back to Alistair, and Jessamy, remembering Mrs Brunt telling her that the women didn't mind Kate making up to the men because she meant no harm, put on a bright face as though she did not mind, either.

When Kate finished the song she blew Alistair a kiss, went back to the platform, gave many bows to the standing ovation from the men and disappeared behind the curtained doorway. Mr Adler promised that Kate would sing them another song later.

Mrs Brunt was over the moon that Kate had sung to her lodger. 'Such an honour,' she said, 'and it'll get you money for your work. I expect that's why she did it. You'll have become special to our ladies.' She turned to Jessamy. 'You weren't jealous, Mrs MacKay, were you?'

'No, no, it was all part of the fun. She really is a very attractive girl, isn't she?'

'She's not beautiful,' Alistair said, his smile broad, 'but my goodness – she has personality! It reaches out to people.'

'Yes, it does,' Jessamy said, her face stiff from smiling. She turned to Mrs Brunt. 'Mind you, I don't know whether I would like to leave her alone with my husband.' She laughed so that Mrs Brunt would know she didn't mean it, of course.

Their landlady patted her hand. 'You would have no worry on that score, my love. Kate is dead straight. She will never be responsible for any broken marriages – that's why she's liked by everyone.'

There were three more turns before Kate came on again: a comedian with a strong Cockney accent that Jessamy found difficult to follow, two young girls who played duets on the pianoforte and a man who recited an endless poem on unrequited love.

The return of Kate was welcomed.

This time Mr Adler announced that all of Kate's songs

were dedicated to Dr MacKay and his wife. He reminded the audience to give generously as the box was about to be passed around, and added that everyone was invited to join in the chorus of all the songs.

Kate began with the *Skye Boat Song* and Jessamy glanced at Alistair and gave him a warm smile. It started with the chorus, 'Speed bonnie boat like a bird on the wing', and with Kate coaxing them all to join in they just about lifted the rafters.

The next song was *My Ain Folk*, and Jessamy thought it the wrong choice. She felt choked and she saw Alistair flick at each eye with a fingertip. Voices were low as they joined in; 'Far frae my hame I wander; but still my thoughts return to my ain folk over yonder, in the sheilng by the burn...'

There must have been a number of Scottish people in the audience because Jessamy saw a few handkerchiefs being used.

For the last song, Kate brought the rest of the cast out on to the stage and asked the baritone and tenor to lead the singing of *I Love A Lassie*, and a fine rousing rendering it was, too.

When the platform was finally emptied, the audience was reluctant to let Kate go. Mr Adler came over to ask Alistair if he and his wife would wait a few minutes. Kate had to leave since she had friends staying with her, but would like a few words with them before she left. Alistair said yes, of course, but was having difficulty himself in coping with all his new lady admirers who were busy offering their services in the dispensary should he need them.

When Kate finally appeared she was wearing a deep turquoise velvet cape with a hood that seemed to make her glow. She seized Jessamy's hands in her own and said, 'How do you do, Mrs MacKay. I hope you didn't think I was really making up to your husband when I was singing to him.' She had a soft, caressing voice.

'No, Miss Keller, of course not.'

'I did it for a purpose, you see. Eustace Adler told me

about your work and I thought if I brought attention to your handsome husband the women at least would give generously.' Her smile had a radiance. The noise had died down while she had been speaking but now it started up again and Kate suddenly yelled, 'Shut up, will you! I'm not finished yet.'

They all laughed, but listened as she addressed them all. 'I want everyone here to spread the word about the new dispensary at Paradise Corner. It's a good cause and some of you might have need of it one day. Tell your friends and remember this, every penny received helps eventually to make a pound.' She turned to Alistair. 'I have to leave now, but I would like to talk to you and your wife again at some time, Doctor. My great-grandfather was an apothecary, you know.'

'He was? Well now, I know that my wife would be as interested in hearing about him as I am, Miss Keller. And may I say how much we've enjoyed this evening.'

'Good. I'll be in touch, then, and see if we can arrange to meet. Oh yes, one more thing.' She brought a linen bag from under her cloak, 'The collection,' and shook hands with them. 'I'm really pleased to have met you both.'

What Jessamy remembered afterwards about the evening was the way Alistair seemed hypnotised by this dark-haired girl, and the thoughtful way in which Kate had looked at him, as though she had suddenly discovered something she had not been aware of before. There was no opportunity for analysing this, however. After they had answered all the questions from people who had stayed behind to talk to them, Mrs Brunt chattered practically non-stop all the way home about the lovely evening. Wait until she told her friends and neighbours about the way Kate had singled out the doctor for her attention. And wasn't Kate nice? She had no airs and graces and fancy her great-grandfather being an apothecary. Well, that was certainly a coincidence and no mistake!

When they arrived home Mrs Brunt insisted on them having some supper of bread and cheese and pickled onions. She was bustling around when she said, 'Oh, I forgot to ask you, Doctor MacKay. How much money did they collect for the dispensary?'

A slow smile spread over Alistair's face. 'I was wondering when someone would ask.' He brought the bag from his pocket. 'I haven't counted it but Mr Adler told me before we left that there was over sixty pounds.'

'*What?*' Jessamy's voice was a squeak. 'I don't believe it.'

Mrs Brunt flopped into a chair. 'Over sixty pounds? It's the most that's ever been collected. I've never known it to be more than thirty. My goodness, they have been generous.'

'And it's all thanks to you,' Alistair said warmly.

'No, don't thank me, I only suggested the idea. It was your presence, Doctor, and your wife's. You are two very nice people. They all liked you and I know many of our group will be only too glad to offer help should you need it.'

'And we shall be pleased to accept, Mrs Brunt.'

In spite of Alistair's teasing earlier on about the punishment of 'stormy loving', he was quiet when they finally went up to bed and she wondered if he had Kate on his mind. He had certainly been taken with her, as were all the other men. It was not for her beauty, since her mouth was large, her nose snub – and yet there was nothing coarse about her. What made this girl so irresistible to men? Was it her wonderful vitality, or an unknown quality with which some people are born?

Alistair was standing gazing into the dying embers of the fire, his fingertips on the edge of the mantelpiece. Jessamy said, 'What are you thinking about – the attractive Kate? She's an interesting person.'

Alistair let his fingertips slip from the mantelpiece then turned. 'What? No, no, I was thinking of the money those people collected tonight. It was quite unexpected, and most generous. I did think we might use some of it to buy linoleum for the main rooms.'

'Linoleum?' Jessamy began to laugh but her voice was a bit shaky. 'Oh, Alistair, you meet a most attractive girl who shows an interest in you and all you can talk about is floor covering.'

'Because it's important – floors must be kept clean. I want the main rooms washed down every day but not by half-starved women getting down on their knees wielding a scrubbing brush and catching splinters in their hands. I've seen the results of this in hospital many times – inflamed fingers...'

'Yes, Alistair. Now can we get off the subject of the dispensary and talk about the entertaining evening we've enjoyed?'

'With pleasure.' He took her in his arms and she rolled her eyes.

'Linoleum!'

They made love but it was not stormy, it was tender, and Jessamy was glad that the delectable Kate had not aroused any wild emotions in him. He was still her Alistair...her very own man.

3

Alistair and Jessamy were up early next morning to start buying stock for the dispensary. Mrs Brunt had kindly made them a map, showing each warehouse and how to get there. They were to start with beds and bedding, and she told them where to board the tram and where to get off. 'I doubt whether you'll get more done this morning than that, as it can be very tiring. You'd best leave crockery and cutlery to the afternoon. When you're hungry there's plenty of little cafés in that area and you'll get cottage pie, a pudding and a cup of tea for ninepence. They're for the working man, you understand, but my husband and I always used them and found the people there a friendly lot.'

They thanked her and left. It was a crisp morning and Jessamy enjoyed the ride on top of the tram. The main roads were busy but when they neared their destination they got off and walked through seedy streets.

They could not have had better treatment, however, when they arrived at the bedding warehouse. A big amiable Cockney called Mr Telfer pulled out chairs for them and asked a woman to bring cocoa. 'On a tray, Sal,' he said, 'and in cups, not mugs.' He then gave them his full attention. So they were opening a dispensary, eh? He took his hat off to them both, but why did they need beds and bedding? He thought that folks came to get medicine. When Alistair explained that he wanted to take patients in and operate on them if necessary, Mr Telfer's eyes opened wide. Well – there was a thing, now – a proper hospital! So they'd be wanting straw paillasses. Oh, no, Jessamy protested. They wanted proper beds. Iron ones, Alistair said. They didn't want to deal with woodworm.

Mr Telfer insisted they would have to have some paillasses. What if there was an epidemic of some kind? There wouldn't be room for everyone in the big hospitals, so they would all come crowding to the dispensary. He made such a big issue of it that Jessamy, remembering all the hints Mrs Brunt had given them, said, 'Do you know what I think, Mr Telfer? I think you have a large stock of paillasses and you want to get rid of them.'

Alistair gave Jessamy a shocked look but Mr Telfer slapped his knee and roared with laughter. 'Doc, I like your missus. She's a woman after me own heart. She's right, I do have a big stock but – ' he turned to Jessamy, sobering, 'I am right in that you'll need the paillasses as well.' So they ordered some and the proper bargaining began, with total embarrassment from Alistair, who took no part in it. Jessamy thoroughly enjoyed herself and was aware that Mr Telford was enjoying it, too. But there came a time when he held up a hand. That was it, he couldn't drop a penny more and and Jessamy accepted the price.

In addition, they bought sheeting, which would be made up to the size needed, and blankets. There was more bargaining and by then, Jessamy was beginning to feel exhausted.

Before they left Mr Telford pushed some coins into Alistair's hand and wished them every success with the dispensary. He had given them four sovereigns! Jessamy said, 'How kind of him. I imagined him to be a hard-headed businessman but there, it's difficult to assess people, isn't it?'

Alistair grunted that he didn't like all this bargaining, but Jessamy insisted it was part of the deal: how much would they have lost, had they accepted the first prices? He finally concurred, but not before Jessamy told him she had no scruples where the dispensary was concerned and neither should he.

They were on their way to buy cutlery when they passed a small café. Alistair stopped. 'That savoury aroma makes me feel ravenous. Should we go in?' Jessamy replied why not and they entered the café, which seemed to be full of working men. At first glance there didn't seem to be any free seats but then two men at a table nearby pulled out chairs, passed the time of day with them then went on talking about their union boss. There was a blackboard on the wall with the menu in white chalk. It said: *Stake and Kid Pie. Cotage Pie. Apple tart. Spotted Dick. With cus.*

Everywhere was spotlessly clean. Although there were no cloths on the tables they were scrubbed to whiteness. They both ordered the steak and kidney pie but Jessamy wanted the apple tart to follow and Alistair the suet pudding with currants; they both pronounced their choice excellent.

When they left, Jessamy said, 'I felt a bit awkward being the only woman in there but I don't think the men noticed.'

'Oh yes they did, my love. They kept giving you quick glances and I heard a man behind me describe you as a natty little piece.'

Jessamy laughed. 'I hope it was meant as a compliment.'

'Of course. Now, shall we go and see about buying the cutlery?'

An elderly Jew attended to them. He had a strong foreign accent and gesticulated a lot. He advised them to buy a cheaper quality but more of them, to allow for theft. 'Oh, yes, yes,' he said, nodding vigorously. 'Staff and patients will take them. They do not want to steal; it is circumstances. But there, we are not here to discuss the politics of the country.'

They bargained over the price and Jessamy thought she would always remember the sad expression on the old man's face when he appealed to Alistair, 'Do you think your wife will allow me one pound for profit?'

It was impossible not to laugh, then they were all laughing. They parted the best of friends.

Alistair suggested they leave the rest of the buying until the next day, but Jessamy pointed out all they still had to do. There were the medical supplies to buy, as well as crockery, pots and pans, and the linoleum to order. For that, they would have to go to Paradise Corner to take measurements.

They went to order the crockery.

A middle-aged woman attended to them and she stated right away that there would be no bargaining. As the crockery was for a dispensary she would quote rock-bottom prices, however, and would give them extra bowls and plates free, to allow for breakages. It was the quickest transaction they had made. When they left Alistair said with firmness, 'And now we go back to Mrs Brunt's.'

Their landlady ushered them into her kitchen and fussed over them, saying they must be done in and were to sit down. She had just made some tea.

Both Alistair and Jessamy were glad to obey. At first Jessamy was sure she would fall asleep in front of the glowing fire, but when Alistair started talking and laughing as he related her prowess at bargaining she was suddenly wide awake. The whole story was told in detail to Mrs Brunt's willing ears. She kept nodding and saying, 'Yes, I know, I know, I've gone through it.'

When all was told she complimented them. They had done very well to achieve all that they had. They could have a nice rest that evening, as they had a busy day ahead of them tomorrow. Then suddenly she jumped up. 'My goodness, I nearly forgot to tell you. There's been a huge mail. Six letters for the Doctor and eleven for you, Mrs MacKay.'

'Eleven?' Jessamy exclaimed. 'I've never had so many at one time. Isn't it exciting?' She hugged her post gleefully to her as they went up to their room.

'And eleven to reply to,' Alistair teased her. 'You are going to have a busy evening, my love.'

'At least I won't be wondering what on earth to tell them. I could fill fifty pages each and not repeat myself.'

Jessamy opened the one from her Cousin Louise first. Her letters were always full of small items of news and also she would get the truth about Romaine. In her mother's letter every small thing Romaine had done would be related in detail, with much exaggeration.

Sure enough, Louise began with news of Romaine. '*She's fine, been up to her usual mischiefs, but she really is a good little soul generally. She's never stopped asking about you and*

Alistair, wanting to know when you would both be home. When I asked her if she wanted to add some kisses to your letters she said she wanted to put proper kisses on to your letter, not just crosses. Your father came up with a solution. He put some carmine on her lips and you have the result on the last page.'

Jessamy turned to the last page and said, 'Ah,' and felt choked. Bless her, and bless Louise for making the kisses possible. With firmness Jessamy went back to the first page, to read the news of the shops she and Louise owned. '*Guess what,*' Louise wrote. '*Flynn told me today that the takings of every shop are up by fifty per cent. He wants us to buy some more. We shall discuss it when you come home.*'

A few months previously, Jessamy and Louise had been persuaded by the Irishman Flynn O'Rafferty to pool their money and invest in a small pharmacy, with Flynn handling the business side. When it was successful, with advice from Flynn they invested in more, Jessamy thinking that the money would come in useful when she and Alistair were free to get married. By then, Alistair had been left a legacy by his aunt and refused to touch it: it was hers to do with as she liked, he said. Sure that Alistair would rather have her dependent on him, she made no further reference to the shops, nor their excellent profits.

Louise gave all sorts of other little snippets of news. Her father, Jessamy's Uncle Bertie, was on again about buying a ship (which he had been doing for years), then there was news of marriages and babies been born. Jessamy felt suddenly homesick, which seemed ridiculous seeing that she and Alistair had been away for only a few days. Then, realising there was a terrible longing in her to see Romaine, she opened her mother's letter.

Esmeralda Every began with the story of Romaine having disappeared for nearly an hour two days before, and the family being utterly frantic. According to her mother, everyone was searching for the child – and where was she? At Mrs Midgin's cottage, that's where, sitting up at the table eating rice pudding with strawberry jam.

'*Oh, Jessamy, I nearly fainted with worry. And do you*

know what the little imp did next? She put a piece of rope round the neck of a sheep and brought it home. The trouble is, of course, she's such a darling it's difficult to be cross with her...'

There were many more escapades, most of them proving to be exaggerated, as Jessamy learned when she read her father's letter. About Romaine he said, '*She toddled off to Mrs Midgin's. Fortunately, I guessed what she had in mind because she'd mentioned she liked the old lady's rice pudding with strawberry jam on it.*' And about the sheep he wrote, '*She did manage to get a piece of rope around its neck, but getting it to move was a different matter. I spoke firmly to her and she's been as good as gold since, bless her little heart.*'

Chadwick then gave her news of the pharmacy, how busy they had been and with the new French perfumes going extremely well. There were bits of news about customers whom Jessamy knew and liked, and he concluded by saying he hoped their plans were going well. He and Mr Blackwell his assistant were looking forward to hearing the results of their venture. Mr Blackwell sent his regards to both of them, and Chadwick signed the letter, '*With kindest regards to Alistair and much love to you, Jessamy dear, from your devoted Papa.*'

Jessamy sat for a while after she had read her father's letter, thinking how much he had meant in her life. He had taught her all she knew about herbs, and about people, too, and the little quirks they had in their natures. He had tried to teach her tolerance – and she had not found this easy.

There was a letter apiece from her cousins Rebecca and Anne. Rebecca was full of the parties she had been to and the boys she had met while Anne talked of nothing but the dispensary, anxious to know when she could come and work with them. Her parents, Edward and Grace Every, who ran the hostelry in St Peel, were being difficult about her leaving home. Please could Alistair and Jessamy talk to them, persuade them it was right for her to do this work. If not, she would run away – she meant it.

Jessamy thought, oh dear, there was trouble ahead and

she wanted no part of it. She had plenty on her mind without worrying about family disagreements. And yet Anne was so dedicated to nursing. She put down those two letters and picking up the others, felt her heartbeats quicken. Four had a Scottish postmark. Were they from Alistair's family?

Only one member of the MacKays had come to the wedding, which was held at a Register Office. Alistair's brother who was two years older than him had stood in as best man. Jessamy liked Dougal at once. He had told them it was too far for his parents to come to the ceremony, but Jessamy knew that they did not approve of their son marrying a divorced woman.

The first letter Jessamy opened was from Alistair's mother.

'*Dear Jessamy*,' she wrote. '*This is a letter of abject apology for thinking you could not be a very nice person because you had been divorced. Dougal told us differently. He said what a warm and loving person you were and how lucky Alistair is to have such a lovely wife. I wish I was near and I could give you a hug and a kiss and beg you to forgive me for my narrow-mindedness. I hope we shall be able to meet in the not-too distant future. We all send our good wishes, Margaret MacKay.*' Jessamy wept over the letter and Alistair, alarmed, asked what was wrong.

'It's a lovely letter from your mother.'

'I know,' he said softly. 'I've had one, too. I'm glad she has no ill-feelings towards you. I think you'll find you have letters from my sisters, too. As soon as it's possible we'll go and visit them, Jessamy.'

'That will be something to look forward to,' she said.

The letters from Alistair's sisters were just as welcoming, and they dispelled the awful guilt that Jessamy had suffered, feeling responsible for severing the close relationship that Alistair had known with his family.

There was only one letter left to read now, from her Aunt Verity and Jessamy sat back to enjoy it. Verity's letters, like her daughter's Louise, were always newsy and without embellishments.

She wrote at first about Jessamy's grandmother Henrietta, saying how much she missed Jessamy and could hardly wait for her to come home. Verity had noticed how the old lady crossed off each day from the calendar as it came along. '*She's looking frail*,' she wrote, '*but my goodness, her eyes are bright with excitement at any small piece of gossip. How alive she becomes. It took me all my time not to tell her that Fabian is back in England. Yes, Jessamy, it's just a visit and as he will still be around at The Montague Acres when you come home I thought I'd better prepare you in case you met unexpectedly.*'

Jessamy sat motionless when she read this news, her heart beating in slow thuds. Alistair would not be pleased to know that Fabian was back in England. And did she want to see him? Would he ask to see Romaine? He had asked if he could keep in contact with her.

Other questions came flooding into Jessamy's mind. After their divorce, had he married Caroline, his ex-fiancée whom he had never really stopped loving? Why had Fabian come back to England? Was Caroline with him? This last thought brought weakness to Jessamy's limbs. Caroline was someone she did *not* want to see.

Why, oh why did he have to come back?

Jessamy went on reading the rest of her aunt's letter, and found the answer to her question. '*I saw Fabian's steward, Mr Stannard. He was telling me that Fabian is going to keep on The Montague Acres, said he needs to come home to England for a change. I'm not sure that it's a good thing, Jessamy. It was home to you for so long. On the other hand you'll be living in London and busy with the dispensary so you're not likely to come into contact with your ex-husband.*

'*Flynn has been a regular visitor lately. I can't understand what Louise intends to do. One minute I think she and Flynn will get together eventually then I think not. She won't talk about him to me, but perhaps she will to you. I would so like to see her married.*'

The rest of the letter was made up of items about the family and the fact that Jeremiah Every, Jessamy's grandfather, was doing his best to persuade Bertie to buy two ships. The act of buying one had caused enough of a furore!

Verity concluded by saying that she too was looking forward to seeing Alistair and Jessamy and hearing all their adventures...

But all that was on Jessamy's mind was her first husband Fabian – and wishing he had stayed in Texas.

After they had had their evening meal, Jessamy and Alistair both settled down to write replies. Then Mr Saunders called round to tell them of the day's progress. Alistair spoke to him about needing measurements of some of the rooms for linoleum, and the builder said he would do that first thing the next morning. Jessamy would have liked to ask about the furniture for the cottage, but decided that they had enough to cope with at that moment. When the old man left she stifled a yawn and said, 'I don't know about you, Alistair, but I'm ready for bed.'

He grinned and said he was ready for bed at any time, but as it turned out Alistair was fast asleep within a minute of laying his head on the pillow. Jessamy smiled and kissed him on the brow. She, too, wanted to sleep but lay wide awake, going over the fact of Fabian visiting England. She kept telling herself it was really no problem at all, but knew it was, because she still had a soft spot in a corner of her heart for the handsome captain.

Before Alistair and Jessamy set off the next morning for their final round of purchasing, they called at Paradise Corner to collect the measurements from Mr Saunders. What astonished Jessamy was the activity going on: the house seemed to be swarming with people. They were introduced to Mr Saunders' three sons, one of whom was cleaning the front windows, one distempering a ceiling and the third building a pulley contraption to transport patients up the stairs.

'It's amazing,' Alistair approved, having been shown the workings. The hall had meanwhile been swept clean of all the rubbish and two women were busy scrubbing it. A cauldron of water was slung over a huge fire in the kitchen and the stove, which had been blackleaded, shone. The ceiling and walls here had been distempered white and a girl and a woman were scrubbing this floor. All the women were introduced as people Mr Saunders could recommend as excellent workers. He said they would be glad to take on the cleaning jobs when the dispensary was open. Jessamy accepted at once. There was hammering going on overhead and on the roof at the front. Loose tiles were being attended to. Mr Saunders said he had taken it upon himself to have all the chimneys swept and the window-frames repainted – he hoped that was all right.

Alistair laughed and said, 'Mr Saunders, you make me feel breathless; my wife and I have felt worn out just doing the shopping these past two days.'

The old man rubbed his chin. 'Ah now, shopping – that's a totally different thing, very wearing.' He pulled up a wooden form and said if Mrs MacKay would care to take a seat, he would ask one of his sons to help him with the measurements. Perhaps the Doctor would let him know which rooms they wanted covering. Jessamy decided to go with them.

With the measurements written down Alistair and Jessamy prepared to leave, and Mr Saunders walked to the front door with them. Tomorrow, he promised, the front steps would be cemented and repaired.

The sun had come out and the weather was surprisingly mild after the recent sharp frosts. When Jessamy remarked what a lovely morning it was Mr Saunders nodded and said in his quiet way, 'It's a morning that gentles the mind.'

When Jessamy left with her husband she repeated the words. ' "A morning that gentles the mind." Who but Mr Saunders would think of such a thing? I feel that all my worries have gone.'

'Worries?' Alistair queried. 'Is there something bothering you?'

'Not any longer,' she said lightly and, unable to tell him that Fabian had been on her mind she added, 'Not now I've seen all the work that is going on in the house.' Alistair seemed happy with the explanation.

It was another busy morning. Alistair dealt with all the medical supplies, which they had left until last. There was no bargaining, but the man who attended to them took them out for a midday meal when the matter was concluded. They went to a small café which catered for businessmen. Although Alistair and Mr West talked business, Jessamy was included in the conversation and Mr West offered a lot of valuable advice regarding the dispensary. Jessamy, stimulated by the talk, felt none of the exhaustion of the two previous days, but when Alistair suggested going to the docks as he wanted to contact one or two captains who carried cargoes of herbs she tensed, remembering Fabian and his ship the *Abercarsis*. She said, with a forced lightness, 'You go. I feel I've had enough buying for a while.'

He linked his arm through hers. 'We'll go back to Mrs Brunt's, then.'

On their way Jessamy was silent and when Alistair asked what was wrong she looked up, startled. 'Oh, I was just thinking that there are many more things to deal with than I had expected.'

'Too true,' he agreed and began to talk about the dispensary, saying that once it opened they would be coping with a totally new way of life. 'There won't be any time for little courtesies, Jessamy. There will probably be occasions when I shout at you and at everyone else in sight. It's so difficult at times to get people to do what you want them to. For instance, a woman will come to the hospital and be given some medicine to take for what ails her. The following week you learn that she hasn't touched it. She says either that she didn't like the taste or that she's sure it won't do her any good. You can imagine the reaction of a doctor or a nurse with hundreds of patients waiting to be seen. Tempers get frayed, but because we are medical people we are supposed to have endless patience. Then you might have a child with sores: you give the mother ointment and tell her to wash the baby before she applies it but no, dirt and ointment are rubbed into open sores. Sometimes you feel you could lash out at these mothers to knock some sense into them, but they wouldn't know why they were being hit.' Jessamy was rather dismayed.

'These are things you haven't mentioned before. I feel you should have told me.'

'I thought it best that you were made aware of them nearer the opening of the dispensary.'

Jessamy looked up at him. 'We are going to be faced with some difficult tasks, aren't we?'

'Yes, Jessamy, and there are some you might think are insurmountable but,' he squeezed her hand and smiled, 'I know you will cope. You've coped with all our other problems that have cropped up over the past few years. The important thing is not to lose one's temper, or at least try not to.'

'How do you get a patient to take medicine if he or she is determined not to?'

'Well, on one occasion when a woman brought her bottle of medicine back untouched I took it from her and said, "That's all right. If you want to die that's your privilege".'

'So what did she say to that?'

'She grabbed the bottle and went storming out. For several weeks she came back for more medicine then one day she deposited an empty bottle on the counter, glared at me, announced she no longer had any pain and off she marched.'

'Without even a word of thanks! Really, people like her don't deserve to have treatment.'

'They do, Jessamy. We don't know the sort of life she lived. She might never have known affection. The fact that she told me her pain had gone was probably her way of saying thanks.'

Jessamy shook her head. 'I'm sure I'll never have your tolerance or your understanding of people.'

'You will, when you work with them and know the conditions under which they live. No, not live – exist – that's all some of them do.'

Alistair went on talking about the poverty and ailments they would have to confront and Jessamy, who had seen the opening of the dispensary as an exciting adventure, knew now she had been living in a fantasy world. She had seen herself as a Florence Nightingale, tending to the sick without accepting the raw realities of life...as Miss Nightingale and her nurses had done during the Crimean War. How could she have been so naive?

When they arrived back at their lodgings the little maid told them Mrs Brunt was out but would be back soon, then added that she would bring up some tea. Jessamy thanked her and they went up to their room.

A few minutes later Maggie knocked on their door to say they had a visitor. She was greatly agitated. It was Miss Keller, the actress – should she ask her to come up?

Alistair said yes of course, and asked Maggie if she would bring an extra cup and saucer. After she had brought them the little maid darted away. Alistair glanced at Jessamy, raised his shoulders and went to the door. Jessamy waited, unsure how she felt about Kate calling. Although she wanted to see how her husband would react at seeing the delectable actress again, she felt too that it could be dangerous.

When Kate came into view Jessamy felt a fluttering in her stomach. She was wearing dark green velvet with a perky matching hat and looked as radiant as she had done before. Alistair greeted her with, 'Miss Keller, what a lovely surprise!'

'I do hope I'm not intruding, Doctor MacKay.'

'No, of course not. It's a pleasure.'

Jessamy went forward then and Kate took both her hands in hers. 'I had a lot of ideas that I felt would help you with the dispensary, Mrs MacKay, and I just couldn't wait to tell you.'

'How interesting,' Jessamy said, wondering if the ideas included getting to know her husband a little better. 'Do sit down, Miss Keller. The maid will be bringing some tea.'

Alistair pulled up a chair and Kate smiled at him. 'This is lovely, I feel so at home with you both. Now, where do I start?'

4

After the tea had been brought up and poured, Kate outlined her ideas. She and other performers did turns at the homes of a number of wealthy people, and she said that many of the daughters were itching to do something to help the poor in order to relieve the boredom of their days. Many of their mothers did charitable work such as running soup kitchens, but did not want their daughters coming into contact with 'unsavoury people'.

Kate pulled a face. 'Some of them are such terrible snobs. They talk about helping the poor but a lot despise them. What most of these women want is praise for doing good work so I thought I could suggest to the daughters that they do some sewing – perhaps make nightdresses and nightshirts for those in hospitals. Our group would supply materials and thread.'

'That would be splendid,' Alistair enthused.

'Some of the girls said they could knit stockings and socks. They really are keen.'

Jessamy said, 'It's good of you to go to this trouble, Miss Keller.'

'Not at all. My family didn't have much money when I was a child but my mother was always begging clothes or boots for families who were worse off. When I asked for cast-off clothes from these wealthy voluntary workers I received three sackfuls of shabby evening gowns, some of them sequinned, tatty silk chemises, satin negligées which were torn and faded and worn-out satin slippers. For men we were given several velvet smoking jackets, minus nap, smoking caps, two overcoats with the fur collars removed, two faded pink hunting jackets, one suit with loud checks – threadbare in parts, and about a dozen pairs of boots, so misshapen they must have belonged to a cripple. One woman did get clippings to help make a rag rug out of the hunting jacket, the smoking jackets and the suit with the loud checks, so all was not entirely lost.'

Jessamy was thoughtful for a moment then said, 'I remember my grandmother telling me once that some of the so-called rich were as poor as some of the just average families.'

Kate nodded. 'I would accept that. My mother, who was a sewing maid at a big house before her marriage, said it was all patch, patch, patch to make do. Any dress with a worn part had to be neatly darned with fancy stitches. And the daily food, she said, was near-starvation level, unless the family were entertaining and then a special show was put on.'

Kate suddenly smiled and it was as though the sun had come out on a dull day. 'Well, at least we've made a start if we can get these girls sewing and knitting. Is there anything else I can ask them to do? As I told you they are really keen.'

Alistair suggested they could do with bandages being rolled and Kate took a notebook from her reticule and wrote this down, saying it was as good as done. Jessamy was aware of her husband watching this vivacious girl intently and could not help wondering what was in his mind.

In less than a minute she had a fair idea of what he was thinking. Kate, who had put her book away, got up, saying she must not take any more of their time and Alistair said immediately, 'Please don't go, Miss Keller. It's a pleasure to have your company.' He was on his feet. 'Please sit down again.'

'Yes, do,' Jessamy echoed and was sincere about it. 'Let me pour you another cup of tea.'

'Well, all right, but I really mustn't encroach on your time. It was good of you to see me. I just barged in on you.'

'You can barge in any time, Miss Keller.' Alistair's smile was warm. 'We are grateful for all you've done for us and will be doing.'

And so Kate sat down again and, in spite of Jessamy

having a few small qualms about her husband's obvious interest in their guest, she did enjoy Kate's stories of her concert work. She told of the evening when she tripped over her parasol and went flat on her face and how the audience all thought it was a part of the show and laughed their heads off. Kate laughed too, at the memory – she had an infectious giggle.

'That was in spite of having a bloodied nose. I looked a sight the next night. Apart from my eye being black and blue I had a cold and my nose was red with wiping it. So, as I couldn't very well sing a nostalgic song to a good-looking man in the audience, I made a comedy of it, chose a fat man with a bulbous nose and sang to him, *Two Luverly Black Eyes*. The audience just about pulled the roof down. I still do a comedy turn, at the right time.'

Alistair and Jessamy laughed and Jessamy asked for more stories.

Kate grinned, 'Are you prepared to sit up all night?'

They didn't sit up all night but it was nearly eleven o'clock when Kate got up to leave. Mrs Brunt, who had joined them, offered to put Kate up overnight but she thanked her and said she shared rooms with another girl who would worry if she didn't come home.

Alistair put on his overcoat saying he would get her a cab but Kate would not hear of it. She would see herself home, she said, and no matter how Alistair insisted she refused. 'I'm going now,' she said, 'and if you follow me I'll never call and see you again. And I mean it, I have a very strong will.'

While Alistair was still trying to persuade her to have company Kate slipped out and must have run down the stairs because when Jessamy went on to the landing she heard the front door closing quietly. She came back into the room with Mrs Brunt smiling in an indulgent way and Alistair looking definitely disappointed.

Jessamy said, 'I admire Miss Keller. She stayed late, but did not expect Alistair to put himself out to see her home.'

'It was the least I could have done,' Alistair protested.

Mrs Brunt shrugged. 'She's a very independent soul,

and so sensible. I enjoyed this evening but now I must go and let you both get to bed.'

When goodnights had been exchanged Alistair, who was still wearing his overcoat, said in a dreamy way, 'What an amazing person Kate is. She's not coquettish in any way, yet she has the ability to draw – '

He paused and Jessamy finished for him, 'The ability to draw men to her? Is she a woman you could love, Alistair?'

He chucked her under the chin. 'I might have done had I not met you, my darling.' He pulled her to him and kissed her and although they did not make love that night Jessamy was satisfied to sleep with his arm around her.

At breakfast the next morning Alistair said suddenly, 'We're due home in two days aren't we, Jessamy? Would you mind if I didn't go with you?'

She stared at him then put her cup down carefully. 'Yes, I would mind, Alistair, I would mind it very much. We are a newly-married couple who are on our honeymoon. The family are looking forward to welcoming us back – a celebration has been arranged. How do you think they would feel if I returned alone? How do you think I would feel, a bride without a bridegroom?' Her voice broke.

'Jessamy, I'm sorry.' He took her hand in his. 'It was thoughtless of me, stupid. Of course we'll go home together.' He paused then went on, 'It's just that there's so much to do. Would you mind if I came back after a couple of days? You can stay on, of course, for as long as you wish.'

Jessamy flicked a fingertip across each eye. 'When you return I shall be with you. I know how much there is to be done, but I just wouldn't have been able to face everyone on my own and see their disappointment, especially Romaine's. She's just living for your return.'

'I know. Forgive me, darling. We'll see how things progress. We still have today and tomorrow. We may be able to stay at home a little longer than two days. We'll see Mr Saunders after breakfast.'

Jessamy prayed that Alistair would agree to their renting the cottage. If he did, the furniture that Mr Saunders had promised would have to be installed, beds would have to be made up and so many, many other things done. When they called in to see Mr Saunders at Paradise Corner they were astonished at what else had been achieved. By now the front steps had been repaired and as the cement was not quite set they had to go round to the back. The store-rooms and laundry room had been distempered as well as the kitchen; floors, shelves and the inside of cupboards scrubbed and aired. All the activity today seemed to come from overhead and in the hall.

When Alistair opened the door that led into the hall he said, 'Good Lord!'

The hall was in the process of being converted into three rooms and a passageway made from the front door to the stairs. Mr Saunders saw them and came to greet them. 'You'll see a difference,' he said, smiling.

'It's amazing. I can't believe so much has been done in such a short time. You must all have been working very late.'

'Not too late. The lads and I knocked off about nine o'clock last night. We're all keen to see the place taking shape. It's sad when a lovely old house like this stands neglected. You can feel it coming to life, can't you? Come and have a look at the panelling. It's gleaming. The women polished it all yesterday.' He moved away and said over his shoulder, 'They love the old house, too.'

The hall had divided well into three rooms and Mr Saunders had been right when he said the panelling was gleaming. Jessamy had felt surprised when the old man remarked that the women loved the house, too, and knew to her shame that she had not expected such a comment simply because these women were poor. Was she then like some of the wealthy who considered the working classes to be without feelings? Heaven forbid.

There was a lot of hammering and sawing going on, so Mr Saunders took them upstairs, running his hand lovingly over the patina of the mahogany balustrade. 'Look at how this beautiful wood responds to love and care. This house will be a boon to the sick – they see so little beauty in their lives. I shall bring flowers from my garden.' Jessamy stored Mr Saunders' words in her mind for a time that might come when she was overtired and impatient and might feel like giving up the work. Alistair had warned her of such a thing happening.

The big room on the first floor that was to be the ward had been completed and Jessamy felt glad she had pressed for this room to have blue linoleum to make it brighter. It was the only room to be completed on this floor but, judging by the sounds of activity, it would not be long before others followed.

Alistair spent a lot of time in the future laboratory and operating room, explaining his needs to Mr Saunders, and Jessamy listened carefully, hoping to be able to spend time in both rooms learning all she could on the operating and scientific sides of the work.

They had come downstairs and Jessamy was plucking up courage to ask Mr Saunders about furniture for the cottage when he mentioned it himself. 'Oh, by the way,' he said. 'I got the lads to put the furniture in the Coachman's Cottage. You might want to move it around but you can do that at your leisure. There's bedding including sheets and we've laid some new linoleum but you'll probably want some rugs, or a carpet.' He handed the key to Alistair. 'Go in when you want. You may have a free hand.'

Jessamy was overwhelming in her thanks, and would have said more but Alistair cut her short; they must not detain Mr Saunders any longer as he had work to do. Jessamy kept her annoyance under control and even when they were outside and Alistair said he wanted to inspect a small hall nearby for its potential as a soup kitchen, she asked quietly if they could take another look at the cottage first. He sighed and said yes, if she must and still she made no complaint but when he walked ahead, she stopped and waited until he missed her.

When he did, and turned and asked in a pained way what was wrong she walked towards him and spoke quietly. 'You know perfectly well what's wrong, Alistair. You will not accept graciously that we shall live in the cottage. Well, when you treat me like a dog and expect me to follow on your heels something has to be done. I'll forget the cottage. We'll move into the house, seeing that is what you want in order to save a few shillings rent a week.'

'Jessamy, you are being purposely awkward. When I walked ahead it was simply that I had other things on my mind.'

'Let me ask you one thing: if it had been Kate Keller with you instead of your wife, would you have walked ahead and ignored her?'

'What in heaven's name has Kate Keller to do with this?' His expression was stormy.

'Answer me — and I want an honest answer.'

'I refuse to answer such a stupid question.' He turned away.

Jessamy, determined not to show her anger, spoke quietly again. 'If I disliked or was jealous of Kate, I would not have asked it, but I do like her, very much, and I have to know how you would have treated her if the position had been similar.'

He turned swiftly. 'I told you my mind was on other things!'

'That is not the truth and you know it. If you'll excuse me I'll go back to Mrs Brunt's and pack my bag. Tomorrow I'll go home, leaving you to get on with all the things you have to do. I won't stay long – two or three days – and when I return I'll try and arrange for us to live in some rooms on the top floor of Paradise Corner.'

'And will you tell Mr Saunders that your husband doesn't want to live in the cottage – make a fool of me?'

'I wouldn't be so petty. I'd simply tell him that after weighing it all up, we feel that it would be best for you to live at the dispensary, to be near any patients who might need constant attention.'

'I think you're behaving absolutely irresponsibly.'

'No, Alistair. I might have done so before I came here, but I've learned more about life in the raw since coming to the East End than I've learned in the rest of my life. I really have grown up during my...honeymoon.' She walked away then to hide the sudden rise of tears.

Alistair caught up with her. 'Jessamy, this is ridiculous, and all because I walked ahead of you!'

'No, Alistair,' she said in a low voice. 'It's because you object to us living in a cottage that was handed to us on a plate, furnished, with bedding – everything for a few shillings rent a week. It would be a perfect place for Romaine to play, away from sick patients, screams of pain and all the rest. Tell me why you are so set against it.'

'I'm afraid I just didn't like it,' he said slowly. 'It had an atmosphere. Oh, look, Jessamy, this is difficult to explain. I only know I didn't want to live in it, but we'll go back together and take another look and if you're really set on it, we'll move in. How's that?'

Jessamy was not sure how she felt. This was all rather a surprise. She had heard many times that some houses did have a strange atmosphere, and Alistair sounded sincere. On the other hand, a determination to live in Paradise Corner might have conveniently created the atmosphere in his mind.

She slipped her arm through his and smiled. 'Perhaps the cottage is haunted.'

Alistair teased her, said she would probably run a mile if she saw a ghost then, suddenly serious again, added, 'Jessamy, to come back to Kate Keller. I don't want you to have any foolish ideas about her. I like her, I'm attracted to her as many men must be but I'm not in love with her. You are my only love and I say that without any sense of melodrama. I hope you believe me.'

'Yes, Alistair, I do and I'm sorry you didn't mention the way you felt about the cottage before this. I had no idea.'

Jessamy felt nothing but pleasure when they stepped inside the Coachman's Cottage again. The furnishings and furniture were a surprise. She had expected rather heavy dark oak furniture for some reason and instead found a walnut table, chairs and sideboard with elegant legs. A large blue Turkish rug all but covered the whole floor of the living room with the surrounds stained in walnut and ready to polish. Velvet curtains in dark orange with fringes of gold hung at the windows and the two armchairs had been replaced by two covered in velvet in the same blue as the carpet. Jessamy turned to Alistair, her eyes alight. 'Alistair, what luxury, it's – ' She stopped as she saw his solemn expression. 'What is it?'

'Nothing. I was miles away for the moment.' He looked around him. 'As you say, it's luxurious. If there were ten ghosts we couldn't refuse to move in. Shall we look at the scullery?'

Blue linoleum had been fitted on the floor here, the same shade as Jessamy had chosen for the ward at the dispensary. There was a large sink and running water and outside a water closet, next to a coalhouse.

Upstairs the bedroom floors were also covered with the blue linoleum and in each room were two sheepskin rugs. Jessamy laughed. 'We are being thoroughly spoilt.' The furniture in the bedrooms was of mahogany – a wardrobe, dressing-table and bed. The larger room had a double bed and the smaller, two single ones. All the bedding looked new, including lovely chintz quilts. Jessamy looked up. 'Oh, Alistair, I can't think there can be anything evil in this house.'

'I'm sure you're right. Look, Jessamy, don't mention what I said to Mr Saunders. I feel foolish now. If you want to browse round for a while I'll just go over and have a word with him, see if he can give me a date when he thinks the dispensary might be ready. We'll also have to arrange with the warehouses for the goods to be delivered.'

When Jessamy opened cupboards in the kitchen she found them fully supplied with crockery, cutlery, pots and pans. There were even sheets and towels in the big wardrobe upstairs. She took off her jacket and started making up the beds and had a wonderful feeling of satisfaction that at last the three of them would be on their own.

Then she felt a little pang. No, Louise would be coming back with them. It would be impossible to do without her once the dispensary was up and running, but how nice it would have been to have spent some time alone with Alistair and Romaine.

Sacrifices were something she had had to get used to while waiting for her divorce to go through, but at least there were times in the cottage on the moors when Alistair was solely hers, and others when she had Romaine all to herself. Times such as this would become a rarity in the future.

Jessamy smoothed a hand over the quilt on the double bed and straightened. Well, no one could say she had not been warned and...she had accepted the challenge. There was no drawing back now.

She felt a small draught of cold air waft through the room as though the window were open, but it was closed. Did she imagine there was a strange atmosphere in the room? Jessamy remembered a party she had been to as a child when a boy had said suddenly, 'There's a horrible little dwarf standing in that corner over there.'

The gaze of every child had gone to the corner and although there was nothing to see there were cries of terror and some children had rushed to get out of the room.

The boy had laughed then and called them fools. He had made up the story. After that Jessamy had tried to rationalise anything that seemed strange and, coming to the conclusion that she had been influenced by Alistair's words, she went confidently downstairs.

After all, everything was going well. Alistair had agreed to taking the cottage and in two days' time they would be going home to see the family before settling down here. At that moment all seemed right with the world.

The homecoming at St Peel was all Jessamy had anticipated. She savoured the feel of Romaine's plump little arms tight about her neck, the smacking kiss on her cheek, the quiet loving welcome of her father and the affection of all the family – her aunts, uncles and cousins. The only jarring note came from her mother, who complained she had been in bed all day with a migraine, and from her

Uncle Digby and Aunt Dorcas, who were their usual dour selves, but then these things were not unusual and would do nothing to spoil the celebratory evening at Beacon Hall.

As the evening was dry they decided to walk to the Hall. Romaine, who would normally be skipping ahead, held Alistair and Jessamy by the hands, as though afraid they would leave her again. Twice she had asked if she could tell the story about the ducks, but because she had asked when grown ups were talking, Alistair had said, 'Later, darling.'

Now she stopped and said she was tired. Alistair picked her up and immediately she took his chin between forefinger and thumb, turned his face to hers and asked, with great patience, if she could now tell them about the ducks. He laughed and said yes.

And so Romaine told a garbled tale about a little duck who was very naughty and always getting into trouble and Jessamy was smiling in an indulgent way until she realised her daughter was talking about the ducks on the pond at The Montague Acres. She froze. Who had taken her to the house, or had she wandered off as she often did and had found it? Supposing Fabian had seen her, taken her into the house? If he had and Alistair found out he would be furious.

Jessamy decided she must put the matter aside for the moment.

When Beacon Hall came into view she felt a wave of nostalgia sweep over her. It was old, a three-storeyed lath and plaster structure. There were no luxuries inside and it was draughty but Jessamy loved it because her grandmother lived there and Jessamy adored her. The old lady could no longer get around, but she was still lively, loved gossip and was full of quaint sayings and philosophies. Jessamy had learned a great deal from Henrietta Every, and maybe she would learn more this evening.

Jeremiah was waiting for them in the hall. He was tall, straight-backed, had a slightly arrogant air and ruled the family, or liked to think he did. Jessamy had been one of the first rebels, and there were others coming up in this new generation.

'Ah, there you are.' He came forward. The only one to get any fuss was Romaine, who had a special place in his heart because she was the only grandchild of his favourite son Chadwick. Jessamy felt a tug at her heartstrings. Romaine really was beautiful. Alistair had told her once that his great-grandfather had run away to marry the daughter of a proud Romany family, who had disowned her. Romaine had dark velvety eyes, hair with the iridescent sheen of a raven's wing and a wanderlust that took her over the moors at times.

Jeremiah stated, 'The rest of the family are waiting. Just give me time to announce you, then come up.'

The sitting room was upstairs and a hubbub of voices came from above as they waited. There was a sudden silence then, as someone began to play *Here Comes The Bride* on the piano, they entered to a burst of applause.

When it died down Jeremiah announced that Henrietta was waiting to greet the honeymooners in her room but they would be back soon. He then said to Jessamy and Alistair, 'I'll take charge of Romaine and will bring her to see my wife in a few minutes.'

They went along the landing to Henrietta's small sitting room and Jessamy choked back a tear when she felt the thin arms around her neck and heard the whispered, 'Oh, my lovely girl. It's so good to see you again.' But the next moment the old lady was smiling through her tears as she greeted Alistair, and said she had been awake from four o'clock waiting to see them.

They talked for a few minutes then Alistair said with a grin that he would leave the two of them to have a good old gossip on their own. This had Henrietta saying to Jessamy, 'You have a jewel of a man, my love. Take good care of him.'

'Oh, I will,' Jessamy said softly.

Henrietta patted the stool in front of her. 'Now then, I want to know all your news.'

Jessamy sighed. 'There's just so much to tell you, Grandma! I'll tell you some of it now and the rest later and I won't miss out a thing. Now, I'll start at the beginning, when we arrived at our lodgings and met Mrs Brunt our landlady...'

Jessamy had covered quite a lot of ground when her grandfather returned with Romaine and said to his wife, 'I'll exchange Jessamy for Romaine. You can have her back later. The others all want to know about London and the East End.'

Jessamy was longing to have a private talk with Louise and her Aunt Verity, but had to be content for the moment to give each of them a hug. When she was asked if the newly-weds had been to a theatre on their honeymoon she hesitated a moment then told them about the evening they had spent with some music hall stars. This delighted the younger element, but brought a look of disapproval from her Uncle Digby whose wife Dorcas said she was surprised that Alistair had taken her to such a den of iniquity.

'Oh no, you're wrong,' Jessamy protested, then catching Alistair's impish grin she went on, 'This was a private party given by wealthy people to raise funds for the dispensary. The performers were high-class artistes, and we were introduced to titled people. The sum we were handed from the collection was magnificent. What is more, these wealthy women have volunteered to run a soup kitchen for us. It was a truly memorable evening.'

Suddenly realising how she had let herself be carried away by her hateful Aunt Dorcas' remark, Jessamy was appalled, but then she thought how her grandmother would enjoy the story. She then spoke of their experiences of stocking up with supplies for the dispensary, and when she told the story of bargaining with the proprietor who had asked Alistair sadly if he thought his wife would allow him a pound profit, the men roared with laughter. Jessamy was complimented on her resourcefulness and this set a light-hearted pattern for the evening.

Rebecca and Anne Every came up, to tell Jessamy that their parents were weakening about allowing them both to go to London. Anne added in her quiet way that she was looking forward to getting some experience in nursing.

What surprised Jessamy was the interest shown in the dispensary by most of her cousins, who seemed to treat the opening of it as though they were setting out on a voyage of discovery. She reminded them, 'We'll be treating sick, poverty-stricken people who have little to look forward to in life,' and gave them some instances of their living conditions. After this there were promises from the young ones that they would get donations from every one there that evening.

When Jessamy did get a chance to speak to Louise her cousin said, 'I've been sent to tell you that Gran wants to speak to you again but she'll have to wait. I want you to myself for a bit.'

They had so many interruptions, however, that they agreed to meet outside in ten minutes, with Louise saying she would bring Jessamy's coat.

Henrietta apologised for taking Jessamy away from the rest of the family again. 'You left me at a most interesting part of your story, my love. You and Alistair were about to go to a music hall.'

Jessamy laughed. 'I've just told the most awful lies about it, but it was Aunt Dorcas' fault.'

She explained the situation and the old lady said, 'Dorcas is such a hypocrite. If she had had the chance to go to the sleaziest of music halls she would have been there first with her big feet. But come on, tell me what happened.'

By the time Jessamy had finished her tale Henrietta was chuckling. 'I wish I had been there to see this Kate Keller singing to Alistair and he lapping it all up. And so he should – he's a handsome fellow. He used to be so quiet, but now he has...an authority – yes, that's it. He'll go far, will yon chappie.'

Jessamy began to tell her about the Coachman's Cottage when she glanced at the clock and said, 'Oh, I'll have to finish this later, Gran. I've promised to have a word with Louise, but I'll be back.'

The old lady patted her arm. 'Don't hurry. I have a lot to mull over and I'll look forward to hearing more about this cottage.'

Louise, who was waiting at the bottom of the steps when Jessamy appeared, held out her coat. 'It's colder than I thought.'

As they moved away Jessamy confided, 'I did want to have a word with you about Romaine. She mentioned seeing ducks on a pond and I realised it was the one at The Montague Acres. Has she been there?'

'Yes, she has. You know what a little imp she is for wandering off. One afternoon last week Mother took her for a walk on the moors, stopped to talk to a friend for a few minutes and when she looked around Romy had disappeared. She came for me and we began a search. Usually it doesn't take long to find her but this time I was getting really worried when who should I see but Fabian? He was with Romy, and she was chatting to him fifteen to the dozen.'

Jessamy's heart skipped a beat. 'Had she gone to the house?'

'She might have made for it. She was near and did ask to see the animals, apparently. Fabian told me he took her to see them but only for a few minutes then he set out to bring her home, knowing we'd be worried stiff.'

Jessamy said firmly, 'I don't want her involved with Fabian. I'm afraid of him, and Alistair would be furious.'

'Jessamy, you must remember that Fabian was good enough to let people think Romaine was his child. I know it was only for a short while but – '

'Did he ever marry Caroline?' Jessamy interrupted.

'I don't know, he didn't mention it. What conversation we had was mostly about you and Alistair. He thought you were doing a splendid thing in opening the dispensary and said I was to tell you he would very much like to contribute financially.'

'Yes, he did offer before when I first talked about our plan, but recently when I mentioned it to Alistair it took me all my time to persuade him that we must not allow pride to stand in the way of accepting funds. But there, let me tell you about the cottage you'll be living in with us. I can fill you in on the rest later as I've hardly seen Romaine since we arrived, nor have I had a talk yet with your mother.'

'You needn't worry about Romaine, she's being utterly spoiled by everyone and Mama is doing her best to stop them. Jessamy, you didn't say much in your letters about the shops making such good profit.'

Jessamy opened a field gate. 'Well, you know that Alistair doesn't like me having this money, even though I'm grateful to Flynn for his expertise. I think he feels it's a husband's right to support a wife – not that I ever mention the shops, but I don't really like the secrecy attached to it. I think the family should know about them, or if not the whole family, then at least Grandpa should be told.'

'No, that would defeat the whole object,' Louise argued. 'I want to prove to Jeremiah that women can also be successful in business, and I am hoping that you'll reinvest your share of the profits in buying up further shops.'

When Jessamy made no reply Louise groaned. 'Oh, don't say you intend to put the money towards the dispensary. Look, I'll go on collecting for that but I want to build a chain of pharmacies – we must, to make an impact.'

Jessamy shook her head. 'Let's leave the business of the shops for the time being. I have a lot on my mind at the moment, dealing with the dispensary, the cottage and keeping my husband from straying.' She laughed as she said it but realised there was a catch in her voice.

Louise immediately seized on this. 'Alistair straying? What on earth are you talking about? You were on your honeymoon, for heaven's sake.'

'I was jesting. We had fun.' Jessamy managed to tell her the story of Kate Keller in a light-hearted way but knew she must be feeling the after-effects of all they had done while they were in London, plus the worry of knowing that Fabian had taken Romaine to The Montague Acres.

She made up her mind she would have to try and see Fabian, talk to him and persuade him not to encourage Romaine to go to their old home. And knew as she thought it that she was secretly glad of an excuse to see him...

5

The next morning Alistair told Jessamy he had promised her father to go to the pharmacy on Every Street and have a talk on medical matters. He asked if she was coming with him.

She said, 'No, I promised to call and see Aunt Verity. We hardly had a chance to talk last night, nor did I have much of a talk with Louise. She is coming back with us, so we'll have to make all the arrangements.'

Although all this was true Jessamy was also hoping to have an opportunity of going to The Montague Acres to see Fabian. She had not wanted to take Romaine with her on this occasion, and her chance came when Esmeralda promised to take the child to visit a neighbour whose cat had had kittens. Romaine, all impatience, rushed upstairs to get her hat and coat and when she came down she wailed, 'Grandma, you're not ready! Please, please, can we go now?'

'This very minute,' Esmeralda replied, with an indulgent smile. She went into the hall, with the child running after her.

Alistair laughed. 'Parents take a back seat where kittens are concerned.'

'Of course.'

The morning was icy but the sun was shining when they left the house. Jessamy took several deep breaths. 'Oh, isn't this air wonderful! I think this is what I shall miss most in London – the open moors, the air, the wildlife.'

Alistair grinned. 'So you stay – I'll engage an assistant.'

'Don't you think you would miss your wife?'

'Well, she did fall asleep on me last night,' he teased.

'Alistair, I am sorry about that but I was so exhausted.'

'I know, my love. Oh, there's Verity at the gate.'

Her aunt was waiting, loose strands of hair blowing

every which way, some of the buttons of her blouse left undone. Jessamy felt a lovely warmth sweep over her. Her aunt might be untidy at times but she was always loving, always caring. Jessamy waved and her aunt opened the gate and came out.

'How nice to see you both. I guessed the time right. I've just made some coffee.'

Alistair said he would call on the way back as he had promised to see Chadwick, and Verity told him that Bertie was expecting him too at the chandlery. She laughed. 'And that should take all morning. When men get talking business they forget everything else.'

'It's nothing to the gossiping that women can do. Enjoy yourselves.' He gave them a broad grin and left.

Jessamy and Verity stood for a moment watching him. Verity said, 'What a fine figure of a man he's become. He has such confidence. Jeremiah was very impressed with him, with his knowledge.' Then she turned to Jessamy and gave her a hug. 'Oh, how I'm going to miss you, and Louise, of course. But there, I can't stand in her way. She's such a restless soul. She's gone to take a fruit cake to Mrs Dobson who's sprained her wrist. She'll be back in a few minutes.'

As they went into the house Verity said, 'I want grandchildren, Jessamy. It's such a delight to have Romy with us.'

'You'll have them, Aunt Verity – stop worrying. Rupert and Francis are both courting.'

Verity shook her head. 'I don't think that either of my sons are serious about their young ladies. Here's Louise coming.'

Louise greeted Jessamy cheerfully. 'I thought you would be sleeping until midday. I've just met Alistair – we've been chatting. Considering all the work the pair of you have been doing in London you look extremely well.' Then, about to take off her coat, she nodded towards the window and gave a groan. 'Oh, heavens, look who's arriving – Aunt Dismal Dorcas. Jessamy, button up your coat, we're leaving. Let's escape through the kitchen.' To her mother she added, 'Sorry, Mama, but after last night I refuse to talk to that woman. You can tell her we've gone sick-visiting, anything. We'll be back...*after* she's gone.'

There was a knock on the front door as the girls hurried through the kitchen.

Once outside Louise said, 'I know I'm letting Mother down, but I just hate that woman. If you could have heard all the snide remarks she made about the family last night...of course, that's nothing new.'

'Didn't anyone protest?'

'All who were listening did, even her own sons, but that didn't stop Dorcas. Oh no, she was enjoying herself too much. Then she began to criticise Henrietta, saying she was sure she could get out of her chair if she wanted to and the reason she didn't was that she liked attention.'

'Oh, no! I can't believe that even Dorcas would say such a spiteful thing.'

'She could and she did. Unfortunately for her, Jeremiah was right behind her. Without a word he marched her out of the room. I don't know what was said but Dorcas disappeared.'

'What about Uncle Digby?'

'He stayed but he was fawning over Jeremiah so much it made me feel sick. I can't wait to get away from here, Jessamy. There's so much hypocrisy among other members of the family. There was Rebecca, sweet as honey to her parents' faces and moaning about them behind their backs because they're delaying giving their consent to her and Anne coming to work in your dispensary.'

Knowing that once Louise got a bee in her bonnet about anything she would go on and on, Jessamy said, 'There's no real malice in Rebecca. It's just that she sees coming to London as an adventure and at the moment feels thwarted.'

'She can't keep her eyes off men, you know, and that means trouble. I hope that neither of them *are* allowed to come.'

'I hope they will be,' Jessamy replied quietly. 'Anne is a born nurse and although I know that Rebecca is a flirt she is a worker, too.'

Louise sighed. 'I'm sorry for going on so, but I really do think you are taking on a big responsibility. If Rebecca gets into trouble Uncle Edward and Aunt Grace are sure to blame you and Alistair.'

'Then we'll have to see that she doesn't, won't we?' Then, to change the subject Jessamy asked Louise if she would come to The Montague Acres with her.

Louise stopped and stared at her. 'Is that wise? You do know that Fabian is living there at the moment.'

'Yes. I need to see him, to ask him not to encourage Romaine to go there.'

Louise's expression changed, become softer. 'Are you being honest with yourself, Jessamy? Isn't it because you want to see him again?'

Colour rose to Jessamy's cheeks. 'Yes, I have to admit that I do want to see him, but at the same time I don't want him to get too fond of Romaine, nor she of him. You know what an affectionate child she is.'

'How can he? You'll be returning to London in a few days' time.'

Jessamy bit on her lip. How stupid, it was something she must have known deep down but ignored. She said in a low voice, 'I want to find out if he ever married Caroline. That's natural, isn't it?'

'Yes, I suppose so. I did ask Mr Stannard once but he said he didn't know, that the master never mentioned anything other than estate business in his letters.'

'I can believe it. Fabian can be as close as an oyster when it pleases him. I do know his faults as well as his good points. Shall we go?'

Louise gave a resigned shrug. 'If you must.'

When they neared the house that had once been her home, Jessamy felt a pang. No wonder the child had wandered back to her roots. There were so many things to draw her – the cows, sheep, the pigs, the ducks on the pond...

Jessamy remembered when Fabian had first taken her to see the house. How excited he had been when he showed her the plans he had drawn and talked about the changes he would make in order to create an ideal environment for their married life. Thanks to him, steps and a terrace had been added, and a drive made where sapling limes would slowly become stately trees. Windows had been enlarged and wrought-iron balconies erected outside the first-floor windows.

In spring the garden was awash with bluebells, purple and yellow crocuses, the gold of daffodils. In summer roses rioted over arbours, fountains played on the front lawn. She had lived in luxury. At that moment Jessamy could feel her bare toes digging into the deep sheepskin rug at the side of the tester bed...and yet, she knew she would not exchange that life for the one in London where she and Alistair would work side by side among the poor and the sick.

As they neared the house Mr Stannard came out. He walked towards them and raised his hat. 'Good morning, ladies.' To Jessamy he added, 'It's good to see you again, ma'am.'

Mr Stannard, usually so stiff, so formal, permitted himself a slight smile. When Jessamy asked if Captain Montague was at home he shook his head. 'Not at the moment, ma'am, but he should be back soon. Would you care to come into the house and wait, or perhaps take a look around the grounds? The master has had an alteration made at the back since you left. He calls it "The Retreat".' Jessamy said they would have a walk around and he touched the brim of his hat, said, 'Very good, ma'am,' and left.

When Jessamy and Louise walked round to the back of the house to see the changes that Fabian had made, the first thing Jessamy noticed was some topiary work in a thick hedge. It had been trimmed in the shape of two birds, standing sideways, their beaks touching. The next thing she noticed was that several beds of sprouting greenery, which in the spring would be a riot of colour, were no longer circular, but heart-shaped. Louise then brought her cousin's attention to the change in direction of the stream. Although it still flowed under bridges and tumbled over ledges of stone and splashed into pools, there were small tributaries where loops had been made. There was also a heart-shaped pool, but it was not until Jessamy noticed the love-seat that she said, in a low voice, 'It's a love garden.'

'A what?' Louise queried.

Jessamy pointed out the flowerbeds, the heart-shaped pool, the seat, then concluded, 'The birds are lovebirds, the tributaries loveknots.'

They stood studying the garden then Louise said at last, 'But why did he want to make one here? Why not in Texas, where he can share it with Caroline?'

'Because – ' Jessamy felt choked for a moment then went on, 'I should imagine he gets homesick for England and needs a break, but at the same time wants to feel that Caroline is here with him.'

'Very romantic,' Louise said dryly.

Jessamy gave a shaky laugh. 'Oh, he is, he's very romantic. When we were engaged he used to write the most beautiful letters from abroad. He once said he was sending me a silver star from the star-spangled sky. It was just cardboard, of course, but I thought it beautiful.'

'Well, I wouldn't dwell on all that.' Louise spoke quietly. 'He belongs to the past.'

'Might I ask who belongs to the past?' The deep, familiar voice had Jessamy turning swiftly and her legs went weak as she met her ex-husband's smiling expression. He was as handsome as ever, his skin bronzed, his eyes that devastating blue.

'Fabian – I, we...Mr Stannard told us we might walk around while we were waiting for you. I hope you don't mind.'

'I'm delighted to see you both. Let me offer you refreshments – come to the house.' As they walked away Louise remarked on the excellent topiary work. Fabian agreed but made no further comment. He asked after Romaine and when Jessamy explained the child's fascination for the kittens Fabian said, 'She loves animals. A darling child, I think of her often.'

His expression was rather sombre and when Jessamy asked him about Caroline he said, 'Caroline and I are not married. We've been too busy building up the business.' He then talked about the work involved in breeding horses until they reached the house.

Once inside, he drew armchairs up to a blazing log fire and Jessamy had a sudden feeling of nostalgia. She had come to the house as a bride...

Fabian ordered coffee then asked Jessamy how she and Alistair were progressing with the dispensary. Not wanting to bore him, she told him briefly about what had been done, but that was not enough for Fabian. He wanted to know how many hospital patients they could cater for, what staff they would have, would Alistair be doing operations at Paradise Corner and whether he was planning to have a private practice, too. Jessamy answered the first three questions then added that Alistair was definitely going into private practice when he could find one available in the right district.

Fabian sat back and rubbed his chin. 'A costly business.' He was silent for a moment then leaned forward. 'Jessamy, I should very much like to buy a house and practice for your husband, if he would accept my sponsorship.'

Jessamy's heart began a slow pounding. 'It's a more than generous offer, but this is separate from the dispensary work and I doubt whether he would accept it, even though most of the money he earns will go towards the dispensary.'

Fabian looked thoughtful. 'I think I can find a way around this. I can get other men involved, men who applaud people who devote their lives to the underprivileged. It can be sent anonymously as a donation from several businessmen. Alistair will never know that I am involved.'

'No, but I will.'

'Jessamy.' He spoke gently. 'Would you deny your husband the means of furthering his career? He's achieved so much by sheer hard work. He set his goal towards being a doctor and ends up a surgeon. It's a wonderful achievement and he's to be congratulated. My share would be submitted through a very good friend who would never disclose the deal.' He paused then added, 'And I'm sure that none of us in this room are likely to do so.'

'I certainly won't,' Louise said firmly.

'Nor I.' Although Jessamy felt obligated to Fabian she knew it would be impossible to raise any objection. 'It's a wonderful gesture and I thank you on behalf of both of us. Please do thank the other people who will be involved. Alistair, I know, will be overwhelmed but overjoyed.'

Fabian acknowledged her words with a nod. 'It's good to know that we can contribute to such an excellent cause.' He then turned to Louise. 'And I understand that you are to help in this venture?'

'Now I wonder what little bird gave you that information,' she answered lightly.

'I know everything there is to know about the district and about the Every family. Both are close to my heart. They're a part of my world and I miss them when I'm away.' He looked at Jessamy as he said it and she was surprised at his expression, surprised at the strength of her feelings for him at that moment.

She got up, saying they really must be going. He offered to drive them home, but they both insisted on walking. He strolled to the end of the drive with them, shook hands, holding Jessamy's hand longer than necessary, and said he hoped that when he was in England again it would coincide with another of their visits home. There was a wistful note in his voice that touched Jessamy but when they left and she mentioned it to Louise her cousin was sceptical.

'I can't weigh him up. Is he genuine or just a good actor?'

'I know one thing – he's genuinely fond of children. You could tell when he mentioned Romaine.'

Louise shot her a quick glance. 'I wouldn't be surprised if the birds in the love garden were meant to represent you and Fabian.'

'Of course not! He's expecting to marry Caroline and

have a family.'

'Jessamy, grow up. If Caroline intended to marry him she would have done so before now, as soon as the divorce came through, like you and Alistair. No, I think what she wanted was a partner to put money into the business. Fabian is obviously homesick for England, but he must still love her or he would not go back. At the same time he kept watching you closely, his expression wistful. Was this genuine or was he wanting to enlist your sympathy? He's a very difficult person to understand. All I can say is that Fabian belongs to the past. Alistair and Romy are your future – don't forget it.'

'Of course I won't forget it!' Jessamy snapped. 'I'm not likely to forget all the years of waiting and then go rushing into Fabian's arms if he held them out. What sort of a person do you think I am?'

'Mostly sensible, capable, loving, but now and again, foolhardy when your heart rules your head. Anyone with half an eye would know by the way you were looking at the handsome Captain Montague that you still have feelings for him.'

Jessamy felt suddenly deflated. 'Oh, Louise, I had no idea I was so vulnerable. Seeing him again brought back the early days before I knew anything about Caroline. I was young, I was in love for the first time, really in love. It was all so romantic. Alistair's and my life is built on a much stronger foundation. We have a mutual interest in medicine, in helping the poor, the sick. There is also our shared deep love for Romaine. Don't think I would ever do anything to destroy our marriage.'

'I don't think you would, consciously, but if you take my advice you'll put Fabian at the back of your mind.'

'Yes, Grandmama,' Jessamy said, a smile in her voice.

'Don't jest about it,' Louise warned. 'Also you should watch your jealousy of Kate Keller. Alistair sees her as someone different, someone to admire, but if you taunt him about her you could drive him straight into her arms.'

Jessamy stopped. 'Taunt him, about Kate Keller?'

'When you told me about her your jealousy was very

evident.' Louise raised her shoulders. 'Oh, heavens, here I am preaching to you as if I had had ten husbands and I haven't even had one.'

Jessamy walked on slowly. 'You speak a lot of sense. You are right about Kate Keller *and* about Fabian. I made the excuse to myself that I must see him to ask him not to encourage Romaine to go to the house, yet I must have known deep down that we would be returning soon to London. Now I'll have to think what to say to Alistair about my going to the house. He doesn't even like Fabian's name being mentioned.'

'Simply tell him that we met Mr Stannard, who mentioned there had been some alterations done to the garden and asked if we would like to see them. That is no lie. We accepted the invitation and then Fabian arrived.'

'If he asks about the alterations I can't very well tell him about the love garden, can I?'

Louise clucked her tongue in irritation. 'Oh, really, Jessamy, you're splitting hairs. Take Henrietta's advice – she always says that if the truth is going to hurt someone then twist it a little.'

As it happened, all Alistair asked when told about the meeting was to enquire if the horse-breeding business in Texas was doing well. Then he moved swiftly on to talk about experiments in medicine that he, Chadwick and Mr Blackwell had been discussing.

Jessamy took Romaine to her father's pharmacy the next morning, where her small daughter began to explore, just as she herself had done as a child. One wall was lined with small drawers containing herbs. Each had the abbreviated name in Latin on the front and Romaine pulled out several, sniffed each one in turn and reeled off, 'Tansy, shepherds' purse, sundew, celandine, meadowsweet...' She then looked at Chadwick and asked, 'Is that right, Grandpa?'

'Every one correct, my love. You are doing splendidly. We'll make a pharmacist of you yet.'

She looked up at him, her face beaming. 'Then I can work with you all day, Grandpa.'

Three customers came in one after the other. The new

young apprentice appeared from the back to help attend to them and as Romaine, who treated everyone as her friend, began to chatter to them, Jessamy said she would take her for a walk and call on the way back.

Once outside, Romaine asked if they could go and see the big waterfall. There was nothing that Jessamy liked better than a brisk walk on the moors so she fastened Romaine's scarf and away they went, with the little girl chatting happily about anything that came into her head. This included the kitten that had one black paw and three white ones; a piece of toffee given her by a customer and coloured crayons promised her by Mr Blackwell who, although retired, often popped into the shop to lend a hand.

It was a lovely morning, crisp with a cloudless blue sky and some high rock formations still touched with frost. Jessamy took a deep breath. On mornings like this it was good to be alive. Romaine suddenly let go of her hand and went skipping ahead, startling a bird preening itself which took off in flight and a rabbit which darted into a burrow. Jessamy thought a little sadly that Romaine too would miss this lovely wilderness when they went to London.

There was a fork in the path ahead. Although the one on the left was a longer and rougher route to the main part of the moor Jessamy had taken it for years because the other conjured up an unhappy incident in her life. Romaine, however, was already on this path and her mother, after hesitating for a moment, let her go ahead. It was time she forgot something that had happened so long ago.

There was a curve in the path and when Jessamy rounded it she found Romaine hitching herself on to a stone slab, on which she herself had sat on that dreadful day. Romaine had hardly settled herself when she slid off and went chasing after a hare.

Jessamy stood looking at the stone slab then deliberately sat on it, wanting to overcome her aversion to it.

It was her Cousin Lillian who had caused all her misery...Lillian, so fair and lovely with her ethereal air.

People spoke of her as an angel, but Jessamy had discovered the evil in her from an early age.

That particular day, however, had been the worst, for Lillian had said, venom in her voice, '*You are illegitimate*!'

Jessamy relived the shock she had experienced and the misery that had followed. And even though her Aunt Verity and her grandma Henrietta had done their best to convince her that Lillian was lying, it was some time before Jessamy had accepted it.

Jessamy got up from the stone, knowing that sitting on it would not erase the memory of her evil cousin. It was Lillian who was partly responsible for the break-up of her first marriage by sending her a poison pen letter on her wedding day, saying that Fabian was still seeing his mistress, Caroline.

Romaine called to her that she wanted to go to the waterfall and Jessamy moved away. She had been told that Lillian was apparently living in America – and she hoped with all her heart that she would stay there.

6

Two days later, after a letter from Mr Saunders telling them that the rooms at Paradise Corner were ready to take beds and furniture, Jessamy and Alistair returned to London with Louise and Romaine. During the following days Jessamy felt that she was living in the middle of a hurricane, being swept from Paradise Corner to the Coachman's Cottage and back again.

She worried about Louise, who seemed restless. At home she was surrounded by her family and had the moorland for exercise, but here in the East End she was confined to the cottage, with only the scrubby park nearby. When Louise had brought Romaine to Paradise Corner the child had raced up and down stairs and in and out of rooms, getting in everyone's way. Jessamy had not said anything to Louise, who was supposed to be looking after her as Louise was helping to make up the many beds and was obviously enjoying having something to do. But then Romaine, in her excitement, fell down the four bottom stairs and cut her knee. While they bandaged it Mr Saunders said, 'I have an idea, Mrs MacKay. My daughter Margaret has young children and your little one needs other children to play with. Margaret has a big garden with swings in it.' He smiled. 'And a play castle.'

Romaine's tears immediately stopped and she was off Jessamy's lap begging to go and play in this garden. Jessamy hesitated, explaining to Mr Saunders in a low voice that it would not be fair to give his daughter the responsibility of looking after Romaine, who was liable to go wandering off.

'Oh, she won't go awandering, ma'am, not with so much to interest her.' There was a twinkle in the old man's eyes as he added, 'Especially when my grandson Daniel is there. He's a real disciplinarian. The children all jump to do his bidding.'

Jessamy also smiled. 'But not Romaine, I'm afraid.'

'I can guarantee that within an hour the little one too will be his slave. They all worship him.'

'He sounds quite a character.'

'Oh, he's a character all right. Although he can get children to obey him he's not nasty with it. In fact, he's a very likable young fellow. He's only eleven years old but already he can charm the birds off the trees. He's clever, too – his teacher says he'll go a long way.' Mr Saunders suddenly chuckled. 'Never did I think I would be guilty of praising my own grandson but there, I just wanted to assure you that with my daughter Margaret and Daniel to look after your little one, she'll come to no harm.'

'I'm sure she won't, and thanks, Mr Saunders.'

Romaine went off happily with the old man and Louise said, 'You have quite a gem there. I liked him on sight.'

'I did, too. Well, Cousin – shall we get on with our chores?'

'What's the next job?'

Free of care they were like children again, chatting and giggling as they unpacked china and cutlery, putting it in cupboards and drawers. Alistair, who had been out to a warehouse to order extra chairs for the waiting room, greeted them with a teasing: 'Might I know the reason for all this hilarity?'

'Well,' Jessamy began, and after explaining about Mr Saunders' grandson, she concluded, 'And without responsibility for a while Louise and I felt like children ourselves.'

'Make the most of it then, as I'm planning to open up here in a week or ten days' time. I've just been interviewing two medical students who are keen to work with us to gain experience, especially as I shall be doing operations. I've also been to see my colleague Doctor Willard Stead who's willing to assist me. He's given me a list of nurses to interview. I'll just go and see how Mr Saunders is getting on.'

Jessamy and Louise worked themselves to a standstill

and at six o'clock, after just a snack at midday they were not only ready for a hot meal but to sit back and relax in the cottage. Alistair had gone out, saying he would not be long and when he returned it was with a meal from the High Street stalls. There were baked pototoes, pig's trotters, pease pudding, black pudding and a small ham shank.

The girls squealed with delight. 'A feast for the gods,' Louise declared and Jessamy said, 'And we didn't have to cook it – what bliss! Oh, Alistair, you're a darling, you're so thoughtful.'

'Of course. I'm the best husband in the world.'

'Mmm, sometimes.' He went out laughing.

It was seven o'clock when Mr Saunders returned to the cottage with Romaine and his grandson Daniel, a sturdy boy with golden hair and an innocent-looking expression.

Romaine, from the moment of entering the room, began jabbering away about what a wonderful time she had had and begging to be allowed to go back to Daniel's house the next day. Alistair picked her up and scolded her gently. They had guests – she could tell them about her day later.

Mr Saunders introduced his grandson and Daniel made a slight bow to Jessamy and Louise and to Alistair he said, 'How do you do, sir,' his voice and manner quiet.

When Jessamy asked if Romaine had behaved herself he said, 'Oh, yes, ma'am. She was no trouble at all. She joined in all the games and later when the children were all a little tired she told us stories, very interesting stories that we had never heard before.'

Romaine's gaze on him was full of adoration. Mr Saunders announced, 'Well, we must go. I'm sure Romaine will be ready for bed after such a busy day. I'll call for her again in the morning, if you wish. My daughter and the children loved having her.'

Romaine was saying, 'Oh, please, please,' when Alistair put a finger to her lips, and told her only if she would go to bed now without any protests. She promised and crossed her heart.

It was not until she was settled into bed that Daniel was discussed, with Jessamy saying what an attractive boy he was, how well-spoken and well-mannered. Alistair then told them that his mother Margaret had been lady's maid to a wealthy family before she married, which had Jessamy enquiring how he had come by this information.

'She came to the house one day with a message for her father. He told me afterwards about her work and said how it had enlarged her knowledge of people. She's an attractive woman, beautifully spoken.'

'Well,' declared Jessamy, 'and you never told me.'

Alistair grinned. 'There's a lot more I could tell you if I had the time.' Jessamy picked up a cushion and threw it at him and Alistair, laughing, said he would go and see if Romaine was asleep.

Jessamy sank into a chair and said to Louise, 'She should be after all the games they played but she was over excited and absolutely besotted with Daniel. Did you see the way she looked at him? He has such an innocent expression, I can't imagine him getting the children to obey him.'

'Oh, I can. Do you remember that boy who used to come and stay with his grandparents during the summer when we were young? They lived at Dene Cottage. He was fair, had an angelic face but a will of iron. Can't you remember how we, and every other girl in the vicinity, were moonstruck with him?'

Jessamy chuckled. 'Fancy you remembering him! He hadn't crossed my mind since his grandmother died.'

Louise glanced at her. 'Shall I tell you something? I watched for him every year, praying he would come to visit his sick grandfather and I ached when he didn't.'

Jessamy could not help thinking how much her cousin had suffered in her love life and hoped that Romaine would not suffer for knowing Mr Saunders' grandson. But although she could not have guessed it, fate already had the lives of this boy and girl entangled, bringing adventure, great joy but also sorrow for their future...

The change in Romaine's life began after the next day, when Mr Saunders and his daughter brought her home, with Margaret offering to look after the child every day while they were putting the finishing touches to the dispensary. She was, as Alistair had said, attractive and beautifully spoken. She was also neatly dressed, with a quiet manner. But when she said with a smile that she was being a little selfish, that Romaine had lightened her life, her whole face beamed. 'She's such a vivacious child, with a fund of information and a flair for storytelling. My children too are entranced by her.'

Mr Saunders spoke up then, assuring Jessamy and Alistair that Romaine would not be spoiled. Margaret was strict with her brood. They all sat down and had a talk about making the play-sessions a regular arrangement, with Louise being asked her opinion because, after all, she had come to look after Romaine and loved her like her own child. She said, 'I think it would be good for her to be with other children, if only for a time, and it would allow me to help with the work at Paradise Corner. I really had no idea there was so much to do.'

And so it was agreed that Romaine would play with Margaret's four younger children, two girls and two boys, and be given lessons in the afternoon by a cousin who used to be a teacher until she had to stay at home to look after her invalid mother. Daniel went to a small private school, his grandfather paying for all lessons.

Margaret at first refused any payment, but when Alistair insisted she eventually accepted a small sum each week to cover Romaine's food and expenses.

The following day Alistair received a letter at Paradise Corner from a solicitor, with the offer from five medical men – who wished to remain anonymous – to buy him a practice. Alistair was so astonished that at first he couldn't get beyond trying to guess who these men were. Jessamy said this was not important and when Alistair realised what it would mean he ran upstairs jubilantly to tell Mr Saunders.

Jessamy shook her head and said wryly to Louise, 'I only hope he won't want to start looking right away for a practice, otherwise I shall look for a cave to hide in. I had no idea Fabian would act so fast.'

A letter from Rebecca came by the next post saying her

parents had finally agreed to Anne and her coming to London: Aunt Verity would bring them as soon as Jessamy said it was convenient. Rebecca's excitement was very apparent.

Jessamy had just handed over the letter to Louise to read when Tom Hansard, the student who would be with them first, came to inspect the dispensary. He appeared to be about nineteen, was slender, dark-haired and full of enthusiasm.

Willard Stead called next; Jessamy later described him as tall, not unattractive, with a quiet pleasant manner.

The third person to arrive was the second student, Richard Mather, who said that although he would not be with them for another few weeks, he thought he had better introduce himself. He had nothing in the way of good looks as his hair was unruly, his nose had been broken at one time and he had a wide mouth, but he had dark impressive eyes, great charm and a wonderful smile that gave the impression he was handsome. One minute he would be lively, jesting and the next deadly serious about his work. Jessamy liked all three men and pushed aside the thought that there might be trouble with Rebecca.

Alistair had set a date for opening the dispensary. Although Jessamy was sure that everything would be ready in time, she found that the days were not long enough. On the day that Verity, Rebecca and Anne arrived, nothing could be accomplished. Anne's main interest lay with the medical side, Verity's in the work involved to convert the house and Rebecca's in the fact that the staff included two students and an assistant doctor! As Jessamy led the way to the top floor to show Verity and the girls their rooms, she thought a little grimly that she would have to have a talk with Rebecca about her attitude towards men.

When Verity brought up this subject later Jessamy said, 'I'm hoping that time will shape her, make her a more responsible person. The fact of working with the sick and knowing of their appalling poverty can be a great leveller.'

Verity nodded. 'You could be right. Still, if she doesn't behave you have one potent weapon: threaten to send her home.' After a pause she said, 'Do you still want to become a doctor yourself?'

'Oh, yes, definitely – but not until Romaine is older. I have gained so much knowledge already, for when Alistair was studying I read all his books. I went over his homework with him and we discussed many illnesses and their cures.'

When Louise asked if she had forgotten those years, when she and Alistair had been parted while they waited for her divorce to come up, Jessamy said sombrely, 'No, I'll never forget them.'

They had been years of meeting and making love in secret, knowing if there was the slightest breath of scandal, her divorce would not go through. She said, 'We'll adjust to our new life, Aunt Verity, as we did then. Our love remained constant.'

On the day that her aunt left there seemed to be a never ending series of people calling at Paradise Corner for various reasons. Alistair brought in two nurses he had engaged on a regular basis. One was young, a plain girl who seemed painfully shy, the other older with a no-nonsense attitude. Jessamy wondered how the latter would fare working with the matron whom Alistair had recruited, for she had a similar manner. Alistair showed them around. The nurses left eventually and Jessamy had just sunk back into a chair, thinking she would have five minutes' rest when Alistair popped his head round the door and said, 'Another visitor – and you'll never guess who!' He was all smiles.

He came in with Kate Keller who said, her tone apologetic, 'I do hope I'm not intruding, Mrs MacKay.'

Jessamy jumped up quickly, untying her apron, not really sure of what her feelings were at that moment on seeing the obvious pleasure on her husband's face. 'No, of course not, Miss Keller, it's nice of you to call. Do please sit down and I'll make you a cup of coffee.'

'Thanks, but I've just had one with Mrs Brunt. She said to tell you she'll get round to see you soon at the cottage. She's had relatives staying and what with looking after them and her lodgers, you know how it is.' Kate pulled a face. 'You of all people should know, Mrs MacKay. Alistair was telling me about all your visitors and all the work still to be done. Actually, I came to offer my help.'

'It's most kind of you, but – '

'Don't you dare refuse, Jessamy.' Alistair smiled. 'My wife hates to put on anyone, but to be honest we need all the help we can get. But what about your own work?'

'It's mostly evening engagements – I can manage both. I'm tough.' She flexed her muscles. 'I once moved a ton of coal, you know.' There was an imp of mischief in her eyes and Alistair and Jessamy both laughed. It was impossible not to like this girl. Kate was dressed in brown velvet this morning, with a tip-tilted velvet hat that made her look about sixteen. 'You'll let me help then, Mrs MacKay?'

'Yes, but please call me Jessamy.'

'I will, if you both stop calling me Miss Keller.' It was agreed, and after that they were chatting away like old friends.

Rebecca and Anne, who had been out to explore the district, came back into the dispensary, their cheeks red from the icy wind. Once Rebecca knew that Kate was a singer, actress and dancer she was all excitement, pestering to know if it was easy to get work as an actress. When Alistair said grimly that Rebecca could forget all about wanting to go on the stage, Kate said gently that it would be wise to let Rebecca know the realities of stage life. She proceeded to explain patiently all the work and upsets it involved.

Anne had passed no remark while Kate and her sister were talking but when Rebecca clasped her hands and declared she would bear any hardships if she could only be an actress, her sister said sharply, 'If you say one more word on the subject I'll see you go back home. We were allowed to come here for the sole purpose of helping Alistair and Jessamy with the dispensary.'

'I know, but I can surely discuss the stage, can't I?'

'Not in my hearing. Talking about an idea or an ambition leads to trying to carry it out.'

When Rebecca told her she was being stupid, Kate said quietly, 'Your sister speaks a lot of commonsense, Rebecca – take note of her. You might think you'll be working hard here, but believe me, it will be heaven to what you would have to put up with, doing stagework. If you're out of work you almost starve, if you're in work and doing well you have to put up with the jealousy of people who will try to stab you in the back by telling the manager dreadful tales about you – and because they are actors and actresses, it will sound true. You'll have male actors mauling you, unless you're strong enough to hold them at bay, and if you're working away and don't have regular lodgings you'll put up with fleas and bedbugs.'

'Oh, stop it!' Rebecca wailed. 'All right, you win.' The next moment she was saying, 'I'll dedicate myself to learning to be a nurse, then I can fall in love with a handsome doctor and live happily ever after.'

'Don't count on it,' Kate warned her again. 'A dedicated doctor does not make a perfect husband.'

'Thank you *very* much,' said Alistair, with an amused smile.

Kate eyed him with dismay. 'I had forgotten for a moment you were there.' She turned to Jessamy. 'I was generalising, of course. Your husband speaks so highly of you I positively drool with envy. It's true,' she insisted when Jessamy just sat smiling. 'Every time he's spoken to me about you pearls of beauty drop from his lips.' She began to laugh then they were all laughing.

It was not until Alistair had taken Kate to look around the newly-restored premises that Jessamy began to wonder when her husband and Kate had met to do so much talking. She had not reached any conclusion when they returned and presented her with another problem: Kate had offered to take charge of a soup kitchen.

Alistair was full of it. 'It's so generous of Kate, with all her other work to do and organising the sewing parties. She says she'll have no difficulty in finding additional volunteers.'

'None at all,' declared Kate. 'There are plenty of bored young girls left to recruit from wealthy families.'

'It's very kind of you,' Jessamy said, 'but it would take an awful lot of your time. Soup would have to be served early morning and at midday.'

Rebecca, with great eagerness, immediately offered to help and it took Jessamy all her time to keep her temper under control. When a dispensary had first been mooted only she and Alistair had been involved: all the planning had come from them. She had pictured them running the soup kitchen together, but now there were so many other people becoming a part of the venture she felt she was being pushed out. It was one thing to like Kate Keller, but quite another when she and Alistair had just about settled the running of a soup kitchen without even consulting her. She said, 'A hall would have to be found before any plans could be made.'

'Kate suggests renovating one of the derelict buildings in Paradise Street or Paradise Road. There are certainly plenty to choose from.'

Kate told Jessamy the choice must be hers, as she knew what would be required, and this mollified Jessamy somewhat.

Before Kate left, Jessamy arranged with her to look at properties the next morning. When Alistair suggested accompanying them, Jessamy said, 'You have enough to do, Doctor MacKay – and anyway, cooking is woman's business.'

Jessamy enjoyed herself the following morning. She had intended to ask Louise to come with them, but her cousin had received a letter from Flynn to say he would be arriving that morning by train, and asking Louise to meet him.

Some of the derelict buildings had once been small warehouses. A few were beyond renovation but they eventually found a vacant hall, its walls strong and only parts of the roof in need of repair. When Jessamy asked Mr Saunders where she should apply to rent it he gave her his lovely warm smile and said, 'I own it. I'll have it repaired and there won't be any rent to pay. It's for a very good cause.' Jessamy said she could not thank him enough and he told her that his thanks would be in seeing the poor having something hot in their bellies on cold winter days.

Kate stayed on at Paradise Corner to help, and Rebecca and Anne worked hard too, Rebecca never far from Kate's side, asking questions when Anne was out of sight. Kate left at six o'clock as she was doing her act at a private house later, but promised to come the next day to lend a hand.

During the afternoon a note had been delivered from Louise saying that Flynn wanted to look for rooms, but they would be back about half-past six. She added that they were not to cook a meal – she and Flynn would bring some food back with them.

At six o'clock when Jessamy, Alistair and the girls returned to the Coachman's Cottage, Jessamy collapsed into a chair, feeling grateful she did not have a meal to cook. She even wondered how she would find the energy to talk when Louise and Flynn came home, but Flynn's arrival was like a tonic. He was carrying a huge hamper which he lugged into the kitchen before greeting them. Then he was all smiles. 'Alistair, you look splendid. Jessamy, you're more beautiful than ever!' He turned to the girls and shook hands with each of them. 'This must be Anne and this Rebecca. How are you? We came in a van, so the food will still be warm.'

Louise laughed. 'In other words, we all have to jump to it!'

'No, no,' Flynn protested. 'Just tell me where everything is and I shall lay the table.' Rebecca said eagerly that she would help and brought out a tablecloth while Anne fetched cutlery and Louise the plates.

Jessamy had expected a meal bought at the market but instead there was chicken, slices of roast pork and beef and dishes of vegetables and roast potatoes.

'Heavens!' she exclaimed. 'Where did all this come from?'

Flynn grinned. 'It's a long story.'

While they tucked in he told them that he had managed to rent a flat above a shop next to this restaurant, where the chef turned out to be the brother of a friend of his, and well...

He kept them entertained and he was so full of humour, so warm and so friendly that Jessamy wondered how Louise had resisted his pleas to marry him over the years. Rebecca hardly took her gaze from him. Her admiration might have flattered any other man but Flynn only had eyes for Louise.

He had just finished telling them about a deal he had made when he suddenly looked around him. 'Hey, where's my gorgeous Romy?' Jessamy explained she was staying overnight with friends and he would see her the next morning. 'Good,' he said, 'I've brought her a doll.'

Alistair chuckled. 'It's a good job she isn't here. She would never have gone to sleep tonight.'

Jessamy was pleased to notice that Alistair was relaxed. He had been tense all day, wanting everything to be ready for Monday when the dispensary was due to open. She had half-expected him to want to go back to the house to work, but he stayed at home until ten o'clock, when he said he would walk the girls over to Paradise Corner. Flynn told him to hurry back and they would have a bedtime drink. Jessamy was pleased about this because Rebecca's adoring gaze on Flynn during the evening had become an embarrassment. If he had been staying in the house, heaven only knows what might have happened.

After Alistair and the girls had gone Flynn teased Jessamy, telling her she would have to watch Rebecca if she didn't want to lose her husband; the girl had never taken her eyes off him.

Louise said wryly, 'It wasn't Alistair she had her eye on, it was you.' When Jessamy nodded Flynn looked from one to the other then became serious.

'If it was both of us then you'll have trouble with that one.' Jessamy told him she would cope and left it at that.

They chatted until Alistair returned. He would have

poured them all a drink but Louise told him she was ready for bed and Jessamy said that she, too, could hardly keep her eyes open. She thanked Flynn for the evening.

'It was lovely, Flynn. You're a marvellous storyteller and we haven't had much to laugh about lately. We'll see you tomorrow.'

'You will – and I promise you won't find me here talking when you get up in the morning.' He gave her a hug, kissed Louise and warned them about chattering until the early hours.

Louise stifled a yawn. 'I hardly have the strength to climb the stairs.'

Flynn shooed them out. 'Off you go the pair of you, sleep well.'

On the way upstairs Louise said in a low voice, 'I'm worried about Rebecca. I think she could be a nymphomaniac.'

'A what?'

Louise repeated the word then explained it meant a female with strong sexual urges. Jessamy said, 'Aren't we all?' then they were stifling giggles.

As it turned out, there was no chance of Jessamy's having a private talk with Rebecca. A final check-up was run through of the stock and Alistair spoke to the staff about records being kept of each patient – strictly kept, he stressed. Later he called them together again and talked generalities with even Rebecca paying rapt attention.

'The people you'll be dealing with will be poorly clad. Many of them will be unwashed, too, but they're human beings and I want them to be treated as such, with respect. Some will never have known any other life but poverty, near-starvation and ill-treatment. Remember this, if any of us here had been born under different circumstances, we might be in the same position as the people we will be tending.' He discussed hygiene and how important it was to the well-being of the patients. Alistair was inclined to go on about certain things and hygiene was one of them. Jessamy, happening to glance at Rebecca, saw that her gaze was fixed adoringly on Richard Mather. When the talk ended she took her young cousin aside and issued an ultimatum; either she stopped concentrating on men, or she would be sent back to St Peel.

Rebecca looked at her with wide-eyed innocence. 'But I don't realise I'm staring at them! I like men, but I wouldn't do any wrong, I promise you that, and I certainly do not want to go back home.'

Jessamy left it at that but felt suddenly worried when she recalled that Romaine wore the same innocent look as Rebecca when she was denying a misdemeanour. She had a sudden unbearable longing to see her small daughter, to feel the plump little arms about her neck. She put on her hat and coat and had just told Louise where she was going when Alistair said quietly from behind her, 'I know how you feel, Jessamy, I ache to see Romy too, but it would be foolish at this stage. She's settled temporarily with Margaret and the family and we are opening the dispensary in the morning. She'll be back home to sleep in a few days' time.'

Jessamy saw the sense of this and reluctantly took off her hat and coat. If Romaine had insisted on coming home with her it could have been chaotic. Opening the dispensary was no occasion for an excited child.

By Sunday evening everyone was restless, not knowing what lay ahead. Louise fretted, 'There might not even be one patient turn up.'

Alistair answered this with a wry smile. 'Or we might find ourselves having to cope with a hundred.'

'Heaven forbid,' declared Anne.

Jessamy and Louise came back to the cottage at half-past nine, leaving Flynn and Alistair still talking at the house. Louise said, 'I hope they don't stay there chatting all night.'

'I doubt it. I told Alistair I would wait up for him, no matter what time it was.'

Louise yawned then said she would bid her goodnight and be off to bed.

Jessamy sat back in the chair and closed her eyes. It was a treat to relax for a while. Tomorrow, the official opening of the dispensary at Paradise Corner, would be a testing day – the first day of their new life.

7

Jessamy had been semi-dozing when a draught of icy air roused her. Thinking it would be Alistair arriving she got up and had called his name when she became aware of a presence in the room. She stood, her body rigid, as she remembered her first day at the cottage and feeling the icy draught...remembered Alistair saying there was something about the cottage he didn't like, but was unable to pinpoint it. She knew that whoever was in the room was behind her. Fear paralysed her for a moment then, knowing she must face the presence or leave the cottage, she turned slowly. At first there was nothing to see and her heart, that had been pounding, began to steady. Perhaps she had been dreaming and had imagined the draught. Then the flame of the lamp flickered and went low and a faint mist appeared in the corner of the room. In it Jessamy could see the outline of a woman. The figure began to develop until she made out a young girl in a hooded cape, the hood thrown back showing dark hair in plaited coils about her head. The features became clear and there was such a desolation in the eyes that Jessamy lost all fear and felt only sympathy.

'Who are you?' she asked in a low voice. The girl put a hand on her thigh, moved it slowly down her leg then held out her hands, the gesture one of pleading.

The flame of the oil-lamp came back to normal and with it girl and mist faded. Jessamy sank into a chair. Who was she and what were her needs? Why the pleading? Did Mr Saunders know about her? Surely not. Romaine could have seen her and been terrified. Jessamy suddenly tensed: someone was coming down the stairs. The door opened and Louise came limping in.

'Oh, Jessamy, I'm in such agony. A pain started here.' She put her hand on her right thigh then moved it down her leg. A coldness touched Jessamy's spine – it was just as the girl had shown. 'I could hardly get out of bed,' Louise went on. 'Would you give me a rub?'

Jessamy swallowed hard. 'Come over to the fire.' She helped her cousin to remove her dressing gown then lifted the nightdress and asked Louise to hold it. 'It sounds like sciatica.' She started at the back and moved her hand slowly over the thigh, trying to find the area of pain.

Louise gave a sigh. 'That's soothing...you have a lovely warmth in your hand. Aunt Catherine said you had the power of healing and so did that gypsy woman on the quayside at Newcastle, do you remember? We paid a penny for the parrot to tell our fortune.'

Jessamy did remember. She drew her hand away, afraid of possessing this power. There was something well, uncanny about it, like seeing the ghost of the girl.

'Will you massage me a little more, Jessamy?' There was a pleading note in Louise's voice. 'I'm sure the pain has eased a little.'

Jessamy protested that it was impossible for the pain of sciatica to ease in that short time, but Louise insisted and so Jessamy gave in, but asked that no mention of healing powers should be made to Alistair. After a few minutes she straightened. 'Well?'

'It's miraculous. My skin is warm, even hot in places, and the pain is almost gone. Why don't you want Alistair to know? Think of all the good you could do, in the dispensary alone.'

Jessamy told her then about the ghost and Louise was wide-eyed as she listened. 'But don't you see, Jessamy, it wasn't coincidence that the girl appeared as I had my pain. There was a purpose in it – a divine purpose to stress to you that you do have the power of healing in your hands. Should you waste this God-given power? I'm not suggesting that you treat Alistair's private patients for money, but think of all the poor people in pain – the cramps that I had were agonising.'

Jessamy gave her reason for not using her power, if indeed she did have it: news of it would inevitably spread and there would be people flocking from all over; the wealthy as well as the poor. She would never know a home life as such.

'Will you now?' Louise asked quietly. 'You have to be dedicated to one thing or another. You wanted to start a dispensary, you still want to be a doctor. Something has to be sacrificed.'

Jessamy wanted to say that she could manage both, but knew deep down that she would have to make a choice. She said, 'Louise, I can't think clearly any more tonight. Seeing the girl upset me. I'll have a word with Mr Saunders tomorrow if I get the chance and find out if he can shed any light on her appearance. I must go to bed now.' As the grandfather clock began to chime the hour of midnight she added, 'I do think it's too bad of Alistair to stay over at the house talking when I told him I would wait up for him here.'

'That's men,' Louise answered wryly. 'Haven't you learned that they consider themselves to be the only important creatures on this earth?' She stifled a yawn. 'Let's go up. We have a busy day ahead of us tomorrow.'

Before they parted Louise, who was not a demonstrative person, put her hand on Jessamy's shoulder and said softly, 'I've had too much to say. Do as you think best, Jessamy. After all, we do have only one life. Why should we make sacrifices for people who probably won't appreciate it anyway.' Then she added with a sudden grin, 'But thanks anyway for getting rid of my pain!'

The next morning Jessamy awoke at half-past seven and realising that Alistair had not been to bed she got up and dressed. She cleared the ashes from the grate, laid the fire, lit it then went up to tell Louise she was going to Paradise Corner and to follow on when she felt like it. Louise said she felt completely better and would get up right away.

It was the kind of damp morning that penetrated the bones, with fog hovering in patches. It was thicker when Jessamy reached the end of the street and when she turned the corner she could see vague outlines of figures. Then she stopped, realising they were huddled groups of people waiting for the dispensary to open. Heavens – it was just after eight and the dispensary was not due to open until nine. She walked on slowly, aware now of outbursts of coughing and that some women had young children at their side or held young babies. When Jessamy drew closer she saw that there must be thirty or more people waiting, as many men as women. The women wore shawls, the men shabby suits with mufflers at their necks. A man with a hollow-sounding cough greeted Jessamy with, 'Mornin', ma'am. A nasty one, ain't it?'

'Yes, it is.' She felt embarrassed that she would be going into the warmth. 'I'll see if it's convenient to open a little earlier, as I know they were working till late last night. My husband didn't even go to bed.' Jessamy felt more embarrassed than ever. Why should she be making excuses? They knew the dispensary was not supposed to open until nine o'clock. More people were arriving as she went to open the door. Warm air met her as she stepped inside and there was a hum of activity. Tom Hansard, looking professional in his white coat, hailed her. 'The Doctor's in the waiting room, Mrs MacKay. He's been up all night. Have you seen the crowd outside? Isn't it encouraging?'

Jessamy said yes and excused herself. She would ask her husband if they could open earlier.

Alistair, who was sitting at the table in the waiting room with a pile of papers in front of him looked up. 'Jessamy, sorry about last night. I catnapped here in a chair.'

'The people outside, Alistair – they must be frozen. Can we open earlier?'

'No, because if we did they would expect us to open early every morning.' Alistair picked up a piece of paper, turned it over then laid it on a growing pile.

'You're all right sitting here – look at that blazing fire.' Her voice rose. 'There are small children out there, babies in arms, people who might not even have had a hot drink before coming out or a bite to eat. Where is all that wonderful feeling you had for the downtrodden and the sick?'

Alistair momentarily closed his eyes. 'Jessamy, there has

to be discipline, yes, even with the poor and sick. I know they're cold but I've been going over all the accounts last night, seeing if it was feasible to start our soup kitchen sooner than planned. I thought we could open the hall early, give the patients something hot to drink and that way they would be sitting in the warmth waiting for the dispensary to open.'

Jessamy, feeling deflated, sank on to a chair. 'I'm sorry, Alistair. I was worried last night when you didn't come home. I imagined you and Flynn sitting chatting instead of getting some sleep.' She got up. 'Can I get Cook to give those waiting a mug of tea or cocoa? There are people out there with graveyard coughs.'

Alistair gave a brief smile. 'You have a way of expressing yourself that makes me feel ashamed I'm sitting here in the warmth. Graveyard coughs, indeed! Yes, see Cook about giving them a hot drink then tell the patients to come in.'

'Thanks, Alistair.' Jessamy was away.

To her relief the cook agreed at once. 'The poor souls, I was just thinking they'd be frozen stiff out there. We've plenty of boiling water. Here's Betsy, she'll get the mugs out.' The little kitchen maid, who was pin-thin, was bringing the enamel mugs from the shelf at great speed.

Jessamy went to the front door to call the people in. There was no rush; one followed another in an orderly fashion and in silence. Even the children were quiet. Alistair asked them to sit down, explained that they would be given a hot drink then told them how the staff at Paradise Corner were hoping to open a soup kitchen soon. He added that in future they could come into the waiting room at half-past eight, but that the dispensary would not open until nine.

There was no reaction, no show of pleasure and Jessamy ached for the hopelessness of their lives. Rebecca, Anne and Betsy served the mugs of cocoa. One woman started to cough and before long it seemed that every patient was coughing.

Although all the work had been completed on the Saturday, one of the cleaners popped in now to see if there was anything further needed. She helped to take round the cocoa, chatting to some of the women. 'Hello there, Nell, 'ow's the stomach – 'aven't got rid of them pains, then? Why, Janey, didn't see yer. Brought the little 'un, 'ave yer. 'E's all skin and bone, bless 'im. Doc'll soon put 'im right. Eh, Maggie, didn't expect to see you 'ere – not carrying again, are yer? Or is it that yer've 'ad too much to eat?' A raucous laugh accompanied this last remark then, 'Just my little joke, gal.'

A baby began to cry, then another to wail, which set off some of the older children. Mothers scolded, threatening smacks should they not shut up, and this was where Rebecca, surprisingly, came into her own. She took one child from its mother's arms and talked softly to it. The child gave a hiccuping sob and was quiet. She talked to other children and gave them a piece each from biscuits she had in her pocket. Men began to eye Rebecca with interest, not all of them young. She did look lovely in a light blue cotton overall, her dark hair fastened back with a matching blue ribbon.

The two nurses came in, having been sent down by Matron to find out what all the activity was about. Jessamy was explaining the position when Louise arrived. The nurses were in uniform – the younger one, Elizabeth Hope, in a dark green dress, white apron and a triangle of linen covering her hair, and the no-nonsense Hannah Fanshaw in a grey dress. Both benefited by wearing uniform. Hannah gave a sniff and said the Doctor should have informed Matron at least of the change. Jessamy, who had disliked the nurse on sight, snapped, 'There's no change as far as you two and Matron are concerned. The dispensary will be open at nine o'clock as arranged, but I shall pass on your complaint.'

'Oh no, ma'am, there is no need. Is there anything we can do at the moment to help?' asked the nurse, hurriedly.

'Yes. Will you carry the empty mugs into the kitchen?' When Hannah hesitated, Jessamy pointed out that others were helping and added, 'Most willingly.'

Louise, watching the two nurses move away, grinned. 'I can't stand that Fanshaw woman, either. I feel she's the type who will try and drop the poison, make snide remarks about other members of staff. Still, I could be wronging her. Now, is there anything that I can be doing?'

'I'm sure there will be when we get under way. For the present go and have some breakfast. I know you won't have had any and fainting staff won't be any use.'

'Faint? You must be jesting. See you later.'

At nine on the dot Alistair called in the first patient. An elderly woman was urged by others to go up. She had been there first.

Jessamy sat on Alistair's left to take down the name and address of patients and Dr Willard Stead sat on his right. The woman's husband who came with her did all the talking. He said his wife had had a pain in her right side for some time and she had been sick. Alistair asked more questions, then after saying something in a low voice to Willard Stead, requested the man to take his wife to the next room where Dr Stead would examine her. He then motioned to Hannah Fanshaw to go with them.

Jessamy, who wanted to take notes for her own satisfaction, wrote in her own little book, 'Appendix?' then filed the woman's record that Alistair handed to her.

The next patient was a man with bronchial trouble. After examining him, Alistair said he would give him some medicine and if he would wait a few minutes, he would make it up for him.

A girl who came to the table carrying a baby whispered to Alistair's questioning that she was twelve years old and the mother of the child. The baby whimpered piteously. The girl said she lived with an aunt. The baby had had a fit and the aunt, who was on her way out to work, told her niece to put the child in a warm bath. She lowered her head and when she said no more Alistair prompted quietly, 'And?'

The girl began to cry. 'I don't know nothing about babies, sir. I put the little tin bath on the fire to get warm but it was hotter than I thought because it burned her bottom.'

Jessamy and Alistair exchanged quick glances then Alistair said, his voice gentle, 'Do you mean there was no water in the bath?'

'No, sir. You see, I didn't know nothing about babies. Me aunt told me I'd get locked up for cruelty, but I wouldn't 'urt a 'air of her 'ead, I reely wouldn't. I love 'er. Me cousin told me to come to you.'

'You did right.' Willard Stead was back. Alistair asked him to take over then told the girl to bring the baby into the back room, leaving Jessamy full of pity yet horrified at such appalling ignorance.

This was not the only case of ignorance they dealt with that morning. Another child, of six years old, who had fallen on a spade and cut her leg had been made to walk two miles for three mornings to take food to her grandmother who was ill. The leg had been bound with a piece of soiled rag and when it was removed the wound was suppurating. Her father brought her in. He had been working away and knew nothing about the accident until he got home. Alistair cleaned and dressed her leg. There was also a man with a carbuncle on the back of his neck, whose wife had kept stabbing at it with a needle to burst it before it was ripe to be lanced; the carbuncle had festered. When Alistair asked the man if his wife had sterilised the needle he said he didn't know nothing about that, it was one his neighbour used to stitch the horse's harness. At this Jessamy winced.

It seemed to her that morning that as one group of patients left, another arrived to take its place. The complaints were numerous. There were those with rheumatism and others with arthritis, whose hands were misshapen and who shuffled along with the aid of sticks. Women worn out with childbearing hoped for a miracle medicine to rejuvenate them, along with others who were worn out from doing factory work and trying to keep a home going at the same time. One woman said all she needed was a pick-me-up and when Alistair recommended rest she gave a short derisive laugh. 'Rest? I don't know the meaning of it! I have a consumptive husband, three children with rickets, one who's not right in the head and another who's nearly two and hasn't yet started to walk. My mother copes with them while I'm at work, but leaves when I come home. No, Doctor, rest is a stranger to me.'

The woman was well-spoken and Jessamy found herself wondering about her earlier background. Many of the men suffered from backache and some were nearly bent double; in almost every case the trouble stemmed from the job they had been doing when they were younger. 'Crippled me, it did,' said one. 'I were carrying loads ten times me own weight.'

What really impressed Jessamy about Alistair on that first Monday was not only his gentleness but the way he instilled hope into every one of his patients – even in the two women that he knew had a terminal illness.

They had intended to close at one o'clock but that first day, with the staff 's consent, they worked until three, with each member taking it in turns to have a sandwich and a hot drink.

Afterwards Alistair called them together and thanked them for their dedication. 'You've all done splendidly. We will in future make a point of closing at one as there's a great deal of work to be got through after we close to the public. There are also operations to be dealt with – some of these will have to be done in the evening. Are there any questions?'

Rebecca's hand shot up. 'Many women who were ill were harassed by having to bring some of their children with them. Do you think it would be possible to set aside a room where they could play while the mothers were being attended to? I would be willing to help.'

'It's a good question, Rebecca, and it was something that had occurred to me. We will discuss this.'

Jessamy had noted several times how good Rebecca was with the children and how her sister Anne, although having a great deal of medical knowledge, seemed to lack sympathy with the patients. As if on cue, Anne asked now if some of the men were not shamming to get out of doing any work.

Alistair shook his head. 'There are the work-shy but I can assure you that every person dealt with today was genuine.'

Hannah Fanshaw said briskly that she objected to all and sundry taking part in this discussion. Matters such as these should be left to the two doctors and qualified staff.

Alistair pointed out that this was a charitable organisation where, although experienced staff had to be employed, other people were giving their services free and had a right to be included in any discussion. Matron, who had been standing at the back, said she agreed, which surprised most people except Jessamy, who had come to realise that although Matron had her own ideas about many things the welfare of her patients was close to her heart.

Alistair said that on that note, they would close the meeting for today. There would be other discussions.

As they all began to disperse, Jessamy overheard Hannah Fanshaw mutter to Willard Stead, 'It's quite ridiculous treating such as you and me in this way. Any doctor, much less a surgeon, who is friendly with his patients and sundry members of the staff is doomed to failure.'

To this Willard replied, 'I prophesy that in time Doctor MacKay will become one of the big names in his field. My faith in him is echoed by people who are already well-known themselves. If you will excuse me, Nurse.'

The tight-lipped Hannah hurried away, with Jessamy silently applauding Dr Stead; at the same time she noted that he had earned himself an enemy – a rather vicious-tongued one – and this was something one ought not to encounter where sickness was concerned.

Louise had gone back to the cottage to get changed ready for Flynn, and although Alistair and Jessamy had promised to follow in half an hour, they were still at Paradise Corner at seven o'clock that evening, going over the patients' notes with Willard Stead when Kate Keller called.

Alistair, who had looked jaded, suddenly perked up. 'Kate, you're like a breath of fresh air.' He introduced her to Willard Stead as their favourite actress and the doctor gave her a bow and told her he was honoured to meet her. Kate laughed and said she was flattered to be welcomed by such exalted company.

She then said, 'I wanted to come earlier as I was anxious to know how everything had gone but felt I couldn't intrude.'

Alistair assured her she would never intrude then gave her a brief outline of their day. 'Heavens,' she said, 'I had no idea there would be so many patients.'

Jessamy nodded. 'And likely to be more. Louise came this morning saying she didn't really know what she could do to help and she was on the go the whole time. We all were.'

A voice called, 'Who is taking my name in vain?' It was Louise who had come in the back way with Flynn.

After Flynn had been introduced he said, 'Look, I'm sure you want to get away from medical matters and I know a nice little restaurant. Let us celebrate – be my guests.'

Alistair and Willard insisted they would share the expense. Then Jessamy exclaimed, 'What about Rebecca and Anne, and the rest of the staff? Have they eaten? Heavens, I'm not a bit organised.'

Louise scolded her and told her to stop worrying. Of course they had eaten – Cook had made a meal for them. Then she added, 'Incidentally, Tom Hansard has taken Rebecca, Anne and Elizabeth Hope out for a walk.'

Alistair grinned. 'You are a veritable mine of information.'

Jessamy said, 'Oh, I hope they'll be all right.'

Flynn, his eyes twinkling, laid a hand on Jessamy's arm. 'The girls will be, but what about Tom? I mean to say, three to one!' He got up. 'Shall we go?'

It was a strange evening, with Jessamy aware of undercurrents. They sat at a round table in the restaurant, with Kate between Willard and Alistair, she next to her husband with Flynn on her other side and Louise beside Flynn and linking up with Willard.

Kate, as usual, sparkled and at first Jessamy was aware

that the gaze of all the men was concentrated on her. Later she saw that Louise kept glancing at Willard and after a while they became deep in conversation, which did not please Flynn. Then Willard turned back to talk to Kate, which seemed to annoy Alistair. Flynn began to tell Jessamy about how he had once trained a little Irish terrier to jump through a hoop and his description was so droll she began to laugh. She caught Alistair glaring at her then Kate turned to him and his manner immediately changed and was all smiles.

Jessamy decided afterwards that the best part of the evening had been the food, which she had enjoyed despite the underlying tensions.

Willard offered to see Kate home, but she insisted there was no need. Once outside the restaurant, she hailed a cab, said a quick goodnight, promised to call the next day and with a wave was away.

'An extraordinary woman,' Willard said. 'Quite fascinating.'

'Yes,' said Alistair stiffly. 'So vivacious.'

'And natural with it,' declared Flynn.

'It was a lovely meal,' said Louise brightly, giving Jessamy a nudge.

'Oh, it was,' Jessamy echoed.

When they arrived home Alistair said he would just walk round to Paradise Corner and check that everything was all right. He smiled and touched Jessamy gently on the cheek. 'I'll be back soon and that is a promise.'

Jessamy wished that the affectionate gesture had not been his way of apologising for paying so much attention to Kate.

Flynn gave Louise a wave. 'See you tomorrow, darlin'. Sweet dreams!'

The girls watched the men walking away then Louise retorted, 'Sweet dreams my foot!' They went into the cottage. 'I've seen a man look at a woman in a besotted way, but not three at the same table. I don't blame Kate, though. She happens to be naturally vivacious.'

Jessamy said, 'I think Flynn was jealous of the way you

and our Doctor were having such an intimate talk.'

'An intimate talk? We were discussing the future of the dispensary.' Louise paused then mused, 'Do you really think he was jealous?'

'Yes, and I don't think he'll wait forever for you to agree to marriage.'

'Mmm, I'll have to think about that. Do you know, Jessamy, I think we both have problems with our men. You'll have to watch Alistair with Kate.'

'I know, but he knows I know. I'm not going to force the issue: I don't think Kate would do anything to hurt us.'

'Don't forget the strength of sexual attraction between male and female.'

'I think the bonds of true love are stronger.'

'And I think you could be deluding yourself,' Louise said quietly. 'Good night, Jessamy. Give me a call in the morning.'

Jessamy, who felt suddenly afraid that she could lose her husband and also afraid that the ghostly apparition of the girl might reappear, followed her cousin upstairs, but bed was no protection from her fears. She was plagued by the thought that the girl might in some way have have been trying to warn her about Alistair and Kate. If only she had had a chance to talk to Mr Saunders, find out if he knew of any history about the ghost girl, but they had been so busy.

Tomorrow she *must* make an opportunity to speak to him...

8

Kate Keller's eyes misted with tears as she sat in the cab on the way home. She was a fool to have come tonight; a fool to have gone to the house on Paradise Corner. She had tried so hard to stay away – but if she did not see Alistair, there would be no point in living. She had known numerous men in her life; many had told her they loved her and she had thought herself to be in love several times. In adolescence, she had sworn undying love to one boy yet had realised how flawed her declaration was, when the boy left town to go to college and she had flitted lightly from one new boy to another.

It was only now that she knew she had never experienced the love of which poets wrote, that other women talked about – the deep love where the man would be her entire world, when she would sacrifice her career to be with him. Over and over again she had been told that she could easily get work in the West End theatres. She had thought about it for a future time, but now it had lost its appeal. All she wanted was to be near Alistair, to help him with his work...and knew, with a feeling of despair, that real love meant making unselfish decisions, such as going out of his life. He and Jessamy were deeply in love, no one could doubt that. Jessamy had made sacrifices – she had waited nearly five years for him to complete his studies.

Kate pulled a handkerchief from her pocket and wiped her eyes, her mind made up. She must prove her love for Alistair and try to stop seeing him. It would help when she started the soup kitchen. But even as she thought it, tears rose once more. She *had* to see him. He wanted to see her, she knew by the look in his eyes. They could be friends – after all, she had remained friends with men who had once said they loved her. Two big tears welled up and ran slowly down her cheeks. Friends? When what she wanted was to be in his arms, to feel his lips on hers...Kate dashed the tears away. No, she must be firm. Tomorrow she would discuss the soup kitchen with Alistair. Once it was opened she would have plenty to occupy her, to stop her from thinking about him.

Meanwhile, in Paradise Corner, Alistair brooded alone, wondering how he could overcome this feeling he had for Kate Keller. He had admired several women in the past apart from Jessamy, had been aroused sexually when thinking about them, but never had he felt what he did for Kate. It had become almost obsessional with him. Tonight, in the presence of his wife, he had actually displayed jealousy when Flynn had laughed and joked with Kate. How could he have behaved so badly? He had seen the hurt in Jessamy's eyes and had hated himself. The last person in the world he wanted to hurt was Jessamy; she had already suffered so much because of his stupidity in making her pregnant when she was still married to Fabian Montague. He *must* stop seeing Kate...but if he did so, would it make any real difference? When he was making love to Jessamy these days, Kate would come unbidden into his thoughts, even though Jessamy was always so loving and could match his passion when he was in one of his wilder moods. Never once had she refused his advances. She was not like some wives, who apparently would make any excuse to avoid sex...they felt unwell, they had a headache.

With a deep sigh, Alistair got to his feet. Last night he had stayed up late, tormented by thoughts of Kate but tonight, he had promised Jessamy he would not be long. He could only pray she was in bed and already asleep, not only because his eyes felt weighted through lack of rest but because if she happened to be in a loving mood he would feel a cheat if he tried to respond.

Upstairs, in the staff bedrooms, Rebecca lay wide awake, full of resentment towards the poker-faced nurse Hannah Fanshaw, who had walked unexpectedly into her room when she and Tom had been laughing and talking in there. She had actually accused them of doing forbidden things!

Tom had gone red in the face and seemed unable to refute this accusation. Rebecca had done all the talking, controlling her temper to point out that she was sitting at one side of the room and Tom the other. This had made no difference to the miserable woman, who called her a 'man-mad menace' and said that if she had her way, Rebecca would not be working in her hospital at all. With that she had swept out, slamming the door behind her.

Rebecca recalled how she had repeated '*Her* hospital!' with indignation, and how Tom had begun to laugh. 'Oh, Rebecca, if you could have seen your face. It was a study in fury. I always feel floored by that type of woman. She had been diminished by Doctor Stead at the meeting so had to take it out on someone.'

'And I became the target – I'll be the one to get into trouble. Oh, Tom, I hope I won't be sent home.'

'You won't. Mrs MacKay said you were a good worker and that you were splendid with the children.'

Rebecca did like the children. She felt so sorry for them, poor little things. The people were to be pitied, too. It wasn't their fault they were so poor. She only wished they were not so smelly. She sighed. She just had to stay, there were so many things she wanted to see. Tom was fun to be with. He knew all the theatres, the names of all the actors and actresses and the words of all the popular songs. He told her he liked Kate Keller who had a vivid personality but was not the kind who was always making eyes at men. Then he had added teasingly, 'Not like you, lovely Rebecca, who are such a dreadful flirt.'

'I'm not!' she exclaimed. 'Cousin Jessamy told me not to look at men the way I do because it gives them the wrong idea. What am I supposed to do?' She paused then went on, her expression earnest. 'I like looking at men. They're so, so...'

'Masculine?' Tom suggested playfully.

'They're strong. They don't say spiteful things, not like women do. They're lovely, kind. I just like looking at them.'

'I hope you like looking at me the best,' Tom teased.

'Doctor Stead is better looking,' she replied with great seriousness.

Tom flung up his hands. 'Rebecca, what am I going to do with you? How can I take you out if you're always looking at other men?'

'But I don't want to go out with them. I don't want to go out with Doctor Stead. I enjoy being with you.'

'Good. We must try and arrange to have a night out at the Music Hall.'

It all sounded exciting but how could she obtain the consent of Jessamy and Alistair? Suddenly she brightened. There were matinées at the theatre, so if she and Tom managed to get the same afternoon off, they could go to one of those. It wouldn't be as exciting as going out in the evening but, as the saying went, 'Beggars can't be choosers'.

At the Coachman's Cottage, Jessamy, too, lay wide awake in bed, feeling utterly miserable. What was going to happen to her marriage? Her first husband had become withdrawn because of another woman who had been in his life when he married. Later he admitted that although Caroline had jilted him, he had never stopped loving her. With Alistair it had been different. She had been the only one in his life. Their love for one another had been deep...and, she had thought, everlasting. He had declared passionately that it would be so.

Jessamy was sure that Alistair had tried to fight his obvious obsession with Kate. He still made love to her, he had even tried to make love to her in the stormy way she liked at times, but something was missing – it had become just an act. Should she approach Kate, ask her to leave them alone? But if Alistair got to know he would hate her for treating him as an adolescent.

Then Jessamy deliberately switched her thoughts back to their day at the dispensary. She wondered how she had ever pictured Alistair and herself running it with the sole help of voluntary workers. The project had developed to an extent she had never visualised. Today she had felt like a lowly paid worker sitting at the table filing the patients' cards...and had been treated as such by the hateful Hannah Fanshaw who, wanting information about a patient, had ignored her and spoken directly to Alistair. He had told her shortly that his wife would give her the information she required and Hannah, her cheeks red with the rebuff, had looked at Jessamy with a cold hatred when she repeated her request.

Was this the sort of thing she would have to endure, as well as her husband's obsession with another woman? No, with her knowledge of medicine she would ask, when things settled down, to be a proper part of the nursing staff. She would also face Alistair eventually about Kate. He could be living in a dream world about the actress, and only need a jolt to bring him to his senses. In the meantime she would try to behave as though everything were normal.

She was about to turn over on to her side when she heard the front door close. Alistair. When he began to climb the stairs she snuggled down and feigned sleep. It would be impossible to talk to him now – she must wait until she felt calmer. He came up to the bed, touched her hair gently then, moving away, began to undress. Jessamy had a job to stop herself from bursting into tears.

Louise had not gone to bed when she went upstairs but stood at the window, knowing a restlessness she had not experienced for a long time. She had been very ready to tell Jessamy about her husband's shortcomings, but had not mentioned her own worry about Flynn. She had been so sure of him. He had teased other women, yes, it was his way, but he had never shown any serious interest in any of them...not until this evening. Then he had been as taken with Kate Keller as Alistair was and Willard Stead, too. Had Jessamy been right when she said that Flynn would not wait for ever for her to say yes to marriage?

Louise found herself wishing she had never come to London. Things were not turning out as expected. She had come mainly because she felt she could not bear to be parted from little Romy, whom she had come to regard almost as her own child. And Romy loved her. Now everything had changed – Louise had lost her to a family she had only just met. It was good for the child to be able to play with other children, but she ached to hold her, to tell her stories and have her put her arms around her neck and say, 'I love you, Aunt Louise.'

Romy, of course, was lavish with her affection. Jessamy had promised that her daughter would be coming back home as soon as they got the dispensary under way, but would she want to come back home? She obviously doted on the boy Daniel.

Louise had started to undo the buttons on her blouse when she heard Alistair arrive home and come upstairs. Would Jessamy be waiting to tackle him about his behaviour that evening? There was no further sound, however, and Louise presumed that Jessamy had fallen asleep. She undressed and got into bed wondering what the next day would bring. Fewer patients for one thing, she hoped.

Jessamy usually woke Louise every morning, but the next day it was the other way around. Louise said, 'Come on, sleepyhead, time to get up. Your husband has already gone but he's laid and lit the fire, a most welcome sight. Look, it's snowing, quite heavily. Ugh! I hate snow.'

Jessamy drew herself up in bed. 'How can you?' She yawned. 'It's beautiful. I hope it won't stop patients coming to be attended to.'

'Well, I hope it does. There were far too many people there yesterday – it was like a madhouse. Well, not exactly, but there really were far too many to deal with.' She went to the door. 'I've put the kettle on for a cup of tea and I think the water should be boiling by now. Don't go back to sleep, will you.' Louise laughed as she went out. It was what Jessamy always said to her.

The snow had eased when they left for Paradise Corner, but there was a sharp wind and the thin layer of snow crunched under their feet. It was not yet eight o'clock and Jessamy was relieved to see that no one was waiting in the icy cold. They were just taking off their coats, however, when there was a hammering on the front door and a woman shouted, 'For God's sake let us in, me 'usband's dying.'

Willard Stead opened the door and the woman rushed in, with two men supporting another man who was fighting for breath. The sick man's face was blue. 'Help him, *please!*' the woman begged.

Alistair, who came hurrying forward, took one look at him and said, 'We must get him upstairs.' It was the first time the chair-lift had been used and Alistair was calling orders as they lifted the man on to it.

Jessamy guessed her husband was going to perform an emergency tracheotomy. She wanted to be there, knowing all the instruments he would need, but after calling to Tom Hansard and Hannah Fanshaw he said to Jessamy, 'I may be some time, it all depends on circumstances.'

It was then that Nurse Fanshaw, her face drained of colour, said shamefacedly, 'Sir, I haven't yet overcome a feeling of faintness in the operating room.'

Looking annoyed, Alistair told Jessamy to come with him, and Elizabeth Hope, too. It was from the nurse Jessamy learned that Matron was in bed with a fever.

After that, it all seemed to go like clockwork. The patient was laid on the table, his wife and friends despatched, hands washed quickly in disinfected water and Alistair was so quick in making an incision and inserting the tube that Jessamy could hardly believe it. Very quickly, the man's colour returned to normal. Tom Hansard said, 'I congratulate you on your speed and efficiency, sir.'

'Both are essential in a case like this, Mr Hansard. Another few minutes and the patient would have choked.' Alistair paused then added, 'My wife is to be congratulated, too. She anticipated my every need.' He turned to Elizabeth Hope. 'Will you ask Nurse Fanshaw if she is *able* to help get the patient to bed?'

It was unlike Alistair to be sarcastic. Jessamy realised how deeply annoyed he must feel, being unable to depend on the services of the older nurse. Jessamy had thought by all her talk that she would have been well able to attend operations. It just showed that most people had a weakness of some kind.

This proved to be another day when every moment was busy and it was not until the afternoon that Jessamy had the chance to talk to Mr Saunders about the ghost girl.

He rubbed the side of his nose. 'Well now, Mrs MacKay, I have heard talk of a ghost, but the incident goes back a long way. It was a lady of over ninety told me about it – and then it was all hearsay. I've never seen any ghost myself nor has anyone I know.'

'What did the old lady say about the girl?'

'Well, if I remember correctly, a young lad got her into trouble and, very much against his mother's wishes, they were married. The mother wouldn't even talk to either of them after that. The baby was a girl, and both wife and husband doted on her. Then the little girl had an accident. I don't know what happened, but it left the child crippled in one leg. Now the mother-in-law was a faith healer but when her son and his wife pleaded with her to try and heal the child, she refused. It was a dreadful thing for her to do, seeing as she had a God-given gift.'

Jessamy was silent for a moment then said, 'I've been told I have the power of healing in my hands. Was the girl trying to plead with me to use that power? I'm afraid of what seems to me to be like black magic.'

Mr Saunders said gently, 'Ah no, ma'am. If the Lord gave you that power, it will be for the good of humanity.'

Jessamy agreed, knowing if she really had a gift she must use it. Time would tell.

9

During the next two days, the dispensary was as busy as ever. Since her talk with Mr Saunders, Jessamy found she was most anxious to test her powers. The opportunity came on the third morning when Alistair and Willard Stead were upstairs examining a patient who seemed in need of an operation. Tom Hansard and Jessamy were downstairs and had just dealt with an elderly man who had a dreadful cough when the next patient, a woman of about forty, came in and asked quietly if Jessamy could attend to her alone; she explained that she was a spinster and could not bring herself to undress in front of a man.

Jessamy hesitated for a moment then said, 'Yes, of course. I can explain your problem to my husband when he returns. Will you come with me, please?'

She took her into the empty room on the other side of the passageway and asked what was the trouble. Even with Jessamy the woman was embarrassed. Her cheeks were tinged with red as she told her about the terrible pain she had in the lower part of her left buttock.

'It's there when I'm standing, but worse when I'm sitting or lying down. In fact it's agony when I'm sitting.' When Jessamy asked if she had had a fall she shook her head. 'No. I just don't know what is causing it.'

'I'll take a look.' Jessamy pulled the couch nearer to the fire and put screens around it. 'There, I'll help you to undress.'

'Thanks, I'll be glad of some help. I have such a job to dress and undress as both my arms are stiff with rheumatism. My mother said it runs in the family.'

When Jessamy enquired if there was someone at home to help her, the woman said, 'No, there's no one. My mother died three weeks ago and she had been bedridden for the last ten years.'

'Haven't you any sisters, or cousins who could help?'

She shook her head. 'No, I have no family and I've lived a reclusive life. I never knew my father and I had no uncles or aunts or grandparents. No friends, either, as Mother would never have people to the house. Please forgive me for talking so much. I haven't spoken to anyone since my mother's funeral.'

Jessamy said gently, 'Please don't apologise, Miss Walters. Talk as much as you wish. Often it helps a doctor to diagnose a pain. You may be suffering from tension...we are apt to hold our buttocks tightly when we are under stress.'

'My mother was heavy and I had to lift her. I felt it a strain at times. Neighbours used to offer to help when she first took to her bed but she wouldn't accept, was rude to them. I know it's wrong to speak ill of the dead, but she was so possessive. I couldn't even talk to anyone because she would get into a rage and shout at me.'

Miss Walters stepped out of her brown cotton knickers. 'There, I'm ready.' She was trembling.

Jessamy asked her to lie face down on the couch and covered her with a blanket, thinking as she did so what awful lives some people led, not to have had a family, or to have known boys, gone to parties. She moved her hand over the left buttock and within seconds of probing to find the area of pain, Miss Walters exclaimed, 'That's it! That's the spot. Oh, how warm your hand is, how soothing.'

Jessamy caught her breath with a feeling of excitement. How rewarding it would be if she could give this poor woman some relief. She went on in gentle massaging movements all over the buttock but coming back time and again to the troublesome area. Twice she pressed on the spot but there was no further indication of intense pain. At last she said, 'Is the pain easier, Miss Walters?'

'I can't feel it at all now. It's amazing.' She glanced over her shoulder. 'Is it likely to come back?'

'That I can't tell you, but I hope not. I will ask you to come again and we'll know more then. It's possible I might have released a trapped nerve. If you will just sit up I'll give your arms a massage to try and help that rheumatism.'

There was no immediate relief this time but Jessamy kept on massaging and was satisfied when Miss Walters said, 'It's astonishing, but the lovely warmth from your hands seems to be getting right inside my arms. The stiffness is definitely easier. How wonderful it will be if I'm able to get a good night's sleep for once.'

'I hope you do, Miss Walters.'

Jessamy had spent so much time with her patient that Anne came to look for her: Alistair wanted to know what she was doing as there were records to attend to. Jessamy was about to retort that someone else could do it then changed her mind. It would be foolish and unprofessional to cause any annoyance. She said quietly, 'Tell Doctor MacKay that I'm coming now.'

She helped her patient to get dressed then told her to come again in a week's time. Miss Walter's last words were, 'I'm glowing, just as if I had been sitting over a hot fire. Thank you so much.' Jessamy felt a glow, too, convinced now that she *had* been given the gift of healing. She went to face her husband who, to her surprise, gave her a brief smile. Jessamy was feeling relieved that she had not upset him when she caught sight of Kate Keller, just leaving. Her heart gave a little lurch – so *that* was the reason for his change of mood. Well, something would have to be said. This feeling of being shut out of his life could not go on.

It was nine o'clock that evening when Alistair arrived home. Apart from the fact that he had said he would be back about seven, Jessamy had worked herself up into an angry state over all the sacrifices she had made while Alistair was away studying. She was ready to explode when he did finally arrive, and before he had even had a chance to take off his hat and coat she shouted, 'This affair has got to stop!'

He looked at her, bewildered. 'What affair?'

'You know perfectly well what I mean. With Kate Keller!'

Alistair removed his hat, took off his coat and hung both

up before replying. He turned to face her. 'Now would you mind telling me what all this is about, without shouting.'

'Oh, I shall tell you all right, but whether I can do so without shouting is another matter. This morning when I was tending to a patient, Anne came in to tell me that you wanted to know where I was, as there were records to be attended to. I expected to find you annoyed, but instead you were smiling. And why? Because Kate had been to see you.'

Alistair sighed. 'Really, Jessamy, how immature can you get? Kate came to see *you*. She wanted to tell you that some people she knew had promised to give free vegetables and meat for the soup when the kitchen gets under way.'

Jessamy might have accepted this explanation, had it not been for the word 'immature'. Her husband was no doubt comparing her with the older and more worldly-wise Kate.

'A likely story,' she snapped. 'If she wanted to see me then why didn't she wait?'

Alistair closed his eyes momentarily. 'Because she had arranged to meet one of these people. She was excited and wanted you to know of the offer.'

'She wanted to see *you*,' Jessamy said stubbornly.

'If that is what you think, Jessamy, then that is your prerogative.'

The anger suddenly drained from her. 'It's not what I want to think, Alistair. It's what I see, and I ask myself why? You've told me so many times that I am the only one you love or will ever love.'

'But you don't believe me,' he said quietly.

'How can I,' she replied piteously, 'when I see the way you look at her? Your whole face is alive with love.'

'Are you perhaps mistaking lust for love?'

She was about to protest that he was not a lustful person when she thought of the times when their coupling was wild and stormy, totally unlike the times when he was gentle and tender with her. Jessamy looked at her husband through different eyes. She said, 'Do you lust after many women?'

He thought about it before answering. 'Now and again, I suppose, as most men do, but with Kate it's a strong emotion. I would never attempt to touch her, though, nor would she want me to, I'm sure.'

'Are you trying to fool me or yourself, Alistair?'

'Kate has strong principles.' He spoke sharply. 'She knows the way you and I feel about one another.'

'That wouldn't stop her from having strong feelings for you. I don't say she would deliberately throw herself at you, but I've found that sexual feelings can overwhelm one. I would say they are the strongest emotion in humans.'

Alistair suddenly grinned. 'Do you realise what you are doing to my feelings at this moment, woman?'

Oh, no, Alistair, she thought, not now. It would be unbearable while she was in this mood. There was so much more that had to be cleared up. She said, 'You know that I like Kate. I would be sorry if she went out of our lives, but at the same time it's like a thorn in my flesh when I see you together. Her eyes light up when she's with you and so do yours when she comes into a room. How can I stand it?'

'We'll talk it over, the three of us.'

Jessamy flared up again. 'Oh, don't be so stupid. It would kill our friendship stone dead.'

'The only other alternative, Jessamy, is for you to accept that I love you and would never do anything to hurt you.'

'How can I? How can I let you make love to me, knowing you are lusting after another woman?'

'Jessamy, you said a few minutes ago that sexual feeling is the strongest emotion in humans. It might be the strongest physical emotion, but people have been known to die for love. I love you so much I would die for you if the occasion arose.' It was said without heroics, a quiet statement that held sincerity.

She said, 'Oh, Alistair,' and burst into tears.

He took her in his arms, held her close for a moment then, sitting down, drew her on to his lap and talked soothingly to her. She was doing too much; she took everyone's worries on to her shoulders and he had not helped by upsetting her over Kate. He would see that she had no cause in future to have this worry. Perhaps it would be best if she rested for a few days.

At this Jessamy's tears stemmed. No, the dispensary was just getting under way. She made to sit up but he drew her down again. 'Do you know what I was thinking about as I walked home this evening? The time I came to visit you in Newcastle when you and Louise were staying with Cornelius and Abigail Black and I found you alone. I don't know why that should so suddenly come into my mind.'

'I had suffered morning sickness. I think it was the first time. I know I looked dreadful.'

'You looked adorable to me,' he said softly. 'I had been aching to see you for weeks. I remembered how dark the day was and how cosy the room, with the flames from the fire dancing on the wall. No place in the world could have been more beautiful to me then. At this moment I can hear the hoots of the tugs on the river; it was a mournful sound, yet somehow wonderful, all part of the mystery of love.'

The mystery of love, Jessamy repeated to herself. How romantic Alistair made it sound. Yes, it had been romantic, in spite of the house being in a rundown area of tenement buildings. The people were warm and friendly and how kind Cornelius and Abigail had been. Jessamy felt full of nostalgia for those days gone by.

Alistair went on talking softly, about the cottage on the moors which had been a sanctuary to them, where they had made love during the long enforced waiting for Alistair to complete his studies...

Jessamy had a feeling of going through a healing process and knew she could meet Kate again without any feeling of animosity towards her. Her eyelids drooped...She was partly conscious that Alistair carried her upstairs, undressed her and put her to bed, but the next morning when she awoke it all seemed part of a dream.

That afternoon when the dispensary closed Kate called again. Alistair greeted her in his usual affectionate way then said, 'I'll leave you two together for a chat.'

Kate, eyes shining, said to Jessamy, 'I've been bursting to tell you my news. I have a number of people who are going to supply meat and vegetables to make the soup, as well as others who have offered to provide all the utensils for cooking. Oh, yes, and some have clubbed together to buy stoves. Isn't it splendid?'

'It certainly is, Kate. You've done very well indeed to get all that arranged.'

Kate laughed her infectious laugh. 'I have a lot more to do yet. I need coal for the stoves, water to be laid on and a covered shelter outside where people can wait for the soup kitchen to open. You know how the people waited outside in the cold for the dispensary to open. When you have a minute I want you to decide where to put the stoves.'

Jessamy took off her overall. 'I may as well come now, as we've finished here. At least I have – Alistair will be working for some time yet. He and Willard have some operations to discuss.'

After Jessamy had told Alistair where they were going, she walked with Kate to Paradise Street and found about ten men working on the building with Mr Saunders giving orders. The old man greeted them with a smile and raised his cap. 'Good day to you, ladies. We need your expert help in planning where to put everything.'

Jessamy had not seen Mr Saunders for several days and the sight of him brought a terrible longing for Romaine. Margaret had kept her with the family while the dispensary had got under way but now Jessamy knew she just had to see her child. When she asked Mr Saunders about her he said, 'She's splendid, ma'am, but I think getting a little homesick. Yesterday she talked a lot about her Papa and Mama. I was going to mention it before I went home.'

'And I'm longing to see her, Mr Saunders. My Cousin Louise is missing Romaine, too. I won't, of course, stop Romy from being with your daughter and children through the day. She loves being with them and enjoys her schooling.' Jessamy smiled. 'She's a veritable mine of information these days.'

Mr Saunders smiled, too. 'I learn from her as well; she's a lovely child.'

Louise, who had spent the day with Flynn, was back when Romaine arrived home later. She came running in shouting, 'Papa, Mama, Aunt Louise,' gave each a hug in turn then began chattering about what she had learned that day. She took a breath then told them about the games they had played, the food they had eaten, then gave them a beaming smile and said, 'I'm hungry.'

The three adults exchanged smiles and Alistair said, 'Well, we were young once.'

At the end of half an hour Jessamy realised how easily a child could become a stranger. Romaine's talk was all of Grandpa Saunders, Auntie Margaret, Daniel and the other children. She exhausted herself and fell asleep while Louise was reading her a story.

Alistair consoled his wife. 'You have to realise that she hasn't even slept at home for nearly a week. You must also take into consideration that she's playing with other children.'

'I don't like it,' Jessamy repeated. 'We'll lose her.'

'No, not now she's started to come home again and remember, she had been asking about us. Family ties are strong.'

'I don't think they are in one so young,' Louise disagreed. 'I remember when Christian and I went to stay with an aunt for a month when we were little. She indulged us and although we both loved our parents we hated it when we had to come home to St Peel.'

'A month is a much longer time. Stop worrying, both of you. She's an affectionate little soul and will always want to come home to us.'

Jessamy wished she could share her husband's confidence. Romaine was a restless child who would always be wanting to seek new horizons. That very evening had demonstrated this. She had talked about Daniel, who had apparently said that when he was grown up he would be going away to make beautiful ceilings in big houses, and

Romaine had added, 'I shall go with him, of course.' It was said with all the aplomb of a grown woman.

Jessamy knew she would have to dismiss this worry from her mind. There were many other, more important matters to discuss. For instance, Louise was worried because Flynn was talking about buying a restaurant, but there had been no chance to go into this because Romaine had arrived. She said now to Louise, who was sunk in gloom, 'Is Flynn definite about wanting to own a restaurant?'

'He seems to be. It means I won't be seeing him so often.' She paused then looked up. 'Now that Romy spends her days with Mr Saunders' daughter and the children, I think I'll go back home.'

Jessamy and Alistair exchanged dismayed glances. Jessamy said, 'We would miss you terribly. So would Romaine, now she's coming home to sleep. She says you're the best story-teller in the whole world.'

'We would miss you at the dispensary, too,' Alistair said sincerely. 'You have a way with the people.'

Louise gave a wan smile. 'Stop it, or I'll think I'm indispensable.'

'We value your help,' Alistair said quietly, 'and I know that Jessamy would be lost without you. You've always been so close.'

Jessamy said, 'Yes, I would, but then we mustn't be selfish. You must do as you wish, Louise.'

Her cousin gave a little sniff. 'I need to be wanted. I'll stay.'

Jessamy jumped up and hugged her and they were both tearful when Alistair came and put his arms around them saying, a slight catch in his voice, 'Can I give a bit of love, too?'

Louise dabbed at her eyes, apologising for behaving so stupidly. They told her she was not being stupid at all, and Alistair suggested they have a glass of wine to celebrate Louise's decision to stay.

When the wine was poured Louise took a sip then looked at Alistair. 'I really must have been mad to even suggest leaving. Do you know that your wife cured me of an agonising pain in my leg the other night simply by putting her hands on it?'

Alistair's gaze went to Jessamy. She said, 'I thought at the time it was just one of those chance things but today, well, I lightly massaged a patient's lower back and she found ease. Of course, it may just have been a trapped nerve.'

'It's a gift,' Louise declared. 'Aunt Catherine swore that Jessamy was responsible for restoring movement in her arm after her stroke and for her regaining speech.'

Alistair sat looking at his hands for a moment then raised his head. 'There have been faith healers from time immemorial and I don't decry this gift, but at the same time, I would not like it to get around that my wife feels she has this power.'

'Why not?' Louise demanded. 'It would be of immense value to poor folks.'

'I know, and I'm not going to object to Jessamy helping to ease their pain if she feels she has this gift, but at the present time the medical profession condemns faith healers as charlatans.'

Realising that Alistair had his reputation to consider, Jessamy suggested, 'I could let the people think I had released a trapped nerve.'

Alistair accepted this then got up. 'I must go over and check that everything is in order at Paradise Corner as Matron is still indisposed. We can talk more later.'

When the front door closed Jessamy said, 'I haven't yet mentioned to him about the ghost girl. We don't seem to have much time for talking these days.'

'You're not leading the lives of an average married couple. Be thankful that you see him every day – sailors' wives don't.' With this philosophy delivered Louise went to tackle the washing up.

When Alistair returned he talked at first about the operations he and Willard had planned, then about the number of people who suffered from malnutrition; the soup kitchen would be a godsend. It was then that Jessamy decided to tell him about their ghost, saying it could account for the strange atmosphere he had experienced in the cottage.

Alistair looked angry. 'I know nothing about the supernatural but it annoys me that Mr Saunders made no mention of all this. We have a young child to be considered.' Jessamy explained hastily that Mr Saunders himself had not experienced anything unusual then told him the story of the people who had once lived in the house.

'All right,' Alistair said, 'I'll accept the story, but if you have any further experiences of the supernatural we'll leave.'

Jessamy made no remark, feeling sure that because of her healing powers the ghost girl would be visible to her alone. To change the subject she asked after Matron and was told she was still running a temperature but that Anne was going to sleep in her room in case she needed anything. Alistair then added, 'Rebecca was studying in her room and Tom has gone home for the evening, so all is well.'

What Alistair did not know was that Rebecca was to meet Tom later to go to the Music Hall, an arrangement that had her full of a nervous excitement. She had put a bolster in her bed and humped the clothes around it, hoping that if Anne did look in she would take it that she was asleep. Rebecca prayed that her deception would not be discovered.

10

Once Rebecca had left the house she had to restrain herself from breaking into a run. Tom had said he would be waiting at the top of Paradise Street. Her main worry now was if he were not there. She could not afford to hang about waiting for him. She had been told she must never venture out alone in the evenings because there were men of dubious character abounding. The stalls in the High Street were still trading, the naphtha flares giving a festive air to the scene.

Although Rebecca tried to walk at a reasonable pace so as not to draw attention to herself she felt out of breath as she neared the top of the street. Tom had said he would be waiting in the doorway of the basketmaker's shop but when she arrived it was empty. She panicked. What should she do? There were a number of youths shouting ribaldries at one another nearby. She was suddenly grabbed from behind and the scream died in her throat as Tom said, 'You managed it!'

'Oh, Tom, what a fright you gave me. Thank goodness you were here.'

He put a hand under her elbow and started urging her forward. 'I have a cab waiting in the next street – I didn't dare come anywhere near the house. I have tickets for the London Pavilion. We'll miss some of the early turns, but they're never very good. Did you have any trouble getting away?'

She told him of her subterfuge and he laughed and called her a clever girl. She said, 'I don't know that I was very clever. If Anne discovers I'm not there that will be the death of my freedom. She's younger than I am but to hear her talk you would think she was my maiden aunt and in charge of me.'

'She's well up in medical matters, though. She told me

she's been interested in nursing since she was small, but there, we are going to forget about medicine for the next few hours. We're going to enjoy ourselves.'

The journey alone was exciting to Rebecca, sitting in close proximity in a hansom cab with a young man amidst all the activity of other cabs and carriages with beautifully dressed women and well-groomed men, all pleasure-bent. Some day she would go to parties, to balls and to theatres where she would sit in a box with a handsome escort and be the envy of all the other women there.

When they reached Piccadilly Circus, Rebecca's excitement grew at the lights, the people milling around, the restaurants and hotels. Oh, this was really living!

She had thought that nothing could have given her a greater thrill than being in the West End, but once in the theatre she was utterly spellbound. There were three storeys that went all around the theatre; the first one contained velvet-curtained boxes, above which were smaller boxes, open with single rows of people occupying them. The third tier was a gallery, where couples strolled around chatting, even though a comedian was on stage, bringing bursts of laughter.

Most eyecatching of all was the beautiful ornamentation inside the theatre – the carvings, tall pillars, gilt decoration and red plush tip-up seats. She squeezed Tom's arm. 'If I die tomorrow I shall go to heaven oozing happiness.'

Her escort grinned. 'We'll go together. I'm already walking on silver clouds.'

By the time they were settled in their seats a group of acrobats were performing. Rebecca watched them open-mouthed. Two young men in tight-fitting silver costumes were swinging a girl in a dress with a short frilly skirt scattered with coloured sequins. They threw her to an older man who caught her then, swinging her round by her ankles, he threw her back to the young men who amazingly caught her, amid tumultuous clapping.

During the next part of their performance there was complete silence from the audience. The acrobats did backward somersaults across the stage then the older man lay down, his legs in the air. The girl lay back on his right foot and the man rolled her over on to the other one. He did this slowly at first, then the motion became quicker until the audience were gasping at the speed. The man suddenly slowed the action again, drew his leg down then shot the girl up in the air where she somersaulted and landed upright on his two feet. The audience went wild and shouted for more. The foursome had to come out again and again, but at last the curtain came down.

The orchestra began to play a lively tune and ten long-legged chorus girls, their nakedness covered with brief feathery costumes and wearing beautiful feathery bonnets, came dancing out, their precision perfect. They high-kicked and tap-danced, and Rebecca was there in spirit dancing and high-kicking along with them. If only she could get a job in the chorus...

Tom had told her that the main turn was a woman called Vesta Tilley, a male impersonator. Rebecca, who was not quite sure what to expect, was more than intrigued to see Miss Tilley immaculate in evening dress, top hat, a cape thrown over her shoulder, and smoking a cigar. How beautifully daring. Rebecca immediately took over this role, singing to the audience and enjoying the adulation. 'The Great Little Tilley', as Vesta was known, sang *After The Ball...Following In Father's Footsteps...The Piccadilly Johnnie With A Little Glass Eye*, with the audience at the actress' invitation singing the chorus of each one.

There was a standing ovation at the end of her turn, with many men calling, 'More, more!' but as Tom explained, she would possibly be going on to another theatre to do a turn and so every minute was crucial.

Rebecca, at first so enraptured at the thought of getting a job in the chorus, was now set on being a star. She could sing, she loved dressing up. She had always been the best in the Christmas plays that she and her cousins performed. She would get to the top, she would.

Still lost in her dreams on the way back in the cab, she said dreamily, 'Thank you, Tom, for a wonderful, wonderful evening. I shall never forget it as long as I live.'

'Nor I,' he said softly. 'My greatest pleasure was in watching your different expressions. We must come again.'

'Oh, yes,' she murmured. 'I've made up my mind to be an actress. A male impersonator, like Miss Tilley.' When Tom chuckled she was furious. 'I will, I'll show you.'

Suddenly serious, Tom said quietly, 'It takes years to reach that kind of standard, Rebecca. Years of hard work and heartbreak.'

Rebecca recalled Kate Keller's advice and even when Tom pointed out that her parents would surely object, she still insisted that an actress was what she was going to be and that was that.

Tom said on her own head be it, then asked if she would like to stop off for a glass of wine. He knew of a café in Covent Garden frequented by theatre people. Although Rebecca knew she was already taking a dreadful risk she said on a note of gaiety, 'Why not? I may as well be hanged for a sheep as a lamb.'

The café was a crowded cellar under a shop, where the rise and fall of voices mingled with laughter. Rebecca looked about her, feeling a joyousness. The people were mixed. They included what Tom called 'stage door Johnnies', with their silk-lined capes and their monocles; some partnered women with painted faces and others were with attractive young girls who might be dancers in the chorus. Older men too were attentive to young women who had an air of belonging to the theatre. There were also couples like Tom and herself who were out for adventure.

Waiters were weaving in and out of the crowds, trays of drinks held high, but Tom drew Rebecca to the bar, saying it would be a job to get a waiter to take an order with the sons of earls and lords calling for attention. The customers were two-deep at the bar and while Tom was trying to elbow his way to the front Rebecca had her bottom pinched by a young man standing next to her. When she turned her head and glared at him he gave her a mischievous grin and said, 'Temptation beckoned and I succumbed to it.'

'Well, you had no right to. You are ill-mannered, sir. It was quite abominable to treat a young lady so.'

He was immediately contrite. 'I'm sorry, do forgive me. You are so beautiful and have such a teasing look in your eyes.'

'I was not teasing anyone. I'm waiting for my fiancé to fetch drinks.' Rebecca looked away then gave him a quick sideways glance. He really was most attractive. As other men tried to make their way to the bar the people in front of her swayed, nearly causing her to lose her balance.

The young man caught her by the arm, steadying her, then he said, 'Your fiancé ought not to have brought you to this mêlé. Come, let me see if I can find you a seat.' His hand tightened under her elbow and he drew her away. Rebecca, feeling a small panic, glanced over her shoulder to see if she could locate Tom, but it was impossible.

The young man soothed her. 'Please do not look so worried. I am not trying to abduct you. Look, here is a seat where you can watch for your fiancé.' It was a single chair facing the bar and Rebecca thanked him and sat down. She expected her escort to leave now but he waited to make sure she came to no harm.

When Tom managed to extricate himself from the crush, holding high a bottle of wine and two glasses, Rebecca jumped up and waved to him. He came over, looking from her to the young man, his expression a mixture of query and annoyance. Rebecca quickly explained how the man had saved her from falling. Tom thanked him a little stiffly, and the young man said it was nothing and withdrew, without having given his name. Tom put the bottle of wine and glasses on the table then scolded Rebecca for being friendly with strange men. She flared up, accusing him of having behaved foolishly in leaving her to cope with a group of men who had been almost fighting their way to the bar. Then Tom was penitent. Yes, of course he should have found her a seat, but he had been afraid she might have been molested had he left her on her own.

When Rebecca pointed out that he *had* left her on her own he said, 'I behaved foolishly and I've apologised. Now may I pour you a glass of wine?'

She smiled at him. 'Yes, of course. I don't want our evening to be spoiled.'

'It won't be. Now then, just let me get this bottle opened.'

The only time that Rebecca had been allowed wine before was at Christmas, and then only one glass. After drinking two glasses, her head was swimming deliciously. What a wonderful feeling. She was no longer annoyed that the young man had pinched her bottom; she took it as a sort of compliment, and every now and then his face would float before her. He was so good-looking, his features noble. Was noble the right word?

Tom said, 'Come back to earth, lovely Rebecca.' He laid a hand over hers and added softly, 'I think I've fallen in love with you. I must have done because you are the first girl I've wanted to take home to meet my parents.'

Rebecca giggled. 'Please don't be serious. I don't want marriage – not yet. Remember, I want to go on the stage.'

Tom made no attempt to argue, knowing it would be useless at this point. He simply filled up her glass and his own. They would enjoy the rest of the evening. At this stage he had no designs on Rebecca; he only wanted to please her, but during the drive back in the cab, with the young girl's head on his shoulder and her warm body close to his, he began to feel very aroused.

He put his hand inside her coat and at first she made no protest as he fondled her breast. Then she drew a quick breath and tried to push his hand away, but when he unbuttoned the bodice of her dress and slipped his hand right inside and touched her flesh she gave a long drawn out, 'Ohhh...' of pleasure.

Tom had had girls from the time he was fourteen, but they had been mostly maids or factory girls. Rebecca was of different stock and he knew he would be playing with fire to try and take her, but his body was aching and he was unable to draw back. Not that he could seduce her in the cab – but if he had her longing for him, he knew of a small derelict building in the middle of Paradise Street where he could love her properly.

Rebecca tried to move away from him but he pulled her back and buried his face against her throat. Her body tensed and she began to moan softly. His mouth covered hers and as he moved his lips sensuously, she put her arms around him, returning his kisses with a great deal of passion. Was she not a virgin, then? The thought made him pause. He would hate it if another man had already taken her. He whispered, 'Has any man ever made love to you, Rebecca?'

She shook her head vigorously. 'No, never. I was too afraid, but I don't feel afraid with you, Tom.'

His breathing quickened. He began to raise her skirt and had his hand on her leg when the cabbie opened the window above and called in a hoarse voice, tinged with humour, 'We're there, guv. D'you need any 'elp, mate?'

Tom pulled himself together. 'We can manage, thank you.'

By the time he had helped Rebecca out of the cab and paid the fare his blood had cooled. They were at the top of Paradise Street. Tom put his arm around Rebecca, who was none too steady on her feet and felt suddenly very protective towards her. He must have been mad to behave the way he had. She was a dear sweet girl, fun-loving but not free with her favours, he was sure of that, even though she had seemed experienced when he kissed her. The problem now was to get her back into the house and up to her room undetected.

He decided to escort her up the back stairs, where there would be less chance of anyone being abroad at this time in the morning. Before they went up, Tom stressed to Rebecca that she must not make a sound and she put a finger to her lips and said, 'Shhh.'

They reached the top floor without mishap and as Rebecca's room was the second one from the top of the stairs, Tom was just beginning to feel relieved when a door opened further along the landing. In the faint light of a lowered gas-jet he made out the figure of her sister, Anne. Fortunately, she turned in the opposite direction, towards the bathroom, and when she was out of sight Tom hurried Rebecca into her room and urged her to get undressed and into bed. A small oil-lamp had been turned low. Rebecca sank on to the bed and made to lie down, fully dressed. Tom jerked her to her feet and spoke in a harsh whisper, explaining that Anne was on the prowl and she was to get undressed at once.

This information finally sank in and Rebecca started to fumble with her buttons. Tom, in a fever of impatience, began to undress her himself, his body ice-cold. He was relieved to find she was not wearing corsets. The only time he faltered was when he got her to step out of her lace-edged drawers. Her nightdress was under the pillow. He pulled it over her head, pushed her arms through the sleeves, threw back the bedcovers and lifted her into bed and covered her. She gave a beatific smile, said, 'Good night,' and closed her eyes. Tom gathered up her clothes, threw them in the wardrobe then tiptoed to the door and opened it. There was not a sound. He slipped outside, closed the door gently, and went down to his room on the floor below. He was sweating heavily.

Never again would he go through such an ordeal. He had no idea even if Rebecca had been missed. Well, he would know in the morning. He threw off his clothes, got into bed and lay thinking how he had undressed her and that she had stood before him naked before he managed to get her nightie over her head; how ludicrous it all seemed that he had not wanted to rape her.

Fear, that was it – fear of discovery. If it ever came out that he had taken her to a theatre, then to a wine bar and brought her home in a state of inebriation he would be finished at the dispensary, dishonoured. It would be something to regret for the rest of his life, a great opportunity missed through his own stupidity. Not only was Alistair MacKay an excellent surgeon, but he was a wonderful tutor, too. And yet, had Tom really learned his lesson? He had only to think of touching Rebecca's flesh for his blood to pound.

Tom spent a restless night, with sexual fantasies tormenting him, but at half-past six when Alistair MacKay came to his room and shook him awake he knew a coldness he had never experienced before.

'Get up, Mr Hansard, I have something to say to you.' Alistair threw Tom his dressing gown, his face looking as if it had been carved in granite. Tom was trembling as he shrugged himself into the dressing gown. He swept his hand over his hair and waited.

'You know why I'm here, Hansard.'

'I can guess, sir.'

'When I interviewed you I stressed that there was to be no intimacy with any member of the female staff. You gave me your word that you would respect the rule. Am I correct?'

'Yes, sir.' Tom stared beyond Alistair.

'Yet in spite of this you spent the latter part of the evening with my wife's cousin and brought her home drunk in the early hours of the morning.'

Tom thought, oh God, Rebecca must have been most explicit about their movements. What else had she told him?

'The only thing in your favour, Hansard, is that Rebecca stressed that you had behaved towards her in the most gentlemanly way. She said that you allowed her to have only a small glass of wine but she admitted she had drunk another one when you went to call a cab. She begged me not to reprimand you in any way, but of course you must be reprimanded. I consider your behaviour deplorable and Rebecca's, too. She is not a child but a grown woman. She is very attractive and has a winning way with her but we simply cannot have such a thing happening again. You must understand this.'

Tom's relief was so great that he was not going to be asked to leave that he wanted to shout his thanks. He managed to say quietly, 'Yes, sir, and I promise it shall not happen again.'

'Good. At the same time, I don't expect you to ignore one another. That would be foolish when we are all working together. I would just stress that if you want entertainment with female company it shall be with someone outside the dispensary.' Tom agreed.

Rebecca was in a state of nerves. Jessamy had woken her at half-past six, saying she had come over to have a serious talk with her. Rebecca guessed, of course, what it would be about but knowing that Tom would be questioned by Alistair, was not sure how much she should say. Jessamy and Alistair had apparently been out visiting Mrs Brunt the night before and had seen Tom more or less holding Rebecca up on their way home.

'I want the truth,' Jessamy had said sternly.

Rebecca tried desperately for Tom's sake to play the incident down. She had no idea whether Tom would be told to leave, or whether she would be sent back home. Jessamy said she would let her know after she had talked to Alistair. A few weeks ago, Rebecca would have thought it the end of the world to be sent home, but her main worry now was that Tom would be dismissed, and that she could not bear. Working at the dispensary with Alistair meant so much to him.

Jessamy kept Rebecca in suspense all day. Tom did, however, pass her a note to say he was being allowed to stay. '*Unhappily*,' he added, '*we will not be allowed to socialise, which will be hell. But remember this, darling Rebecca, I love you and always will. Yours, Tom*.'

Rebecca choked back tears. She loved him, too, she was sure of it. Look how caring he had been – what other man would have undressed her and not forced himself on her? Dear, kind Tom.

It was seven o'clock that evening when Jessamy called Rebecca into the waiting room and told her that they would allow her to stay. Rebecca was in tears when she thanked her. 'It's been such an ordeal and I'm grateful that you've allowed Tom to stay. I was the one at fault.'

'You were both at fault, Rebecca.' Jessamy spoke gently, but was firm when she went on, 'I must stress that any more escapades and you both go, which may mean the end of Tom's career.'

'I know and I won't do anything more to jeopardise it,

on that I give you my word.'

Looking at the earnest expression on the lovely young face, Jessamy wished she could have more faith in her cousin's promise. Rebecca was so mercurial: she was sincere at this moment, but in another two weeks' time would she even remember this incident? Jessamy gave a deep sigh when, after five minutes, Rebecca was all effervescent again, praising her for not having told Anne what had happened.

Later that evening when Jessamy was telling Louise all about it her cousin said, 'It might end there for Tom but not for Rebecca. She's a tease, she can't help it. Wait until she gets her hooks into Richard Mather. He may not be handsome but he has great charm. But there, it's no use anticipating trouble. How did you find Mrs Brunt last night? Is she still poorly?'

'Yes, so out of sorts she's talking of giving up taking in lodgers. Kate was there and seemed concerned about her. She's very fond of Mrs Brunt and I think treats her as a mother figure.' Jessamy tried to sound casual when mentioning Kate, but her voice was none too steady. Yet neither Kate nor Alistair had behaved in any way but that of simple good friends. She gazed into the fire for a moment then looked up. 'Has Flynn settled this business about buying a restaurant?'

'I don't think he's quite so set on going into that line, after all. He said tonight that if he ran a restaurant it would defeat his object of coming to London, which was to see me more often.' Louise gave a quick grin. 'I think he might be back in the fold again.'

'Don't be too complacent.' Jessamy spoke quietly. 'Yes, we both have to look to our men. When I married Alistair it never occurred to me that I would have to work to make our marriage a success. Now I know I have competition, and so may you, Louise. You can't keep on putting off your marriage and expect Flynn to wait around forever. He has appetites like any other man.'

Louise eyed her with a solemn expression. 'I *have* taken Flynn for granted. Perhaps I'll need to do some rethinking.'

The evening before the soup kitchen was due to open Kate, Jessamy, Alistair, Louise, Flynn, Mr Saunders and two of his sons helped to prepare and make the soup, arrange forms for the people to sit on and set up a trestle table to hold bowls and spoons. It meant quite a lot of work but it was fun, too. Flynn kept them lively. 'Well now,' he said, eyeing the table. 'Wouldn't you say there was some valuable stuff there? Valuable to those who have nothing, I mean. I had better do something about it.'

He disappeared, was away about ten minutes and came back with a large piece of cardboard and some coloured crayons. 'Don't you worry now,' he said as he started to draw bunches of posies around the edge. 'I'll be nice to them, I wouldn't hurt their feelings for the world.' They all watched with some bewilderment until he started to write a message in the middle, which said, *Dear friends, would you be so kind as to return your bowls and spoons so that others too can partake of the delicious soup. Thank you. Yours sincerely, Dr MacKay*.

Alistair protested, 'Now just a minute, Flynn. If a tin bowl or a cheap metal spoon disappears, what does it matter?'

'Ah, now, it would not matter if only one bowl and spoon were missing, but supposing that ten of each disappeared per day. At the end of a year it would amount to around three thousand six hundred bowls and spoons to be replaced.'

Jessamy gasped. 'Heavens, so it would.'

Louise cautioned, 'I doubt if half the people will be able to read.'

'They'll ask the other half who can,' Flynn replied with a gentle smile. 'Many are honest and although poverty-stricken, have their pride and won't want their good name sullied. They will watch the others to see that bowls and spoons are returned.'

Alistair said smiling, 'You really are quite a character, Flynn. You admit to getting the best out of business acquaintances and yet you – '

Flynn held up a hand. 'I only do that to those who have cheated others and tried to cheat me. As my old grandmother used to say, there has to be bad as well as good in a man otherwise he'll have no understanding of his fellow men.'

Mr Saunders said he agreed with that. 'No man is perfect in the sight of God, but many think they are and are insufferable. But there, as *my* old mother used to say,' he gave a mischievous grin, 'talking won't get the work done. What do we do next?'

They were busy until about nine o'clock and when Alistair returned from a trip outside he said, 'Mmm! The appetising aroma of that soup will bring folks flocking from far and wide in the morning.'

Jessamy thought afterwards that it was the first time she had been in Kate's company when she had not dominated the proceedings. She wondered if her jealousy had exaggerated Kate's charm, but when she happened to look up, sure enough Flynn and Alistair were watching Kate and so were Mr Saunders' two sons, the younger one wearing a quite besotted expression. Kate began to ladle out bowls of soup. 'We must all have a taste.'

The soup was declared to be excellent by all, with Flynn saying that if he decided to open a restaurant, would Kate give him the recipe. Jessamy sensed Louise's disapproval.

After the stoves were banked up to keep the shed warm for the morning, they all left, with Kate saying she would be there again at half-past six. She wished them goodnight and within seconds seemed to have vanished into thin air. When Alistair said that someone should have accompanied her home, Jessamy forced herself to say lightly, 'You know how Kate is – she never wants anyone to do her a favour.' Then she added, 'I don't know about anyone else but I am ready for bed. I'll have to be up early in the morning in case Kate's helpers don't turn up.'

Alistair went to do his nightly round at the dispensary and Louise said she would just have a few words with Flynn. Jessamy was asleep before Alistair or Louise came home. She overslept the following morning and when she called at the soup kitchen Kate was there already, drinking tea with her three helpers – a bright, friendly woman and her two nieces. The girls were painfully shy, but when Jessamy mentioned that a crowd of people were already waiting outside, Kate busily handed out long white pinafores and the girls, as they donned theirs, were as excited as though they were getting dressed up for their first ball.

Jessamy had called Louise before she left and her cousin now looked in to say she would see to the patients' records at the dispensary if Jessamy wanted to stay on to see the soup kitchen 'launched'.

'Yes, I would,' she said gratefully. 'It will be interesting to see people's reaction to our special soup.'

11

On the day the soup kitchen opened, Richard Mather arrived. Jessamy was not quite sure which caused the most stir, the student with his charm or the new soup kitchen.

Louise said, 'It's not a charm that's acquired, it's something he was born with. Heaven help us, not only with Rebecca drooling over him, but Anne, too, as well as Elizabeth Hope and even the tight-lipped Fanshaw. Thank goodness I at least am immune!'

What pleased Jessamy was the way that the patients now talked freely in the waiting room, instead of sitting silent, wrapped in their own private world of pain and hopelessness. The soup kitchen had started them off. One elderly man said, as he picked at his teeth, 'Never tasted anything like that soup. It had real meat in it, duck.'

The woman sitting next to him nodded. 'I know. Last time I had such good soup was when I was in service. Started at twelve, I did. Some skivvies had scraps thrown to them, but Cook was good to me, told me I needed fattening up.'

A woman in the row in front gave a sniff. 'But how long will it last, eh? I'll give 'em abaht a coupla weeks and then, you mark my words, it'll be like bloomin' dishwater.'

Immediately she was verbally attacked by several other patients; she did not know when she was well off. Look at them – they had a good doctor, they sat in a warm room, the doctor's missus kept an eye out for clothes and boots for them and their kiddies and now there was the soup kitchen, too. She should keep her big mouth shut. The woman did.

Although Jessamy was exhausted as usual that evening she felt it had been one of the most rewarding days she had known. The patients had found a voice, which relieved their tensions, the soup kitchen was a success, and she had been able to ease the backache of four women, one who cried in gratitude, saying she had not been free of pain for the past ten years.

What is more, although Richard Mather attracted women to him he not only had a wide knowledge of medicine but got on well with Tom Hansard and Willard Stead. The soup kitchen was so busy that Jessamy had stayed to help until the early-morning session was over; she went back again at midday. The helpers were all very willing, but not having done a day's work in their lives they got a little flustered every now and again. The two girls, their cheeks flushed with excitement, begged to be allowed to come again and Kate said their names would be on the rota.

Kate was indefatigable. She kept up a lively chatter and the people loved it. Even when they were finished for the day she was still bright. 'And do you know something,' she said to Jessamy, 'I would say that every bowl and spoon has been returned. Isn't that good?'

Jessamy asked her to come for a meal later, but Kate refused. 'Thanks for asking me, Jessamy, but I'm doing a show at a private house this evening.' She put a hand on Jessamy's arm and smiled. 'Some other time, perhaps.'

'Of course, and thank you for all you have done.' On an impulse she leaned forward and kissed Kate on the cheek. 'You were splendid.'

Kate seemed touched. 'So were you and all the helpers. I'll see you in the morning, Jessamy.'

Jessamy had a sudden lost feeling. Louise was out with Flynn, Alistair had stayed to have a long talk with Richard Mather and Romaine had begged to stay with Mr Saunders' daughter and family, because a relative was going to put on a shadow show. Romaine had been full of it the night before. She explained how this man made all sorts of things with his hands. 'Birds, dogs, cats, houses, people with funny faces, trees, flowers...' She paused for breath. 'You see it all on a white sheet. Daniel can make things as well. He said he would show me how to do it. I must go, Mama, I must. *Please.*'

Jessamy had smiled and given her consent, but her heart ached. Was this to be her life for ever more? A child she hardly ever saw, a husband who recently had been too tired to make love to her, or at least gave that reason. It was not that she was desperate for sex but she needed to be wanted. Jessamy had just thought back to her first marriage when there was a knock at the front door followed by Rebecca calling, 'Are you there, Jessamy?'

Jessamy got up. 'Yes, come in.'

A rather dejected-looking Rebecca entered slowly and looked at Jessamy with tear-filled eyes. 'I think I'm homesick.'

'Ah.' Jessamy gave her a hug. 'Sit down. I'll make us a cup of tea then we can have a talk.'

'I didn't want to bother you, but Anne and that awful Hannah Fanshaw have suddenly become as close as two peas in a pod; Elizabeth has gone to see a friend, Tom is with Alistair and Richard Mather discussing medical matters and I had no one to talk to.'

'I'm sorry, Rebecca. I should ask you to the cottage more often.'

'I don't want to be wet-nursed. I want to be independent, free.'

Jessamy sighed. 'I don't think one can ever be really free. We are all dependent on someone. Now, what do you think of our Richard Mather?'

Rebecca's depression vanished. 'Oh, he's lovely! He's like a god with his unruly dark hair and sea-blue eyes. He has such charm and he's the same with everyone, even the patients with their shabby clothes. Today he put his arm around an old crone and led her gently to the reception desk. She was toothless and you could see she just loved him.'

The lid of the kettle began to rattle and Jessamy made the tea. 'Well, take care that you don't fall in love with him.'

'Oh, I have already – how could I do otherwise? The strange thing is that he seems only to have eyes for our Anne, and she's just so plain. What does he see in her?'

There was no malice in Rebecca's voice, just curiosity. Jessamy poured out the tea, saying wryly, 'One minute you're in love with Tom Hansard and now it's Richard Mather.'

'Oh, I love Tom, too!'

'Rebecca – ' Jessamy sat down. 'You *must* listen to me. This falling in love with nearly every man you meet has got to stop. Do you realise what might have happened when you sneaked out to the theatre with Tom the other night? You could have been seduced.'

'Oh, no, Tom just wanted to kiss me.' Rebecca's expression was one of wide-eyed innocence and Jessamy became angry.

'You were drunk and didn't realise what you were doing. You could have become pregnant, and what then?'

'I would quite like to have a baby,' Rebecca replied, a wistful note in her voice.

Jessamy gave a despairing sigh. 'Rebecca, I don't think I can cope with you.'

'Oh, I wouldn't want one until I'm married. And I won't – I give you my word.' She gave a small sigh. 'I only wish I could go to the theatre without any fuss being made. It was such fun, Jessamy. You see, I thought it would be different living in London, but I'm watched over all the time, more so than when I was at home. I quite like Matron, but she has an eagle eye. I was glad when she ran a fever – I felt beautifully free. Perhaps I ought to go back home. I don't think I'm any good at nursing people.'

Jessamy, who only a minute ago had been feeling unable to cope with her man-crazy cousin found herself saying, 'You're good with children, Rebecca, very good indeed. You can soothe them when their mothers can't.'

'I don't mind smelly babies but I hate smelly adults. Some of them stink. They never wash.'

'I know, but how would you like to get up in the morning in a freezing cold room, without fuel for a fire, without anything to eat for breakfast and then strip off and wash in ice-cold water?'

'No, I...oh, I didn't know people lived like that. How

awful.'

'They do, Rebecca, that is why we opened the soup kitchen.'

Rebecca started to say something then Alistair came in smiling. 'Hello, I've brought a visitor.'

He ushered in Richard Mather and Rebecca immediately sat up, on the alert. Jessamy welcomed the student then offered him a drink. He thanked her but said they had just had some cocoa. He had a low voice, with warm undertones. He acknowledged Rebecca and took the proffered chair opposite her. Rebecca never took her gaze off him.

Alistair, Jessamy and their guest discussed the work of the dispensary and Jessamy quickly realised that although Richard Mather might be a breaker of hearts, he was certainly knowledgable about medicine and serious in his aim to become a surgeon.

When he got up to leave Rebecca stood up too, saying she must be getting back to the house. To Jessamy's relief Alistair said he would walk with them as there were some papers he had forgotten to pick up. Rebecca looked disappointed. Richard Mather thanked Jessamy for her hospitality then they left.

When Alistair returned he sank back into an armchair and gave a deep sigh. 'It's been quite a day. I don't know whether you realise it, but with the opening of the kitchen we had nearly twice as many patients.'

Jessamy's eyebrows went up. 'I knew there were more than usual, but I hadn't realised it was that many. Still, I was at the shed most of the time. I'll have to leave Kate to deal with that side.'

'She said she was glad of your help. Poor Kate, I thought she looked very tired indeed when she had finished.'

Jessamy felt a rise of anger. In her opinion Kate had looked full of energy. There was no mention from Alistair that his wife looked tired, that she had helped at the soup kitchen, dealt with the records of the patients, massaged the backs of several women and looked in at the ward to see how the patients were progressing.

Alistair put his hands over his face and she said, 'Are you all right?'

He rubbed his eyes. 'Just tired. I did intend to do some paperwork, but I think I'll have to leave it for tonight. I'll go up to bed, if you don't mind.'

'No, of course not. It's sensible. I'll just clear up and follow.'

Alistair said goodnight and after he had gone Jessamy sat in the chair he had vacated, feeling dispirited and hurt. Alistair had often gone to bed early because of tiredness, but never once had he gone without asking her if she was coming too, saying, 'Not because I want to make love to you, my darling, but I want you to give me one of your lovely warm cuddles.'

How willingly and lovingly she had gone with him. Was he so desperately in need of sleep tonight – or was he so far removed from her that he wanted to be alone to think about Kate? Jessamy thought it sad that their dedication to help heal the sick could indirectly be responsible for bringing a rift in their marriage. A rift was certainly there. Alistair had not even given her a goodnight kiss...

She was sitting rocking slowly to and fro in the old velvet-cushioned chair when the lamp suddenly lowered and a small draught touched her cheek. She brought the chair to a stop, her heart beating fast, knowing that the ghost had appeared. She got up and looked behind her and there was the girl, motionless, looking distressed.

Jessamy said, 'I have tried to help some women who had backache.'

The girl nodded quickly then pulled the hood of her cloak closely about her face.

'Are you telling me about a shawled figure?' Jessamy queried hesitantly.

The girl nodded vigorously then spread her hands as though pushing someone away.

'A person I must avoid?' Again came the vigorous nodding. There was the sound of the front door opening. The girl vanished and the lamplight became normal.

Louise bounced in. 'I'm glad you're still up, Jessamy. I

have something to tell you!'

'And I have something to tell you,' Jessamy replied, a quiver in her voice. 'Our ghost girl has just paid another visit.'

'My news will keep. What happened? Here, sit down. You look awful.'

'I feel it.'

Jessamy related what had happened and Louise said, 'How are you going to pick out a shawled figure? About eighty per cent of the women around here wear shawls, including those who come to the dispensary. What could anyone have against you? You're very well-liked among the patients.'

They discussed a number of vague possibilities without reaching any conclusion and in the end Jessamy said, 'Let's leave it for now. What is your news? Has Flynn bought a restaurant?'

'No, we're...well, we're going to be married.' Louise was as solemn as if she were relating bad news.

Jessamy stared at her for a moment then a smile spread over her face. 'Oh, Louise, this is wonderful news.' She gave her a hug. 'It is so unexpected – Flynn must be the happiest man in the world. He's waited so long for you to say yes.'

'He seems to be, although I have confessed to him about my past. Jessamy, I couldn't marry him without telling him about my poor dead baby, and that my father was its father, too.' She gulped with emotion. 'Flynn accepted it all without any hesitation. He just said it was life and he would never mention the subject again. Oh Jessamy, I feel as though an enormous burden has been lifted from me.'

'Your mother will be over the moon when she knows – she's been longing for you to be married.' Jessamy felt very emotional. 'I think it will help to heal the wounds of the past. When is the wedding to be?'

'Soon, but it's to be quiet. We'll live in Flynn's flat until we can find a house we like. I still want to look after Romy when necessary.'

'No, Louise, you'll be having your own children.'

'There'll be no family – that was the arrangement.'

'Is that fair to Flynn? He loves children, you know the fuss he makes of Romaine.'

'Jessamy, will you do me a favour and keep off the subject? We both love Romaine and she loves us. I couldn't love her more if she was my own child.'

Although Jessamy had no wish to spoil her cousin's good news, she was disturbed that Louise seemed to be totally disregarding the fact that she, Jessamy, was Romaine's mother. She would have to put this right, but this was not the time. She said, 'Where is the honeymoon to be?'

'We haven't decided, but Flynn seems to want to go to Paris.'

Jessamy was lost momentarily in a world of nostalgia. Paris was where she and Fabian should have gone for their honeymoon, but things had not worked out that way.

Louise talked briefly about her wedding clothes then said with a wry smile that she was not exactly bride material. She was pleased that she and Flynn were getting married but she felt no nervous flutters. Jessamy simply said that everything would be different on the day.

The following morning Jessamy went to the soup kitchen, just to check that Kate's helpers had shown up, and they had. On the rota today were three middle-aged women from the upper classes, one of whom, a tall arrogant-looking female, was making her tongue go about making a charge for the soup. Everyone could manage to pay a penny. It was quite ridiculous that they got it for nothing.

Kate, usually so even-tempered, had bright spots of colour on her cheeks as she answered, 'Many people who come here, Mrs Moljoy, don't even have one penny in their pocket. What's more, Doctor MacKay made the rule and I and other helpers are abiding by it.'

Jessamy came forward..'It's the whole point of opening the soup kitchen, to give some food to people who would otherwise go without.'

Kate introduced her to Mrs Moljoy who acknowledged Jessamy with a brief nod then proceeded to state that some people would say anything in order to get something for nothing; Mrs MacKay was being rather naive if she believed their lies.

Seeing that Kate looked ready to explode Jessamy said quietly, 'We are definitely not going to charge for soup, Mrs Moljoy, so if you have no wish to do voluntary work in our kitchen then we will understand.'

The aristocratic head went up. 'I don't think you realise who I am, Mrs MacKay. I think your attitude is deplorable and I shall see that you get no more contributions from *my* circle of friends!'

Although Jessamy was furious she forced herself to speak calmly. 'I deplore *your* attitude, Mrs Moljoy, and if that is also the attitude of your circle of friends then I feel we shall be better off without your contributions.'

The woman sneered. 'You'll be sorry.'

'You might be sorry too, Mrs Moljoy. Lord Felby is a great friend of my husband, and his friends have been more than generous to our project. I shall acquaint him with your meanness and I think in future you may find yourself ostracised in his social circle.'

The wretched woman, although taken aback by this, grabbed her coat and shrugged herself into it. Jessamy said to the others, 'If you wish to go with your friend I will understand.' One of the women gave a sniff and said Mrs Moljoy was no friend of theirs – they were staying.

Mrs Moljoy stormed out and slammed the door.

Seconds later Mr Saunders came in, and glanced over his shoulder. 'Someone is in a bad mood.'

Jessamy recounted the incident and the old man shook his head. 'When a woman wants to be boss and enjoys hearing herself talk then commonsense flies out of the window. Oddly enough I looked in to see if you needed any extra help. Our next door neighbour, who was widowed a few months ago, needs to be busy. She's a good worker.'

Kate looked at Jessamy. 'I say, send her along?' Jessamy agreed, wanting to go to the dispensary to see if she could solve the warning given by the ghost girl. She promised to look in later.

At Paradise Corner there seemed to be as much bustle as in a big hospital. Alistair came out of the waiting room, crossed into the room opposite, called some instructions then came out again and went upstairs. Tom Hansard and Richard Mather, each with notes in their hands, passed him on the way down, exchanging brief nods. Anne and Rebecca emerged from the direction of the kitchen, accompanied by Louise who, catching sight of Jessamy said, 'Hello, are you here to stay?' When Jessamy said yes, Louise passed her a patient's record card. 'Alistair asked me to find the notes on a Thomas Hamilton, but there must be two men of that name as this is not the one.'

Rebecca seemed inclined to linger but Anne caught hold of her arm. 'Come on, we have work to do. There's patients to be washed and fed. They should have been attended to earlier.'

Rebecca sighed, cast an appealing look in Jessamy's direction then went off with her sister. Louise grunted, 'Huh – Rebecca will never make a nurse.'

Willard Stead came down the stairs with the no-nonsense Hannah Fanshaw in tow, whose usually cold face wore a slight look of animation.

Louise commented, 'Silly cow – she's trying to look coy.'

Alistair came running downstairs again. 'Jessamy, hello. Louise, have you found the notes I want?'

She told him that Jessamy was going to look for them and drifted away. 'Honestly,' Alistair said, 'I asked her to look for them ten minutes ago!'

Jessamy went to hunt for them in the files and brought out a card. 'The one Louise gave you was for Hamilton, Thomas A. This one is Thomas G. It's easy to make a mistake.'

'There is no room for error where illness is concerned,' Alistair replied shortly. 'One has prostate trouble and the other, kidney problems. If I had operated on the wrong one...' He strode away.

Louise appeared looking contrite and Jessamy sighed. 'Somehow I think it's going to be one of those days.' She told her cousin about the fracas with Mrs Moljoy and

Louise said, 'I'm glad you stood up to the wretched woman.' After a pause she added, 'I was awake half the night thinking of the ghost's warning. I know the Moljoy woman doesn't fit into the description but could she be the one?'

Jessamy gave a firm shake of her head. 'No, I'm sure I still have that to face.' Louise promised to be on the lookout.

During the morning there was trouble from two men and three women who were abusive over their treatment, loudly accusing Alistair of incompetence. Jessamy guessed by the similarity of their complaints that someone had deliberately put them up to it; that someone must surely have been Mrs Moljoy. When she told Alistair of the trouble at the soup kitchen he said, 'Right. We'll soon get this sorted out.'

The haranguing by the five had taken place in the dispensary and before Alistair even had a chance to tackle them there were patients on their feet, women as well as men, who demanded that the aggressors should be bashed up and thrown out. Things were looking ugly and the five became suddenly scared when a woman shouted that they had been paid to do it. Some men were already advancing towards them when Alistair held up his hand and said he knew who the person was; the one responsible would be severely dealt with.

There was some cheering at this and the now-cringing troublemakers were led away by Willard Stead and Richard Mather. The incident had certainly provided plenty to talk about and it was some time before the patients settled down.

At about half-past eleven an elderly woman who announced herself as a Mrs Weldon asked in a hoarse voice for the lady doctor to examine her. Alistair gave Jessamy a quick nod and she took the woman into the room across the passage. The woman, badly stooped, a shawl over her head, mumbled that she had womb trouble. Jessamy had knowledge of most womanly complaints, although if it was serious, Alistair would have to examine her as well. In the meantime she could have a talk with the patient.

She drew out a chair and the woman eased herself on to it, giving a deep sigh as she did so. It was then Jessamy realised that the woman had the shawl so closely drawn round her face that she was unable to make out her features. Her heartbeats quickened. Could this be...?

'Well, get on with it,' the woman said on a tetchy note.

Jessamy sat opposite her. 'Now then, Mrs Weldon, what exactly is your trouble?' Jessamy was glad her voice was firm.

'Revenge. I've suffered from it for years.'

'Pardon?' Jessamy wondered if she had heard correctly.

'Revenge. Don't say you haven't heard of it?'

'Of course I have, but what has revenge to do with womb trouble?'

'Because I never got married, never had children and I wanted them.'

'I'm sorry, but I still don't understand how...'

'Well you should, because you were the one who took the man I loved away from me. No, not your present husband, the first one – *Captain Fabian Montague*. Now there was a man, and he would have married me if you hadn't snatched him away!'

Jessamy was becoming more and more bewildered until the woman suddenly pushed the shawl back, snatched off a grey wig then drew a handkerchief over her face, wiping off make-up.

Jessamy sat staring at her, a terrible coldness inside her. 'Lillian,' she breathed.

'That's right – your very dear cousin whom you never expected to see again.' The words were rapped out, the expression vicious.

Jessamy thought of all the awful poison pen letters that Lillian's mother had sent to members of the Every family and how Lillian herself had sent one to Jessamy on the day she had married Fabian; a letter that had been indirectly responsible for the break up of their marriage. She said in a low voice, 'Haven't you done enough? What more do you want?'

'I want you to suffer as I suffered. Fabian Montague was the only man I really and truly loved and you stole him from me!'

'Lillian, you're so wrong. Fabian had never stopped loving Caroline, his ex-fiancée, the girl who jilted him. She married someone else and when her husband died, she and Fabian got together again. I might add that he would never have loved you; he disliked women who ran after men.'

'I didn't run after him! You told lies about me, that's why he turned from me. You said terrible things – you told him I was a prostitute.'

Jessamy stared at her. 'How could I? I didn't even know you were.'

'I wasn't, I wasn't! I was always particular who I went with.' She spat the words out and there was a wildness in her eyes that Jessamy had seen before, on the night on the moors when she had stepped from behind a rock and threatened her with a pair of scissors. Her heart began an uncomfortable pounding. She rose slowly. 'I have no more to say to you, Lillian. I must go now, I have sick patients to attend to.'

'Oh, no you don't, not till I've done what I came to do. Rid the world of vermin like you.' There was a froth of spittle on her lips.

Realising there was the same madness in her cousin as there had been on that night on the moors, Jessamy backed away. Lillian suddenly lunged forward and grabbing Jessamy's arm with her left hand brought a knife out from under her shawl and put the point at her throat. Jessamy stood frozen, feeling that her life's blood would soon be draining away.

A sudden anger flooding through her gave her the impetus to push Lillian away. She made for the door but Lillian grabbed her and swung her away from it. Jessamy tried to shout but her throat felt locked. She backed away with her cousin stalking her, the knife thrust out, like a fencer seeking to demolish a weaponless opponent. When Lillian suddenly lunged forward and Jessamy felt the point of the knife on her throat again she panicked and ran back to the door, but before she could even thump on the panel Lillian swung her away again with such force that this time she fell to the floor; she heard, rather than saw, her mad cousin turn the key in the lock. Before Jessamy could get to her feet her cousin had pushed her down again and, standing over her, eyes bloodshot, saliva running onto her chin, she said with menacing softness, 'You first, then your child.'

The mention of Romaine was the impetus this time to give Jessamy the strength to punch her cousin in the windpipe. As Lillian staggered, Jessamy was up and pounding on the door, yelling, 'Help! Help! Murder! She's trying to kill me!'

When Lillian ran at her again, Jessamy managed to trip and throw her to the ground. Footsteps came hurrying and when Jessamy shouted that the door was locked, there was a lot of noise as many people seemed to be making an onslaught on it.

Panting, streaming with sweat and tears, Jessamy thought she had Lillian pinned to the floor but she had misjudged the strength of madness. She was thrown aside and Lillian, issuing bloodcurdling yells, brought the knife down with all her strength – and missed as Jessamy rolled away and was upright, gasping with relief, when she felt the knife rip down the top of her left arm. It sliced through her overall sleeve, taking flesh with it – she could feel the warm blood running down her fingers. As faintness overtook her, she heard Lillian give a maniacal laugh and scream, 'That's just a start,' when the door crashed down and people rushed in. Jessamy, unable to move, saw Alistair reaching towards her saying, 'Jessamy, oh my God,' then there was a merciful blackness.

12

Jessamy came to in a room where a lamp was burning low and flames from a fire danced on the walls. The room was unfamiliar and she wondered in an idle way where she could be. She made to move and winced with pain. Her arm hurt. What had happened? Why was she in this strange room? Remembrance came slowly, then as she relived the horror of the frenzied attack she cried out and tried to sit up. Gentle hands restrained her.

'You're all right, Mrs MacKay, lie still. Your husband will be with you soon.'

'My cousin...Lillian...?'

'She's been taken care of. Your husband has seen to that.'

A mist blurred Jessamy's vision. Although the voice was vaguely known to her, she could not make out its owner's features. She closed her eyes and opened them, then focused on Richard Mather. She plucked at the bedclothes. 'They won't allow her to come back, will they?'

Richard laid his hand gently over hers. 'No, she won't be back. The doctors will put her in an asylum, where she belongs.'

Jessamy became agitated. 'My arm, she stabbed my arm! Will it be all right? Will I be able to use it?'

'Of course, your husband attended to it.' Richard Mather's smile reassured Jessamy. She felt sleepy and closed her eyes.

When next she awoke it was to see Alistair standing by her bed. He was talking to Willard Stead, saying in a low voice, 'There'll be shock to contend with. It was something so totally unexpected. The last we heard of her cousin, she was in America. We hoped she would stay there.'

Jessamy moved; Alistair sat down and took her good hand in his. 'Darling, how are you feeling?' Willard Stead moved silently away.

Aware of the constant dull ache in her bandaged arm she said, 'She ripped my arm, she ripped it.'

'I've stitched it, Jessamy. You must calm down, my love. I know it's not easy, you've had a dreadful experience, but I don't want you to get more agitated.' He leaned over and kissed her on the brow, on her cheeks, her lips. 'I ache for you, I feel I should have noticed there was something strange about the shawled figure.'

Jessamy noticed then the strain on his face. 'How could you? No one could have guessed her identity. I'll be all right. Please don't blame yourself.' She felt sleepy again and guessed she was drugged.

Through the following hours she would awake to find someone sitting with her. Once it was Anne, another time it was Hannah Fanshaw and she was surprised at how gentle and caring the tight-lipped nurse was in comparison with Anne. Her cousin was all efficiency, plumping up her pillows, lifting her up on to them, disregarding the searing pain it brought to her wounded arm. Hannah Fanshaw asked if there was anything she could get for her, and when Jessamy said her lips were dry Nurse Fanshaw moistened them, rather than raise her to drink the water. She brought another pillow so Jessamy could rest the injured arm on it and talked soothingly, of the farm where she had been brought up, describing the countryside, the heather-clad hills, the sunrises and sunsets until Jessamy's eyelids drooped and she was asleep again.

The others who sat with her were like visions appearing then fading away. Louise, Tom Hansard, Richard Mather, Willard Stead, Alistair...

It was daylight when Rebecca brought her breakfast. 'I asked to bring it so that I could say how sorry I was about what happened. I've been told not to talk about it and I won't, but I'm so glad you're all right, Jessamy. I know about your arm but, there, I mustn't talk about that either. Do you think you can manage a little porridge? Cook has made it nice and milky. I'll feed it to you.'

For all the talk about Anne having the makings of a

good nurse, Rebecca was much better at handling her. She managed to sit her up without causing any discomfort, fed her painstakingly and washed her hands and face and tidied her hair without causing Jessamy any undue distress. She said, 'You are a good nurse, Rebecca. Whose room is this? I don't recognise it.'

'Doctor Stead's. He has moved into a little attic room for the time being. He's nice, I like him. Oh, here's Nurse Fanshaw – I'd better go.'

Jessamy slept most of the day, waking only when Alistair came to dress her arm. He announced it was doing splendidly and she was asleep again before Hannah Fanshaw had finished bandaging it.

During the next few days she let the hours wash over her, uncaring about the dispensary, the soup kitchen or Rebecca, who Anne said was behaving irresponsibly by gazing at every man in sight. Sometimes she would hear people talking in low voices by her bed. Once Alistair said (she thought it was Alistair), 'She's been badly shocked. She's rejecting any kind of responsibility...which is good. When she's well I think it might be a good idea to send her home for a week or two to convalesce.'

Home? She *was* home – what was he talking about?

Louise came to see her and so did Kate, while Anne and the other two nurses continued to tend to her needs. When Alistair came Willard Stead was always with him, no doubt to compare notes. Tom Hansard looked in briefly but when Richard Mather came to see her he always stayed for a while. He was such a kind person, so gentle.

One day Alistair asked her if she would like to see Romaine. Jessamy became agitated. 'No, no, I don't want her to see me with a bandaged arm. She's so sensitive, she would be upset.'

'It's all right, darling, don't get in a state.' Alistair was gentle with her. 'I thought you might be missing her, that's all. Perhaps in another few days. Mr Saunders sends his kind wishes, by the way.'

It was on this particular day that Jessamy started to acknowledge that there was a world outside the room she was in, and she had no liking for it. She wanted to stay cocooned. She wanted to ignore Elizabeth Hope's complaint that Hannah Fanshaw treated her like dirt; she tried to close her ears to talk of how frantically busy they had been in the dispensary and how they thought that Matron was not as poorly as she tried to make out. She had no wish to know that Rebecca had been found trying to sneak out late one night to meet someone, nor that she would not say whom.

What was more, Jessamy certainly did not want to know from Nurse Fanshaw that poor Dr MacKay was working himself into the ground and that Kate Keller had come two evenings running to try and persuade him to do less.

When Louise came to sit with her for a while and asked if there was anything she wanted she said, 'Yes, I want to run into a forest and hide.' Then she burst into tears. Louise put her hand on hers and said quietly that they must try and arrange it. The result of this was Alistair telling her that as soon as she was well enough Louise and Flynn would take her back to St Peel for a few weeks. He said, 'Your parents have been so worried about you and I know they will be delighted to have you with them for a while.'

Louise added lightly, 'It will be a lovely change and I can tell the family that Flynn and I are going to get married.'

'Yes,' Jessamy said, apathy setting in again.

The next morning, however, she saw the visit as a chance to talk to her grandmother. Henrietta, she felt, was the only one who would understand her state of mind.

The following day Alistair took out the stitches in her arm. The skin was puckered and the stitchmarks angry-looking, but Alistair and Willard Stead were well pleased with the result.

Alistair put his arm around Jessamy. 'The marks will fade in time, my love.'

'It doesn't matter if they don't,' she said drearily.

Alistair glanced at Willard and gave a despairing shrug. There was talk of Romaine going with them, but apart from the fact that Alistair did not agree with this, saying that Romaine would be excited and unmanageable, Jessamy said it would be wrong to take her; she had made the East End her home now and it would be wrong to unsettle her again so soon. Louise and Flynn, who had both wanted the child with them, had to accede to this but Louise warned Jessamy that grandparents, great-grandparents and the rest of the family were going to be disappointed.

'I don't care,' Jessamy replied. 'It's what is best for Romaine that counts, not what the family want. Did you know that Lillian was wanting to kill Romaine, too?' Her voice broke and she gave way to tears. Would this feeling of lethargy and weakness ever disappear?

Louise looked at Alistair who had come up and shook her head.

It was another two weeks before Jessamy was strong enough to travel. In that time she had shown little interest in anything and Alistair said to Louise and Flynn, 'I'm hoping that once she's home something will trigger off her desire to live a normal life again.'

Flynn had wanted to borrow a friend's limousine and drive them North but Alistair said it would be too long a journey, so they went by train and Flynn insisted on buying the tickets and booked First Class.

As Louise said afterwards, the journey was just something to be endured. Jessamy remained in a world of her own. At first, Flynn and Louise had been chatty but when Jessamy showed no interest or response and eventually went to sleep, they talked in low voices about the situation.

'It seems as though Jessamy has sunk into a deep depression and is now unreachable. It could be the after-effects of shock still. The first time Lillian attacked her all those years ago was bad enough, but this would be worse because with Lillian in America she must have thought, as we all did, that she would stay there.' Louise looked at her cousin worriedly.

Flynn whispered, 'I think what surprises me the most is her refusal to see Romaine. We all know how she adores her.'

'The mind is a strange thing. Perhaps Jessamy feels that as long as she has no contact with her, Romy might be safe. Lillian did threaten to kill the child.'

Jessamy, who was feigning sleep so she would not have to make an effort to join in the conversation, thought how wrong they both were. Her purpose in keeping apart from Romaine was so that her daughter would gradually forget her and not miss her when she died. Alistair would be all right because he had Kate to turn to, and Kate would make a lovely mother. She wanted children. Jessamy did want Alistair to be happy. He had looked so sad when he came to the station with them and she wished she had not turned her cheek away when he kissed her. But then it would make it easier for him if he thought she no longer loved him when the time came to part. She listened to the rhythm of the wheels on the track and it lulled her to sleep.

Flynn had brought a picnic basket full of good things like chicken, ham and wine and although Jessamy had no appetite, she ate some at lunchtime to please him. When they arrived at the Central Station, her father and Aunt Verity were there to meet them. There were tears in the eyes of both when they hugged her. Chadwick explained that the whole family had wanted to come but thought it would be too overwhelming. Her father put his arm around her and said, 'Your mother wanted to be at home to greet you.'

A carriage was waiting and they all got into it, but Jessamy could remember nothing of that part of the journey. She could not even recall seeing her mother again. Later, Louise told her that she had refused to have anything to do with Esmeralda.

'All you talked about last night was wanting to see Grandma and insisting we walk to Beacon Hall. So, I am going to take you today. You're strong enough now, after that long walk we had over the moors yesterday.'

'We did? Why don't I remember it?'

'Because I think you wanted to shut out memories of Lillian. But we have to talk about her: she's in a mental home, now, she's safe and she can't ever do you any more harm. Is that clear, Jessamy?' Jessamy nodded and her cousin went on, 'Talking to Grandma is obviously important to you and we're hoping you'll be able to get rid of your fears and be your normal self again.'

'I won't be, I'm going to die.'

'Rubbish.'

Jessamy's eyes widened. 'But I am, I know it.'

'I repeat, that's rubbish. I think you've been treated far too gently for far too long. Now it's time for some straight talking. You're enjoying the little world you've locked yourself into, where everyone is so kind, so very understanding.'

'Don't you have any idea what I suffered? I was being attacked by a madwoman whose intention it was to kill me!' Jessamy's voice had risen and Louise was pleased.

She goaded her yet further by saying, 'I can only guess what you suffered, but what I *do* know is that you're so wrapped up with yourself that you just dismiss Alistair and Romy. What does it matter if they break their hearts if you die? Why should you worry – someone else will comfort them in their grief. I suppose you already have Alistair married to Kate and her acting as stepmother to Romy, never even considering that the child has had little contact with Kate, kind though she is.'

'No, I – well, yes, after all, Alistair *is* in love with Kate.'

'Why won't you get it into your fat head that you are his one and only love! Yes, he's attracted to Kate, but...'

'I don't want to discuss it.' Jessamy hurried ahead and Louise smiled to herself. It was a start, and if she knew her grandmother, Jessamy was in for another jolt to bring her down to earth.

Louise caught her up when they were in sight of Beacon Hall. Jessamy's footsteps slowed and she said, 'I don't know whether I want to see Grandma today. Perhaps tomorrow.'

'Jessamy, listen to me and listen carefully.' Louise stopped. 'As you well know, Henrietta is housebound and lives for little snippets of news. She hears the same kind of thing from the family day after day. She's been keyed up waiting for you to arrive but now, because of your selfishness, you decide you don't want to see her. All right, you do what you like, I shall go for a walk.'

Jessamy opened her mouth to speak, closed it again and marched ahead towards Beacon Hall, slowing as she neared the old house with its great beams infilled with lath and plaster, emotion stirring in her. How many times had she come to her grandmother for advice and comfort?

Louise caught her up in the hall and as they crossed the stone-flagged floor Henrietta called from upstairs, 'Jessamy, is that you?' There was a soft note in the old lady's voice, instead of the usual excitement, and Louise answered, 'It's both of us, Grandma. We're coming up.'

When they went into Henrietta's sitting room she held out her arms. 'How good to see you, my love.' As the bird-bone arms held Jessamy close she thought of the many times they had held her like that and how happy she had been to visit her. Louise said she would go for her walk and leave them to their chat, and when she had gone Henrietta nodded towards the stool. 'Sit down, Jessamy dear, and we'll have a talk. Now – how are you feeling?'

'A little better, Grandmama. It's nice to have some lovely fresh air.'

She fell silent and Henrietta said gently, 'Tell me about Lillian. It may help to rid you of your awful experience.'

Jessamy spoke briefly of Lillian in a desultory way, concluding, 'But she's being cared for now.' When Jessamy was silent again the old lady asked her what else had upset her and when Jessamy said, 'Nothing, nothing at all,' Henrietta put her hand over hers.

'You've never needed to lie to me before, Jessamy dear.'

In a rush of words Jessamy blurted out, 'Alistair has fallen in love with Kate and Romaine no longer needs me. She's happy with Margaret and her family and if I die Alistair can marry Kate. She's a lovely person, she adores children and would be good to Romaine.'

'Well, well,' said Henrietta. 'I think we had better try and get all this sorted out. First let me say that if I had a sovereign for every time I thought that your grandfather was in love with another woman, I would be rich. He likes flirting, yes, even at his age, but I know that he loves me and I never question what he does when he's not at home.' Henrietta paused then went on softly, 'You know, Jessamy dear, it is possible for a man to love two women and for a woman to love two men, but in different ways.'

Jessamy's head went up. 'I would no longer love Alistair if I knew he was making love to another woman.'

'Then you've never been in love with him. It's not something you can turn on and off at will. Fabian divorced you for another woman. Can you honestly say you no longer have any love for him? Be honest.'

'No, I don't. I – ' An image of her first husband came to Jessamy so vividly at that moment he might have been standing in front of her. He was a big handsome Viking of a man and she knew then she could feel emotional thinking about him. Was it love? Yes, but different from the kind of love she felt for Alistair. She looked at her grandmother.

'Yes, I think I do, but even if Alistair was living with Kate I wouldn't want Fabian to make love to me.'

Her grandmother's eyebrows went up. 'Are you quite sure about that?'

'Of course I'm sure. I do have some principles!'

'Someone once said that principles fly out of the window when sexual emotions are aroused.'

Slow colour rose to Jessamy's cheeks as she recalled the wild love that she and Alistair had shared at the cottage on the moors. She said in a low voice, 'I let Alistair make love to me when I was still married to Fabian. I behaved like a whore.'

'No, my love, a whore charges for her favours. Put it down to nature. Although, mind, I don't know that the Lord will accept that as an excuse on Judgment Day.'

Henrietta spoke lightly and Jessamy gave a wan smile. 'Oh, Grandmama.' Her voice broke. Tears welled up and ran slowly down her cheeks, then she was sobbing in genuine grief, releasing the knot that had been tied so tightly inside her for weeks. Henrietta put her arms around her grand-daughter and held her close.

When the storm was over Jessamy wiped her eyes and murmured, 'I'm sorry.'

'I'm glad. A good cry is what you needed. Now I'll ring for some tea. We both need it.' Henrietta talked quietly to her, pointing out how long Alistair had loved her, adding that that kind of love did not disappear in a day. Then, after a pause, she went on, 'Of course he's attracted to an appealing woman, what man isn't, but the fact that you think Kate a lovely person makes me believe she's no threat to your life. Forget Lillian, my love, forget your jealousy of Kate, concentrate on showing Alistair how much you love him. Trust him. In the meantime, enjoy walking on the moors and seeing all the family again. You know the old saying, "Physician heal thyself". Well, you have healing in your hands to help other people, but you must have healing in your heart to cure what ails you. Ah, here's the tea.'

Later, when Jessamy walked home with Louise she said, 'I realise now how badly I have behaved to Mama. I don't know what made me ignore her.'

'Oh, don't worry about Esmeralda, she's resilient. The only person she's interested in is herself, always has been and always will.'

'She loves Ralph.'

'Jessamy, it's not love your mother has for her bastard son. She wanted him all to herself and was almost suicidal when he told her he was getting married. It was a good job that he and his wife went to America to live, otherwise she would have plagued their lives. She was madly jealous when Romy showed more affection to your father than to her when you went to London. It's a good job that you and Alistair live far away from all the family.'

'I'll have to visit them all. I didn't want to at first but now I know I won't mind, apart from Uncle Digby and Aunt Dorcas, that is. They have such an unbearable manner.'

'Then don't. Just visit who you want – you're here to

recuperate. Shall we call in at the shop and see your father now, or would you rather see him at home? Perhaps it would be wise to wait until lunchtime.'

Jessamy agreed, knowing that if her uncles and aunts from the other businesses in St Peel happened to catch sight of her, she would be bombarded with questions and she was not yet ready for them.

Chadwick caught them up just before they reached home and when Jessamy greeted him with a smile he put his arm around her. 'I'm glad to see you looking so much better, my love.'

Esmeralda seemed tearful at first when she found that Jessamy no longer ignored her but seconds later she was talking about a wealthy family which had come to live on the moors and how she had become friendly with the wife. Her conversation from then on dealt with her social life. When Chadwick tried to change the subject and failed he gave Jessamy a rueful glance and raised his shoulders. She smiled in understanding.

The following morning, knowing that her mother was having coffee with her wealthy friend, that Louise and Flynn were visiting one of his friends and that her Aunt Verity was to be involved with local charitable work, Jessamy had a wonderful sense of freedom as she set out to wander the moors on her own. She made in the direction of the waterfall, revelling in the sharp March wind which stung her cheeks. She saw Mrs Lane going into her cottage and remembered the old lady telling her once when she was young, that she heard fairies singing when the wind was strong. Jessamy always listened for them when it was windy and often imagined she heard them. There had been gales in the area recently and a yew tree, one of four, had been blown down. Someone had started to cut it up, but had not completed the task, probably because the wood, being harder than oak, had defeated the saw. Suddenly the morning seemed filled with sound. A grouse cock skimmed over the ground, its bronze breast and red comb lovely in a shaft of sunlight, its strident cries of *cok, cok, cok* mingling with the croaking and bubbling of frogs in a nearby pool.

Although Jessamy had purposely put Romaine to the back of her mind, she found herself thinking how much she would have enjoyed being with her.

She could now hear the thunder of the waterfall; the sound brought back all sorts of thoughts, of walking with Fabian...walking with Alistair on Saturday afternoons, discussing medicine, listening to his homework and correcting his answers from a book. All that seemed a world away now.

Had life been less complicated then, or was she just imagining there were no upsets? She put both men firmly to the back of her mind as the waterfall came into view. With the heavy rains it was in full spate and as the weak sun made rainbows in the gossamer cloud of rising spray Jessamy felt moved by the magnificence of nature. She stepped back from the waterfall but could still feel the dampness on her cheeks as the wind tossed the rising spray in every direction. Suddenly she jumped as someone took her by the arm and drew her further back still. When she looked at her rescuer, her heart began a slow pounding. It was Fabian...

He spoke her name but she could only tell by the movements of his lips. He drew her further away still from the water and when they were able to speak and be understood he said, 'What a surprise, Jessamy! I thought you were in London.'

'I was...I've – been ill. I came home to recuperate.' The blue of his eyes were emphasised by the bronze of his skin and it was impossible not to be impressed by his good looks and virility. 'You look well. I didn't know you were back in St Peel again.'

'I arrived late last night. Is this a coincidence? During the voyage I kept thinking about you, wondering how you were. And how is lovely Romaine?' His expression and voice had softened. 'I often think of her, too. She's such a dear, winsome little girl.'

'Yes, she's an imp at times, but lovable.'

'Would you like to walk back to The Montague Acres,

Jessamy? We could have coffee.'

Jessamy's instinct was to refuse but she found herself accepting the invitation. Fabian cupped a hand under her elbow and smiled down at her as they walked on. It was a devastating smile that aroused all sorts of emotions in her. He said, 'I just can't believe that we're walking together. Do you remember the snowy afternoon when we went into the fisherman's church? I was due to sail the following morning.'

'Yes, I do.' She remembered the icy cold, how he had unfastened his overcoat, drawn her inside it and how he had told her he had fallen in love with her. She imagined she could feel again the warmth of his body as he had held her close. Tremors went through her. She said, 'Is Caroline with you?'

'No, I can't get her away from her beloved horses. How is Alistair, and how is the work at the dispensary?' She told him that Alistair was well and described the work they were doing. Her husband was still looking for a private practice.

'Ever since he received the news of the generous financial help you arranged, Fabian, he's been on tenterhooks trying to find suitable accommodation, but it's not easy getting just the right district,' Jessamy went on. 'I'm sure he'll be doing too much.'

'Just as you have obviously been doing.' He spoke gently. 'You must take better care of yourself.'

Jessamy, feeling that Alistair was under censure for having neglected her, related the story behind her breakdown. Fabian stopped and searched her face. 'What an appalling experience. You could have been killed. And as for poor Lillian...what torment she must have suffered. I once knew terrible jealousy but I never felt murderous, thank heaven.'

He walked on and Jessamy, assuming that he had been jealous of Caroline, changed the subject by asking if he was still enjoying life in Texas.

'Yes, I am, but – ' He nodded in the direction of The Montague Acres which had just come into view. 'This will always be home to me. I feel constantly drawn back to it.' There was nostalgia in his voice. The Montague Acres had been Jessamy's home once but although she was determined not to get sentimental about it, she had to admit the place did look beautiful with its sweep of lawns and landscaped gardens, the foliage in the tubs on the balconies spilling over. Later the red and pink of geraniums would mingle with the greenery there. In sheltered places there were snowdrops, and purple and yellow crocuses. The lovely yellowy curled leaves of the oak tree were beginning to unfurl and when she saw an ash tree, which was ahead in growth, she quoted the old saying, 'If the oak's before the ash there'll be a splash, but if the ash is before the oak there'll be a soak.'

Fabian laughed. 'We've certainly had a soak according to Mr Stannard. Shall we walk to the back of the house? The stream is in full spate...a raging torrent!' He smiled as he made the last remark.

Although Jessamy agreed to the walk she felt reluctant to see the love garden again, with its topiary birds representing Caroline and Fabian. They were sheltered from the wind at the side of the house and Jessamy could hear the clucking of hens, the quacking of ducks and the grunting of pigs, which brought back memories of Fabian playing the Pied Piper, leading the ducks to the pond and of Romaine, helpless with laughter at his antics. The memories hurt and she stared straight ahead and concentrated on the heart-shaped beds of spring flowers, which were just beginning to show colour. The heart-shaped pool was all but overflowing, the water deeply ruffled by the wind. The stream was rushing madly, tumbling over stones and spilling over where the small tributaries formed love-knots. For a time Jessamy kept her eyes averted from the lovebirds but when she gave a surreptitious glance in their direction she looked again, surprised to see an addition to the topiary work – a small bird which stood between the parents. She turned to Fabian, who had stopped to examine the bark of a tree.

'Fabian, you didn't tell me you and Caroline now have

a child.'

'Mmm?' he queried, fingering a broken fragment of bark.

'The hedge, the two birds – there's an addition, a young one.'

Fabian looked towards the hedge. 'No, we don't have a child. It was just a bit of whimsy on my part.' He paused then added softly, 'I call her Romaine because I love her and wish I had a daughter like her.'

Colour rose to Jessamy's cheeks. She turned away. 'That is not fair, Fabian.'

He shrugged. 'Perhaps I am indulging myself, but I'm not harming anyone.'

'Yes, you are, you've upset me. I think you brought me here with the intention of telling me that. You'll be saying next that you and I are the parent birds.' He was silent but he looked distressed, and Jessamy's heart gave a lurch.

She turned a reproachful gaze on him. 'Oh, Fabian, how could you? You know that Alistair and I are happily married and if Alistair – ' She stopped, remembering how she had been pouring out her troubles to her grandmother about Alistair and Kate. She moved away and Fabian followed her.

'Jessamy, I'm sorry. I wouldn't consciously do anything to hurt you, or Alistair. Please believe me. It's just that...well, I wanted to feel I had a family. It's something you perhaps can't understand. You have everyone here, as well as Alistair and Romaine.'

'You have Caroline. You divorced me so you could marry her. Perhaps you've forgotten that.' Jessamy spoke harshly.

'There's only one thing that matters in Caroline's life and that is her horses. We are business partners, nothing more now. All that is over.'

'Fabian, don't ask for my sympathy.'

'I'm not.'

'You are, indirectly. You're an attractive virile man, and you have had women almost swooning over you. If you stop feeling sorry for yourself and look around there could be someone you could fall in love with, a woman who would be happy to give you children.'

'I don't want *any* woman. There's only one woman I want – and no other will do. I only ask that we can remain friends. Surely it's not too much to ask?' When she hesitated he coaxed, 'We are not likely to meet often.'

'No, that's true. I don't know how long I shall be staying but I will promise to call before I leave.'

Fabian wanted her to come into the house for coffee, but she refused, saying she really ought to be getting back. He then offered to walk her home but she said it would not be wise. She gave a wry smile. 'You know what people are. We would only have to be seen walking together for them to conjure up a story that I had left Alistair and had come back to you.'

'And if I kissed you,' he teased, 'that would verify it.'

'Heaven forbid. If my mother heard such a thing it would put her in bed for days.'

'Then I shall be circumspect and only shake hands with you when I leave you at the gates.'

As they walked down the drive he talked about the grounds and how he was hoping to come back in the summer when everything would be in full bloom and the fountains on the lawn, playing.

His handclasp was firm as they said goodbye and Jessamy felt rather emotional. 'You *will* see me before you leave?' he asked in a low voice.

'Yes, I promise.' She withdrew her hand, said goodbye and left. When she looked back he was still watching her. He raised a hand and she was aware of a great sadness in him. She felt sad, too, but unsure whether Louise had been right when she said that Fabian was an actor. Then she thought no – he was just a man who wanted a wife and children. His affection for Romaine was genuine. He had been surprised and pleased, as she had been, that fate should bring them to St Peel at the same time.

After all, they had loved once...and as her grandmother had said, love does not die in a day.

13

The next day Jessamy could not get Fabian's sad expression out of her mind, but after that her days were fully occupied with visiting, being invited out, going for drives with Flynn and Louise and helping to serve in her father's shop when the apprentice was ill and Mr Blackwell, who normally would have helped out, was away.

This she thoroughly enjoyed. It was a tonic to have a customer come in and greet her with a beaming smile and remarks such as, 'Why, Miss Jessamy, isn't this a treat now? Eeh, how we've missed you and the little one, too.'

It was at the shop where she and her father had their longest talks, for at home her mother dominated the conversation. Jessamy was able to discuss topics like the poverty in the East End and the kind of people they dealt with at the dispensary. She described Alistair's patience with even the most awkward of them, and spoke of her worry that when he eventually set up his private practice it would prove too much for him to handle. Chadwick put her mind at rest: doctors and surgeons were always overworked, but they coped. Alistair was strong, the kind of person who needed to be stretched.

Jessamy had not thought of this, but realised it was true. No matter how busy Alistair was he kept his promise to write to her every day, even though it was just a few scribbled lines to tell her that all was well at Paradise Corner and that he loved her very much.

Kate wrote every few days, long letters, full of humour about some of the helpers at the soup kitchen, the 'toffs', who coming for the first time, were surprised at the bareness of the shed and the tin bowls. '*I think they expected Aubusson carpets, silverware and crystal, but I soon put them right, bless them, and I'm sure in time they'll make good workers. Incidentally, with permission from Alistair, I took Rebecca and Anne to a wealthy home, where we gave a show for funds for the dispensary. Over a hundred pounds was collected. Rebecca was in her element. To my surprise Anne was full of praise for the evening. One is always getting surprises. I do miss you, Jessamy, but I was so pleased to hear from Alistair that you are feeling so much better. The day you come home we'll get the flags out and have the band playing! Love, Kate.*'

Jessamy had been in St Peel for two weeks when she became homesick for London. When she told Louise, her cousin said that she was ready to leave and, in fact, Flynn would have to go back soon anyway on account of some business deal that was in the offing. After her parents had been told there was a running around saying goodbyes. Remembering her promise to see Fabian before she left, Jessamy made a quick visit...only to learn he had gone to Scotland to visit friends. Jessamy thought it was perhaps just as well. She left word with Mr Stannard to tell Fabian she would write.

The parting with her grandmother was hardest to bear. The old lady seemed suddenly to be more frail than ever and, although both tried to hold back tears, there was a quiver in Henrietta's voice when she said, 'Come again soon, my darling girl, and do take care of yourself.'

'And you, Grandmama. Thanks for making me come to my senses. I love you very much.' The tiny hand clung to hers for a moment then she released it and Henrietta, managing a smile, said to give dear Romy a kiss and hug from her and love to Alistair.

Chadwick and half the family saw them off at the station. Esmeralda, who said she hated goodbyes, bade her daughter farewell at home – she did not even come to the door to wave the three of them away. Although Jessamy was used to her mother's ways she still felt hurt.

Alistair was there to meet them at St Pancras with Romaine, Rebecca and Anne. The child pulled away from her father and ran towards her, calling, '*Mama! Mama!*' Jessamy picked her up and laid her cheek to her daughter's, tears stinging her eyes. 'Mama, I saw the big puffing engine!'

Louise said, 'And don't I get a kiss?' Romaine wriggled down and flung herself into Louise's arms.

Alistair drew Jessamy to him. 'I've missed you so much, my darling.' He held her away from him and gently wiped her tears with his thumb. 'You look blooming.'

'So she should,' Louise said, laughing. 'Flynn has taken us everywhere, along the pier at Tynemouth where we had a good blow, then along the seafront to Cullercoats and on to Whitley Bay. We've been to Seahouses and...'

Rebecca broke in to tell them about the concert she and Anne had been to, then Alistair interrupted in turn to suggest it might be a good idea if they talked on the way home as Kate would have a meal ready for them. He added to Jessamy, 'She offered and I accepted. I thought it very kind of her.'

'Very kind indeed,' Jessamy murmured, her heart sinking. Why did Kate always have to be on the scene. And yet, it was more than generous of the actress, who led such a busy life. There was a time during the drive to Paradise Corner when everyone seemed to be talking at once and Jessamy wanted to shout, 'Stop, calm down!'

Rebecca announced, 'Jessamy, did Alistair tell you that Matron has left? She got better but decided to retire. We have a new one, at least she's not a matron, she's a housekeeper. I quite like her but she's got her eyes on everything.'

Anne, angry-looking, said, 'Rebecca, it's not your place to discuss the business of the dispensary. I thought you would have been more interested in asking how our parents were.'

Rebecca looked crushed. 'I spoke without thinking. I intended to ask about them later.'

There was a silence. Even Romaine sat quiet. Jessamy said, 'Your father and mother are fine, Rebecca. I'll tell you all the news when we get settled in.'

When they arrived at the Coachman's Cottage Kate came out and ran to the gate, waving and calling, 'Right on cue! The meal is ready to serve.'

Jessamy thanked her for her good deed. Kate hugged her. 'I couldn't wait for you to get back. My goodness, you look splendid, doesn't she Alistair?'

'She certainly does. She looks as if she's been out in the sun.'

'I'm weatherbeaten.' Jessamy tried to speak lightly.

During the meal she had an odd feeling that something was different, had changed, but she was unable to place it. Everyone seemed in a party mood. Jessamy gave Rebecca and Anne news of their parents, said how they were missing them both, then talked about the rest of the family. Romaine became over-excited so Flynn told her stories about the fairies and the leprechauns, which quietened and enchanted her.

Rebecca was eager to know what the family had said about their engagement. Flynn grinned. 'I was welcomed into the family like royalty. We're to be married in the summer but the date's not set yet.'

Romaine was looking sleepy and Jessamy said, 'Bedtime, my love, I'll take you up.' Romaine drew away and began to whinge. She wanted Aunt Louise to take her to bed, she told the best stories.

It was like a blow to the stomach but Jessamy managed to force a smile. 'Yes, she does,' and turning to Louise, asked if she minded taking her up.

'No, of course not.'

Flynn said he would go up too and after Romaine had said goodnight all round and the three of them had disappeared upstairs, Jessamy said brightly, 'Well, I think I'll start clearing away.'

'Oh, no you won't,' declared Kate. 'That is our job. Rebecca, Anne – how about lending a hand?'

They agreed at once and as they cleared the table Alistair gripped Jessamy's hand and smiled. 'Aren't we lucky to have all these helpers.' Then when Kate and the girls went into the scullery Alistair sat in the armchair, drew Jessamy on to his lap, laid his cheek to hers and whispered, 'Don't be upset, darling, you know what children are when they're overtired. Tomorrow Romy will be smothering you with her love. She's done nothing but chatter about you since last night. Remember how long it's been – and be patient.'

Jessamy knew he was doing his best to lessen her hurt but even when Louise came down saying that Romy wanted to say goodnight to her Mama, it only emphasised the slight, for she guessed that Romaine had been coaxed into asking for her.

Flynn came out of the bedroom as Jessamy reached the landing and he whispered, 'She's nearly asleep.'

Romaine did manage to murmur, 'Goodnight, Mama,' and hold up her face for a kiss, but the next moment she was asleep. Jessamy stood looking at the lovely young face and wondered how, only a few weeks ago, she had been reconciled to dying and to leaving her child. Now here she was, fully recovered from her breakdown but feeling ill with sorrow and fear because she felt she was losing her. Why, oh why, had she not taken her daughter to St Peel? They would have been together all the time, cementing their love, their closeness.

Or was this a selfish attitude? She was thinking only of herself, not of her child. When Lillian had threatened to kill Romaine she had been willing to sacrifice herself to save her, yet here she was, jealous of her Cousin Louise, who had loved and helped to care for Romaine since the day she was born.

Jessamy dropped a kiss on her daughter's brow and went out. Alistair and Flynn were down in the scullery with Kate and the girls. There was a burst of laughter, followed by Flynn saying, 'I know you don't believe me, but that is what the man said, so help me.'

In the normal way Jessamy would have gone right in and shared in the fun, but now she stood in the sitting room feeling as isolated as though she were on a desert island.

Alistair came in, his laughter dying away as he saw her. 'Jessamy, are you all right?'

'Yes, just tired, I think.'

Louise who had followed Alistair in said, 'Of course you are. It's been an emotional day. Saying goodbye to the family this morning, coming home, the little party, then all that talking...' She called to the others, 'Come along, folks, we must leave these two lovebirds on their own.'

There was a clatter of crockery, of cutlery being put away, then they were all in the room, laughing and saying goodnight. When Alistair came back after seeing them off and suggested gently that Jessamy ought to go up to bed she said no, she wanted to talk. 'I want to know about the new housekeeper and catch up on everything that's been happening at the dispensary.'

Alistair drew the settee up to the fire and they sat together, his arm around her. He told her that the housekeeper's name was Mrs Cotter; she had done some nursing and seemed competent. Then, giving her a loving glance he added, 'We can talk about the dispensary later. I must tell you my other news – I've been saving it until you were home. You are the first to know.' He paused then announced dramatically; 'I've bought a practice. It's in Devonshire Street, near Wimpole Street in the West End.' He grinned. 'A *most* prestigious address, my dear!'

'Oh, Alistair, that's wonderful.' Jessamy gave him a hug.

'You'll love the place. It's furnished and is quietly elegant, a bit larger than I envisaged but I do need a good address to draw the right patients.' When Jessamy made no comment he went on, 'I need those wealthy patients, to provide funds for the dispensary and for any more improvements we might want to make. You do agree?'

'Yes, but will you be able to keep on the work at Paradise Corner *and* the practice? Do you want us to leave the cottage and live in Devonshire Street?'

'Yes to your first query, and I must add that when I'm settled into the practice I shall also be doing operations at Guy's Hospital.'

'Alistair, it's too much,' Jessamy protested, feeling dismayed.

He explained the schedule he had worked out then said, 'As for leaving the cottage, I'm not sure about that. You like it, it is handy for Paradise Corner and furthermore, Romaine is happy with Margaret. She not only has the other children to play with but is getting educated at the same time.'

Greatly relieved at not having to leave the cottage, Jessamy said she fully agreed.

'Good.' Alistair drew her head to his shoulder. 'Oh, how I've missed you, my darling.'

Jessamy, suddenly feeling brighter, teased him. 'I didn't miss you at all. I had such a lovely time.'

He sat up, startled, then seeing the mischief in her eyes pulled her to her feet and kissed her throat and eyelids, saying in sensuous tones, 'You'll pay for that, my girl.'

Her body began to throb and she said a little shakily, 'When does the punishment start, master?'

Within seconds they were reliving the evening in his lodgings when they had made wild love...Alistair turned down the lamp and after frantically undressing one another they made love on the rug in the firelight, Alistair speaking her name over and over again in a ragged voice, while Jessamy gave little moans and now again small yelps of delight. Tender love could be satisfying but this stormy loving took them to unbelievable peaks of ecstasy where everything was a fiery, golden splendour and where intimate phrases were used, phrases not used at any other time.

And it was only during these stormy sessions that, when the peak was reached and the throbbing died away, it was a mere few seconds before the body was being replenished for a further onslaught.

At last, satiated, they fell asleep upstairs in one another's arms.

When Jessamy woke the next morning Alistair had gone from the bed. Usually she felt a little ashamed after a night of stormy lovemaking, but this morning she lay drowsy and contented as a well-fed kitten. Alistair was wholly hers. A tiny doubt had crept into her mind once or twice while she was away that Alistair and Kate might have been unable to resist their mutual attraction, but now she had no more worries on that score. No man could have made love so many times if he had been sexually active with another woman.

Within the next hour Jessamy was back in the old routine. Mr Saunders collected Romaine, who was all loving again towards her mother, giving her hugs and smacking kisses and telling her how much she loved her. Louise called her traitor and Romy, guessing by the teasing in her aunt's voice that it was meant to be funny, chuckled. On their way over to the dispensary, Jessamy and Louise looked in at the soup kitchen to see Kate who greeted them with a cheerful smile, saying she had a surfeit of helpers. Three of the women had got the date wrong, but they wanted to stay. 'I've agreed,' she said, raising her eyebrows in a comical way.

'Poor Kate,' Jessamy said when she and Louise left. 'She copes at times with impossible odds.'

To which Louise replied wryly, 'Don't we all.'

At Paradise Corner Jessamy was introduced to Mrs Cotter, the new housekeeper and liked her instantly; she also received a big welcome from Willard Stead and the two students. Some of the patients, too, said they had missed her. 'You're like a bit of sun come out,' declared one elderly man. 'I feel better already, me duck.'

Alistair smiled and squeezed Jessamy's hand when she sat down at the table to take up her old job of keeping the records.

When Louise and Flynn were told about Alistair's new practice, they were eager to see the house. It was decided that they would all go together the following evening. Rebecca promised to stay in with Romaine. 'If she does wake,' she said, 'I have some lovely stories to tell her.'

Although Jessamy had no wish to live at Devonshire Street, she could not help but be impressed by the simple Georgian elegance that Alistair had described. Louise and Flynn were also very taken with the place. Flynn half-jokingly suggested that he and Louise could move in when they were married and rent some rooms.

Alistair smiled. 'Why not? There are plenty to choose from, and it's uneconomic to leave them empty.'

Jessamy, dismayed, looked quickly at Louise, wondering

who would look after Romaine when necessary.

Louise shook her head. 'It's tempting, but for one thing I want to stay near Romy and for another, I would rather live within easy reach of the dispensary. I'm beginning to like the work there. I could never be a stay-at-home wife.'

Flynn shrugged his shoulders and grinned. 'It was just a thought. Come along, let's have something to eat. It will be my treat, a celebration.'

Jessamy went with mixed feelings. One moment she had been worried that she might no longer have Louise to look after Romaine and the next, she was madly jealous when her cousin said she wanted to be near the child, as though she belonged to her.

The men were busy talking about the new practice and the work it would involve, and Louise said to Jessamy, 'It is a lovely house, but I think you're wise to stay at the cottage. Romy would miss so much if you moved, and you would find it more difficult to get over to Paradise Corner. It's only recently that I've appreciated how much the dispensary means to you. I had never realised it could be so rewarding helping the poverty-stricken. We are lucky, aren't we? We've always been well cared for, well-clothed.'

Jessamy felt suddenly ashamed for having such mean thoughts about her cousin. Louise only had Romaine's welfare at heart, as she had. She said, 'Yes, very lucky. We had love too, at home, which a lot of the children we deal with lack, poor little souls. Have you noticed how caring Rebecca always is to the children at the dispensary? And they seem to love her in return.'

While Rebecca was being discussed she was sitting curled up in an armchair at the cottage, dreamily reliving the two weeks when her cousin had been away. She was very fond of Jessamy, but she had enjoyed herself so much during her absence that she wished she had stayed away for longer. On the other hand, of course, the situation had been ideal, with Matron confined to her room and Anne busy tending to her at night. Now with Matron gone she not only had Anne's eagle eyes to contend with, but those of the new housekeeper.

Rebecca gave a small, ecstatic sigh. Even if she had no more wonderful outings to look forward to for a while, nothing could take away the lovely excitement of her trips to the theatre with both Tom Hansard and Richard Mather. Neither man knew about the other taking her out, but both seemed ready to take the risk of discovery by Alistair, and the serious repercussions that would follow. Was she, then, worth this risk? Rebecca smiled secretly. It had all been so thrilling – the performances and the drinks afterwards. There were, of course, the rather dreadful parts when she had allowed Tom and Richard to...Rebecca closed her eyes tightly as though trying to blot out the fact that she had allowed both men to have their way with her.

She sat up slowly. They had both sworn that nothing would happen to her, but supposing she had a baby? She couldn't, she couldn't! She would be sent home, disgraced for ever. Then she suddenly brightened. Why was she worrying? Tom and Richard were medical students and knew everything there was to know about the body. If they said she would not conceive, then she wouldn't.

With this worry off her mind she allowed herself to dwell on the actual act. Although she had known what a man and a woman did to make a baby, she had been unprepared for the strong feelings it aroused in her. The first time it had been with Tom, who had taken her to one of the derelict buildings in Paradise Street, the second with Richard who had borrowed a motor car. In both cases she had had a lot to drink – three or four glasses of wine. On the next two occasions she had had less to drink and enjoyed the lovemaking more. It had been so exciting... Tom had fumbled a lot but Richard seemed to be more experienced. Both men, in their different ways, had been tender and yet, although Richard was better-looking, she felt she loved Tom best.

Tonight she had told Richard she would be sitting with Romaine and he had asked what time Jessamy and Alistair were due back. She said late, possibly around ten o'clock and Richard had whispered that he would try and call in about half-past eight. It was nearly that now. Emotions stirred in her. Would he come? He was on duty at nine o'clock. Rebecca got up and going to the front door, peeped out. To her surprise fog blotted out the buildings opposite. Should she draw the curtains back a little, show some light? She shivered and hurried back to the blazing fire. It was wrong to have invited Richard here. This was Jessamy and Alistair's home. It was cheating – and risky, too.

She glanced at the curtains then drew them apart a fraction, her heart thumping. Never had she imagined that feelings could be so rampant. Oh, why didn't he come? Tom would have been here before now. Three times she went to the front door again and at the third time, seeing a dim shape coming in her direction, she closed the door quickly and leaned against it, waiting. Footsteps came closer, slowed then passed. Her shoulders went slack. It would be best if Richard did not come. There would not be enough time to make love. After all, he was not likely to come in and jump on her right away!

But Rebecca was wrong. When there came a gentle tap on the door she raced to open it, then she was in his arms and his hand was inside her blouse in seconds. 'Oh, my love, I am hungry for you.' His voice was ragged. 'I had a job to get away. Mrs Cotter wanted to talk.' He walked Rebecca in front of him to the sitting room, his hand caressing her breast.

She moaned, 'Oh, Richard, I want you, too.'

By the time he had her in front of the fire he had her blouse off and was unfastening his trouser buttons. It was over so quickly she could hardly believe it. She begged him not to stop but he said, 'Sorry, precious, I couldn't wait. Next time it'll be different – we'll have a proper evening out, I promise.'

Richard was already putting himself to rights and Rebecca, feeling disillusioned, had picked up her blouse when there was a knock at the front door. Richard, quite calm, asked in a low voice if there was a back way out. Rebecca, in a panic, nodded towards the scullery door while she struggled to put on her blouse. She was buttoning it up with trembling fingers when the knock came again, this time sharp and imperative.

Richard dropped a kiss on her nose, whispered, 'Say you were lying down,' and vanished.

His calmness had the desired effect. She went to the door, saw it was her sister Anne and said, as she fastened the last button. 'Oh, it's you. I had a headache coming on and I went to lie down beside Romy. Actually, she's been quite restless. Is something wrong?'

'No, I just thought I would keep you company for a while.' She went into the sitting room and Rebecca followed, trying hard to stay calm. Anne's eyes were everywhere before she sat down. Then she gave a sniff and asked who had been smoking cigars. Rebecca told her Flynn and Alistair, then looked around quickly to see if there was any evidence that Richard Mather had paid a visit. There was nothing. She sat back in the chair wishing that Anne would leave, wanting to think over the interlude with Richard, but her sister was in no hurry. She sat staring at her and when Rebecca asked what was wrong she snapped, 'What were you doing before I arrived? Your hair is tousled and your face is all flushed.'

Rebecca, feeling safe, gave a deep sigh. 'Will you for heaven's sake stop watching me like a hawk! I told you – I lay down on Romy's bed. I feel I have a temperature.'

'You have a temperature all the time, gazing at every man in sight.'

'Well, it's better than gazing in the way that you do at Hannah Fanshaw!'

Hot colour rushed to Anne's face. 'What exactly do you mean by that?'

'Just what I say. You look at her as if she were some god you worshipped. Ugh, she's so plain, she's...'

Anne jumped to her feet. 'She's a very clever woman and I happen to admire her dedication to medicine, which you will never have in a million years because you haven't the brains. All you can think of is men, men, men. One of these days you'll get yourself into real trouble.'

'No, one of these days I'll get married and have a home and children while you will turn out to be a plain-looking, tight-lipped spinster like your dear friend Nurse Fanshaw, without ever knowing a man's love. I feel sorry for you.'

'I know your type!' Anne shouted. 'You're the kind of person who ends up on the streets. Well, when you're riddled with disease don't come running to me for advice because you won't get it.' With that Anne swept out, slamming the door behind her.

Rebecca sank into a chair, shocked at the way things had turned out. She and Anne had never been really close, but they had rubbed along together well enough, never had a big quarrel like this. What had happened to sour her sister so? Anne had never had a young man to walk out with – was that the reason?

Rebecca felt suddenly ashamed of that thought, and of her own behaviour just now. Fancy telling her sister she would become a plain, tight-lipped spinster like Hannah Fanshaw. How had all this come about? Had she been aware of Richard Mather's visit? But how could she? What a fiasco the evening had been. She would never speak to Richard Mather again. He came from a wealthy family and no doubt thought he could use her like some sons of the rich treated their servant girls. Oh, yes, she had been told all about it. Well, he would never have his way with her again. Rebecca had a weep, but had pulled herself together again by the time Alistair and Jessamy returned.

Anne was not in the room they now shared when Rebecca returned to Paradise Corner so, presuming she was with the Fanshaw woman, telling her all about their quarrel, Rebecca undressed and got into bed, feeling more miserable than she could ever remember.

When she awoke the next morning, Anne was there getting dressed. Rebecca immediately apologised for what she had said the night before. Anne told her she had been as much to blame then went on, 'To save you from feeling that I'm watching you all the time, I'm going to share Hannah's bedroom from now on and Elizabeth will move in with you. She is very pleasant.'

'Anne, I – you don't bear me a grudge, do you? I wouldn't want – '

'No, don't worry. Hannah showed me the error of my ways.' There was a wryness in Anne's voice. 'It seems we're never too old to learn. Now come along, get up.' Normally Rebecca would jump to her sister's commands but now when Anne went out she lay back, puzzled. Why this turnabout attitude? Not that she minded sharing with Elizabeth, she welcomed it in fact. She got on well with her. It just seemed strange that after sharing a bedroom with Anne since they were small her sister should be willing to go in with someone else. Slowly, Rebecca began to see the pleasant change it would make in her life. She would be able to sneak out and be with Tom at least for a while, even if they could not have any more visits to the theatre. By the time Rebecca was up and dressed she decided she might marry Tom. Not right away, of course, but one day. She closed her mind completely to thoughts of Richard Mather.

At least, she did then...but when she saw him downstairs and he gave her one of his devastating smiles her heart skipped a beat. A friend at home had told her that men suffered if they couldn't make love when they wanted to. Perhaps that was why he had been in such a hurry the night before. No doubt when he had a chance he would explain all this to her.

It was not until the afternoon that Rebecca had the chance of a talk with Richard and then it was he who approached her. She was in the ward tending to the needs of the patients when he came in. He drew her aside. 'Rebecca, precious, I'm sorry about last night. Please forgive me.' He spoke in a low persuasive voice. 'I was aching for you and when I saw your dear sweet face when you opened the door it was all too much for me. I had to take you there and then.'

She looked up at him with a worshipping gaze and whispered, 'It's all right. I understand how a man suffers if he can't...can't...'

'*Mather.*' It was Dr Stead's voice. 'You're wanted in the

dispensary.'

'Yes, sir.' Richard gave Rebecca a quick warm glance and left.

Willard Stead turned to Rebecca. 'Don't let Mather distract you from your duties, Rebecca.'

'No, I won't. He doesn't. He had promised to lend me a medical book and had forgotten to give it to me. He was just telling me he would bring it in this afternoon.' An elderly patient began to moan and Rebecca, excusing herself, went over to the woman, feeling elated that everything was all right again with Richard. He really did love her. Perhaps they could arrange to meet again when he was off-duty...

Jessamy had been puzzled about Rebecca the night before. It was obvious her cousin had been crying but she denied it, said she thought she had the beginnings of a cold. Then this morning, here she was almost bursting with happiness. But of course, that was her volatile nature. Still...

Jessamy forgot about Rebecca and everything else when Alistair told her he was going to do some dissecting that evening and asked if she would like to attend. 'Oh, yes, please,' she enthused, as though she was being asked to an exclusive party rather than going to see a cadaver cut up. Alistair told her they would meet in the operating room at seven o'clock and that Willard Stead, the two students, Elizabeth Hope and Hannah Fanshaw would also attend. Although Jessamy was doubtful that Nurse Fanshaw, with her queasiness about operations, would want to be there she kept her doubts to herself. Jessamy always had an odd feeling going into the operating room, even when it was empty. Now, with a dead body on the trolley, she had a feeling of awe. Here was a man who had lived in poverty for the last years of his life and yet in death was to provide valuable medical knowledge for those who nursed, who saved lives. She stood beside Hannah in case she felt faint.

Alistair began the proceedings on the same lines along which Jessamy had been thinking. 'There should be dignity in death,' he said. 'It may seem that this body is being violated but the soul is gone and the knowledge we gain from dissection is invaluable. I like to think that the person involved somehow knows that he could be responsible for giving help to other sufferers. This patient had a cirrhotic liver caused by excessive drinking and when you see the organ, gentlemen,' he glanced at the two students with a wry smile, 'it may cause you to limit your intake of alcohol.'

When he made the first incision Jessamy felt Hannah sway. She was paper-white. Jessamy gripped her arm tightly and the nurse steadied. 'I'm all right,' she whispered. 'Thanks.'

Jessamy looked across at the two students. Tom was pale but Richard seemed totally absorbed in the proceedings. Jessamy had drunk wine in small quantities but when she saw the damaged liver she felt she never wanted to touch another drop of alcohol again.

Alistair was not only expert in dissecting but was an excellent lecturer. Being shown parts of the body and having them described could have been gruesome, even horrifying, yet he made them aware that there was a delicacy in the bone structure and in the arrangement of veins, nerves and sinews. By the end of the session, Jessamy felt she had been initiated into the beginning of time: it was an awesome experience.

Tom and Richard thanked Alistair for the knowledge they had gained. So did Hannah Fanshaw, adding, 'And thanks to your wife, I'm over my problem of feeling faint.'

Later, Alistair said to Jessamy, 'So you didn't feel faint?'

'No, I was too fascinated. You taught us all a lot, Alistair. You have a wonderful way of imparting knowledge.'

During the next few weeks Jessamy felt she was living life to the full. A big improvement had taken place in the health of the patients; many of them thanked Alistair for his help and for the nourishing soup served at the kitchen. There were also grateful thanks for the clothes and boots that Kate had distributed. She now had a strong team of regular helpers, not only for the kitchen but for collecting clothes and footwear to be supplied to the patients. There was also the deep personal satisfaction Jessamy obtained from easing the pain of many people by healing with her hands. She insisted on maintaining the explanation that she employed some form of massage, and in this way, protected herself and the dispensary from unwanted publicity. The grateful patients praised her deft fingers. In some cases, she effected cures.

Then, one day, Alistair asked her if she would visit a house where apparently a woman and her children were poorly. A neighbour had reported it but said she had to go to work and couldn't care for them. Jessamy was shocked to discover a mother and her four children huddled in one bed in an unheated basement room, its walls running with damp. Their only coverings were rags and they were all suffering badly from malnutrition. Jessamy told the woman she would be back and ran all the way to the dispensary. In less than half an hour she had installed then in the ward, where they were washed and fed and settled in warmed beds. Within a few days they were recovering. The problem then was where to house them, at which point Mr Saunders came to their aid. He and his sons worked on a derelict house to make it habitable and installed the ground floor with a collection of odd pieces of furniture. The woman wept in gratitude at such comfort. The incident sparked off another charitable project, of getting the most poverty-stricken people into better living conditions.

It was not until Jessamy came into contact with this family that she realised she had only touched on the fringe of poverty. On another occasion, she found children left alone in a bare room with rats running around while their mother did slave labour in a factory. The father had been killed in an accident at work. Then there was an elderly, eccentric woman in a hovel, who would not allow anyone in to attend to her. A neighbour reported to Jessamy, 'I think she's dead. There's an awful stink when you push the letter-box open.' Jessamy got a workman to break the door down and he said, 'Oh, Gawd.' The woman, who had gangrene in both legs, lay in absolute squalor on the verge of death. For the first time in years Jessamy vomited.

Alistair had leaflets printed and distributed in the neighbourhood, asking people to report such cases. The list grew. Eventually district nurses were employed to do regular visits and Mr Saunders and his sons set up a crêche in a derelict building where working mothers could leave their children in warm, safe conditions during the day. Rebecca asked if she could be one of the nursery nurses and was immediately given a responsible post.

Helping to administer this project increased Jessamy's workload enormously, but she didn't mind. She felt full of energy and fulfilment, oddly happy, even though she and Alistair rarely made love these days. He was often late home and would sometimes fall asleep in the armchair, when she would gently rouse him with a kiss and coax him to go up to bed.

Then one evening, about six weeks after she had managed to get the woman with the four children rehoused, she suffered a blow that made her feel her life had come to an end.

14

Flynn had invited Alistair and Jessamy out to dinner with Louise and himself. Alistair said it would be impossible that evening, as he had a lot of paperwork to catch up on so the Irishman asked Jessamy to come on her own; with persuasion from all three she accepted.

When Alistair asked what time they would be back Flynn told him that at the earliest it would be eleven o'clock, then with a grin added, 'It could be midnight, so don't wait up – I have a very attractive escort in mind for your lovely wife.'

Alistair laughed. 'Oh, I shall definitely wait up in that case. I might have to fight a duel with this prince of men!'

It was all so light-hearted and Jessamy thoroughly enjoyed the evening. At ten o'clock, however, Louise complained of a headache and they left. When they reached home Jessamy said goodnight to Flynn and Louise, who were going to the dispensary to fetch something for her cousin's headache, and let herself quietly into the cottage in case Alistair was asleep. Suddenly, she froze. There were voices coming from the sitting room – low, intimate voices. Then she heard Alistair say, 'You *must* stay, Kate. We couldn't do without you and I couldn't bear not to see you.' With a feeling of having a leaden weight inside her, Jessamy went forward and pushed the door open gently.

Alistair and Kate were standing in front of the fire, Alistair's hands on Kate's shoulders, looking soulfully into each other's eyes. It was reminiscent of the scene on the night she had found Fabian and Caroline together, and Jessamy felt sick.

'So,' she said.

The pair jumped guiltily apart. Alistair said, 'Jessamy... you're back early.'

'Yes. I'm so sorry to interrupt your big love scene.' Did this ice-cold voice belong to her?

'It wasn't like that,' Kate said, distressed.

'Perhaps I was mistaken. I thought I heard Alistair say he couldn't bear not to see you.'

'We were not making love.' Alistair spoke earnestly.

'Tell me one thing, *have* you ever made love?'

'Only once,' he said quickly.

'I see. So you think that mitigates the offence? I presume this happened when I was away.'

There was a silence then Alistair spread his hands. 'Everyone is open to temptation.'

'Oh, yes, we both know about temptation, don't we? But when we succumbed to it I was unhappy with my husband and then you were not married with a wife and child... whom you pretended to love.'

'I didn't pretend, Jessamy, you know I didn't.'

'He does love you,' Kate said quietly, 'that is why I was telling him I wanted to leave.'

'And I loved you as a friend, Kate. You betrayed me. So did Alistair. That is unforgivable.'

'Yes, it is.' Kate's eyes were brimming with tears. 'It's not enough to say I'm sorry. I can only hope that in time you might find it in your heart to forgive me. I'll go home and pack, leave London.'

'That won't be necessary. I shall be the one to leave. You do excellent work here – don't let the people suffer because of what's happened.'

'So do you, Jessamy!'

'There are a hundred people who could do my job, but only one you. You run the soup kitchen, find helpers, collect money, all of which is so important. I won't be missed.' Jessamy spoke the last four words with great bitterness.

Kate picked up her coat. 'I'll stay until I can find someone to take charge of the kitchen.' Then she was gone. When Jessamy made to follow her Alistair caught her arm.

'I'll speak to her later. Now we must talk – we have to. We can't go to bed with this situation hanging fire.'

Jessamy stood looking at him, feeling oddly detached. 'I had no intention of going to bed. I'm leaving you, Alistair. I won't be here in the morning to go to the dispensary. Louise will see to the records.'

'Jessamy, for God's sake be reasonable!'

'I *am* being reasonable. You can't bear to live without Kate; I can't bear to live with you.'

Alistair thrust his fingers through his hair in a despairing way. 'I've tried to explain to you before that one can love different people in different ways. My love for you is on a different plane to what I feel for Kate.'

'Oh, yes, I am there for your convenience when Kate is not around.'

'No! Why won't you try and understand?'

'Why won't you? I'm leaving you and nothing will make me change my mind.'

'It's all very well for you to say you're leaving me, but you have no right to deprive me of Romy.'

'I'm not. I won't be taking her away from all she's familiar with. There are plenty of people who love her here. Louise would be only too pleased to take over as mother.'

Alistair eyed Jessamy with alarm. 'Jessamy, you obviously haven't recovered from the shock of being attacked by Lillian.'

'I'm fully recovered from that ordeal, but I was certainly shocked to find you in an almost loving embrace with Kate.'

'We were not in a loving embrace, but forget that for the moment. You talk about leaving. Where would you go – what about money?'

'That is no problem. I have an income from the shops that Louise and I own. I'm not sure yet where I shall go – certainly not home. I may take this opportunity to train as a doctor.'

'Oh, I see. It's something you've always wanted to do and now you are seizing this situation as an excuse.' Alistair spoke harshly.

'No. As a matter of fact I think it will have to come

later. There must be thousands of people in other areas who need the sort of care we've been providing here. I may carry on this work elsewhere.'

'Look, Jessamy, you go to bed. I'll sleep on the sofa. I'm sure you'll feel differently in the morning.'

'I won't. You go to bed, I'll sleep with Romaine. In the meantime I want to wait to have a talk with Louise.'

'Well pray heaven that *she* will be able to talk some sense into you, because I obviously can't!' He stormed out.

Jessamy had just sunk into an armchair when Louise came in quietly. 'What is all the shouting about?'

When Jessamy had explained the situation, Louise stared at her. 'You must be mad, leaving because your husband transgressed...only once.'

'That is all they admit to, but apart from that how could I trust a man again who makes wild, passionate love to me when I return, tells me how much he has missed me, when all the time he and Kate have been – cavorting.'

Louise drew up a chair. 'Jessamy, listen to me. No one is perfect. Alistair admitted before to being drawn to Kate. She's in love with him – it's obvious. You are away, Alistair is lonely, he and Kate get together, the situation becomes emotional. They make love – only once. I believe them. Kate, not wanting to get involved again, sensibly decides to leave.'

'And what does Alistair do? Not only does he beg her to stay but he tells her he can't exist without her! Tell me, is that the reaction of a man who loves only his wife?'

Louise was silent for a moment, studying Jessamy, then she said, 'You asked Alistair and Kate to be truthful with you regarding their lovemaking. I'm asking you to be honest with me: was Alistair right when he implied that you were making their little affair an excuse to pave the way for you to go into medicine? I know you told him you were not planning it for the present time, but is it your aim eventually?'

Jessamy looked at her squarely. 'During the past few weeks I've been strangely happy. I had a feeling of fulfilment. When I was watching the dissection the other evening I felt awed. It seemed that I had been taken to the beginning of time, that I had seen some of the mysteries of creation. No, the affair with Alistair and Kate is not an excuse to leave my home, my husband and child. It will tear my heart to leave Romaine, but I must for her sake. I know you love her as if she were your own. Will you look after her, Louise?'

Until that moment the situation had seemed unreal and Jessamy had felt almost detached but now, when Louise got up, put her arms around her and said of course she would look after Romaine, Jessamy began to weep, big slow tears that made her feel as if her lifeblood was draining away.

Although they talked for another half hour Jessamy did not alter her decision to leave. She did say, however, that she would stay on for a few days to settle her affairs and decide where to go.

At the end of a week she was still at the cottage, for the simple reason that she could not decide what to do for the best. It was a wretched time, unnatural, not being able to talk freely to Alistair or be friendly with Kate when she called every morning at the kitchen to see if she needed anything. One morning Kate said, a pleading in her voice, 'Jessamy, can't we forget what happened and start all over again?'

Jessamy declared firmly, 'Never,' and left.

It was Louise who suggested that if Jessamy had definitely made up her mind to go, she could recommend lodgings in Poplar, another area of East London where she would find poverty enough. Flynn knew the landlady, a widow who would be willing to rent her two rooms.

At first Jessamy rejected this idea, saying bitterly that when she did leave it would have to be somewhere where she could lose herself. To this Louise replied wryly she could lose herself in London very easily, but did point out that if Romaine was ill in the future and asked for her, at least she could be contacted and was within reach.

'She's a healthy child.'

'Oh, for heaven's sake, Jessamy, I'm speaking of realities.

You're living in a little world of your own, and it's time someone told you what may be in store.' Louise walked to the door. 'I'll go upstairs and leave you to think it over.'

Jessamy sat sunk in misery. It seemed so unfair that she should have to be the one to leave, when Alistair was the transgressor. There was a sudden thumping on the front door, a continuous series of thuds that grew weaker as they went on. When she opened the door, Rebecca stumbled in. Her face was colourless and beads of perspiration lined her upper lip and brow.

Jessamy caught her before she fell. 'Rebecca, what on earth?'

'I was...pregnant. I had an...abortion. I'm – bleeding...It hurts.'

An abortion? Oh my God. Jessamy, just managing to support her, called up the stairs, 'Louise, *Louise!* Come quickly, I need your help.'

Her cousin came to the top of the stairs and Jessamy shouted to bring sheets and towels, quickly. After Jessamy had explained the situation Louise spread sheets on the floor of the sitting room, helped Jessamy with Rebecca then leaving her to pack the girl with towels to staunch the bleeding, departed to fetch Alistair. As Jessamy put a kettle of water on the fire and brought a bowl and fresh towel, questions raced through her mind. Who was responsible for this pregnancy? And who had done the abortion? An amateur, obviously. Rebecca was haemorrhaging badly. She seemed to be unconscious but suddenly she opened her eyes and whispered, 'The father of the baby is not known to anyone here. I won't say who he is.' When Jessamy asked who had done the abortion, she mouthed, 'A woman,' then closed her eyes.

Alistair and Louise entered, both breathless. Alistair said, 'I'll have to lift her up on the table. Get me some blankets and more hot water in a bowl.'

Louise went for blankets while Jessamy poured water into the bowl and added the disinfectant that Alistair had brought. As he washed his hands he said, 'I'll need your help, Jessamy – we don't want anyone else to know about this. She'll have to stay here afterwards. We'll put her in our bed. I'll sit up with her.' Their relationship at that moment was one of surgeon and nurse and Jessamy was glad she was there to assist.

When Alistair examined Rebecca he said, 'Oh God, who did this and what in heaven was used?'

Rebecca whispered, 'She had a metal hook.'

Alistair went pale with anger. 'These back-street butchers should be imprisoned for life.' He added to Jessamy in a low voice, 'She's torn the membranes.'

Jessamy knew enough about abortionists to know that dirty, crude instruments could be responsible for a girl dying or at the least, being left infertile. She prayed that Rebecca, loving children, would not be denied them through this criminal action.

Jessamy threaded and handed sutures to Alistair while Louise mopped his brow as he perspired in the heat of the room. He worked quickly but it took a long time to repair the internal damage.

Louise had put a warming pan over the bed and Alistair carried his limp patient upstairs. He stayed with Rebecca for a time and when he came downstairs Jessamy handed him a cup of tea.

'So,' he said. 'Who was the one who made her pregnant?'

When Jessamy repeated what Rebecca had said he dismissed it as a likely story, then went on, 'Hazarding a guess, I would say it was Tom Hansard.'

Louise said quietly, 'According to what I overheard she's also been seeing Richard Mather.'

Jessamy looked up quickly. 'Was this while I was away?'

Louise nodded. 'I think quite a lot has been going on behind our backs. I understand that Rebecca has been seen late at night with Tom Hansard and on another occasion with Richard Mather.'

'Why didn't you tell me?' Alistair demanded. 'Jessamy and I are supposed to be responsible for the girl!'

'Because I only heard about it this morning! Now don't try putting the blame on me – I was against Rebecca coming in the first place. You know how she is about men.'

Alistair apologised and Jessamy said, 'I feel terribly responsible too but we'll have to remain calm. The thing is done and can't be undone. I don't even think this should be mentioned to Tom or Richard, or we'll raise gossip. We'll keep Rebecca until she's well, then she'll have to go home.'

'Let's hope she gets well,' Alistair said quietly. 'Septicaemia is a real danger in these cases – and it can be fatal.'

Jessamy's heart began a slow painful thudding. 'Shouldn't her parents be told?'

'I'm hoping to save them that worry. We'll just have to hang on and see. I'll go up and take another look at her now.' Alistair, grim-faced, went upstairs. When he came down he said that Rebecca was holding her own then he added, 'I'm going back to the dispensary now. I shall say that Rebecca is running a temperature and we are keeping her here. This will be accepted, as we do have a minor influenza epidemic at the moment. Will you keep an eye on her, please? I won't be too long.'

When Alistair returned later he said, 'I'm convinced that either Hansard or Mather is responsible. They were both so concerned about Rebecca and their expressions were avid with curiosity...and guilt. It took me all my time not to accuse them and give them a damn good hiding, the blackguards, but I felt you were right, Jessamy. It wouldn't do to discuss the situation with anyone. One spark can set off a forest fire. I saw Anne and although she said she would come and sit with Rebecca she seemed relieved when I told her that we would take charge for the time being, until "the infection" had cleared.'

Jessamy insisted that she and Louise would share the patient-care and eventually Alistair agreed, when Jessamy pointed out to him that he had a full day to face the following morning.

He took the first shift, however, and when Jessamy took over from him, Rebecca's temperature had dropped. 'Although it's a little early to tell, I think she's going to pull through,' he said with a sigh.

'Pray heaven she will,' Jessamy responded fervently.

Alistair nodded, gave his wife's shoulder a squeeze and went to catnap on the sofa downstairs.

During her vigil all sorts of thoughts went through Jessamy's mind. Rebecca was a loving person who had let herself be carried away by the promise of adventure. Should she be blamed for the strength of her emotions which, after all, were God-given? Should Alistair be blamed for being drawn to Kate? Jessamy, who felt she had hated him a week ago, felt close to him again because he had needed her help. She was beginning to think she might stay and accept the situation, when it occurred to her that people had also been given willpower and it was up to the individual to control it. Alistair had told Kate he could not live without seeing her. Well, he could see her every minute of the day if he wished; why should she be a slave to his whims? She would tell Louise when Rebecca was well that she would accept the rooms she had mentioned...start a new life for herself.

Rebecca stirred and Jessamy touched her hand, feeling again a deep grief that this attractive girl, usually brimming over with the joy of living might never know the pleasure of bearing a child.

Rebecca's recovery was slow. Alistair would still not allow visitors, pointing out that if staff went down with the influenza there would be no one to care for the patients. His rule was accepted, since a number of people had succumbed to the infection.

When Rebecca was over the worst she said one day, with a pathetic air, that she would like to go home for a visit. Jessamy, seizing this opportunity, suggested it might be better if she stayed at St Peel and, to her surprise, the girl agreed. Looking up she said, 'I'm afraid of my own feelings if I stayed here, and I'm scared that someone might get to know what has happened. Thank you for saving my life and for protecting my reputation.'

It was decided that Louise and Flynn would take her back up North. Jessamy told Louise that when she came back, she would take up the offer of the rooms in Poplar, if they were still available.

'Yes, they're still available.' Louise sighed. 'I had hoped you might have changed your mind about leaving, but as you've had plenty of time to make a decision, I won't try and press you to stay.'

On the day that Rebecca left, no one would have guessed what had happened. She was full of good spirits, telling everyone she would soon be back and she laughed with Tom Hansard and Richard Mather, but Jessamy knew by their sheepish expressions that they both guessed what had taken place and felt guilty.

It was when Jessamy said goodbye to her cousin that she caught a glimpse of her inner pain and held her close. Rebecca whispered her thanks and was bright again.

The following evening Jessamy went to see Mr Saunders' daughter Margaret, to tell her she was going to take up charity work in another part of London. She asked her if she would continue their arrangement to look after Romaine. Margaret said yes of course she would, they all loved having her. Romy was part of the family now. Although Alistair paid Margaret a regular sum for Romaine's keep, Jessamy often contributed gifts of cakes and groceries. Now she pressed a lump sum of money into the woman's hand and begged her, a catch in her voice, to accept it, as a token of Jessamy's gratitude. 'You've been so kind, all of you.'

Margaret said, 'You make it very difficult, Mrs MacKay. I promise you that Romy will be well looked after and Daniel, bless him, will continue to keep her in order.' Margaret was normally a very quiet person, but perhaps sensing there was more to this situation than met the eye, tactfully went on talking.

'Daniel is having lessons in decorative plasterwork at the moment. He's most interested in it, despite his youth. I have some of his designs here, and some of Romy's work – but no doubt you've seen these before.'

Jessamy felt a pang, remembering the time Romaine had come home all excited, wanting to show her mother her 'draw-rings'. Jessamy had been busy, so had told her 'later' – and Romaine had not mentioned them since.

When Jessamy confessed this to Margaret, the other woman said pensively, 'Romy is a strange little soul. I've found, like you, that if I don't look at something straight away when she wants me to, I don't get to see it at all. But then one can't give in to a child's whims all the time, otherwise they would be the rulers. Anyway, let me show you their work now.'

Daniel certainly had a gift. He had drawn designs for ceilings, columns and friezes, decorated with cherubs, acanthas leaves, roses, vines, figures of Neptune and mermaids, and intricate trelliswork. He apparently copied them with enormous care from one of his grandfather's books on architecture.

Margaret said, 'At the moment Daniel is drawing from books, but Romaine draws strange creatures from her own imagination. Look at this!' She showed Jessamy a horse with wings and a man on its back, a long beard flowing out behind him. Sitting in the chariot behind was a woman with one eye in the middle of her forehead; she wore a broad-brimmed hat laden with flowers.

Margaret smiled at Jessamy. 'One has to admit that your small daughter is a thinker. I feel she has artistic talent, and it will be interesting to see how it develops as she matures.'

Jessamy felt a terrible ache. She would miss this stage of her daughter's development, but then sacrifices had to be made if she were to help other children and their parents to a better life.

At this moment the golden-haired Daniel arrived and Jessamy was as impressed with his manners as she had been on the first occasion. He gave her a slight bow and said, 'How do you do, Mrs MacKay.' He was nearly twelve now, but seemed older. He had a sturdy build and an air of confidence and authority. She could imagine him being firm, not only with Romaine but with his younger brothers and sisters, too. When Jessamy told him that his mother had been showing her some of his drawings and one done by Romaine he said, 'I showed that one to my drawing-master. He thought that Romy showed great promise and

I think so, too.' A smile touched his lips. 'She can also be very trying at times but we all love her.'

'I'm glad,' Jessamy said softly, feeling as though another big problem had been solved.

She felt so relaxed when she left their little house that she had put the fact that she would be leaving Alistair soon to the back of her mind. She came down to earth, however, when he marched in a few minutes after her arrival, looking stern.

'Jessamy, what is all this nonsense about you leaving? I thought you had put that foolishness behind you, but Louise tells me otherwise.'

'Why should you think it's nonsense? I told you and Kate I would be leaving when I discovered what you two had been up to behind my back. Nothing has changed since then.'

'No, one thing has not changed, Jessamy – my love for you. It goes deep. Kate and I know that we can live apart without it affecting us.'

'How nice for you,' Jessamy replied sarcastically. 'Well, I can live without you as well, and I have nothing more to say.' She turned to leave and he told her to wait, he had plenty to say to her.

Their confrontation ended with an almighty row, both of them shouting things that would haunt them for a long time to come. It did, however, make it easier for Jessamy to pack up and leave the following day.

When Flynn and Louise arrived to take her to her lodgings Alistair was nowhere in sight.

It was a silent threesome which drove away.

15

After Jessamy moved into the rooms she had rented in Poplar and found that poverty was rife in the district, just as Louise had foretold, she decided to postpone applying to become a doctor and concentrate on the needs of the people around her. During that long first year alone, using her own money and with the aid of willing helpers, she opened a dispensary and a soup kitchen, distributed clothing and managed to get some families rehoused. Her experience at Paradise Corner was invaluable, and so was her healing gift.

During the second year, she planned to open another soup kitchen. When Louise, who visited her regularly, learned about this she said worriedly, 'Jessamy, you must ease up.'

'I can't. I have too much to do.'

'You take a few days off – go back to the Coachman's Cottage and relax.'

'Thanks, but no.' Jessamy went into the kitchen and made tea.

Louise, Flynn, Alistair and Romaine had all eventually moved into the big house in Devonshire Street. They had, however, kept on the cottage so that Louise could relax there in between shifts at the dispensary.

Louise followed her cousin into the kitchen. 'You must have some rest, you've worked like a Trojan this year.'

'So have the volunteers. I can't rest: I *must* open another soup kitchen.'

Louise banged a cup down on to the tray. 'What are you trying to prove? To show Alistair that you can beat his record? He has one dispensary and one soup kitchen but you have to have two of them.'

'I'm not trying to compete,' Jessamy said quietly. 'We need another desperately. I only wish I could supply five or six. There are men, women and children who come to us in the morning without a hot drink or crust of bread having passed their lips. There are also people with jobs who can't afford to have anything for breakfast because they're on starvation wages. I feel I must do something for them.'

'Jessamy, Jessamy, you can't feed the world.'

'I'm not trying to feed the world. I only want to help ease the malnutrition around here. It's appalling. Children and their parents are dying from it. It's heartbreaking. I know I can only play a small part in what should be done, but I do at least feel fulfilled, that I'm helping.' She moved away. 'I'll bring the tea.'

When it was poured Louise said sadly, 'Fulfilled? With a child longing for you? You are becoming just a name to Romy, Jessamy, not a flesh and blood mother.'

Jessamy tensed. 'That is the only way I can help the poor. She does have a home life, which I cannot give her. She has all the love she needs, as well. She has Alistair, you, Flynn, Margaret, Kate...'

'Jessamy, she needs her *own* mother. You of all people should know that. Your mother lavished all her love on your half-brother. You had the love of other people, yes, but it didn't stop you from longing to feel your mother's arms around you. You told me you felt rejected.'

'It was different for Mama. She was never allowed to have Ralph to live with her. I was close to Romaine until I left: she knows that I love her.'

Louise sighed. 'Soon it will be her eighth birthday. No doubt you will send her a card and presents when what she really needs is to feel your arms around her. How can you fool yourself like this?'

'And can't you understand that I have a vocation? There's so much that still needs to be done. When I've accomplished more I shall let Romaine back into my life.'

'Oh, how kind of you.'

'Louise, don't be cruel to me! At times I ache to hold her, I ache with loneliness. What I'm doing is something I *have* to do; it's as though some Supreme Being is guiding me.'

'Rubbish. You are just trying to show Alistair that you too can be successful. It's the same as me wanting to own a string of pharmacies so I could prove to Grandfather Every that I, a mere woman, could succeed in business like his precious sons. Thank heavens I've realised since then that there is more to life than trying to match the achievements of men.'

'Louise.' Jessamy spoke quietly. 'If women had not fought for equality in the past there would be no women in the medical world, people like Sophia Jex-Blake, Edith Pochey, Elizabeth Blackwell, Elisabeth Garrett and many more. They became doctors against great odds and fought all their lives for women to be recognised in medicine. There would have been no Florence Nightingale and her nurses, either. Might I also point out that if there were no dispensaries, with no women to help run them, or soup kitchens run mainly by women, there would be many more deaths of adults and children.' Jessamy suddenly ran out of steam and felt exhausted.

'I agree,' said Louise calmly. 'All I ask is that you consider being a mother again. You could still do your good deeds, working with Alistair. Won't you think about it?'

'I can never go back to him. Can't even *you* understand my feelings? I feel so humiliated, Louise. First Fabian left me for another woman and then Alistair. I ask myself over and over again where I went wrong that two men should abandon me.'

'You didn't go wrong, Jessamy. You were unfortunate that Fabian was still in love with Caroline when he met you and as for Alistair, for a start, he didn't leave you – it was the other way round. I think it was fate that Kate came into your lives. Perhaps it was to test your love for him.'

'I'll repeat a word that you often use – rubbish! Alistair is a grown man, not a callow youth.'

'Then why don't you visit Romy?'

'I did once in the first few months after leaving Alistair,

don't you remember? Don't you remember how she cried, sobbed brokenheartedly when she knew I wasn't staying? I couldn't put her through that again, and it made me ill. Anyway, I don't want to discuss it any more.'

Louise got up and put on her coat. 'Very well, but think over what I've said before it's too late. Don't think that you can put Romaine out of your life indefinitely then reappear when it suits you.' She gave Jessamy a quick peck on the cheek, said she would see her in a few days' time and left, leaving Jessamy tearful.

She flopped into an armchair and looked around her. The sitting room was comfortably furnished as her landlady had allowed her to bring what furniture she wished. She was a kindly woman, but kept herself to herself, never prying into Jessamy's life. At first Jessamy had appreciated that, but lately she wished she would come in at times for a chat. There were evenings when the loneliness was unbearable, the room a cage.

She could have made a social life for herself but was reluctant to become too involved with people. There was the young doctor who was in charge of the dispensary...(it was just a dispensary, with no hospital treatment attached), who had often asked her out. Some of the volunteers in the soup kitchen, who were from the upper classes, had invited her to their homes, but she had always made excuses. Jessamy had craved solitude, wanted to nurse her grievances about the way life had treated her.

She sat now mulling over Louise's accusation that she just wanted to match Alistair's achievements. It might have been that way at first, she admitted, but not now. There were so many people who needed her help. In time she could qualify as a doctor – but what then? She might be able to help to cure more ailments but what would happen to her dispensary, her soup kitchens? They must be kept going. Would she always have to go on begging for money to run them? Her own income could not finance one quarter of the project at its present size.

Tears welled up. Was she to go on being denied the closeness and love of her own child in order to help the poor and the sick? Jessamy thought of the gratitude shown her by people who cried when she helped to ease or cure pain they had endured for years, using the God-given gift of healing in her hands.

She thought of the mother who had knelt at her feet for giving her warm clothes, boots and stockings in the winter for her children, who had gone barefooted other winters. She thought of all those who relied on the soup kitchen...the dispensary, people who were sick, were lame. She thought finally of those who now slept in dry rooms, in beds, instead of on damp floors, bundled in rags. Her tears stemmed. This work *must* go on. It had to – even if it meant sacrificing her ambition to become a doctor. She would have to wait until she could find someone as dedicated as herself to take over the responsibility.

Jessamy put work to the back of her mind and thought of Romaine's imminent birthday. She was still having lessons with Margaret's children but Alistair had told Louise he planned to send her to a private school in a few months' time. She would be upset at having to part from a family she had been close to and loved. Surely it would be better to wait until she was older? Yes, she was sure it would. Should she write to her husband and suggest it? After all, Romaine was her daughter, too. She would sleep on it.

It was in the middle of the night that Jessamy made the decision to ask to see Alistair and...to ask to see Romaine on her birthday. Once she had made up her mind, Jessamy's heart began a wild beating. She tried to visualise a meeting with her daughter. Louise said she was still full of high spirits, still warm and loving, but could throw a tantrum when things didn't please her, despite her age.

'Flynn can get her out of one, so can young Daniel. Flynn coaxes or teases but Daniel will simply say, "Stop that!" and she stops at once. She worships that boy. He may only be a youngster, but he has the air of an adult. He's clever, talks freely about many things. I think he could go far academically, but he is still set on becoming a professional stuccoist doing decorative plasterwork in big houses. He has the artistic talent for it.'

It occurred to Jessamy that there would come a time one day when Romaine would fall in love and marry. It seemed unthinkable. She had sent her games and a doll last birthday. Should she send clothes this time, a party dress and handkerchiefs? Romy had liked pretty handkerchiefs. Finding it impossible to go to sleep again Jessamy got up and wrote her letter to Alistair, feeling a pang as she remembered the little love notes he had sent every day when she went home to St Peel after her Cousin Lillian had attacked her. And that seemed a decade away. Then she hardened her heart. Love notes! Huh – when all the time he had been making love to Kate Keller.

She posted the letter the next day...and although she felt renewed hatred for Alistair, for what he had done, she watched the post after that for a reply as eagerly as a child would do.

When the reply came she was shaking as she opened it. It was short and to the point. '*Dear Jessamy, I shall be pleased to see you again on Romy's birthday and she is looking forward to seeing you, too. We shall expect you for tea at four. Alistair.*'

There was no mention of Romaine being excited at her visit, but then this was something Alistair would avoid saying in order to keep the reply impersonal.

Louise called the following day, saying she was delighted to hear that Jessamy was coming to Devonshire Street for the party. She had not seen Romy since the letter had come as the child was staying over with Margaret and her family for a few days. She often did this if Louise and Flynn had to be away from Devonshire Street.

When Jessamy mentioned the idea of buying a party dress Louise said, 'Romaine has quite a few already, but then you know what children are for changes.' Jessamy spent some time choosing a dress and eventually bought a delicate blue silk one, caught up in loops at the hem with pink ribbon bows. She also bought handkerchiefs and a big box of chocolates, and prayed she had done the right thing.

On the afternoon of her eighth birthday Romaine stood watching from the window of her father's surgery for her mother. Would she recognise her? It seemed an age since she had seen her. Romaine was not sure how she felt about the visit. She wanted to feel pleased, but resented the fact that she lived somewhere else. Her father had explained, 'Your mother helps poor people, Romaine. She finds proper homes for them and gives them clothes and footwear. This is especially important for the children, who otherwise would go about in rags and barefooted, yes, even in winter.'

Romy felt sorry for the children, but also sorry for herself because she had no mother. Daniel and his brothers and sisters had a mother and so had the children who came to the dispensary. They would cry for their mothers if the nurses took them away for a few minutes to put bandages on them. She had cried once for her mother, who had come to see her and then left again. Surely her own daughter should have been more important to her than other children? Why didn't someone else look after them?

She wasn't even allowed to have Daniel and the rest of his family to her party because Aunt Louise said that her mother might want her all to herself. Aunt Margaret was giving another little party for her tomorrow, with Daniel and the younger children, but she had wanted him to see her mother again.

Jessamy had worked herself up into such a state of nerves that when she stepped out of the cab in Devonshire Street she was actually trembling. The day was warm and she was wearing a silver-grey walking dress and a grey straw hat trimmed with apple-green ribbon. For a moment she caught a glimpse of a young face peeping from behind the lace curtains, then it was gone. Romaine? She picked up her parcels and walked to the front door. She lifted the brass door knocker and let it fall.

A middle-aged woman opened the door but before she had a chance to say anything Romaine was there. She seemed to have appeared from nowhere – a taller Romaine than Jessamy had visualised. She was beautiful, but distant.

She had pictured her daughter hurrying towards her, arms outstretched ready to hug her, instead of which she held out a hand and said politely, 'Good afternoon. Will you come in, please? Papa will be here in a moment.'

Alistair came down the stairs slowly, solemn-looking. Jessamy swallowed hard.

'Hello, Jessamy.' He too held out a hand. 'It was good of you to come. Mrs Bland will take your hat. Here, shall I hold your parcels?'

Jessamy was trembling so much she could hardly unpin her hat. After she had handed it and her handbag to the housekeeper she took the presents from Alistair and held them out to Romaine. 'Happy birthday, darling.'

Romaine thanked her politely, omitting the 'Mama'; Jessamy felt choked and wished herself miles away.

'Shall we go into the sitting room?' Alistair led the way. Jessamy prayed that Louise would follow but the three of them remained alone. She was invited to sit down, then Alistair took a seat opposite. After Romaine had put the parcels tidily on a nearby table she, too, sat down and folded her hands on her lap. Oh, God, why had she come? She could think of nothing to say and it seemed that Alistair was determined that she would be the first to speak. Her desperate gaze went to the mantelpiece where the birthday cards were arranged and after clearing her throat and forcing a smile she said, 'You have a lot of cards, Romaine.'

'Yes, thank you for yours. My name is Romy.'

Alistair said sternly, 'Romy!' Then added quietly, 'Aren't you going to open your presents?'

'Yes.' Romaine's voice was almost inaudible. Her mother seemed different from how she remembered her. She was lovely, yet not as Romy had pictured her. She had always thought of her mother as loving and happy, but when this woman saw her she had stared at her and looked as if she didn't like her. She was a stranger.

Romaine undid the ribbons on the parcels then opened the largest one. It was a dress – beautiful, but too small.

Jessamy felt dismayed. She had not allowed for Romaine

getting taller. The situation was getting worse and worse. She said, a catch in her voice, 'Oh dear, it's too small. I can get it changed. It will be no trouble. You can choose something else, another colour...' Her voice trailed off.

'But I like it. It needs to be a little longer, that's all. The dressmaker will know how to alter it.' Romaine undid the second parcel and showed some animation. 'Chocolates – oh, thanks!' Then she opened the package containing the six embroidered handkerchiefs and admired them. There were more thanks, but no acknowledgment that Jessamy was her mother. Suddenly, there was a commotion outside and Alistair, excusing himself, went to find out what it was. Jessamy looked across at Romaine. She was sitting with her head bowed, and Jessamy had a sudden feeling that she was crying. She got up quickly and going over to her, knelt down. 'Romaine...Romy, I'm sorry if you're upset about the dress.'

The child's head jerked up and her big dark eyes were brimming with tears. 'It doesn't matter about the dress. It's just that I – I expected you to be different.'

Jessamy felt a tug at her heart. 'Different in what way?'

'I thought you would cuddle me like a mother, and love me.'

'Oh, Romy.' She was about to do just that when there were voices and some laughter. She rose to her feet as Alistair, Flynn and Louise came in. Flynn was holding out a big box. 'I dropped the cake. Oh, hello there, Jessamy. They sent the wrong one, we went back to change it and I've dropped it.' He turned to Romaine. 'But it's all right, sweetheart. Just a little piece of icing is knocked off.'

Louise came over to Jessamy and whispered, 'Are you all right?' Jessamy managed a wan smile and nodded, then looked at Romaine, who had wiped away her tears and was giggling at something Flynn had said.

Jessamy began to feel more confident. During the birthday tea, however, she became more and more angry at Alistair's behaviour. He did nothing whatsoever to acknowledge her or to bring her into the conversation. Flynn was telling Romaine about the women icing the cakes at the bakery, exaggerating as he so often did: 'They work so fast that one minute the cakes are all bare and the next, they are covered with icing in all fancy patterns and little rosebuds and other things added.'

Louise teased him. 'Oh, Flynn, you do exaggerate. It must have taken them hours.'

Romaine wanted to know how the icing was put on and Flynn described the proceedings in great detail. Romaine laughed and said she would like to ice a cake and Flynn declared, 'So you shall.'

Several times Louise and Flynn made an attempt to bring Jessamy into the conversation but Alistair always seemed to divert the attention from her. For instance, when Louise suggested that Romaine show her mother her recent drawings later on, Alistair picked up a plate of lemon-curd tarts and held them out. 'You must all have one. Do pass them around – they're a speciality of the bakery and absolutely delicious.'

On another occasion when Flynn said he had his eye on a limousine he was thinking of buying, and added that he would take them all for a ride, Alistair stood up and said brightly, 'I think it's time for Romy to cut the cake and make a wish.'

Romaine was self-conscious about blowing out the candles and when she was teased afterwards about the wish she had made, she said quietly that a wish repeated would never come true. She glanced at Jessamy as she said this.

Later on, when Flynn suggested a run down to Brighton for the day soon, Alistair said with a rueful smile, 'I'm afraid you would have to count me out. I have too tight a schedule for frivolities.'

His tone sharp for once, Flynn retorted, 'You know the old adage, my friend: "All work and no play makes Jack a dull boy".'

Alistair spread his hands. 'So I'm dull – but the work still has to be done.'

'I'm quite sure you could take one day off if you wished.'

Louise said sweetly, 'May I remind you two gentlemen that this is Romy's birthday tea.'

They apologised then Alistair wiped his mouth with his napkin and said he was sorry but he had to leave.

Jessamy looked up and asked if she could have a word with him before he left. Alistair said of course and took her up to his study on the first floor. When he drew out a chair for her she said she would rather stand. What she had to say would only take a minute.

She attacked him at once. How could he treat her in such an odious way! Every time Flynn or Louise tried to include her in the conversation he had blocked her replies.

Alistair looked at her in what she assumed was feigned surprise. He had not been aware of doing it, he said.

'Oh, yes you were,' she exclaimed. 'You did it deliberately to prevent me from having any contact with Romaine, to punish me!'

He raised his shoulders. 'Perhaps I was doing it unconsciously. After all, it is nearly two years since you have attempted to even see her. How long will it be before you decide to see her again? Another two, three years, four? I wanted to save her from suffering any more hurt at your hands.'

'Strange how opinions differ, isn't it?' Jessamy said wryly. 'Louise asked me to get in touch with Romaine – and why? To save her heartache. You behaved despicably, Alistair, trying to demean me in the eyes of our daughter. Yes, *ours*. I carried her, brought her up while you were at college studying.'

'Then loving her, why did you abandon her?'

'Because I didn't want her to be involved in the tangle of our lives, didn't want her to find out that we had parted because her father had a mistress.'

'I don't consider Kate my mistress,' he said coldly. 'You asked me how I could behave in such an odious way – I ask you now how you could behave like God in condemning us for our weakness. Even God forgives sinners.'

'I am not an almighty being,' she retorted. 'Just a trusting wife who believed her husband when he said he would love her forever.'

'I've never stopped loving you.' Alistair spoke quietly.

Jessamy looked at her husband, saw the pain in his eyes, noticed a few grey hairs among the dark curly locks and felt a wave of love sweep over her. It did not, however, cause her to weaken in any way. Kate still worked with him. She could be sleeping with him for all she knew. Louise had said she thought not, but did intimate in a roundabout way that there was still a bond between them.

She said, changing the subject abruptly, 'I understand you want to send Romaine to a private school. Is that wise? She feels secure with Margaret's family and is being educated by an excellent teacher.'

Alistair's mouth tightened. 'Romaine will go to a private school in a month's time and as you take no part in her upbringing, I suggest you do nothing to disrupt my authority.' Seeing the jut of the strong chin Jessamy said no, she would not intrude and, after thanking him for allowing her to come to the birthday tea, hurried out, suddenly unable to bear any more.

Louise, who met her in the hall said, 'Well?'

Jessamy whispered, 'My hat, my bag, I'm leaving.'

From the sitting room window Romaine watched her mother hurrying along the street, her head down, her Aunt Louise following and trying to catch her up. Was her mother crying? If so, she hoped it wasn't because she had not been very nice to her. It was only because she had stayed away so long. Actually, she was just beginning to like her when she and Papa had gone upstairs.

Alistair stood at his study window, watching Louise catch Jessamy by the arm and bring her to a stop. He had almost gone after her but stopped himself in time, knowing it would not have achieved anything. Jessamy had a strong stubborn streak.

God, how he loved her, how he missed her. His feelings for Kate were different. They *had* only made love once when Jessamy had gone up North, but since Jessamy left him, Kate slept with him occasionally, which had become more a need for both of them than an overwhelming love. With Jessamy he had been able to let passion go rampant. She understood his nature and matched it. Although Kate seemed to be the more worldly wise of the two, she was inclined to withhold herself. He sensed a virginal streak in her.

He had been able to talk about his troubles, too, to Jessamy and she would always put her arms around him and cuddle him to her, talking in the soothing way she would to a child. 'Now it'll be all right, darling, you'll see.' Then she would add, 'You're too big a man to let anything get you down.'

Kate never gave him praise, yet he was glad of her company, her liveliness. At one time it used to torment him when men showed their admiration for her; now it no longer bothered him. What *did* upset him was the thought of Jessamy with another man. He was always picturing her in bed with someone, gasping in intimate abandon...Louise said there was no one else, but how could she be sure?

When Kate learned from Louise what had happened at the birthday party she was terribly distressed, having prayed that Jessamy would come back to Alistair. It was not that she loved him any the less, but she had allowed herself to become much too involved. Apart from the fact that she suffered for having been partly responsible for the couple parting she found herself weighed down by being unable to leave him. How could she walk out on him when he seemed so lost? They had vowed they would not make love again after that one night, but when Jessamy had not come back they had been drawn together again by a need for affection. There had been almost a desperation on Alistair's part and she had not been able to respond to him as she would have wished – and knew it was guilt.

If only he and Jessamy would get together again she would go right out of their lives, live abroad if necessary. Kate sighed. She couldn't see it happening, somehow. There was an awful stubbornness in both of them that neither she nor Louise had envisaged, and yet they had always seemed so amenable.

When Jessamy got back to her lodgings she broke down

and wept bitterly. She had not expected Alistair to be gushing, but had thought he might make an effort to be pleasant, for Romaine's sake. Even though Louise made excuses for him, saying he was under an awful lot of pressure, it did nothing to alter Jessamy's decision never to pay another visit. Neither he nor Romaine wanted her – and it was her daughter's attitude that cut deepest.

The day after the party when Louise came to see Jessamy and found her in a seriously depressed state, she announced, 'Something has to be done – you can't go on like this. I know that Alistair behaved badly but you must make allowances for him. No,' she said, 'let me finish. You must look at things from his point of view. You walk out on your husband and child, ignore them completely and never bother to ask to see Romy until now. I didn't know until this morning but apparently when she knew you were coming she told Alistair she didn't want to see you. He had to talk her into it.'

Jessamy looked up and said sharply, 'That is what *he* told you. Did Romy say anything to you?'

'No, but I believe Alistair. Incidentally, she hasn't spoken a word to anyone since you left yesterday. Alistair said to just leave her – she'll come out of her mood eventually.'

Jessamy began to cry and Louise sighed and got up. 'Oh dear. I'll make us a cup of tea then we've got to have a talk about the future.'

By the time Louise brought in the tea Jessamy had dried her eyes. 'I'm sorry, Louise. I'm all right now.'

'Good, then perhaps we can have a down to earth talk. I have a suggestion to make and I hope you won't reject it without at least thinking it over. You've been overdoing things and I suggest that for the next few months you have two days off a week and take a complete rest.'

'Two days?' Jessamy looked at her, appalled. 'I couldn't possibly do that. Everything would come to a stop.'

Louise poured the tea and said calmly, 'It might if you suddenly had another breakdown and that is right where you are heading.' Jessamy was silent and Louise went on,

'This is my plan – and don't interrupt until I've explained it. You could spend those two days at the cottage and I might, I repeat might, be able to persuade Romy to come and visit you there.'

Jessamy immediately brightened. 'Oh, if only she would.'

'Well, are you willing to try?'

Jessamy said hesitantly that she could perhaps manage one day but Louise insisted it had to be two days to do any good.

'Two days out of a week is a long time. I would have to try and find someone to take my place.'

Louise closed her eyes momentarily. 'Will you stop putting obstacles in the way! I know you were the one to start the dispensary but Doctor Draycott, being qualified, is technically in charge. He'll easily find someone to help. He was the one to bring in those two very efficient voluntary workers.'

'I know, but there's something else.'

Jessamy was about to say that she would have less time to use her healing powers when Louise concluded with, 'You must look after your own health, Jessamy, otherwise you'll be of no use to anyone.'

She gave in, the one compensation being that Romaine might come and visit her.

16

Jessamy chose the middle of the following week to go and relax at the Coachman's Cottage for the first time. A fire had been lit ready, and the sitting room was warm. A kettle on the hob was singing. It was a homely scene but Jessamy felt a chill. She had just moved closer to the fire when Louise arrived. 'So you came, Jessamy. Good! I thought you might have changed your mind. How do you feel?'

'Strange. It's as though I've never lived here.' Her teeth chattered.

'Don't worry – after we've had a cup of tea the cottage will have wrapped itself around you. I told Alistair I wanted to slip out for ten minutes. I did mention last night about you being here and he said he thought it was a good idea to have a rest. I told Romy, too.'

The lid of the kettle began to rattle and Louise said she would make the tea. She made it, brought cups and saucers, milk and sugar and when she said no more Jessamy prompted, 'And?'

Louise turned. 'Oh, Romy. She didn't say anything much. She did bid us good morning at breakfast, but she's still so withdrawn, which as you know isn't like her. She can be in a bad mood one minute and sunny the next.'

'Do you think you could persuade her to come and see me tomorrow? She could travel with you in the morning when you come over to Paradise Corner. Will she be going to Margaret's as usual?'

'No, there's a wedding in the family as it happens. I can ask her, but I can't promise she'll agree to see you.' Louise poured the tea. 'I'll have a quick drink then I must go. Duty calls. I've brought a ham and egg pie, it's in the pantry. I'll come and share it with you when the dispensary closes. Incidentally, don't expect to be relaxed the whole day. You'll have to adjust.'

'I know, that is why I've brought books to study.' When Louise scolded her Jessamy said, 'I couldn't possibly sit here all day twiddling my thumbs after the frantically busy life I've been leading. Anyway, I become relaxed while I'm studying.'

'Well, just see you don't overdo it. Remember that the brain needs a rest as well as the body.'

Jessamy grinned. 'Yes, Doctor.'

Louise giggled. 'I've become very medically minded, not to say bossy!' She drank some of the tea then put the cup down. 'I'm away, see you later.'

Left on her own, at first Jessamy was terribly restless. She roamed around, went upstairs from room to room and came down again, thinking it had been a mistake to come to the cottage, it held too many memories. Eventually she pulled a chair up to the fire, sat back and made an effort to relax. She must, otherwise she would be wasting her time.

It was impossible, however, to let go. Too many regrets rose to torment her. If only she and Alistair had taken a dispensary elsewhere they would never have met Kate Keller...if only she had not made Kate so welcome, Alistair might not have fallen in love with her...if only...

Jessamy sighed. It was no use regretting the past: it had happened and nothing could change it. She picked up a medical book but after reading three paragraphs and realising she had not taken in one word, she put it down again. Was she simply wasting time here – should she go back to her work in Poplar? No, she must wait until tomorrow in case Romaine came to see her...She stared into the heart of the fire and made out figures as she had done as a child. Then they had been fairy-tale figures – a princess, a handsome prince on a charger, Little Red Riding Hood...Now they were men in cloth caps marching, carrying banners. No, they were women in shawls...The figures began to merge, became blurred.

It was Louise who woke her and when Jessamy realised it was half-past one she could hardly believe it. 'I never sleep during the day, never!'

'Which proves how much you need the rest. It can only do you good. Come on – the meal is ready.'

As they ate, Louise talked about the patients, some of whom still asked after Mrs MacKay. After a pause she said, 'I told Kate you were here. She would like to come and see you.'

'No.' Jessamy spoke firmly. 'It would serve no purpose. I don't even want to talk about her.'

'It serves no purpose either to ignore her. She does a good job. Heavens, she works hard enough in the soup kitchen and has done her share for a good two years.'

'She stole my husband.'

'Kate did not steal him. You walked out on Alistair.'

'I think a wife has every right to walk out on a husband if he takes a mistress.'

'Kate is not Alistair's mistress.' Louise spoke patiently. 'They seldom even see one another these days. But there, I won't say any more. I'm sorry I mentioned Kate, it was just that I hate to see two lives spoiled because of obstinacy.' Louise glanced at the clock. 'How time flies. I'm going back to the dispensary for half an hour as I have some filing to finish. I'll get a cab to Devonshire Street, check that everything's all right then come back and stay with you until bedtime.' When Jessamy protested that there was no need, Louise said, 'It will help to get the first day over. Tomorrow should be easier.'

Jessamy was surprised to feel more settled after Louise's visit and wondered if it was because her cousin had said that Alistair and Kate were not often together. Perhaps their mutual attraction had faded at last. Not that she would go back to him, but if she could get friendly with Romaine it would make it easier to visit her. She decided to get down to some studying.

She worked until dusk, got up to light the lamp and draw the curtains then sat back for a while to read over her notes. She had built up the fire. The room was cosy, the atmosphere soporific and she found it difficult to concentrate. She began stifling yawns then her eyelids began to droop...

It was a cold draught that roused Jessamy from her semi-stupor. Had Louise come back? As she drew herself up in the chair the lamp flickered and suddenly she was wide awake, an icy finger touching her spine.

The ghost girl!

She was afraid to look round. The last time she had seen the apparition was the eve of Lillian's murderous attack. The light steadied and then Jessamy, worried in case she had missed a warning that was important, found the courage to stand up and turn. The light began to flicker: the girl took form. Her right arm was held at her side and her lips were moving as though she were speaking to a child.

'My child?' Jessamy queried. Then frantically, 'Is she in danger?'

The girl shook her head, put her hand over her shoulder and began to rub between her shoulderblades, wincing as she did so.

'My daughter's in pain?'

She nodded. Suddenly there was the sound of a key turning in the front-door lock then Louise calling, 'I'm back!'

The lights steadied; the ghost girl vanished.

Louise came in, started to explain why she was early then stopped. 'What is it, Jessamy? What's wrong – are you ill?' She came quickly over to her. When Jessamy explained what had happened Louise gave a shiver. 'It's strange because I had a feeling that Romy was in pain this morning, but when I asked her she denied it. I persisted, told her if she was she ought to see her father and at that she went flouncing out. I was about to follow her when I heard her bedroom door bang, which means Keep Out. What should we do?'

'Bring her here in the morning. Tell her about the ghost girl.'

'Jessamy, I couldn't! It would frighten her to death.'

'It wouldn't, not Romaine. She's full of curiosity, and she would come here for that reason. We have to know what is wrong.'

'Yes, I suppose you're right. I'll bring her then at about half-past eight.'

It was a rather pale-looking Romaine whom Louise deposited on the doorstep the following morning. The child said in a low voice, 'Aunt Louise said to tell you she'll call later.' Jessamy invited her in and Romaine went on, 'She told me that you had been visited by a ghost who had spoken to you about me.'

'Not spoken, Romy, but conveyed by gestures. Take your hat and coat off and sit down and I'll describe what happened.'

By the time Jessamy had told the story Romaine's eyes were wide with wonder. 'Fancy seeing a real live ghost. I do have a pain, but how could she possibly know?'

'This pain,' Jessamy asked gently, 'where is it?'

'Where the ghost girl said.' Romaine reached a hand behind to indicate the area of her upper spine.

When Jessamy asked why she hadn't told her father, as he would have given her something to ease it, a closed look came over Romaine's face. 'He couldn't. He was the cause of it. And you too,' she added accusingly.

Jessamy looked at her, bewildered. 'How do you mean?'

'The pain started the night after the party when I overheard two of the servants talking. Prue said to Meg, "Poor Miss Romy, 'er mother walked out on 'er and the Doctor ain't 'er real father. It's a man up North called Montague".'

Jessamy tensed and her heart began a slow, painful beating. 'Romy, this isn't true! Your Papa is your real father, I promise.'

'He isn't, he isn't! Meg asked her how she knew and Prue said she had an aunt who worked in a big house near The Montague Acres at St Peel. We *lived* there once. She also said you married Uncle Fabian and he divorced you. You and Papa are liars. I hate you both!'

Romaine's voice broke then and she began to cry, big tears rolling down her cheeks. Jessamy tried to take her in her arms but Romaine struggled away from her. The rejection brought a constriction to Jessamy's throat and she swallowed hard.

'Romy, listen to me and listen carefully. Prue has her story all wrong. That's the trouble with gossip – every person who repeats a story is inclined to exaggerate so that the original is magnified out of all proportion. After I married Fabian Montague he discovered he was still in love with a young lady who had once jilted him. It was he who suggested that I divorce him.'

Romaine, who had been listening intently, dried her eyes. 'And then did you marry Papa?'

'Yes, and afterwards you were born, and we loved you and were very happy.' Jessamy prayed that she would be forgiven the lie about the birth.

Romy asked why they had lived at The Montague Acres. Jessamy took a quick breath. 'Your Uncle Fabian, who was going to live abroad, told us we could go on living there while your father was studying to be a doctor.'

Romaine, her expression now full of curiosity, asked, 'Did Uncle Fabian marry that lady he was in love with?'

'Not yet. They live in Texas in America and are in partnership breeding horses.'

Romaine thought this all very exciting and her troubles seemed to be forgotten as she asked a torrent of questions. What kind of horses were they? Did they have a ranch? Grandpapa Chadwick knew a man who owned a ranch, he had told her all about it when she was staying at St Peel. 'I would like to ride!' Romaine made a pretence of riding and as she made the movements she suddenly gave an ouch of pain and sat back very still.

Her mother said gently, 'I feel you are suffering from tension, my darling. If you would allow me I think I could ease it.' When Romaine seemed hesitant she went on, 'I have helped many people by simple massage. Why not let me try? Come to the fire and take off your dress, then lie down on your tummy on the sofa.'

Romaine did so rather reluctantly, but within a few minutes was saying, 'Oh, that's lovely, Mama. How warm your hand is.'

Jessamy felt a rush of joy. Romaine had accepted her; at last she had called her Mama.

The gentle rhythmic movements of Jessamy's hand over the painful area brought constant murmurs of pleasure from Romaine; the pain was easing, it was wonderful, wonderful.

After a while Jessamy told her that that was all for now, and Romaine gave her a hug. 'How clever you are, Mama. Does Papa know you can cure pain?'

'Yes, but my way of healing is not altogether accepted in the medical world so it might be best not to mention it.' It took a lot of persuasion on Jessamy's part to convince her daughter to keep the knowledge to herself but she knew if Romaine gave her word she would never break it.

A few minutes later Louise looked in, her expression showing her uncertainty but when she saw Romaine's happy face she was all smiles. 'So you've had a nice talk, you two.'

'Oh, yes,' said Romaine. 'I had a pain, but it's gone.' She glanced at Jessamy with a smile of conspiracy.

Louise said to the child, 'Come on – I'll take you to the soup kitchen. I know you enjoy helping Aunt Kate. Then after the dispensary is closed I'll collect you and we'll have a nice lunch with your mother.' To Jessamy she added, 'I'll bring the food.' Romaine was outside and Louise about to follow when she paused and whispered to Jessamy, 'Success! Splendid. I'll hear all about it later.'

At that moment Jessamy felt that the warmth she had generated in Romaine was circulating in her own body. Not only had she and Romaine become reconciled but she had helped to ease the pain of her own flesh and blood, which seemed to her a great achievement.

She began to daydream, seeing herself visiting Romaine at Devonshire Street. Would Alistair object? Surely not – he had Romaine's welfare at heart.

Her daydream expanded. Was it possible that she and Alistair could get together again? She would be willing to make the first approach. It was not that she wanted to give up her work, but she would be able to see Romaine in the evenings. After all, Alistair was out all day and often in the evenings, too. He would probably be pleased for Romaine to be with her mother.

Kate had been the biggest stumbling block to their reconciliation but according to Louise, she and Alistair rarely saw one another these days. In fact Kate, from the very beginning, had promised to go right out of their lives if they would get together again. Perhaps she should talk to Kate after all: they had been good friends once...

Jessamy was still in this magnanimous mood when Louise and Romaine came back. Romaine's talk was all of the patients at the soup kitchen and dispensary, and how awful it was that they were so poor and hungry. Then she complained about some of them being dirty and smelly; her attitude reminded Jessamy of Rebecca, who had made the same complaint. She said, 'So you don't think you would like to work in a soup kitchen when you grow up?'

'Oh, no. I want to be married to Daniel and have children.'

'And live in a nice clean home?' Louise teased her.

'Of course.' The little girl was thoughtful for a moment then went on, 'But I would like to travel the world first, or be a lady's maid or – or something.'

Jessamy and Louise exchanged amused glances, then Jessamy objected, 'Now hang on a minute. I thought you had made up your mind to marry Daniel. Do you think he'll wait for you to travel around the world?'

'Yes, because he loves me.'

'Oh, to be young,' Louise murmured.

After they had finished their lunch Louise said she would leave them while she went over to Paradise Corner briefly to see one of the post-operative patients who was elderly and not too well.

Jessamy cleared the table and stacked the dirty dishes with Romy's help. The child chattered happily about this and that, until she suddenly went quiet.

'What is it, my love?'

'Mama, you said that you were married to Uncle Fabian and then you married Papa.' Jessamy froze. What was on her mind? Dates? She said yes, and waited. 'So is Aunt Kate now married to Papa?'

Relief flooded over Jessamy. She gave a shaky laugh. 'No, of course not. She's just a friend.'

'Then why does she sometimes sleep with Papa in his bed?'

The words had such a massive and unexpected impact on Jessamy that it was some time before she was able to speak. 'I think you must be mistaken, Romy.'

'No. Sometimes when Aunt Louise and Uncle Flynn have gone away for the night, Aunt Kate comes to sleep with Papa and look after him.'

Anger suddenly swamped Jessamy. How could they all have contrived such a thing? How could Louise have lied when she said that Alistair and Kate seldom saw one another! Sanity suddenly took over. Louise wouldn't lie, she was the soul of honesty. She said, 'You must have dreamt it, Romy.'

'No, she was there in Papa's bedroom. I heard them talking.'

Jessamy was in a dilemma. She could hardly ask how many times her daughter had heard them talking, nor could she warn her not to repeat such a thing in front of other people. Then Romaine said, 'I haven't told anyone else, Mama, only you.' Although this solved one part of Jessamy's problem she was worried that her small daughter sensed there was something not quite right about the situation. She did not want to think that Romy had become an adult before she had known full childhood.

Romaine touched her arm. 'Mama, will you be coming home to live?' There was a pleading in her voice.

Jessamy might have said, 'Possibly,' had not the recent conversation taken place. Instead she put her off with, 'Not at the moment, Romy. I have my work to do and it's important.'

'*I* am important,' the child retorted. 'I haven't got a mother. Everyone else I know has one. Let someone else look after the poor.'

Jessamy said quietly, 'I promise I'll try and see you as

often as I can. We can have long talks.'

'I don't want long talks when *you* feel like it. I want you at home so you're always there.'

'Please, Romy, let me explain.'

'No!' She was shouting now. 'You go and live with your dirty smelly patients. I hate you, I don't ever want to see you again. I'll go and live with Aunt Margaret who loves me!'

Louise, who had come in unnoticed, said, 'Well, and what is this all about?'

'Take me away, Aunt Louise,' Romaine said in a pitiful voice that tore at Jessamy's emotions. Louise looked at Jessamy who nodded. Before they left Louise mouthed, 'I'll be back.'

Jessamy wept bitter tears, feeling that the beautiful new world she had begun to build up was in ruins. When Louise did return she said, 'Mr Saunders is keeping an eye on her at Margaret's place. I couldn't get a word out of her. What on earth happened?'

After the story was told Louise said, 'Oh, Lord, what a mix up. Flynn and I do go away sometimes, I suppose, and we stay at the cottage occasionally if we've been to a party where he's drunk too much and is boisterous. It doesn't happen often, though. As for Alistair and Kate sleeping together I don't believe it: he wouldn't be such a fool. You can imagine the servants talking, and he does have his reputation to consider.'

'Romy seemed positive about it.'

'She has a vivid imagination and could have misinterpreted an innocent situation. Once when Alistair felt poorly when he was at the dispensary Kate went home with him. He was sick and Kate and one of the servants got him up to bed and stayed with him until he fell asleep. Kate left in the early hours and I remember how we laughed when she told me how she had crept out the back way, in case any of the neighbours should see her and put a wrong interpretation on it. So you see how certain things can be misleading?'

'Yes. I'm only sorry that I've turned Romy against me.'

'So am I but you know, Jessamy, you only have yourself to blame. You want the best of both worlds.'

Jessamy was silent for a moment then she said, 'I won't come and stay at the cottage again. I'm going to fulfil my childhood ambition and apply to train as a doctor. My husband and daughter don't want me and I've realised now that other people can handle the dispensary and the soup kitchens.' Jessamy gave a wan smile. 'I used to feel so important, but I'm just a little cog in a big wheel.'

'What do you hope to gain by qualifying?'

'Prestige, respect. At the moment I'm just a charity worker and would be considered a charlatan by some members of the medical profession if they knew of my healing powers.'

Louise's eyebrows went up. 'Does that really bother you? Surely you must get satisfaction from your gift!'

'Yes, but without the status of becoming Doctor Jessamy MacKay I feel I haven't achieved anything on my own. I have no husband, no child – I'm nothing.'

'Oh, Jessamy, Jessamy.' Louise reached out a hand to her. 'We all love you.'

Her cousin's lips trembled. 'I know, but I have to have something else. I need to be recognised. That's the way I am, I can't help it.'

That night Jessamy wrote to The London School of Medicine for Women, feeling there would be a better chance of being accepted there than at a college where male students predominated. Two days later she heard that their intake of students was full at the moment but they would let her know if a place became available for the next academic year. She was prepared to wait but when four months passed without any word she began to despair. Then one morning she received a letter asking her to come for an interview. Although the interview went quite well, the long waiting period had prepared her for failure so when she learned that she had been accepted, Jessamy felt a quiet pleasure rather than wild joy.

It was Louise who was excited; she included Alistair's congratulations along with those of Flynn and herself.

'They really are pleased for you and say you deserve the chance after all your hard work. What does your training entail?'

'The study of anatomy, physiology, chemistry, botany, "matera medica", mental pathology, surgery, midwifery and so on. The list is endless!'

'Do you study in hospitals?'

'Not until the fourth year. I was told that this can be the most taxing part of the course because of the opposition from all the male doctors who are still against women entering their profession. It's so foolish, because think of all the women who are too embarrassed to have a man examine them.'

Louise agreed, but cautioned, 'I only hope it won't be too much for you. You still look peaky.'

'Give me time and I shall be a new woman.'

It was only a few months later that Louise was saying, 'Jessamy, the change in you is miraculous! You are positively glowing – I've never seen you looking more beautiful. What's your recipe? Is it that you know you will eventually achieve your ambition of becoming a doctor?'

'I would say it's because I'm learning something new every day that is going to be of direct benefit to mankind. Each subject is so absorbing. I wish now that I had applied to the School earlier. No, that's not true. Everything I did was a step towards it. I was gaining experience all the time.'

It was not that everything was rosy at the School: Jessamy's looks and ability made her several enemies. Two of the older tutors disliked her because she was a favourite with an attractive senior surgeon, who came in to give lectures and there was also a clique of students younger than herself who hated her because she could answer questions that defeated them. They called her 'Uppity MacKay' within her hearing and when Jessamy failed to respond to this childishness they dropped poison about her behind her back.

It was another student with whom Jessamy had made friends who told her what they were saying. 'You must do something about it, Jessamy,' she urged, 'or it could affect your career later. This sort of gossip sticks.'

The following day Jessamy came upon the clique in a corridor. They sniggered behind their hands when they saw her and there were sneers on their faces as she approached. One of them said loudly, 'In the olden days she would have been put in the stocks and pelted with rotten fruit.'

Jessamy stopped and looked from one to the other, her gaze steady and appraising. Then she said, 'Slander is an offence punishable by law. I would like to give you my own version of a speech that Mr Shakespeare wrote for Othello. "To steal a purse is to steal trash; to steal one's good name is to steal everything." You are slandering *my* good name when you tell people I was quoted as being a loose woman in court when my divorce came up. No such quote was made in court or anywhere else and, for your information, my husband did not divorce me, I divorced him.'

Jessamy paused then went on, 'I have only to go to the Committee with your accusations and the careers of all of you will be ended before they have begun.' She turned away then came back. 'Oh, yes, I want a written apology, signed by all of you, before bedtime.' There was dead silence when she left them. Her stomach was trembling but she walked away with her head held high.

She told her friend Jane what had transpired but begged her not to say anything and Jane gave her word. That same evening Jessamy was approached by a number of students who said they applauded her for what she had done. When she blamed Jane for breaking her word, Jane held up her hands. 'Not guilty. It was one of the clique who was full of remorse for what had happened. I can understand it, you know. I was drawn into a similar group while at boarding school. I was an only child and terribly lonely and was so grateful to have anyone notice me that I told all sorts of lies about other girls to curry favour and make myself interesting.'

She pulled a face. 'Terrible, isn't it? Fortunately for me,

an elderly teacher took me under her wing and taught me a lot about people and their ways and said that I should feel sorry for this type of person. They lived in a small closed world.'

After this she and Jessamy often had lengthy discussions, especially after lectures.

Some lecturers gave the impression that they were doing the students a big favour by imparting knowledge, but there was one elderly doctor, named Innes, who explained things in simple terms so that even the layman could understand.

He began his talk one day by saying, 'Many an illness stems from an unhappy childhood. Insecurity is the worst thing that can happen to a child, and this may occur in any walk of life. A person may become a hypochondriac through lack of parental affection when young. They crave attention and will resort to complaining about all sorts of disorders. In quite a number of cases a woman, when she marries and has children, will show excessive love to a son and deny a daughter affection.'

At this, Jessamy tensed. It was Esmeralda all over again.

'These people are to be pitied,' the doctor went on. 'They've suffered in their tender years when a child needs affection, needs someone to cling to, which is so important. Even animals suffer if they are neglected. A baby chimpanzee, abandoned by its mother, clung to a broom and cried piteously when the broom was taken away. When a family is orphaned and are split up they're like little lost souls.'

Jessamy felt she loved this man who was so full of compassion.

Dr Innes went on to speak of the case of a small boy whose mother had constantly beaten him. The authorities had him sent to an orphanage, but he ran away, to try to find his mother. She and his home had meant security to him, despite the beatings. The mother as it turned out had been badly treated herself when young. She promised to mend her ways and was given another chance to bring up her son. There was no wondrous change in her, of course: she still beat the lad, only less regularly, and he grew up strong and was a good worker.

'Now,' he said, 'every case does not end up in this way. Which brings us to the genes that we inherit from our forbears...'

After the lecture Jessamy said to Jane, 'My mother is a hypochondriac but I'm afraid I can't feel any pity for her. My father loves her, just as I did when I was younger and was always trying to please her. I made her a sampler for her birthday once, working painstakingly on it and then she just threw it aside, said she hated embroidery.'

'Then don't you think it was all the more reason why you should have been sorry for her?' Jane said gently. 'She must be a very unhappy woman.'

'Jane, my mother has been pampered. My father has given her everything he could afford but she's never satisfied. She's always wanting more. I know that she was denied affection from her parents but she's a grown woman now, for heaven's sake.'

Jane said quietly, 'You were lucky to have the love of your father and all your other relatives. My parents had no time for me; they were all in all to one another. You see, my mother ran away to marry my father and was disowned by her parents, so I never knew my grandparents, uncles, aunts or cousins. I was brought up by nannies, each one a martinet. But there, I'm free now and will be delighted if I can qualify.'

Jessamy felt guilty afterwards that she had not told Jane about her illegitimate half-brother Ralph and how her mother, loving the child, had wanted to keep him but had been forced by her parents to have him adopted. Perhaps when she knew Jane better she would tell her. Unfortunately, there was no opportunity. Three days later Jane had word to say that her father had died and she had to go back home. In a low voice, she told Jessamy she would not be coming back.

Jessamy was dismayed. 'Oh, Jane, I'm so sorry. Why not?'

'My father died a bankrupt, apparently, and there's no

money for my fees.'

Jessamy could only offer sympathy to her new-found friend and say she hoped that once she was home she might find that the situation was not so bad as she expected, but Jane simply shook her head.

When Jessamy saw Louise next she said, 'It seems so unfair. She hasn't had a happy life and was so looking forward to the course. If only I could have helped her financially, but I need every penny we make from the shops. I'll miss her in spite of knowing her such a short time. But,' she squared her shoulders, 'I shall just have to try and get on with my studies.'

Louise said, 'I admire your dedication. I enjoy working at the dispensary but I must admit it's because I need to have something to do that gets me out of the house. I'm not a born housewife.'

Jessamy said softly, 'Don't belittle yourself, Mrs O'Rafferty. Flynn has no complaints and I have so much to thank you for.'

'You've done as much for me.'

'No, you've done much, much more, Louise. I've always had your shoulder to cry on, you've given me endless good advice, you've been a second mother to Romy, you've kept me informed about her and Alistair. You're my lifeline and I don't know what I would do without you.'

Louise, embarrassed as always when sentiment was involved, mumbled that anyone would think Jessamy was about to emigrate to Australia.

Her cousin gave a shaky laugh. 'I'll let you know if I am.' That ended the rather emotional scene but Jessamy knew she could carry on this new phase of her life knowing that nothing could destroy the closeness between her cousin and herself.

At the end of Jessamy's first year at medical school, Fabian Montague came unexpectedly back into her life. She was walking along the Strand during one of the breaks in her studies, thinking she would like to buy some new clothes, when someone stepped in front of her and laughed softly.

'Jessamy.'

She looked up, a pulse beating in her temple at the familiar voice. 'Fabian! What are *you* doing here?'

'I arrived in London four hours ago. I had some business to attend to and if it had not taken longer than I expected, I would have been well on my way to St Peel by now. I had just decided to have some lunch when I caught sight of you.' His smile was heartwarming. 'How is that for fate? Will you have lunch with me? The Savoy is only steps away.'

Jessamy said, 'Thank you, that would be nice,' then thought how banal that sounded. *Nice* – to have lunch with the man to whom she had once been married, and had not seen for years? As he cupped her elbow and they walked away she told him she was surprised that he had recognised her among so many people.

'You haven't changed. If anything you are more beautiful than ever.'

'Fabian, you were never a flatterer. I must have changed. I've known sorrow and bitterness.'

'If you hadn't known them how could you appreciate the sweeter things in life?'

When she queried, 'Such as?' he replied, 'Meeting me,' and she laughed. 'Now I consider *that* the cherry on the cake.'

She was impressed with the Savoy; there was a mass of flowers everywhere, voices were subdued, the music muted. It was a haven. The people in the dining room were so well-dressed she felt self-conscious in her light brown costume with its darker velvet trim but soon realised that the attention of the diners was drawn to the handsome and distinguished-looking man at her side. A deferential waiter ushered them to a table for two and drew out the chairs. A menu was given to each but Jessamy said she would leave the choice to Fabian. She watched him as he studied the dishes on offer. Although his brow was puckered in concentration he had an air of well-being, of virility. His skin was deeply bronzed and his dark hair had a bleached streak at the front. He looked up, his smile mischievous. 'Well, ma'am, do I meet with your approval?'

Warm colour rose to Jessamy's cheeks. 'I was thinking how well you looked. Life on the ranch certainly agrees with you. Are you and Caroline – ?'

'Caroline is married, yes, but not to me. I'm pleased for her – she's happier than I've ever seen her. I sold her my share of the ranch some time ago and since then I have been globetrotting and enjoying every minute of it. Now, Jessamy, tell me all your news. How is Alistair? Is the private practice a success? Do you both still run the dispensary, and how is dear little Romy?'

'Romaine is nearly eleven.' Jessamy paused then added, 'Louise tells me she's tall for her age.'

Fabian laid down the menu. '*Louise tells you?* What has happened since I saw you last?' His voice was quiet, concerned.

She moved a knife a fraction. 'It's a very long story.'

'I have time.' The wine waiter came and after wine and food had been ordered Jessamy told the whole story, making it as brief as possible. Fabian sat, his fingers steepled under his chin, listening but asking no questions.

When she concluded, 'And that is the whole sorry tale,' he sat back.

'Mmm. I must admit to feeling astonished, Jessamy, that you not only find it impossible to forgive your husband his one small lapse but that you actually abandoned your adorable child.'

Jessamy bridled. 'Isn't it a typical male attitude to blame the wife when it's the husband who has sinned?'

'Not sinned, my dear. Just succumbed to a momentary weakness.'

She picked up her bag and gloves and made to go. 'I'm sorry, but I don't think I want to stay.'

He laid his hand over hers. 'Sit down, Jessamy.' He spoke gently, but when she tried to draw her hand away he held it tightly. 'Please stay.' She gave in.

He leaned forward. 'When I first met you, you were a very lovable and vulnerable young lady.'

'I was only sixteen! At that time I trusted people – since

then...I've grown up.'

He inclined his head. 'I deserved that rebuke. Who am I to condemn you? Forgive me. It's just that I find it sad you felt it necessary to desert those you love.'

'There are compensations. I have been able to help others who are poverty-stricken and ill. I will also be able to give more help if I get my M.D. No, I should say *when* I get it because that is my aim. Now, how about you? If you've sold your part of the ranch what are you planning to do now?'

'Oh, I have my finger in many pies. Tell me, what exactly does your training involve?'

Jessamy, who wanted to know more about his life, simply mentioned a few of the subjects she was studying and added that she was also mastering the basics of Greek and Latin.

When Fabian asked her if she had much free time she said yes, but she used it for study as there was so much to learn.

Fabian shook his head. 'You must have some pleasure, too.'

The waiter brought the hors d'oeuvre and after he had served them and left, Fabian gazed at Jessamy for a moment then said, 'When you used to talk about the dispensary and your work among the East End people there was such warmth in your voice, such sympathy. Now, although there's an eagerness in you to learn more about medicine there's also a coldness in your determination to achieve your ambition.' His expression suddenly softened. 'I do wish you could combine your home life with your career. Do you think you might be able to in the future?'

'I've stopped thinking about the future,' she said shortly. 'Things seldom turn out as planned.'

'No, they don't, do they?' There was sadness in his eyes.

Jessamy said, 'I'm sorry I was so brusque, Fabian. Forgive me. I'm not a very nice person these days.'

'Perhaps we can meet again, Jessamy. I think it will do us both good to talk.' He smiled suddenly. 'Do you know what I was thinking about the other day? That time you had a bad back and I massaged you with some oil a geisha girl gave me when I was in Japan.'

Jessamy pulled a face. 'Oh, dear. I had no idea then of the true profession of a geisha girl. What an innocent I was.'

'And lovely,' he said softly, as he reached out to cover her hand with his. 'Jessamy, can we meet again? I will be coming back to London in a fortnight's time. Actually, now that I'm settling at The Montague Acres for some time I shall be paying regular visits to business acquaintances down here.'

Although Jessamy did not withdraw her hand she did say she thought it would not be wise to meet.

'Why not? Surely we can be friends. I do have a lot to tell you about my travels, especially in Egypt. I could tell Mr Stannard, but he's only interested in his work and who else is there to talk to?'

Seeing a look of mischief in his eyes she answered lightly, 'You could tell all the women who practically swoon for your favours.'

He laughed, said the swooning type did not appeal to him, then added in serious vein, 'There's only one woman I'm wholly comfortable with and that is you, Jessamy. I ask only friendship.'

There had been times in the past when she had thought of him as a lonely man and, knowing the ache of loneliness herself, she agreed. After that they talked with an easy companionship as they ate their succulent roast duckling followed by Pêche Melba, drank wine and lingered over coffee. Fabian did suggest a walk afterwards along the Embankment but Jessamy said some other time perhaps, as she had a lecture at four o'clock.

They parted outside the Savoy. Fabian saw her into a cab that would take her to the College while he was to go for his train to St Peel. He leaned forward as though about to kiss her then drew back. 'Au revoir, Jessamy.'

During the following year Jessamy saw Fabian many times, but their relationship remained on a platonic basis.

Often, she would long to feel his arms around her and knew that he wanted to make love to her, but she also knew if they went beyond the basis of friendship she would be lowering the standard that she had set for Alistair.

During their times together Jessamy, at Fabian's prompting, talked at greater length about her studies, fellow students and lecturers, and Fabian, with his many business ventures and trips abroad, was never short of conversation. He suggested once that Jessamy should come to St Peel to see her family, then they could spend a whole day together in the privacy of The Montague Acres. Knowing what Fabian meant by privacy, Jessamy felt tremors go through her, but she told him it would be impossible. The College authorities would not take kindly to her having time off at such an important stage of her training.

Then one day Jessamy received a letter from her Cousin Rebecca, to say that she and Tom Hansard were getting married. '*I know you'll be surprised,*' she wrote. *'We've corresponded for some time, and have exchanged visits to meet each other's parents, then Tom proposed and I accepted. It was all so sudden and lovely. You must come, Jessamy. You and Alistair were so kind to me when I was at Paradise Corner...*'

Jessamy lowered the letter, her heartbeats quickening. Family weddings were considered a valid reason for having time off at the medical school. Why should she go on longing to be loved when Alistair had Kate? Although Jessamy had believed the explanation Louise had given about Kate's presence in Alistair's room, with the passage of time she was more ready to believe Romaine's version of events.

Jessamy read the rest of the letter. The wedding was to be quiet – both Rebecca and Tom wanted it that way. Anne was to be the only bridesmaid. They were going to be married in church but Rebecca was not to be a white bride. She had put in brackets (*you know why, Jessamy!*). She concluded her letter: *'Please try and write back to say you'll be with us on our big day!'*

Louise too had had an invitation and she came that

evening to her cousin's rooms, full of talk of the wedding and what she and Jessamy should wear.

Jessamy wrote to Fabian the next day to tell him she would be in St Peel in three weeks' time and he replied by return of post, saying he hoped they would be able to spend some time together.

Jessamy closed her eyes and went into a fantasy world where Fabian picked her up in his powerful arms and carried her upstairs to make love to her in the big four-poster. Annoyingly, when she was in bed that night and tried to continue the fantasy, Alistair intruded; no matter how she tried to dismiss him, he remained with her until she slept.

The following morning, remembering this, she said aloud, 'Oh, no you don't, Alistair MacKay! You enjoy a love life and so shall I.'

For the wedding Jessamy bought a pale rose costume and matching hat with a delicate green feather that curled on to her cheek. Louise had chosen a deep blue dress and coat with a cream straw hat with cornflowers on the brim. When the two of them dressed up to show Flynn, two days before the wedding, he said, 'Well, now, isn't that a lovely sight, neither of them looking a day over sixteen!'

Louise replied, 'And isn't my husband the biggest liar in the world!' Then the three of them were laughing, which set the mood for the forthcoming journey.

They were going by car this time and Verity had written to ask Louise and Flynn to bring Jessamy home with them as Chadwick and Esmeralda would be there. They would all have a nice meal together.

The wedding was to take place the morning after at nine o'clock. Alistair and Romy had also been invited, but Alistair had refused owing to pressure of work and Romy had told Louise she had no wish to go. Jessamy was surprised by this, knowing how her daughter loved her old home and all the family. At the same time, however, Jessamy felt relieved. Much as she longed to see Romy it would have been difficult to travel together, knowing the child's hostility towards her.

Flynn shortened the long journey with his constant lively chatter and flow of anecdotes so that by the time they approached St Peel Jessamy had a childish feeling of pleasure at coming home. Although she had not seen the family since she had started her studies, she had kept in touch with her father, her Aunt Verity and her grandmother, the three people she most wanted to see. Now she lowered the window and took a deep breath of the fresh sea air. 'Isn't it lovely after London? I'm looking forward to a long tramp over the moors.'

'Right now?' Flynn teased, 'or shall I take you to Uncle Bertie's first?'

'Uncle Bertie's, please,' she said softly.

When they drew up outside the house Louise said to Jessamy, 'Race you to the door!' as she used to when they were children. They arrived together, laughing and breathless.

Jessamy had expected the door to be flung open and her father and Verity to be there to greet them, but it was some moments before the door was opened and then it was by the maid who said to Louise, her expression sombre, 'The family are in the sitting room, ma'am.'

Louise stepped quickly inside. 'Whatever is wrong, Sarah?'

Sarah's lips quivered then she began to cry. 'It's terrible, ma'am, terrible. Miss Rebecca has taken her own life. Well, we can't believe it, we can't take it in. And now the family have just heard that your grandmother Mrs Henrietta Every has died. It's like a nightmare, ma'am.'

Louise, Flynn and Jessamy just stood there stunned, then Chadwick came into the hall, his face grey. He drew Jessamy and Louise to him and said, an agony in his voice, 'I'm sorry, I'm so sorry...'

17

Chadwick took the three of them into the breakfast room, saying they could be alone there. So many people had called after hearing of the tragedy. To Louise he said, 'Your mother will be here soon. She's taking old Mrs Taylor home. She brought Rebecca into the world.' He drew his fingertips across his eyes.

'Forgive me. It's all been so harrowing, with my dear mother going, too. She was so excited about the wedding; you know how Henrietta loved these occasions.'

Jessamy, who had never seen her father so distressed said gently, 'Sit down, Papa. Don't talk any more just now. We'll hear what happened later.'

His back straightened. 'No, I shall tell you now. You have to know eventually.' He stirred the fire into a blaze and drew chairs closer to it. When they were seated he began, 'It started last night when your Cousin Anne apparently said a very nasty thing to Tom about Rebecca. She said that her sister...well, that she had been...intimate with a number of men.'

'That's a dreadful thing to say,' Jessamy protested, 'and it just can't be true.'

'It certainly isn't,' declared Louise.

Chadwick held up his hand. 'I have to tell you as it was told to me.' He paused then went on, 'Tom was very angry and told Anne that he wouldn't listen to such things. Rebecca was not that sort of person. Anne sneered and suggested that he ask Rebecca how many times a man called Richard Mather had made love to her.'

Verity came quietly into the room as Chadwick made this last statement. She embraced the visitors, sat down then motioned to Chadwick to continue.

'Apparently, Tom went straight away to see Rebecca and faced her with the accusation. She made no reply at first then he told her he wanted to know only one thing: had Richard Mather ever made love to her? She denied it but when Tom kept on at her she eventually admitted that he had. Tom, naturally, was stunned then he shouted "Whore", told her the wedding was off and stormed out.'

'How terrible,' Jessamy murmured.

'It's more than that.' This from Louise. 'That wicked, evil Anne deserves to be horsewhipped. And she was supposed to be the bridesmaid!'

Chadwick nodded to Verity and said gently, 'I think that you can tell them the next part.'

'Yes. Tom was staying with us overnight so that he and Rebecca wouldn't meet before the wedding. When he came back in a terrible state Bertie and I talked to him, pointing out that Anne might have said what she did from jealousy. Rebecca, being pretty and affectionate, had always come in for a lot of fuss. After a time Tom calmed down and said he would go and see Rebecca and apologise – but she was not in the house or at the hostelry. The men got up a search party – '

Verity's lip trembled and Chadwick, his voice not quite steady, took up the tale. 'It was not until early this morning that Rebecca was found, by her father...drowned in the river.'

'Could it have been an accident?' Louise asked. 'Sarah told us she had taken her own life.'

'It appears that this is the case. Her footprints were in the mud leading from the bank into the water. We're trying to keep this quiet. The fact that Rebecca was found in the river must have made Sarah put her own interpretation on events. I must have a word with her – no one else suggested it could be suicide. We are the only ones who know about the quarrel.'

Jessamy looked at her father. 'There'll have to be a post mortem. The footprints – '

Chadwick looked at her steadily. 'Your Uncle Bertie and I smoothed them over. There are parts of the bank where it crumbles away, and after these recent heavy rains, someone could possibly lose their footing and fall in. We did it for Tom, your Uncle Edward and your Aunt Grace's sakes. We have no regrets.'

Louise shivered. 'God, what a dreadful shock it must have been for all three of them. What a terrible end to a love story.'

'They were devastated – I think we all were. Then, a few minutes before you and Louise arrived, we were given the news of your grandmother. I can only say we're thankful that she was spared Rebecca's death.' Chadwick got up. 'You must excuse me. I'll have to go and see my father. Jeremiah will be feeling so lost. Although he would never admit it, Mother was his anchor. Still, knowing my father, he'll put a brave face on it.'

When Chadwick and Verity had gone from the room, accompanied by Flynn, Jessamy turned to Louise. 'Did we do wrong in not telling Rebecca's parents about the – ' she lowered her voice ' – the abortion?'

'Definitely not. What purpose would it have served? It would only have been more for them to have endured. Tom must bear his part of the blame for that. Rebecca was such a fool to go out with both him and Richard Mather. She played with fire, and was burnt badly once. I never thought she'd have to suffer for it again. Damn Anne and her spiteful, jealous tongue! Just wait till I see her...'

Verity reappeared. 'Sarah will bring us some tea in a minute. While I think about it, there's something else I must tell you. Tom, not wanting Edward and Grace to know what Anne had said about Rebecca, told them that he and Rebecca had had a quarrel and that she had taken his words the wrong way and run out. I think it was very courageous of him to take the blame. The stigma will always be with him.'

'What will he do?' Louise asked.

'Take up private practice. He'll need to work to take his mind off the tragedy.'

Verity sighed. 'Poor Tom, poor Rebecca. She always had this infatuation with men. Many people prophesied that she would come to a bad end, but I'm sure that no one imagined such a tragic one.'

When Jessamy asked if her mother was coming round Verity said no and spread her hands. 'We all know Esmeralda – she can't stand trouble. She has one of her migraines according to Chadwick. When she learns about Henrietta I imagine she'll be in bed for a week. I'm sorry, Jessamy, for sounding so mean, but your father needs her support right now. It was a terrible thing, and as for your Uncle Edward finding Rebecca's body...Oh, here's the tea.'

At the end of that day Jessamy wondered if she would ever know a more unhappy one. She grieved over the tragedy of Rebecca but her grief for the loss of her grandmother was greater because she had been so much a part of her life. At times she could almost feel the bony arms holding her close, hear her chuckling at some funny incident or imparting one of her quiet philosophies. Henrietta had taught her so much. In death she appeared to be smiling, as though she were enjoying the anticipation of the wedding. How good it was that she had been taken knowing nothing of the dreadful tragedy.

When Jessamy went home with her father that night they found a note from Esmeralda to say that she had gone to stay with a friend. She had been told about Henrietta and knew she would be ill if she had to contend with any part of it all.

Chadwick tore up the note and threw it on the fire, saying with an air of sadness, 'There is only one Esmeralda.'

He looked utterly drained and Jessamy said gently, 'I think we would both benefit from having an early night.'

'I think so, too.' He came to kiss her goodnight and held her tight for a moment. 'I'm glad to have you home, my love. Try not to blame your mother too much for leaving. She's so highly strung. Her headaches are mostly genuine, but I must admit she does rather tend to fall back on them as an excuse if she wants to get out of certain things.' After a pause he said, 'I still love her,' and Jessamy felt choked, realising his loneliness.

According to what her Aunt Verity said in her letters,

her father was often on his own in the evenings in recent months and Jessamy was grateful to her and to Uncle Bertie, who often looked in on him and had a game of cards with him after the day's work was done.

In bed she found herself thinking of Fabian and of the fantasy she had created of being swept up in his arms and carried upstairs. It brought the words of Robert Burns to her mind: '*The best laid schemes o' mice an' men Gang aft a-gley.*' Her planning, her fantasy, had certainly gone a-gley. But she still wanted to see Fabian. He would learn of the tragedy, know that she would be here, needing comfort. Perhaps she could slip away for an hour some time, without being missed.

There was little opportunity, however, until the third day when her father asked her if she would deliver some medicine to two of his patients who were temporarily housebound. He followed the request up by telling her not to hurry back. 'Take a walk on the moor, my love, get some fresh air. You've been in a depressed atmosphere for too long.'

Jessamy welcomed the break. The talk for the past three days had been solely of death. Once she had delivered the medicine she would go to The Montague Acres. It would be wonderful to see Fabian – not that they could make love under the circumstances, but just to have contact with him would be wonderful, to feel his comforting strong arms around her, his cheek against hers.

With the medicine delivered, Jessamy set off in the direction of Fabian's estate, taking a narrow side road, sheltered by bushes and trees, that led to the side of the house.

As she opened the wooden gate she felt an almost childish sense of anticipation. She prayed that he would be at home. Yes, she could hear him talking, he was at the front of the house. Was he about to depart or to go back in? Jessamy crept along the side of the wall, stopped and peeped around the corner...and froze. Fabian was coming down the steps, his arm about a woman who was smiling up at him as he said, laughing, 'No, darling, the

choice must be yours. I know the kind of bed that I like...'
Jessamy pressed back against the wall. Caroline! There was no mistaking that elegant figure, the flirtatious way she had of looking up at Fabian.

Dear God. What treachery, telling her how much he loved her and all the time Caroline was still in the background. It couldn't be happening again – it couldn't! Jessamy felt as though her body was being slowly encased in ice, gradually closing off all feeling.

How long she stood there she had no idea. When she did move she felt stiff and walked as though someone else was controlling her limbs. At times she had felt a great loneliness. Now, without Fabian, her life would be completely barren. Since Sunday evening she had stayed at her Aunt Verity's during the day and now she made her way back there, not wanting to talk to anyone. The maid came to see if she needed anything and Jessamy told her no. Without taking off her hat and coat she sat in an armchair in front of the fire and was unaware of anything until Louise arrived.

'I've been looking everywhere for you – where on earth have you been? Chadwick said you had gone to deliver some medicine, but that was about two hours ago.'

'Was it? I went for a walk.'

'Jessamy, what's happened? Did you meet Fabian?'

'No, I didn't meet him.'

Louise left the room and when she returned, Verity was with her. Her aunt said gently, 'I think you may be suffering from delayed shock, Jessamy. I've brought you a mild sedative. I didn't want to worry your father, as he's not too well himself at the moment. If you drink this,' she held out a medicine glass, 'you'll soon feel better.'

It was the thought of worrying her father that penetrated the fog by which Jessamy seemed to be surrounded. 'It's all right, Aunt Verity. I think it was just a temporary lapse. I don't really need anything. I'll come with you – didn't you say we were going to see Uncle Edward and Aunt Grace? Look, I'm ready.'

Verity and Louise exchanged glances. Louise said, 'We

too are ready.' For the remainder of the day they visited relatives and the talk was of death. Jessamy let it wash over her.

Her father received a letter of condolence from Fabian and she, too, had a short note saying how sorry he had been to hear the dreadful news. He asked if there was a possibility of them meeting for half an hour before she returned to London. Trembling with rage, and disillusion, she wrote back to say it was impossible; she also said she doubted whether she would be able to see him again in the future.

On the day of the double funeral, Jessamy never shed a tear and wondered whether she would ever be able to cry again. Something had dried up inside her.

She forced herself to try and appear normal, but on the day of her departure with Louise and Flynn her father said to her, 'Jessamy dear, if you have any problems, will you share them with me? I know your life hasn't been easy now for a long time, but a trouble shared *is* a trouble halved.'

She put her arms around him. 'Yes, Papa, I will. And you take care of yourself.' She smiled. 'I've told Aunt Verity and Uncle Bertie to keep an eye on you.' Jessamy made no mention of her mother, who had not even troubled to come and say goodbye.

She had rather dreaded the journey back, undertaken in such different spirits from the week before, but Flynn had been to a number of places around St Peel with Louise's two brothers Rupert and Francis, and had the usual fund of chatter.

Anne was not coming back to the dispensary; she had decided to live for a time with a distant relative in Durham. Tom Hansard had left right after the funeral, to take up his practice. Jessamy had had a talk with him and knew he was hoping to find solace in helping other people; she had been able to assure him that this would certainly help to heal his own wounds.

Jessamy had always hated coming back to the loneliness of her rooms, but this time she felt curiously indifferent, and was able to promise Louise and Flynn that she would be perfectly all right. She settled back at medical school with a greater determination than ever to get her degree.

It was a week later when Fabian turned up on her doorstep in the evening, wanting to know what was wrong. She nearly shut the door in his face but then invited him in and told him briefly the reason why she wanted nothing more to do with him.

He looked at her, astonished. 'Caroline and her husband are moving house in Texas. She came over here to see friends and to buy some English furniture to be shipped out there. I invited her up to The Montague Acres, certainly, but only on a friendly basis. You must have overheard us talking about a choice of bed.'

'Like yours? No doubt she's slept in it.'

'No, she hasn't.'

'Fabian, in case you don't know, you had your arm around her, you called her "Darling" and laughingly told her you knew the kind of bed that *you* liked...'

'Yes, I did, and if you see any wrong in that then your mind is warped.'

'My mind wasn't warped the time I found you and Caroline in the early hours of the morning gazing soulfully into each other's eyes. We were engaged at the time, if you remember.'

'Jessamy, that belongs to the past.' He paused, then added gently, 'I think perhaps you're suffering from the aftermath of the awful tragedy. I'll call again when you've had a chance to recover.'

'I have recovered. I don't want to see you ever again.'

He said quietly, 'I'll respect your wishes, Jessamy. Goodbye, my dear.' With that he left.

The finality of the words suddenly made her want to say 'Wait!' but she found it impossible to say.

And so she went back to a life where her only visitor was Louise, who kept loyally seeking to find a way of bringing back the warmth that had been a part of her cousin. When she told Alistair about it he said, 'Give her time. Delayed shock can have devastating results. It can last for a year or two, before the mind can be freed.'

Jessamy's attitude had one good result: she began to think in a coldly clinical way that impressed her tutors, and later, when she worked in various hospitals, she won the acclaim of fellow doctors, even those who were the most antagonistic towards women in the profession. In spite of her attitude, however, she always retained sympathy for her patients, and this gave Louise hope that Jessamy would one day be restored to her former self.

When Jessamy eventually qualified she showed no particular pleasure, but set about buying a small house and setting up a practice. She charged a fee according to the patients' ability to pay, as she needed funds to keep her charitable ventures going. She also continued to use her healing gifts, which were especially effective in alleviating rheumatism.

Louise had got into the habit of calling to see Jessamy about three times a week for an hour in the afternoon, to give her news of Alistair and Romaine, and anything else she thought might interest her. At times Jessamy would be unresponsive and once she returned home so annoyed she told Flynn she was staying away for a week.

'It's maddening when she sits like a tailor's dummy, so you've no idea whether she's interested in what you're saying or not. We've been very close all our lives, shared everything, yet she's never mentioned what happened that day on the moors when she came back in that strange mood. I feel sure that Fabian Montague was involved in some way.'

'Ask her,' Flynn suggested. 'I'm sure she does listen to what you say and would miss you terribly if you abandoned her too.'

The following day Louise delivered an ultimatum to Jessamy. Either she responded to her when she called or she would stay away. She was sick of talking to a piece of wood.

Jessamy said, a pleading in her voice, 'Please don't stay away, Louise. You are my only link with the family. I *do* listen.'

'Right, then tell me about Fabian. Some time after we left St Peel he apparently moved out of The Montague Acres and according to Mother, is planning to travel the world, by sea. Why? I thought he wanted to stay and enjoy his home. You said you hadn't spoken to him that day on the moors, but did you *see* him?'

'Oh yes, I saw him all right – with Caroline.' Jessamy told the story in a low voice and concluded, 'Don't tell me I was a fool to keep this to myself. I didn't want to talk about it and I don't now. Some day, perhaps.'

Louise, who felt they had progressed a little, laid her hand over Jessamy's and smiled. 'Some day.'

Not long after this Romaine ran away from home. She had often wandered off exploring when she was young, but had never got very far. This time, Louise said, she had gone further afield to Kent. When Jessamy asked, why Kent, Louise said it was to be with Daniel. 'She's still besotted with him. I told you he was apprenticed to his Uncle Frederick who is a Master Decorative Plasterer. They do all this lovely work in big houses. Alistair has gone after her and is furious at having to cancel appointments. Daniel will be furious, too. He allows nothing to come between him and his work.'

Jessamy said, 'Well, Romy hasn't caused Alistair too much trouble thus far, considering that she is a rebel at heart.'

'And you haven't been troubled by her either, have you?' Louise retorted. 'After all, you are her mother, or have you forgotten?'

'No, I haven't forgotten but I must remind you, Louise, that you have enjoyed being a mother to Romy, since you made the decision not to have children of your own. You've been a good mother and I'm grateful.'

'I've always loved her as if she were my own child, but I'm sure that even after all these years there's still a longing in her to have you living at home. She's at a difficult age and still needs you.' She gave Jessamy a quick kiss on the cheek. 'I'll let you know what happens tomorrow.'

When Louise arrived the following afternoon she said, 'Well, you'll be pleased to know that Romy is back safe and sound, but she's living in a dream world of being married to Daniel and travelling with him from place to place.'

'So he wasn't angry with her for going to Kent?'

'He was very angry – wouldn't even speak to her at first, apparently – told her to go back home. Then he gave her a lecture about consideration for other people and told her she was not to even write to him again. But,' Louise smiled, 'you know Romy. She did get his permission to write to him but he said her letters must be sent through his mother from now on, so she need never know his address. And although she doesn't usually get around Daniel he has also agreed to write to her occasionally.'

'So what did Alistair have to say to all this?'

'He lectured her too and explained that because of her stupidity he had been unable to see patients who were quite ill. He told her she must promise not to run away again. Romy managed in a devious way to get out of actually promising, but if Daniel does write to her it might keep her at home. I hope so.'

Daniel did keep his promise to write to Romy. They were only short notes, but to Romaine they were love letters and she tied them up with blue ribbon.

After a time, Daniel found himself looking for the postman on a Thursday when he always received Romy's weekly letter and began to wish she would write more often. Now in her teens, she had a lively style and a way of writing about people so that he could see them in front of him clearly. Often she would enclose a drawing she had done, and he never failed to be astonished at her talent.

For her part, Romaine lived for the times when Daniel came home. Sometimes he would be away for two or three months and when he did get back he had so many relatives to visit she would see him for just a short time, and then invariably in the presence of someone else.

Then came a day when he arrived unexpectedly. They

met in the lane that led to the back door of his home, where Romy was visiting Margaret. He stopped and she stopped, and Romaine's heart was a wild thing. She smoothed a hand over her pale blue cotton dress. He came forward slowly and when he reached her he slung the bag he had been carrying over his shoulder to the ground and stood staring at her, feeling hot blood stirring in him. How lovely she was. He said, 'You look different, Romy. It's your hair.'

She put a hand to it. Margaret often did her hair in various styles when they had fun pretending she was a wealthy young lady and Margaret her maid. This time her hair was swept up in curls on top of her head and tied with a piece of cherry-coloured satin ribbon. Romaine said, 'Your mother did it.' She suddenly looked upset. 'You don't like it.'

She made to untie the ribbon and he said hastily 'No, leave it! I do like it – your hair looks lovely. The style suits you. It was just that it seemed to put you out of my reach. You look like a lady, well, you *are* a lady.'

She was dismayed. 'Oh, no I'm not. I'm just me, Romy, and I love you.' She started to tug at the ribbon to loosen it and he stayed her hand.

'Leave it. I like it – but you mustn't talk about love. Come along, let's give Mother and the family a surprise.'

Daniel linked his arm through hers and they stepped out towards the back door with Romy in a seventh heaven on this sunny summer day. The lane could not exactly be termed romantic, not in the East End, but when Daniel opened the door that led into their garden Romaine thought she would always associate the sweet smell of honeysuckle with this particular homecoming.

Unfortunately, however, it would also remind her of the time he told her he would be going away for a year.

'A whole year?' She looked at him with an agonised expression. 'I can't bear it. It's such a long time. All I have to look forward to is seeing you.'

'Romy, stop talking such nonsense, you know that's not true. When you write to me you tell me all the things you've been doing, like going to parties and acting in plays at school.'

'They are ordinary things. Life is only exciting when you are home.'

Daniel said, 'Romy, the things that are apparently unattainable create the most interest. I was once in love with a girl whose parents were wealthy. I was miserable if I didn't catch just a glimpse of her every day.'

Romaine felt a sudden surge of jealousy. 'Who was she?'

'It doesn't matter – someone you don't know. The thing was, that when I *did* get to know her and she even flirted with me, I didn't want her any more.' Romaine tried to argue that it was different with them but Daniel dismissed this. 'You haven't got the point. Supposing, just supposing we married, we would be as other couples are and slip into an everyday existence.'

'It doesn't happen if the couple are really in love.' Romaine spoke earnestly but Daniel dismissed this, too.

'My parents were in love, still are, but romance and excitement fly out of the window when there isn't much money and there are children to feed.' When Romaine was inclined to argue Daniel held up his hand. 'When you are a few years older we might discuss this again.'

'Oh, you, you!' she fumed. 'You're so arrogant, so big-headed. I hate you.'

'You don't, you know,' he said softly.

She looked him straight in the eye. 'At this moment I do, Daniel and possibly, if I don't see you for a year, I might fall in love with someone else.'

'If you do,' he teased, 'will you still write to me?' She looked for something to throw at him and finding nothing, kicked him on the ankle. He just laughed and said, 'Temper, temper!'

Romaine wondered afterwards how she would have fared with Daniel away for a year if she had not had several changes of scene herself. Her Aunt Louise and Uncle Flynn had taken her with them for several holidays: they went twice to St Peel, and once to Scotland and to Brighton, which she had really enjoyed. All the same, she hoped that Daniel's Uncle Frederick would get some big commissions nearer home, and then she would see Daniel more often.

18

During the next two years, Romaine led what she thought of as a frustrated life. Apart from the times that Daniel was away working in various parts of England, he also spent a total of fourteen months in France and Italy. The awful part of it was that each time he came home from abroad she was away on holiday, the last time in Paris with Aunt Louise and Uncle Flynn – a special treat for her sixteenth birthday. It was not until Romaine found out that Daniel had been home from Italy during this time that she became convinced her holidays had been deliberately arranged to keep her and Daniel apart.

This was refuted, with Daniel's mother saying that even they had no idea when he would be home, but Romaine was still not convinced. Even when he came back from shorter trips in England she hardly saw him, and when she did there was always someone else there at the same time.

Daniel had been in Devon for six weeks when his mother, Margaret, told Romaine excitedly that her son would be home the following weekend; as he would be arriving on his nineteenth birthday, they were going to have a party.

Although Romaine was delighted by this news she wished she would not have to share him with so many people. She so longed to know of his personal life when he was away. It was always of his work he talked in his letters.

On the morning of the party Margaret did Romaine's hair for her, at her request repeating the style she had worn on the day she and Daniel had met in the lane; the only difference being that this time, the curls were circled by rose-coloured velvet ribbon to match the tiny bows on her sprigged muslin dress. Margaret had said, stepping back, 'Romy, you look truly lovely. You'll have many admirers at the party.'

Romaine wanted only one admirer – Daniel – and as the time for his arrival drew near, she was in a fever of uncertainty. Supposing he had met someone else and brought the girl home with him? She would die. There was no special girl with him when he arrived, however, but there were plenty of others who rushed to greet him, and so many relatives crowding round that Romaine thought as far as the party was concerned it was going to be an utter failure.

When he did get round to greeting her he held her at arms' length. 'Romy! You're beautiful.' The next moment he was hugging one of his aunts. 'Aunt Miriam, you look positively blooming!'

Some more of his relatives came up then and Romaine moved away. She was just wishing she were back home, when a young man she had never met before spoke to her and told her he found her most attractive. He was only one of a number of young men who approached her and Romaine hoped that Daniel would notice. Daniel, however, was constantly the centre of attention.

Feeling utterly miserable by now she had made up her mind to sneak away when Daniel caught her by the arm. 'Romy, I'm sorry I couldn't get back to you. Come into the garden, away from the noise.'

There was a mist outside and it was refreshingly cool after the heat of the room. She took a deep breath then said, 'I was just about to go home. I was aching to see you after so long but was beginning to feel like an intruder.'

Daniel stopped and tilted her face towards him. '*You* an intruder? Never. I just lived for your letters.'

'It seems as though you've been away a lifetime.' She searched his face in the light from a window. He always did have an air of authority, even as a boy; now he seemed a mature man. She went on, 'You've never talked about the people you met when you were abroad. Did you get to know many foreign girls?'

'Dozens. The Italian girls especially are very beautiful and very romantic.'

Romaine felt a stab of jealousy. 'Could you converse with them?'

He grinned. 'I could, but one didn't need to know the language. All the girls talked with their hands and their eyes.'

'Not with their lips?' she asked in a tart voice.

'Of course.'

'I'm surprised you bothered to come home.'

His expression became serious. 'I needed to see my family and I also needed to see you, Romy. While I was in Devon I realised that I was falling in love with you. When I finish my apprenticeship we can – '

'Oh, Daniel, I've always been in love with you! I'll follow you wherever you go.'

'No! Don't even think of such a thing.' He spoke sharply and it was like a slap on the face to her. 'You're too young to do anything so foolish. It would be stupid to follow me only to have your father bring you back. He was really angry when he had to fetch you from Kent.'

'I was much younger then.'

'You are still only sixteen and obviously haven't learned much more sense.'

She stared at him. 'A few moments ago you said you loved me.'

'I do, but you must grow up. You are still behaving like a child.'

'I have a woman's feelings.'

'But not the sense of a woman, Romy.'

'I suppose all the girls you met were sensible.'

'Yes, they were. I made love to some of them.'

'How generous of you. I am really surprised you came home.'

She was near to tears and about to leave when Daniel touched her arm gently. 'I said I *made* love, not that I was *in* love with any of them. You have pride of place in my heart.'

Her head went up. 'Is that so? I would never have

guessed.' The next moment she was saying, a catch in her voice, 'Daniel, I love you. Why are you being so cruel to me?'

'How am I cruel – because I speak the truth? I'm not in a position to rush into anything. We must be patient.'

'I have no patience. You go gallivanting over to France and Italy while I am stuck here bored to death.'

'Romy, I was working, and long hours, too. I wasn't gallivanting anywhere. You went to Paris with Louise and Flynn, saw all the wonderful sights that most girls would give their right arm for, but you behave like a shrew and a shrewish wife is something I could not abide.'

'I wouldn't be a shrew,' she retorted. 'You wouldn't let me.'

'Romy, let me say something.'

'I have a few words I want to say first. Two weeks ago I saw some peacocks on a lawn. They were strutting about looking as if they owned the world and everything in it. The peahens were drab, subservient-looking creatures. Well, I'm not going to be like those peahens. I have a voice and I want to use it.'

'Oh, you do,' he said drily. 'There's no doubt about that, but you are using it in the wrong way. You were five years old when I first met you and I was taken with your high spirits and bright chatter. You had a way with you as though you were hugging life and enjoying every minute of it. You've lost that. I want you to get it back.'

'Before you decide to marry me? No, thank you. I'll live my life the way I want it to be, not as you dictate.' Turning from him she ran across the grass, pulled open the gate and sped up the road. She heard Daniel call to her but ran on, tears streaming down her cheeks. What a fiasco! She had been longing, aching to see him – now she had ruined everything. She slowed to a walk, then stopped to pull herself together. She would have to go back: Flynn was coming to collect her at eleven o'clock. She dried her eyes and, head up, walked back to the house. Daniel was leaning against the railings.

'So, the wanderer returns.'

'Only because Flynn will be calling, expecting me to have had a wonderful time.'

'And I spoilt it for you,' he said softly.

'No, I learned something tonight. I learned that Lord Byron was right when he said that "Man's love is of man's life a thing apart – " '

' " 'Tis woman's whole existence",' Daniel finished for her.

'But not in my mother's case,' Romy said. 'She did what she wanted to do – she became a doctor. I don't want to do anything as ambitious as that, but now that you have abandoned me – '

'I have not abandoned you. I ask only that you be patient.'

'You do what you want. I shall become an – an artist.'

'You can't become one overnight.'

'I don't expect to.' As the faint strains of a violin came from the house Romaine picked up her skirt. 'Excuse me, Daniel. I promised one of my admirers a dance.' She prayed that Daniel would demand that she danced with him, but he made no attempt to follow.

She suddenly felt surprisingly calm. She would leave home. No one really wanted her, so she would make a new life for herself elsewhere. Perhaps she would even go to Paris again, for her French was fluent, thanks to her private schooling.

By the time Romaine was in bed that night, however, she knew she would try to go somewhere near the area where Daniel was working. Even if she never saw him, she needed that close link. He was a part of her being, just as her great-grandfather Jeremiah had been to her great-grandmother Henrietta. Sometimes she could *feel* Daniel in the room beside her – and was sure he would be thinking about her. He loved her, she knew that; she also knew he was too stubborn to give in to her. Until he was ready to marry her, she must not sit around and waste her life. They would get together some time. Romaine found herself thinking of her mother. At one time she had hated her for leaving home to live her own life, hated her for preferring to look after poor people, instead of caring for her own daughter. Now she was beginning to admire Jessamy for having the courage to break away from all restrictions and get what she wanted from life. Not many women would have tackled what she had. Romaine did not want to follow in her mother's footsteps, but she would like to become an artist...possibly a portrait painter. Daniel's tutor had told her recently that she really did have talent. Perhaps some day she would be a famous artist. In the meantime she would make plans to leave home. She did have some money, which she had saved from past Christmases and birthdays.

As though thoughts had gone winging through the air, Jessamy was thinking of Romaine that same evening. It was one of those times when she suffered from a dreadful longing to see her daughter. Normally when her longing became unbearable, she would go to the private school Romy attended and from a short distance wait for her to come out. Always she would be with a group of laughing girls and every time she seemed more beautiful. Then Jessamy would wonder what her daughter's future held. Would she still want to marry Daniel? Was he the right person for her?

All that evening Jessamy felt restless, and before she went to bed she had a sudden urge to go to the Coachman's Cottage. This was puzzling enough, but when the urge became stronger she was worried. Had the ghost girl something to tell her? She went to bed knowing there was nothing she could do now, but she tossed and turned, and at seven o'clock when she got up, Jessamy had made up her mind to go over to the cottage that evening.

Louise came in the afternoon for one of her usual visits, and when Jessamy told her about her instinct her cousin gave a shiver. 'Oh, I feel all goose-pimply.'

Jessamy said, 'I hope no one is going to die, or anything like that. I shall stay at the cottage tonight, I'll have to.'

'I'll get a fire going.' Louise gave another shiver. 'I'll stay with you, if you like.'

'No, I'd rather be alone, Louise, and you don't want to have to tell Flynn that I'm expecting a ghost for tea.'

Jessamy made an attempt at a smile that didn't quite come off.

When Louise left Jessamy she promised to call at the cottage early the next morning and find out how things had gone.

Jessamy had a sick feeling when she let herself into the cottage but felt better when she saw the cheerful fire in the sitting room and a note from her cousin saying there was food in the pantry.

After a meal she settled herself in the armchair with a rug over her knees for her vigil. All sorts of thoughts went through her mind; she remembered her life when they had all lived here and were happy, before Alistair had taken up with Kate Keller. She semi-dozed and when she roused, the fire had burned low. Jessamy put on some more logs and coal, and settled back again. It had occurred to her that she might have built the whole thing up through being over-emotional, but something told her she had been right to come.

It was a long vigil, and at half-past two in the morning, feeling a longing to sink into the deep featherbed, she threw back the rug and was about to get up when the lamp began to flicker. It went low and she felt the draught. She tensed. *The ghost girl had come*.

In the dim light the apparition took shape. She was wearing the cloak, as before, but the hood was pushed back from her face. Jessamy got up. The ghost girl stood rubbing her arms from shoulder to hand, a look of pain in her eyes. She then held out her arms and clasping her hands seemed to be drawing someone to her. Afterwards she began to massage the back of her hand gently.

Jessamy said, 'Is it a woman who needs my help?'

The girl shook her head.

'A man and he...' The girl nodded vigorously then rubbed under her breast. 'A man who needs my help and my love?'

The girl gave a quick nod, seemed to hesitate then her expression began to change. The lights flickered, she faded and the next moment was gone.

Jessamy tried to visualise the ghost girl's expression but

found it impossible. She felt suddenly drained, her eyelids weighted. She sank back into the chair and pulled the rug over her. Who was it who was ill and needed her help? Her father? Mist surrounded her.

It was Louise who awoke her the next morning. 'Jessamy, what happened? You haven't been to bed!'

Jessamy had a job to get her eyes opened. She tried to move and felt stiff.

Louise said, 'It's only half-past seven but I had to come early because I've received a letter from my mother. Fabian has had an accident, apparently, and he's been quite ill. I wondered if the feeling you had about the cottage...?'

Jessamy was now wide awake. She drew herself up in the chair. 'What sort of accident?'

'He was on the clifftop at St Peel throwing a ball to a dog. The ball bounced over the cliff and Fabian went after it, then fell. He has a broken wrist, pulled muscles in his arm and had to have stitches for a cut on his head. He also has severe bruising all over his body. Although he's home from hospital, she says he's still in a lot of pain.'

Jessamy told Louise about the ghost girl's actions, then said, 'It fits in with Fabian, doesn't it? I feel she was asking my help. I would go to him, but I need to find a reliable doctor first to take over my practice. I can't even call on Dr. Draycott since he bought his own practice.'

'Would Willard Stead do?'

'Willard? Surely he's in America?'

'He was, but you remember he lost his wife a while ago? Well, he felt he wanted to come back to England after that so he's staying with his brother. He came to see us yesterday at Paradise Corner and says he misses not being busy. I know he would be only too pleased to help out. I'll ask him and let you know what he says.'

The result of this was that Willard Stead came back to Jessamy's lodgings with Louise to say he would be glad to take over her workload. He still had that quiet, gentle manner which Jessamy knew would appeal to her patients. They talked for a long time, about her work in Poplar and about the old days, when they had all been at the dispensary together. It was arranged that she would leave for St Peel that afternoon.

'Don't worry,' Willard said with a boyish grin. 'I'll have all your patients cured by the time you come back.'

'If you do,' she teased, 'I will offer you a partnership!' To which he laughingly replied, 'And I shall probably accept.'

On this bright note Jessamy went upstairs to pack. When Louise followed her she said, 'Where will you stay, with the family away?'

Jessamy's parents, Louise's parents and Jeremiah were going to the golden wedding of Henrietta's brother and his wife at Dover, and were intending to stay for a week. Jessamy said, 'Actually, I think it's for the best. Can you imagine how Mama's tongue would be going if she knew I was visiting Fabian! I'm hoping to avoid meeting any of the family.'

Louise eyed her with some curiosity. 'Are you intending to stay at The Montague Acres?'

'Heavens, no – I would never live that down. I'll stay with Fabian during the day and sleep at home. If I come back late I needn't even light a candle.'

'A secret assignation,' Louise said, half-teasing.

'It has to be, Louise. I don't even know that Fabian will want me there all day but I must be, to do any good.'

'On the contrary, I feel sure he will be glad to have your company. He's been away such a lot that he hasn't really made friends up there.'

While Jessamy was folding nightclothes and underwear ready to pack, Louise talked about her cousin's power to pick up the waves of the ghost girl. 'It's amazing, really. These waves must travel through the air. Fabian was probably going over his life with you and longed to see you.'

'Perhaps. I only hope I can ease his pain.'

Louise went to the station with her. Unfortunately, the cab was held up in traffic and Jessamy only had seconds to board the train. She shouted to Louise, who was enveloped in steam from the engine, 'I'll write...' And back came a disembodied voice through all the noise. 'Don't rush back, we'll manage.'

Jessamy had thought that the train journey might prove an ordeal, but after the bad night she had spent she slept a good part of the way. It was when she arrived at Newcastle Central and stepped on to the platform with no one to meet her that she had a bereft feeling.

She felt better, however, when she arrived home. It was strange going into a cold, empty house. The curtains in her old bedroom were heavy velvet. She drew them, lit the lamp, turned it down low and put a match to the kindling of the fire already laid in the grate. Within a short time the cold air had gone from the room. She ate food she had brought with her, boiled a kettle of water on the fire, made a hot drink and when the fire was glowing had a feeling of satisfaction at what she had achieved.

She slept soundly and after having some breakfast, set out for The Montague Acres, taking a roundabout route.

There was a mist over the moors and Jessamy found something mournful in hearing the baa-ing of sheep before a group was disclosed as the mist drifted. Yet it was something that had amused her when she lived here. Had she become acclimatised to London life, then, or was it an omen that Fabian was really ill?

Her ex-husband's steward, Mr Stannard, opened the door to her. 'Good morning, ma'am,' he said in a formal way, as though she came every morning to call. 'The master is indisposed but I'm sure he will be pleased to see you. I'll enquire. Will you take a seat?' He pulled a chair closer to the fireplace in the hall where a huge log fire burned.

It was several moments before Mr Stannard reappeared. He held the door of the study open and invited her to enter. When Jessamy went in the door was closed quietly behind her. Fabian, in a dressing gown with a rug over him, was propped up by pillows on a sofa. He looked dreadful. His face was badly bruised, his right foot was in plaster, there was a cut on his brow that had been stitched and he was obviously in pain.

'Jessamy,' he said, giving her a smile of welcome. Even that seemed to cause him pain. He motioned her to a chair. 'Such a surprise. How wonderful to see you.' He paused. 'I understand that your parents and some of the family are away. What brought you here?'

'You did.' She brought the chair closer and sat down. 'I was told about your accident.'

'The ball is recovering.' There was the trace of a boyish grin.

'But you, I'm told, are bruised all over.'

'My body is a study in shades of blue and black. It could have been worse – I could have broken many bones. Jessamy, it's a tonic seeing you.' He reached out a hand to touch her, then winced. 'It's bruised inside. It's the most painful part of me – keeps me awake at night.'

'Perhaps I can help to ease it.' She told him about her gift and although he looked a little sceptical, she took his hand, laid hers over the back of it for a while then began a gentle massaging.

'Your hand is warm,' he said. 'Comforting.' They sat in silence for a while, then Fabian said softly, 'I've missed you, Jessamy. I went abroad, thinking I could forget you, but there wasn't a country I visited when you weren't with me. Couldn't we be friends again?'

There was still a closed feeling inside her but because of his pain and because of the pleading in his voice she said, 'Yes, but I must apologise first about Caroline.'

'That's all in the past, Jessamy, long since done with these many years.' In the next breath he said, surprise in his voice, 'My hand is hot. I can hardly feel any pain. It's wonderful.'

'You'll need some more treatments, Fabian.' She tried to speak in a matter-of-fact way, but he lay smiling at her.

'Very good, Doctor.'

'I'm serious,' she said.

He sobered. 'I'll never forget that you came when I needed you desperately.' He picked up her hand and kissed the palm. At one time this gesture, those words, would have moved her deeply. Now they aroused no emotion, not even a tiny spark. Sensing this perhaps, Fabian asked after the family. He especially wanted to know about Romaine, and Jessamy, not wanting to bring any sentiment into the visit, talked at great length about her daughter.

When the physician came, Jessamy left the room. After he had gone and she returned to Fabian he was all smiles. 'Doctor Jones was patting himself on the back for the improvement in me. I didn't enlighten him that a very attractive lady was responsible.' Fabian paused then said, in more serious vein, 'Could you stay here, Jessamy? My days suddenly seem very bleak without you.'

'I could stay during the next few days but I must go home at night.' She gave a wry smile. 'To fulfil the proprieties.'

'I'll accept your terms, ma'am,' he answered light-heartedly.

But Jessamy didn't go home. She was persuaded to stay and she slept in one of the spare rooms, which was warm and cosy.

During the next few days Fabian improved so much he was able to get up for an hour in the morning, afternoon and in the evening. He was like a child in the pleasure he showed.

On the fifth morning Jessamy awoke feeling she was running a temperature. She guessed the reason. Every night, as soon as it was dark, she had gone for a walk over the moors. The weather had been bad – strong winds with heavy rain, which had never bothered her in the past; in fact she had revelled in walking in stormy weather. She dosed herself and hoped she would be able to throw off the chill.

In the afternoon Fabian had just remarked that Jessamy looked flushed when there was the sound of angry voices in the hall. The next moment the door was flung open and to Jessamy's astonishment, her mother rushed in, anger in every line of her.

'Surprised you, haven't I? You didn't expect us to be home for another few days, did you? You're a slut. How dare you come up here and sully our good name?'

Mr Stannard, who had followed Esmeralda in, apologised to Fabian, then Chadwick was there and taking his wife by the arm, he said, 'Esmeralda, for heaven's sake!'

She shook him off and pointing at Fabian, screamed at Jessamy, 'He walked out on you, went off with another woman. You're divorced and yet you come crawling back to him for his favours. You're a whore, yes, a whore!'

Chadwick looked at Jessamy in appeal and suddenly furious, she went up to her mother and slapped her hard across the face. 'Stop your filth! Fabian has been ill, as you well know. I came to help nurse him.'

Her mother, a hand to her face, stood staring at Jessamy for a moment then she said in a vicious tone, 'No, you are the filthy one and I don't ever want to see your face again.' With that she stormed out.

Chadwick, distressed, turned to Jessamy. 'I'm sorry, love. Your mother doesn't mean it. She's not well – it's her age.'

Jessamy thought no, she's just a terribly spoiled woman who's always been allowed to have her own way. She said drearily, 'Go after her, Papa. I'll be all right. I'll go back to London tomorrow.'

He kissed her, gave her a hug and looking near to tears, left.

Jessamy felt terrible. She sank into a chair and Fabian, who had poured some brandy, brought it to her. 'Drink this, my dear.'

She sipped at it then looked up at him. 'I did a terrible thing. I struck my mother.'

'I think you did right,' he said gently. 'She was hysterical and had to be brought to her senses. Now, why don't you lie down?'

'No, I'm going to pack. I must leave, Fabian. I can't stay now, not after what has happened. You are on the mend, at least.'

Fabian tried all ways to persuade her to stay, at least until the next day, but Jessamy's mind was made up. Her chill might grow worse and she just had to go home now, while she could still travel.

19

While Jessamy was on her way back to London, Romaine was making plans to leave home. After much thought she decided to go to Bedford first, then make her way gradually to Leicestershire, so that she would not be easily traced. She packed a bag with several changes of clothes and wrote two notes, one to her father and the other to Louise and Flynn, thanking them for all they had done and saying she was sorry to be running away, but she had to. She needed some freedom, and if they found her and brought her home, she would simply run away again.

That night she catnapped in a chair until five o'clock, gathered her things together and crept out of the house, taking a cab to St Pancras station. It was a bitterly cold morning, with frost prettying the branches of the trees. She gave a little shiver but knew it was partly due to excitement.

At St Pancras, finding she would have a wait of an hour and a half before the first train to Bedford, she went into the waiting room and warmed her hands at the fire. Five minutes later, a woman dressed in a flowing black cloak and a large-brimmed black straw hat sporting a feather, came breezing in, greeting Romaine with a cheerful, 'Good morning!'

Romaine murmured a greeting and sat down. The woman came and sat beside her, informing her that she was going to Bedford and had a while to wait for a train, which was really rather annoying as she had just had word to say that her brother was dying. She did want to get there before he died.

Romaine, intrigued by this flamboyant character who didn't seem in the least distressed, said, 'Why?'

The woman eyed her in surprise. 'I suppose because it's the thing to do. My name, by the way, is Pettinfor. Adele.

Widow.'

Romaine gave her name and had to restrain herself from adding, 'Spinster. Runaway.'

Mrs Pettinfor began to tell Romaine about her brother. 'I never liked George much, he was always penny-pinching and a liar, too. All my family were penny-pinching and so was my husband. When he died, though, I found I was rich and this has allowed me to realise my ambition – to travel.'

When Romaine asked if she had been abroad she replied, 'I've travelled the world, my dear. It gives one a lovely feeling of freedom. So where are you bound at this ungodly hour?'

'I'm going to Bedford, too,' said Romaine.

'Do you live there?'

'No. As matter of fact I'm running away from home.'

Mrs Pettinfor beamed at her. 'I applaud you. When I was young I longed to run away but I had no money. What made you want to leave?'

'A need to be free.'

'Ah, I know that feeling. After my husband died it was wonderful to do exactly as I pleased without having to ask permission first. Mind you, after a time freedom can be a lonesome thing. Even though I detest my family, I was quite glad to see them all again. At least, I was for a time. I have kept my house on in London, so I can be alone if I wish, but no doubt in another couple of months I'll be away again.'

She talked about how she had accepted an arranged marriage, hoping for some independence and how her husband had turned out to be even more dominant and more stingy than her father. 'That man,' she said, 'did not have an ounce of romance in him. I'll offer you some advice, my dear: if you meet a romantic, penniless rogue, marry him. Even if he leaves you later for someone else, you have at least for a time known heaven. I only knew hell with my dear departed.'

Romaine said she would remember and the woman told her if there was anything she could do to make her freedom easier, Romaine had only to ask. Romaine did think of something and decided she would mention it during their train journey.

On the way to Bedford Romaine wrote a note to her father saying she was staying with a friend and was in good spirits, and Mrs Pettinfor agreed to post the letter when she returned to London. At Bedford station, a carriage was waiting for the older woman, to take her to her brother's house. He lived out of town, and when Mrs Pettinfor offered Romaine a lift she accepted.

She alighted at the beginning of a country lane. Mrs Pettinfor wished her luck, and Romaine said she hoped she would find her brother improved. She smiled to herself when the widow waved her umbrella from the carriage window and called, 'Enjoy your freedom!'

It was still early and although the skies were grey the sun was trying to get through the clouds. Smoke rose lazily from the chimneys of cottage and farm and the smell of woodsmoke hung on the chill air. When Romaine passed a small farm and the appetising aroma of bacon cooking drifted out, she realised how hungry she was.

After hesitating she went round to the back and asked a young woman who was sweeping the yard if she could give her some breakfast; she would pay for it. The woman wiped her hands down her apron and gave a nod. 'Ay, come in.'

They went into the kitchen and the woman, who said her name was Mrs Watson, disappeared into a back room and returned with two slices of bacon which she put on a griddle and swung over the fire. A kettle was boiling on the hob and she made a pot of tea. During this nothing was said. Romaine, feeling a little uncomfortable, asked if she had children.

The woman brought a loaf from a bin and cut a slice. 'We've had two but they both died.' Romaine said she was sorry, it was sad to lose children, and Mrs Watson cut another slice of bread then looked up. 'It's life, isn't it?'

No more conversation passed between them at this stage. Romaine sat down to a plate of bacon, egg, two sausages and fried bread. Mrs Watson went out and left her to it, with Romaine still hearing the toneless voice and thinking how awful life was for some people.

In spite of the morose atmosphere she thoroughly enjoyed her breakfast. When the farmer's wife came back and Romaine asked how much she owed and was told nothing, she took a half crown from her purse and laid it on the table. 'I insist. I was grateful for the meal – it was delicious.'

Mrs Watson dropped the coin into a vase on the mantelpiece and said it would come in for a rainy day. She went out again. Romaine picked up her bag and followed. The woman was finishing sweeping the yard. Romaine called, 'Thank you for your kindness,' but there was no reply.

There were no men in the fields. Was Mrs Watson a widow?

The sun had come out and although it was weak Romaine was glad of a little brightness. Would she meet many people like the farmer's wife? She had not even asked her where she was bound.

About a mile further on Romaine stopped, and taking a sketchpad and pencil from her bag, began to draw first Mrs Watson then Mrs Pettinfor. With the farmer's wife she had captured an awful hopelessness in her eyes, which did not surprise her. She was surprised, however, when she found she had also portrayed a sadness in the eyes of her lively, eccentric travelling companion. Romaine put her pad and pencil away and moved on, determined to enjoy her freedom.

At midday she came across a gypsy encampment in a spinney. Several people seemed to be at work. There were tents but caravans, too. The latter were brightly painted and, feeling curious, she went to have a peep in one nearby. It was scrupulously clean and quite well furnished. She had taken another step forward when a voice said behind her, 'Can I offer you refreshments?'

Romaine turned to see a tall, dignified woman in black eyeing her with some curiosity. 'Oh, no, no thanks. I was interested in the caravan. It looks...attractive, colourful.'

'Come in, have a look around. Visitors are always welcome, especially another Romany.'

Romaine stared at her. 'My father's great-grandmother was a Romany, but how did you know?'

'One Romany can always recognise another. Do come in.'

They climbed the steps into the caravan and Romaine looked about her, entranced. There were many silver-framed photographs on the walls and as many porcelain ornaments on the shelves. A rich red patterned rug covered the floor. Chairs were upholstered in a matching red velvet. There were cushions in jewel colours.

'It's beautiful!' Romaine exclaimed.

She was invited to sit down at a small table where a pack of Tarot cards lay on a blue plush tablecoth. The woman gave her a small glass of fruit juice. Romaine thanked her then, touching the pack of cards, asked if she told fortunes.

'I use them for my own guidance,' the woman said quietly.

'Could you give me guidance?'

'Do you want it?'

Romaine said, 'I'm in love. The young man is in Leicestershire at the moment, and I want to be near him. Sometimes I feel he is in the room with me. I would like to know if we will get married.'

The woman's gaze met hers steadily. 'Is there a doubt?'

'Well, we can't get married until he's completed his apprenticeship. I needed to be free to be near him.'

'The path to freedom can be rough; it has many pitfalls.'

'I'll accept them,' Romaine said earnestly. 'All I want to know is if Daniel will marry me.'

'Do you really want to know the future? If I were to tell you that you would be very poor and quarrelsome and that he would die early in your marriage, would you still want to know?'

Romaine stared at her, shocked. 'Is Daniel going to die?'

'I have no idea. I'm simply putting an imaginary situation to you. If you know the future there is no excitement, no anticipation.'

'But you use the cards to know *your* future!'

The woman smiled and shook her head. 'As I said, I only use them for guidance, to learn what course of action will be best for my people. For instance, there was a time when the cards warned me of fire. It was a hot summer and the undergrowth was as dry as tinder. I warned everyone to look out for smoke and thus we were able one day to prevent a tiny fire from spreading.'

'Can you honestly say you've never wanted to know your own future?' Romy queried.

'I have never been tempted. My mother lived her life on what the cards told her and died of worry at thirty.'

'But gypsies make a living telling fortunes.'

'Some do, my people don't. We earn a living making articles for general use. I can only offer this advice: if you expect sunny paths all the time and no storms you will know disillusionment, but if you are prepared for rough paths and storms you will cope and will know the pleasure of achievement. Your man is masterful and you like to rule, so you must learn to compromise.'

Romaine's eyes widened. 'Daniel *is* masterful but I don't think that I want to rule.'

A man came to the caravan and called something in a foreign tongue. The woman answered in the same language then said to Romaine, 'I must go now. A child is ill.'

She walked to the edge of the spinney with her guest then said gently, 'I'm pleased to have met you. May peace and truth go with you.'

Romaine left with mixed feelings, unsure whether she was pleased or sorry that the gypsy woman had not read the cards for her.

Further along the road she stopped and sketched her, and found she had portrayed her with an aura of mysticism, something she had not been able to catch when drawing fairy creatures from her imagination.

The gypsy had known that Daniel was masterful, but she was wrong when she said that Romaine liked to rule.

Or was she? Louise had scolded her often for wanting her own way. Romaine walked on, thinking that in one short morning she had met three people with totally diverse characters and ways of life.

For the next few days she roamed the countryside, staying one night only at each cottage or farmhouse, enjoying meeting different people yet not wanting to get involved. To those who queried the wisdom of travelling alone she told the same story, that she was an orphan going to live with an aunt and uncle at Kettering, but wanted a little freedom first. Surprisingly, most women, older ones as well as younger ones, sympathised with her. They would have enjoyed some freedom in their lives.

The number of sketches of these people she had done made Romaine realise she was weaving a canvas of life, some of it colourful, some drab. There was the elderly spinster who had lived with her sister for forty years; they had both been in love with the same man. 'He married someone else,' she said, 'and we each blamed the other for losing him. When my sister died I realised how we had wasted precious years quarrelling. How I wish we could have those years over again.' In that spinster's eyes was a world of longing.

Romaine moved around for two weeks in all and was beginning to get restless to go even further afield when the impetus to do so came one Friday evening when she knocked on the door of a whitewashed cottage.

A young woman opened the door and when Romaine asked if she knew of anyone who would put her up for the night she said, 'I could, but my husband Tom and I will be leaving early in the morning to go to Market Harborough. It's the yearly Fair.'

Romaine smiled. 'I think I too would like to go to the Fair.'

The day, for October, was mild and sunny, the road from the station at Market Harborough packed with wagons, carts, barrows, vans and cattle, the path crammed with people of all ages. The air was filled with sounds – bright chatter, the lowing of the animals, the crunch of hooves and wheels on the rough stone road and the scraping of a fiddler playing a lively tune.

Romaine, her eyes shining, said, 'Isn't this all wonderful?' Tom laughed and told her to wait until she got to the marketplace. Once they reached the square and Romaine heard fairground music she was caught up in the atmosphere. The lively tune of the organ mingled with the changing pitch of voices, the lowing of penned cattle for sale, the baa-aing of sheep and the grunting of pigs. Romaine accepted that cattle were sold to the highest bidders, but when she knew that people lined up on a platform were workers being bid for by farmers and others, she was shocked.

'It's awful, so demeaning. They're human beings, after all.'

Maggie and Tom eyed her in surprise. Tom said, 'It's the hirings, Romy. The people are hired by farmers and others. It's the accepted thing – employers need workers and the people up there need to be employed or they'll starve.'

On the platform were men and women of varying ages and young girls and boys. All of them but one had a defeated air, the exception being a girl of about sixteen who had a saucy look.

When Romaine said that some of the older men and women didn't look as if they had the strength to work, Maggie nodded. 'That's the sad thing. Many of them don't have homes, you see. They're a moving population and if they don't get work today, they'll probably end up in the workhouse.'

Tom said gently, 'Don't look so distressed, Romy, it's life. Let's enjoy the Fair.'

Romaine, knowing it was not right to spoil the day for this couple who had been so kind to her, agreed but it was a while before she could get the faces of the hirelings out of her mind. Then, catching sight of brightly painted caravans among the stationary carts, wagons and barrows, she exclaimed, 'Oh, look. Gypsies!'

As she made to move toward them Maggie caught her

arm. 'Don't go near them, Romy, they're dirty.'

Tom added, 'And they're thieves.' Then he remarked with a chuckle, 'They'd steal *you* and sell you if they had the opportunity.'

Romaine knew otherwise but refrained from saying so. They were not the gypsies she had met, anyway. They walked on. People milled around, causing congestion when groups stopped to watch certain entertainers. There were the usual jugglers, dancing dervishes, actors performing a play, singers and a sword-swallower who made Jessamy's throat feel raw.

After the three of them had stood for a while watching Tom became impatient. 'Come on, you two, let's move on. I know the Fair is here for over a week, but we only have today and anyway, the first day always seems the best.'

'I agree,' Maggie said, then she turned to Romy. 'Tom and I have to be back at work on Monday and will be leaving on the Sunday evening train, but if you want to stay on I'm sure my parents will be glad to put you up.'

She had hardly finished speaking when they were surrounded by numerous people, who turned out to be Tom and Maggie's families. There were squeals of delight and hugs. Romaine was introduced and when Maggie told her parents she was needing accommodation, offers came from all sides. Maggie's parents claimed her, with her father saying with a broad grin, 'There's room for three on the floor.' The roly-poly figure and three chins of his wife wobbled as she laughed and told Romy he was a joker. There was a bed for her.

'It's too big for one,' a cousin of Maggie teased, and his twin brother added, 'And you'll never sleep with the church bells chiming. Why not come and stay at *our* house?'

Romaine laughed. 'I like a big bed and I could sleep through an earthquake.'

Mrs Brempster beamed. 'Isn't she nice? I can see we'll get on like a house afire.'

The family split up then, with a promise to meet again

later.

Maggie said as they walked away, 'They're a big-hearted lot. They let their hair down on Fair Day but they're all hardworking during the week. They work at Symington's. We'll show it to you in a few minutes, but first you must see our Grammar School.'

Romaine was intrigued by the school 'on stilts' in the square, with a Butter Market underneath. Tom explained that the builder had wanted it constructed that way so that people could shelter under it during bad weather. He then pointed out the church with its beautiful tall spire which he said, went back to the twelfth century.

Romaine looked up at it with awe. 'That's a long time ago.'

Maggie teased her husband, saying that one minute he was moving them on to see more of the Fair and the next giving a history lesson.

Tom grinned. 'It's for the benefit of our lovely guest. To our right,' he went on, flinging his arm out in a dramatic gesture, 'we have the Dragon Inn, where 'tis said that a part of it housed a vicar in the seventeenth century.' Tom chuckled. 'I bet the poor man is constantly turning in his grave at the thought of having been connected with an inn.' He waved his arm again.

'And beyond our Grammar School there is...guess what? Another inn, the Green Dolphin. There it is, wedged between the two Symington buildings. They provide work for several hundreds of people.'

Maggie said, 'On the right is the corset factory, where nearly all the women in the family work, including our mothers. The other factory deals with coffee, tea and general goods. Symington's are a good firm to work for. I was there before I married. If you fancied a job there, Romy, my mother would speak for you.'

'Thanks, I'll certainly think about it.'

When they had passed the Green Dolphin Tom took over again. 'Yonder is Sun Yard where Maggie's parents live and over there is Adam and Eve Street where,' he added, with an impish light in his eyes, 'Eve tempted

Adam with the apple.'

Maggie chuckled. 'What? Close to Tripe Lane?' Then she became suddenly serious. 'Oh dear, we're being blasphemous.'

Tom suggested, 'Let's get back to the Fair. We can show Romy other places later.'

A brass band began playing a lively march, which put them back into the mood of the Fair. They bought hot pasties from a stall and washed them down with homemade lemonade then stopped at a sideshow, where a man was shouting, 'Step inside and see the two-headed lamb!' People were lining up to pay their sixpences to go in. Romaine wanted to go in too but Tom said the lamb did not have two heads; it was a trick done by mirrors and was a waste of money. Maggie agreed. Romaine had no idea what Tom meant by it being 'done by mirrors' and thought she might come another day and find out.

There were stalls of all kinds, selling homemade cakes, secondhand clothes, pots and pans, books and bric-à-brac. They were endless. At the sides of the High Street, restless cattle were railed off from people and traffic. Carts, wagons and traps were still coming in a constant stream. The crowd was dense. Among the milling throng were a few well-dressed people, but the majority were working people wearing, according to Maggie, their Sunday best. There were also poverty-stricken people, whose children were bare-footed.

A number of these children were eyeing the sweetmeats and buns with such a hungry longing that Maggie and Romaine decided to slip a copper into their hands. The wonder, the joy this brought had Romaine looking for more children to treat but she was checked by Maggie, who said ruefully, 'Sorry, love, it has to end there otherwise we would have a horde of children chasing us.'

Although Romaine saw the sense of this she wished she had a lot of money so she could give treats to poor parents, too. Some friends of Tom hailed him then and when they started discussing cattle Maggie suggested she take Romaine to see her parents' house then meet again at the

Grammar School.

The Brempsters' house was under an archway with a yard that widened at the top with the far houses having small gardens in front. Maggie said, 'The people around here may be poor, but they tend their gardens lovingly and they're alive with colour in the summer.' She opened the door of the house where they had stopped and went straight in to a room with a glowing fire. There was colour, too, in this room that seemed cluttered with furniture – a crimson plush cloth on the table and an assortment of cushions on the sofa and armchairs, all richly embroidered. Maggie said, 'It's all Mother's work. She used to do beautiful embroidery on the corsets, but her hands are a little stiff now, so she works on the machines.'

A neighbour looked in and called, 'Your man's waiting for you, Maggie. His nails are bitten down to the quick.'

'Oh, thanks, I'd forgotten all about him.' Maggie grinned at Romaine. 'Don't tell him I said that. Come along.'

'Thought you'd both gone to Leicester,' Tom greeted them, still his cheery self. 'I thought it might be a good idea to show Romy the layout of the town so she'll be able to find her own way around.'

They showed her the roads that led out of the town then took her to the various yards. First they went to Quaker's Yard where the chimney sweeps and their families lived, then told her she must avoid the next yard where vagrants congregated, and then went on to see the others. Some were clean, while others had open sewers on the outside walls of the houses; they stank, but Tom said she had to see the bad as well as the good.

Afterwards they met up with the family again and had another joyous reunion as if they had not met for years. Someone suggested they should all go round the Fair again. After that the women were ready to go home and the men to go for a drink.

It was dusk and the air had grown cold. Mrs Brempster said, 'We three'll put our feet up and have a nice cup of tea.' To Maggie she added, 'I got your father to pop home and build up the fire.'

It was dark in the narrow alleyway and the brightly burning fire was a welcome sight. Mrs Brempster went in first, saying, 'We have gas laid on but I can't stand the hissing of the jets.' She lit a lamp. 'There, that's more homely.'

More homely? For the first time since leaving London Romaine felt a wave of homesickness. Maggie said gently, 'You're tired, aren't you? We've walked you off your feet. I'm tired, too. We'll just sit easy and have an early night.'

But they were denied the early night. When Mr Brempster and Tom arrived there were six more men from the family with them, all in a merry mood.

Although Romaine had boasted she could sleep through an earthquake, revellers in the streets and the church clock chiming every quarter of an hour competed to keep her awake, and made Sunday a day to be got over rather than enjoyed. She went with the family to church, visited Tom's relatives in the afternoon, went to church again in the early evening and afterwards visited Maggie's side of the family.

Maggie said, 'All this activity only happens when Tom and I come home. When we've gone back you can settle down with the parents. And Romy, if ever you feel like coming back to Bedford, you'll be more than welcome.'

'Thanks, Maggie, thanks to both of you for everything.'

They embraced, all a little tearful, with Romaine wondering what the next few days would have in store for her.

20

When Jessamy returned from St Peel she not only felt emotionally drained but had such a heavy cold that Louise insisted she went straight to bed. She ran a fever and had spells of delirium in which Fabian figured. Although, with the attention of Willard Stead, who stayed on to help, she improved quite quickly, he insisted she took things easy for a while.

Jessamy gave a weak smile. 'I know what you are trying to do, steal my patients from me.'

'I couldn't – they're all asking when you'll be back.' He paused then added gently, 'You have no idea how much they all love you.'

'What is love?' she queried.

Willard and Louise exchanged glances then Louise said, 'Now that would fill a book. We can talk about it when you are better. It's medicine time.'

When Willard and Louise went downstairs he said, 'She really will have to slow down. Apart from all the work she does here this healing gift of hers wears her out. Then there's the emotional side. She felt compelled to go rushing off to St Peel to help Captain Montague. She told you when she came back that she was not in love with him any more, yet in her delirium she talked about him all the time.'

'A lot of it didn't make any sense, of course, but I got the impression that she wanted to remain friends with him but was finding it difficult.' Louise sat thoughtful for a few moments then she said, 'After her Cousin Lillian tried to kill her the first time Jessamy suffered a profound shock. I wondered at the time if she would pull through. Even after we thought she had recovered, she said she felt that something cold was locked inside her and I don't think it's been unlocked, even after all these years.'

Willard nodded slowly. 'That's very possible. It may sound foolish, but another shock could be the key. The fact that she talked about Fabian a lot during her delirium suggests she was shaken at hearing about his accident; this might be the answer to her problem. Time will tell.'

Although Jessamy appeared to have made a quick recovery from her illness, it was another three weeks before Willard would allow her to take her surgery on her own. And it was then that Jessamy learned for the first time about Romaine running away.

'Fortunately,' Louise consoled her, 'we know she's all right. A woman in London who met her on her travels forwarded a letter that Romy had written and enclosed a note of her own to say she was all right. The woman had made enquiries and found she was settled with a very caring family. She did say, however, that she was unable to give the address as she had to respect Romy's need for privacy.'

'Well,' said Jessamy, 'it was good of her to go to so much trouble.'

'I thought so, too. Romy obviously left to find Daniel. When she does, and knowing Romy's determination she will, Daniel will let us know and send her back.'

Jessamy thought – and then she would run away again, for this is what Romy had told Louise and Alistair in the notes she had left for them. There was the same wanderlust in her as she herself had known when she was young. Jessamy prayed that her daughter's life would not turn out as hers had done.

Her mind slipped back to the five days she had spent at St Peel helping Fabian. She was still not over the awful altercation she had had with her mother. Louise had written to Chadwick Every to tell him Jessamy was ill and couldn't write, and she received a letter back saying how terribly sorry he was about the incident; he hoped that Jessamy would soon recover. Verity had also written, saying that Chadwick, for the first time she could remember, had completely lost his temper with Esmeralda and told her that if she did not alter her ways he would leave her. This, said Verity, had completely subdued Esmeralda, but for how long she had no idea.

Louise had also informed Fabian that Jessamy had a heavy cold and would write when she was well again. Fabian wrote to Jessamy, told her how much her visit had meant to him and said he would look forward to hearing from her when she was well again. Jessamy began a letter to him when she was up and about but never finished it, for the simple reason that she was not sure of her feelings towards him. She had enjoyed his company when they were together, but once away from him she was afraid of becoming involved, afraid of allowing that kind of emotion to come into her life ever again. 'Dear God,' she whispered, 'let my daughter love one man and he love her forever.'

Romaine kept coming into Jessamy's mind and two days later when Louise called she said, in a pensive way, 'I know that Romy is all right and I can understand her wanting to be near Daniel, but I would have expected her to have been homesick by now, wouldn't you?'

'For what?' Louise demanded. 'A home where she lives, not with her mother but myself and Flynn, and a father who leads a frantically busy life.'

'Doesn't Alistair want Romy at home?'

'Of course he does but he knows if he was able to bring her back she would only run away again. Romy does what she wants to do, just like her mother.' Louise got up. 'I'll see you some time.'

'You will come back?' The pleading in her cousin's voice made Louise weaken. She dropped a kiss on Jessamy's brow. 'Yes, of course I will.'

When Louise had gone Jessamy leaned back in her chair, wishing she could overcome this awful feeling of wanting to burst into tears and yet be unable to cry.

She had been prone to moods like this ever since she had been ill after her return from St Peel. She must try to pull herself together. She couldn't go on depending on Willard Stead popping in and lending a hand, even though he did enjoy being occupied.

She thought of Romaine once more in the care of strangers. Was her daughter, until recently only a schoolgirl, just being defiant in leaving home – or was she truly happy in her lodgings?

As it happened, Romaine had settled in with the Brempsters as though she had always known them. Mrs Brempster left for work at six o'clock in the morning, came home for breakfast at half-past seven, brought her a cup of tea and left her a cooked breakfast of bacon and egg in the oven.

The fire was always burning brightly and Romy would plan her destination for the day. She had told her landlady about Daniel and his work and how she wanted to find and be near him. Fortunately, she still had some money left.

Mrs Brempster had been alarmed at first. Leicestershire covered a wide area and there were many, many big houses where Daniel could be working. Romy had told her cheerfully that she had all the time in the world and she enjoyed walking, no matter how bad the weather. Then she had added, 'Don't worry. I've told you that I wrote to my father telling him I was all right.'

This had settled Mrs Brempster's mind but she warned Romy that while it would be all right to accept a lift from a farmer or on a carrier's cart, she was never to get into a motor car unless a chauffeur was driving. Romy had promised and set out every morning to find a big house where decorative plasterwork was in progress.

At the end of a week she had had no luck but she did have one interesting experience.

She was walking along the road to Bowden when she heard a child screaming; the noise held terrible pain. It came from a stone-built cottage on the edge of a wood and as Romaine stopped a woman, greatly agitated, came running out and begged her to go for a doctor.

'My little girl's been burned,' she sobbed. 'Her dress is stuck to her back. My husband is trying to pull it off but it's taking her skin with it.'

'Oh, he mustn't do that. Take me to her.' When the

woman stood looking bewildered, Romaine repeated, 'Take me to her! I know what to do.' The woman turned and ran into the cottage and Romaine followed.

A child of about two was lying on her stomach on a rug, her screams agonising as the father, tears running down his face, was trying to pull away the pieces of material. Romaine shouted, 'Stop it, it's the worst thing you could do.' To the mother she added, 'Bring me some sheeting, a pair of scissors and some oil, any kind – olive oil, castor oil – but *be quick*. And send someone for the doctor.'

Romaine's authoritative manner steadied them both. The father said he would get the doctor while the mother brought oil from a cupboard, a sheet from a clean-laundry basket and scissors from the dresser drawer. Romaine swiftly cut a piece of the linen, soaked it with castor oil and, spreading it over the child's back, talked soothingly. 'There, there, sweetheart. This will ease the pain.'

The mother, fist to mouth said, 'The pieces – stuck to her?'

A middle-aged, well-dressed woman came into the room but was silent. Romaine poured more oil on to the linen. 'The oil will loosen them eventually. I can't do more now. The doctor must see her.'

The woman spoke then, saying softly, 'What happened, Mrs Dolman?'

'Oh, ma'am, she was sitting on the fender. I forgot I'd taken the guard away. A piece of coal must have exploded, shooting out hot cinders. It does that sometimes. Oh, God, I'll never forgive myself. I'd just gone up the garden when I heard her screaming.'

'I met your husband. The doctor is up at the house; he should be here any minute.' The screaming of the child had subsided to hiccupping sobs. Romaine knelt down beside her, took a tiny hand in hers and carried on talking soothingly. The next moment there were voices outside then a stockily-built man came bustling in. Romaine stood up and the doctor leaned over and raised the oil-soaked cloth. He looked up. 'Who put this on?'

'I did,' Romaine said.

'Oh, and who are you to usurp my authority? I should have been called at once.'

Furious, Romaine said, 'As you must know, sir, speed is essential when dealing with burns. You could have been miles away.'

'And what credentials do you possess, young woman, to take it upon yourself to deal with *my* patient?' he demanded.

'None, but I feel myself qualified in dealing with an emergency. My father is a surgeon and my mother a doctor.'

There was a sudden stillness then he snapped, 'It's a pity you were not taught how to speak to your elders.'

'Oh, I was, but I was not taught how to deal with anyone as unpleasant as yourself.' Romaine turned to Mrs Dolman. 'I'll go now. I hope your little girl will recover soon.'

'Thank you very much for your help,' she replied in a low voice.

Romaine left, the doctor's anger almost a tangible thing. A minute later the smartly-dressed woman caught up with her. She said, 'Congratulations, my dear. You were splendid. People tend to fear our aggressive Doctor Plumbee, and I personally detest him. My name, by the way, is Dorothea Cerralden.'

Romaine stared straight ahead. 'Mine is Romy.'

Mrs Cerralden gave her a quick glance. 'You said, Miss Romy, that your father is a surgeon and your mother a doctor?'

'That's right, Mrs Cerralden, but I would rather not discuss it.'

'I understand. Would you care to come up to the house and have coffee? I would like you to meet my father-in-law.'

When Romaine, still ruffled, asked why, Mrs Cerralden replied with a wry smile, 'He's an irascible old man who enjoys getting the best of people. He was a colonel in the army and still likes to be addressed as such, and I would very much like to see how he would react to meeting someone as forthright as yourself.' When Romaine hesitated she pointed out that it had started to rain and so Romaine accepted.

They cut diagonally through the woods with Mrs Cerralden talking about the Dolmans. 'They're a very willing couple and the husband is a hard worker, but in some ways they're, well, a little backward. I'll get a nurse to keep an eye on young Daisy, she's a dear little girl.'

The house was three-storeyed, brick-built, the rooms spacious and tastefully furnished. A manservant came forward to take their outdoor clothes then Mrs Cerralden led the way upstairs. They went into a room at the back, where the windows overlooked a large garden.

A bony-faced man with sparse silver hair, who was seated near the window, a rug over his knees, grumbled that the coffee was already two minutes late. Mrs Cerralden said, 'I've brought a visitor to meet you, Colonel.'

He banged the arm of the chair and said tetchily, 'I told you I didn't want to see anyone today. Why don't you ever listen?'

She said quietly, 'I have no control when circumstances alter plans.' She explained about the burnt child and related the conversation that had been exchanged between the doctor and Romaine. At this the old man gave a gleeful chuckle. 'She bested old Plumbee, eh! Where is she?' Romaine was introduced and he eyed her up and down. 'Well, fancy a youngster like you out-talking Doc. He'll be livid. Sit down, tell me about yourself. Who are your people, where do you come from?'

Mrs Cerralden intervened, 'Her father is a surgeon and her mother a doctor but the rest is a closed book, I'm afraid.'

The old man's head went up. 'I was not addressing you, Dorothea. Speak when you are spoken to.'

Romaine's hackles were instantly up. She said to Mrs Cerralden, 'Why do you allow him to speak to you in this demeaning way? It's appalling.'

'And you are very rude,' he snapped. 'You are a guest in this house.'

'I was.' Romaine got up. 'Excuse me.'

She had taken a few steps when he sighed. 'Oh, do sit down. If I held a normal conversation it would be so boring.'

'If you had something interesting to say,' she retorted, 'you wouldn't be bored.'

'And what inspiring subject would you suggest?' He made a pretence at stifling a yawn.

'People?'

'Oh, and what interesting things have you learned about them in your *short* life, *Miss* Romy?'

'I've learned many interesting things, Colonel. I've learned that some people are unhappy because they don't know how to be pleasant, or because of petty jealousy, and there are some who think that people in lesser circumstances are void of brains.'

'Oh, clever, clever, Miss Romy,' he said with a sneer.

'Not clever, I've learned by experience.'

'So, because you were able to ease the pain of a burnt child and because your father is a surgeon and your mother a doctor you no doubt think you are qualified to enter the medical profession?'

'Not at all. I would like to become an artist. It's surprising what one can learn about people from sketching them.'

He gave a harsh laugh. 'What a field day you would have sketching the "abominable" Doctor Plumbee and myself.'

'Oh, I shall certainly do sketches of you both!'

A maid came in with the coffee and after she had been roundly scolded for her tardiness by the Colonel, Mrs Cerralden poured it then suggested to Romaine, 'Why don't you come and stay with us for a few days? I know my husband would love to have a sketch of his father.'

When Romaine said she would think about it the Colonel snapped, 'I haven't invited you.'

Mrs Cerralden looked angry and was about to make a retort when Romaine stood up for a second time. 'It's all right, Mrs Cerralden. I appreciate it that you asked me. I'll go now.'

The old man threw up his hands. 'Heaven preserve me from witless women. Did I say I would not give you permission?'

Romaine turned to him and grinned. 'I might agree to come if you asked nicely.'

'Never.' She picked up her gloves and he said, 'All right, all right. Will you come and stay with us for a few days?'

'Thank you, I accept. Now, please excuse me.'

Mrs Cerralden said as they went downstairs, 'He's the most infuriating man I know. He vents his temper on me because I haven't been able to give him grandchildren. I get so lonely at times. My husband is away for weeks at a time.'

'Why don't you get a companion?'

She sighed. 'I have thought about it, but I know the Colonel would demand attention from her, too. And who would put up with his snide remarks?'

'I would,' Romaine said. 'Not that I'm looking for a job at the moment, although I might need one in the future.'

They had reached the hall and Mrs Cerralden stopped and turned to her. 'I know he enjoyed his battle with you – not that he would ever admit it.'

Romaine laughed. 'I enjoyed it, too. I found it stimulating.'

'You wouldn't consider – ?' She shook her head. 'No, I have no right even to think of it. I'm grateful that you're coming to visit us.'

Romaine stood hesitant. 'I wouldn't mind the job but I would need some time free.'

Mrs Cerralden smiled. 'Let's talk. Come this way.'

The result of the talk was the agreement that Romaine would come every morning, stay for lunch and if she could, stay later also. A generous wage was offered, which Romaine gratefully accepted. She could hardly wait to tell Mrs Brempster her news.

Mrs Brempster oohed and aahed when told about the job and laughed herself silly when she heard Romaine's account of her conversation with the Colonel. 'I wish I could have been there. Mind you, I think that kind of man is lonely.'

'I think so, too.' Romaine told her about Mrs Cerralden driving her round the countryside visiting churches, adding, 'They're everywhere!'

Mrs Brempster chuckled. 'Like pubs. You know what they say, "Pubs to rot your guts and churches to save your souls". Now tell me again about the poor little girl who was burned.'

Romaine did tell her that she and Mrs Cerralden had called to enquire about Daisy later and found her sleeping. 'All the family had rallied round and were going to take turns sitting up with little Daisy so she would not turn over on to her back.'

The night clouds had brought deluging rain, which lashed against the window panes. Mr Brempster was working late and his wife and Romaine sat in the kitchen with the lamp turned low and the fire casting dancing flames on the walls. Mrs Brempster began reminiscing about the times when the floods were really bad.

'On one occasion the water was three feet deep in Coventry Road and eight to ten feet deep in the Square. It broke shop windows. My uncle who was in the Constabulary thought he saw bodies floating, but they were only tailors' dummies. We younger ones thought this very funny, but the damage was awful.' Then she exclaimed, 'Oh, heavens, we're getting morbid. Do you skate?'

Romaine, who had to switch her mind from floods to ice said, 'Yes.'

'Good. When the real winter comes you can go skating on the canal or on Folly's Pond. You'll have a wonderful time. I loved it when I was thinner. Yes, I was like a willow wand, believe it or not.' She chuckled. 'Now I'd go through the ice if it was five feet thick.' As though determined to let Romaine know that things would not be dull she talked about the big party they had every Christmas and about when the circus came to Harborough. Oh, she would love the circus. The feats they performed!

Romaine thought how lucky she was to be with such lovely warm people and wished, not for the first time, that she had grown up in the care of her own mother.

The next morning when she went to Cerralden House, Mrs Cerralden greeted her with genuine pleasure. 'How lovely to see you again, Miss Romy, do come in. I've just been to enquire about little Daisy. She has had quite a good night. You got back safely?'

'Yes, I did. What did the Colonel say when he knew I was coming to be your companion?'

'He grumbled, of course, but I know he was pleased. We had better go up.'

The old man glared when they went in and said to Romaine, 'Don't think you can boss me around because I won't have it. I get enough from that old battle axe of a nurse.'

'I know my place, sir,' Romaine said demurely, trying not to smile at the interested gleam in his eyes.

'Good, then we both know how we stand.'

After the coffee had been brought and poured he talked disparagingly about a new invention that had been introduced by a Mr John Fleming of London University; it was supposed to work wonders for the wireless in the future. 'Who wants to listen to people screeching on that wretched contraption. Marconi should be shot for inventing it.'

Mrs Cerralden said in soothing tones, 'But you were interested in listening to the crystal set that Henry brought, Colonel.'

'Crystal sets, cat's whiskers! A load of rubbish. Why don't they leave things as they are.'

Romaine said, 'If there had been no improvements over the centuries we would all still be living in caves.'

'Oh, Miss Clever speaks. Did you think that out all by yourself?'

'No, a teacher mentioned it.'

'So, tell me what good you think it's going to do to have a wireless in every home, with people's ears glued to them.'

'Surely to be able to communicate is an improvement. The invention is in its infancy. We'll learn, in time, what people in other countries are doing.'

He gave a 'Humph!', which Romaine came to accept after several visits to the house as the signal that the current subject was at an end and he was ready to have a grumble at something else.

She came to enjoy these sessions and knew by the glint in his eyes that he was enjoying them, too. Sometimes Mrs Cerralden would complain that he was claiming too much of Romaine's time. Once when she mentioned it, he said in an imperious way, 'I pay the wages, I call the tune.' Colour rose to Mrs Cerralden's cheeks. She turned and left, closing the door quietly behind her. When Romaine asked him if it was jealousy that made him humiliate his daughter-in-law he roared, 'Jealousy is for weaklings!'

Romaine met his glare steadily. 'Exactly.' She picked up a book. 'Shall I continue reading to you?'

'No! Get out of my sight.'

'If I go, I won't come back.'

'God damn you, girl! That woman Dorothea stole my son from me.'

'Surely you're a little mixed up. I would say that the only reason she puts up with your ill-temper is because you happen to be the father of the man she loves.' The old man said, 'Humph!' and Romaine opened the book at the bookmark and began to read.

This conversation in no way softened his manner, but Romaine did notice for the rest of that day at least that he did not make any more snide remarks to his son's wife.

One day Mrs Cerralden said, 'My husband Henry will be home for Christmas – I can't wait! By the way, I must try and arrange transport for you. The days are getting colder.'

Romaine demurred. 'I love walking. The stormier the weather the better I like it.'

The weather was wet, the sleet like needles of ice. Although Romaine roamed the countryside seeking big houses without any news of Daniel, she always found a pleasure in returning to the Brempsters' house in Sun Yard with its cosy fires. Some nights Mrs Brempster and Romaine would have long talks. Mrs Brempster enjoyed describing her work at Symington's factory and Romaine liked hearing about all the beautiful corsets of silks and satin, and all the intricate stitching and lovely hand embroidery.

'I used to be a dab hand at embroidery one time,' the older woman said, 'but with these puddingy things – ' she held out her hands ' – I'm not so good any more. But then I like working the machines.'

She spoke highly of her employees, who had provided recreation rooms and a gymnasium and who, when ponds and canal were frozen over, gave the workers an afternoon off and took those who wanted to skate to a special pond. Mrs Brempster sighed. 'Oh, for my skating days. Still, we can't have everything, can we?'

One time she said, 'Romy, I don't want to probe into your life but you never get any letters from your parents. They *do* know where you are?'

'They know I'm all right. I'll be in touch with them soon.'

When Mrs Brempster asked her if she ever felt homesick Romaine said, 'I ache to go back at times, but I have to be near Daniel. One of these days I'll find him, I know I will.'

One afternoon a week later, Romaine was coming down the High Street on the righthand side, about to get some shopping for her landlady when she suddenly tensed at the sight of a young man emerging from one of the big houses. He stopped, checked a pocket, patted it and came on, whistling.

It was dusk, and at first Romaine thought she was mistaken, but as he drew near, her body began to go hot then cold. There was no way of mistaking that jaunty walk, nor the way he wore his cap cocked to one side. He glanced at her, passed by, stopped then turned. '*Romy?*'

She had always dreamed of seeing a joyousness in Daniel at first recognition, even though she knew he would be annoyed with her later. But what she saw was cold accusation, and with a sob she made to cross the road. She stepped off the curb and was yanked back. There was shouting, a horse neighing and Daniel yelling, 'What are you trying to do, kill yourself?'

She tried to pull away from him but he held her firmly and, as people stopped to see what all the commotion was about, he said, 'Let's get out of this.' He walked her to the other side of the High Street. They had passed three shops when Romaine said quietly, 'Will you please let go of my arm, Daniel. You're hurting me.'

He released her and stopped. 'Romaine, we must talk.' The coldness had gone from his eyes and although he showed no signs of affection he was calmer.

She was shivering inside and, thinking of the cosy fire at the Brempsters' she said in a low voice, 'I lodge near here, and my landlady won't mind if we talk there. She and her family have been very kind to me.'

Romaine walked on and Daniel fell in step beside her. 'You make it sound as though your own family had not been kind to you.'

'I'm not suggesting they were deliberately unkind, but they all have someone, and I felt left out. My father has Kate, Aunt Louise has Uncle Flynn, and your mother, although she is always loving towards me, has her own family to care for. Even my own mother deserted me to help the sick and the poor. Have you any idea, Daniel, what it is to want to belong to someone, to be important in their life?'

'Romy.' Daniel spoke quietly. 'Have *you* any idea what it's like to love someone and to have that person run away and not know what is happening to them? Your father was nearly out of his mind when you disappeared this time. He left everything and spent a whole week searching for you, trying to get some hint where you might be.'

When Romaine said she had sent a letter saying she was with a friend and was all right, Daniel flung out his hands. 'And can you imagine the furore that caused! Who was the person? It could have been a man.'

'My father knows perfectly well that you are the only one I love.'

'And a fine way you have of showing it,' Daniel retorted.

'You come here, seeking me out, knowing I have work to do.'

Romaine shook her head. 'All I wanted was to be near you. I would not have intruded in your life.' She stopped and added with a quiet dignity, 'Would you leave me, please. I give you my word that if I see you again I shall walk on the other side of the street.' She moved away and Daniel made no attempt to follow. She was glad, knowing she would have been unable to say any more for the terrible ache in her throat.

How she got through that evening and the next two days she had no idea. She put on a bright face and talked a lot. Then, on the afternoon of the third day as she was about to open the Brempsters' front door, she heard a voice say softly, 'Romy, I love you. I've never stopped loving you.'

The next moment she was in Daniel's arms, sobbing her heart out.

21

Jessamy had reached a stage when, after each evening surgery, she felt like crawling straight into bed. She had fought against it but one evening as she was seeing the last patient out she made up her mind that after she had had something to eat she would give in to her weariness and take a book with her to bed.

She had called goodnight to her patient when she noticed a man crossing the road a little further up the street. There was something familiar about him and she waited. He was limping a little. He was coming in her direction and, as he moved under the light of a street lamp, her heart began a slow pounding. Fabian! He was following the numbers and as he stopped at her gate and saw her outlined against the hall light he said, uncertainly, 'Jessamy?'

She walked down the path and opened the gate. 'Fabian, what a surprise!'

'Oh, it is you. I wasn't sure. A friend who was driving to London offered me a lift and I couldn't refuse.'

'I'm glad you didn't. Come in. I was just going to make a meal.' Her weariness had gone. 'Will you share it? It's nothing exotic – cold meat and cheese and potato fritters.'

He laughed. 'I was going to ask you out to dinner, but the fritters have won me over. No one makes them better than you. Do you remember the night we – no, no, I mustn't reminisce.'

As they went into the house Jessamy smiled over her shoulder at him. 'Come into the kitchen then we can talk while I'm cooking.' She pulled out a chair for him. 'There, now you can tell me if you've been to any more faraway places while I make dinner.'

Fabian told her he had been to Brittany for three weeks recently, and spoke of the peace of the tiny village where he owned some property. He described it all in great detail and she felt he was trying to skim over the time she had been with him at St Peel. During her stay there he had told her several times he still loved her, and although she had agreed to be friends she knew he had been disappointed that she was unable to offer more.

She brought out a basin and ingredients for the fritters then, realising he had fallen silent she said, 'I'm sorry I didn't get a letter written to you, Fabian. I tried but I wasn't well at the time then later I was so busy it just...' Her voice trailed off.

'It's all right, Jessamy. I thought perhaps you didn't want to have anything more to do with me. How are you feeling now?'

'Oh, not bad. I must say that you are looking much better.'

'Thanks to you,' he said softly. 'Yes, yes, it was,' he went on when she made to protest.

Jessamy put finely-grated onion and herbs into the potato and cheese mixture, shaped it into cakes, dipped them into batter and dropped them into the sizzling beef fat. Fabian closed his eyes, a beatific smile on his face. 'I can taste them already.' Jessamy, who had been a little tense, began to relax. Fabian said, 'You're still working too hard, Jessamy. You should ease up, have a holiday. Come to Brittany with me. We can have separate rooms,' he added, smiling.

'It sounds tempting, but there's so many people here who need my help. At the moment I'm trying to place four orphaned children with a caring couple so that they won't have to be split up and go into a soulless Home.'

'Jessamy, you can't be responsible for all these children.'

'They have no one else,' she said earnestly. 'If you could see them, bewildered, lost-looking, huddled together, clinging to the only ones they're familiar with, your heart would ache too. There are tiny children dying of malnutrition because no one cares. One woman brought in a baby who was dying and asked if I could do anything for the child. She said her husband spent all their money on drink and when I asked why she hadn't brought the baby sooner she said because he wouldn't let her – he didn't like accepting charity! Then she added, in a loving way, "It's his pride, see".'

Jessamy flung out her hands. 'What can you do with people like that? But there, I'm talking too much about myself. How about you, are you planning any more sea voyages?'

'Not for the moment, but I will when you decide to come with me.' His voice held a teasing.

Jessamy said, 'Fabian, that is a taboo subject.'

'All right, tell me about Romy instead.'

Jessamy explained what had happened, concluding, 'And don't tell me it's because she's been neglected. She has so many people who love her. Romy has always been seeking adventure – it's something built into her. I used to go wandering off too when I was young.'

'You know why,' he said gently. 'Your mother never had any time for you either.'

'That was different and you know it. I gave Romy a lot of love. I cuddled her, read her stories, was sympathetic when she was hurt. Then Louise took over the role of mother and could not have been more affectionate. My mother never once gave me a kiss or a cuddle. When she took me up to bed she would tell me to say my prayers and get into bed, then she would take the lamp away and leave me in darkness.'

Fabian laid his hand over hers. 'Forgive me Jessamy. I had no right to say what I did.'

She said in a low voice, 'I felt terrible when my mother forced her way into your house and said such dreadful things.'

'Did you ever get the chance to tell her that at that time I wasn't capable of making love?' A wry smile touched his lips.

'No, but I don't think she would have believed it anyway. I had a letter from my father the other day and apparently my mother has been very subdued since he lost his temper and told her he would leave her if she didn't mend her ways. I didn't think that anyone could have subdued Esmeralda.'

Fabian grinned. 'Ah, the masterful touch.' Then serious, he went on, 'Jessamy, I've shared a part of your life once, long ago. I hope that some time in the future I might be able to share it again.'

'I'm sorry that I can't give you an answer to that, Fabian. Not now, anyway. I enjoyed visiting you, I've enjoyed seeing you this evening, but I can't say more.'

His smile was gentle. 'I'm a patient man, Jessamy. I can wait.'

Before Fabian left he and Jessamy agreed they would keep in touch and Jessamy also agreed that he could call when he next came to London.

That evening in bed, for the first time since her Cousin Lillian's attack on her, Jessamy longed to have a man's arms around her but even then, she was not quite sure whether it was Fabian's arms or Alistair's for which she longed.

For Romaine, life had changed dramatically the moment she invited Daniel into the Brempsters' kitchen. He waited until Mrs Brempster came in and left with an invitation to come to tea the following Sunday.

'A lovely young man,' her landlady enthused. 'So mannerly, so protective. I think you're a very lucky girl.' Romaine happily agreed with her.

On the Sunday Mr Brempster gave Daniel a warm welcome and over tea asked about his work. As Daniel began to describe some of the designs he was using, Romaine was back in Daniel's home in the East End, listening as his Uncle Frederick described the changes in style over the centuries. Not that she understood everything, when he talked about the Renaissance style with its jumble of French and Italian patterns being transferred to England, and how the Elizabethans abandoned themselves to a riot of robust and vulgar styles. But the words 'robust' and 'vulgar' made it sound exciting.

What she did understand and was intrigued by were the

terms strapwork, interlacing and fretwork on ceilings, and she loved hearing about the decorations of swags, scrolls, cherubs, flying angels, warriors in chariots, foliage, shells and beautiful figures. Later she said to Daniel, 'I saw some medieval gargoyles on a church the other day that were really horrible. Do you think the mason was trying to portray the evils that are in humans, like greed, envy, and jealousy?'

'I would say so.'

Mrs Brempster said, 'Our Romy is a thinker, isn't she? She's done some very good sketches of people. Bring them down, my love. Show them to Daniel.'

He went through them with Romy, who said, 'I felt I had learned a lot about people's characters as I sketched them.'

Daniel studied the portraits carefully then sat back. 'They're good, Romy, very good. You've widened your horizons.' He turned to the Brempsters. 'Romy showed promise when she was quite young. I remember showing some of her work to my tutor and he said then that she had talent.'

Mr Brempster teased Romaine. 'Well, one of these days we'll be boasting that the famous artist Romaine MacKay stayed here.'

Daniel laughed and shook his head. 'No, she'll be too busy looking after me and bringing up our children.'

Romaine's smile was stiff as she replied lightly, 'I'll have servants and shall sketch or paint portraits in my spare time.'

Daniel chuckled. 'Servants? I haven't even got through my apprenticeship yet.'

Mrs Brempster said quietly, 'I think that everyone should have dreams, even housewives.'

'Yes, I think I'll agree with that, but reality must come into it as well.'

Mr Brempster changed the subject by saying, 'What do you think about the Queen donating money in aid of the jobless? I bet she hasn't the faintest idea how the poor live.'

His wife said sharply, 'Now then, we'll have no calling of royalty in this house. Queen Alexandra is a good woman.'

Her husband gave Daniel a wink. 'I reckon we'd better make ourselves scarce and have a drink.'

Daniel said, 'I'm sorry, Mr Brempster, I can't. I'll have to go, I have some studying to do.'

Mrs Brempster beamed at him. 'How sensible of you.'

Daniel left with an invitation to come again any time he wished. Romaine went outside with him.

He tapped her lightly on the tip of her nose. 'Nice to know that I can call and see you. I'll come again as soon as I can. I must go, Romy.' He kissed her briefly, then added, 'Mind you behave yourself,' and was gone.

Romaine could hardly believe it. She could understand Daniel being careful when they had been in the house alone – anyone could have popped in. It was open house in the Yard. But outside, saying goodnight...

She went slowly into the house and Mrs Brempster asked if something was wrong. She said, 'I don't think I'll ever understand the behaviour of some people.'

'I wouldn't try if I were you. I'm sure that the Lord Himself who made us must be a little mystified at times. Why is it that I love my husband one minute and hate him the next?' She laughed. 'Aren't we women awful?' Jessamy laughed with her.

From then on, Daniel called two or three times a week in the evenings but always when Mrs Brempster, her husband, or both of them were there. The only time they had alone was when Romaine would see Daniel to the door; always, he would kiss her briefly and leave. When Romaine complained about this and asked if he could come earlier, when she was alone, he told her it was impossible then said, a teasing in his voice, that it was perhaps just as well, seeing how he felt towards her. He had promised her father she would come to no harm.

She stared at him. 'My father? How does he know about me?'

'I wrote to him. I felt he had a right to know you were

safe and well. I didn't give him your address, and I stressed it would be no use trying to contact you because you had no intention of coming home.'

Romaine then accused him of being a traitor and when she went ranting on about how impossible it was to trust anyone Daniel said coldly, 'That's it – there'll be no more meetings. You know how I feel about shrewish women.' He made to leave and Romaine panicked.

'Daniel, if you don't want to see me I'll understand, but I'll still stay here. I just want to be near you.'

He gave a deep sigh. 'What am I going to do with you? I don't want to be a master who cracks the whip, but – '

'And I don't want to be a slave!'

A slow smile spread over his face. 'I'll allow you to shout now and then, how's that?' He put his arms around her, held her close and when he kissed her this time, there was real passion in it. But the moment she responded he drew away. 'See you soon.'

She listened to his firm steps, waited until his sturdy figure could be glimpsed in the light of the lamp at the entrance to the alleyway, then he was lost in the darkness. Romaine, with a resigned air, went back into the house.

Daniel continued his three times a week visiting, came twice for tea on consecutive Sundays, and told her on the second visit that his uncle had said that he could bring Romaine to the Hall to see their work. This would be when the family resident there left for a long weekend in London.

This had Romaine as excited as if she were to visit one of the royal palaces. Daniel said, 'And if there happens to be a hard frost we can do some skating on the lake.'

Mrs Brempster laughed at this. 'If we have a hard frost you can do some skating here on Folly Pond, and I can watch you.'

Now that Romaine was able to see Daniel, it helped her to cope with the Colonel, who could be quite nasty at times. He was never without a complaint. One day he waved the newspaper. 'It says here that pills called Aspirin are on the market and a professor – a *professor*, mark you, says they will counter headaches due to strain and overwork.' He threw the paper down. 'Yesterday I read that the pills cause stomach trouble, sweating and sickness. Fools, fools!'

Romaine argued with him to keep him happy. 'You must be fair, Colonel. Experiments are going on all the time; it'll take some while to get the pills right.'

To which he replied, 'You, Miss, are as stupid as the rest of 'em!'

This really annoyed Romaine. Why should she put up with such insults? She would leave – there must be other houses where she could find work. She brooded about this during the long afternoon at home then, at five o'clock the Colonel and his insults flew out of the window when Daniel arrived unexpectedly to take her to see the stuccowork. The family had just left.

The visit to Felcy Hall was an event to remember. Not only was there the joy of seeing the beautiful stuccowork and paintings, but Daniel's Uncle Frederick had his men show her how moulds were made and how the plaster was mixed. He also told her that someone must paint her portrait one day; she had grown into a beautiful young lady.

Daniel said, 'And that is praise indeed coming from Uncle Frederick. He has never been known to flatter.'

Although Romaine had seen drawings of stucco decoration and photographs of rooms, she had never seen the actual work. Each doorway they went through was flanked by tall decorated columns, with statues at either side. At one entrance there were Grecian figures of a man and a woman, at another, warriors. A third displayed elderly men with flowing beards, each looking at a book. 'The philosophers,' Daniel explained. 'Look at their expressions. Every time I see them I think what a lot I could learn if only I could meet them today.'

Romaine studied them then said, 'I think we just keep on learning as we grow up. Old people have a lot of philosophy.'

Daniel smiled. 'You could be right.'

Each room at Felcy Hall was different. In one, all four walls were painted with frescoes of Biblical scenes, the sombre colours highlighted by the friezes of stuccowork. In the centre of one ceiling was a circular painting of a woman in draperies, and surrounding it were plaster rings of flowers, cherubs, doves and in the corners, groups of angels blowing trumpets. The white stucco was touched with gold. Romaine thought that this room would be a favourite with her until she saw another, its walls and ceiling decorated with the most exquisite designs, some interlaced with delicate tracery. There were arches in the walls that formed balconies with twisted rails down which tiny ivy leaves trailed. The walls curved at the top to form a dome with fan shapes spreading to the centre, each one containing a sunburst.

'Oh, Daniel,' she breathed. 'I never imagined such beauty. Now I can understand your absorption with your work and I'm prepared to make sacrifices.'

Daniel said softly, 'You're a darling,' and had just drawn her to him when a jovial voice called, 'Oh, to be young again!' They sprang apart to see the foreman grinning broadly. 'The boss said to tell you that there's a drink of cocoa ready.'

Later that evening after Romaine had described to Mrs Brempster the detail of every room she had seen, she gave an ecstatic sigh. 'I don't think I could be happier than I am at this moment. Could I possibly experience anything more beautiful or so – so awesome?'

Mrs Brempster smiled tenderly and gave her hand a gentle pat. 'You will when you hold your first baby in your arms.'

'Babies,' Romaine said dreamily. 'I want lots – five boys and five girls.'

Mrs Brempster laughed. 'And possibly get five sons and one girl as I did.'

'I wouldn't mind.' Romaine turned her head. 'It seems strange that only days ago I was thinking I would like to study to be a portait painter. I imagined myself getting commissions from wealthy people and travelling abroad.

Now all I want is Daniel, a home and children.'

Mrs Brempster said, a wistful note in her voice, 'We all have our dreams. My ambition was to have my own dressmaking business and work with lovely silks, satins, velvets and brocades.' She spread her hands. 'And what happens? I fall in love, get married and the children come along. Not that I've regretted any part of it,' she hastened to add. 'I love them all.'

In bed that night Romaine thought of her visit to Felcy Hall, of all the beauty there must be in the world and how she must have just touched the fringe of it.

22

When Romaine arrived at Cerralden House the next morning she found Mrs Cerralden in a state of agitation. The Colonel had apparently invited his godson for a visit and he had only just informed her now that he would be arriving this afternoon at four o'clock.

'Four o'clock,' she repeated. 'There's a meal and a room to be prepared before then. Cook and Agnes will be upset – they like a full day's notice. I'll have to go and tell them.'

Mrs Cerralden was at the door when she turned. 'The Colonel said he had invited André because he wants him to take a look at your sketches. André Guerlain is a well-known portrait painter. He lives in Paris.'

Romaine stared at her. 'Why would a well-known artist want to look at *my* sketches?'

'The Colonel says you have talent. He often takes out your work to look at it when you're not here. He is a connoisseur. Oh, yes, there's something else I have to tell you: he says it's too cold for you to walk here in this weather. From now on, Bates will collect you every morning and drive you back after lunch.'

When Romaine made an 'Oh' of surprise, Mrs Cerralden put her hand over her mouth to stifle a girlish giggle. 'He doesn't want you to catch cold. Neither do I – he would be like a bull with a sore head. You'd better go up to him, but don't mention André. He wants it to be a surprise.'

The Colonel was not exactly in a good mood, just less rude than usual. At odd times he gave her sly looks and Romaine wondered if, childlike, he was itching to tell her his news. When she was ready to leave he reminded her that the chauffeur would be there waiting for her. She thanked him for his kind thought and he mumbled that there was a hard frost and he didn't want her to fall and break a leg.

Bates was a dour man with little conversation but Romaine was happy just to sit and enjoy the comfort of riding in the limousine. He set her down at the church in Market Harborough and told her he would pick her up there in the morning. Romaine was only sorry that Mrs Brempster would not be in to hear her news.

When she was told later she said, 'Well, we never know what is going to happen, do we? Not only is a famous artist going to look at your sketches, but you have been travelling in a limousine!'

Romaine said, 'I was quite glad of the ride – the wind's cutting.'

'Too cutting to go skating?' her landlady asked with a teasing smile. 'We're making up a party tonight to go to Folly's Pond. Daniel will be here soon. We'll find skates for you both.'

'Oh, that will be wonderful! One day at Felcy Hall and now Folly's Pond.' Romaine suddenly sobered. 'I think it might be wise not to say anything about the sketches to Daniel. He just won't take my work seriously.'

'He might if he knows you have exceptional talent. On the other hand, men are unpredictable. Best leave it for now.'

Daniel was as enthusiastic as Romaine about the skating, and before long the Brempsters' kitchen was alive with the chatter of workmates and relatives. They all set off in high spirits and when they reached Leicester Road they met more skaters bound for the pond.

The full moon silvered the icy roads and trees and every now and again there was the crackling of ice as the younger ones jumped on the frozen pools at the road edge. The strains of a brass band drifted on the night air and the orange and red lights of naphtha flares could be glimpsed through the trees. By the time they arrived, there were many people already on the pond, some tumbling about, others skating steadily. There was a hot potato stand, the charcoal glowing red. The wind tossed the flames of the naphtha flares hither and thither and the appetising smell of the baked potatoes mingled with the pungent smell of paraffin.

Daniel helped Romaine with her skates, put on his own then held out his hand. 'Shall we have a go?'

It was Daniel who had taught Romaine to skate on a pond about half a mile from his home near Paradise Corner. She had taken to it right from the start and while he had been away, other young men had taught her how to waltz. This she had kept to herself, wanting to surprise Daniel when the time came.

They stepped onto the ice and were soon away, arms crossed, skating joyously. The icy wind stung their cheeks but they were both too exhilarated to mind. They had circled the pond several times, taking long sweeps, when Daniel said, 'Now I shall teach you to waltz.'

When she went into an easy rhythm he was annoyed at first and said she had made a fool of him, but when she laughed he laughed too and reversed. Romaine matched his steps and her spirits soared as they moved in perfect harmony. It was heaven.

Other partners claimed her after this but she skated best with Daniel. Mrs Brempster confirmed this when Romaine went to where she was sitting on a tree stump. 'You and Daniel are a perfectly matched couple. You skate as if you were floating on clouds.'

Romaine, dreamy-eyed, responded with, 'That's exactly how I felt. Oh, I wish the night would go on for ever.'

By eleven o'clock, however, people were beginning to leave. They had to be up early the next morning. The potato stands and the band had gone and the naphtha flares were being extinguished when the Brempster party left. The older people walked in front, the younger ones behind. There was no bright chattering among the latter, just secretive whispers. Daniel slipped an arm around Romaine's waist. 'Enjoyed it?'

'Oh, yes, it was wonderful. Look at the stars twinkling and the lovely moon – I've never seen it brighter.'

'A night for romance,' Daniel whispered close to her ear. 'Do you think we can slip away for a few minutes?

You can say you left your gloves behind.'

She pulled them off and pushed them into her pocket, her heart a wild thing. Daniel called about the gloves and at this there was a burst of laughter from the older ones. They had used the same excuse when they wanted a bit of canoodling during their young days.

Romaine, nothing daunted, began to run and Daniel sprinted after her. When the moon went behind the clouds she darted into a clump of trees and seconds later Daniel had her in his arms. They stood, laughing helplessly, then both suddenly sobered. Daniel cupped Romaine's face between his palms. 'We only have a few minutes but I had to hold you close.' His mouth covered hers and they kissed with a rising passion. Both were trembling. The next moment Daniel drew away. They must go. Romaine protested and made to put her arms around him but he pressed them to her sides. Then, taking her by the hand, he walked her back to the road.

The moon was bright again and although she was disappointed Romy knew that Daniel was right. The Brempsters had stopped and were waiting for them. Mr Brempster called to ask if she had found her gloves and she waved them. The older couple walked on.

Romaine grumbled that they were treating her like a daughter and Daniel said, 'They feel responsible for you. They made me think of my responsibility after we had sneaked into the wood. If we're to meet in future, we must avoid a repetition of this evening. Sneaking away to be alone, I mean.'

'But why, Daniel? We love each other.'

'I promised Doctor MacKay that no harm would come to you.'

'No harm has.'

'But I can no longer promise that unless you help me. I always thought I would be able to control my feelings, but I was wrong. I'm like the people in your sketches who turn out differently from what you expected.'

'No, you've proved yourself strong. It's the way I've always thought of you – I don't want you to change.'

He gave her a squeeze. 'I'm glad. I love you very much, Romy.'

Romaine whispered that she loved him very much, too. Before they parted she told him about the Colonel's godson coming for a visit but nothing more, and felt guilty.

By the following morning, however, when she was on her way to Cerralden House she had grown excited. Very soon now she would be meeting this wonderful artist who probably had women swooning all over him. She thought about asking Bates what André was like then changed her mind. Let it be a surprise...

And surprise it was. She had imagined him to be tall and handsome, with a flamboyant air, instead of which he was small and quite ordinary-looking. When Romaine was introduced to him, however, and he bowed, kissed the back of her hand and said in a low, caressing voice, 'I am delighted to meet you, M'mselle,' her heart gave a little flutter.

She murmured, 'And I am pleased to meet you, Mr Guerlain.'

Dorothea Cerralden suggested they go and have coffee with the Colonel and on the way up André said to Romaine, 'My godfather told me that you have talent, M'mselle, and after looking at your portfolio last night, I agree with him.'

Romaine protested that she was just an amateur and the artist smiled. 'Allow me to be a judge of that.'

Her second surprise of the morning came when the Colonel bade her a cheerful good day and said he was glad she had met his godson. Then he spoilt it by adding, 'Aren't you lucky?'

Feeling that she was being treated like a poor relation, Romaine forced herself to say coolly, 'I shall be better qualified to comment on that after I've become acquainted with him, sir.'

André chuckled. He said to the Colonel, 'I would say that *we* are the lucky ones to know such a beautiful and intelligent young lady.' He gave Romaine the most devastating smile.

Mrs Cerralden began to talk about the change in the weather but the Colonel said irritably, 'André has not come all this way to discuss the weather. Art is his subject.' He turned to the other man. 'Perhaps you would give us your opinion of my very intelligent and beautiful companion.'

André spread his hands. 'But of course.' He sat up, his gaze on Romaine. 'You do have talent, M'mselle. Your work is vibrant, it is original, but you need tuition. I know of an excellent school in Paris you could attend. I am sure my mother would be delighted to put you up. She – '

Romaine interrupted. 'Mr Guerlain, you're going too fast. You make me feel breathless. I couldn't possibly go to live in Paris – my father would never allow it.'

André eyed her in astonishment. 'But why?' He flung out his hands and his head went up. 'I, André Guerlain, am offering you the opportunity of a superb training and the chance to be my protégée. This is something I have not done for any other student. My mother would chaperone you.'

The Colonel, tight-lipped, said, 'I asked you to assess her work, my lad, not steal her from me.'

André leaned over, picked up Romaine's portolio from the side of the chair, opened it and began to go through the sketches. He pulled one out and held it up. 'This is a sketch of a benign-looking elderly gentleman. *You*, Godfather – but do not feel smug. Look at the mouth, there is meanness there, while in the eyes we find – '

'A sadness,' Romaine said quietly.

'Exactly.'

'Nonsense!' declared the Colonel. 'I am smiling.'

André nodded slowly. 'Oh yes, and *that* is why I say M'mselle Romaine has a talent worth cultivating.' He brought out several more sketches, talking all the time. 'See this lady with the roses on her hat? She has a merry air, but inside her is a cruel streak. The gypsy lady who looks so autocratic is steeped in gentle mysticism – and regard this man who puts fear in people...yet has a constant fear inside himself.'

He turned to Romaine. 'Am I correct, my dear?'

Embarrassed, she whispered, 'Yes.'

'That is why I want you to have the best tutors.'

The Colonel, his feathers ruffled, said, 'It will have to be talked over, but not now. There are some business matters I want to discuss with you alone.'

André shrugged. Mrs Cerralden got up, saying to Romaine that they would leave the men to their talk. When they were downstairs, she said, 'Oh dear, what a quandary André has put you into, Romy.'

'Not really. As much as I would love to go to Paris, it just isn't possible and I shall have to accept it.'

Although Romaine had tried to treat the incident in a matter-of-fact way she went about the house in a dreamlike state for the rest of the morning. Just to be in Paris would be heaven enough but to be tutored by a top art teacher...If only a way could be found. The more she thought about it, the more determined she became.

She did not see the painter again that day. After being closeted with the Colonel for some time he left to visit friends. Mrs Cerralden did tell her, however, that he was determined to get Romaine to Paris. 'He says that you are truly beautiful, and he must get you to sit for him.'

Romaine felt little shivers of pleasure go through her.

Daniel might object but this opportunity was something she could not refuse. It was also something she would keep to herself until it was settled.

For the next three days André was away and with each day Romaine knew a greater longing to see him again, which was something she was unable to understand. She hardly knew the man, had been in his company for no more than twenty minutes.

The Colonel remarked on her abstraction and said in his snide way, 'Don't tell me you are besotted with my famous godson. I gave you credit for more sense.'

Romaine, who was annoyed, did manage to say quietly, 'I have much more important things on my mind than to become besotted with your godson – or anyone else,' which brought a 'Humph' from the Colonel, to show the subject was closed.

Romaine was grateful for one thing; it made her realise she must give full attention to Daniel when she saw him next. He had been working late for the past three evenings.

André returned the next day. After greeting her with his devastating smile, he approached her about the possibility of her posing for him.

Romaine's heart began to pound. 'I am willing, but I must get the Colonel and Mrs Cerralden's permission.'

'I already have it. I suggested two o'clock for our first session. Dorothea has agreed to stay with you.' When Romaine asked what she should wear, he stepped back, studied her a moment then said, 'What you are wearing now will be perfect.' When Romaine left him she ran into the cloakroom that led from the hall and studied her reflection in the cheval mirror.

She was wearing a dark green velvet dress that fitted at the waist and buttoned up the front. At the neck was a cream frill that she felt was a contrast to her dark hair, which for her work she wore tied back. Now she felt she would like it swept up, the curls falling over a band of velvet ribbon, as Margaret had dressed it for parties. Romaine had almost mastered the style and decide to try again for the portrait.

It was a very nervous Romaine who went to Mrs Cerralden's room at ten minutes to two and asked if she looked all right.

'Romy, you look as if you have stepped out of a portrait. Wait until André sees you.'

André's pleasure showed in his dark eyes. 'Excellent!' They went to an attic room that had been converted into a studio. The only contents of the room, apart from the easel, canvases and paints, were three chairs and a stool. The floorboards were bare and the room would have seemed very cold had it not been for the blazing fire in the tiled fireplace.

André seated Romaine, arranged the skirt of her dress, adjusted the frill around her neck, fiddled with the curled ends of her hair then stepped back and told her to relax. Although he had not touched her skin, every move had seemed an intimacy to Romaine and she found herself trembling. It seemed an age before he was ready to start.

Although Romaine began to calm down, André was still not at ease. Time and again he was up and placing her in a different position. Then at last he started. Twice Romaine glanced from the corners of her eyes to see if Mrs Cerralden was comfortable and was sharply reprimanded by André. Would she please pay attention!

After what seemed an age but could have been no more than half an hour, he put down palette and brush, lifted the canvas to the floor then gave a sigh. 'It is useless today. The mood is wrong. Tomorrow we can try again.' No, no, he assured Romaine, the fault was not hers. It happened often. Tomorrow might be better.

Some progress was made the following day, but André would not show them what he had achieved. He suggested they miss a day and try the next.

The following afternoon, Mrs Cerralden had gone visiting, the Colonel was resting and Romaine was preparing to leave when André called to her. 'M'mselle, I feel in a good mood – would you sit for me?'

Romaine explained that Mrs Cerralden was out, then, seeing his disappointment she added hesitantly, 'I don't mind her not being there if you...'

'Splendid. Her presence was rather distracting.'

Romaine put her hand to her hair. 'I must put it up.'

He told her this was unnecessary – it was the dress he wanted to alter.

She thought he wanted to rearrange the skirt and was startled when he began to undo the bodice. She put up her hand to stop him but he went on unfastening the buttons, saying softly, 'I want *this* portrait for me.' When the buttons were undone he slipped the top half of the dress off her shoulders. She caught her breath and his touch on her skin and his caressing voice as he told her to relax sent tremors through her.

He then lifted her breasts from the confines of her chemise and kissed each one. As she moaned, he pulled the chemise up, allowing the lace edge just to cover the nipples.

'There,' he said softly, 'that is much more tempting. Will you stay still while I capture your beauty? You are proud of your beauty, you thrill to your power over men. Lift your head, thrust your body forward, tempt them... That is it!'

Romaine felt her power. She *was* a temptress desired by all men, and as André ran his fingertips lightly over her skin, she experienced the most delicious sensation that was just building to an ecstasy when voices intruded. Men's voices outside, calling to one another. They penetrated her dream world, bringing a coarseness to it.

She became aware of André at the easel, sketching quickly, and of a man in the grounds shouting, 'Bring that sow ower 'ere, Jake.'

Reality took over and, horrified at her wanton state, she pulled the front of her dress together and with trembling fingers began to try and fasten the buttons. She had managed two when André challenged her.

'What are you doing? I am not finished. Sit down, Romaine.'

'No! I must have been mad to come up here alone.'

'Chérie, you are all right, no harm will come to you. I have not attempted to seduce you, have I? You cannot learn to be an artist until you have experienced all the emotions.'

'I no longer want to be an artist,' she said with a sob. 'I feel degraded.'

He told her it was all in the mind. She was beautiful, she had a lovely body. At first there was a coaxing in his voice but when she resisted all his reasoning it became hard. She was being foolish – acting childishly; he wanted nothing more to do with her. He then threatened her, saying that if she should tell the Colonel or Mrs Cerralden she would be in trouble.

Romaine said bitterly, 'All I want to do is to forget it ever happened. And now, if you'll excuse me...'

She hurried out, clutching her dress to her. The house was quiet and she crept downstairs and went into the cloakroom to finish tidying herself. Although she felt utterly drained and would have appreciated a drive home with Bates she decided instead to walk, needing to sort out her thoughts.

Pray heaven that Daniel would never get to know...It was unlikely he would, as André wanted to keep the incident quiet. Although Romaine longed to unload her guilt to someone she knew she must not tell even Mrs Brempster.

The wind was strong and when it began to rain there were icy particles of sleet in it that stung her cheeks. She welcomed it as punishment for her stupidity.

When she arrived at the Brempsters' she found a note from Daniel saying he would be unable to get round that evening as they were trying to complete the work at Felcy Hall before Christmas. She felt suddenly homesick and this on top of the upset with André had her in tears. In the end, not wanting to face her landlady when she returned, she left a note saying she had a headache and had gone to bed.

She spent an almost sleepless night and felt terrible. Mrs Brempster had been in the habit of calling her just before she left for the factory. This morning Romaine replied as usual that she would be down, but instead lay still. How could she possibly face André Guerlain again? It was impossible. She would have to stay away, but if she did, Mrs Cerralden would send someone to find out what was wrong. The Colonel would not want to be without one of his puppets, because that is what she had become. Romaine dragged herself out of bed, dressed, went downstairs, washed at the kitchen sink and made herself a cup of tea. She did toast herself a piece of bread but was unable to eat it.

Bates was waiting for her as usual and as usual she bade him a good morning and had a mumbled reply. They drove in silence and Romaine began to think she was crazy to have come. How on earth was she going to appear normal when she faced the Frenchman? As it turned out it wasn't André she had to face, but Daniel.

She had got out of the car at the back of the house and was walking along the narrow path that led to the front when he stepped out of the bushes and faced her, his eyes blazing with anger.

'You certainly deceived me! All sweet innocence to my face and whoring with your Frenchie lover behind my back.'

Romaine, shocked at the sudden attack and accusations, was trembling so much she could hardly stand. 'It's just not true. Whoever told you that is lying.'

'No one needed to lie,' he retorted. 'I saw the proof with my own eyes.' He held out a piece of paper that had been torn, but the part of the sketch he showed her was of her sitting with her head up, her body outthrust in a brazen way. She felt sick. 'And do you know where I got it?' he demanded. 'From one of your lover's friends as he passed it around in the local inn last night.'

Romaine, seizing at a straw that would break this horror, exclaimed, 'You told me you couldn't see me last night because you were working!'

'We finished late and went for one drink, but don't change the issue. I would have killed your miserable lover had I not been pulled off him by my workmates.'

'He's not my lover!'

'I can tell you this, you'll not want to set eyes on him again. His face is not a pretty sight, nor those of his fancy friends. We had nothing to do with it. The locals did the job and warned the bloodied ones if they told anyone they would find themselves at the bottom of the canal.'

Daniel paused and his anger suddenly died. 'I couldn't believe it of you, Romy. I ached at times to make love to you, but not only had I given my promise to take care of you, I also wanted you to be a virgin on our wedding night.'

'I'm still a virgin,' she said earnestly. 'You must believe me. I know I behaved foolishly but I got carried away. I had posed for Colonel Cerralden's godson several times already, but only with Mrs Cerralden in attendance. Oh, I wish I had told you about it, Daniel. He offered to sponsor me at art school in Paris. I thought you might be jealous...Oh, and now I've ruined everything by my stupidity. Please forgive me – such a thing would never happen again.'

'That's what you say, Romy,' he said sadly, 'but unfortunately, I could never trust you again. I'm sorry.' He turned and walked away, a droop to his shoulders and Romaine felt she would die of a broken heart.

When she went into the house she made straight for the cloakroom in order to pull herself together before meeting anyone, but before she reached the door, Mrs Cerralden came hurrying to her. 'Oh, Romaine, I'm so glad I saw you before you went upstairs. The Colonel's in a *terrible* temper. There were such goings on last night with André.'

Romaine stood rigid. Oh God, how much did they know? Dorothea went on, 'André and some of his friends got into a fight with some men in the local inn. Mind you, I blame André. He always acts in such an arrogant way and like my father-in-law, is inclined to make snide remarks. I don't know what was said last night to cause the fracas, but he came in looking absolutely awful. His face was badly bruised, he was limping and looked frightened. He tidied himself up and after the Colonel had called him all sorts of fools, he packed and left early this morning.' Mrs Cerralden sighed. 'I can't say I'm sorry. I don't like trouble. Only one good thing came out of his visit – your portrait. He left it for you.'

Romaine said, a tremor in her voice, 'I didn't know that he had finished it.'

'He must have been working on it in secret, and for long hours, too. It is completed and it really is truly beautiful. It's in the attic on the easel – come and have a look at it. Later, when the Colonel calms down, I'll have it brought to his room.'

Romaine, who had no option but to view it, was glad afterwards to have had the privilege of seeing the expertise of André Guerlain. In the portrait, she was alive – even her dress seemed real. She felt if she ran her fingers over the canvas she would feel the soft silky plush of the velvet.

Mrs Cerralden nodded in approval. 'It's you, Romy, with that lovely pensive look you have when you're sitting quietly.'

A maid called up to tell them they were wanted by the Colonel and Mrs Cerralden lifted the painting carefully from the easel. She gave Romaine a wink. 'Let's see if this will rid him of his temper.'

The Colonel studied the portrait for some time then eyed Romaine over the top of his glasses. 'Well, and what is your opinion of Monsieur Guerlain's work?'

'I can certainly see why he's acknowledged as a famous artist.'

'Oh, you praise yourself, do you?'

'I was not passing any remark about myself. It was his expertise I was praising.'

'Same thing,' he snapped. 'Trust a woman to twist everything round to suit herself.'

Romaine said, 'Have you ever been known to say anything good about anything or anyone?'

'I tell the truth,' he retorted.

'Then you may go on telling what you think of as the truth, but I don't want to hear any more of it. I've had enough.' She turned and left with Mrs Cerralden following her.

'Romy, please wait!'

Romaine stopped at the foot of the stairs. 'I'm sorry, Dorothea. I have nothing against you. It's just that I have troubles of my own and I want to try and sort them out.'

Mrs Cerralden begged only one thing, that she would not desert them altogether. 'Have a rest, my dear, and then think about it again.' They parted on that note.

When Romaine told Mrs Brempster that she was not going back to Cerralden House and why, her landlady said, 'We really ought to feel sorry for the old gentleman. He is a lonely soul, but then he should realise he can't boss people around. Cheer up, love, Daniel will be here later.'

Romaine, not wanting to mention their quarrel, said, 'He's working every night at the moment. I'll have an early night again. Catch up on my beauty sleep.'

She lay in bed in utter misery. She was trembling, not with cold, but with the nerve-wracking experience she had gone through. She had seen paintings of nude women in galleries and had thought of them as art, but when a girl at the private school she attended once brought in post-cards of paintings of naked girls in various poses, obtained by her older sister in Paris, the other girls had giggled and it had made the nudes seem dirty.

Romaine's face and body now burned with shame. She could imagine André and his friends making sly remarks about her, putting her in the category of a mindless prostitute. No wonder Daniel wanted nothing more to do with her.

As she pictured him in his anger, she knew it was not this so much that had upset her as the sadness in his voice when he said he had wanted her to be a virgin on their wedding night.

The tragic part of it was that she was still a virgin, even though her image had been sullied. Tears welled up and rolled slowly down the sides of her face.

Without Daniel she had nothing to live for.

23

When Louise arrived at Jessamy's house unusually early one morning, before breakfast, she felt alarmed. 'What's wrong? What's happened?'

Louise pulled off her gloves and unwrapped her scarf. 'I have a problem that I need to discuss. I could do with a cup of tea.'

'I've just made some. Come into the kitchen.'

When the tea was poured Louise took a sip then looked up. 'It's Alistair, I'm worried about him. He's not well.'

Knowing that Louise would not be here to report any ailment that could be cured with rest or pills, Jessamy said quietly, 'What do you feel is wrong?'

'I think he has cancer.'

Icy claws clutched at Jessamy's spine.

'He's lost a lot of weight recently. I didn't pay much attention to it because he's always on the go, then I noticed he kept rubbing at his shoulder, his arm and the back of his hand. When I mentioned it he put it down to twinges of rheumatism and I accepted it.' Louise paused and when she continued she was emotional, which was unusual for her. 'It was when he admitted that he had cramp in his hand and there was a hoarseness in his voice that I became really worried.'

'His lungs,' Jessamy whispered.

Louise nodded and brushed a hand across her eyes. 'But he still wouldn't admit to there being anything wrong. He said I was making mountains out of molehills. What was a little touch of rheumatics and cramp? He's been making copious notes. He wants to write a medical book.'

'What does Kate say?'

'She's in Huddersfield, has been for the past fortnight, helping to nurse an elderly relative. I wondered if you would come and talk to him, Jessamy. Perhaps try to ease his pain.'

'I will gladly come, but I doubt whether Alistair would take notice of anything I had to say.'

'I feel he would, Jessamy. Lately he's been talking about you, reminiscing about your early days together. That's something he's never done before. He spoke with affection, with love.'

'How will Kate take it?'

'I think she would be pleased. She still grieves that she was partly responsible for you and Alistair parting. Alistair said he would be home at seven tonight and that for once, he would not be going out again. Please come, Jessamy. This evening if you can.'

Jessamy promised.

It was Alistair who opened the door to her. Jessamy had been prepared to see a change in him, but was so shocked at his gaunt face and his thinness that she was unable to speak for the constriction in her throat.

He had obviously been expecting her because he showed no surprise. 'Come in, Jessamy.' Sadly, the huskiness in his voice was attractive. 'Will you come up to my study? Louise will have some coffee sent up.'

When they were seated he said quietly, 'It's good to see you, Jessamy, even though it's not under the best of circumstances. Louise is behaving like a mother hen, insisting that I'm ill.'

'You are ill, Alistair. You must see someone.'

'I have but...it's too late.'

Too late? A chill crept over her and she knew an almost unbearable agony. Then suddenly an earnest expression came over his face. 'There's still so much I want to do.' He got up and began to move around the room. 'There's so much knowledge still to be gained, with experiments going on all the time.'

He began to cough and Louise, who had come in with a tray, put it down hastily and taking his arm led him back to the chair. 'Now calm down, Alistair. I'll pour you some coffee.' After she had given him his cup she said to Jessamy, 'I'll leave you. See if you can knock some sense into him.'

The hot drink had stemmed Alistair's cough but he looked so drained. He said softly, 'I'm glad you came, Jessamy. I've longed many times to see you, to apologise for being so stubborn. Kate has been on at me time and again to write to you, but pride prevented me.' A sadness came into his eyes. 'How unimportant our differences have become.'

'I've been just as stubborn, Alistair. Look, you are not one for giving up. You must seek other advice.'

'I've seen the three top men in their field. They all gave the same verdict: it's gone too far to operate.'

It was difficult for Jessamy not to put her arms around him, not to tell him that she still loved him, that she had never stopped loving him. He said, 'I would have liked to have had a few more years, to have written my book, to pass on the knowledge that I've gained during my career.'

'Louise said you had copious notes. I can help you go through them, sort them into sections. With your guidance, I could even write the book.'

'No, you have your own work to deal with.'

'I can manage it, Willard Stead will help me. He's staying in England until after Christmas and he needs to be working.'

'Oh, Jessamy, if we *could* manage it.' His eyes were bright with unshed tears.

'We'll do it, Alistair. Where do we start?'

They talked about medical matters and for a while there was the same closeness between them they had known before Kate Keller had come into their lives. Then a friend called to see Alistair and Jessamy went downstairs to find Louise.

Louise said, 'Well, what do you think?'

'He's dying, Louise, and he knows it.' She had to swallow hard. 'Three top men have seen him, but it's too late to operate – he could last six months, or it could be only a matter of weeks. He – ' Jessamy stopped suddenly and looked wide-eyed at Louise. 'Something's just occurred to me. *The ghost girl*...When I last saw her at the cottage, I thought it was Fabian she was trying to tell me about, but it wasn't. It was Alistair! She was rubbing her left arm and hand – so was he. With Fabian it was his right. Oh, Louise, she was telling me that Alistair needed my love and I failed him.'

'You helped Fabian instead. He had no one. Alistair does have Kate.'

Yes, he had Kate. Jessamy felt a terrible bleakness. All those years wasted because of pride. She said, 'She should be told, and so should Romy.'

'Kate is due home soon, and Daniel said in the letter we had last week that Romy might come here for Christmas. Do we tell her now or wait?' They agreed to wait a week to give Alistair a chance to at least start the book, which was so important to him.

When Alistair's condition became known, Jessamy had several offers of help at her dispensary, which left her most of the day free to be with Alistair. At other times she helped Willard with the morning and evening surgeries, which were drawing more and more patients. Willard said once, 'When Alistair has the book under way I could look in on him for a short chat, just to break the working schedule.'

'I think it might be a good idea to give him a call now. He's working with a feverishness, feeling that time is running out, and if he's not careful he'll burn himself out completely.'

Whatever it was that Willard said to Alistair, it was effective and the sick man calmed down.

Within five days they had covered a surprising amount of preparatory work. Alistair said it was because he and Jessamy were working as a team. One day when he was rubbing his hand and arm and Jessamy suggested giving him a gentle massage, her husband agreed, saying he would be glad to try it.

Afterwards he said he couldn't praise the treatment highly enough – the warmth was such a comfort. Jessamy was so pleased she had been able to help him she could have wept.

Jessamy had been at the house in Devonshire Street for a week when Kate came home. Louise had gone to meet her at the station and Jessamy was in the sitting room when they returned. Kate's lips trembled. Jessamy held out her arms and she went into them.

'Oh, Jessamy, I'm so glad you're here. I was a coward. I knew, and I couldn't face up to it.'

Alistair came in and put his arms around both of them and Jessamy was aware of the love in his eyes when he greeted Kate. It was impossible to feel jealous in such a tragic situation, but she still felt an ache, nevertheless, and knew a longing to regain the deep love that she and Alistair had once shared. Then she recalled him saying the day before, 'Knowing that death is hovering in the wings is a great leveller. We regret so many things – and yet what does it matter in the end? We can't change anything.'

How true, she thought, and with this acceptance she felt she had reached another dimension in her life.

24

Romaine awoke early the next morning and unable to go to sleep again she got up, put on her dressing gown and went downstairs. Mrs Brempster, who had just come in for breakfast, said, 'Romy, you're up early.' She smiled. 'You must have known there was a letter for you. Perhaps it's from Daniel.'

Romaine took it eagerly then shook her head. 'No, it's from my mother's Cousin Louise. How did they know my address? Daniel must have told them.' There were two separate pages in the envelope. To her surprise one note was from her mother. She read this first.

'*Dear Romy,*

'*Now I am writing to you, I'm sorry to convey bad news. Your father has been working too hard and is terribly exhausted. He talks about you a great deal and I know it would give him immense pleasure to see you. He loves you very much. Try to come and see him as soon as you can. Love from Mama.*'

Romaine's heart began a slow beating. She unfolded the second note. Her aunt was more direct.

'*Your father has cancer, Romy, and is not expected to live. I've enclosed train times. Send a telegram to say when you expect to arrive and I shall meet you at St Pancras. Love, Aunt Louise.*'

Romaine looked at Mrs Brempster and said in an agonised whisper, 'My father is dying.'

'Oh, Romy, no – surely not!' Romaine gave her Louise's letter to read, and afterwards Mrs Brempster took the girl in her arms and held her close. 'I'm so sorry.'

When Romaine began to blame herself for her father's illness, she soothed her. 'No, my love, it's the Lord's will. If it's our time to die then nothing can stop it.'

Romaine drew away. 'I must decide on which train to

take and I'll have to send a telegram.'

Mrs Brempster took over. 'You go upstairs to pack. I'll see to everything.'

When Romaine came down, a neighbour was wrapping up sandwiches, someone else had gone to send a telegram to Devonshire Street and Mrs Brempster's nephew was waiting with a wagon to take her to the station. The landlady said, 'Now don't worry, my love, you'll be in plenty of time. Dave will see you on to the train.' She gave her a hug. 'Write to me when you can. Take care of yourself.' By then Mrs Brempster too was tearful.

The journey was a nightmare to Romaine. Would she get there in time? Would her father forgive her for staying away? If only she had known he was ill. If only she had written to him. *If only...*The two words drummed in her brain to the rhythm of the wheels until she felt she would scream.

When she arrived at St Pancras she looked for Louise, but instead it was her mother she saw. They walked hesitantly towards one another, as though unsure of a welcome. Then Romaine dropped her bag and they went wordlessly into one another's arms.

The moment they drew apart a porter came up and asked if they wanted a cab. Jessamy dabbed at her eyes. 'Yes, please.' To Romaine she said, 'We'll talk later.'

Two things about her mother impressed themselves on Romaine as they walked across the street – her beauty and her lovely voice, which was musical, low-keyed. Had she forgotten this, or had she been so absorbed in her own importance she had never noticed?

Once in the cab, Romaine asked about her father.

'He's very poorly, Romy, so be prepared to see a big change in him. He's lost a great deal of weight. He's so looking forward to seeing you – he wanted to get up to welcome you, but he's not strong enough.'

'Oh, Mama, I'm so sorry. I've behaved badly. I was selfish.'

Jessamy laid a hand over hers. 'We're both tormented people. I regret so many things and keep thinking if only

I could have forgotten my stupid pride. But regrets, as your great-grandmother Henrietta once said, are useless commodities as they don't change anything. All your father wants now, Romy, is your love.'

Romaine felt choked. Jessamy told her how she was helping Alistair to compile his medical notes so that they could be published one day in book form, and this gave Romaine a chance to get over her emotion.

When Jessamy asked about Daniel, Romy said they were not very friendly at the moment, then went on quickly to ask about Kate. 'Is she still with...Papa?'

'Yes, Romy, and don't feel uncomfortable. There's no atmosphere. She went to the soup kitchen today as someone was ill, but you'll see her this evening.' Jessamy talked about other members of the family until they arrived.

Louise opened the door, and after greeting Romaine she said with a forced lightness to Jessamy, 'I suggest you take Romy straight up, otherwise we shall have our patient defying doctor's orders and trying to negotiate the stairs.'

Her aunt's cheery manner had given Romaine hope that her father was not as ill as everyone feared, but when she went into the bedroom and saw him she was too deeply shocked to speak. He was propped up by pillows, his face as small as a child's, his skin yellow against the snowy-white linen. He seemed a stranger until he smiled and held out a hand to her. She went to him, unable to control her tears.

He stroked her hair. 'There, there, my love, you're home and that's all that matters.' He patted the other side of the bed. 'Come round and climb up beside me and I can put my arm around you.'

Romaine took off her shoes and when she was on the bed, her head against his shoulder, she said with a shaky laugh, 'It's like old times, isn't it, when I used to climb in between you and Mama.'

It was not until her mother got up quickly, saying she would bring coffee that Romaine realised how gauche she had been. How could she have reminded her mother of happier days? When she gave her father a dismayed glance he squeezed her shoulder and whispered, 'Don't worry, Romy baby, it's inevitable under the circumstances. Now then, I want to hear all your adventures.'

Romy baby...it was a long time since he had called her that.

She tried to remember all the amusing parts of her life away from home and began with meeting the eccentric Mrs Pettinfor then, skipping a great deal, she told him about lodging with the Brempsters and how kind they had been to her.

'You've been so lucky,' Alistair said, 'and I'm grateful to the Lord for that.'

His voice had suddenly gone hoarse and when Louise and Jessamy came up with coffee and cakes Louise quickly poured him a drink and took it to him. By then Alistair looked drained, and his eyes were closed. Jessamy motioned to Romaine to stay still, but when he had fallen asleep she slid off the bed and put on her shoes. They went downstairs.

This, she was told, was the pattern of his days. He and Jessamy worked part of the morning on his notes, then he slept during the afternoon and would be a little brighter in the early evening again.

When Louise went upstairs to look in on Alistair Romaine said to her mother, 'Have you forgiven Kate for taking Papa from you?'

Jessamy said, 'I left him. A common grief has drawn us very close. Kate loves your father too, Romy – and he loves her.'

'I'm afraid this is something I cannot understand.'

'Neither could I at first. Now I do, but it's not something I can explain readily. There are different kinds of love. I loved your Uncle Fabian when I married him – still do, in a way, but I don't think I could love anyone more than I love your father.'

'Yet you left him.'

'Yes. There was more than one reason, but that is something I don't want to go into at the moment.'

Romaine had kept a little aloof from Kate when the

actress had stayed on to run the soup kitchen after her mother's departure from Paradise Corner; she was prepared to remain like that now, but when Kate arrived that evening Romaine felt a wave of affection for her and greeted her with warmth, to which Kate readily responded.

Within a few minutes, all four women were talking like long-lost friends. Kate had them laughing about some of the people who came to the soup kitchen and tried to get extra helpings. She described the man who turned up four times, each time wearing a different hat.

'It's true,' she said. 'He must have thought we'd never notice that the backs of his hands were covered with tattoos!'

Although Louise and Jessamy tried to keep the atmosphere as bright as possible, it was Kate with her little anecdotes who made the most impact. And yet Romaine knew the effort it must have cost her because whenever Alistair was discussed there was pain in her eyes.

Romaine wrote to Mrs Brempster and to Mrs Cerralden, and by return had letters from both, as well as one from the Colonel. Mrs Brempster's was full of affection; she said how much Romy was missed and hoped to hear better news of her father soon.

Dorothea Cerralden wrote to say she had never known her father-in-law to be so upset over anyone. He was writing himself but she just wanted to say she was thinking of them all and concluded that miracles did happen.

The Colonel had written, '*My dear girl, what sad news we received. Your father is too young, too valuable to humanity to be taken. Why not me instead, who is so insufferable and no good to anyone? I miss your sharp tongue and impish smile. I don't ask anything of the Lord, but I will break my rules and do so by asking Him to spare your papa. But don't count on it, He seems to have His rules too. Affectionately yours, Edward Cerralden.*'

Romaine shed tears over the letters, feeling she didn't deserve such affection. She must apologise to the Colonel for walking out of her job. She had behaved childishly.

The days went by quickly after that, not only because

of the many people who called to ask after Dr MacKay but also because she was constantly aware of an urgency in her mother to get the medical notes compiled. Each time she would say to herself, 'Before Papa dies,' and feel a terrible ache of loss.

When she mentioned this feeling of urgency to Louise, saying she felt that her father was being pushed too hard, Louise said, 'Alistair told us he wanted to share Christmas with us. He also said he would live until all his notes were compiled. According to your mother, they'll be finished by Christmas Eve.'

Every day Jessamy set aside a time to massage Alistair's hand and arm, and each time he talked of the wonderful ease and comfort it gave him. Jessamy sent up a little prayer, thanking the Deity for having given her this gift.

As Christmas drew near Alistair was so frail he could hardly speak, but his pleasure was obvious when they dressed a Christmas tree in his room. 'It's beautiful,' he whispered, his gaze on the angel. 'Thank you.'

Usually they gave the presents out on Christmas Eve and made a party of it, but this year they were unable to do so because of his condition. They did, however, invite a close friend of Alistair, a prominent surgeon, and he went first into the room when they went upstairs.

'Sedgefield,' Alistair whispered, a smile lighting his eyes. 'How good it is to see you.'

The others all stood in the background while the surgeon went over to him and took his hand.

'Dear friend,' he said, 'I have a task to perform which gives me the greatest pleasure. Your wife let you think she was still working to get the notes of your work compiled. Well, with help from a number of people and a publisher friend of old Walters, I would like to present you with a bound early copy of your book, which is to be published later.'

Alistair mouthed, 'Published?' with an expression of disbelief, then looked from one to another of his family, who all nodded and smiled an assurance.

The surgeon then brought the book from behind his

back. 'It's entitled, as you wished, *A Medical Treatise.*'

Alistair's eyes filled with tears, but there was a radiance in his expression that Romaine had never seen before in anyone. When he whispered his thanks to all of them, holding the book to him, there was not a dry eye in the room. They kissed him in turn then his nurse, who had warned them not to stay too long, hustled them out. He must rest.

Later, when Romaine was alone with Flynn she said, 'I wish I could have a long talk to Papa, find out how he feels about life in general, how he feels about...dying.'

'I think he told us tonight, Romy girl,' Flynn said gently. 'There's a glow in him. He had something to leave behind – medical knowledge that will benefit people all over the world. Plenty of wealthy folk hoard their money, thinking it'll earn them a place in Heaven, but it won't because there's no pockets in shrouds.'

Flynn paused then went on, 'I do know, however, that me old grandfather earned himself a place in Heaven, not that he'd done anything great. He played the flute, you see, lively tunes that set folk's feet going. He played it on his deathbed then gave it to me, saying, "Flynn, me boy, play that when I'm gone, play it whenever you see long faces. It won't cure their troubles but it will make them forget them for a time".'

'And do you play it?' Romaine asked. 'I have never heard you.'

'Oh, I played it at times when I was on the moors at St Peel. Recently I've played it for your father when we were alone, at his request.'

'Why not to us?'

Flynn grinned. 'Ah, now, there's a story. I'm not the best of flute players. I make your Aunt Louise wince. She tells me, in the kindest possible way, that I don't have an ear for music, but your father seems to like it.'

'I would, too,' Romy grinned. 'I have no ear for music either.'

Flynn patted her hand. 'You're a lovely girl me darlin' and so you shall hear it one of these days and you can dance a jig.'

That night she awoke from sleep and thought she heard the sound of a flute, but although she sat up and listened intently, everywhere was quiet. She lay back, deciding she must have been dreaming.

The following day, after Jessamy had given Alistair his massage, he whispered that he wanted her to read something. She said yes, of course, then was taken aback when she saw it was his will. He pressed her hand and nodded. It was important. He wanted to discuss it with her. Jessamy didn't think he was strong enough to discuss anything but to please him she sat down and read it.

The gist of it was that Romaine would receive a substantial bequest on her twenty-first birthday. Large bequests would also be made to herself and Kate. The house would be left to Louise and Flynn, with the proviso that if they sold it he would prefer a medical man to occupy it. There was money set aside to open more soup kitchens and dispensaries, and a list of charities which were to benefit. Alistair was a wealthy man.

When Jessamy had finished reading the will and protested that she should not receive anything he said, 'You are my wife, Jessamy, my first and true love,' and she wept inwardly for their lost years.

Then Alistair whispered, 'Romy must decide who she wants to live with. She has a roving spirit.' His eyes closed and Jessamy thought he was sleeping, but he had gone into a coma. They sat with him, but at two in the morning he slipped away. The book was clasped to him and there was a smile on his lips, which had all of them, apart from Romaine, murmuring it was good to know he had died peacefully.

It was Romaine's first encounter with death. It seemed so final and she found it difficult to accept that she would not be able to speak to her father again.

There was a lot of whispering among the adults, and when the nurse asked them to leave while she attended to the master, Jessamy put an arm about Romaine's waist and said gently, 'Why don't you go to bed, my love? We'll be up for a while yet. Certain things have to be discussed.'

She agreed, needing to be alone to think. The lamp was on low and the firelight threw shadows on the walls. She stood in front of the fire for a long time, finding it unbearable that her father would be buried in the ground. Why couldn't they embalm him like the Egyptians did so he would be there forever?

She undressed slowly and got into bed. The maid had put the warming pan over the sheet, but she lay rigid, feeling she would never be warm again. If only Daniel had forgiven her and she could have told him how she felt about her father.

Romaine was not sure if she had drifted into sleep but she suddenly felt wide awake and was aware of music.

This time she *knew* it was her Uncle Flynn playing the flute, a toe-tapping lively jig that was not spoilt by a few discordant notes. She thought of his old grandfather telling him on his deathbed to play the flute and suddenly a warmth crept into Romaine. She knew, without any doubt whatsoever, that her father could hear it, too.

She whispered, 'Thanks, dear Uncle Flynn, I love you,' and when the music ended she slept.

The following day was one of activity. There was a constant stream of visitors come to pay their last respects, and many letters to be written. One of the hardest for Jessamy to write was to Alistair's family, as she had not been in touch with the MacKays since she and Alistair had parted.

The letter she had by return, however, was heartwarming. It said how lovingly Alistair had spoken of her and how much he had praised her for all the work she had done for the poor and the sick. It concluded that three of his brothers would be coming to the funeral. Jessamy was deeply touched by her husband's praise of her – it was so unexpected.

Margaret came over from the East End and was not only distressed about Alistair, but also upset that Daniel had refused to accompany her.

'He and Romy have fallen out,' she said, 'and according

to Daniel, there's no hope of reconciliation. I can't believe it. They love each other, have done since they were children. What has happened?'

Jessamy soothed her. She was not to worry – it was no more than a lovers' tiff. Given time they would get together again, she was sure of it.

When Margaret left she promised that Daniel would be at the funeral with his father.

Chadwick had written to say that he and Verity would be coming the day before the funeral but that they would have to return afterwards. Bertie was not well and neither was Esmeralda. None of them were getting any younger. Louise said, 'Father is seldom ill but I would have been surprised if Esmeralda did not have one of her famous headaches.'

For Jessamy it was lovely to see her father and her aunt, and to have a talk without any other members of the Every family being there. Chadwick said, 'Jeremiah talked of coming with us then changed his mind. He still bosses us around, or tries to, but he's not the same since he lost Henrietta. He's become rather frail recently.'

Verity gave all the news of the family but when she and Jessamy were alone for a while she said, 'I saw Fabian yesterday, love. He had just come back from Egypt and was shocked when he knew about Alistair. He sends his condolences but said he would write to you.' Verity paused then went on, her voice gentle, 'I suppose you know he's still in love with you, Jessamy. It may not seem the time to tell you but I feel there's been so much you've missed. Yes, I know you had your work, but you haven't had a proper home life for so long. You haven't had the pleasure of seeing Romy grow up, either. She's a beautiful girl but has such a lost look.'

'Romy is a wanderer. She'll always be moving from place to place. I wanted her to come and live with me, but she won't. She won't live with Louise and Flynn either. She says she'll keep in touch with us, but she wants to go back to Market Harborough. She has a job she likes there and excellent lodgings.'

Verity raised her shoulders. 'Who am I to lay down laws? I couldn't keep Louise at home, but I am glad she settled down with Flynn. He's a lovely person – and so is Fabian when you really get to know him. I feel he's so lonely, Jessamy.'

'He's a wanderer too. The sea will always draw him.'

Verity shook her head. 'Not any more. He wants to settle down...with you, Jessamy. Think about it.'

They were interrupted then and Jessamy was glad, not wanting to admit that Fabian had been on her mind. She, too, had been lonely many times. The trouble was that in spite of all she had gone through, the ache of Alistair suffering, there was still something locked inside of her that kept a part of her frozen.

The day of the funeral was bitterly cold. Only the men were to attend. There were eight carriages and about fifty people walking behind the cortège, men well-clad. What touched Jessamy deeply was when Chadwick told her that many poor people, who had been attended by Alistair in hospital and at Paradise Corner, had travelled all the way to the cemetery in the icy wind to pay their respects; some of them crippled. Chadwick said he had spoken to one man who said, 'Nothing would have kept us away. We've lost a much-loved friend, who always listened to our troubles and never once lost his patience. He was a true gentleman.'

'And no man,' concluded Chadwick, 'could have a better accolade than that.'

On the evening after the funeral, when the house was strangely quiet after all the activity, Flynn suggested they all get down to business. He began by saying that he and Louise had decided to sell the house in Devonshire Street. The amount received would be divided between Louise, Jessamy and Kate.

Jessamy and Kate refused. Alistair had willed it to the O'Raffertys.

Louise spoke then. 'We've decided to go back to live in the Coachman's Cottage. I want to return to Paradise Corner and feel I need to live nearby.'

Kate said, 'I want to keep on at the soup kitchen and would like to buy a small house within walking distance.'

Romaine, who had been quiet until then, sat up. 'You've all offered me a home but although I'll keep in touch and will try and visit I still want to go back to Market Harborough. My mind is made up. Please don't try and change it.'

No one challenged her.

Although Romaine's head was up in a defiant way Jessamy was aware of the lost look that Verity had mentioned and when they were alone later she said quietly, 'Romy, I know you were terribly upset about your father but I feel there's something else troubling you. I understand that Daniel was at the funeral with his father but he hasn't been to see you. When Margaret called she said she knew that you had fallen out with Daniel but he refused to say why. Can you tell me?'

Several times Romaine had been surprised to feel that the only person who would understand her behaviour with André, was her mother. She began to cry and when Jessamy drew her into her arms, the whole story came out.

'I feel dirty,' she sobbed. 'Daniel despises me and wants nothing more to do with me. I love him, always have. I always will.' Jessamy talked to her, explained about the strength of sexual feelings, the temptations.

'You must give Daniel time. He'll be consumed with jealousy that another man had looked at your body. He's a very strong person, he proved it to you. He's loved you too long to stay away forever. His mother said he was going abroad again in a few weeks' time. I feel sure he won't leave without seeing you.'

'Oh, Mama, I hope he does. I'm glad I told you – I feel it's a weight off my mind. I would like to stay on with you and Aunt Louise and Uncle Flynn for a few more days, if I may, but I do want to go back to the Brempsters and to work for Mrs Cerralden and the Colonel.'

The following morning Jessamy had a letter from Fabian. He asked to be forgiven for not having kept in touch with her. He had thought he had been doing it for the best and realised, when he heard about Alistair, that he had been wrong. He told her he was coming to London in five or six days' time and asked if they could meet.

Jessamy wrote back to say that she was returning to her home in Poplar and asked him to call there, between surgeries if possible. It was not excitement Jessamy felt at the thought of seeing Fabian, more the pleasure of meeting an old friend again.

Willard Stead, who had been taking her surgeries while Alistair had been ill, welcomed her the next morning, and so did the patients. Some of the comments were just gruff remarks such as, 'Glad you're back, Missus,' or 'I feel better for seeing you, Doc,' but it made Jessamy feel wanted. While Alistair had been alive and she was nursing him, she had had the feeling of being needed. When he died she felt alone again. Even Romaine had chosen to return to the people with whom she lodged.

Jessamy liked Willard Stead, he was a quiet man, absorbed in his work. After surgery they would have a coffee and discuss the problems of the various patients and afterwards, talk generalities, somehow avoiding any talk of his private life. This morning, to Jessamy's surprise, he spoke about Kate, said what a nice person she was and how she had helped him to accept the death of his wife. It was not that Jessamy felt any jealousy of Kate, more a curiosity to know why the actress should get to know so much about Willard's private life when she knew practically nothing and yet had known him for years. Willard unconsciously answered her question.

'Kate is a most unusual person in that she has great talent, I was told, and could have been at the top of her profession by now. Yet she would not allow it to dominate her life.' He paused. 'Not like me, Jessamy, who lives in a world of medicine. I couldn't believe how I, a qualified doctor with so much experience, had not been able to diagnose my wife's illnes. Kate asked me if it was an illness that was easy to spot. I told her no, and that it was not until the post mortem that I learned she had contracted a rare tropical virus. How, we don't know. Kate then said,

"And therein lies your answer, Doctor Stead. You are not God. Let your heart tell you if you are guilty".'

Willard nodded slowly. 'She was right. I had let the world of medicine dominate my commonsense. After that I knew peace.'

'I'm glad,' Jessamy said. Later, she thought that if Kate could help Willard, surely she could help Romy. She sat down and wrote to Daniel.

'Dear Daniel,

'Romy is heartbroken. She loves you, has done since she was five years old and in all that time, has never been interested in anyone else. She enjoyed drawing, later doing sketches. She has talent, as you know. Then along comes a famous artist who praises her work. She was hypnotised by him and was horrified when she realised what she was doing. She ran from him. She told me so and Romy doesn't lie. I write this only because I made one big mistake in my life and pride prevented me from admitting it.

'If you feel you can never forgive her, Daniel, please tell her then she can readjust her life. She has great determination. It's the uncertainty that is so painful.

'She doesn't know that I'm writing to you and I wouldn't want her to know. Incidentally, my daughter is going back to Market Harborough. She knows you are going abroad but she likes working at Cerralden House. I wish you well in your work, Daniel. Yours sincerely, Jessamy MacKay.'

Two days later she had a reply.

'Dear Mrs MacKay,

'Thank you for your letter. It brought me to my senses. Pride was preventing me from climbing down from my lofty pinnacle. I love Romy dearly, but could not accept that she would even think of looking at another man. Such arrogance! I shall call on her. I want to marry your daughter when I finish my apprenticeship and hope to have your permission. Thank you again for your advice. Yours sincerely, Daniel.'

A few days later, Jessamy learned of the fruits of her intervention in a letter from Romaine.

'Dear Mama,

'You'll never guess! Daniel and I are together again. I

went for a walk in the direction of Felcy Hall, but not intending to call on him, when who should I see crossing a field but Daniel himself. He saw me, waved and began to run. I ran too and we met outside an old barn. It was snowing and we went inside. It smelled of cattle and mice but to me it could have been the Hanging Gardens of Babylon. We talked and talked and Daniel said he had never stopped loving me. It had been his pride that prevented him from coming to me. He wants to marry me when he's finished his apprenticeship. He said we would be fighting all the time because I had a wanderlust and he wants a home and children, but that is what I want too, Mama. I've learned from the awful incident with André that fame is not important. It's loving and being loved that's important.

'I'm sending you the beautiful portrait that André did of me. I wouldn't be able to hang it in our future home because of Daniel, but I feel that you would like it. I'm so very happy and I want you to be too. Perhaps some day you will meet someone you could marry. I hope so. I shall try and visit you soon. Your loving daughter, Romy.'

Jessamy stared out of the window. *Your loving daughter... it's loving and being loved that's important...*

When Fabian came to visit he took both of Jessamy's hands in his and said again how sorry he was to hear about Alistair. He added, 'He'll be a great loss to the medical world.'

She withdrew her hands. '*And* to his family.'

'Of course, forgive me.'

Jessamy saw then that he looked drawn and she drew a chair forward. 'Sit down, Fabian. I've made some coffee, I'll pour it.' As she attended to this she asked if he had enjoyed his latest trip to Egypt.

It was several seconds before he replied. 'Yes, there's always something new to explore. It's just that – '

'There was no one to share it with you,' she said gently.

'Oh, we were in a party, people were very kind, they – ' He paused again. 'No, you're right, it's not the same. They were mostly couples this time, and the others in the party were families.' Fabian gave a wry smile. 'There weren't even any elderly widows to mother me.'

Jessamy saw a world of loneliness in her ex-husband then. He had no one who cared for him to come home to, he sought escape by constantly travelling yet becoming more lonely than ever. She, too, had known great loneliness. She said, trying to speak in a casual way, 'I've been promising myself a trip abroad for some time. The trouble was getting someone to take over my practice. Willard Stead has been helping out recently. He's decided now to stay in England until the spring.' She smiled. 'He and Kate Keller have become good friends. I might ask him if he would take over and let me have a break.'

Fabian leaned forward, his expression eager. 'Jessamy, would you come to Brittany with me? Remember, I have property there. It's beautiful, so isolated. There are just the seabirds, the beach, the – '

'No, Fabian, I couldn't. That wasn't in my mind.'

'I meant it on a purely platonic basis. There's a four-roomed cottage a hundred yards away where servants lived when the family came to stay at the larger house. I would sleep at the small one.'

Jessamy shook her head. 'For a moment I thought it a good idea. Now I'm not so sure.'

'Don't you trust me? You loved me once.'

'I was a child. You did leave me for Caroline.'

'And found I no longed loved her. Caroline complained that I was forever talking about you. She told me to go home but I couldn't. Pride wouldn't let me.'

Pride, Jessamy thought bitterly. It was responsible for so much.

Fabian said in a low voice, 'I must admit I thought when we met again and got on so well together that we might...'

'Marry again? It's out of the question. I still love Alistair.'

'Wouldn't you have stayed with him if you had?' he asked quietly.

'I had my pride too,' she retorted. 'I also found work to do that was rewarding.'

'I found solace in building the Love Garden. Childish

perhaps, but we all have our weaknesses. When I had my accident and you came at once and helped to ease my pain I dreamed again of making a life together. And, knowing how much your charitable work means to you, I thought I could organise a dispensary at St Peel, perhaps a soup kitchen, too. I would work with you. There's a lot of poverty in that area, just as there is elsewhere.'

Jessamy was silent for moment then she said, 'I'm sorry, Fabian, I'm not the person I was when we married. There's a coldness in me now.'

'There's a warmth there too, Jessamy,' he said softly, 'otherwise you would not have come to me when I needed you, nor would you be caring for the sick and needy.'

'It wouldn't work. Think of the gossip, for one thing. People have long memories. I went to The Montague Acres as a bride and was still living there when we divorced.'

His eyebrows went up. 'I would have thought that with all you've gone through you would have been above gossip. If you didn't want to live with your parents your Aunt Verity would be pleased to have you. We could meet only at the dispensary at first, or the soup kitchen, then when the gossip died down we could get married.'

Jessamy was silent, considering this, then she shook her head. 'No, I've told you, I have this awful coldness in me. It wouldn't be fair to you.'

Fabian got up. 'Very well. I won't trouble you ever again, but I suggest that you cut out the canker inside of you and try to be a woman again. And do it soon, for time is running out. Don't get up. I'll see myself to the door.'

Jessamy had tensed at the word canker. Now she thought yes, Fabian was right. That was exactly what it was. She had let it grow, blaming Alistair and Kate for the separation. The recent phrase of Willard Stead suddenly came into her mind. 'I allowed the world of medicine to dominate my commonsense.'

It was what she had done.

The front door closed and still she sat.

Then, noticing Fabian's scarf, she picked it up and held

it to her cheek. There had been such resignation in his voice as he took his leave. No, it had been despair...

She jumped up and ran into the hall. By the time she had opened the door Fabian was crossing the road. She called to him and he turned, hesitated, then came hurrying back.

She held up the scarf. 'You forgot this.'

'Oh, thanks. I didn't realise.' His voice was flat.

'Fabian, I want to look around the Love Garden again.'

'You do?'

'Yes,' she whispered. 'And in the not-too distant future I should like to walk around it with you...every morning.'

'Oh, Jessamy, Jessamy.'

He drew her into his arms and she felt the lovely warmth of his body. And when his lips touched hers the coldness in her was released and began to dissolve.